INKSPELL

INKSPELL

CORNELIA FUNKE

*Translated from the
German by Anthea Bell*

Chicken House

Scholastic Inc. / New York

Published in Germany as *Tintenblut* by Cecilie Dressler Verlag 2005.
Original text copyright © 2005 by Dressler Verlag.
English translation copyright © 2005 by Anthea Bell.

Cover, map, and chapter-head illustration copyright © 2005 by Carol Lawson.
Chapter-ending illustrations copyright © 2005 by Cornelia Funke.

Library of Congress Cataloging-in-Publication data available

ISBN-13: 978-0-439-93611-8
ISBN-10: 0-439-93611-X

10 9 8 7 6 5 4 3 2 1   09 10 11 12 13/0

Printed in the U.S.A.   23

This edition first printing, August 2009

The text type was set in Horley Old Style MT at 11 pt.
Display type hand-lettered by David Coulsen
Book design by Elizabeth B. Parisi and Leyah Jensen

If I knew where poems came from,
I'd go there.

— **Michael Langley,** *Staying Alive*

To Brendan Fraser,
whose voice is the heart of this book.
Thanks for inspiration and enchantment.
Mo wouldn't have stepped into my writing room without you,
and this story would never have been told.

To Rainer Strecker,
who is both Silvertongue and Dustfinger.
Every word in this book is just waiting for him to read it.

And of course, as almost always, last but for sure not least,
for Anna, wonderful, wonderful Anna, who had this
story told to her on many walks, encouraged and advised me,
and let me know what was good and what could still be
improved. (I very much hope that the story of Meggie and Farid
has its fair share of the book now?)

TABLE OF CONTENTS

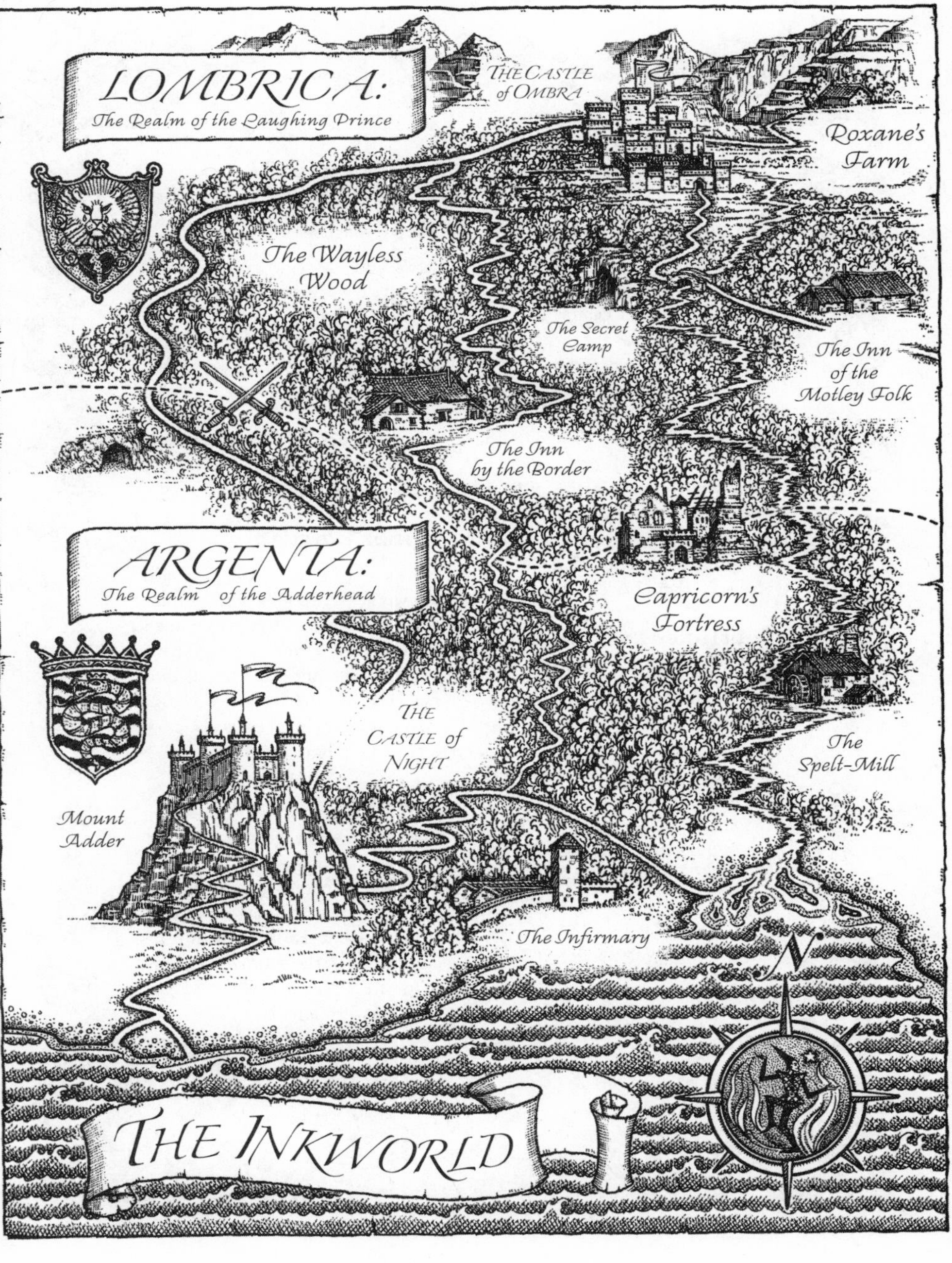

LOMBRICA:
The Realm of the Laughing Prince

THE CASTLE of OMBRA

Roxane's Farm

The Wayless Wood

The Secret Camp

The Inn of the Motley Folk

The Inn by the Border

ARGENTA:
The Realm of the Adderhead

Capricorn's Fortress

THE CASTLE of NIGHT

Mount Adder

The Spelt-Mill

The Infirmary

THE INKWORLD

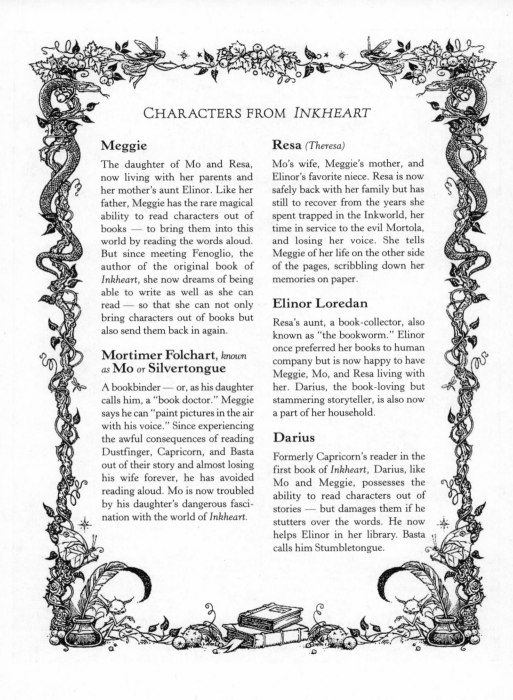

CHARACTERS FROM *INKHEART*

Meggie

The daughter of Mo and Resa, now living with her parents and her mother's aunt Elinor. Like her father, Meggie has the rare magical ability to read characters out of books — to bring them into this world by reading the words aloud. But since meeting Fenoglio, the author of the original book of *Inkheart*, she now dreams of being able to write as well as she can read — so that she can not only bring characters out of books but also send them back in again.

Mortimer Folchart, *known* as Mo *or* Silvertongue

A bookbinder — or, as his daughter calls him, a "book doctor." Meggie says he can "paint pictures in the air with his voice." Since experiencing the awful consequences of reading Dustfinger, Capricorn, and Basta out of their story and almost losing his wife forever, he has avoided reading aloud. Mo is now troubled by his daughter's dangerous fascination with the world of *Inkheart*.

Resa *(Theresa)*

Mo's wife, Meggie's mother, and Elinor's favorite niece. Resa is now safely back with her family but has still to recover from the years she spent trapped in the Inkworld, her time in service to the evil Mortola, and losing her voice. She tells Meggie of her life on the other side of the pages, scribbling down her memories on paper.

Elinor Loredan

Resa's aunt, a book-collector, also known as "the bookworm." Elinor once preferred her books to human company but is now happy to have Meggie, Mo, and Resa living with her. Darius, the book-loving but stammering storyteller, is also now a part of her household.

Darius

Formerly Capricorn's reader in the first book of *Inkheart*, Darius, like Mo and Meggie, possesses the ability to read characters out of stories — but damages them if he stutters over the words. He now helps Elinor in her library. Basta calls him Stumbletongue.

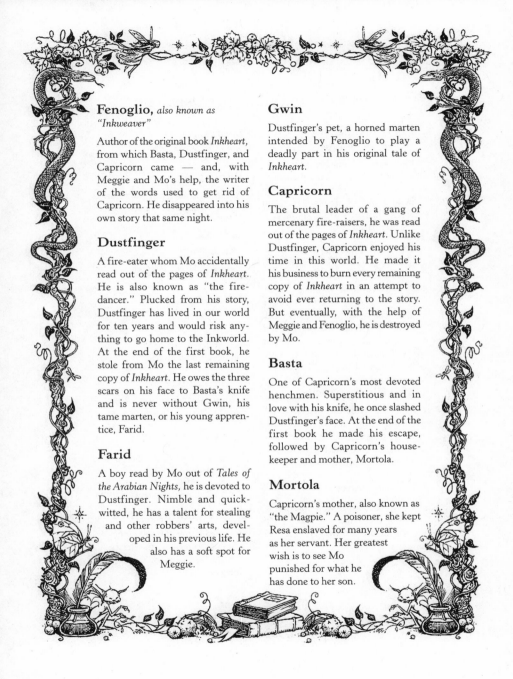

Fenoglio, *also known as "Inkweaver"*

Author of the original book *Inkheart*, from which Basta, Dustfinger, and Capricorn came — and, with Meggie and Mo's help, the writer of the words used to get rid of Capricorn. He disappeared into his own story that same night.

Dustfinger

A fire-eater whom Mo accidentally read out of the pages of *Inkheart*. He is also known as "the fire-dancer." Plucked from his story, Dustfinger has lived in our world for ten years and would risk anything to go home to the Inkworld. At the end of the first book, he stole from Mo the last remaining copy of *Inkheart*. He owes the three scars on his face to Basta's knife and is never without Gwin, his tame marten, or his young apprentice, Farid.

Farid

A boy read by Mo out of *Tales of the Arabian Nights,* he is devoted to Dustfinger. Nimble and quick-witted, he has a talent for stealing and other robbers' arts, developed in his previous life. He also has a soft spot for Meggie.

Gwin

Dustfinger's pet, a horned marten intended by Fenoglio to play a deadly part in his original tale of *Inkheart.*

Capricorn

The brutal leader of a gang of mercenary fire-raisers, he was read out of the pages of *Inkheart*. Unlike Dustfinger, Capricorn enjoyed his time in this world. He made it his business to burn every remaining copy of *Inkheart* in an attempt to avoid ever returning to the story. But eventually, with the help of Meggie and Fenoglio, he is destroyed by Mo.

Basta

One of Capricorn's most devoted henchmen. Superstitious and in love with his knife, he once slashed Dustfinger's face. At the end of the first book he made his escape, followed by Capricorn's house-keeper and mother, Mortola.

Mortola

Capricorn's mother, also known as "the Magpie." A poisoner, she kept Resa enslaved for many years as her servant. Her greatest wish is to see Mo punished for what he has done to her son.

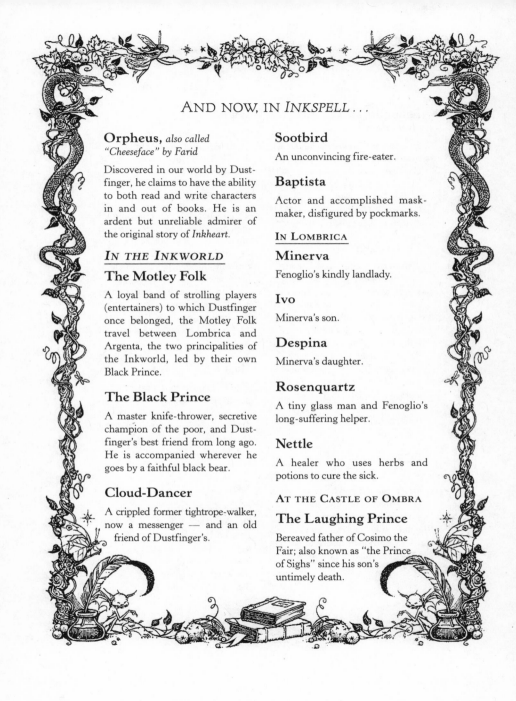

AND NOW, IN *INKSPELL* . . .

Orpheus, *also called* "Cheeseface" *by Farid*

Discovered in our world by Dustfinger, he claims to have the ability to both read and write characters in and out of books. He is an ardent but unreliable admirer of the original story of *Inkheart*.

IN THE INKWORLD

The Motley Folk

A loyal band of strolling players (entertainers) to which Dustfinger once belonged, the Motley Folk travel between Lombrica and Argenta, the two principalities of the Inkworld, led by their own Black Prince.

The Black Prince

A master knife-thrower, secretive champion of the poor, and Dustfinger's best friend from long ago. He is accompanied wherever he goes by a faithful black bear.

Cloud-Dancer

A crippled former tightrope-walker, now a messenger — and an old friend of Dustfinger's.

Sootbird

An unconvincing fire-eater.

Baptista

Actor and accomplished maskmaker, disfigured by pockmarks.

IN LOMBRICA

Minerva

Fenoglio's kindly landlady.

Ivo

Minerva's son.

Despina

Minerva's daughter.

Rosenquartz

A tiny glass man and Fenoglio's long-suffering helper.

Nettle

A healer who uses herbs and potions to cure the sick.

AT THE CASTLE OF OMBRA

The Laughing Prince

Bereaved father of Cosimo the Fair; also known as "the Prince of Sighs" since his son's untimely death.

Violante, *"Her Ugliness"*

The unhappy wife of Cosimo, daughter of the Adderhead, mother of Jacopo — the heir to the realms of both Lombrica and Argenta.

Balbulus

An illuminator (illustrator), brought to the library of the Castle of Ombra by Violante.

Brianna

The willful daughter of Roxane and Dustfinger, maid to Her Ugliness.

Cosimo the Fair

The deceased son of the Laughing Prince.

AT ROXANE'S FARM

Roxane

Dustfinger's beautiful wife, formerly a minstrel who now grows herbs for the healers.

Jehan

The son of Roxane and her deceased second husband.

Jink

Another horned marten.

IN ARGENTA

AT THE INFIRMARY

The Barn Owl

The physician who looked after Dustfinger when he was a child.

IN THE CASTLE OF NIGHT

The Adderhead, *also known as "the Silver Prince"*

A warmongering tyrant who fears only death itself. Capricorn and his fire-raisers were in his pay.

Slasher

Formerly Capricorn's fire-raiser, now in the Adderhead's service.

The Piper, *also known as "Silvernose"*

Formerly Capricorn's fire-raiser, he, too, now sings his dark songs for the Adderhead.

Firefox

Capricorn's successor, chief bodyguard and herald to the Adderhead.

Taddeo

The librarian of the Castle of Night.

WORDS MADE TO MEASURE

He has been trying to sing
Love into existence again
And he has failed.

Margaret Atwood, "Orpheus 2," *Eating Fire*

Twilight was gathering, and Orpheus still wasn't here.
Farid's heart beat faster, as it did always when day left him alone with the darkness. *Curse that Cheeseface! Where could he be?* The birds were falling silent in the trees, as if the approach of night had stifled their voices, and the nearby mountains were turning black. You might have thought the setting sun had singed them. Soon the whole world would be black as pitch, even the grass beneath Farid's bare feet, and the ghosts would begin to whisper. Farid knew only one place where he felt safe from them: right behind Dustfinger, so close that he could feel his warmth. Dustfinger wasn't afraid of the night. He liked it.

"Hearing them again, are you?" he asked, as Farid pressed

close to him. "How many times do I have to tell you? There aren't any ghosts in this world. One of its few advantages."

Dustfinger stood there leaning against an oak tree, looking down the lonely road. In the distance, a streetlamp cast its light on the cracked asphalt where a few houses huddled by the roadside. There were scarcely a dozen of them, standing close together as if they feared the night as much as Farid.

The house where Cheeseface lived was the first on the road. There was a light on behind one of its windows. Dustfinger had been staring at it for more than an hour. Farid had often tried standing motionless like that, but his limbs simply would not keep still.

"I'm going to find out where he is!"

"No, you're not!" Dustfinger's face was as expressionless as ever, but his voice gave him away. Farid heard the impatience in it . . . and the hope that refused to die, although it had been disappointed so often before. "Are you sure he said Friday?"

"Yes, and this is Friday, right?"

Dustfinger just nodded, then pushed his shoulder-length hair back from his face. Farid had tried growing his own hair long, but it was so curly, tangled, and unruly that in the end he cut it short again with his knife.

" 'Friday outside the village at four o'clock,' that's what he said. While that dog of his growled at me as if it really craved a nice crunchy boy to eat!" The wind blew through Farid's thin sweater, and he rubbed his arms, shivering. A good warm fire, that's what he'd have liked now, but Dustfinger wouldn't let him light so much as a match in this wind. Four o'clock . . . Cursing quietly, Farid looked up at the darkening sky. He knew it was well past four, even without a watch.

"I tell you, he's making us wait on purpose, the stuck-up idiot!"

Dustfinger's thin lips twisted into a smile. Farid was finding it easier and easier to make him smile. Perhaps that was why he'd promised to take Farid, too . . . supposing Orpheus really did send Dustfinger back. Back to his own world, created from paper, printer's ink, and an old man's words.

Oh, come on! thought Farid. How would Orpheus, of all people, succeed where all the others had failed? So many had tried it . . . the Stammerer, Golden Eyes, Raventongue. Swindlers who had taken their money.

The light went out behind Orpheus's window, and Dustfinger abruptly straightened up. A door closed. The sound of footsteps echoed through the darkness: rapid, irregular footsteps. Then Orpheus appeared in the light of the single streetlamp. Farid had privately nicknamed him Cheeseface because of his pale skin and the way he sweated like a piece of cheese in the sun. Breathing heavily, he walked down the steep slope of the road, with his hell-hound beside him. It was ugly as a hyena. When Orpheus saw Dustfinger standing by the roadside he stopped, smiled broadly, and waved to him.

Farid grasped Dustfinger's arm. "Look at that silly grin. False as fool's gold!" he whispered. "How can you trust him?"

"Who says I trust him? And what's the matter with you? You're all jittery. Would you rather stay here? Cars, moving pictures, canned music, light that keeps the night away —" Dustfinger clambered over the knee-high wall beside the road. "You like all that. You'll be bored to death where I want to go."

What was he talking about? As if he didn't know perfectly well that there was only one thing Farid wanted: to stay with him. He was about to reply angrily, but a sharp crack, like boots treading on a twig, made him spin around. Dustfinger had heard it, too. He had stopped and was listening. But there was nothing to be seen among the trees, only the branches moving in the wind, and a moth, pale as a ghost, that fluttered in Farid's face.

"I'm sorry, it took longer than I expected!" cried Orpheus as he approached them.

Farid still couldn't grasp the fact that such a voice could emerge from that mouth. They had heard about Orpheus's voice in several villages, and Dustfinger had set out at once in search of it, but not until a week ago had they found the man himself in a library, reading fairy tales to a few children. None of the children seemed to notice the dwarf who suddenly slipped out from behind one of the shelves crammed with well-thumbed books. But Dustfinger had seen him. He had lain in wait for Orpheus, approaching him just as he was about to get into his car again, and finally he'd shown him the book — the book that Farid had cursed more often than anything else on earth.

"Oh, I know that book!" Orpheus had breathed. "And as for you," he had added almost devoutly, looking at Dustfinger as if to stare the scars from his cheeks, "I know you, too! You're the best thing in it. Dustfinger! The fire-eater! Who read you here into this saddest of all stories? No, don't say anything! You want to go back, don't you? But you can't find the door, the door hidden among the letters on the page! Never mind! I can build you a new one, with words made to measure! For a special price, between friends — if you're really the man I take you for."

A special price between friends? What a laugh! They'd had to promise him almost all their money, and then wait for him for hours in this godforsaken spot, on this windy night that smelled of ghosts.

"Is the marten in there?" Orpheus shone his flashlight on Dustfinger's backpack. "You know my dog doesn't like him."

"No, he's finding something to eat." Dustfinger's eyes

wandered to the book under Orpheus's arm. "Well? Have you . . . done it?"

"Of course!" As Orpheus spoke, the hellhound bared its teeth and glared at Farid. "To start with, the words were rather hard to find. Perhaps because I was so excited. As I told you at our first meeting, this book, *Inkheart*" — Orpheus stroked the volume — "was my favorite when I was a child. I was eleven when I last saw it. I kept borrowing it from our run-down library until it was stolen. Unfortunately, I hadn't been brave enough to steal it myself, and then someone else did, but I never forgot it. This book taught me, once and for all, how easily you can escape this world with the help of words! You can find friends between the pages of a book, wonderful friends! Friends like you, fire-eaters, giants, fairies . . . ! Have you any idea how bitterly I wept when I read about your death? But you're alive, and everything will be all right! You will retell the story —"

"I?" Dustfinger interrupted him with an amused look. "No, believe me, that's a task for others."

"Well, perhaps." Orpheus cleared his throat as if he felt embarrassed to have revealed so much of his feelings. "However that may be, it's a shame I can't go with you," he said, making for the wall beside the road with his curiously awkward gait. "But the reader has to stay behind, that's the iron rule. I've tried every way I could to read myself into a book, but it just won't work." Sighing, he stopped by the wall, put his hand under his ill-fitting jacket, and brought out a sheet of paper. "Well — this is what you asked for," he told Dustfinger. "Wonderful words, just for you, a road of words to take you straight back again. Here, read it!"

Hesitantly, Dustfinger took the sheet of paper. It was covered with fine, slanting handwriting, the letters tangled like thread. Dustfinger slowly ran his finger along the words, as if he had to show each of them separately to his eyes. Orpheus watched him like a schoolboy waiting to be told the mark his work has earned.

When Dustfinger finally looked up again, he sounded surprised. "You write very well! Those are beautiful words. . . ."

Orpheus turned as red as if someone had spilled mulberry juice over his face. "I'm glad you like it!"

"I like it very much! It's all just as I described it to you. It even sounds a little better."

Orpheus took the sheet of paper back with an awkward smile. "I can't promise that it'll be the same time of day there," he said in a muted voice. "The laws of my art are difficult to understand, but believe me, no one knows more about them than I do. For instance, I've discovered that if you want to change or continue a story, you should only use words that are already in the book. Too many new words and nothing at all may happen, or, alternatively, something could happen that you didn't intend. Perhaps it's different if you wrote the original story —"

"In the name of all the fairies, you're fuller of words than a whole library!" Dustfinger interrupted impatiently. "How about just reading it now?"

Orpheus fell silent as abruptly as if he had swallowed his tongue. "By all means," he said in slightly injured tones. "Well, now you'll see! With my help, the book will welcome you back like a prodigal son. It will suck you up the way paper absorbs ink."

Dustfinger just nodded and looked down the empty road. Farid sensed how much he wanted to believe Cheeseface — and how afraid he was of another disappointment.

"What about me?" Farid went up to him. "He did write something about me, too, didn't he? Did you check it?"

Orpheus gave him a rather nasty look. "My God," he said

sarcastically to Dustfinger, "that boy really does seem fond of you! Where did you pick him up? Somewhere along the road?"

"Not exactly," said Dustfinger. "He was plucked out of his story by the man who did me the same favor."

"Ah, yes! That . . . Silvertongue!" Orpheus spoke the name in a disparaging tone, as if he couldn't believe that anyone really deserved it.

"Yes, that's what he's called. How do you know?" There was no mistaking Dustfinger's surprise.

The hellhound snuffled at Farid's bare toes. Orpheus shrugged. "Sooner or later you get to hear of everyone who can breathe life into the letters on a page."

"Indeed?" Dustfinger sounded skeptical, but he asked no more questions. He just stared at the sheet of paper covered with Orpheus's fine handwriting. But Cheeseface was still looking at Farid.

"What book do you come from?" he asked. "And why don't you want to go back into your own story, instead of his, which has nothing to do with you?"

"That's none of your business!" replied Farid angrily. He liked Cheeseface less and less. He was too inquisitive — and far too shrewd.

But Dustfinger just laughed quietly. "His own story? No, Farid isn't in the least homesick for that one. The boy switches from story to story like a snake changing its skin." Farid heard something like admiration in his voice.

"Does he indeed?" Orpheus looked at Farid again, so patron- izingly that the boy would have liked to kick his fat shins, but the hellhound was still glaring hungrily at him. "Very well," said Orpheus, sitting down on the wall. "I'm warning you, all the same! Reading you back is easy, but the boy has no business in your story! I can't put his name into it, I can only say 'a boy,' and as you know, I can't guarantee that it will work. Even if it does, he'll probably just cause confusion. He may even bring you bad luck!"

Whatever did the wretched man mean? Farid looked at Dustfinger. *Please,* he thought, *oh, please! Don't listen to him. Take me with you.*

Dustfinger returned his gaze. And smiled.

"Bad luck?" he said, and his voice conveyed the certainty that no one could tell him anything he didn't already know about bad luck. "Nonsense. So far the boy has brought me nothing but good luck instead. And he's not a bad fire-eater. He's coming with me. And so is this." Before Orpheus realized what he meant, Dustfinger picked up the book that Cheeseface had put down on the wall beside him. "You won't be needing it anymore. And I shall sleep considerably more easily if it's in my possession."

Dismayed, Orpheus stared at him. "But . . . but I told you, it's my favorite book! I really would like to keep it."

"And so would I," was all Dustfinger said as he handed the book to Farid. "Here, take good care of it."

Farid clutched it to his chest and nodded. "Now for Gwin," he said. "We must call him." But just as he took a little dry bread from his trouser pocket and was about to call Gwin's name, Dustfinger put his hand over Farid's mouth.

"Gwin stays here," he said. If he had announced that he was planning to leave his right arm behind, Farid couldn't have looked at him more incredulously. "Why are you staring at me like that? We'll catch ourselves another marten once we're there, one that's not so ready to bite."

"Well, at least you've seen sense there," said Orpheus, his voice sounding injured.

Whatever was he talking about? But Dustfinger avoided the boy's questioning gaze. "Come on, start reading!" he told Orpheus. "Or we'll still be standing here at sunrise."

Orpheus looked at him for a moment as if he were about to say something else. But then he cleared his throat. "Yes," he said. "Yes, you're right. Ten years in the wrong story — that's a long time. Let's start reading."

Words.

Words filled the night like the fragrance of invisible flowers. Words made to measure, written by Orpheus with his dough-pale hands, words taken from the book that Farid was clutching tightly and then fitted together into a new meaning. They spoke of another world, a world full of marvels and terrors. And Farid, listening, forgot time. He didn't even feel that there was such a thing. Nothing existed but the voice of Orpheus, so ill-suited to the mouth it came from. It obliterated everything: the potholed road and the run-down houses at the far end of it, the streetlamp, the wall where Orpheus was sitting, even the moon above the black trees. And suddenly the air smelled strange and sweet. . . .

He can do it, thought Farid, *he really can do it,* and meanwhile the voice of Orpheus made him blind and deaf to everything that wasn't made of the written letters on the sheet of paper.

When Cheeseface suddenly fell silent, Farid looked around him in confusion, dizzy from the beautiful sound of the words. But why were the houses still there, and the streetlamp, all rusty from wind and rain? Orpheus was still there, too, and his hell-hound.

Only one thing was missing. Dustfinger.

But Farid was still standing on the same lonely road. In the wrong world.

FOOL'S GOLD

For plainly this miscreant had sold himself to Satan, and it would be fatal to meddle with the property of such a power as that.

Mark Twain, *Tom Sawyer*

"No!" Farid heard the horror in his own voice. "No! What have you done? Where has he gone?"

Orpheus rose ponderously from the wall, still holding that wretched piece of paper, and he smiled. "Home. Where else?"

"But what about me? Go on reading. Go on!" Everything was blurred by the tears in his eyes. He was alone again, alone as he had always been before he found Dustfinger. Farid began trembling so hard that he didn't even notice Orpheus taking the book from his hands.

"And here's the proof of it once again," he heard the man murmur. "I bear my name by right. I am the master of *all* words, both written and spoken. No one can compete with me."

"Master of words? What are you talking about?" Farid shouted in such a loud voice that even the hellhound flinched. "If you know so much about your trade, then why am I still here? Go on, start reading again! And give me that book back!" He reached for it, but Orpheus avoided him with surprising agility.

"The book? Why should I give it to you? You probably can't even read. Let me tell you something! If I'd wanted you to go with him, then you'd be there now, but you have no business in his story, so I just left out what I'd written about you. Understand? And now be off before I set my dog on you. Boys like you threw stones at him when he was a puppy, and he's enjoyed chasing your sort ever since!"

"You brute! You liar! You traitor!" Farid's voice broke. Hadn't he known it? Hadn't he told Dustfinger? Cheeseface was as false as fool's gold.

Something made its way between his bare feet, something furry and round-nosed with tiny horns between its ears. The marten. *He's gone, Gwin,* thought Farid. *Dustfinger's gone. We'll never see him again!*

The hellhound lowered its bulky head and took a hesitant step toward the marten, but Gwin bared his needle-sharp teeth, and the huge dog withdrew its nose in astonishment. Its fear gave Farid fresh courage.

"Come on, give it to me!" He rammed his thin fist into Orpheus's chest. "That piece of paper, and the book, too! Or I'll slit you open like a carp. I swear I will!" But he couldn't help sobbing, which made the words sound nowhere near as impressive as he had intended.

Orpheus patted his dog's head as he stowed away the book in the waistband of his trousers. "Dear me, that really scares us, Cerberus, doesn't it?"

Gwin pressed close to Farid's ankles, his tail twitching uneasily back and forth. Even when the marten ran across the road and disappeared into the trees on the other side, Farid thought it was because of the dog. *Deaf and blind,* he kept thinking later, *you were deaf and blind, Farid.* But Orpheus smiled, like someone who knows more than his opponent.

"Let me tell you, my young friend," he said, "it gave me a terrible fright when Dustfinger wanted the book back. Luckily, he handed it to you, or I couldn't have done anything for him. It was hard enough persuading my clients not to just kill him, but I made them promise. Only on that condition would I act as bait . . . bait for the book, because in case you haven't caught on yet, this is all about the book. The book and nothing else. They promised not to hurt a hair on Dustfinger's head, but I'm afraid no one said a word about you."

And before Farid realized what Cheeseface was talking about, he felt the knife at his throat — sharp as the edge of a reed, colder than mist among the trees.

"Well, well, who have we here?" a well-remembered voice murmured in his ear. "Didn't I last see you with Silvertongue? It seems you helped Dustfinger steal the book for him, isn't that so? What a fine little fellow you are!" The knife scratched Farid's skin, and the man breathed peppermint into his face. If he hadn't known Basta by his voice, then that stinking breath would have identified the man. His knife and a few mint leaves — Basta was never without them. He chewed the leaves and then spat out what remained. He was dangerous as a rabid dog and not too bright, but how did he come to be here? How had he found them?

"Well, how do you like my new knife?" Basta purred into Farid's ear. "I'd have liked to introduce the fire-eater to it, too, but Orpheus here has a weakness for him. Never mind, I'll find Dustfinger again. Him and Silvertongue, and Silvertongue's witch of a daughter. They'll all pay. . . ."

"Pay for what?" said Farid. "Saving you from the Shadow?"

But Basta only pressed the blade more firmly against his neck. "Saving me? They brought me bad luck, nothing but bad luck!"

"For heaven's sake, put that knife away!" Orpheus interrupted, sounding sickened. "He's only a boy. Let him go. I have the book as we agreed, so —"

"Let him go?" Basta laughed aloud, but the laughter died in his throat. A snarling sound came from the woods behind them, and the hellhound laid back its ears. Basta spun around. "What the devil . . . ? You damned idiot! What have you let out of the book?"

Farid didn't want to know the answer. He felt Basta loosen his grip for a moment. That was enough: He bit the man's hand so hard that he tasted blood. Basta screamed and dropped the knife. Farid jerked back his elbows, rammed them into the man's narrow chest, and ran. But he had entirely forgotten the little wall by the roadside; he stumbled on it and fell to his knees, so hard that he was left gasping for breath. As he picked himself up he saw the paper lying on the asphalt, the sheet of paper that had carried Dustfinger away. The wind must have blown it into the road. With quick fingers, he reached for it. *I just left out what I'd written about you. Understand?* Orpheus's words still rang in his head, mocking him. Farid clutched the sheet of paper to his chest and ran on, over the road and toward the dark trees waiting on the other side. The hellhound was growling and barking behind him. Then it howled. Something snarled again, so fiercely that Farid ran even faster. Orpheus screamed, fear making his voice shrill and ugly. Basta swore, and then the snarl came again, wild as the snarling of the great cats that had lived in Farid's old world.

Don't look around, he thought. *Run, run!* he told his legs. *Let the cat eat the hellhound, let it eat them all, Basta and Cheeseface included, just keep running.* The dead leaves lying under the trees were damp and muffled the sound of his footsteps, but they were slippery, too, and made him lose his balance on the steep slope. Desperately, he caught hold of a tree trunk, pressed himself against it, knees trembling, and listened to the sounds of the night. Could Basta hear him gasping?

A sob escaped his throat. He pressed his hands to his mouth. The book, Basta had the book! He'd been supposed to look after it — and how was he ever going to find Dustfinger again now? Farid felt the sheet of paper that held Orpheus's words. He was still holding it tight. It was damp and dirty — and now it was his only hope.

"Hey, you little bastard! Bite me, would you?" Basta's voice reached him through the quiet night air. "You can run, but I'll get you yet, do you hear? You, the fire-eater, Silvertongue and his hoity-toity daughter — and the old man who wrote those accursed words! I'll kill you all! One by one! The way I've just slit open the beast that came out of the book."

Farid hardly dared to breathe. *Go on,* he told himself. *Go on! He can't see you!* Trembling, he felt for the next tree trunk, sought a handhold, and was grateful to the wind for blowing through the leaves and drowning out his footsteps with their rustling. *How many times do I have to tell you? There aren't any ghosts in this world. One of its few advantages.* He heard Dustfinger's voice as clearly as if he were still following the fire-eater. Farid kept repeating the words as the tears ran down his face and thorns gashed his feet: *There are no ghosts, there are no ghosts!*

A branch whipped against his face so hard that he almost cried out. Were they following him? He couldn't hear anything except the wind. He slipped again and stumbled down the slope. Nettles stung his legs, burrs caught in his hair. And something jumped up at him, furry and warm, pushing its nose into his face.

"Gwin?" Farid felt the little head. Yes, there were the tiny horns. He pressed his face into the marten's soft fur. "Basta's back, Gwin!" he whispered. "And he has the book! Suppose Orpheus reads him into it again? He's sure to go back into the book sometime, don't you think? How are we going to warn Dustfinger about him now?"

Farid twice found himself back at the road that wound down the mountain, but he dared not walk along it and instead made his way on through the prickly undergrowth. Soon every breath he drew hurt, but he did not stop. Only when the first rays of the sun made their way through the trees, and Basta still hadn't appeared behind him, did he know that he had gotten away.

Now what? he thought as he lay in the damp grass, gasping for breath. *Now what?* And suddenly he remembered another voice, the voice that had brought him into this world. Silvertongue. Of course. Only Silvertongue could help Farid now, he or his daughter, Meggie. They were living with the bookworm woman these days. Farid had once been there with Dustfinger. It was a long way to go, particularly with the cuts on his feet. But he had to get there before Basta did. . . .

DUSTFINGER COMES HOME

"What is this?" said the Leopard, "that is so 'sclusively dark,
and yet so full of little pieces of light?"
Rudyard Kipling, *Just So Stories*

For a moment Dustfinger felt as if he had never been away —
as if he had simply had a bad dream, and the memory of it
had left a stale taste on his tongue, a shadow on his heart, nothing
more. All of a sudden everything was back again: the sounds, so
familiar and never forgotten; the scents; the tree trunks dappled
in the morning light; the shadow of the leaves on his face. Some
were turning color, like the leaves in that other world, so autumn
must be coming here, too, but the air was still mild. It smelled of
overripe berries, fading blossoms, a thousand or more flowers
dazing his senses — flowers pale as wax glimmering under the
shade of the trees, blue stars on stems so thin and delicate that
he walked carefully so as not to tread on them. Oaks, planes, tulip
trees towering to the sky all around him! He had almost forgotten
how huge a tree could be, how broad and tall its trunk, with a leaf
canopy spreading so wide that a whole troop of horsemen could

16

shelter beneath it. The forests of the other world were so young, their trees still children. They had always made him feel old, so old that the years covered him like cobwebs. Here he was young again, just a child among the trees, not much older than the mushrooms growing among their roots, not much taller than the thistles and nettles.

But where was the boy?

Dustfinger looked around, searching for him, calling his name again and again. "Farid!" It was a name that had become almost as familiar to him as his own over these last few months. But there was no reply. Only his own voice echoing back from the trees.

So that was it. The boy had been left behind. What would he do now, all alone? *Well*, thought Dustfinger as he looked around in vain one last time, *what do you think? He'll manage better in that world than you ever did. The noise, the speed, the crowds of people, he likes all that. And you've taught him enough of your craft, he can play with fire almost as well as you. Yes, the boy will manage very well.* But for a moment the joy of his homecoming wilted in Dustfinger's heart like one of the flowers at his feet, and the morning light that had welcomed him only a moment ago now seemed wan and lifeless. The other world had cheated him again: Yes, it had let him go after all those years, but it had kept the only beings there to whom he had given his heart. . . .

Well, and what does that teach you? he thought, kneeling in the dewy grass. *Better keep your heart to yourself, Dustfinger.* He picked up a leaf that glowed red as fire on the dark moss. There hadn't been any leaves like that in the other world, had there? So what was the matter with him? Angry with himself, he straightened up again. *Listen, Dustfinger, you're back!* he told himself firmly. *Back! Forget the boy — yes, you've lost him, but you have your own world back instead, a whole world. You're back, can you finally believe it?*

If only it wasn't so difficult. It was far easier to believe in unhappiness than in happiness. He would have to touch every flower, feel every tree, crumble the earth in his fingers and feel the first gnat-bite on his skin before he really believed it.

But yes, he was back. He really was back. At last. And suddenly happiness went to his head like a glass of strong wine. Even the thought of Farid couldn't cloud it anymore. His ten-year nightmare was over. How light he felt, light as one of the leaves raining down from the trees like gold!

He was happy.

Remember, Dustfinger? This is what it feels like. Happiness.

Sure enough, Orpheus had read him to the very place he had described. There was the pool, shimmering among gray and white stones, surrounded by flowering oleander, and only a little way from the bank stood the plane tree where the fire-elves nested. Their nests seemed to cluster more densely around the trunk than he remembered. A less practiced eye might have taken them for bees' nests, but they were smaller and rather paler, almost as pale as the bark peeling from the tall trunk to which they clung.

Dustfinger looked around, once again breathing the air he had missed so much these last ten years. Scents he had almost forgotten mingled with those that could be found in the other world, too. And you could find trees like the ones around the pool there, too, although smaller and much younger. Branches of eucalyptus and alder reached out over the water as if to cool their leaves. Dustfinger cautiously made his way through the trees until he reached the bank. A tortoise made off at a leisurely pace when his shadow fell on its shell. The tongue of a toad, sitting on a stone, shot out and swallowed a fire-elf. Swarms of them were whirring about over the water, with their high-pitched buzzing that always sounded so angry.

It was time to raid their nests.

Dustfinger kneeled down on one of the damp stones. Something rustled behind him, and for a moment he caught himself looking for Farid's dark hair and Gwin's head with its little horns, but it was only a lizard pushing its way out of the leaves and crawling up onto one of the stones to bask in the autumn sunlight. "Idiot!" he muttered, leaning forward. "Forget the boy — and as for the marten, he won't miss you. Anyway, you had good reasons for leaving him behind. The best of reasons."

His reflection trembled on the dark water. His face was the same as ever. The scars were still there, of course, but at least he had suffered no further injuries, his nose hadn't been smashed in, he didn't have a stiff leg like Cockerell in the other story, everything was in the right place. He even still had his voice — so the man Orpheus obviously knew his trade.

Dustfinger bent lower over the water. Where were they? Had they forgotten him? The blue fairies forget every face, often just minutes after seeing it, but what about these others? Ten years is a long time, but did they count years?

The water moved, and his reflection mingled with other features. Toadlike eyes were looking up at him from an almost human face, with long hair drifting in the water like grass, and equally green and fine. Dustfinger took his hand out of the cool water, and another hand stretched up — a slender, delicate hand almost like a child's, covered with scales so tiny that you could scarcely see them. A damp finger, cool as the water from which it had risen, touched his face and traced the scars on it.

"Yes, it's not easy to forget my face, is it?" Dustfinger spoke so quietly that his voice was scarcely more than a whisper. Loud voices frighten water-nymphs. "So you remember the scars. And do you remember what I asked you and your sisters to do for me, when I was here before?"

The toadlike eyes looked at him, black and gold, and then the water-nymph sank and vanished as if she had been a mere illusion. But a few moments later, three of them appeared together in the dark water. Shoulders white as lily petals shimmered beneath the surface, fishtails with rainbow scales like the belly of a perch flicked, barely visible, in the water below. The tiny gnats dancing above the water stung Dustfinger's face and arms, as if they had been waiting just for him, but he hardly felt it. The nymphs hadn't forgotten him — neither his face nor what he needed from them to help him summon fire.

They reached their hands up out of the water. Tiny air bubbles rose to the surface, the sign of their laughter, as silent as everything else about them. They took his hands between their own, stroked his arms, his face, his bare throat, until his skin was almost as cool as theirs and covered with the same fine, slimy deposit that protected their scales. Then, as suddenly as they had come, they disappeared again. Their faces sank down into the dark pool, and Dustfinger might have thought, as always, that he had only dreamed them, but for the cool sensation on his skin, the shimmering of his hands and arms.

"Thank you!" he whispered, although only his own reflection now quivered on the water. Then he straightened up, made his way through the oleander bushes on the bank, and moved toward the fire-tree as silently as possible. If Farid had been here, he'd have been prancing through the wet grass like a foal in his excitement.

Cobwebs wet with dew clung to Dustfinger's clothes as he stood under the plane tree. The lowest nests hung so far down that he could easily reach into one of the entrance holes. The first elves came swarming angrily out when he put in the fingers that the water-nymphs had covered with moist slime, but he calmed them by humming quietly. If he could hit the right note, their agitated swirling soon turned to a tumbling flight, their own humming and buzzing becoming drowsy, until their tiny, hot bodies settled on his arms, burning his skin and leaving a tiny deposit of soot. However much it hurt he must not flinch, mustn't scare them away, must reach even farther into the nest until he found what he was looking for: their fiery honey. Bees stung, but fire-elves burned holes in your skin if the water-nymphs hadn't touched it first. And even with their protection, it was prudent not to be too greedy when you stole the elves' honey. If a robber took too much they would fly in his face, burn his skin and hair, and wouldn't let him go until he was writhing in pain at the foot of their tree.

But Dustfinger was never greedy enough to annoy them. He took only a tiny piece of honeycomb from the nest, scarcely larger than his thumbnail. That was all he needed for now. He went on humming quietly as he wrapped the honey in some leaves.

The fire-elves woke as soon as he stopped humming. They whirred around him faster and faster, while their voices rose to a sound like bumblebees buzzing angrily. However, they did not attack him. You had to ignore them, act as if you hadn't even seen them as you turned and walked away at your leisure, slowly, very slowly. They went on whirling in the air around Dustfinger for some time, but in the end they fell behind him, and he followed the small stream that flowed out of the water-nymphs' pool and wound slowly away through willows, reeds, and alders.

He knew where the stream would take him: out of the Wayless Wood, where you hardly ever met another soul of your own kind, and then on northward, to places where the forest belonged to human beings, and its timber fell to their axes so fast that most trees died before their canopies could offer shelter to so much as a single horseman. The stream would lead him through the valley as it slowly opened out, past hills where no man had ever set foot because they were full of giants and bears and creatures that had never been given a name. At some point the first charcoal-burners' huts would appear on the slopes, Dustfinger would see the first patch of bare earth among the dense green, and then he would be reunited not just with fairies and water-nymphs but, he hoped, with some of those human beings he had missed for so long.

He moved into cover when a sleepy wolf appeared between two trees in the distance and waited, motionless, until its gray muzzle had disappeared. Yes, bears and wolves — he must learn to listen for their steps again, to sense their presence nearby before they saw him — not forgetting the big wildcats, dappled like tree trunks in the sunlight, and the snakes as green as the foliage where they liked to hide. They would let themselves down from the branches with less sound than his hand would make brushing a leaf off his shoulder. Luckily, the giants generally stayed in their hills, where not even he dared go. Only in winter did they sometimes come down. But there were other creatures, too, beings less gentle than the water-nymphs, and they couldn't be lulled by humming as the fire-elves could. They were usually invisible, well hidden among timber and green leaves, but they were no less dangerous for that: Tree-Men, Trows, Black Bogles, Night-Mares . . . some of them even ventured as far as the charcoal-burners' huts.

"Take a little more care!" Dustfinger whispered to himself. "You don't want your first day home to be your last." The sheer intoxication of being back gradually died down, allowing him to think more clearly again. But the happiness remained in his heart, soft and warm like a young bird's downy plumage.

He took off his clothes beside a stream and washed the water-nymphs' slimy deposit off his body, together with the fire-elves' soot and the grime of the other world. Then he put on the clothes he hadn't worn for ten years. He had looked after them carefully, but there were a few moth holes in the black fabric all the same, and the sleeves had already been threadbare when he first took them off in that other world. These garments were all red and black, the colors worn by fire-eaters, just as tightrope-walkers clothed themselves in the blue of the sky. He stroked the rough material, put on the full-sleeved doublet, and threw the dark cloak over his shoulders. Luckily, everything still fitted; getting new clothes made was an expensive business, even if you just took your old clothes to the tailor to be patched up again, as the strolling players usually did.

When twilight fell he looked around for a safe place to sleep. Finally, he climbed up onto a fallen oak with its root-ball towering so high into the air that it offered good shelter for the night. The root-ball was like a great rampart of earth, yet some of the roots still clung to the ground as if unwilling to let go of life. The crown of the fallen tree had put out new shoots, although they now pointed to the ground and not the sky. Dustfinger nimbly clambered along the mighty trunk, digging his fingers into its rough bark.

When he reached the roots, which were now thrusting up into the air as if they could find nourishment there, a few fairies flew up, chattering crossly. They had obviously been looking for building materials for their nests. Of course: It would soon be autumn, time for a more weatherproof sleeping place. The blue fairies took no particular trouble over the nests they built in spring, but as soon as the first leaf turned color they began improving them, padding them with animal fur and birds' feathers, weaving more grass and twigs into the walls, sealing cracks with moss and fairy spit.

Two of the tiny blue creatures didn't fly away when they saw him. They stared avidly at his sandy hair as the evening light, falling through the treetops, tinged their wings with red.

"Ah, of course!" Dustfinger laughed softly. "You want some of my hair for your nests." He cut off a lock with his knife. One of the delighted fairies seized the hair in her delicate, insectlike hands and fluttered quickly away with it. The other fairy, so tiny that she could only just have hatched from her mother-of-pearl egg, followed her. He had missed those bold little blue creatures, he'd missed them so much.

Down below among the trees, night was falling, but in the light of the setting sun the treetops overhead were turning red as sorrel in a summer meadow. Soon the fairies would be asleep in their nests, the mice and rabbits in their holes and burrows. The cool of the night would make the lizards' legs stiff, the birds would fall silent, predators would prepare to go hunting, their eyes like yellow lights in the darkness. *Let's hope they don't fancy a fire-eater for dinner,* thought Dustfinger, stretching his legs out on the fallen trunk. He thrust his knife into the cracked bark beside him, wrapped himself in the cloak he hadn't worn for ten years, and stared up at the leaves. They were growing darker and darker now. An owl rose from an oak and swooped away, little more than a shadow among the branches. A tree whispered in its sleep, words that no human ear could understand.

Dustfinger closed his eyes and listened.

He was home again.

SILVERTONGUE'S DAUGHTER

Was there only one world after all, which spent its time
dreaming of others?

Philip Pullman, *The Subtle Knife*

Meggie hated quarreling with Mo. It left her shaking inside,
and nothing could comfort her — not a hug from her
mother, not the licorice candies Resa's aunt Elinor gave her if
their loud voices had carried to the library, not Darius, who
firmly believed in the miraculous healing powers of hot milk and
honey in such cases.

Nothing helped.

This time it had been particularly bad, because Mo had really
only come to see her to say good-bye. He had a new job waiting,
some sick books too old and valuable to be sent to him. In the
past Meggie would have gone with him, but this time she had
decided to stay with Elinor and her mother.

Why did he have to come to her room just when she was reading the notebooks again? They'd often quarreled over those

26

notebooks recently, although Mo hated a quarrel as much as she did. Afterward, he usually disappeared into the workshop that Elinor had had built behind the house for him, and a time would come, once Meggie couldn't bear to be angry with him anymore, when she would follow him there. He never raised his head when she slipped through the doorway, and without a word Meggie would sit down beside him on the chair that was always ready for her and watch him at work, just as she had done even before she could read. She loved watching his hands free a book from its shabby dress, separate stained pages from each other, part the threads holding together a damaged quire, or soak rag paper to mend a sheet of paper worn thin. It was never long before Mo turned and asked her a question of some kind: Did she like the color he'd chosen for a linen binding, did she agree that the paper pulp he'd mixed for repairs had turned out slightly too dark? It was Mo's way of apologizing, of saying: Don't let's quarrel, Meggie; let's forget what we said just now.

But that was no good today. Because he hadn't disappeared into his workshop, he'd gone away to see some book collector or other and give the collector's printed treasures a new lease on life. This time he wouldn't come to her with a present to make up for the quarrel — a book he'd found in a secondhand bookshop somewhere, or a bookmark decorated with blue jay feathers found in Elinor's garden. . . .

So why couldn't she have been reading some other book when he came into her room?

"Good heavens, Meggie, you seem to have nothing in your head but those notebooks!" he had said angrily. It had been the same every time, these last few months, whenever he had found her like that in her room — lying on the rug, deaf and blind to all that went on around her, eyes glued to the words with which she had written down what Resa told her — tales of what she had seen "there," as Mo bitterly called it.

There.

Inkworld was the name Meggie gave to the place of which Mo spoke so slightingly and her mother sometimes with such longing. Inkworld, after the book about it, *Inkheart*. The book was gone, but her mother's memories were as vivid as if not a day had passed since she was there — in that world of paper and printer's ink where there were fairies and princes, water-nymphs, fire-elves, and trees that seemed to grow to the sky.

Meggie had sat with her mother for countless days and nights, writing down what Resa's fingers told her. Resa had left her voice behind in the Inkworld, so she talked to her daughter either with pencil and paper or with her hands, telling the story of those years — those terrible magical years, she called them. Sometimes she also drew what her eyes had seen but her tongue could no longer describe: fairies, birds, strange flowers, conjured up on paper with just a few strokes, yet looking so real that Meggie almost believed she had seen them, too.

At first Mo himself had bound the notebooks in which Meggie wrote down Resa's memories — and each binding was more beautiful than the last — but a time came when Meggie noticed the anxiety in his eyes as he watched her reading them, completely absorbed in the words and pictures. Of course she understood his uneasiness; after all, for years he had lost his wife to this world made of words and paper. How could he like it if his daughter thought of little else? Oh yes, Meggie understood Mo very well, yet she couldn't do as he asked — close the books and forget the Inkworld for a while.

Perhaps her longing for it wouldn't have been quite as strong if the fairies and brownies had still been around, all those strange creatures they had brought back from Capricorn's accursed village. But none of them lived in Elinor's garden now. The fairies' empty nests still clung to the trees, and the burrows that the brownies had dug were still there, but their inhabitants were gone. At first Elinor thought they had run away or been stolen, but then the ashes had been found. They covered the grass in the garden, fine as dust, gray ashes, as gray as the shadows from which Elinor's strange guests had once appeared. And Meggie had realized that there was no return from death, even for creatures made of nothing but words.

Elinor, however, could not reconcile herself to this idea. Defiantly, desperately, she had driven back to Capricorn's village — only to find the streets empty, the houses burned down, and not a living soul in sight. "You know, Elinor," Mo had said when she came back with her face tearstained, "I was afraid of something like this. I couldn't really believe there were words to bring back the dead. And besides — if you're honest with yourself — you must admit they didn't fit into this world."

"Nor do I!" was all Elinor had replied.

Over the next few weeks, Meggie often heard sobbing from Elinor's room when she slipped into the library one last time in the evening to find a book. Many months had passed since then — they had all been living together in Elinor's big house for nearly a year, and Meggie had a feeling that Elinor was glad not to be alone with her books anymore. She had given them the best rooms; Elinor's old schoolbooks and a few writers she no longer much liked had been banished to the attic to make more space. Meggie's room had a view of snow-topped mountains, and from her parents' bedroom you could see the distant lake with its gleaming water, which had so often tempted the fairies to fly in that direction.

Mo had never simply gone off like that before. Without a word of good-bye. Without making up the quarrel . . .

Perhaps I should go down and help Darius in the library, thought Meggie as she sat there wiping the tears from her face. She never cried while she was quarreling with Mo; the tears didn't come until later . . . and he always looked terribly guilty when he saw her red eyes. She was sure that yet again everyone had heard them quarreling! Darius was probably making the hot milk and honey already, and as soon as she put her head around the kitchen door Elinor would begin calling Mo, and men in general, names. No, she'd better stay in her own room.

Oh, Mo. He had snatched the notebook she was reading out of her hand and taken it with him! And that one was the book where she had collected ideas for stories of her own: beginnings that had never gotten any further, opening words, crossed-out sentences, all her failed attempts . . . How could he just take it away from her? She didn't want Mo to read it; she didn't want him seeing how she tried in vain to fit the words together on paper, words that came to her tongue so easily and with such power when she read aloud. Meggie could write down what Resa described to her; she could fill pages and pages with the stories her mother told her. But as soon as she tried to make something new of them, a story with a life of its own, her mind went blank. The words seemed to fly out of her head — like snowflakes leaving only a damp patch on your skin when you put out your hand to catch them.

Someone knocked on Meggie's door.

"Come in!" she snuffled, looking in her trouser pockets for one of the old-fashioned handkerchiefs that Elinor had given her. ("They belonged to my sister. Her name began with an M, like yours. Embroidered in the corner there, see? I thought it would be better for you to have them than let the moths eat holes in them.")

Her mother put her head around the door.

Meggie tried a smile, but it was a miserable failure.

"Can I come in?" Resa's fingers traced the words in the air faster than Darius could have said them aloud. Meggie nodded. By now she understood her mother's sign language almost as easily as the letters of the alphabet — she knew it better than Mo and much better than Elinor, who often called for Meggie in desperation when Resa's fingers went too fast for her.

Resa closed the door behind her and sat down on the window-sill with her daughter. Meggie always called her mother by her first name, perhaps because she hadn't had a mother for ten years, or perhaps because, for the same inexplicable reason, she had always called her father just Mo.

Meggie recognized the notebook as soon as Resa put it on her lap. It was the one that Mo had taken. "I found it lying outside your door," said her mother's hands.

Meggie stroked the patterned binding. So Mo had brought it back. Why hadn't he come in? Because he was still too angry, or because he was sorry?

"He wants me to put them away in the attic. At least for a while." Meggie suddenly felt so small. And at the same time so old. "He said, 'Perhaps I ought to turn into a glass man or dye my skin blue, since my wife and daughter obviously think more of fairies and glass men than of me.'"

Resa smiled and stroked Meggie's nose with her forefinger.

"Yes, I know, of course he doesn't really think that! But he always gets so angry when he sees me with the notebooks. . . ."

Resa looked out through the open window. Elinor's garden was so large that you couldn't see where it began or ended, you just saw tall trees and rhododendron shrubs so old that they surrounded Elinor's house like an evergreen wood. Right under Meggie's window was a lawn with a narrow gravel path around it. A garden seat stood to one side of the lawn. Meggie still remembered the night when she had sat there watching Dustfinger breathe fire. Elinor's ever-grumpy gardener had swept the dead leaves off the lawn only that afternoon. You could still see the bare patch in the middle where Capricorn's men had burned Elinor's best books. The gardener kept trying to persuade Elinor to plant something in that space, or sow more grass seed there, but Elinor just shook her head energetically. "Who grows grass on a grave?" she had snapped the last time he suggested it, and she told him to leave the yarrow alone, too. It had grown luxuriantly around the sides of the blackened patch ever since the fire, as if to make its flat flower heads a reminder of the night when Elinor's printed children were swallowed up by the flames.

The sun was setting behind the nearby mountains, so red that it was as if it, too, wanted to remind them of that long-extinguished fire, and a cool wind blew from the hills, making Resa shiver.

Meggie closed the window. The wind blew a few faded rose petals against the pane; they stuck to the glass, pale yellow and translucent. "I don't want to quarrel with him," she whispered. "I never used to quarrel with Mo. Well, almost never . . ."

"Perhaps he's right." Her mother pushed back her hair. It was just as long as Meggie's, but darker, as if a shadow had fallen on it. Resa usually held it back with combs. Meggie often wore her hair like that, too, and sometimes when she looked at her reflection in the mirror of her wardrobe she seemed to be seeing not herself but a younger version of her mother. "Another year and she'll be towering over you," Mo sometimes said when he wanted to tease Resa, and the shortsighted Darius had confused Meggie with her mother several times already.

Resa ran her forefinger over the windowpane as if tracing the rose petals that clung to it. Then her hands began speaking again, hesitantly, just as lips can sometimes hesitate. "I do understand your father, Meggie," she said. "Sometimes I myself think the two of us talk about that other world too often. Even I don't understand why I keep coming back to the subject. And I'm always telling you about what was beautiful there, not the other things: being shut up, Mortola's punishments, how my hands and knees hurt so much from all the work that I couldn't sleep . . . all the cruelty I saw there. Did I tell you about the maid who died of fright because a Night-Mare stole into our bedroom?"

"Yes, you did." Meggie moved very close to her mother, but Resa's hands fell silent. They were still roughened from all her years of toil as a maid, working first for Mortola and then for Capricorn. "You've told me about everything," said Meggie. "The bad things, too, even if Mo won't believe it!"

"Because all the same he feels that we dream only of the wonderful part. As if I ever had much of that!" Resa shook her head. Again her fingers fell silent for a long time before she let them go on. "I had to steal it for myself, in seconds, minutes . . . sometimes a precious hour when we were allowed out in the forest to gather the plants Mortola needed for her black potions."

"But there were the years when you were free, too! When you disguised yourself and worked in the markets as a scribe." Disguised as a man . . . Meggie had pictured it over and over again: her mother with her hair cut short, wearing a scribe's tunic, ink on her fingers from the finest handwriting to be found in the Inkworld. So Resa had told her. It was the way she had earned a living in a world that didn't make it easy for women to work. Meggie would have liked to hear the story again now, even if it had a sad ending, for after that Resa's years of unhappiness had begun. But wonderful things had happened during that time, too, like the great banquet at the Laughing Prince's castle to which Mortola had taken her maids, the banquet where Resa saw the Laughing Prince himself, and the Black Prince and his bear, the tightrope-walker called Cloud-Dancer. . . .

But Resa hadn't come into her room to tell all those stories again. She said nothing in reply. And when her fingers did begin to speak once more, they moved more slowly than usual. "Forget the Inkworld, Meggie," they said. "Let's both of us forget it, at least for a little while. For your father's sake — and for yours. Or one day you may be blind to the beauty around you here." She looked out of the window again at the gathering dusk. "I've told you all about it already," said her hands. "Everything you wanted to know."

So she had. And Meggie had asked her many questions, thousands and thousands of them. *Did you ever see one of the giants? What sort of clothes did you wear? What did the fortress look like, in the forest where Mortola took you, and that prince you talk about, the Laughing Prince — was his castle as huge and magnificent as the Castle of Night? Tell me about his son, Cosimo the Fair, and the Adderhead and his men-at-arms. Was everything in his castle really made of silver? How big is the bear that the Black Prince always keeps beside him, and what about the trees, can they really talk? And that old woman, the one they all call Nettle, is it true that she can fly?*

Resa had answered all these questions as well as she could, but even a thousand answers did not add up to a whole ten years, and there were some questions that Meggie had never put to her.

She had never asked about Dustfinger, for instance. But Resa had talked about him all the same, telling her that everyone in the Inkworld knew his name, even many years after he had disappeared. Of course, he was known as the fire-dancer, too, so Resa had recognized him at once when she met him for the first time in this world. . . .

There was another question that Meggie didn't ask — although it often came into her mind — for Resa couldn't have answered it: What about Fenoglio, the writer of the book that had drawn first her mother and finally even its own author into its pages? How was Fenoglio now?

More than a year had passed since Meggie's voice had cast the spell of Fenoglio's own words over him — and he had disappeared as if they had swallowed him up. Sometimes Meggie saw his wrinkled face in her dreams, but she never knew if it looked sad or happy. Not that it had ever been easy to read the expression on Fenoglio's tortoiselike face, anyway. One night, when she woke suddenly from one of these dreams and couldn't get to sleep again, she had begun a story in which Fenoglio was trying to write himself home again, back to his grandchildren and the village where Meggie had first met him. But as with all the other stories she'd started to write, she never got past the first three sentences.

Meggie leafed through the notebook that Mo had taken away from her, then closed it again. Resa put a hand under her chin and looked into her face.

"Don't be cross with him!"

"I never am, not for long! He knows that. How much longer will he be away?"

"Ten days, maybe more."

Ten days! Meggie looked at the shelf beside her bed. There

they were, neatly arranged side by side: the Bad Books, as she secretly called them, full of Resa's stories: tales of glass men and water-nymphs, fire-elves, Night-Mares, White Women, and all the other strange creatures that her mother had described.

"All right. I'll phone him and say he can make them a box. But I'll keep the key to it."

Resa dropped a kiss on her forehead. Then she carefully passed her hand over the notebook in Meggie's lap. "Does anyone in the world bind books more beautifully than your father?" her fingers asked.

Meggie shook her head with a smile. "No," she whispered. "No one, in this world or any other."

When Resa went downstairs again to help Darius and Elinor with supper, Meggie stayed by the window to watch Elinor's garden filling with shadows. When a squirrel scurried over the lawn, its bushy tail stretched out behind it, she was reminded of Dustfinger's tame marten, Gwin. How strange that she now understood the yearning she had so often seen on his master's scarred face.

Yes, Mo was probably right. She thought about Dustfinger's world too much, far too much. She had even read some of Resa's stories aloud a few times, although didn't she know how dangerous her voice could be when it spoke the words on the page? Hadn't she — to be perfectly honest, more honest than people usually are — hadn't she cherished a secret hope that the words would take her to that world? What would Mo have done if he'd known about these experiments? Would he have buried the notebooks in the garden or thrown them into the lake, as he sometimes threatened to do with the stray cats that stole into his workshop?

Yes, I'll lock them away, thought Meggie, as the first stars appeared outside. *As soon as Mo has made them a new box.* The box with her favorite books in it was crammed full now. It was red, red as poppies; Mo had only recently repainted it. The box for the notebooks must be a different color, perhaps green like the Wayless Wood that Resa had described so often. Yes, green. And didn't the guards outside the Laughing Prince's castle wear green cloaks, too?

A moth fluttered against the window, reminding Meggie of the blue-skinned fairies and the best of all the stories that Resa had told her about them: how they healed Dustfinger's face after Basta had slashed it, in gratitude to him for the many times he had freed their sisters from the wire cages where peddlers imprisoned them to be sold at market as good-luck charms. And deep in the Wayless Wood he . . . no, that's enough!

Meggie leaned her forehead against the cool pane.

Quite enough.

I'll take them all to Mo's workshop, she thought. *At once. And when he's back I'll ask him to bind me a new notebook for stories about this world of ours.* She had already begun writing some: about Elinor's garden and her library, about the castle down by the lake. Robbers had once lived there; Elinor had told her about them in her own typical storytelling style, with so many grisly details that Darius, listening, forgot to go on sorting books, and his eyes widened in horror behind his thick glasses.

"Meggie, suppertime!"

Elinor's call echoed right to the top of the stairs. She had a very powerful voice. Louder than the *Titanic*'s foghorn, Mo always said.

Meggie slipped off the windowsill.

"Coming!" she called down the corridor. Then she went back into her room, took the notebooks off the shelf one by one until her arms could hardly hold the stack, and carried the precarious pile down the corridor and into the room that Mo used as an office. It had once been Meggie's bedroom; she had slept there when she first came to Elinor's house with Mo and Dustfinger, but all you could see from its window was the gravel forecourt, some spruce trees, a large chestnut, and Elinor's gray station wagon, which stood outdoors in all weather, because it was Elinor's opinion that cars living in luxury in a garage rusted more quickly. But when they had decided to come and live there, Meggie had wanted a window with a view of the garden. So Mo, surrounded by Elinor's collection of old travel guides, did his paperwork in the room where Meggie had slept before she ever went to Capricorn's village, when she still had no mother and almost never quarreled with Mo. . . .

"Meggie, where are you?" Elinor's voice sounded impatient. Her joints often ached these days, but she refused to go to the doctor. ("What's the point?" was her only comment. "They haven't invented a pill to cure old age, have they?")

"I'll be down in a minute!" called Meggie, carefully lowering the notebooks onto Mo's desk. Two of them slipped off the pile and almost knocked over the vase of autumn flowers that her mother had put by the window. Meggie caught it just before the water spilled over Mo's invoices and receipts for gasoline. She was standing there with the vase still in her hand, her fingers sticky with drifting pollen, when she saw the figure between the trees where the path came up from the road. Her heart began to thud so hard that the vase almost slipped out of her fingers again.

Well, that just went to prove it. Mo was right. "Meggie, take your head out of those books, or soon you won't know the difference between reality and your imagination!" He'd told her that so often, and now it was happening. She'd been thinking about

Dustfinger only a moment ago, hadn't she? And now she saw someone standing out there in the night, just like the time, more than a year ago, when she'd seen Dustfinger waiting outside their house, motionless as the figure she saw there at this moment. . . .

"Meggie, for heaven's sake, how many more times do I have to call you?" Elinor was wheezing from climbing all the stairs. "What are you doing, standing there rooted to the spot? Didn't you say — good heavens, who's that?"

"You can see him, too?" Meggie was so relieved she could have hugged Elinor.

"Of course I can."

The figure moved. Barefoot, it ran over the pale gravel.

"It's that boy!" Elinor sounded incredulous. "The one who helped the matchstick-eater steal the book from your father. Well, he's got nerve, turning up here. He looks somewhat worse for wear. Does he think I'm going to let him in? I daresay the matchstick-eater's out there, too."

Elinor came closer to the window, looking anxious, but Meggie was already out the door. She ran downstairs and raced through the entrance hall. Her mother came along the corridor leading to the kitchen.

"Resa!" Meggie called. "Farid's here. It's Farid!"

5

FARID

He was stubborn as a mule, clever as a monkey, and nimble as a hare.

Louis Pergaud, *The War of the Buttons*

Resa took Farid into the kitchen and tended his feet first. They looked terrible, cut and bleeding. While Resa cleaned them and put bandages over the cuts, Farid began telling his story, his tongue heavy with weariness. Meggie did her best not to stare at him too often. He was still rather taller than she was, even though she'd grown a great deal since they last met . . . on the night when he had gone off with Dustfinger. Dustfinger and the book. She hadn't forgotten his face, any more than she could forget the day when Mo first read him out of his own story in *Tales from the Thousand and One Nights*. She'd never met another boy with such beautiful eyes, almost like a girl's. They were as black as his hair, which was cut a little shorter than it had been in the old days and made him look more grown-up. Farid. Meggie felt her tongue relishing his name — and quickly turned her eyes away when he raised his head and looked at her.

Elinor stared at him all the time without any embarrassment and with as much hostility as she had shown in scrutinizing Dustfinger when he had sat at her kitchen table, feeding his marten bread and ham. She hadn't let Farid bring the marten into the house with him. "And if he eats a single songbird in my garden he'd better watch out!" she said as the marten scurried away over the pale gravel. She had bolted the door after him, as if Gwin could open locked doors as easily as his master.

Farid played with a book of matches as he told his tale.

"Look at that!" Elinor whispered to Meggie. "Just like the matchstick-eater. Don't you think he looks a lot like him?"

But Meggie did not reply. She didn't want to miss a word of the story Farid had to tell. She wanted to hear everything about Dustfinger's return, about the man with the hellhound who read aloud so well, about the snarling creature that could have been one of the big cats from the Wayless Wood — and about the words that Basta had shouted after Farid: *"You can run, but I'll get you yet, do you hear? You, the fire-eater, Silvertongue and his hoity-toity daughter — and the old man who wrote those accursed words! I'll kill you all! One by one!"*

While Farid told his story, Resa's eyes kept straying to the grubby piece of paper he had put down on the kitchen table. She looked at it as if she were afraid of it, as if the words on that paper could draw her back again. Back to the Inkworld. When Farid repeated the threat Basta had shouted, she put her arms around Meggie and held her close. But Darius, who had been sitting next to Elinor in silence all this time, buried his face in his hands.

Farid didn't waste much time describing how he had gotten to Elinor's house on his bare, bloody feet. In answer to Meggie's questions, he just muttered something about getting a lift from a truck driver. He ended his account abruptly, as if he had suddenly run out of words, and when he fell silent it was very quiet in the big kitchen.

Farid had brought an invisible guest with him. Fear.

"Put more coffee on, Darius!" said Elinor as she looked gloomily at the table laid for supper. No one was taking any notice of it. "This could be iced tea, it's so cold."

Darius set to work at once, busy and eager, like a bespectacled squirrel, while Elinor gave Farid a glance as cold as if he were personally responsible for the bad news he had brought. Meggie still remembered just how alarming she had once found that look. "The woman with pebble eyes," she had secretly called Elinor. Sometimes the name still fitted.

"What a terrific story!" exclaimed Elinor as Resa went to give Darius a hand; Farid's news had obviously made him so nervous that he couldn't measure out the right amount of ground coffee. He had just begun counting the spoonfuls he was tipping into the filter for the third time when Resa gently took the measuring spoon from his hand.

"So Basta's back with a brand-new knife and a mouth full of peppermint leaves, I suspect. Bloody hell!" Elinor was apt to swear when she was anxious or annoyed. "As if it wasn't bad enough waking up every third night drenched in sweat because I've seen his foxy face in my dreams . . . not to mention his knife. But let's try to keep calm! Look at it like this: Basta knows where *I* live, but obviously it's Mo and Meggie he's after, not me, so this house ought really to be safe as — well, safe as houses, for you. After all, he's not likely to know you've moved in here, is he?" She looked at Resa and Meggie triumphantly, as if this were a conclusive argument.

But Meggie's response made Elinor's face darken again at once. "Farid knew," she pointed out.

"So he did," growled Elinor, her glance turning to Farid again. "You knew, too. How?"

Her voice was so sharp that Farid instinctively flinched. "An old woman told us," he said in a wavering voice. "We went back to Capricorn's village after the fairies Dustfinger took with him turned to ashes. He wanted to see if the same thing had happened to the others. The whole village was deserted, not a soul in sight, not even a stray dog. Only ashes, ashes everywhere. So we went to the next village and tried to find out just what had happened, and . . . well, that was when we heard how a fat woman had been there, saying something about dead fairies, but at least, she said, luckily the human beings hadn't died on her, too, and they were living with her now. . . ."

Elinor lowered her gaze guiltily and collected a few crumbs from her plate with one finger. "Damn it," she muttered. "Yes. Perhaps I did say rather too much in that shop when I phoned you from there. I was in such a state after seeing the empty village! How could I guess those gossips would tell Dustfinger about me? Dustfinger, of all people! Since when do old women talk to someone like him?"

Or to someone like Basta, thought Meggie.

But Farid just shrugged his shoulders, rose to his feet, which were now covered with bandages, and began limping up and down Elinor's kitchen. "Dustfinger thought you'd all be here in any case," he said. "We even passed this way once because he wanted to see if *she* was all right."

He jerked his head Resa's way. Elinor snorted scornfully. "Oh, did he, indeed? How good of him." She had never liked Dustfinger, and the fact that he had stolen the book from Mo before disappearing had done little to lessen her dislike. Resa, however, smiled at Farid's words, though she tried to hide her smile from Elinor. Meggie still clearly remembered the morning when Darius had brought her mother the strange little bundle he'd found outside the front door — a candle, a few pencils, and a box of matches, all tied up with stems of blue speedwell. Meggie had known at once who the bundle came from. And so did Resa.

"Well," said Elinor, drumming on her plate with the handle of her knife, "I'm delighted to hear that the matchstick-eater's back where he belongs. The very idea of him slinking around my house by night! It's just a pity he didn't take Basta, too."

Basta! When Elinor said his name Resa suddenly rose from her chair, went out into the corridor, and came back with the telephone. She held it out to Meggie with a look of entreaty in her eyes and began gesticulating so excitedly with her other hand that even Meggie had difficulty in reading the signs she traced in the air. But finally she understood.

Resa wanted her to call Mo. Of course.

It seemed forever before he came to the phone. He'd probably been working. When Mo was away he always worked late into the night, so that he could get home sooner.

"Meggie?" He sounded surprised. Perhaps he thought she was calling because of their quarrel, but who'd be interested in that stupid argument now?

It was some time before he could make anything of the words she was hastily stammering out. "Slowly, Meggie!" he kept saying. "Take it slowly." But that was easier said than done when your heart was in your mouth, and Basta might be waiting at Elinor's garden gate this very minute . . . Meggie didn't even dare to think this idea through to its logical conclusion.

Mo, on the other hand, remained strangely calm — almost as if he had expected the past to catch up with them again. "Stories never really end, Meggie," he had once told her, "even if the books like to pretend they do. Stories always go on. They don't end on the last page, any more than they begin on the first page."

"Has Elinor switched on the burglar alarm?" he asked now.

"Yes."

"Has she told the police?"

"No. She says they wouldn't believe her, anyway."

"She ought to call them, all the same. And give them a description of Basta. You can describe him between you, right?"

What a question! Meggie had tried to forget Basta's face, but it would live on in her memory for the rest of her life, as clear as a photograph.

"Listen, Meggie." Perhaps Mo wasn't quite as calm as he pretended. His voice didn't sound the same as usual. "I'll drive back tonight. Tell Elinor and your mother. I'll be with you by tomorrow morning at the latest. Bolt everything and keep the windows closed, understand?"

Meggie nodded, forgetting that Mo couldn't see her over the phone.

"Meggie?"

"Yes, I understand." She tried to sound calm and brave, even if she didn't feel that way. She was scared, badly scared.

"See you tomorrow, Meggie!"

She could tell from his voice that he was going to set out right away. And suddenly, seeing the moonlit road in her mind's eye, the long road back, a new and terrible thought came into her mind. . . .

"What about *you?*" she exclaimed. "Mo! Suppose Basta's lying in wait for *you* somewhere?" But her father had already hung up.

Elinor decided to put Farid where Dustfinger had once slept: in the attic room, where crates of books were stacked high around the narrow bedstead. Anyone who slept there would surely dream of being struck dead by printed paper. Meggie was told to show Farid the way, and when she wished him good night he just nodded abstractedly. He looked very lost sitting on the narrow bed — almost as lost as on the day when Mo had read him into Capricorn's church, a thin, nameless boy with a turban over his black hair.

That night, before she went to sleep, Elinor checked the burglar alarm several times to make sure it really was switched on. As for Darius, he went to find the rifle that Elinor sometimes fired into the air if she saw a cat prowling under one of the birds' nests in her garden. Wearing the orange bathrobe that Elinor had given him last Christmas — it was much too big for him — he settled down in the armchair in the entrance hall, the rifle on his lap, staring at the front door with a determined expression. But when Elinor came to check the alarm for the second time he was already fast asleep.

It was a long time before Meggie could sleep. She looked at the shelves where her notebooks used to stand, stroked the empty wood, and finally kneeled down by the red-painted box that Mo had made long ago for her favorite books. She hadn't opened it for months. There wasn't room in it for a single extra book, and by now it was too heavy for her to take it when she went away. So Elinor had given her the bookcase to hold more of the books she loved. It stood beside Meggie's bed, and it had glass doors, and carvings that twined over the dark wood, making it look as if it hadn't forgotten that it was once alive. And the shelves behind the glass doors were well filled, for by now Resa and Elinor, as well as Mo, gave Meggie books, and even Darius brought her a new one now and then. But her old friends, the books Meggie had already owned before they had moved in with Elinor, still lived in the box, and when she opened the heavy lid it was almost as if half-forgotten voices met her ears and familiar faces were looking at her. How well worn they all were. . . . "Isn't it odd how much fatter a book gets when you've read it several times?" Mo had said when, on Meggie's last birthday, they were looking at all her dear old books again. "As if something were left between the pages every time you read it. Feelings, thoughts, sounds, smells . . . and then, when you look at the book again many years later, you find yourself there, too, a slightly younger self, slightly different, as if the book had preserved you like a pressed flower . . . both strange and familiar."

Slightly younger, yes. Meggie picked up one of the books lying on top and leafed through it. She had read it at least a dozen times. Ah, here was the scene she had liked best when she was eight, and there was the one she had marked with a red pencil when she was ten because she thought it was so beautiful. She ran her finger down the wobbly line. There'd been no Resa in her life then, no Elinor, no Darius, only Mo . . . no longing to see blue fairies, no memories of a scarred face, a marten with little horns, and a boy who always went barefoot, no memory of Basta and his knife. A different Meggie had read that book, very different . . . and there she would stay between its pages, preserved as a memento.

With a sigh, Meggie closed the book again and put it back with the others. She could hear her mother pacing up and down next door. Did she, like Meggie, keep thinking of the threat that Basta had shouted after Farid? *I ought to go to her,* thought Meggie. *Perhaps our fear won't be so bad if we're together.* But just as she was getting up Resa's footsteps died away, and it was quiet in the room next door, quiet as sleep. Maybe sleep wasn't a bad idea. Mo certainly wouldn't arrive any sooner just because she was awake and waiting for him. . . . Oh, if only she could at least have called him, but he was always forgetting to switch his cell phone on.

Meggie closed the lid of her book box softly, as if the sound might wake Resa again, and blew out the candles that she lit every evening although Elinor was always telling her not to. As she was taking her T-shirt off over her head, she heard a knock at her door, a very quiet knock. She opened the door, expecting to see her mother outside because she couldn't sleep after all, but it was Farid. He went scarlet in the face when he saw that she was wearing only her underclothes. He stammered an apology and before Meggie could say anything limped away again on his lavishly bandaged feet. She almost forgot to put the T-shirt back on before going after him.

"What's the matter?" she whispered anxiously as she beckoned him back into her room. "Did you hear anything downstairs?"

But Farid shook his head. He was holding the piece of paper in his hand: Dustfinger's return ticket, as Elinor had tartly described it. Hesitantly, he followed Meggie into her room, and looked around it like someone who doesn't feel comfortable in enclosed spaces. Ever since he had disappeared with Dustfinger, leaving no trace behind, he had probably spent most of his days and nights in the open air.

"I'm sorry," Farid stammered, staring at his toes. Two of Resa's bandages were already peeling off. "I know it's late, but —" And for the first time he looked Meggie in the eye, turning red again as he did so. "But Orpheus says he didn't read it all," he went on, his voice hesitating. "He just left out the words that would have taken me into the book, too. He did it on purpose, but I have to warn Dustfinger, so . . ."

"So, what?" Meggie pushed the chair from her desk over to him and sat down on the windowsill herself. Farid sat down as hesitantly as he had entered her room.

"You must get me there, too. Please!" He held the dirty piece of paper out to her again, with such a pleading expression in his black eyes that Meggie didn't know where to look. How long and thick his eyelashes were! Hers were nowhere near as beautiful.

"Please! I know you can do it!" he stammered. "I remember that night in Capricorn's village . . . I remember all about it, and you had only a single sheet of paper then!"

That night in Capricorn's village. Meggie's heart always began to thud when she thought of it: the night when she had read the Shadow into appearing, and then hadn't been able to make him kill Capricorn until Mo did it for her.

"Orpheus wrote the words, he said so himself! He just didn't read them aloud — but they're here on this paper! Of course my actual name isn't there or it wouldn't work." Farid was speaking faster and faster. "Orpheus says that's the secret of it: If you want to change the story you must only use words that are already in the book, if possible."

"He said that?" Meggie's heart missed a beat, as if it had stumbled over Farid's information. *You must only use words that are already in the book, if possible* . . . Was that why she'd never been able to read anything out of Resa's stories — because she'd used words that weren't in *Inkheart*? Or was it just because she didn't know enough about writing?

"Yes. Orpheus thinks he's so clever because of the way he can read aloud." Farid spat out the man's name like a plum pit. "But if you ask me, he's not half as good at it as you or your father."

Maybe not, thought Meggie, *but he read Dustfinger back. And he wrote the words for it himself. Neither Mo nor I could have done*

49

that. She took from Farid the piece of paper with the passage that Orpheus had written. The handwriting was difficult to decipher, but it was beautiful — very individual and curiously ornate.

"When exactly did Dustfinger disappear?"

Farid shrugged. "I don't know," he muttered, abashed. Of course — she had forgotten that he couldn't read.

Meggie traced the first sentence with her finger. *Dustfinger returned on a day fragrant with the scent of berries and mushrooms.*

Thoughtfully, she lowered the piece of paper. "It's no good," she said. "We don't even have the book. How can it work without the book?"

"But Orpheus didn't use the book, either! Dustfinger took it away from him before he read the words on that paper!" Farid pushed his chair back and came to stand beside her. Feeling him so close made Meggie uneasy; she didn't try to figure out why.

"But that can't be so!" she murmured.

Dustfinger had gone, though.

A few handwritten sentences had opened the door between the words on the page for him — the door that Mo had tried to batter down so unsuccessfully. And it was not Fenoglio, the author of the book, who had written those sentences, but a stranger — a stranger with a curious name. Orpheus.

Meggie knew more than most people about what waited beyond the words. She herself had already opened doors, had lured living, breathing creatures out of faded, yellowing pages — and she had been there when her father read this boy out of an Arabian fairy tale, the boy of flesh and blood now standing beside her. However, this Orpheus seemed to know far, far more than she did, even more than Mo — Farid still called him Silvertongue — and suddenly Meggie was afraid of the words on that grubby piece of paper. She put it down on her desk as if it had burned her fingers.

"Please! Do please at least try!" Farid's voice sounded almost pleading. "Suppose Orpheus has already read Basta back after all? Dustfinger has to learn that they're in league with each other. He thinks he's safe from Basta in his own world!"

Meggie was still staring at the words written by Orpheus. They sounded beautiful, enchantingly beautiful. Meggie felt her tongue longing to taste them. She very nearly began reading them aloud. Horrified, she clapped her hand to her mouth.

Orpheus.

Of course she knew the name, and the story that surrounded it like a tangle of flowers and thorns. Elinor had given her a book with a beautiful poem about him in it.

Orpheus with his lute made trees
And the mountaintops that freeze,
  Bow themselves when he did sing:
To his music plants and flowers
Ever sprung; as sun and showers
  There had made a lasting spring.

Everything that heard him play,
Even the billows of the sea,
  Hung their heads, and then lay by.
In sweet music is such art,
Killing care and grief of heart
  Fall asleep, or hearing die.

She looked at Farid with a question in her eyes. "How old is he?"

"Orpheus?" Farid shrugged. "Twenty, twenty-five, how should I know? Difficult to say. His face is like a child's."

So young. But the words on the paper didn't sound like a young man's words. They sounded as if they knew a great many things.

"Please!" Farid was still looking at her. "You will try, won't you?"

Meggie looked out of the window. She couldn't help thinking of the empty fairies' nests, the glass men who had vanished, and something Dustfinger had said to her long ago: *Sometimes, when you went to the well to wash early in the morning, those tiny fairies would be whirring above the water, hardly bigger than the dragonflies you have here, and blue as violets . . . they weren't very friendly, but by night they shone like glowworms.*

"All right," she said, and it was almost as if someone else were answering Farid. "All right, I'll try. But your feet must get better first. The world my mother talks about isn't a place where you'd want to be lame."

"Nonsense, my feet are fine!" Farid walked up and down on the soft carpet as if to prove it. "You can try right away as far as I'm concerned!"

But Meggie shook her head. "No," she said firmly. "I must learn to read it fluently first. That's not going to be easy, given his handwriting — and it's smeared in several places, so I'll probably copy it out. This man Orpheus wasn't lying. He did write something about you, but I'm not quite sure that it will do. And if I try it," she went on, trying to sound very casual, "if I try it, then I want to come with you."

"What?"

"Yes, why not?" Meggie couldn't keep her voice from showing how hurt she felt by his horrified look.

Farid did not reply.

Didn't he understand that she wanted to see it for herself? She wanted to see everything that Dustfinger and her mother had told her about, Dustfinger in a voice soft with longing: the fairies swarming above the grass, trees so high that you thought they would catch the clouds in their branches, the Wayless Wood, the strolling players, the Laughing Prince's castle, the silver towers of the Castle of Night, the Ombra market, the fire that danced for him, the whispering pool where the water-nymphs' faces looked up at you. . . .

No, Farid didn't understand. He had probably never felt that yearning for a completely different world, any more than he felt the homesickness that had broken Dustfinger's heart. Farid wanted just one thing: He wanted to find Dustfinger, warn him of Basta's knife, and be back with him again. He was Dustfinger's shadow. That was the part he wanted to play, never mind what story they were in.

"Forget it! You can't come, too." Without looking at Meggie he limped back to the chair she had given him, sat down, and pulled off the bandages that Resa had so carefully put on his toes. "People can't read themselves into a book. Even Orpheus can't! He told Dustfinger so himself: He's tried it several times, he said, and it just won't work."

"Oh no?" Meggie tried to sound more sure of herself than she felt. "You said yourself that I read better than he does. So perhaps I can make it work!" *Even if I can't* write *as well as he does,* she added to herself.

Farid cast her an uneasy glance as he put the bandages in his trouser pocket. "But it's dangerous there," he said. "Particularly for a g —" He didn't finish the word. Instead he began inspecting his bloodstained toes intently.

Idiot. Meggie's anger tasted bitter on her tongue. Who did he think she was? She probably knew more about the world she'd be reading him into than he did. "I know it's dangerous," she said, piqued. "Either I go with you or I don't read aloud from this sheet of paper. You must make up your mind. And now you'd better leave me alone. I have to think."

Farid cast a final glance at the piece of paper with Orpheus's words on it before he went to the door. "When will you try?" he asked before he went back out into the corridor. "Tomorrow?"

"Perhaps," was all Meggie would say.

Then she closed the door behind him and was alone with the words that Orpheus had written.

THE INN OF THE
STROLLING PLAYERS

"Thank you," said Lucy, opening the box and taking out a match. "WATCH, EVERYONE!" she cried, her voice echoing round the White Flats. "WATCH! THIS IS GOODBYE TO BAD MEMORIES!"

Philip Ridley, *Dakota of the White Flats*

It took Dustfinger two whole days to get through the Wayless Wood. He met very few people on the way: a few charcoal-burners blackened with soot, a ragged poacher with two rabbits slung over his shoulder and hunger written large on his face, and a group of the prince's game wardens, armed to the teeth, probably on the trail of some poor devil who had shot a deer to feed his children. None of them saw Dustfinger. He knew how to pass unseen, and only on the second night, when he heard a pack of wolves howling in the nearby hills, did he dare to summon fire.

Fire. So different in this world and the other one. How good it would be to hear its crackling voice again at last, and to be able to answer. Dustfinger collected some of the dry wood lying around among the trees, with wax-flowers and thyme rambling over it. He carefully unwrapped the fire-elves' stolen honey from the leaves that kept it moist and supple and put a tiny morsel in his mouth. How scared he had been the first time he tasted the honey! Scared that his precious booty would burn his tongue forever and he would lose his voice. But that fear had proved groundless. The honey did burn your mouth like red-hot coals, but the pain passed away — and if you bore it long enough, then afterward you could speak to fire, even with a mere human tongue. The effect of a tiny piece lasted for five or six months, sometimes almost a year. Just a soft whisper in the language of the flames, a snap of your fingers, and sparks would leap crackling from dry wood, damp wood, even stone.

At first the fire licked up from the twigs more reluctantly than it had in the old days — as if it couldn't really believe he was back. But then it began to whisper and welcomed him more and more exuberantly, until he had to rein in those wildly leaping flames, imitating the sound of their crackling until the fire sank lower, like a wildcat that will crouch down and purr if you stroke its fur carefully enough.

While the fire devoured the wood and its light kept the wolves away, Dustfinger found himself thinking of the boy again. He couldn't count the many nights when he'd had to tell Farid how fire spoke, for the boy knew only mute and sullen flames. "Heavens above," he muttered to himself as he warmed his fingers over the glowing embers, "you're still missing him!" He was glad that the marten at least was still with the boy, to keep him company as he faced the ghosts he saw everywhere.

Yes, Dustfinger did miss Farid. But there were others whom he had been missing for ten long years, missing them so much that his heart was still sore with longing. It was with those people crowding his mind that he strode out, more impatiently with every passing hour, as he approached the outskirts of the forest and what lay beyond it — the world of humans. It was not just his longing for fairies, little glass men, and water-nymphs that had tormented him in the other world, nor his desire to be back in the silence under the trees. There weren't many human beings he had missed, but he had missed those few all the more fiercely.

He had tried so hard to forget them since the day he came, half-starved, to Silvertongue's door, and Silvertongue had explained that there could be no way back for him. It was then he had realized that he must choose. *Forget them, Dustfinger* — how often he had told himself that! — *forget them, or the loss of them all will drive you mad.* But his heart simply did not obey. Memories, so sweet and so bitter . . . they had both nourished and devoured him for so many years. Until a time came when they began to fade, turning faint and blurred, only an ache to be quickly pushed away because it went to your heart. For what was the use of remembering all you had lost?

Better not remember now, either, Dustfinger told himself as the trees around him became younger and the canopy of leaves above grew lighter. *Ten years — it's a long time, and many may be lost and gone by now.*

Charcoal-burners' huts appeared among the trees more and more often now, but Dustfinger did not let the soot-blackened men see him. Outside the forest, people spoke of them slightingly, for the charcoal-burners lived deeper in the forest than most dared to go. Craftsmen, peasants, traders, princes: They all needed charcoal, but they didn't like to see the men who burned it for them in their own towns and villages. Dustfinger liked the charcoal-burners, who knew almost as much about the forest as he did, although they made enemies of the trees daily. He had sat by their fires often enough, listening to their stories, but after all these years there were other stories he wanted to hear, tales of what had been going on outside the forest, and there was only one place to hear those: in one of the inns that stood along the road.

Dustfinger had one particular inn in mind. It lay on the northern outskirts of the forest, where the road appeared among the trees and began to wind uphill, past a few isolated farms, until it reached the city gate of Ombra, the capital city of Lombrica, the Laughing Prince's realm.

The inns on the road outside Ombra had always been places where the strolling players called the Motley Folk met. They offered their skills there to rich merchants, tradesmen, and craftsmen, for weddings and funerals, for festivities to celebrate a traveler's safe return or the birth of a child. They would provide music, earthy jokes, and conjuring tricks for just a few coins, taking the audience's minds off their troubles large and small. And if Dustfinger wanted to find out what had been happening in all the years he was away, then the Motley Folk were the people to ask. The players were the newspapers of this world. No one knew what went on in it better than these travelers who were never at home anywhere.

Who knows? thought Dustfinger as he walked down the road, with the autumn sun, by now low in the sky, on his face. *If I'm lucky I may even meet old acquaintances.*

The road was muddy and full of puddles. Cartwheels had made deep ruts in it, and the hoofprints left by oxen and horses were full of rainwater. At this time of year it sometimes rained for days on end, as it had yesterday, when he had been glad to be under the trees where the leaves caught the rain before it drenched him to the skin. The night had been cold, all the same, and his clothes were clammy even though he had slept beside his fire. He was glad that the sky was clear today, apart from a few shreds of cloud drifting over the hills.

Luckily, he had found a few coins in his old clothes. He hoped they would be enough for a bowl of soup. Dustfinger had brought nothing with him from the other world. What would he do here with the printed paper they used for money in that world? Only gold, silver, and ringing copper counted in this one, with the local prince's head on the coins if possible. As soon as his money was gone he'd have to look for a marketplace where he could perform, in Ombra or elsewhere.

The inn that was his destination hadn't changed much in the last few years, either for better or for worse. It was as shabby as ever, with a few windows that were hardly more than holes in the gray stone walls. In the world where he had been living until three days ago, it was unlikely that any guests at all would have crossed such a grubby threshold. But here the inn was the last shelter available before you entered the forest, the last chance of a hot meal and a place to sleep that wasn't damp with dew or rain . . . *and you got a few lice and bugs thrown in for free,* thought Dustfinger as he pushed open the door.

It was so dark in the room inside that his eyes took a little while to adjust to the dim light. The other world had spoiled him with all its lights, with the brightness that made even night into day there. It had accustomed him to seeing everything clearly, to thinking of light as something you could switch on and off, available whenever you wanted. But now his eyes must cope again with a world of twilight and shadows, of long nights as black as charred wood, and houses from which the sunlight was often shut out, because its heat was unwelcome.

All the light inside the inn came from the few sunbeams falling through the holes that were the windows. Dust motes danced in them like a swarm of tiny fairies. A fire was burning in the hearth under a battered black cauldron. The smell rising from it was not particularly appetizing, even to Dustfinger's empty stomach, but that didn't surprise him. This inn had never had a landlord who knew the first thing about cooking. A little girl hardly more than ten years old was standing beside the cauldron, stirring whatever was simmering in it with a stick. Some thirty guests were sitting on rough-hewn benches in the dark, smoking, talking quietly, and drinking.

Dustfinger strolled over to an empty place and sat down. He surreptitiously looked around for a face that might seem familiar, for a pair of the Motley trousers that only the players wore. He immediately saw a lute-player by the window, negotiating with a much better dressed man than the musician himself, probably a rich merchant. No poor peasant could afford to hire an entertainer, of course. If a farmer wanted music at his wedding he must play the fiddle himself. He couldn't have afforded even the two pipers who were also sitting by the window. At the table next to them, a group of actors were arguing in loud voices, probably about who got the best part in a new play. One still wore the mask behind which he hid when they acted in the towns' marketplaces. He looked strange sitting there among the others, but then all the Motley Folk were strange — with or without masks, whether they sang or danced, performed broad farces on a wooden stage or breathed fire. The same was true of their companions — traveling physicians, bonesetters, stonecutters, miracle healers. The players brought them customers.

Old faces, young faces, happy and unhappy faces, there were all of those in the smoke-filled room, but none of them seemed familiar to Dustfinger. He, too, sensed he was being scrutinized, but he was used to it. His scarred face attracted glances everywhere, and the clothes he wore did the rest — a fire-eater's costume, black as soot, red as the flames that he played with, but that others feared. For a moment he felt curiously strange amid all this once-familiar activity, as if the other world still clung to him and could be clearly seen: all the years, the endless years since Silvertongue plucked him out of his own story and stole his life without intending to, as you might crush a snail-shell in passing.

"Hey, who have we here?"

A hand fell heavily on his shoulder, and a man leaned over him and stared at his face. His hair was gray, his face round and beardless, and he was so unsteady on his feet that for a moment Dustfinger thought he was drunk. "Why, if I don't know that face!" cried the man incredulously, grasping Dustfinger's shoulder hard, as if to make sure it was really flesh and blood. "So where've you sprung from, my old fire-eating friend? Straight from the realm of the dead? What happened? Did the fairies bring you back to life? They always were besotted with you, those little blue imps."

A few men turned to look at them, but there was so much noise in the dark, stuffy room that not many people noticed what was going on.

"Cloud-Dancer!" Dustfinger straightened up and embraced the other man. "How are you?"

"Ah, and there was I thinking you'd forgotten me!" Cloud-Dancer gave a broad grin, baring large, yellow teeth.

Oh no, Dustfinger had not forgotten him — although he had tried to, as he had tried to forget the others he had missed. Cloud-Dancer, the best tightrope-walker who ever strolled around the rooftops. Dustfinger had recognized him at once, in spite of his now gray hair and the left leg that was skewed at such a curiously stiff angle.

"Come along, we must drink to this. You don't meet a dead friend again every day." He impatiently drew Dustfinger over to a bench under one of the windows. A little sunlight fell through it from outside. Then he signaled to the girl who was still stirring the cauldron and ordered two goblets of wine. The little creature stared at Dustfinger's scars for a moment, fascinated, and then scurried over to the counter. A fat man stood behind it, watching his guests with dull eyes.

"You're looking good!" remarked Cloud-Dancer. "Well fed, not a gray hair on your head, hardly a hole in your clothes. You even still have all your teeth, by the look of it. Where've you been? Maybe I should set out for the same place myself — seems like a man can live pretty well there."

"Forget it. It's better here." Dustfinger pushed back the hair from his forehead and looked around. "That's enough about me. How have you been yourself? You can afford wine, but your hair is gray, and your left leg . . ."

"Ah, yes, my leg." The girl brought their wine. As Cloud-Dancer searched his purse for the right money, she stared at Dustfinger again with such curiosity that he rubbed his fingertips together and whispered a few fire-words. Reaching out his forefinger, he smiled at her and blew gently on the fingertip. A tiny flame, too weak to light a fire but just bright enough to be reflected in the little girl's eyes, flickered on his nail and spat out sparks of gold on the dirty table. The child stood there enchanted, until Dustfinger blew out the flame and dipped his finger in the goblet of wine that Cloud-Dancer pushed over to him.

"So you still like playing with fire," said Cloud-Dancer, as the girl cast an anxious glance at the fat landlord and hurried back to the cauldron. "My own games are over now, sad to say."

"What happened?"

"I fell off the rope, I don't dance in the clouds anymore. A market trader threw a cabbage at me — I expect I was distracting his customers' attention. At least I was lucky enough to land on a cloth-merchant's stall. That way I broke my leg and a couple of ribs, but not my neck."

Dustfinger looked at him thoughtfully. "Then how do you make a living now that you can't walk the tightrope?"

Cloud-Dancer shrugged. "Believe it or not, I can still go about on foot. I can even ride with this leg of mine — if there's a horse available. I earn my living as a messenger, although I still like to be with the strolling players, listening to their stories and sitting by the fire with them. But it's words that nourish me now, even though I can't read. Threatening letters, begging letters, love letters, sales contracts, wills — I deliver anything that can be written on a piece of parchment or paper. And I can be relied upon to carry a spoken message, too, when it's been whispered into my ear in confidence. I make quite a good living, although I'm not the fastest messenger money can hire. But everyone who gives me a letter to deliver knows that it really will reach the person it's meant for. And a guarantee of that is hard to find."

Dustfinger believed him. *For a few gold pieces you can read the prince's own letters*, that was what they used to say even in his own time. You just had to know someone who was good at forging broken seals. "How about our other friends?" Dustfinger looked at the pipers by the window. "What are they doing?"

Cloud-Dancer took a sip of wine and made a face. "Ugh! I should have asked for honey in this. The others, well" — he rubbed his stiff leg — "some are dead, some have just disappeared like you. Look over there, behind the farmer staring so gloomily into his tankard," he said, jerking his head at the counter. "There's our old friend Sootbird, with a laugh fixed on his face like a tattoo, the worst fire-eater for miles around, although he still tries to copy you and wonders why fire would rather dance for you than him."

"He'll never find out." Dustfinger glanced surreptitiously at the other fire-eater. As far as he remembered, Sootbird could juggle burning torches well enough, but fire didn't dance for him. He was like a hopeless lover rejected again and again by the girl of his choice. Long ago, feeling sorry for the man's futile efforts, Dustfinger had given him some fire-elves' honey, but even with its aid Sootbird hadn't understood what the flames were telling him.

"I've heard that he works with powders bought from alchemists now," Cloud-Dancer whispered across the table, "and that's an expensive pastime, if you ask me. The fire bites him so often that his hands and arms are quite red from it. But he doesn't let it get at his face. Before he performs he smears it with grease until it shines like bacon fat."

"Does he still drink after every show?"

"After the show, before the show, but he's still a good-looking fellow, don't you think?"

Yes, so he was, with his friendly, ever-smiling face. Sootbird was one of those entertainers who lived on the glances of others, on laughter and applause, on knowing that people will stop to look at them. Even now he was entertaining the others who were leaning against the counter with him. Dustfinger turned his back; he didn't want to see the old mixture of admiration and envy in the other man's eyes. Sootbird was not one of those he had missed.

"You mustn't think times are any easier now for the Motley Folk," said Cloud-Dancer across the table, low-voiced. "Since Cosimo's death the Laughing Prince doesn't let the likes of us into the markets except on feast days, and as for going up to the castle itself, that's only when his grandson demands entertainers loudly enough. Not a very nice little boy — he's already ordering his servants around and threatening them with whipping and the pillory. Still, he loves the Motley Folk."

"Cosimo the Fair is dead?" Dustfinger nearly choked on the sour wine.

"Yes." Cloud-Dancer leaned over the table, as if it wasn't right to speak of death and misfortune in too loud a voice. "He rode away scarcely a year ago, beautiful as an angel, to prove his princely courage and finish off the fire-raisers who were haunting the forest then. You may remember their leader, Capricorn?"

Dustfinger had to smile. "Oh yes. I remember him," he said quietly.

"He disappeared about the same time you did, but his gang carried on the same as ever. Firefox became their new leader. There wasn't a village nor a farm this side of the forest that was safe from them. So Cosimo rode away to put an end to their evil deeds. He smoked out the whole band, but he didn't come home himself. Since then, his father, who used to like eating so much that his breakfast alone could have fed three whole villages, has become known as the Prince of Sighs, too. For the Laughing Prince does nothing but sigh these days."

Dustfinger held his fingers in the dust motes dancing above him in the sun. "The Prince of Sighs!" he murmured. "Well, well. And what about His Noble Highness on the other side of the forest?"

"The Adderhead?" Cloud-Dancer looked around uneasily. "Hmm, well, I'm afraid *he's* not dead yet. Still thinks himself lord of the whole world. When his game wardens find a peasant in the forest with a rabbit he has the man blinded; he enslaves folk who don't pay their taxes and makes them dig the ground for silver until they're coughing up blood. The gallows outside his castle are always in use, and he likes to see a pair of Motley trousers dangling there best of all. Still, few speak ill of him, because he has more spies than this inn has bedbugs, and he pays them well. But you can't bribe Death," added Cloud-Dancer softly, "and the Adderhead is growing old. It's said that he's afraid of the White Women these days, and terrified of dying, so terrified that he falls to his knees by night and howls like a beaten dog. And they say his cooks have to make him calves' blood pudding every morning, because that's supposed to keep a man young, and he keeps a hanged man's finger bone under his pillow to protect him from the White Women. He's married four times in the last seven years. His wives get younger and younger, but still none of them has given him what he wants most dearly."

"So the Adderhead has no son yet?"

Cloud-Dancer shook his head. "No, but all the same his grandson will rule us some day, because the old fox married one of his daughters off to Cosimo the Fair — Violante, known to everyone as Her Ugliness — and she had a son by Cosimo before he went away to die. They say her father made her acceptable to the Laughing Prince by giving her a valuable manuscript to take for her dowry — and the best illuminator at his court into the bargain. Yes, the Laughing Prince was once as keen on written papers as on good food, but now his precious books are moldering away! Nothing interests him anymore, least of all his subjects. There are rumors that it's all gone exactly as the Adderhead planned, and that he himself made sure his son-in-law would never return from Capricorn's fortress, so that his grandson could succeed to the throne."

"The rumors are probably true." Dustfinger looked at the crowd in the stuffy room. Strolling peddlers, physicians, journeymen, craftsmen, players with darned sleeves. One man had an unhappy-looking brownie sitting on the floor beside him. Many looked as if they didn't know how they were going to pay for the wine they were drinking. There were few happy faces to be seen here, few faces free of care, sickness, and resentment. Well, what had he expected? Had he hoped that misfortune would have stolen away while he was gone? No. He had wanted to come back — that was all he'd hoped for in ten long years — not back to paradise, he'd just wanted to come home. Doesn't a fish want to be back in the water, even if there's a perch lying in wait for it?

A drunk staggered against the table and almost spilled the wine. Dustfinger reached for the jug. "And what about Capricorn's men? Firefox and the rest? Are they all dead?"

"In your dreams!" Cloud-Dancer laughed bitterly. "All the fire-raisers who escaped Cosimo's attack were welcomed to the Castle of Night with open arms. The Adderhead made Firefox his herald, and these days the Piper, Capricorn's old minstrel, sings his dark songs in the Castle of Silver Towers. He wears silk and velvet, and his pockets are full of gold."

"The Piper's still around?" Dustfinger passed his hand over his face. "Heavens, have you no good news at all to tell me? Something to make me glad to be home again?"

Cloud-Dancer laughed, so loudly that Sootbird turned and glanced at him. "The best news is that you're back!" he said. "We've missed you, Master of the Fire! They say the fairies sigh as they dance by night, since you left us so faithlessly, and the Black Prince tells his bear stories about you before falling asleep."

"So the Prince is still around, too? Good." Relieved, Dustfinger took a sip of the wine, although it really did taste vile. He hadn't dared to ask about the Prince, for fear he might hear something like Cosimo's sad story.

"Oh, he's doing fine!" Cloud-Dancer raised his voice as two peddlers at the next table began to quarrel. "Still the same — black as pitch, quick with his tongue and even quicker with his knife, never seen without his bear."

Dustfinger smiled. Yes, this was good news indeed. The Black Prince: bear-tamer, knife-thrower, probably still fretting angrily at the way of the world. Dustfinger had known him since they were both homeless, orphaned children. At the age of eleven they'd stood side by side in the pillory over on the far side of the forest, where they were born, and they'd still smelled of rotten vegetables two days later. They had both been born in Argenta, the Silver Land, the realm of the Adderhead.

Cloud-Dancer looked at his face. "Well?" he asked. "When are you finally going to ask the question you've been wanting to ask since I clapped you on the shoulder? Go on! Before I'm too drunk to answer you."

Dustfinger had to smile; he couldn't help it. Cloud-Dancer had always known how to see into other people's hearts, though you might not have thought so from his face. "Very well. What shall I . . . how is she?"

"At last!" Cloud-Dancer smiled with such self-satisfaction that two gaps in his teeth showed. "Well, first, she's still very beautiful. Lives in a house now, doesn't sing and dance anymore, doesn't wear brightly colored skirts, pins up her hair like a farmer's wife. She tends a plot of land up on the hill behind the castle, growing herbs for the physicians. Even Nettle buys from her. She lives on that, sometimes well, sometimes not so well, bringing up her children."

Dustfinger tried to look indifferent, but Cloud-Dancer's smile told him that he wasn't succeeding. "What about that spice merchant who was always after her?"

"What about him? He left years ago; he's probably living in some big house by the sea, growing richer with every sack of pepper his ships bring in."

"Then she didn't marry him?"

"No. She chose another man."

"Another man?" Once again Dustfinger tried to sound indifferent, and once again he failed.

Cloud-Dancer enjoyed keeping him in suspense for a while, and then went on. "Yes, another man. He soon died, poor fellow, but she has a child by him, a boy."

Dustfinger said nothing, listening to his own thudding heart. His stupid heart. "What about the girls?"

"Oh, the girls. Yes, them — I wonder who their father can have been?" Cloud-Dancer was smiling again, like a little boy who has pulled off a mischievous trick. "Brianna's as lovely as her mother already. Although she's inherited your red hair."

"And Rosanna, the younger?" Her hair was dark, like her mother's.

The smile on Cloud-Dancer's face disappeared as if Dustfinger had wiped it away. "The child has been dead a long time," he said softly. "There was a fever, two winters after you went away. Many died of it. Even Nettle couldn't help them."

Dustfinger drew bright, damp lines on the table with his forefinger, which was sticky from the wine. Dead. Much might be lost in the space of ten years. For a moment he tried desperately to remember her face, such a little face, but it blurred, as if he had spent too long over the attempt to forget it.

Amid all the noise, Cloud-Dancer sat with him in silence for a long time. Then at last he rose, ponderously; it wasn't easy to get up from the low bench with his stiff leg. "I must be off, my friend," he said. "I still have three letters to deliver, two of them up there in Ombra. I want to be at the city gate before dark, or the guards will have their little joke again and refuse to let me in."

Dustfinger was still drawing lines on the dark wood of the table. *Two winters after you went away* — the words stung like nettles in his head. "Where are the others camping at the moment?"

"Just outside the city wall of Ombra. Our prince's beloved grandson celebrates his birthday soon. Every entertainer and minstrel is welcome at the castle on that day."

Dustfinger nodded without raising his head. "I'll see. Maybe I'll go along, too." He abruptly rose from the hard bench. The girl by the hearth looked at them. His younger daughter would have been about her age now if the fever hadn't carried her off.

Together with Cloud-Dancer, he made his way past the crowded benches and chairs to the door. It was still fine outside, a sunny autumn day, clad in bright foliage like a strolling player.

"Come to Ombra with me!" Cloud-Dancer laid a hand on his shoulder. "My horse will carry two, and we can always find a place to sleep there."

But Dustfinger shook his head.

"Later," he said, looking down the muddy road. "It's time I paid a visit."

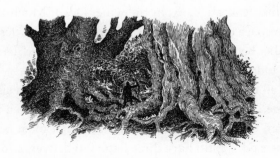

MEGGIE'S DECISION

> The idea hovered and shivered delicately, like a soap bubble,
> and she dared not even look at it directly in case it burst. But
> she was familiar with the way of ideas, and she let it shimmer,
> looking away, thinking about something else.
>
> **Philip Pullman,** *Northern Lights*

Mo came home just as they were all sitting down to breakfast, and Resa kissed him as if he'd been away for weeks. Meggie hugged him harder than usual, too, relieved that he had come back safe and sound, but she avoided looking him straight in the eye. Mo knew her too well. He would have spotted her guilty conscience at once. And Meggie's conscience was very guilty.

The reason was the sheet of paper hidden among her schoolbooks up in her room, closely written in her own hand, although the words were by someone else. Meggie had spent hours copying out what Orpheus had written. Every time she got something wrong she had begun again from the beginning, for fear that a single mistake could spoil everything. She had added just three words — where the passage mentioned a boy, in the sentences left unread by Orpheus, Meggie had added "and the girl." Three nondescript, perfectly ordinary words, so ordinary that it was overwhelmingly likely that they occurred somewhere in the pages of *Inkheart*. She couldn't check, however, because the only copy of the book she would have needed to do that was now in Basta's hands. Basta . . . the mere sound of his name reminded Meggie of black days and black nights. Black with fear.

Mo had brought her a present to make peace between them, as he always did when they had quarreled: a small notebook bound by himself, just the right size for her jacket pocket, with a marbled paper cover. Mo knew how much Meggie liked marbled patterns; she had been only nine when he had taught her how to color them for herself. Guilt went to her heart when he put the notebook down by her plate, and for a moment she wanted to tell him everything, just as she had always done. But a glance from Farid prevented her. That glance said, "No, Meggie, he won't let you go there — ever." So she kept quiet, kissed Mo, whispered, "Thank you," and said no more, quickly bending her head, her tongue heavy with the words she hadn't spoken.

Luckily, no one noticed her sad expression. The others were still anxious about Farid's news of Basta. Elinor had gone to the police, on Mo's advice, but her visit to them had done nothing to improve her mood.

"Just as I told you," she said crossly, working away at the cheese with her knife as if it were the cause of all this trouble. "Those fools didn't believe a word I said. A couple of sheep in uniform would have listened better. You know I don't like dogs, but maybe I ought to get some after all . . . a couple of huge black brutes to tear Basta apart the moment he comes through my garden gate. A Dobsterman dog, yes. A Dobsterman or two. Isn't a Dobsterman the dog that eats people?"

"You mean a Doberman." Mo winked across the table at Meggie.

It broke her heart. There he was winking at her, his deceitful daughter who was planning to go right away, to a place where he probably couldn't follow her. Perhaps her mother would understand, but Mo? No, not Mo. Never.

Meggie bit her lip so hard that it hurt, while Elinor, still in a state of agitation, went on. "And I could hire a bodyguard. You can do that, can't you? One with a pistol — no, not just a pistol, armed to the teeth: knives, rifles, everything, and so big that Basta's black heart would stop at the mere sight of him! How does that sound?"

Meggie saw Mo suppress a smile with difficulty. "How does it sound? As if you'd been reading too many thrillers, Elinor."

"Well, I *have* read a lot of thrillers," she said, injured. "They're very informative if you don't usually mix much with criminals. What's more, I can't forget seeing Basta's knife at your throat."

"Nor can I, believe me." Meggie saw his hand go to his throat as if, just for a moment, he felt the sharp blade against his skin again. "All the same, I think you're worrying unnecessarily. I had plenty of time to think it all over on the drive back, and I don't believe Basta will come all the way here just to get revenge. Revenge for what? For being saved from Capricorn's Shadow — and by us? No. He'll have had this Orpheus read him back by now. Back into the book. Basta never liked our world half as much as Capricorn did. Some things about it made him very nervous."

He spread jam on top of his bread and cheese. Elinor watched this, as usual, with horror, and Mo, also as usual, ignored her disapproving glance.

"So what about those threats he shouted after the boy?"

"Well, he was angry that he'd gotten away, wasn't he? I don't have to tell you the kind of things Basta says when he's angry. I'm only surprised he was actually clever enough to find out that Dustfinger had the book. And I'd like to know where he found this man Orpheus, too. He seems to be better than me at reading aloud."

"Nonsense!" Elinor's voice sounded cross but relieved, too. "The only one who may be as good at it as you are is your daughter."

Mo smiled at Meggie and put another slice of cheese on top of the jam. "Thanks, very flattering. But, however that may be, our knife-happy friend Basta has gone! And I hope he's taken the wretched book with him and put an end to that story forever. There'll be no more need for Elinor to jump when she hears something rustling in the garden at night, and Darius won't have to dream of Basta's knife — which means that the news Farid has brought is in fact very good news! I hope you've all thanked him warmly!"

Farid smiled shyly as Mo raised his coffee cup to him, but Meggie saw the anxiety in his black eyes. If Mo was right, then by now Basta was in the same place as Dustfinger. And they all thought Mo *was* right. You could see the relief in Darius's and Elinor's faces, and Resa put her arms around Mo's neck and smiled as if everything was fine again.

Elinor began asking Mo questions about the books he had so shockingly abandoned to answer Meggie's phone call. And Darius was trying to tell Resa about the new system of classification he had thought up for Elinor's library. But Farid looked at his empty plate. Against the background of its white china, he was probably seeing Basta's knife at Dustfinger's neck.

Basta. The name stuck in Meggie's throat like a pebble. She kept thinking the same thing: If Mo was right, Basta was now where she soon hoped to be herself. In the Inkworld.

She was going to try it that very night, she would try to use her own voice and Orpheus's words to make her way through the thicket of written letters, into the Wayless Wood. Farid had pleaded with her to wait no longer. He was beside himself with anxiety for Dustfinger, and Mo's remarks had certainly done nothing to change that. "Please, Meggie!" He had begged her again and again. "Please read it!"

Meggie looked across the table at Mo. He was whispering something to Resa, and she laughed. You heard her voice only when she laughed. Mo put his arm around her, and his eyes sought Meggie. When her bed was empty tomorrow morning he wouldn't look as carefree as he did now. Would he be angry or merely sad? Resa laughed when, for her and Elinor's benefit, he mimicked the horror of the collector whose books he had abandoned so disgracefully when Meggie had phoned, and Meggie had to laugh, too, when he imitated the poor man's voice. The collector had obviously been very fat and breathless.

Elinor was the only one who didn't laugh. "I don't think that's funny, Mortimer," she said sharply. "Personally, I'd probably have shot you if you'd simply gone off leaving my poor books behind, all sick and dirty."

"Yes, I expect you would." Mo gave Meggie a conspiratorial look, as he always did when Elinor lectured him or his daughter on the way to treat books or the rules of her library.

Oh Mo, if only you knew, thought Meggie, *if only you knew.* . . . She felt as if he would read her secret in her face any minute now. Abruptly, she pushed back her chair, muttered, "I'm not hungry," and went off to Elinor's library. Where else?

Whenever she wanted to escape her own thoughts, she went to books for help. She was sure to find something to keep her mind occupied until evening finally came and they all went to bed, suspecting nothing.

Looking at Elinor's library, you couldn't tell that scarcely more than a year ago it had contained nothing but a red rooster hanging dead in front of empty shelves, while Elinor's finest books burned on the lawn outside. The jar that Elinor had filled with some of their pale ashes still stood beside her bed.

Meggie ran her forefinger over the backs of the books. They were ranged side by side on the shelves again now, like piano keys. Some shelves were still empty, but Elinor and Darius were always out and about, visiting secondhand bookshops and auctions, to replace those lost treasures with new and equally wonderful books.

Orpheus . . . where was the story of Orpheus?

Meggie was on her way over to the shelf where the Greeks and Romans whispered their ancient stories when the library door opened behind her, and Mo came in.

"Resa says you have the sheet of paper that Farid brought with him in your room. Can I see it?" He was trying to sound as casual as if he were just asking about the weather, but he'd never been any good at pretending. Mo couldn't pretend, any more than he could tell lies.

"Why?" Meggie leaned against Elinor's books as if they would strengthen her backbone.

"Why? Because I'm curious, remember? And what's more," he added, looking at the backs of the books, as if he could find the right words there, "and what's more, I think it would be better to burn that sheet of paper."

"Burn it?" Meggie looked at him incredulously. "But why?"

"I know it sounds as if I'm seeing ghosts," he said, taking a book off the shelf, opening it, and leafing absentmindedly through it, "but that piece of paper, Meggie . . . I feel it's like an open door, a door that we'd be well advised to close once and for all. Before Farid tries disappearing into that damn story, too."

"What if he does?" Meggie couldn't help the cool note that crept into her voice. As if she were talking to a stranger. "Why can't you understand? He only wants to find Dustfinger! To warn him about Basta."

Mo closed the book he had taken off the shelf and put it back in its place. "So he says. But suppose Dustfinger didn't actually want to take him along, suppose he left him behind on purpose? Would that surprise you?"

No. No, it wouldn't. Meggie said nothing. It was so quiet among the books, so terribly quiet among all those words.

"I know, Meggie," said Mo at last, in a low voice. "I know you think the world that book describes is much more exciting than this one. I understand the feeling. I've often imagined being right inside one of my favorite books. But we both know that once imagination turns to reality things feel quite different. You think the Inkworld is a magical place, a world of wonders — but believe me, your mother has told me a lot about it that you wouldn't like at all. It's a cruel, dangerous place, full of darkness and violence, ruled by brute force, Meggie, not by justice."

He looked at her, searching her face for the understanding he had always found there before but did not find now.

"Farid comes from a world like that," said Meggie. "And he didn't choose to get into this story of ours. You brought him here."

She regretted her words the moment they were out. Mo turned away as if she had struck him. "Yes. You're right, of course," he said, going back to the door. "And I don't want to quarrel with you again. But I don't want that paper lying around your room, either. Give it back to Farid. Or else, who knows, there could be a giant sitting on your bed tomorrow morning." He was trying to make her laugh, of course. He couldn't bear the two of them to be on bad terms again. He looked so depressed. And so tired.

"You know perfectly well nothing like that can happen," said Meggie. "Why do you always worry so much? Things don't just come out of the words on the page unless you call them. You should know that better than anyone!"

His hand was still on the door handle.

"Yes," he said. "Yes, no doubt you're right. But do you know what? Sometimes I'd like to put a padlock on all the books in this world. And as for that very special book . . . I'd be glad, now, if Capricorn really had burned the last copy back there in his village. That book brings bad luck, Meggie, nothing but bad luck, even if you won't believe me."

Then he closed the library door after him.

Meggie stood there motionless until his footsteps had died away. She went over to one of the windows looking out on to the garden, but when Mo finally came down the path leading to his workshop he didn't look back at the house. Resa was with him. She had put her arm around his shoulders, and her other hand was tracing words, but Meggie couldn't make them out. Were they talking about her?

It was sometimes an odd feeling suddenly to have not just a father but two parents who talked to each other when she wasn't with them. Mo went into his workshop alone, and Resa strolled back to the house. She waved to Meggie when she saw her standing at the window, and Meggie waved back.

An odd feeling . . .

Meggie sat among Elinor's books for some time longer, look-ing first at one, then at another, searching for passages to drown out her own thoughts. But the letters on the pages remained just letters, forming neither pictures nor words, and finally Meggie went out into the garden, lay down on the grass, and looked at the workshop. She could see Mo at work through its windows.

I can't do it, she thought, as the wind blew leaves off the trees and whirled them away like brightly painted toys. *No. I can't! They'll all be so worried, and Mo will never, ever say a word to me again.*

Meggie thought all those things, she thought them over and over again. And at the same time she knew, deep down inside her, that she had made up her mind long ago.

THE MINSTREL WOMAN

The minstrel must go on his way,
As he has done so long,
And so a note of sad farewell
Lingers around his song.
Ah, will I e'er come back again?
My dear, alas, who knows?
The heavy hand of death is laid
On many a budding rose.

E. von Monsterberg, quoted from
Musikanten, Gaukler und Vaganten

It was just getting light when Dustfinger reached the farm that Cloud-Dancer had described to him. It lay on a south-facing slope, surrounded by olive trees. The soil, said Cloud-Dancer, was poor and stony there, but it suited the herbs that Roxane grew. The house stood alone, with no village nearby to protect it. There was only a wall, hardly chest-high, and a wooden gate. You could see the rooftops of Ombra in the distance, the castle towers rising high above the houses, and the road winding toward the city gate — so near, and yet too far to be a refuge if highwaymen or soldiers coming home from war thought it a good idea to loot this lonely farm, where only a woman and two children lived.

Perhaps at least she has a farmhand, thought Dustfinger as he stood behind some bushes of broom. Their branches hid him, but he had a good view of the house.

It was small, like most farmhouses — not as poor as many of them but not much better, either. The whole house would have fitted a dozen times over and more into one of the great halls where Roxane had once danced. Even the Adderhead used to invite her to his castle, poorly as he thought of the Motley Folk, for in those days everyone had wanted to hear her sing. Rich traders, the miller down by the river, the spice merchant who had sent her presents for more than a year . . . so many men had wanted to marry her, had given her jewelry and costly dresses, offered her fine apartments in their houses, and every one of those apartments was certainly larger than the little house where she lived now. But Roxane had stayed with the Motley Folk. She had never been one of those women among the strolling players who would sell their voices and their bodies to a lord and master for a little security, a settled home. . . .

However, the day had come when she, too, had tired of traveling and had wanted a home for herself and her children. For no law protected those who lived on the road, and that meant the Motley Folk as well as robbers and highwaymen. If you stole from a player you need not fear any punishment, if you did violence to one of their women you could safely go back to your comfortable home, and even if you killed a traveler you need not fear the hangman. All his widow could do in revenge was strike the killer's shadow as the sun cast it on the city wall, only his shadow, and she had to pay for her husband's funeral, too. The Motley Folk were fair game. People called them the Devil's decoys, they liked to be entertained by them, listened to their songs and stories, watched their clever tricks — and barred their doors and gates to them when evening came. The players had to camp outside towns and villages, outside the protection of the walls, always on the move, envied for their freedom, yet despised because they served many masters for money and bread.

Not many strolling players ever left the road — the road and the lonely paths. But that was obviously what Roxane had done.

There was a stable beside the house, a barn, and a bakehouse, and between them a yard with a well in the middle of it. There was a garden, fenced off to keep chickens and goats from uprooting the young plants, and a dozen narrow fields on the slope beyond. Some had been harvested, while in others the herbs stood high, bushy, and heavy with their own seed. The fragrance borne across to Dustfinger on the wind made the morning air both sweet and bitter.

Roxane was kneeling in the farthest field, among plants of flax, comfrey, and wild mallow. She seemed to have been at work for a long time already, although the morning mist still hung in the nearby trees. A boy of perhaps seven or eight kneeled beside her. Roxane was talking to him and laughing. How often Dustfinger had summoned up her face in his memory, every part of it: her mouth, her eyes, her high forehead. It had been more difficult with every passing year, and with every year the picture had dimmed, desperately as he had tried to remember more clearly. Time had blurred her face and covered it with dust.

Dustfinger took a step forward — and two steps back. He had thought of turning back three times already, of stealing away again as silently as he had come, but he had stayed. A wind blew through the broom bushes, catching him in the back as if to give him fresh heart, and Dustfinger plucked up his courage, pushed the branches aside, and walked toward the house and the fields.

The boy saw him first, and a goose rose from the tall grass by the stable and came toward him, cackling and beating her wings. Peasants were not allowed to keep dogs, that was a privilege reserved for princes, but a goose was a reliable guard, too — and just as alarming. But Dustfinger knew how to avoid the gaping beak and stroked the excited bird's white neck until she folded her wings like a freshly ironed dress and waddled peacefully away, back to her place in the grass.

Roxane had risen to her feet. She wiped the earth off her hands onto her dress and looked at him, just looked. She had indeed pinned up her hair like a farmer's wife, but it was obviously as long as ever and still as black, apart from a few gray strands. Her dress was as brown as the earth where she had been kneeling, no longer brightly colored like the skirts she used to wear. But her face was still as familiar to Dustfinger as the sight of the sky, more familiar than his own reflection.

The boy picked up the rake lying on the ground beside him. He clutched it with a grimly determined air, as if he were used to protecting his mother from strangers. *Clever lad*, thought Dustfinger, *never trust anyone, certainly not a scar-faced man like me suddenly emerging from the bushes.*

What was he going to say when she asked him where he'd been?

Roxane whispered something to the boy, who reluctantly lowered the rake. Suspicion still lingered in his eyes.

Ten years.

He'd often been gone a long time — in the forest, in the towns on the coast, among the isolated villages lying in the hills around — like a fox that visited farmyards only when its stomach rumbled. "Your heart's a vagabond," Roxane always said. Sometimes he'd had to search for her when she had moved on with the others. They lived together in the forest for a while, in an abandoned charcoal-burner's hut, and then in a tent with other strolling players. They even managed to hold out within the solid walls of Ombra all one winter. He was always the one who wanted to move on, and when their first daughter was born and Roxane wanted to stay put more often — in some reasonably familiar place, with the other women among the strolling players, close to the shelter of walls — he would go off alone. But he always came back to her and the children, much to the annoyance of all the rich men who flocked around her wanting to make an honest woman of her.

What had she thought when he stayed away for a whole ten years? Had she, like Cloud-Dancer, thought him dead? Or did she believe he had simply left without a word, without saying good-bye?

He could not find the answer in Roxane's face. He saw bewilderment there, anger, perhaps love, too. Perhaps. She whispered something to the boy, took his hand, and made him walk beside her. She went slowly, as if she must prevent her feet from going faster. He longed to run to her, leaving one of those years behind him at every step, but he had used up all his courage. He stood there as if rooted to the spot, looking at her as she came toward him after all those years, all the years for which he had no explanation . . . except one that she wouldn't believe.

Only a few paces still separated them when Roxane stopped. She put her arm around the boy's shoulder, but he pushed it away. Of course. He didn't want his mother's arm reminding him how young he still was. How proudly she thrust out her chin. That was the first thing he had noticed about Roxane — her pride. He couldn't help smiling, but he bowed his head so that she couldn't see the smile.

"Obviously, no living creature can withstand you to this day. My goose has always driven everyone else off." When Roxane spoke there was nothing special about her voice, none of the strength and beauty it had when she sang.

"Well, nothing's changed there," he said. "In all these years." And suddenly, as he looked at her, he finally, truly knew that he had come home. It was so strong a sensation that he felt weak at the knees. How happy he was to see her again, how dreadfully, terribly happy! *Ask me,* he thought. *Ask me where I've been.* Although he didn't know how he would explain.

But she only said, "You seem to have been well off, wherever you've been."

"It only looks like that," he replied. "I didn't stay there of my own free will."

Roxane examined his face as if she had forgotten what it looked like and stroked the boy's hair. It was as black as hers, but his eyes were the eyes of another. They looked at him coldly. Dustfinger rubbed his hands together and whispered fire-words to his fingers until sparks fell from them like rain. Where they landed on the stony ground flowers sprang up, red flowers, each petal a tongue of flame. The boy stared at them with mingled delight and fear. In the end he crouched down beside them and put his hand out to the fiery flowers.

"Careful!" warned Dustfinger, but it was already too late. The boy, taken by surprise, put his burned fingertips in his mouth.

"So the fire still obeys you," said Roxane, and for the first time he detected something like a smile in her eyes. "You look hungry. Come with me." And without another word she walked toward the house. The boy was still staring at the fiery flowers.

"I've heard you grow herbs for the healers." Dustfinger stood indecisively in the doorway.

"Yes, even Nettle buys from me."

Nettle, small as a moss-woman, always surly, sparing of her words as a beggar with his tongue cut out. But there wasn't a better healer in this world.

"Does she still live in the old bear's cave on the outskirts of the forest?" Hesitantly, Dustfinger walked through the doorway. It was so low that he had to duck his head. The smell of freshly baked bread rose to his nostrils. Roxane placed a loaf on the table, brought cheese, oil, olives.

"Yes, but she isn't often there. She's getting more eccentric all the time, she roams the forest talking to the trees and to herself, looking for plants still unknown to her. Sometimes you don't see her for weeks, so people come to me more and more often these days. Nettle has taught me things these last few years." She didn't look at him as she said that. "She's shown me how to grow herbs in my fields that usually thrive only in the forest. Butterfly clover, jinglebell leaf, and the red anemones where the fire-elves get their honey."

"I didn't know those anemones could be used for healing, too."

"They can't. I planted them because they reminded me of someone." This time she did look at him.

Dustfinger put out his hand to one of the bunches of herbs hanging from the ceiling and rubbed the dry flowers between his fingers: lavender, where vipers hide, and helpful if they bite you. "I expect they grow here only because you sing for them," he said. "Didn't folk always say: When Roxane sings, the stones burst into flower?"

Roxane cut some bread, poured oil into a bowl. "I sing only

for the stones these days," she said. "And for my son." She handed him the bread. "Here, eat this. I baked it only yesterday." Then, turning her back to him, she went over to the fire. Dustfinger watched her surreptitiously as he dipped a piece of bread into the oil. Two sacks of straw and a couple of blankets on the bed, a bench, a chair, a table, pitchers, baskets, bottles and bowls, bundles of dried herbs under the ceiling, crammed close together the way they used to hang in Nettle's cave, and a chest that looked strangely fine in this otherwise sparsely furnished room. Dustfinger still remembered the cloth merchant who had given it to Roxane. It was a heavy load for his servants to carry, and it had been full to the brim with silken dresses embroidered with pearls, the sleeves edged with lace. Were they still there in the chest? Unworn, useless for working in the fields?

"I went to Nettle when Rosanna first fell ill." Roxane did not turn to him as she spoke. "I didn't know anything, not even how to draw the fever out of her. Nettle showed me all she knew, but nothing helped our daughter. So I rode to see the Barn Owl with her, while her fever rose higher and higher. I took her into the forest, to the fairies, but they didn't help me, either. They might have done it for you — but you weren't there."

Dustfinger saw her pass the back of her hand over her eyes. "Cloud-Dancer told me." He knew these were not the right words, but he could find no better.

Roxane just nodded and passed her hand over her eyes again. "Some say that you can see the people you love even after death," she said quietly. "They say the dead visit you by night, or at least in your dreams; your longing for them calls them back, if only for a little while. . . . Rosanna didn't come. I went to women who said they could speak to the dead. I burned herbs whose fragrance was supposed to summon her, and I lay awake long nights hoping that she would come back, at least once. But it was all lies. There's no way back. Or have you been there? Did you find one?"

"In the realm of the dead? No." Dustfinger shook his head with a sad smile. "No, I didn't go quite so far. But believe me, if I had, then even from there I'd have sought some way to get back to you. . . ."

How long she looked at him! No one else had ever looked at him like that. And once again he tried to find words, the words that could explain where he had been, but there were none.

"When Rosanna died," Roxane's tongue seemed to shrink from the word, as if it could kill her daughter a second time, "when she died and I held her in my arms, I swore something to myself: I swore that never, never again would I be so helpless when death tried to take away someone I love. I've learned a great deal since then. Perhaps today I could cure her. Or perhaps not."

She looked at him again, and when he returned her glance he did not try to hide his pain, as he usually would.

"Where did you bury her?"

"Behind the house, where she always used to play."

He turned to the open door, wanting at least to see the earth under which she lay, but Roxane held him back. "Where have you been?" she whispered, laying her forehead against his chest.

He stroked her hair, stroked the fine gray strands like silken cobwebs running through the sooty black, and buried his face in it. She still mixed a little bitter orange into the water when she washed her hair. Its perfume brought back so many memories that he felt dizzy. "Far away," he said. "I've been very, very far away." Then he just stood there holding her tightly, unable to believe that she was really there again, not just a figment of his dreams, not just a memory, blurred and vague, but a woman of flesh and blood with fragrant hair . . . and she was not sending him away.

How long they simply stood there like that, he didn't know.

"What about our older girl? How is Brianna?" he asked at last.

"She's been living up at the castle for four years now. She serves Violante, the prince's daughter-in-law, known to everyone as Her Ugliness." She came out of his arms, smoothed her pinned-up hair, and reached for his hands. "Brianna sings for Violante, looks after her spoiled little son, and reads to her," she said. "Violante adores books, but her eyesight is bad, so she can't easily read them for herself — let alone that she must do it in secret because the prince thinks poorly of women who read."

"But Brianna can read?"

"Yes, and I've taught my son to read, too."

"What's his name?"

"Jehan. After his father." Roxane went over to the table and touched the flowers standing on it.

"Did I know him?"

"No. He left me this farm — and a son. The fire-raisers set light to our barn, he ran in to save the livestock, and the fire consumed him. Isn't it strange — that you can love two men and fire protects one of them but kills the other?" She was silent for some time before she spoke again. "Firefox was leader of the arsonists then. They were almost worse than under Capricorn. Basta and Capricorn disappeared at the same time as you, did you know?"

"Yes, so I've heard," he murmured, unable to take his eyes off her. How lovely she was. How beautiful. It almost hurt to look at her. When she came toward him again every movement reminded him of the day he had first seen her dance.

"The fairies did very well," she said quietly, stroking his face.

"If I didn't know better, I'd think someone had simply painted those scars on your face with a silver pencil."

"A lie, but a kind one," he said just as softly. No one knew better than Roxane where the scars came from. They would neither of them forget the day when the Adderhead had commanded her to dance and sing before him. Capricorn had been there, too, with Basta and all the other fire-raisers, and Basta had stared at Roxane like a tomcat eyeing a tasty bird. He had pursued her day after day, promising her gold and jewels, threatening and flattering her, and when she rejected him again and again, alone and in company, Basta made inquiries to discover the identity of the man she preferred to him. He lay in wait for Dustfinger on his way to Roxane, with two other men, who held him down while Basta cut his face.

"You didn't marry again after your husband died?" *You fool,* he thought, *are you jealous of a dead man?*

"No, the only man on this farm is Jehan."

The boy appeared in the doorway as suddenly as if he had been listening behind it, just waiting for his name to be spoken. Without a word he made his way past Dustfinger and sat down on the bench.

"The flowers are even bigger now," he said.

"Did you burn your fingers on them?"

"Only a little."

Roxane pushed a jug of cold water over to him. "Here, dip them in that. And if it doesn't help I'll break an egg for you. There's nothing better for burns than a little egg white."

Jehan obediently put his fingers in the jug, still looking at Dustfinger. "Doesn't he ever burn himself?" he asked his mother.

Roxane had to smile. "No, never. Fire loves him. It licks his fingers, it kisses him."

Jehan looked at Dustfinger as if his mother had said that fairy and not human blood ran in his veins.

"Careful, she's teasing you!" said Dustfinger. "Of course it bites me, too."

"Those scars on your face — they weren't made by fire?"

"No." Dustfinger helped himself to more bread. "This woman, Violante," he said. "Cloud-Dancer told me the Adderhead is her father. Does she hate the strolling players as much as he does?"

"No." Roxane ran her fingers through Jehan's black hair. "If Violante hates anyone, it's her father himself. She was seven when he sent her here. She was married to Cosimo when she was twelve, and six years later she was a widow. Now there she sits in her father-in-law's castle, trying to care for his subjects, as he has long neglected to do in his mourning for his son. Violante feels for the weak. Beggars, cripples, widows with hungry children, peasants who can't pay their taxes — they all go to her, but Violante is a woman. Any power she has is only because everyone's afraid of her father, even on this side of the forest."

"Brianna likes it at the castle." Jehan wiped his wet fingers on his trousers and looked at their reddened tips with concern.

Roxane dipped his fingers back in the cold water. "Yes, I'm afraid so," she said. "Our daughter likes to wear Violante's cast-off clothes, sleep in a soft four-poster bed, and have the fine folk at court pay her compliments. But I don't care for it, and she knows I don't."

"The Ugly Lady sends for me, too, sometimes!" There was no mistaking the pride in Jehan's voice. "To play with her son. Jacopo pesters her and Brianna when they're reading, and no one else will play with him because he always starts screaming when you have a fight with him . . . and when he loses he shouts that he's going to have your head chopped off!"

"You let him play with a prince's brat?" Dustfinger cast Roxane an anxious glance. "Whatever their age, princes are never friends to anyone. Have you forgotten that? And the same is true of their daughters, especially if the Adderhead is their father."

Roxane made her way past him in silence. "You don't have to remind me what princes are like," she said. "Your daughter is fifteen years old now; it's a long time since she took any advice from me. But who knows, maybe she'll listen to her father, even if she hasn't seen him for ten years. Next Sunday the Laughing Prince is holding festivities to celebrate his grandson's birthday. A good fire-eater is sure to be welcome at the castle, since Sootbird is the only one they've had to entertain them all these years." She stopped in the open doorway. "Come along, Jehan," she said, "your fingers don't look too bad, and there's plenty of work still to do."

The boy obeyed without protest. At the door he cast a last, curious look at Dustfinger, then ran off — and Dustfinger was left alone in the little house. He looked at the pots and pans near the fire, the wooden bowls, the spinning wheel in the corner, and the chest that spoke of Roxane's past. Yes, it was a simple house, not much bigger than a charcoal-burner's hut, but it was a home — something that Roxane had always wanted. She had never liked to have only the sky above her by night . . . even if he made the fire grow flowers for her, flowers to watch over her sleep.

MEGGIE READS

"Don't ask where the rest of this book is!" It is a shrill cry that comes from an undefined spot among the shelves. "All books continue in the beyond . . ."

Italo Calvino, *If on a Winter's Night a Traveler*

When all was quiet in Elinor's house, and the garden was bright in the moonlight, Meggie put on the dress that Resa had made for her. Several months ago, she had asked her mother what kind of clothes women wore in the Inkworld.

"Which women?" Resa had inquired. "Farmers' wives? Strolling players? Princes' daughters? Maidservants?"

"What did *you* wear?" Meggie asked, and Resa had gone into the nearest town with Darius and bought some dress material there: plain, coarsely woven red fabric. Then she had asked Elinor to bring the old sewing machine up from the cellar. "That's the sort of dress I wore when I was living in Capricorn's fortress as a maid," her hands had said, putting the finished dress over Meggie's head. "It would have been too fine for a peasant woman, but it was just about good enough for a rich man's

93

servant, and Mortola was very keen that we shouldn't be much worse dressed than the prince's maids — even if we only served a gang of fire-raisers."

Meggie stood in front of her wardrobe mirror and examined herself in the dull glass. She looked strange to herself. And she'd be a stranger in the Inkworld, too; a dress alone couldn't alter that. A stranger, just as Dustfinger was here, she thought — and she remembered the unhappiness in his eyes. *Nonsense,* she told herself crossly, pushing back her smooth hair. *I'm not planning to spend ten years there.*

The sleeves of the dress were already a little too short, and it was stretched tight over her breasts, too. "Good heavens, Meggie!" Elinor had exclaimed when she realized, for the first time, that they weren't as flat as the cover of a book anymore. "Well, I imagine your Pippi Longstocking days are over now!"

They hadn't found anything suitable for Farid to wear, not in the attic or in the trunks of clothes down in the cellar that smelled of mothballs and cigar smoke, but he didn't seem to mind. "Who cares? If it works we'll start out in the forest," he said. "No one will be interested in my jeans there, and as soon as we come to a village or town I'll steal myself something to wear!"

Everything always seemed so simple to him. He couldn't understand that Meggie felt guilty because of Mo and Resa any more than he understood her anxiety to find the right clothes. When she confessed that she could hardly look Mo and her mother in the eye after deciding to go with him, he had just asked "Why?" looking at her blankly. "You're thirteen! Surely they'd be marrying you off to someone quite soon anyway?"

"Marrying me off?" Meggie had felt the blood rise to her face. But how could she talk about such things to a boy out of a story in the *Thousand and One Nights*, where all women were servants or slave girls — or lived in a harem?

"Anyway," added Farid, kindly ignoring the fact that she was still blushing, "you're not intending to stay very long, are you?"

No, she wasn't. She wanted to taste and smell and feel the Inkworld, see fairies and princes — and then come home again to Mo and Resa, Elinor and Darius. There was just one problem: The words Orpheus had written might take her into Dustfinger's story, but they couldn't bring her back. Only one person could write her back again — Fenoglio, the inventor of the world she wanted to visit, the creator of glass men and blue-skinned fairies, of Dustfinger and Basta, too. Yes, only Fenoglio could help her to return. Every time Meggie thought of that, her courage drained away and she felt like canceling the whole plan, striking out those three little words she had added to what Orpheus had written: "*. . . and the girl.*"

Suppose she couldn't find Fenoglio, suppose he wasn't even in his own story anymore? *Oh, come on! He* must *still be there,* she told herself whenever that thought made her heart beat faster. He can't simply write himself back, not without someone to read what he's written aloud! But suppose Fenoglio had found another reader there, someone like Orpheus or Darius? The gift didn't seem to be unique, as she and Mo had once thought.

No, he's still there! I'm sure he is! thought Meggie for the hundredth time, reading her good-bye letter to Mo and Resa once more. She herself didn't know why she had chosen to write it on the letterhead that she and Mo had designed together. That was hardly going to mollify him.

Dearest Mo, dear Resa. Meggie knew the words by heart.

Please don't worry. Farid has to find Dustfinger to warn him

*about Basta, and I'm going, too. I won't stay long, I just want to
see the Wayless Wood, the Laughing Prince, and Cosimo the Fair,
and perhaps the Black Prince and Cloud-Dancer. I want to see the
fairies again, and the glass men — and Fenoglio. He'll write me
back here. You know he can do it, so don't worry. Capricorn isn't in
the Inkworld anymore, after all.*

See you soon, lots of love and kisses, Meggie.

*P.S. I'll bring you back a book, Mo. Apparently, there are
wonderful books there, handwritten books full of pictures, like the
ones in Elinor's glass cases. Only even better. Please don't be angry.*

She had torn up this letter and rewritten it three times, but
that had made matters no better. Because she knew that there
were no words that could stop Mo from being angry with her and
Resa from weeping with anxiety — the way she did the day
Meggie came home from school two hours later than usual. She
put the letter on her pillow — they couldn't miss seeing it
there — and went over to the mirror again. *Meggie,* she thought,
what are you doing? What do you think you're doing? But her
reflection did not reply.

When she let Farid into her room just after midnight he was
surprised to see her dress. "I don't have shoes to go with it," she
said. "But luckily it's quite long, and I don't think my boots show
much, do they?"

Farid just nodded. "It looks lovely," he murmured awkwardly.

Meggie locked the door after letting him in, and took the
key out of the lock so that it could be unlocked again from
outside. Elinor had a second key, and though she probably
wouldn't be able to find it at first, Darius would know where it
was. Meggie glanced at the letter on her pillow once more. . . .

Over his shoulder, Farid had the backpack she had found in
Elinor's attic. "Oh, he's welcome to it," Elinor had said when

Meggie asked her. "It once belonged to an uncle of mine. I hated him! The boy can put that smelly marten in it. I like the idea!"

The marten! Meggie's heart missed a beat.

Farid didn't know why Dustfinger had left Gwin behind, and Meggie hadn't told him, although she knew the reason only too well. She herself, after all, had told Dustfinger what part the marten was to play in his story. He was to die a dreadful, violent death because of Gwin — if what Fenoglio had written came true.

But Farid just shook his head sadly when she asked him about the marten. "He's gone," said the boy. "I tied him up in the garden, because the bookworm woman kept on at me about her birds, but he gnawed through the rope. I've looked for him everywhere, but I just can't find him!"

Clever Gwin.

"He'll have to stay here," said Meggie. "Orpheus didn't write anything about him, and Resa will look after him. She likes him."

Farid nodded and glanced unhappily at the window, but he didn't contradict her.

The Wayless Wood — that was where Orpheus's words would take them. Farid knew where Dustfinger had meant to go after arriving in the forest: to Ombra, where the Laughing Prince's castle stood. And that was where Meggie hoped to find Fenoglio, too. He had often told her about Ombra when they were both Capricorn's prisoners. One night, when neither of them could sleep because Capricorn's men were shooting at stray cats outside again, Fenoglio had whispered to Meggie, "If I could choose to see one place in the Inkworld, then it would be Ombra. After all, the Laughing Prince is a great lover of books, which can hardly be said of his adversary the Adderhead. Yes, life must surely be good for a writer in Ombra. A room in an attic somewhere, perhaps in the alley where the cobblers and saddlers work — their trades don't smell too bad — and a glass man to sharpen my quills, a few fairies over my bed, and I could look down into the alley through my window and see all life pass by. . . ."

"What are you taking with you?" Farid's voice startled Meggie out of her thoughts. "You know we're not supposed to bring too much."

"Of course I know." Did he think that just because she was a girl she needed a dozen dresses? All she was going to carry was the old leather bag that had always gone with her and Mo on their travels when she was little. It would remind her of Mo, and she hoped that in the Inkworld it would be as inconspicuous as her dress. But the things she'd stuffed into it would certainly attract attention if anyone saw them: a hairbrush made of plastic, modern like the buttons on the cardigan she had packed; also a couple of pencils, a penknife, a photograph of her parents, and one of Elinor. She had thought hard about what book to take. Going without one would have seemed to her like setting off naked, but it mustn't be a heavy book, so it had to be a paperback. "Books in beach clothes," Mo called them, "badly dressed for most occasions but useful when you're on vacation." Elinor didn't have a single paperback on her shelves, but Meggie herself owned a few. In the end she had decided on one that Resa had given her, a collection of stories set near the lake that lay close to Elinor's house. That way she would be taking a little bit of home with her — for Elinor's house was her home now, more than anywhere else had ever been. And who knew, maybe Fenoglio would be able to use the words in it to write her back again, back into her own story. . . .

Farid had gone to the window. It was open, and a cool wind was blowing into the room, moving the curtains that Resa had made. Meggie shivered in her new dress. The nights were still very mild, but what would the season be in the Inkworld? Perhaps it was winter there. . . .

"I ought to say good-bye to him, at least," murmured Farid. "Gwin!" he called softly into the night air, clicking his tongue.

Meggie quickly pulled him away from the window. "Don't do that!" she snapped. "Do you want to wake up everyone? I've already told you, Gwin will be fine here. He's probably found a female marten by now. There are a few around the place. Elinor's always afraid they'll eat the nightingale that sings outside her window in the evening."

Farid looked very unhappy, but he stepped back from the window. "Why are you leaving it open?" he asked. "Suppose Basta . . ." He didn't finish his sentence.

"Elinor's alarm system works even if there's an open window," was all Meggie said, while she put the notebook Mo had given her in her bag. There was a reason why she didn't want to close the window. One night in a hotel by the sea, not far from Capricorn's village, she had persuaded Mo to read her a poem. A poem about a moon-bird asleep in a peppermint wind. Next morning the bird was fluttering against the window of their hotel bedroom, and Meggie couldn't forget how its little head kept colliding with the glass again and again. Her window must stay open.

"We'd better sit close to each other on the sofa," she said. "And sling your backpack over your back."

Farid obeyed. He sat down on the sofa as hesitantly as he had on her chair. It was an old, velvet, button-backed sofa with tassels, its pale green upholstery very worn. "You need somewhere comfortable to sit and read," Elinor had said when she asked Darius to put it in Meggie's room. What would Elinor say when she found that Meggie had gone? Would she understand?

She'll probably swear a lot, thought Meggie, kneeling beside her schoolbag. *And then she'll say, "Damn it, why didn't the silly girl take me, too?"* That would be Elinor all over. Meggie suddenly wanted to see her again, but she tried not to think of any of them anymore — not Elinor or Resa or Mo. Particularly not Mo, for she might have only too clear an idea of what he'd look like when he found her letter . . . *No, stop it,* she told herself.

She quickly reached into her schoolbag and took out her geography book. The sheet of paper that Farid had brought with him was in there, beside her own copy of it, but Meggie took out only the copy in her own handwriting. Farid moved aside as she sat down next to him, and for a moment Meggie thought she saw something like fear in his eyes.

"What's the matter?" she asked. "Have you changed your mind?"

But he shook his head. "No. It's just . . . it hasn't ever happened to you, has it?"

"What?" For the first time Meggie noticed that he had a beard coming. It looked odd on his young face.

"Well, what — what happened to Darius."

Ah, that was it. He was afraid of arriving in Dustfinger's world with a twisted face, or a stiff leg, or mute like Resa.

"No, of course not!" Meggie couldn't help the note of injury that crept into her voice. Although — could she really be sure that Fenoglio had arrived unharmed on the other side? Fenoglio, the Steadfast Tin Soldier . . . she had never seen people again after sending them away into the letters on the page. She'd seen only those who came *out* of the pages. Never mind. *Don't think so much, Meggie. Read, or you may lose courage before you even feel the first word on your tongue. . . .*

Farid cleared his throat, as if he, and not Meggie, must start reading.

So what was she waiting for? Did she expect Mo to knock on her door and wonder why she had locked it? All had been quiet next door for some time. Her parents were asleep. *Don't think of them, Meggie! Don't think of Mo or Resa or Elinor, just think of the words — and the place where you want them to take you. A place of marvels and adventures.*

Meggie looked at the letters on the page, black and carefully shaped. She tried the taste of the first few syllables on her tongue, tried to picture the world of which the words whispered, the trees, the birds, the strange sky. . . . Then she began to read. Her heart was thudding almost as violently as it had on the night she had been meant to use her voice to kill. Yet this time she had to do so much less. She had only to open a door, nothing but a door between the words, just large enough for her and Farid to pass through. . . .

A fresh fragrance rose to her nostrils, the scent of thousands and thousands of leaves. Then everything disappeared: her desk, the lamp beside her, the open window. The last thing that Meggie saw was Gwin, sitting on the windowsill, snuffling and looking at them.

10

THE INKWORLD

Thus sharply did the terrified three learn the difference
between an island of make-believe and the same island come
true.

J. M. Barrie, *Peter Pan*

It was bright. Sunlight filtered through countless leaves.
Shadows danced on a nearby pool, and a swarm of tiny red
elves was whirring above the dark water.

I can do it! That was Meggie's first thought when she sensed
that the letters on the page really had let her through and she
wasn't in Elinor's house anymore, but somewhere very, very
different. *I can do it. I can read myself into a story.* She really had
slipped through the words, as she'd so often done in her mind.
But this time she wouldn't have to slip into the skin of a character
in the story — no, this time she would be in the story herself, part
of it. Her very own self. Meggie. Not even that man Orpheus had
done it. He had read Dustfinger home, but he couldn't read himself into the book, right into it. No one but Meggie had ever done
it before, not Orpheus, not Darius, not Mo.

Mo.

Meggie looked around almost as if she hoped he might be standing behind her, as usual when they were in a strange place. But only Farid was there, looking around as incredulously as she was. Elinor's house was far, far away. Her parents were gone. And there was no way back.

Quite suddenly, Meggie felt fear rise in her like black, brackish water. She felt lost, terribly lost, felt it in every part of her. She didn't belong here! What had she done?

She stared at the paper in her hand, so useless now, the bait she had swallowed. Fenoglio's story had caught her. The sense of triumph that had carried her away just now was gone as if it had never been. Fear had extinguished it, fear that she had made a terrible mistake and it could never be put right. Meggie tried desperately to find some other feeling in her heart, but there was nothing, not even curiosity about the world now surrounding her. *I want to go back!* That was all she could think.

But Farid turned to her and smiled.

"Look at those trees, Meggie!" he said. "They really do grow right up to the sky. Look at them!"

He ran his fingers over his face, felt his nose and mouth, looked down at himself, and on realizing that he was obviously entirely unharmed began leaping around like a grasshopper. He made his way over the tree roots that wound through the moss that grew thick and soft between them, jumped from root to root — and then turned around and around, laughing, arms outstretched, until he was dizzy and staggered back against the nearest tree. Still laughing, he leaned against its trunk, which was so vast that five grown men with their arms stretched out could hardly have encompassed it, and looked up into the tangle of twigs and branches.

"You did it, Meggie!" he cried. "You did it! Hear that, Cheeseface?" he shouted at the trees. "She can do it, using your words. She can do what you've tried thousands of times! She can do it, and you can't!" He laughed again, as gleefully as a small child. Until he noticed that Meggie was perfectly silent.

"What's the matter?" he asked, indicating her mouth in alarm. "You haven't . . . ?"

Lost her voice, like her mother? Had she? Her tongue felt heavy, but the words came out. "No. No, I'm all right."

Farid smiled with relief. His carefree mood soothed Meggie's fears, and for the first time she really looked around her. They were in a valley, a broad, densely wooded valley among hills with trees standing so close together on their slopes that the crowns grew into one another. Chestnut and oak on the hillsides, ash and poplar farther down, mingling their leaves with the silvery foliage of willows. The Wayless Wood deserved its name. It seemed to have no end and no beginning, like a green sea where you could drown as easily as in the wet and salty waves of its sister the ocean.

"Isn't this incredible? Isn't it amazingly wonderful?" Farid laughed so exuberantly that an animal of some kind, invisible among the leaves, snarled angrily down at them. "Dustfinger told me about it, but it's even better than he said. How can there be so many different kinds of leaves? And just look at all the flowers and berries! We won't starve here!" Farid picked a berry, round and blue-black, sniffed it, and put it in his mouth. "I once knew an old man," he said, wiping the juice from his lips, "who used to tell stories at night by the fire. Stories about paradise. This is just how he described it: carpets of moss, pools of cool water, flowers and sweet berries everywhere, trees growing up to the sky, and the voices of their leaves speaking to the wind above you. Can you hear them?"

Yes, Meggie could. And she could see elves, swarms of them, tiny creatures with red skins. Resa had told her about them. They were swirling like midges above a pool of water, only a few steps away, which reflected the leaves of the trees. It was surrounded by bushes that bore red flowers, and the water was covered with their faded petals.

Meggie couldn't see any blue fairies, but she did see butterflies, bees, birds, spiders' webs still silvery with dew although the sun was high in the sky, lizards, rabbits . . . There was a rustling and a rushing all around them, a crackling and a scratching and a pulsing; there was a hissing and a cooing and a chirping. This world seemed to be bursting with life, and yet it seemed quiet as well, wonderfully quiet, as if time didn't exist, as if there were no beginning or end to the present moment.

"Do you think he came here, too?" Farid looked around wistfully, as if hoping that Dustfinger would appear among the trees at any moment. "Yes, of course. Orpheus must have read him to this very place, don't you think? He told me about that pool, and the red elves, and the tree over there with the pale bark where you can find their nests. 'And then you must follow a stream,' he said, 'a stream going north. For in the south lies Argenta where the Adderhead rules, and you'll be hanged from a gallows there quicker than you can say your name.' But I'd better take a look from up there!" Quick as a squirrel, he climbed a sapling, and before Meggie knew it he had caught hold of a woody vine and was hauling himself up to the top of a gigantic tree.

"What are you doing?" she called after him.

"You can always see more from farther up!"

Farid was hardly visible among the branches now. Meggie folded up the sheet of paper with Orpheus's words on it and put it in her bag. She didn't want to see the letters anymore; they seemed to her like poisonous beetles, like Alice in Wonderland's bottle saying, "Drink me!" Her fingers touched the notebook with its marbled paper cover, and suddenly she had tears in her eyes.

"When you come to a charcoal-burner's hut, Dustfinger said, then you know you're out of the Wayless Wood." Farid's voice came down to her like the sound of a strange bird. "I remember every word he said. If I want them to, words stick in my memory like flies sticking to resin. I don't need paper to put them on, not me! You just have to find the charcoal-burners and the black patches they leave on the forest floor, he said, and then you know the world of humans isn't far off. Follow the stream that springs from the water-nymphs' pool. It will lead you straight to Lombrica and the Laughing Prince's realm. Soon you'll see his castle on the eastern slope of a hill, high above a river. It's gray as a wasp's nest, and the city is all around it, with a marketplace where you can breathe fire right up to the sky. . . ."

Meggie was kneeling among the flowers — violets and purple bellflowers — most of them fading now, but they were still fragrant and smelled so sweet that she felt dizzy. A wasp was zooming around among them — or did it just look like a wasp? How much had Fenoglio copied from his own world and how much had he made up? It all seemed so familiar and yet so strange.

"Isn't it lucky he told me about everything in such detail?" Meggie saw Farid's bare feet. He was swinging through the leaves at a dizzy height. "Dustfinger often couldn't sleep at night. He was afraid of his dreams. I used to wake him up when they were bad, and then we sat by the fire and I asked him questions. I do that very well. I'm brilliant at asking questions. You bet I am!"

Meggie couldn't help smiling at the pride in his voice. She

looked up at the canopy of foliage and saw that the leaves were turning color, as they had been in Elinor's garden, too. Did the two worlds keep time with each other? And had they always kept time, or did their stories become inextricably linked only on the day when Mo brought Capricorn, Basta, and Dustfinger from one into the other? She would never find out the answer, for who could know?

There was a rustling under one of the bushes, a thorny shrub, heavy with dark berries. Wolves and bears, cats with dappled fur — Resa had told her about them, too. Involuntarily, Meggie stepped back, but her dress caught on some tall thistles white with their own downy seed heads.

"Farid?" she called, angry with herself when she heard the fear in her voice. "Farid!"

But he didn't seem to hear her. He was still chattering away to himself high among the branches, carefree as a bird in the sunshine, while she, Meggie, was down here among the shadows. Shadows that moved, had eyes, growled . . . Was that a snake? She freed her dress with such a violent tug that it tore, and stumbled farther back until she came up against the rough trunk of an oak tree. The snake slid past quickly, as if the sight of Meggie had made it mortally afraid, too, but there was still something moving under the bush, and finally a head pushed out from the prickly twigs. It was furry and round-nosed, and it had tiny horns between its ears.

"No!" whispered Meggie. "Oh no!"

Gwin stared at her almost reproachfully, as if he thought it was her fault that his fur was full of fine prickles.

Farid's voice above her was more distinct now. Obviously, he was finally coming down from his lookout post. "No hut, no castle, nothing in sight!" he called. "It'll be a few days before we get out of this forest, but that's how Dustfinger wanted it. He wanted to take his time coming back to the world of humans. I think he was almost more homesick for the trees and fairies than for other people. Well, I don't know about you — and the trees are beautiful, very beautiful — but personally I'd like to see the castle, too, and the other strolling players, and the men-at-arms."

He jumped down on the grass, hopped on one leg through the carpet of blue flowers — and let out a cry of delight when he saw the marten. "Gwin! Oh, I knew you'd heard me! Come here, you son of a devil and a snake! Won't Dustfinger be surprised to see we've brought him his old friend after all!"

Oh, won't he just! thought Meggie. *Fear will take his breath away — he'll go weak at the knees.*

The marten jumped onto Farid's knee as the boy crouched down in the grass, and affectionately licked his chin. He would have bitten anyone else, even Dustfinger, but with Farid he acted like a young kitten.

"Shoo him away, Farid!" Meggie's voice sounded sharper than she had intended.

"Shoo him away?" Farid laughed. "What are you talking about? Hear that, Gwin? What have you done to offend her? Left a dead mouse on one of her precious books?"

"Shoo him away, I said! He'll be all right on his own, you know he will. Please!" she added, seeing his horrified expression as he looked at her.

Farid straightened up, the marten in his arms. His face was more hostile than she had ever seen it before. Gwin jumped up on his shoulder and stared at Meggie as if he had understood every word she said. Very well, then, she'd just have to tell Farid — but how?

"Didn't Dustfinger tell you?"

"Tell me what?" He looked at her as if he'd like to hit her.

Above them, the wind blew through the leaf canopy like a menacing whisper.

"If you don't shoo Gwin away," said Meggie, although each word was difficult to utter, "then Dustfinger will. And he'll chase you away, too."

The marten was still staring at her.

"Why would he do a thing like that? You don't like him, that's what it is. You never liked Dustfinger, and you don't like Gwin, either."

"That's not true! You don't understand!" Meggie's voice was loud and shrill. "He's going to die because of Gwin! Dustfinger dies, that's how Fenoglio wrote the story! Perhaps it's been changed, perhaps this is a new story we're in and everything in the book is just a pile of dead words, but all the same . . ."

Meggie hadn't the heart to go on. Farid stood there shaking his head again and again, as if her words were like needles digging into it, hurting him.

"He's going to die?" His voice was barely audible. "He dies in the book?"

How lost he looked standing there with the marten still perched on his shoulder! He looked at the trees around them with horror, as if they were all intent on killing Dustfinger. "But — but if I'd known that," he stammered, "I'd have torn up Cheeseface's wretched piece of paper! I'd never have let him read Dustfinger back!"

Meggie just looked at him. What could she say?

"Who kills him? Basta?"

Two squirrels were chasing around overhead. They had white spots as if someone had shaken a paintbrush over them. The marten wanted to go after them, but Farid seized his tail and held it tight.

"One of Capricorn's men. That's all Fenoglio wrote!"

"But they're all dead!"

"We don't know that." Meggie would have been only too glad to comfort him, but she didn't know how. "Suppose they're still alive in this world? And even if they aren't — Mo and Darius didn't read all of them out. Some are still sure to be here. Dustfinger tries to save Gwin from them, and they kill him. That's what it says in the book, and Dustfinger knows it. That's why he left the marten behind."

"Yes, so he did." Farid looked around as if seeking some solution, a way he could send the marten back again. Gwin nuzzled his cheek with his nose, and Meggie saw the tears in Farid's eyes.

"Wait here!" he said, and he turned abruptly and went off with the marten. He had gone only a few paces before the forest swallowed him up like a frog swallowing a fly, and Meggie stood there on her own among the flowers. Some of them grew in Elinor's garden, too, but this wasn't Elinor's garden. This wasn't even the same world. And this time she couldn't just close the book and be back again: back in her own room, on the sofa that smelled of Elinor. The world beyond the words on the page was wide — hadn't she always known it? — wide enough for her to be lost there forever. Only one person could write her out of it again — an old man — and Meggie didn't even know where he lived in this world he had created. She didn't even know if he was still alive. Could this world live if its creator was dead? Why not? Books don't stop existing just because their authors have died, do they?

What have I done? thought Meggie as she stood there waiting for Farid to come back. *Oh Mo, what have I done? Can't you fetch me back again?*

11

GONE

I woke up and knew he was gone. Straightaway I knew he was gone. When you love somebody you know these things.
David Almond, *Skellig*

Mo knew at once that Meggie was gone. He knew it the moment he knocked on her door and only silence replied. Resa was down in the kitchen with Elinor, laying the table for breakfast. The clink of the plates made its way upstairs to him, but he hardly heard it, he just stood there outside the closed door, listening to his own heart. It was beating far too loudly, far too fast. "Meggie?" He pressed down the handle, but the door was locked. Meggie never locked her door, never.

His heart beat even faster, as if to choke him. The silence behind the door sounded terribly familiar. Just such a silence had met his ears once before, when he had called Resa's name again and again. He had waited ten years for an answer.

Not again, please God, not again. Not Meggie.

It seemed as if he heard the book whispering on the other side of the door: Fenoglio's accursed story. He thought he heard the pages rustling, greedy as pale teeth.

"Mortimer?" Elinor was standing behind him. "The eggs are getting cold. Where are you and Meggie? Oh heavens!" She looked at his face with concern and reached for his hand. "What's the matter with you? You're pale as death."

"Do you have a spare key for Meggie's door, Elinor?"

She understood at once. Just like Mo, she guessed what had happened behind that locked door, presumably last night when they were all asleep. She pressed his hand. Then she turned without a word and hurried downstairs. But Mo just stood there leaning against the locked door, heard Elinor call Darius and begin to search for the key, cursing, and he stared at the books standing side by side on her shelves all down the long corridor. Resa came running upstairs, pale-faced. Her hands fluttered like frightened birds as she asked him what had happened. What was he to say?

"Can't you imagine? Haven't you told her about the place often enough?" He tried the handle again, as if that could change anything. Meggie had covered the whole door with quotations. They looked to him now like magic spells written on the white paint in a childish hand. *Take me to another world! Go on! I know you can do it. My father has shown me how.* Odd that your heart didn't simply stop when it hurt so much. But his heart hadn't stopped ten years ago, either, when the words on the page swallowed up Resa.

Elinor pushed him aside. She was holding the key in her trembling fingers, and she impatiently put it in the lock. Crossly, she called Meggie's name, as if she, too, hadn't guessed long ago that nothing but silence waited behind that door: the same silence as on the night that had taught Mo to fear his own voice.

He was the last to enter the empty room, and he did so hesitantly. There was a letter on Meggie's pillow. *Dearest Mo . . .* He didn't read on; he didn't want to see the words that would only pierce him to the heart. As Resa picked up the letter he looked around the room — his eyes searching for another sheet of paper, the one the boy had brought with him — but it was nowhere to be found. *Well, of course not, you fool,* he told himself. *She's taken it with her; after all, she must have been holding it while she read.*

Only years later would he discover from Meggie that the original sheet of paper with Orpheus's writing on it had been there in her room all the time, hidden between the pages of a book — where else? Her geography book. Suppose he had found it? Would he have been able to follow Meggie? No, probably not. The story had another path in store for him, a darker and more difficult path.

"Perhaps she's only gone off with the boy! Girls of her age do that kind of thing. Not that I know much about it, but . . ." Elinor's voice reached him as if from very far away. In answer, Resa handed her the letter that had been waiting on the pillow.

Gone. Meggie was gone.

He had no daughter anymore.

Would she come back, like her mother? Fished out of the sea of words again by some other voice? If so, when? In ten years' time, like Resa? She'd be grown-up by then. Would he even recognize her? Everything was blurred before his eyes: Meggie's school things on the desk in front of the window, her clothes, carefully hanging over the back of the chair as if she really meant to come back, her soft toys beside the bed, their furry faces kissed threadbare, although it was a long time since Meggie had needed them to help her get to sleep. Resa began crying without a sound, one hand pressed to her mute mouth. Mo wanted to comfort her, but how could he with such despair in his own heart?

He turned, pushed aside Darius, who was standing there in the open doorway with a sad, owl-like gaze, and went to his study, where those damned notebooks were still stacked among his own papers. He swept them off the desk one by one, as if he could silence the words that way — all the accursed words that had bewitched his child, luring her away like the Pied Piper in the story, to a place where he had already been unable to follow Resa. Mo felt as if he were dreaming the same nightmare all over again, but this time he didn't even have a book whose pages he could have searched for Meggie.

Later, he couldn't say how he had gotten through the rest of that day without going crazy. All he remembered was wandering for hours through Elinor's garden, as if he might find Meggie somewhere there among the old trees where she liked to sit and read. When darkness fell and he set out to look for Resa, he found her in Meggie's room. She was sitting on the empty bed, staring at three tiny creatures circling just below the ceiling, as if they were looking for the door they had come through. Meggie had left the window open, but they didn't fly out, perhaps because the strange, black night frightened them.

"Fire-elves," said Resa's hands when he sat down beside her. "If they settle on your skin you must shake them off, or they'll burn you."

Fire-elves. Mo remembered reading about them in the book. Something always came back in return. There seemed to be just that one book in the whole world.

"Why three of them?" he asked. "One for Meggie, one for the boy . . ."

"I think the marten went, too," said Resa's hands.

Mo almost laughed out loud. Poor Dustfinger, he obviously couldn't shake off his bad luck — but Mo could feel no sympathy for him. Not this time. Without Dustfinger the words on the sheet of paper would never have been written, and he would still have a daughter.

"Do you think at least she'll like it there?" he asked, laying his head in Resa's lap. "After all, you liked it, didn't you? Or, at any rate, you told her so."

"I'm sorry," said her hands. "So very sorry."

But he held her fingers tight. "What are you talking about?" he said softly. "I was the one who brought the damned book into the house, remember?" And then they were both silent. In silence, they watched the poor, lost elves. At some point they did fly through the window, and into the strange night. As their tiny red bodies disappeared into the blackness like sparks going out, Mo wondered whether Meggie was wandering through an equally black night at this moment. The thought pursued him into his dark dreams.

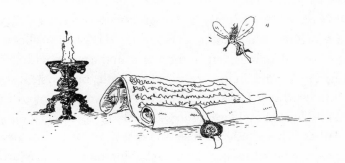

UNINVITED GUESTS

"You people with hearts," he said once, "have something to guide you, and need never do wrong; but I have no heart, and so I must be very careful."

L. Frank Baum, *The Wizard of Oz*

On the day when Meggie disappeared, silence moved back into Elinor's house, but not the silence of the old days when only her books lived there with her. The silence that now filled the rooms and corridors tasted of sorrow. Resa wept a great deal, and Mortimer said nothing, as if paper and ink had swallowed up not just his daughter, but all the words in the world with her. He spent a lot of time in his workshop, ate little, hardly slept — and on the third day Darius, looking very anxious, went to Elinor and told her that Silvertongue was packing up all his tools.

When Elinor entered his workshop, out of breath because Darius had been tugging her along behind him so fast, Mortimer was throwing the stamps he used for gold leaf into a crate, pell-mell — tools that he normally handled as carefully as if they were made of glass.

"What the devil are you doing?" inquired Elinor.

"What does it look like?" he replied and began clearing away his sewing frame. "I'm going to find another profession. I never want to touch a book again, curse them all. Other people can listen to the stories they tell and mend the clothes they wear. I want nothing more to do with them."

When Elinor went to fetch Resa to help her, Resa just shook her head.

"Well, I can understand why those two are useless just now," commented Elinor, as she and Darius sat at breakfast by themselves yet again. "How could Meggie do a thing like that to them? What was her idea — did she want to break her poor parents' hearts? Or prove once and for all that books are dangerous?"

Darius had no answer but silence. He had been the same all these last few sad days.

"For heaven's sake, all of you silent as the grave!" Elinor snapped at him. "We must do something to get the silly creature back. Anything. Good God, it can't be as difficult as all that! After all, there are no fewer than two Silvertongues under this roof!"

Darius looked at her in alarm and choked on his tea. He had left his gift unused for so long that no doubt it seemed like a dream to him, and he didn't want to be reminded of it.

"All right, all right, you don't have to read aloud," Elinor assured him impatiently. Good God, that owlish gaze of horror! She could have shaken him. "Mortimer can do it! But what should he read? Think, Darius! If we want to fetch her back, should it be something about the Inkworld or about our own world? Oh, I'm all confused. Perhaps we can write something like: *Once upon a time there was a grumpy middle-aged woman called Elinor who loved nothing but her books, until one day her niece moved in with her, along with the niece's husband and daughter. Elinor liked that, but one day the daughter set off on a very, very stupid journey, and Elinor swore that she would give all her books away if only the child would come home. She packed them up in big crates, and as she was putting the last book in, Meggie walked through the doorway. . . .* Heavens above, don't stare at me in that sympathetic way!" she snapped at Darius. "I'm trying to do something, at least! And you yourself keep saying: 'Mortimer is a master, it takes him only a couple of sentences!' "

Darius adjusted his glasses. "Yes, only a couple of sentences," he said in his gentle, uncertain voice. "But they must be sentences describing a whole world, Elinor. The words must make music. They must be so closely interwoven that the voice doesn't fall through."

"Oh, for goodness' sake!" Elinor said brusquely — although she knew he was right. Mortimer had once tried to explain it to her in almost the same way: the mystery of why not every story would come to life. But she didn't want to hear about that, not now. *Damn you, Elinor,* she thought bitterly, *damn you three times over for all those evenings you spent with the silly child imagining what it would be like to live in that other world, among fairies, brownies, and glass men.* There had been many such evenings, very many, and Mortimer had often put his head around the door and asked, sarcastically, if they couldn't discuss something other than Wayless Woods and blue-skinned fairies just for once.

Well, at least Meggie knows all she needs to know about that world, thought Elinor, wiping the tears from her eyes. *She realizes she must be careful of the Adderhead and his men-at-arms, and she mustn't go too far into the forest or she'll probably be eaten, torn to pieces, or trodden underfoot. And she'd be well advised not to look up when she passes a gallows. She knows she must bow when a prince rides by, and that she can still wear her hair loose because she's only a girl* . . . Damn it, here came the tears again! Elinor was mopping the corners of her eyes with the hem of her blouse when someone rang the front doorbell.

Many years later, she was still angry with herself for the stupidity that didn't warn her to look through the spy hole in the door before opening it. Of course she had thought it was Resa or Mortimer outside. Of course. Stupid Elinor. Stupid, stupid Elinor. She had realized her mistake only when she opened the door, and there stood the stranger in front of her.

He was not very tall and rather too well fed, with pale skin and equally pale fair hair. The eyes behind his rimless glasses looked slightly surprised, almost innocent like a child's. He opened his mouth to speak as Elinor put her head around the door, but she cut him short.

"What are you doing here?" she barked. "This is private property. Didn't you see the sign down by the road?"

He had come in a car; the impudent fool had simply brought it up her drive! Elinor saw it, a dusty, dark blue vehicle, standing beside her own station wagon. She thought she saw a huge dog on the passenger seat. That was the last straw!

"Yes, of course I did!" The stranger's smile was so innocent that it suited his childish face. "Why, no one could miss seeing the sign, and I really do apologize, Signora Loredan, for my sudden and unannounced arrival."

Heavens above — it took Elinor's breath away. The moonfaced man's voice was almost as beautiful as Mortimer's, deep and velvety like a cushion. Coming from that round face with its childlike eyes, it was so incongruous that you felt almost as if the stranger had swallowed its real owner and taken over his voice.

"Never mind the apologies!" said Elinor abruptly, once she had gotten over her surprise. "Just get out." And so saying, she was about to close the door again, but the stranger only smiled (a smile that no longer looked quite so innocent) and jammed his shoe between the door and the frame. A dusty brown shoe.

"Do forgive me, Signora Loredan," he said softly, "but I've come about a book. A truly unique book. I have heard, of course, that you have a remarkable library, but I can assure you that you don't yet have this book in your collection."

With an almost reverent expression on his face, he put a hand under his pale, creased linen jacket. Elinor recognized the book at once. Of course. It was the only book that made her heart beat faster not because it was a particularly fine edition or because she longed to read it. No. At the sight of that book Elinor's heart beat faster for only one reason: because she feared it like a ferocious animal.

"Where did you get that from?" She answered her question herself, but unfortunately a little too late. Suddenly, very suddenly, the memory of the boy's story came back to her. "Orpheus!" she whispered — and she wanted to shout, loud enough for Mortimer to hear her in his workshop, but before a sound could come out of her mouth someone slipped out of the cover of the rhododendron bushes by the front door, quick as a lizard, and put his hand over her mouth.

"Well, my lady bookworm," a man's voice purred in her ear. Elinor had so often heard that voice in her dreams, and every time she found herself fighting for breath at the sound of it! Even in broad daylight the effect was just as bad. Basta pushed her roughly back into the house. Of course, he had a knife in his hand; Elinor could as easily imagine Basta without a nose as without a knife. Orpheus turned and waved to the strange car. A man built like a wardrobe got out, strolled around the car at a leisurely pace, and opened the back door. An old woman stuck out her legs and reached for his arm.

Mortola. The Magpie.

Another regular visitor to Elinor's nightmares.

The old woman's legs were thickly bandaged under her dark stockings, and she leaned on a stick as she walked toward Elinor's house on the wardrobe-man's arm. She hobbled into the hall with a grimly determined expression, as if she were taking possession of the whole house, and the look she gave Elinor was so openly hostile that its recipient felt weak at the knees, hard as she tried to hide her fear. A thousand dreadful memories came back to her — memories of a cage stinking of raw meat, a square lit by the beams of glaring car headlights, and fear, dreadful fear. . . .

Basta closed the door of the house behind Mortola. He hadn't changed: the same thin face, the same way of narrowing his eyes, and there was an amulet dangling around his neck to ward off the bad luck that Basta thought lurked under every ladder, behind every bush.

"Where are the others?" Mortola demanded while the wardrobe-man looked around him with a foolish expression. The sight of all those books seemed to fill him with boundless astonishment. He was probably wondering what on earth anyone would do with so many.

"The others? I don't know who you're talking about." Elinor thought her voice sounded remarkably steady for a woman half dead with terror.

Mortola's small, round chin jutted aggressively. "You know

perfectly well. I'm talking about Silvertongue and his witch of a daughter, and that maidservant, the one he calls his wife. Shall I get Basta to set fire to a few of your books, or will you call the three of them for us of your own accord?"

Basta? Basta's afraid of fire, Elinor wanted to reply, but she refrained. It wasn't difficult to hold a lighted match to a book. Even Basta, who feared fire so much, would probably be capable of that small action, and the wardrobe-man didn't look bright enough to be afraid of anything. *I just have to keep stalling,* thought Elinor. *After all, they don't know about the workshop in the garden, or about Darius, either.*

"Elinor?" she heard Darius call at that very moment. Before she could reply, Basta's hand was over her mouth again. She heard Darius come down the corridor with his usual rapid tread. "Elinor?" he called again. Then the footsteps stopped as abruptly as his voice.

"Surprise, surprise!" purred Basta. "Aren't you glad to see us, Stumbletongue? A couple of old friends come to pay you a visit!" Basta's left hand was bandaged, Elinor noticed when he took his fingers away from her mouth, and she remembered the hissing creature that Farid said had slipped through the words in Dustfinger's place. *What a pity it didn't eat more of our knife-happy friend,* she thought.

"Basta!" Darius's voice was little more than a whisper.

"That's right, Basta! I'd have been here much sooner, believe you me, but they put me in jail for a while on account of something that happened years ago. No sooner was Capricorn gone than all the people who'd been too scared to open their mouths suddenly felt very brave. Well, never mind. You could say they did me a favor, because who do you think they put in my cell one fine day? I never could get him to tell me his real name, so let's call him by the name he's given himself: Orpheus!" He slapped the man so hard on the back that he stumbled forward. "Yes, our good friend Orpheus!" Basta put an arm around his shoulders. "The Devil did me a real favor when he made Orpheus, of all people, my cellmate — or perhaps our story is so keen to have us back that it sent him? Well, one way or another, we had a good time, didn't we?"

Orpheus did not look at him. He straightened his jacket in embarrassment and inspected Elinor's bookshelves.

"Hey, just look at him!" Basta dug his elbow roughly into Orpheus's ribs. "You wouldn't believe how often I've told him there's nothing to be ashamed of in going to jail, particularly when your prisons here are so much more comfortable than our dungeons at home. Come on, tell them how I found out about your invaluable gifts. How I caught you one night reading yourself that stupid dog out of the book! Reading himself a dog! Lord knows, I could think of better ideas."

Basta laughed nastily, and Orpheus straightened his tie with nervous fingers. "Cerberus is still in the car," he told Mortola. "He doesn't like it there at all. We ought to bring him in!"

The wardrobe-man turned to the door. He obviously had a soft spot for animals, but Mortola stopped him with an impatient gesture.

"The dog stays where it is. I can't stand that creature!" Frowning, she looked around Elinor's hall. "Well, I expected your house to be bigger than this," she said, with assumed disappointment. "I thought you were rich."

"So she is!" Basta flung his arm so roughly around Orpheus's neck that his glasses slipped down his nose. "But she spends all her money on books. What would she pay us for the book we took from Dustfinger, do you think?" He pinched Orpheus's round cheeks. "Yes, our friend here made good juicy bait for the fire-eater. He may look like a bullfrog, but even Silvertongue can't make the words obey him so well, let alone Darius. Ask Dustfinger — Orpheus sent him home as if nothing could be easier! Not that the fire-eater will —"

"Hold your tongue, Basta!" Mortola interrupted him abruptly. "You've always liked the sound of your own voice. Well?" She impatiently tapped her stick on the marble tiles that were Elinor's pride and joy. "Where are they? Where are the others? I shan't ask again!"

Come on, Elinor told herself, *lie to them. Lie yourself blue in the face! Quick!* But she hadn't even opened her mouth when she heard the key in the lock. *Oh no! No, Mortimer!* she prayed silently. *Stay where you are! Go back to the workshop with Resa, shut yourselves up there, but please, please don't come in just now!*

Of course her prayers made not the slightest difference.

Mortimer opened the door, came in with his arm around Resa's shoulders — and stopped abruptly at the sight of Orpheus. Before he had entirely grasped what was going on, the man built like a wardrobe had closed the door behind him in obedience to a signal from Mortola.

"Hello there, Silvertongue!" said Basta in a menacingly soft voice, as he snapped his knife open in front of Mortimer's face. "And isn't this our lovely mute Resa? Excellent! Two birds with one stone. All we need now is the little witch."

Elinor saw Mortimer close his eyes for a moment, as if hoping that Basta and Mortola would have disappeared when he opened them again. But, naturally, no such thing happened.

"Call her!" ordered Mortola, as she stared at Mortimer with such hatred in her eyes that Elinor felt afraid.

"Who?" he asked, without taking his eyes off Basta.

"Don't pretend to be more stupid than you are!" Mortola said crossly. "Or do you want me to let Basta cut the same pattern on your wife's face as he did on the fire-eater's?"

Basta ran his thumb lovingly over the gleaming blade.

"If by 'little witch' you mean my daughter," replied Mortimer huskily, "she isn't here."

"Oh no?" Mortola hobbled toward him. "Be careful what you say. My legs are aching after that endless drive to get here, so I'm not feeling particularly patient."

"She isn't here," Mortimer repeated. "Meggie has gone away, with the boy you took the book from. He asked her to take him to Dustfinger, she did it — and she went with him."

Mortola narrowed her eyes incredulously. "Nonsense!" she exclaimed. "How could she have done it without the book?" But Elinor saw the doubt in her face.

Mortimer shrugged. "The boy had a handwritten sheet of paper with him — the one that sent Dustfinger back, apparently."

"That's impossible!" Orpheus looked at him in astonishment. "Are you seriously saying your daughter read herself into the story, using my words?"

"Oh, so you're this Orpheus, are you?" Mortimer returned his glance, not in a very friendly way. "Then you're responsible for the loss of my daughter."

Orpheus straightened his glasses and gave Mortimer an equally hostile look. Then, abruptly, he turned to Mortola. "Is this man Silvertongue?" he demanded. "He's lying! I'm sure of it! He's lying! No one can read themselves into a story. He can't, his daughter can't, no one can. I've tried it myself, hundreds of times. It doesn't work!"

"Yes," said Mortimer wearily. "That's just what I thought, too. Until four days ago."

Mortola stared at him. Then she signaled to Basta. "Shut them up in the cellar!" she ordered. "And then look for the girl. Search the whole house."

FENOGLIO

"I do practice remembering, Nain," I said. "Writing and reading and remembering."

"That you should!" said Nain sharply. "Do you know what happens each time you write a thing down? Each time you name it? You sap its strength."

Kevin Crossley-Holland, *The Seeing Stone*

It wasn't easy to get past the guards at the gate of Ombra after dark, but Fenoglio knew them all. He had written many love poems for the heavily built oaf who barred his way with his spear tonight — and very successful they were, he had been told. Judging by the fool's appearance, he'd be needing to call on Fenoglio's services again.

"But mind you're back before midnight, scribbler!" the ugly fellow grunted before letting him pass. "That's when the Ferret takes over from me, and he's not interested in your poems, even though his girl can read."

"Thanks for the warning!" said Fenoglio, giving the stupid fellow a false smile as he pushed past him. As if he didn't know that the Ferret was not to be trifled with! His stomach still hurt when he remembered how that sharp-nosed fellow had dug the shaft of his spear into it, when he'd tried pushing past him with a couple of well-chosen words. No, there'd be no bribing the Ferret, not with poems or any other written gifts. The Ferret wanted gold, and Fenoglio didn't have too much of that, or at least not enough to waste it on a guard at the city gates.

"Midnight!" he cursed quietly as he stumbled down the steep path. "As if that wasn't just when the strolling players wake up!"

His landlady's son carried the torch ahead of him. Ivo was nine years old and full of insatiable curiosity about all the wonders of his world. He was always fighting his sister for the honor of carrying the torch when Fenoglio went to visit the strolling players. Fenoglio paid Ivo's mother a few coins a week for a room in the attic. The price included the washing, cooking, and mending that Minerva did for him, too. In return, Fenoglio told her children bedtime stories and listened patiently as she told him what a stubborn oaf her husband could be at times. The fact was, Fenoglio had struck lucky.

The boy scurried along ahead of him with increasing impatience. He could hardly wait to reach the brightly colored tents, where music played and firelight shone among the trees. He kept looking around reproachfully, as if Fenoglio were taking his time on purpose. Did he think an old man could go as fast as a grasshopper?

The Motley Folk had pitched camp where the ground was so stony that nothing would grow on it, behind the cottages where the peasants who farmed the Laughing Prince's land lived. Now that the prince of Ombra no longer wanted to hear their jests and songs, they came less often than before, but luckily the prince's grandson wanted players to entertain him on his birthday, so this Sunday they would at last come streaming through the city gates:

fire-eaters and tightrope-walkers, animal-tamers and knife-throwers, actors, buffoons, and many a minstrel whose songs came from Fenoglio's pen.

For Fenoglio liked writing for the Motley Folk: merry songs, sad songs, songs to make you laugh or weep, as the spirit moved him. He couldn't earn more than a few copper coins for those songs; the strolling players' pockets were always empty. If his words were to earn gold then he must write for princes or for a rich merchant. But when he made the words dance and pull faces, when he wanted to write tales of peasants and robbers, of ordinary folk who didn't live in castles or eat from golden plates, then he wrote for the strolling players.

It had taken some time for them to accept him into their tents. Only when more and more wandering minstrels were singing Fenoglio's songs, and their children were asking for his stories, did they stop turning him away. And now even their king invited Fenoglio to sit beside his fire, as he had tonight. Although not a drop of royal blood ran in his veins, this man was known as the Black Prince. The Prince took good care of his Motley subjects, and they had chosen him to lead them twice already. It was better not to ask where all the gold he gave so generously to the sick and crippled came from, but Fenoglio knew one thing: He himself had invented the Prince.

Oh yes, I made them all! he thought, as the music came more clearly through the night air. He had made up the Prince and the tame bear that followed him like a dog, and Cloud-Dancer who, sad to say, fell off his rope, and many more, even the two rulers who believed that they laid down the law in this world. Fenoglio had not yet seen all his creations, but every time he suddenly met one in flesh and blood it made his heart beat faster — although he couldn't always remember whether any particular one of

them had really sprung from his own pen, or came from somewhere else. . . .

There were the tents at last, bright as windblown flowers in
the black night. Ivo began running so fast that he almost fell over
his own feet. A dirty boy with hair as unkempt as an alley cat's
fur came out to meet them, hopping on one leg. He grinned
challengingly at Ivo — and ran away on his hands. Lord, these
players' children performed such contortions, you might think
they had no bones in their bodies!

"Off you go, then!" growled Fenoglio when Ivo looked pleadingly at him. After all, he didn't need the torch anymore. Several
fires were burning among the tents, which often consisted of little more than a few grubby lengths of cloth stretched over ropes
between the trees. Fenoglio looked around with a sigh of satisfaction as the boy raced away. Yes, this was just as he'd imagined
the Inkworld as he wrote his story: bright and noisy, full of life.
The air smelled of smoke, of roast meat, of rosemary and thyme,
horses, dogs and dirty clothes, pine needles and burning wood.
Oh, he loved it! He loved the hurry and bustle, he even loved the
dirt. He loved the way life here was lived before his very eyes, not
behind locked doors. You could learn anything in this world: how
the smith shaped the metal of a sickle in the fire, how the dyer
mixed his dyes, how the tanner removed hair from leather and
how the cobbler cut it to shape to make shoes. Nothing happened
behind closed doors. It was all going on, in the alleyways, on the
road, in the marketplace, here among shabby tents, and he,
Fenoglio — still as curious as a boy — could watch, although the
stench of the leather was mordant and the dye tubs sometimes
took his breath away. Yes, he liked this world of his. He liked it
very much — although he couldn't help seeing that not everything was working out the way he had intended.

It was his own fault. *I should have written a sequel,* thought Fenoglio, making his way through the crowd. *I could still write one, here and now, and change everything, if only I had someone to read it aloud!* Of course he had looked for another Silvertongue, but in vain. No Meggie, no Mortimer, not even someone like that man Darius who was more than likely to botch the job . . . and Fenoglio could play only the part of a writer whose fine words didn't exactly keep him in luxury, while the two princes he had invented ruled his world after their own fashion. Annoying, extremely annoying.

One of those princes above all gave him cause for concern — the Adderhead.

He reigned to the south of the forest, high above the sea, sitting on the silver throne of the Castle of Night. As an invented character, not by any means a bad one. A bloodhound, a ruthless slave driver — but after all, the villains are the salt in the soup of a story. If you can keep them under control. It was for this purpose that Fenoglio had thought up the Laughing Prince, a ruler who would rather laugh at the broad jokes of the strolling players than wage war, and his magnificent son, Cosimo. Who could have guessed that Cosimo would simply die, and then his father would collapse with grief like a cake taken out of the oven too soon?

Not my fault! How often Fenoglio had told himself that. *Not my idea, not my fault!* But it had happened all the same. As if some diabolical scribbler had intervened, going on with the story in his place and leaving him, Fenoglio, the creator of this whole world, with nothing but the role of a poor writer!

Oh, stop that. You're not so poor, Fenoglio, he thought as he stopped beside a minstrel sitting among the tents, singing one of Fenoglio's own songs. No, he wasn't poor. The Laughing Prince, who was now the Prince of Sighs, would hear only Fenoglio's laments for his dead son, and Balbulus, the most famous illuminator far and wide, had to record the stories Fenoglio wrote for the prince's grandson, Jacopo, in his own hand, on the most costly of parchment. No, he really wasn't so poor!

And moreover, didn't his words now seem to him better in a minstrel's mouth than pressed between the pages of a book, to lie there gathering dust? He liked to think of them as free, owing no one allegiance. They were too powerful to be given in printed form to any fool who might do God knew what with them. Looked at that way, it was reassuring to think that there were no printed books in this world. Books here were handwritten, which made them so valuable that only princes could afford them. Other folk had to store the words in their heads or listen to minstrels singing them.

A little boy tugged at Fenoglio's sleeve. His tunic had holes in it, and his nose was running. "Inkweaver!" He brought out a mask from behind his back, the kind of mask worn by the actors, and quickly put it over his eyes. There were feathers, light brown and blue, stuck to the cracked leather. "Who am I, Inkweaver?"

"Hmm!" Fenoglio wrinkled his lined brow as if he had to think hard about it.

The mouth below the mask drooped in disappointment. "The Bluejay! I'm the Bluejay, of course!"

"Of course!" Fenoglio pinched the child's red little nose.

"Will you tell us another story about him today? Please!"

"Maybe! I must admit, I imagine his mask as rather more impressive than yours. What do you think? Shouldn't you look for a few more feathers?"

The boy took off his mask and looked at it crossly. "They're not very easy to find."

"Take a look down by the river. Even blue jays aren't safe from the cats that go hunting there." He was about to move away, but the boy held on tight. Thin as the children of the strolling players might be, they had strong little hands.

"Just one story. Please, Inkweaver!"

Two other children joined him, a girl and a boy. They looked expectantly at Fenoglio. Ah, yes, the Bluejay stories. He'd always told good robber tales — his own grandchildren had liked them, too, back in the other world. But the stories he thought up here were much better. You heard them everywhere these days: *The Incredible Deeds of the Bravest of Robbers, The Noble and Fearless Bluejay.* Fenoglio still remembered the night he had made up the Bluejay. His hand had been trembling with rage as he wrote. "The Adderhead's caught another of the strolling players," the Black Prince had told him that night. "It was Crookback this time. They hanged him at noon yesterday."

Crookback — one of his own characters! A harmless fellow who could stand on his head longer than anyone else. "Who does this prince think he is?" Fenoglio had cried out into the night, as if the Adderhead could hear him. "*I* am lord of life and death in this world, I, Fenoglio, no one else!" And the words had gone down on paper, wild and angry as the robber he created that night. The Bluejay was all that Fenoglio would have liked to be in the world he had made: free as a bird, subject to no lord, fearless, noble (sometimes witty, too), a man who robbed from the rich and gave to the poor, and protected the weak from the tyranny of the strong in a world where there was no law to do it. . . .

Fenoglio felt another tug at his sleeve. "Please, Inkweaver! Just *one* story!" The boy was really persistent. He loved listening to stories and would very likely make a famous minstrel someday. "They say the Bluejay stole the Adderhead's lucky charm!"

whispered the little boy. "The hanged man's finger bone to protect him from the White Women. They say the Bluejay wears it around his own neck now."

"Do they indeed?" Fenoglio raised his eyebrows, always a very effective move, thick and bushy as they were. "Well, I've heard of an even more daring deed, but I must have a word with the Black Prince first."

"Oh, please, Inkweaver!" They were clinging to his sleeves, almost tearing off the expensive braid he'd had sewn on the coarse fabric for a few coins, so as not to look as poverty-stricken as the scribes who wrote wills and letters in the marketplace.

"No!" he said sternly, freeing his sleeve. "Later, maybe. Now go away!"

The boy with the runny nose looked at him so sadly that, for a moment, Fenoglio was reminded of his grandson. Pippo always used to look like that when he brought Fenoglio a book and put it on his lap with a hopeful expression. . . .

Ah, children! thought Fenoglio, as he walked toward the fire where he had seen the Black Prince. *Children, they're the same everywhere. Greedy little creatures but the best listeners in the world — any world. The very best of all.*

THE BLACK PRINCE

> "So bears can make their own souls . . . ," she said. There was
> a great deal in the world to know.
>
> Philip Pullman, *Northern Lights*

The Black Prince was not alone. Of course not; his bear was with him, as usual. He was crouching by the fire behind his master, like a shaggy shadow. Fenoglio still remembered the words he had used when he first created the Prince at the very beginning of *Inkheart*. He recited them quietly to himself as he approached him: "An orphan boy with skin almost as black as his curly hair, as quick with his knife as his tongue, always ready to protect those he loved — his two younger sisters, a maltreated bear, or his best friend, his very best friend, Dustfinger. . . .

". . . who would have died an extremely dramatic death if it had been left to me, all the same!" added Fenoglio quietly as he waved to the Prince. "But luckily my black friend doesn't know that, or I don't suppose I'd be very welcome at his fireside!"

The Prince returned his greeting. He probably thought he was called the Black Prince because of the color of his skin, but

Fenoglio knew better. He had stolen the name from a history book in his old world. A famous knight once bore it, a king's son who was a great robber, too. Would he have been pleased to think that his name had been given to a knife-thrower, king of the strolling players? *If not, there's nothing he can do about it,* thought Fenoglio, *for his own story came to its end long ago.*

On the Prince's left sat the hopelessly incompetent physician who had almost broken Fenoglio's jaw pulling out a tooth, and to the right of him crouched Sootbird, a lousy fire-eater who knew as little of his trade as the physician knew of drawing teeth. Fenoglio was not quite sure about the physician, but there was no way he had invented Sootbird. Heaven knew where he had come from! All who saw him inefficiently breathing fire, in terror of the blaze, instantly found another name springing to mind: the name of Dustfinger the fire-dancer, tamer of the flames. . . .

The bear grunted as Fenoglio sat down by the fire with his master and scrutinized him with little yellow eyes, as if to work out how much meat there was left to gnaw on such old bones. *Your own fault,* Fenoglio told himself: *Why did you have to make the Prince's companion a tame bear?* A dog would have done just as well. The market traders told anyone who would listen that the bear was a man under a spell, bewitched by fairies or brownies (they couldn't decide which), but Fenoglio knew better. The bear was just a bear, a real bear who loved the Black Prince for freeing him, years ago, from the ring through his nose and from his former master, who beat him with a thorny stick to make him dance in marketplaces.

Six more men were sitting beside the fire with the Black Prince. Fenoglio knew only two of them. One was an actor whose name Fenoglio kept forgetting. The other was a professional strong man who earned his living performing in marketplaces:

tearing apart chains, lifting grown men into the air, bending iron bars. They all fell silent as Fenoglio joined them. They tolerated his company, but he was not by any means one of them. Only the Prince smiled at him.

"Ah, the Inkweaver!" he said. "Do you have a new song about the Bluejay for us?"

Fenoglio accepted the goblet of hot wine and honey that one of the men gave him at a sign from the Prince and sat down on the stony ground. His old bones didn't really like hunkering down there, even on a night as mild as this, but the strolling players did not care for chairs or other forms of seating.

"I really came to give you this," he said, putting his hand into the breast of his doublet. He looked around before handing the Prince the sealed letter, but in this milling throng it was difficult to see if anyone who didn't belong to the Motley Folk was watching them.

The Prince took the letter with a nod and tucked it into his belt. "Thank you," he said.

"You're welcome!" replied Fenoglio, trying to ignore the bear's bad breath. The Prince couldn't write, any more than most of his Motley subjects could, but Fenoglio was happy to do it for him, particularly when it was something like this he wanted. The letter was for one of the Laughing Prince's head foresters. His men had attacked the strolling players' women and children on the road three times. No one else seemed to mind, neither the Laughing Prince in his grief nor the men who were supposed to do justice in his place, for the victims were only strolling players. So the king of the players himself was going to do something about it: The forester would find Fenoglio's letter on his doorstep that very night. Its contents would prevent him from sleeping in peace and with luck would keep him away from women wearing the brightly colored skirts of the Motley Folk in the future. Fenoglio was rather proud of his threatening letters, almost as proud as he was of his robber songs.

"Have you heard the latest, Inkweaver?" The Prince stroked his bear's black muzzle. "The Adderhead has put a price on the Bluejay's head."

"The Bluejay?" Fenoglio swallowed his wine the wrong way, and the physician thumped him on the back so hard that he spilled the hot drink over his fingers. "That's a good one!" he gasped, once he had his breath back. "Well, don't let anyone say words are just noise and hot air! The Adder will have to search a long time for that particular robber!"

How oddly they were looking at him! As if they knew more than he did. But more about what?

"Haven't you heard yet, Inkweaver?" said Sootbird quietly. "Your songs seem to be coming true! The Adderhead's tax-gatherers have already been robbed twice by a man in a bird mask, and one of his game wardens, a man famous for enjoying every kind of cruelty, is said to have been found dead in the forest with a feather in his mouth. Guess what bird the feather came from?"

Fenoglio glanced incredulously at the Prince, but he was looking at the fire, stirring the embers with a stick.

"But . . . but that's astonishing!" cried Fenoglio — and then hastily lowered his voice as he saw the others looking anxiously around. "Astonishing news, I mean!" he went on in an under-tone. "Whatever's going on — well, I'll write another song this minute! Suggest something! Go on! What would you like the Bluejay to do next?"

The Prince smiled, but the physician looked at Fenoglio with scorn. "You talk as if it were all a game, Inkweaver!" he said.

"You sit in your own room, scribbling a few words on paper, but whoever's playing the part of your robber risks his neck, for he's certainly made of flesh and blood, not just words!"

"Yes, but no one knows his face, because the Bluejay wears a mask. Very clever of you, Inkweaver. How is the Adderhead to know what face to look for? A mask like that is very useful. Anyone can wear it." It was the actor speaking. *Baptista. Yes, of course, that was his name. Did I make him up?* Fenoglio wondered. Well, never mind; no one knew more about masks than Baptista, perhaps because his face was disfigured by pockmarks. Many of the actors got him to make them leather masks showing laughter or tears.

"The songs give a detailed description of him, though." Sootbird gave Fenoglio a searching look.

"So they do!" Baptista leaped to his feet, put his hand to his shabby belt as if he wore a sword there, and peered around as if looking for an enemy. "He's said to be tall. That's no surprise. Heroes usually are." Baptista began prowling up and down on tiptoe. "His hair," he said, stroking his own head, "is dark, dark as moleskin, if we're to believe the songs. Now, that's unusual. Most heroes have golden hair, whatever you take golden hair to look like. We know nothing about his origins, but one thing's for sure" — and here Baptista assumed a haughty expression — "none but the purest princely blood flows in his veins. How else would he be so brave and noble?"

"No, you're wrong there!" Fenoglio interrupted him. "The Bluejay is a man of the people. What kind of a robber gets born in a castle?"

"You heard the poet!" Baptista looked as if he were wiping the haughtiness right away from his brow with his hand. The other men laughed. "So let's get to the face behind the feathered mask." Baptista ran his fingers over his own ruined face. "Of course he's handsome and distinguished — and pale as ivory! The songs don't say so, but we know that a hero's skin is pale. With due respect, Your Highness!" he added, bowing mockingly to the Black Prince.

"Oh, don't mind me! I've no objection!" was all the Prince said, his expression unchanged.

"Don't forget the scar!" said Sootbird. "The scar on his left arm where the dogs bit him. It's mentioned in every song. Come along, roll up your sleeves. Let's see if the Bluejay is by any chance here among us!" He looked challengingly around him, but only the Strong Man, laughing, pushed up his sleeve. The others sat in silence.

The Prince smoothed back his long hair. He had three knives at his belt. The strolling players, even the man they called their king, were forbidden to carry arms, but why should they keep laws that failed to protect them? Folk said the Prince was so skillful with a knife that he could aim at the eye of a dragonfly and hit it. Just as Fenoglio had once written.

"Whatever he looks like, this man who's making my songs come true, I drink to him. Let the Adderhead search for the man I described. He'll never find him!" Fenoglio raised his goblet to the company. He was feeling in the best of moods, almost intoxicated, and certainly not with the terrible wine. *Well,* he thought, *and who says so, Fenoglio? You do! You write something, and it comes true! Even without anyone to read it aloud. . . .*

But the Strong Man spoiled his mood. "To be honest, Inkweaver, I don't feel like celebrating," he growled. "They say the Adderhead is paying good silver these days for the tongue of every minstrel who sings songs mocking him. And they also say he has quite a collection of tongues already."

"Tongues?" Instinctively, Fenoglio felt his own. "Does he mean my songs, too?"

No one answered him. The men said nothing. The sound of a woman singing came from a tent behind them — a lullaby as sweet and peaceful as if it came from another world — a world of which one could only dream.

"I'm always telling my Motley subjects: Don't go near the Castle of Night!" The Prince put a piece of meat dripping with fat in the bear's mouth, wiped his knife on his trousers, and returned it to his belt. "To think that we're just food for crows to the Adderhead — mere carrion! But since the Laughing Prince took to weeping instead of laughing, they've all had empty pockets and empty bellies. That's what sends them over there. There are many rich merchants in Argenta, far more than on this side of the forest. It's not for nothing they call it the Silver Land."

Devil take it. Fenoglio rubbed his aching knees. What had become of his good mood? Vanished — like the fragrance of a flower trodden underfoot. Gloomily, he took another sip of honeyed wine. The children came flocking around him again, begging for a story, but Fenoglio sent them away. He couldn't make up stories when he was in a bad temper.

"And there's another thing," said the Prince. "The Strong Man picked up a boy and a girl in the forest today. They told a strange story: They said Basta, Capricorn's knife-man, was back, and they're here to warn an old friend of mine about him — Dustfinger. I expect you've heard of him?"

"Mmph?" Fenoglio nearly choked on his wine with surprise. "Dustfinger? Yes, of course, the fire-eater."

"The best there's ever been." The Prince cast a quick glance at Sootbird, but he was just showing the physician a sore tooth. "He was thought to be dead," the Prince went on, lowering his voice. "No one's heard anything of him for over ten years. There were countless tales of how and where he died, but luckily none of them seem to be true. However, Dustfinger's not the only man the boy and girl are looking for. The girl was also asking about an old man, a writer with a face like a tortoise. You, by any chance?"

Fenoglio couldn't find a word in his head that would do for an answer. Saying no more, the Prince took his arm and pulled him to his feet. "Come along!" he added, as the bear lumbered along behind them, grunting. "The two of them were half-starved, said something about being deep in the Wayless Wood. The women are just feeding them now."

A boy and a girl . . . Dustfinger . . . Fenoglio's thoughts were racing, although unfortunately his head was not at its clearest after two goblets of wine.

More than a dozen children were squatting in the grass under a lime tree on the outskirts of the camp. Two women were ladling out soup for them. The children greedily spooned the thin brew up from the wooden bowls that had been put into their dirty hands.

"See how many they've rounded up again!" the Prince whispered to Fenoglio. "We shall all go hungry because of their soft hearts."

Fenoglio just nodded as he looked at the thin faces. He knew how often the Black Prince himself picked up hungry children. If they turned out to have any talent for juggling, standing on their heads, or other tricks that would bring a smile to people's faces and lure a few coins out of their pockets, then the Motley Folk took them in and let them join the company of the strolling players, going from market to market, from town to town.

"There they are." The Prince pointed to two heads bending particularly low over their bowls. When Fenoglio moved toward them, the girl raised her head as if he had called her name. Incredulously, she stared at him — and put down her spoon.

Meggie.

Fenoglio returned her gaze with such astonishment that she had to smile. Yes, it really was Meggie. He remembered that smile very well, even if she hadn't often had reason to show it when they were imprisoned together in Capricorn's house.

She leaped up, pushed past the other children, and flung her arms around his neck. "Oh, I knew you were still here!" she cried, between laughter and tears. "Did you really have to write those wolves into your story? And then the Night-Mares and the Redcaps — they threw stones at Farid and went for his face with fingers like claws. It was a good thing Farid could make a fire, but still . . ."

Fenoglio opened his mouth — and closed it again, helplessly. His head was full of a thousand questions. How did she get here? What about Dustfinger? Where was her father? And what about Capricorn? Was he dead? Had her plan worked? If so, why was Basta still alive? The questions drowned each other out like humming insects, and Fenoglio dared not ask any of them while the Black Prince stood there, never taking his eyes off him.

"I see you know these two," he remarked.

Fenoglio just nodded. Yes, where had he seen the boy sitting beside Meggie before? Wasn't he with Dustfinger on that strange day when, for the first time, he met one of his own creations face-to-face?

"Er . . . they're relations of mine," he stammered. What a pitiful lie for a storyteller!

The Prince's mocking eyes sparkled. "Relations . . . well, imagine that! I must say they don't look very like you."

Meggie unwound her arms from Fenoglio's neck and stared at the Prince.

"Meggie," said Fenoglio, "may I introduce the Black Prince?"

With a smile, the Prince made her a bow.

"The Black Prince! Oh yes." Meggie repeated his name almost reverently. "And that's his bear! Farid, come here. Look!"

Farid, of course. Fenoglio remembered him now. Meggie had often talked about him. The boy stood up, but not before hastily swallowing the very last of the soup in his bowl. He kept well behind Meggie, at a safe distance from the bear.

"She absolutely insisted on coming!" he said, wiping his greasy mouth on his arm. "Really! I didn't want to bring her, but she's as obstinate as a camel."

Meggie was obviously about to make some sharp retort, but Fenoglio put his arm around her shoulders. "My dear boy," he told Farid, "you have no idea how glad I am to see Meggie here! I could almost say she's all I needed in this world to make me happy!"

He hastily took his leave of the Prince and drew Meggie and Farid away with him. "Come with me!" he whispered, as they made their way past the tents. "We have a great deal to talk about, a very great deal, but we can do it better in my room without strange ears to overhear us. It's getting late, anyway, and the guard at the gate won't let us back into the city after midnight."

Meggie just nodded abstractedly and looked at the hurry and bustle all around her, wide-eyed, but Farid pulled his arm away from Fenoglio's grasp. "I can't come with you. I have to look for Dustfinger!"

Fenoglio looked disbelievingly at him. So it was really true? Dustfinger was —

"Yes, he's back," said Meggie. "The women said Farid might

find him at the house of the minstrel woman he once lived with. She has a farm up there on the hill."

"Minstrel woman?" Fenoglio looked the way Meggie's finger was pointing. The hill she meant was only a black outline in the moonlit night. Of course! Roxane. He remembered her. Was she really as wonderful as he had described her?

The boy was shifting impatiently from foot to foot. "I have to go," he told Meggie. "Where can I find you?"

"In Cobblers' and Saddlers' Alley," replied Fenoglio, answering for Meggie. "Just ask for Minerva's house."

Farid nodded. He went on looking at Meggie.

"It's not a good idea to start a journey by night," said Fenoglio, although he had a feeling that this boy wasn't interested in his advice. "The roads here aren't what you'd call safe. Particularly not at night. There are robbers, vagabonds . . ."

"I can look after myself." Farid took a knife from his belt. "Take care, Meggie." He reached for her hand, then turned abruptly and disappeared among the strolling players. It did not escape Fenoglio that Meggie turned to look back at him several times.

"Heavens, poor lad!" he growled, shooing a couple of children out of the way as they came flocking up to beg him for a story again. "He's in love with you, am I right?"

"Oh, don't!" Meggie let go of his hand, but he had made her smile.

"All right, I'll hold my tongue! Does your father know you're here?"

That was the wrong question. Her guilty conscience was plain to see in her face.

"Dear me! Very well, you must tell me all about it. How you came here, what all this talk of Basta and Dustfinger means, everything! You've grown! Or have I shrunk? My God, Meggie, I'm so glad you're here! Now we can get this story back under control! With my words and your voice —"

"Under control? What do you mean?" She suspiciously examined his face. She had often seen him look just like that in the past, when they were Capricorn's prisoners — his brow wrinkled, his eyes as clear as if they could look straight into your heart. But this wasn't the place for explanations.

"Later!" whispered Fenoglio and drew her on. "Later, Meggie. There are too many ears here. Damn it, where's my torchbearer now?"

STRANGE SOUNDS ON A STRANGE NIGHT

How silent lies the world
Within fair twilight furled,
Bringing such sweet relief!
A quiet room resembling,
Where, without fear or trembling,
You sleep away day's grief.

Matthias Claudius, *Evening Song*

Later, when Meggie tried to remember the way they went to Fenoglio's room, she could see only a few blurred pictures in her mind's eye — a guard who tried to bar their way with his spear, but sullenly let them pass when he recognized Fenoglio, dark alleys down which they followed a boy with a torch, then a steep flight of steps, creaking underfoot as it led them up the side of a gray wall. She felt so dizzy with weariness as she followed Fenoglio up these steps that he felt quite anxious and took her arm a couple of times.

"I think we'd better wait until morning to tell each other

what's happened since we last met," he said, propelling her into his room. "I'll ask Minerva to bring you up a straw mattress later, but you'll sleep in my bed tonight. Three days and nights in the Wayless Wood. Inky infernos, I'd probably have died of sheer fright!"

"Farid had his knife," murmured Meggie. The knife had indeed been a comfort when they were sleeping in the treetops by night, and those growling, grating noises came up to them from below. Farid had always kept it ready at hand. "And when he saw ghosts," she said sleepily, as Fenoglio lit a lamp, "he made a fire."

"Ghosts? There aren't any ghosts in this world, or at least none that I wrote into it. What did you eat all that time?"

Meggie groped her way over to the bed. It looked very inviting, even if it was only a straw mattress and a couple of coarse blankets. "Berries," she murmured. "Lots of berries, and the bread we took with us from Elinor's kitchen — and rabbits, but Farid caught those."

"Good heavens above!" Fenoglio shook his head, incredulous. It was really good to see his wrinkled face again, but right now all Meggie really wanted to do was sleep. She took off her boots, crept under the scratchy blankets, and stretched out her aching legs.

"What gave you the crazy idea of reading yourself and Farid into the Wayless Wood? Why not arrive here? Dustfinger must have told the boy a few things about this world."

"Orpheus's words." Meggie couldn't help yawning. "We only had Orpheus's words, and Dustfinger had gotten Orpheus to read him into the forest."

"Of course. Sounds just like him." She felt Fenoglio pulling the blankets up to her chin. "I'd better not ask you who this Orpheus is. We'll talk again tomorrow. Sleep well. And welcome to my world!"

Meggie just managed to open her eyes once more. "Where are you going to sleep?"

"Don't worry about me. A few of Minerva's relations come in every night to share the family's beds downstairs, and one more won't make much difference. You soon get used to a little less comfort, I assure you. I only hope her husband doesn't snore as loud as she says."

Then he closed the door behind him, and Meggie heard him laboriously making his way down the steep wooden staircase, cursing quietly to himself. Mice scurried through the rafters over her head (at least, she hoped they were mice) and the voices of the sentries guarding the nearby city wall drifted in through the only window. Meggie closed her eyes. Her feet hurt, and the music from the strolling players' camp was still ringing in her ears. *The Black Prince,* she thought, *I've seen the Black Prince . . . and the city gate of Ombra . . . and I've heard the trees whispering to one another in the Wayless Wood.* If she could only have told Resa all about it. Or Elinor. Or Mo. But more than likely Mo never wanted to hear another word about the Inkworld.

Meggie rubbed her tired eyes. Fairies' nests clung to the beams in the roof above the bed, just as Fenoglio had always wanted, but nothing moved behind the dark entrance holes where the fairies flew into them. Fenoglio's attic room was a good deal larger than the one where he and Meggie had been kept prisoner by Capricorn. As well as the bed he had so generously let her have, there was a wooden chest, a bench, and a writing desk made of dark wood, gleaming and adorned with carvings. It did not go with the rest of the furniture: the roughly made bench, the simple chest. You might have thought it had strayed here out of another story, just like Meggie herself. An earthenware jug stood on it, containing a whole set of quill pens, there were two inkwells . . .

Fenoglio was looking happy. He really was.

Meggie passed her arm over her tired face. The dress Resa had made her still smelled of her mother, but now it smelled of the Wayless Wood, too. She put her hand inside the leather bag that she had almost lost twice in the forest and took out the notebook Mo had given her. The marbled binding was a mixture of deep blue and peacock green — Mo's favorite colors. It was good to have your books with you in strange places. Mo had told her that so often, but did he mean places like this? On their second day in the forest Meggie had tried to read the book she had brought with her, while Farid went hunting for a rabbit. She couldn't get past the first page, and finally she had forgotten the book and left it lying as she sat beside a stream with swarms of blue fairies hovering over it. Did your hunger for stories die down when you were in one yourself? Or had she just been too exhausted? *I should at least write down what's happened so far,* she thought, stroking the cover of her notebook again, but weariness was like cotton wool in her head and her limbs. *Tomorrow,* she thought. *And tomorrow I'll tell Fenoglio that he must write me back home, too. I've seen the fairies, I've even seen the fire-elves, and the Wayless Wood and Ombra. Yes. Because, after all, it will take him a few days to find the right words. . . .*

Something rustled in one of the fairies' nests above her. But no blue face looked out.

It was chilly in this room, and everything was strange — so strange. Meggie was used to strange places; after all, Mo had always taken her with him when he had to go away to cure sick books. But she could rely on one thing in all those places: She knew he was with her. Always. Meggie pressed her cheek against the rough straw mattress. She missed her mother and Elinor and Darius, but most of all she missed Mo. It was like an ache tugging at her heart. Love and a guilty conscience didn't mix. If only he had come, too! He'd shown her so much of her own world, how she would have loved to show him this one! She knew he'd have liked it all: the fire-elves, the whispering trees, the camp of the strolling players. . . .

Oh, she did miss Mo.

How about Fenoglio? Wasn't there anyone he missed? Didn't he feel at all homesick for the village where he used to live, for his children, his friends, and neighbors? What about his grandchildren? Meggie had often raced around his house with them! "I'll show you everything tomorrow!" Fenoglio had whispered to her as they hurried after the boy ahead of them, carrying the torch that had almost burned down, and his voice had sounded as if he were a prince informing his guest that he would show him around the palace the next day. "The guards don't like people roaming the streets by night," he had added, and it was indeed very quiet among the close-crammed houses. They reminded Meggie of Capricorn's village so much that she half expected to see one of the Black Jackets around some corner, leaning against the wall with a rifle in his hand. But all they met were a few pigs grunting as they wandered in the steep alleys, and a ragged man sweeping up the garbage that lay among the houses and shoveling it into a handcart. "You'll get used to the smell in time!" Fenoglio had whispered, as Meggie put her hand over her nose. "Think yourself lucky I'm not lodging with a dyer, or over there with the tanners. Even I haven't gotten used to the stink of their trades."

No, Meggie felt sure that Fenoglio didn't miss anything. Why would he? This was his world, born from his brain, as familiar to him as his own thoughts.

Meggie listened to the night. There was another sound as well as the rustle of the scurrying mice — a faint snoring. It seemed to come from the desk. Pushing back her blanket, she made her way cautiously over to it. A glass man was sleeping beside the jug of quill pens, his head on a tiny cushion. His transparent limbs were spattered with ink. Presumably he sharpened the pens, dipped them in the bulbous inkwells, sprinkled sand over the wet ink . . . just as Fenoglio had always wanted. And did the fairies' nests above his bed really bring good luck and sweet dreams? Meggie thought she saw a trace of fairy dust on the desk. Thoughtfully, she ran her finger over it, looked at the glittering dust left clinging to her fingertip, and rubbed it on her forehead. Did fairy dust cure homesickness?

For she was still homesick. All this beauty around her, yet she kept thinking of Elinor's house and Mo's workshop . . . Her heart was so stupid! Hadn't it always beat faster when Resa told her about the Inkworld? And now that she was here, really here, it didn't seem to know just what it ought to feel. *It's because the others aren't here, too,* something inside her whispered, as if her heart were trying to defend itself. *Because they're none of them here.*

If only Farid at least had stayed with her. . . . How she envied him the way he had slipped from one world to another as if he were just changing his shirt! The only longing he seemed to know was for the sight of Dustfinger's scarred face.

Meggie went to the window. There was only a piece of fabric tacked over it. Meggie pushed it aside and looked down into the narrow alley. The ragged refuse collector was just pushing his cart past with its heavy, stinking load. It nearly got stuck between the buildings. The windows above it were almost all dark; a candle burned behind only one of them, and a child's crying drifted out into the night. Roof stood next to roof like the scales of a fir cone, and the walls and towers of the castle rose dark above them to the starry sky.

The Laughing Prince's castle. Resa had described it well. The moon stood pale above the gray battlements, outlining them in silver, them and the guards pacing up and down on the walls. It seemed to be the same as the moon that rose and set over the mountains behind Elinor's house. "The prince is holding festivities for his spoiled grandson," Fenoglio had told Meggie, "and I'm supposed to go up to the castle with a new song. I'll take you with me. We'll have to find you a clean dress, but Minerva has three daughters. They're sure to have a dress among them to fit you."

Meggie took one last look at the sleeping glass man and went back to the bed under the fairies' nests. *After the celebrations,* she thought as she pulled off her dirty dress over her head and slipped under the coarse blanket again, *first thing after the celebrations I'll ask Fenoglio to write me home.* As she closed her eyes, she once again saw the swarms of fairies who had swirled around her in the green twilight of the Wayless Wood, pulling her hair until Farid threw fir cones at them. She heard the trees whispering in voices that seemed to be half earth, half air, she remembered the scaly faces she had seen in the water of dark pools, and the Black Prince, too, and his bear. . . .

There was a rustling under the bed, and something crawled over her arm. Meggie sleepily brushed it off. *I hope Mo isn't too angry* was the last thing she thought before she fell asleep and dreamed of Elinor's garden. Or was it the Wayless Wood?

16

ONLY A LIE

The blanket was there, but it was the boy's embrace that covered and warmed him.

Jerry Spinelli, *Maniac Magee*

Farid soon realized that Fenoglio was right. It had been stupid just to go off like that in the middle of the night. It was true that no robber leaped out at him from the darkness, and not even a fox crossed his path as he climbed the moonlit hill that the strolling players had pointed out to him, but which of the run-down farms lying among the black nocturnal trees was the right one? They all looked the same: a gray stone house, not much bigger than a hut, surrounded by olive trees, a well, sometimes a cowshed, a few narrow fields. Nothing stirred in the farmhouses. Their inhabitants were asleep, exhausted by hard work, and with every wall and every gate that he crept past Farid's hopes dwindled. Suddenly, and for the first time, he felt lost in this strange world, and he was about to curl up and go to sleep under a tree when he saw the fire.

It was burning brightly high up on the slope of the hill, red as a hibiscus flower opening and then fading even as it unfurls. Farid quickened his pace and hurried up the slope, his gaze fixed on the place where he had seen the blossoming flames. Dustfinger! It shone among the trees again, sulfur yellow this time, bright as sunlight. It must be Dustfinger! Who else would make fire dance by night?

Farid went faster, so fast that he was soon struggling for breath. He came upon a path winding uphill, past the stumps of trees that had been felled only recently. The path was stony and wet with dew, but his bare feet were glad to be spared the prickly thyme for a while. There, another red flower blossoming in the darkness! Above him, a house emerged from the night. Beyond it the hill climbed on, terraced fields rose up the slope like steps, with stones piled up along their edges. The house itself looked as poor and plain as all the others. The path ended at a simple gateway and a wall of flat stones just high enough to reach Farid's chest. As he stood at the gate a goose went for him, flapping her wings and hissing like a snake, but Farid took no notice of her. He had found the man he was looking for.

Dustfinger was standing in the yard, making flowers of flame blossom in the air. They opened at a snap of his fingers, spread their fiery petals, faded, put out stems of burning gold, and burst into flower yet again. The fire seemed to come out of nowhere; Dustfinger had only to call it with his hands or his voice, he fanned the flames with nothing but his breath — no torches now, no bottle from which he filled his mouth — Farid could see none of the aids he had needed in the other world. He just stood there setting the night ablaze. More and more flowers swirled around him in their wild dance, spitting sparks at his feet like golden seed corn, until he stood there bathed in liquid fire.

Farid had noticed often enough how peaceful Dustfinger's

face became when he was playing with fire, but he had never seen him look so happy before. Just plain happy. The goose was still cackling, but Dustfinger seemed not to hear her. Only when Farid opened the gate did she scold so shrilly that he turned — and the fiery flowers went out as if night had crushed them in black fingers. The happiness in Dustfinger's face was extinguished, too.

At the door of the house, a woman stood up; she had probably been sitting on the doorstep. There was a boy there, too; Farid hadn't noticed him before. The boy's gaze followed Farid as he crossed the yard, but Dustfinger still hadn't moved from the spot where he was standing. He just looked at Farid as the sparks went out at his feet, leaving nothing but a faint red glow behind.

Farid sought that familiar face for any welcome, any hint of a smile, but it showed only bewilderment. At last Farid's courage failed him, and he just stood there, with his heart trembling in his breast as if it were freezing cold.

"Farid?"

Dustfinger was coming toward him. The woman followed. She was very beautiful, but Farid ignored her. Dustfinger was wearing the clothes he always carried with him in the other world but had never worn. Black and red . . . Farid dared not look at him when he stopped a pace away. He just stood there with his head bent, staring at his toes. Perhaps Dustfinger had never meant to take him along at all, perhaps he'd fixed it from the start that Cheeseface wouldn't read those final sentences, and now he was angry because Farid had followed him from one world to another all the same. . . . Would he beat him? He'd never beaten him yet, although he'd come close to it once when Farid accidentally set fire to Gwin's tail.

"How could I ever have believed that anything would stop you from chasing after me?" Farid felt Dustfinger's hand raise his chin, and when he looked up, he saw at last what he had been hoping for in Dustfinger's eyes: joy. "Where have you been hiding? I called you at least a dozen times, I looked for you . . . The fire-elves must have thought me crazy!" He was scrutinizing Farid's face anxiously, as if he wasn't sure whether there was some change in it. It was so good to feel his concern. Farid could have danced for joy, the way the fire had danced for Dustfinger just now.

"Well, you seem to be the same as ever!" said Dustfinger at last. "A skinny dark-eyed little devil. But wait — you're so quiet! It didn't cost you your voice, did it?"

Farid smiled. "No, I'm all right!" he said, glancing quickly at the woman, who was still standing behind Dustfinger. "But it wasn't Cheeseface who brought me here. He simply stopped reading the moment you were gone! Meggie read me here, using Cheeseface's words."

"Meggie? Silvertongue's daughter?"

"Yes, but what about you? You're all right, aren't you?"

Dustfinger's mouth twisted into the wry smile that Farid knew so well. "As you can see, the scars are still there. But there's no more damage done, if that's what you mean." He turned around and looked at the woman in a way that Farid didn't like at all.

Her hair was black, and her eyes were almost as dark as his own. She really was very beautiful, even if she was old — well, much older than Farid — but he didn't like her. He didn't like either her or the boy. After all, he hadn't followed Dustfinger to his own world just to share him.

The woman came up beside Dustfinger and placed her hand on his shoulder. "Who's this?" she asked, sizing up Farid in much the same way as he had looked at her. "One of your many secrets? A son I don't know about?"

Farid felt the blood rise to his face. Dustfinger's son. He liked the idea. Unobtrusively, he stole a look at the strange boy. Who was his father?

"My son?" Dustfinger affectionately caressed the woman's face. "What an idea! No, Farid's a fire-eater. He was my apprentice for a while, and now he thinks I can't manage without him. Indeed, he's so sure of it that he follows me everywhere, however far he has to go."

"Oh, stop it!" Farid's voice sounded angrier than he had intended. "I'm here to warn you! But I can go away again if you like."

"Take it easy!" Dustfinger held him firmly by the arm as he turned to go. "Heavens above, I forgot how quickly you take offense. Warn me? Warn me of what?"

"Basta."

The woman's hand flew to her mouth when he said that name — and Farid began to tell his story, describing everything that had happened since Dustfinger disappeared from that remote road in the mountains as if he had never existed. When he had finished, Dustfinger asked just one question. "So Basta has the book?"

Farid dug his toes into the hard earth and nodded. "Yes," he muttered ruefully. "He put his knife to my throat. What was I to do?"

"Basta?" The woman reached for Dustfinger's hand. "He's still alive, then?"

Dustfinger just nodded. Then he looked at Farid again. "Do you believe he's here now? Do you think Orpheus has read him here?"

Farid shrugged helplessly. "I don't know! When I got away from him he shouted after me that he'd be revenged on

Silvertongue, too. But Silvertongue doesn't believe it, he says Basta was just in a rage. . . ."

Dustfinger looked at the gate, which was still standing open. "Yes, Basta says a lot of things when he's in a rage," he murmured. Then he sighed and trod out a few sparks that were still glowing on the ground in front of him.

"Bad news," he said softly. "Nothing but bad news. All we need now is for you to have brought Gwin with you."

Thank heaven it was dark. Lies weren't nearly as easily spotted in the dark as by day. Farid did his best to sound as surprised as possible. "Gwin? Oh no! No, I didn't bring him with me. You said he was to stay there. And Meggie said so, too — she said I mustn't bring him."

"Clever girl!" Dustfinger's sigh of relief went to Farid's heart.

"You left the marten behind?" The woman shook her head, as if she couldn't believe it. "I always thought you loved that little monster more than any other living creature."

"Oh, you know my faithless heart!" replied Dustfinger, but his lighthearted tone of voice couldn't deceive even Farid. "Are you hungry?" he asked the boy. "How long have you been here?"

Farid cleared his throat; his lie about Gwin was like a splinter lodged in it. "For four days," he managed to say. "The strolling players gave us something to eat, but I'm still hungry, all the same. . . ."

"Us?" Dustfinger's voice suddenly sounded distrustful.

"Silvertongue's daughter. Meggie. She came with me."

"She's here?" Dustfinger looked at him in astonishment. Then he groaned and pushed the hair back from his forehead. "Oh, how pleased her father will be! Not to mention her mother. Did you by any chance bring anyone else, too?"

Farid shook his head.

"Where is she now?"

"With the old man." Farid jerked his head back the way he had come. "He's living near the castle. We met him in the strolling players' camp. Meggie was very glad to see him. She was going to look for him, anyway, to get him to take her back. I think she's homesick. . . ."

"What old man? Who the devil are you talking about now?"

"Well, that writer! The one with the face like a tortoise — you remember, you ran away from him back then in —"

"Yes, yes, all right!" Dustfinger put his hand over Farid's mouth as if he didn't want to hear another word, and stared toward the place where, somewhere in the darkness, the walls of Ombra lay hidden. "Heavens above, what next?" he murmured.

"Is that . . . is it more bad news?" Farid hardly dared to ask.

Dustfinger looked away, but all the same Farid had seen his smile. "Oh yes," he said. "I suppose there never was a boy who brought so much bad news all at once. And in the middle of the night, too. What do we do with bearers of bad tidings, Roxane?"

Roxane. So that was her name. For a moment Farid thought she would suggest sending him away. But then she shrugged. "We feed them, what else?" she said. "Even if this one doesn't look too starved."

A PRESENT FOR
CAPRICORN

"If he has been my father's enemy, I like him still less!"
exclaimed the now really anxious girl. "Will you not speak
to him, Major Heyward, that I may hear his tones? Foolish
though it may be, you have often heard me avow my faith in
the tones of the human voice!"

J. Fenimore Cooper, *The Last of the Mohicans*

Evening drew on, night fell, and no one came to unlock
Elinor's cellar. They sat there in silence among tubes of
tomato purée, cans of ravioli, and all the other provisions stacked
on the shelves around them — trying not to see the fear on one
another's faces.

"My house isn't all that large!" said Elinor once, breaking the
silence. "By now even that fool Basta should have realized that
Meggie really isn't here."

No one replied. Resa was clinging to Mortimer as if that
would protect him from Basta's knife, and Darius was cleaning
his already spotless glasses for the hundredth time. By the time

footsteps finally approached the cellar door, Elinor's watch had stopped. Memories flooded into her weary mind as she rose, with difficulty, from the container of olive oil on which she had been sitting — memories of blank, windowless walls and musty straw. Her cellar was a more comfortable prison than Capricorn's sheds, let alone the crypt under his church, but the same man opened the door — and Elinor was just as much afraid of Basta in her own house.

When she had last seen him, he had been a prisoner himself, shut up in a cage by the master he adored. Had he forgotten that? How had Mortola persuaded him to serve her again in spite of it? The stupid idea of asking Basta didn't even cross Elinor's mind. She gave herself the answer: because a dog needs a master.

Basta had the man built like a wardrobe with him when he came to fetch them. There were four of them, after all, and Basta remembered only too well the day when Dustfinger had escaped him. "Well, Silvertongue, I'm sorry it's taken some time," he said in his soft, catlike voice, as he pushed Mortimer down the corridor to Elinor's library. "But Mortola just couldn't decide what kind of revenge to take, now that your witchy daughter really has run for it."

"And what has she thought up?" asked Elinor, although she was afraid of the answer. Basta was only too willing to tell her.

"Well, first she was going to shoot you all and sink you in the lake, although we told her just burying you somewhere under the bushes out there would do. But then she decided it would be too merciful to let you die knowing the little witch has gotten away from her. No, Mortola really didn't fancy that idea."

"Oh, didn't she?" Fear made Elinor's legs so heavy that she stopped walking until the wardrobe-man impatiently pushed her on. But before she could ask what Mortola was planning to do instead of shooting them, Basta was already opening the door of her library and ushering them in with an ironic bow.

Mortola was sitting enthroned in Elinor's favorite armchair. Scarcely a pace away from her lay a dog with running eyes and a head broad enough for you to rest a plate on it. Its forelegs were bandaged, like Mortola's own legs, and there was a bandage around its belly, too. A dog! In her library! Elinor tightened her lips. *This is probably the least of your worries right now, Elinor,* she told herself. *You'd better just ignore it.*

Mortola's stick was leaning against one of the glass cases in which Elinor kept her most valuable books. The moon-faced man stood beside the old woman. Orpheus — what did the fool think he was doing, claiming such a name for himself? Or had his parents in all seriousness given it to him? At any rate, he looked as if he, too, had passed a sleepless night, which gave Elinor a certain grim satisfaction.

"My son always said revenge was a dish best eaten cold," observed Mortola, as she looked at her prisoners' exhausted faces. There was a pleased expression on her own. "I admit I wasn't in any mood to take that advice yesterday. I'd have liked to see you all dead there and then, but the little witch's disappearing act has given me time to think, and I've decided to postpone my revenge for a while, so that I can enjoy it all the more, and in cold blood."

"Hear, hear!" muttered Elinor, earning a thrust from the butt of Basta's rifle. But Mortola turned her birdlike gaze on Mortimer. She seemed to be seeing no one else: not Resa, not Darius, not Elinor, just him.

"Silvertongue!" She spoke the name with scorn. "How many have you killed with your velvet voice? A dozen? Cockerell, Flatnose, and finally, your crowning achievement, my son." The bitterness in Mortola's voice was as raw as if Capricorn had died only last night, instead of over a year ago. "And you will die for killing him. You will die as sure as I'm sitting here, and I shall watch, as I had to watch the death of my son. But since I know from personal experience that nothing hurts more, in this or any other world, than the death of one's own child, I want you to see your daughter die before you die yourself."

Mortimer stood there and didn't turn a hair. Usually you could see all his feelings in his face, but at this moment even Elinor couldn't have said what was going on inside him.

"She's gone, Mortola," was all he said, hoarsely. "Meggie's gone, and I don't think you can bring her back, or you'd have done it long ago, wouldn't you?"

"Who said anything about bringing her back?" Mortola's narrow lips twisted into a joyless smile. "Do you think I intend to stay in this stupid world of yours any longer now that I have the book? Why should I? No, I'm going to look for your daughter in my own world, where Basta will catch her like a little bird. And then I'll give the two of you to my son as a present. There'll be more festivities, Silvertongue, but this time Capricorn will not die. Oh no. He'll sit beside me and hold my hand while Death takes first your daughter, and then you. Yes, that's how it will be!"

Elinor glanced at Darius and saw in his face the incredulous astonishment that she herself felt. But Mortola was smiling superciliously.

"Why are you staring at me like that? You think Capricorn is dead?" Mortola's voice almost cracked. "Nonsense. Yes, he died here, but what does that mean? This world is a joke, a masquerade such as the strolling players perform in marketplaces. In our world, the real world, Capricorn is still alive. That's why I got the book back from that fire-eater. The little witch said it herself, the night you killed him: He'll always be there as long as the book exists. Yes, I know she meant the fire-eater, but what's true of him is most certainly true of my son! They're still there, all of them: Capricorn and Flatnose, Cockerell and the Shadow!"

She looked triumphantly from one to another of them, but they all remained silent. Except for Mortimer. "That's nonsense, Mortola!" he said. "And you know it better than anyone. You were in the Inkworld yourself when Capricorn disappeared from it, together with Basta and Dustfinger."

"So? He went away, that's all." Mortola's voice was shrill. "And then he didn't come back, but that means nothing. My son was always traveling on business. The Adderhead sometimes sent him a messenger in the middle of the night when he needed his services, and then he'd be gone the next morning. But he's back now. Back and waiting for me to bring his murderer to his fortress in the Wayless Wood."

Elinor felt a crazy urge to laugh, but fear closed her throat. *There's no doubt about it*, she thought, *the old Magpie's lost her wits!* Unfortunately, that didn't make her any less dangerous.

"Orpheus!" Mortola impatiently beckoned the moon-face to her side. Very slowly, as if to show that he obeyed her by no means as willingly as Basta did, he strolled over to her, taking a sheet of paper out of the inside pocket of his jacket as he did so. With a self-important expression, he unfolded it and laid it on the glass case with Mortola's stick leaning on it. The dog, panting, watched every movement he made.

"It won't be easy!" observed Orpheus as he leaned over the dog, affectionately patting its ugly head. "I've never tried reading so many people over all at once before. Perhaps it would be a better idea to do it one by one —"

"No!" Mortola brusquely interrupted him. "No, you'll read us all over at once, as we agreed."

Orpheus shrugged. "Very well, just as you like. As I said, it's risky because —"

"Be quiet! I don't want to hear this." Mortola dug her bony fingers into the arms of the chair. (*I'll never be able to sit in it again without thinking of her,* thought Elinor.) "May I remind you of that cell? I was the one who paid for its door to open. A word from me and you'll end up back there, without books or so much as a single sheet of paper. And, believe me, I'll make sure you do just that if you fail. After all, you read the fire-eater over without much trouble, according to Basta."

"Yes, but that was easy, very easy! Like putting something back in its proper place." Orpheus looked out of Elinor's window as dreamily as if he were seeing Dustfinger vanish again, this time from the lawn outside. Frowning, he turned back to Mortola. "It's different with him," he said, pointing to Mortimer. "It's not his story. He doesn't belong in it."

"Nor did his daughter. Are you saying she reads better than you?"

"Of course not!" Orpheus stood up very straight. "No one reads better than me. Haven't I proved that? Didn't you yourself say Dustfinger spent ten years looking for someone to read him back?"

"Yes, very well. No more talk, then." Mortola picked up her stick and rose to her feet, with difficulty. "Wouldn't it be amusing if a ferocious cat slipped out of the pages, like the one that came through when the fire-eater left? Basta's hand hasn't healed yet, and *he* had a knife and the dog to help him." She gave Elinor and Darius a nasty look.

Elinor took a step forward, ignoring the butt of Basta's rifle. "What do you mean? I'm coming, too, of course!"

Mortola raised her eyebrows in mock surprise. "Oh, and who do you think decides that? Why would I want you with us? Or that stupid bungler Darius? I'm sure my son would have no objection to feeding you two to the Shadow as well, but I don't want to make things too difficult for Orpheus." She pointed her stick at Mortimer. "We're taking him with us. No one else."

Resa was clinging to Mortimer's arm. Mortola went over to her, smiling. "Yes, little pigeon, I'm leaving you here, too!" she said, pinching her cheek hard. "It will hurt if I take him away from you again, won't it? When you've only just gotten him back. After all those years . . ."

Mortola signed to Basta, who reached roughly for Resa's arm. She struggled, still clinging to Mortimer, with a desperate expression on her face that went to Elinor's heart. But as she went to try and help Resa, the wardrobe-man barred her way. And Mortimer himself gently removed Resa's hand from his arm.

"It's all right," he said. "After all, I'm the only one in this family who hasn't been to the Inkworld yet. And I promise you I won't come back without Meggie."

"Very true, because you won't come back at all!" Basta mocked, as he pushed Resa hard toward Elinor. And Mortola was still smiling. Elinor would have loved to hit her. *Do something, Elinor!* she thought. But what *could* she do? Hold on to Mortimer? Tear up the sheet of paper that the moon-face was so carefully smoothing out on her glass case?

"Well, can we begin now?" asked Orpheus, licking his lips as if he could hardly wait to demonstrate his skill again.

"Of course." Mortola leaned heavily on her stick and beckoned Basta to her side.

Orpheus looked at him suspiciously. "You'll make sure he leaves Dustfinger alone, right?" he said to Mortola. "You promised!"

Basta passed a finger over his throat and winked at him.

"Did you see that?" Orpheus's beautiful voice broke. "You promised! That was my one condition. You leave Dustfinger in peace or I don't read a single word!"

"Yes, yes, all right, don't shout like that or you'll ruin your voice," replied Mortola impatiently. "We have Silvertongue. Why would I be interested in that wretched fire-eater? Go on, start reading!"

"Hey, wait a minute!" This was the first time Elinor had heard the wardrobe-man's voice. It was curiously high for a man of his size — as if an elephant were speaking in a cricket's chirping voice. "What happens to the others when you're gone?"

"How should I know?" Mortola shrugged. "Let whatever comes here to replace us eat them. Make the fat woman your maid and Darius your bootboy. Anything you like, it's all the same to me. Just start reading!"

Orpheus obeyed. He went over to the glass case where the sheet of paper with his words on it was waiting, cleared his throat, and adjusted his glasses.

"*Capricorn's fortress lay in the forest where the first tracks of giants could be found.*" The words flowed over his lips like music. "*It was a long time since anyone had seen the giants, but other and more alarming beings haunted the walls by night — Night-Mares and Redcaps, creatures as cruel as the men who had built the fortress. It was all of gray stone, as gray as the rocky slope behind it. . . .*"

Do something! thought Elinor. *Do something, it's now or never. Snatch that piece of paper from the moon-faced man's hand, kick the Magpie's stick away . . .* But she couldn't move a muscle.

What a voice! And the magic of the words — they slowed her brain, making her drowsy with delight. When Orpheus read of prickly woodbine and tamarisk flowers, Elinor thought she could smell them. *He really does read as well as Mortimer!* That was the only thought of her own that would form in her head. And the others were no better off; they were all staring at Orpheus's lips, as if they could hardly wait for the next word: Darius, Basta, the wardrobe-man, even Mortimer — why, even the Magpie. They listened motionless, caught up in the sound of the words. Only one of them moved. Resa. Elinor saw her struggling against the magic as you might struggle in deep water, finally coming up behind Mortimer and flinging her arms around him.

And then they had all disappeared: Basta, Mortola the Magpie — and Mortimer and Resa.

18

MORTOLA'S REVENGE

I do not dare,
I do not dare to write it,
if you die.
Pablo Neruda, "The Dead Woman," *The Captain's Verses*

It was as if a transparent picture, like stained glass, came down over what Resa had just been seeing — Elinor's library, the backs of the books so carefully classified by Darius and arranged side by side — blurring it all, while the other picture itself became clearer. Stones eroded the books; soot-blackened walls replaced the bookshelves. Grass sprouted from Elinor's wooden floorboards, and the white plaster of the ceiling gave way to a sky covered by dark clouds.

Resa's arms were still wound around Mo. He was the only thing that didn't disappear, and she wouldn't let go of him for fear of losing him again after all, as she had lost him once before. So long ago.

"Resa?" She saw the alarm in his eyes as he turned and realized that she had come, too. Quickly, she put her hand over his mouth.

Honeysuckle climbed up the black walls on their left. Mo put out his hand to the leaves, as if his fingers must feel what his eyes had already seen. Resa remembered that she had once done the same, touching everything, bewildered to find the world beyond the letters on the page so real.

If she hadn't heard the words Orpheus had spoken for herself, Resa wouldn't have known where Mortola had made him read them all. Capricorn's fortress had looked so different when she had last stood in its courtyard. There had been men everywhere, armed men on the flights of steps, at the gate, on the wall. Where the bakehouse had stood there was nothing now but charred beams, and it was by the stairway over there that she and the other maids used to beat the dust from the tapestry hangings, tapestries that Mortola placed on the walls of the bare rooms only on special occasions.

Those rooms were gone. The walls of the fortress were crumbling and black from fire. Soot covered the stones as if someone had painted them with a black brush, and yarrow grew all over the once bare courtyard. Yarrow loved burned earth; it grew everywhere. Where a narrow stairway had once led up to the watchtower, the forest was now making its way into Capricorn's den. Young trees had taken root among the ruins, as if they had been just waiting to reclaim the place occupied by this human abode. Thistles grew in the gaping cavities of the windows, moss covered the ruined stairs, and ivy climbed to the charred wooden stumps that had once been Capricorn's gallows. Resa had seen many men hanging on them.

"What's this?" Mortola's voice echoed from the dead walls. "What are these miserable ruins? This isn't my son's fortress!"

Resa drew closer to Mo's side. He still seemed numbed, almost as if he were waiting for the moment when he would wake up and see Elinor's books again instead of the stones. Resa knew only too well how he was feeling. It was not so bad for her this second time; after all, she wasn't alone now, and she knew what had happened. But Mo seemed to have forgotten everything: Mortola, Basta — and why they had brought him here. Resa, however, had not forgotten, and she watched with a thudding heart as Mortola stumbled through the yarrow to the charred walls and felt the stones, as if she were running her fingers over her dead son's face.

"I'll cut that man Orpheus's tongue out with my own hands and serve it for supper!" she exclaimed. "With chopped foxglove! Is this supposed to be my son's fortress? Never!"

Her head moved frantically back and forth like a bird's as she looked around her. But Basta just stood there in silence, pointing his rifle at Resa and Mo.

"Well, say something!" shouted the Magpie. "Say something, you fool!"

Basta bent down and picked up a rusty helmet lying at his feet. "What do you expect me to say?" he growled, throwing the helmet back into the grass with a gloomy expression and giving it a kick that sent it clattering against the wall. "Of course it's our castle. Didn't you see the figure of the goat on the wall there? Even the carved devils are still standing, though they wear ivy crowns now — and look, there's one of the eyes that Slasher liked to paint on the stones."

Mortola stared at the red eye to which Basta was pointing. Then she hobbled over to the remains of the wooden gate, now splintered, torn off its hinges, and barely visible under the brambles and tall stinging nettles. She stood there in silence, looking around her. As for Mo, he had finally come back to his senses.

"What are they talking about?" he whispered to Resa. "Where are we? Was this where Capricorn used to hide out?"

Resa just nodded. However, the Magpie turned at the sound of Mo's voice and stared at him. Then she came over to him, stumbling as if she felt dizzy.

"Yes, this is his castle, but Capricorn isn't here!" she said in a dangerously low voice. "My son is not here. So Basta was right after all. He's dead, here and in the other world, too, dead, and what killed him? Your voice, your accursed voice!" There was such hatred in her face that Resa instinctively tried to draw Mo away, somewhere, anywhere he would be safe from that glance. But there was nothing behind them but the sooty wall with the figure of Capricorn's goat still displayed on it, a red-eyed goat with burning horns.

"Silvertongue!" Mortola spat out the word as if it were poison. "Killertongue suits you better. Your daughter couldn't bring herself to utter the words that killed my son, but you — oh, you didn't hesitate for a moment!" Her voice was little more than a whisper as she went on: "I can still see you before me, as if it had happened only last night — taking the piece of paper from her hand and putting her aside. And then the words came out of your mouth, fine-sounding as everything you say, and when you'd finished my son lay dead in the dust." For a moment she put her fingers to her mouth as if to suppress a sob. When she let her hand drop again, her lips were still quivering.

"How — how can this be?" she went on, in a trembling voice. "Tell me, how is it possible? He didn't belong in your false world at all. So how could he die there? Was that the only reason you lured him over with your wicked tongue?" And again she turned and stared at the burned walls, her bony hands clenched into fists.

Basta bent down again. This time he picked up an arrow point. "I'd really like to know what happened!" he muttered. "I always said Capricorn wasn't here, but what about the others? Firefox, Pitch-Eater, Humpback, the Piper, Slasher . . . Are they all dead? Or are they in the Laughing Prince's dungeon?" He looked uneasily at Mortola. "What are we going to do if they're all gone?" Basta sounded like a boy afraid of the dark. "Do you want us to live in a cave like brownies until the wolves find us? Have you forgotten the wolves? And the Night-Mares, the fire-elves, all the other creatures crawling around the place . . . I for one haven't forgotten them, but you *would* come back to this accursed spot where there are three ghosts lurking behind every tree!" He reached for the amulet dangling around his neck, but Mortola did not deign to look at him.

"Oh, be quiet!" she said, so sharply that Basta flinched. "How often must I tell you that ghosts are nothing to be afraid of? As for wolves, that's why you carry a knife, isn't it? We'll manage. We managed in their world, and we know our way around in this one a good deal better. And, don't forget, we have a powerful friend here. We're going to pay him a visit, yes, that's what. But first I have something else to do, something I should have done long ago." And again her eyes were on Mo. On him and no one else. Then she turned, walked steadily up to Basta, and took the rifle from his hand.

Resa reached for Mo's arm and tried to pull him aside, but Mortola was too quick on the draw. The Magpie had some skill with a rifle. She had often shot at the birds who pecked the seed from her garden beds, back in Capricorn's yard. Blood spread over Mo's shirt like a flower blossoming, red, crimson. Resa heard herself scream as he fell and suddenly lay there motionless, while the grass around him turned as red as his shirt. She flung herself down on her knees, turned him over, and pressed her hands to the wound, as if she could hold back the blood, all the blood carrying his life away. . . .

"Come along, Basta!" she heard Mortola say. "We have a long way to go, and it's time we found safe shelter before it gets dark. This forest is not a pleasant place by night."

"You're going to leave them here?" That was Basta's voice.

"Why not? I know you were always attracted to her, but the wolves will take care of them. The fresh blood will bring them this way."

The blood. It was still flowing so fast, and Mo's face was white as a sheet. "No. Oh, please, no!" whispered Resa. Aloud, in her own voice. She pressed her fingers to her shaking lips.

"Well, what do you know? Our little pigeon can speak again!" Basta's mocking voice hardly penetrated the rushing in her ears. "What a pity he can't hear you anymore, eh? So long, Resa!"

She did not look around. Not even when their footsteps died away. "No!" she heard herself whispering again and again. "No!" like a prayer. She tore a strip of fabric from her dress — if only her fingers weren't shaking so badly — and pressed it to the wound. Her hands were wet with his blood and her own tears. *Resa,* she told herself sternly, *crying won't do him any good. Try to remember! What did Capricorn's men do when they were wounded?* They cauterized the wound, but she didn't want to think of that. There had been a plant, too, a plant with hairy leaves and pale mauve flowers, tiny bells into which bumblebees flew, buzzing. She looked around, through the veil of tears over her eyes, as if hoping for a miracle. . . .

Two blue-skinned fairies were hovering among the twining honeysuckle. If Dustfinger had been here now, he'd surely have known how to entice them. He'd have called to them softly, persuaded them to give him some of their fairy spit, or the silvery dust that they shook out of their hair.

She heard her own sobbing again. She lifted the dark hair back from Mo's brow with her bloodstained fingers, called him by name. He couldn't be gone, not now, not after all those years. . . .

Over and over she called his name, put her fingers on his lips, felt his breath, shallow and irregular, coming with difficulty as if someone were sitting on his chest. *Death*, she thought, *it's Death*. . . .

A sound made her jump. Footsteps on soft leaves. Had Mortola changed her mind? Had she sent Basta back to fetch them? Or were the wolves coming? If only she at least had a knife. Mo always carried one. Feverishly, she put her hands in his trouser pockets, feeling for the smooth handle. . . .

The footsteps grew louder. Yes, they were human footsteps, no doubt about it. And then suddenly all was still. Menacingly still. Resa felt the handle in her fingers. She quickly removed the knife from Mo's pocket and snapped it open. She hardly dared to turn, but at last she did.

An old woman was standing in what had once been Capricorn's gateway. She looked as small as a child among the pillars that still stood erect. She had a sack slung over her shoulder and was wearing a dress that looked as if she had woven it from nettles. Her skin was burned brown, her face furrowed like the bark of a tree. Her gray hair was as short as a marten's fur, and had leaves and burrs clinging to it. Without a word, she came toward Resa. Her feet were bare, but she didn't seem to mind the nettles and thistles growing in the courtyard of the ruined fortress. Her face expressionless, she pushed Resa aside and bent over Mo. Unmoved, she lifted the bloody scraps of fabric that Resa was still pressing to the wound.

"I never saw a wound like that before," she remarked, in a voice that sounded hoarse, as if it wasn't often used. "What did it?"

"A rifle," replied Resa. It felt strange to be speaking with her tongue again instead of her hands.

"A rifle?" The old woman looked at her, shook her head, and bent over Mo again. "A rifle. What may that be?" she murmured as her brown fingers felt the wound. "Dear me, these days they go inventing new weapons faster than a chick hatches from its egg, and I have to find out how to mend what they stab and cut." She put her ear to Mo's chest, listened, and straightened up again with a sigh. "Are you wearing something under that dress?" she asked abruptly, without looking at Resa. "Take it off and tear it up. I need long strips." Then she put her hand into a leather bag at her belt, took out a little bottle, and used its contents to soak one of the strips of fabric that Resa was offering her. "Press that down on it!" she said, handing the fabric back to Resa. "This is a bad wound. I may have to cut or cauterize it, but not here. The two of us can't carry him on our own, but the strolling players have a camp not far off, for their old and sick people. I may find help there." She dressed the wound with fingers as nimble as if she had never done anything else. "Keep him warm!" she said as she rose to her feet again and slung the sack over her shoulder. Then she pointed to the knife that Resa had dropped in the grass. "Keep that with you. I'll try to be back before the wolves get here. And if one of the White Women turns up, make sure she doesn't look at him or whisper his name."

Then she was gone, as suddenly as she had come. And Resa knelt there in the courtyard of Capricorn's fortress, her hand pressed down on the blood-soaked dressing, and listened to Mo's breathing.

"Can you hear me? My voice is back," she whispered to him. "Just as if it had been waiting for you here." But Mo did not move. His face was as pale as if the stones and grass had drunk all his blood.

Resa didn't know how much time had passed when she heard the whispering behind her, incomprehensible and soft as rain. When she looked around, there stood the figure on the ruined stairway. A White Woman, blurred as a reflection on water. Resa knew only too well what such an apparition meant. She had told Meggie about the White Women often enough. Only one thing lured them, and faster than blood lured the wolves: failing breath, a heart beating ever more feebly . . .

"Be quiet!" Resa shouted at the pale figure, bending protectively over Mo's face. "Go away, and don't you dare look at him. He isn't going with you, not today!" They whisper your name if they want to take you with them, so Dustfinger had told her. *But they don't know Mo's name,* thought Resa. *They can't know it, because he doesn't belong here.* All the same, she held her hands over his ears.

The sun was beginning to set. It sank inexorably behind the trees. Darkness fell between the charred walls, and the pale figure on the stairs stood out more clearly all the time. It stood there motionless, waiting.

BIRTHDAY MORNING

"Nay, not without a wound in the spirit shall I leave this city . . . Too many fragments of the spirit have I scattered in these streets, and too many are the children of my longing that walk naked among these hills . . ."

Khalil Gibran, *The Prophet*

Meggie woke with a start. She had been dreaming, and her dreams had been bad, but she didn't remember what they were about, only the fear they left behind like a knife wound in the heart. Noise came to her ears, shouting and loud laughter, children's voices, the barking of dogs, the grunting of pigs, hammering, sawing. She felt sunlight on her face, and the air she was breathing smelled of dung and freshly baked bread. Where was she? Only when she saw Fenoglio sitting at his writing desk did she remember. Ombra — she was in Ombra.

"Good morning!" Fenoglio had obviously slept extremely well. He looked very pleased with himself and the world in general. Well, who should be pleased with it if not the man who made it up? The glass man Meggie had seen last night, asleep beside the jug of quill pens, was standing beside him.

"Say hello to our guest, Rosenquartz!" Fenoglio told him.

The glass man bowed stiffly in Meggie's direction, took Fenoglio's dripping pen, wiped it on a rag, and put it back in the jug with the others. Then he bent to look at what Fenoglio had written. "Ah. Not a song about this Bluejay for a change!" he snapped. "Are you taking this one up to the castle today?"

"I am indeed," said Fenoglio loftily. "Now, do please make sure the ink doesn't run."

The glass man wrinkled his nose, as if he had never allowed such a thing to happen, put both hands into the bowl of sand standing next to the pens, and scattered the fine grains over the freshly written parchment with practiced energy.

"Rosenquartz, how often do I have to tell you?" snapped Fenoglio. "Too much sand, too much energy. That way you'll smudge everything."

The glass man brushed a couple of grains of sand off his hands and folded his arms, looking injured. "Then you do better!" His voice reminded Meggie of the noise you make tapping a glass with your fingernails. "I'd certainly like to see that!" he added sharply, examining Fenoglio's clumsy fingers with such scorn that Meggie had to laugh.

"Me, too!" she said, pulling her dress on over her head. A few withered flowers from the Wayless Wood still clung to it, and Meggie couldn't help thinking of Farid. Had he found Dustfinger?

"Hear that?" Rosenquartz cast her a friendly glance. "She sounds like a clever girl."

"Oh yes, Meggie's very clever," replied Fenoglio. "The two of us have been through a lot together. It's thanks to her that I'm sitting here now, trying to tell a glass man the right way to scatter sand over ink."

Rosenquartz looked curiously at Meggie, but he didn't ask what Fenoglio's mysterious comment meant. Meggie went up to the desk and looked over the old man's shoulder. "Your hand-writing's easier to read these days," she said.

"Thank you very much," murmured Fenoglio. "You should know. But look — do you see that smudged P?"

"If you are seriously suggesting that I'm to blame for it," said Rosenquartz in his ringing little voice, "then this is the last time I hold your pens for you, and I'm going straight off to look for a scribe who won't expect me to work before breakfast."

"All right, all right, I'm not blaming you. I smudged the P myself!" Fenoglio winked at Meggie. "He's easily offended," he whispered confidentially to her. "His pride is as fragile as his limbs."

The glass man turned his back on Fenoglio without a word, picked up the rag he had used to clean the pen, and tried to wipe a still-damp inkspot off his arm. His limbs were not entirely colorless, like those of the glass people who had lived in Elinor's garden. Everything about him was pale pink, like the flowers of a wild rose. Only his hair was slightly darker.

"You didn't say anything about my new song," Fenoglio pointed out. "Wonderful, don't you agree?"

"Not bad," replied Rosenquartz without turning around, and he began polishing up his feet.

"Not bad? It's a masterpiece, you maggot-colored, ink-smudging pen-holder!" Fenoglio struck the desk so hard that the glass man fell over on his back like a beetle. "I'm going to market today to get a new glass man, one who knows about these things and will appreciate my robber songs, too!" He opened a longish box and took out a stick of sealing wax. "At least you haven't forgotten to get a flame for the wax this time!" he growled.

Rosenquartz snatched the sealing wax from his hand and held it in the flame of the candle that stood beside the jug. His face expressionless, he placed the melting end of the wax on the parchment roll, waved his glass hand over the red seal a couple of times, and then cast Fenoglio an imperious glance, whereupon Fenoglio solemnly pressed the ring he wore on his middle finger down onto the soft wax.

"F for Fenoglio, F for fantasy, F for fabulous," he announced. "There we are."

"B for breakfast would sound better just now," said Rosenquartz, but Fenoglio ignored this remark.

"What did you think of the song for the prince?" he asked Meggie.

"I . . . er . . . I couldn't read it all because you two were quarreling," she said evasively. She didn't want to make Fenoglio even gloomier by saying that the lines struck her as familiar. "Why does the Laughing Prince want such a sad poem?" she asked instead.

"Because his son is dead," replied Fenoglio. "One sad song after another, that's all he wants to hear since Cosimo's death. I'm tired of it!" Sighing, he put the parchment back on his desk and went over to the chest standing under the window.

"Cosimo? Cosimo the Fair is dead?" Meggie couldn't conceal her disappointment. Resa had told her so much about the Laughing Prince's son: Everyone who saw him loved him, even the Adderhead feared him, his peasants brought their sick children to him because they believed anyone as beautiful as an angel could cure all sicknesses, too. . . .

Fenoglio sighed. "Yes, it's terrible. And a bitter lesson. This story isn't my story anymore! It's developed a will of its own."

"Oh no, here we go again!" Rosenquartz groaned. "His story! I'll never understand all this talk. Maybe you really ought to go and see one of those physicians who cure sick minds."

"My dear Rosenquartz," Fenoglio replied, "all this talk, as you call it, is above your transparent little head. But believe me, Meggie knows just what I'm talking about!" He opened the chest, looking cross, and took out a long, dark blue robe. "I ought to get a new one made," he muttered. "Yes, I definitely ought to. This is no robe for a man whose words are sung up and down the land, a man commissioned by a prince to put his grief for his son into words! Just look at the sleeves! Holes everywhere. In spite of Minerva's sprigs of lavender, the moths have been at it."

"It's good enough for a poor poet," remarked the glass man in matter-of-fact tones.

Fenoglio put the robe back in the chest and let the lid fall into place with a dull thud. "One of these days," he said, "I am going to throw something really hard at you!"

This threat did not seem to bother Rosenquartz unduly. The two went on wrangling about this and that; it seemed to be a kind of game they played, and they had obviously forgotten Meggie's presence entirely. She went to the window, pushed aside the fabric over it, and looked out. It was going to be a sunny day, although mist still lingered above the hills surrounding the city. Which was the hill where the house of the minstrel woman stood, the place where Farid hoped to find Dustfinger? She had forgotten. Would he come back if he actually found the fire-eater, or would he just go off with him, like last time, forgetting that she was here, too? Meggie didn't even try to work out just how that idea made her feel. There was enough turmoil in her heart already, so much turmoil that she'd have liked to ask Fenoglio for a mirror, just to see herself for a moment — her own familiar face amid all the strangeness surrounding her, all the strange feelings in her heart. But instead she let her gaze wander over the misty hills.

How far did Fenoglio's world go? Just as far as he had described it? "Interesting!" he had whispered, back when Basta had dragged the two of them off to Capricorn's village. "Do you know, this place is very like one of the settings I thought up for *Inkheart?*" It must have been Ombra he meant. The hills around Ombra really did look like those over which Meggie had escaped with Mo and Elinor when Dustfinger set them free from Capricorn's dungeons, except that these seemed even greener, if that was possible, and more enchanted. As if every leaf suggested that fairies and fire-elves lived under the trees. And the houses and streets you could see from Fenoglio's room might have been in Capricorn's village, if they hadn't been so much noisier and more colorful.

"Just look at the crowds — they all want to go up to the castle today," said Fenoglio behind her. "Traveling peddlers, peasants, craftsmen, rich merchants, beggars, they'll all be going there to celebrate the birthday, to earn or spend a few coins, to enjoy themselves, and most of all to stare at the grand folk."

Meggie looked at the castle walls. They rose above the russet rooftops almost menacingly. Black banners on the towers flapped in the wind.

"How long has Cosimo been dead?"

"Hardly a year yet. I'd just moved into this room. As you can imagine, your voice took me straight to where it plucked the Shadow out of the story: the middle of Capricorn's fortress. Fortunately, all was hopeless confusion there because the monstrous Shadow had disappeared, and none of the fire-raisers noticed an old man suddenly standing among them looking foolish. I spent a couple of dreadful days in the forest, and unfortunately I didn't, like you, have a clever companion who could use a knife, catch rabbits, and kindle fire with a couple of dry twigs. But the Black Prince himself finally picked me up — imagine how I stared when he was suddenly there in front of me. I didn't think I knew any of the men who were with him, but I'll admit that I could never remember the minor characters in my stories very clearly — only vaguely, if at all.

"Well, be that as it may, one of them took me to Ombra, ragged and destitute as I was. But luckily I had a ring that I could sell. A goldsmith gave me enough for it to allow me to rent this room from Minerva, and all seemed to be going well. Very well indeed, in fact. I thought up stories, and stories about stories, better than any I'd made up for a long time. The words came pouring out of me, but when I'd only just made my name with the first songs I wrote for the Laughing Prince, when the strolling players had just begun to find that they liked my verses, Firefox goes and burns down a few farms by the river — and Cosimo the Fair sets out to put an end to Firefox and his gang once and for all. *Good,* I thought, *why not?* How was I to guess that he'd get himself killed? I had such plans for him! He was to be a truly great prince, a blessing to his subjects, and my story was going to give them a happy ending when he freed this world from the Adderhead. But instead he gets himself killed by a band of fire-raisers in the Wayless Wood!"

Fenoglio sighed.

"At first his father wouldn't believe he was dead. For Cosimo's face was badly burned, like those of all the other dead who were brought back. The fire had done its work, but when months passed, and still he didn't return . . ." Fenoglio sighed

185

again, and once more looked in the chest where the moth-eaten robe lay. He handed Meggie two long, pale blue woolen stockings, a couple of leather straps, and a much-washed, dark blue dress. "I'm afraid this will be too big for you — it belongs to Minerva's second daughter, and she's the same size as her mother," he said, "but what you're wearing now urgently needs a wash. You can keep the stockings up with those garters — not very comfortable, but you'll get used to it. Good Lord, you really have grown, Meggie," he said, turning his back to her as she changed her clothes. "Rosenquartz! You turn around, too!"

It was true that the dress didn't fit particularly well, and Meggie suddenly felt almost glad that Fenoglio had no mirror. At home she had been studying her reflection quite often recently. It was odd to watch your own body changing, as if you were a butterfly coming out of its chrysalis.

"Ready?" asked Fenoglio, turning around. "Ah well, that'll do, although such a pretty girl really deserves a prettier dress." He looked down at himself and sighed. "I think I'd better stay as I am; at least this robe doesn't have any holes in it. And what does it matter? The castle will be swarming with entertainers and fine folk today, so no one will take any notice of the two of us."

"Two? What do you mean?" Rosenquartz put down the blade he had been using to sharpen a pen. "Aren't you going to take me with you?"

"Are you crazy? Just for me to carry you back in pieces? No. Anyway, you'd have to listen to that bad poem I'm taking to the prince."

Rosenquartz was still grumbling as Fenoglio closed the door behind them. The wooden staircase that Meggie had hardly been able to climb last night, exhausted as she was, led down to a yard surrounded by houses, with pigsties, woodsheds, and vegetable plots competing for what little space was left. A narrow little stream wound its way through the yard, two children were shooing a pig away from the vegetable beds, and a woman with a baby in her arms was feeding a flock of skinny hens.

"A wonderful morning, isn't it, Minerva?" Fenoglio called to her, as Meggie hesitantly followed him down the last steep steps.

Minerva came to the foot of the stairs. A girl of perhaps six was clinging to her skirt and stared suspiciously at Meggie. She stopped, feeling unsure of herself. *Perhaps they can see it,* she thought, *perhaps they can see I don't belong here. . . .*

"Watch out!" the little girl called, but before Meggie realized what she meant, something was pulling her hair. The little girl threw a clod of earth, and a fairy fluttered away empty-handed, scolding crossly.

"Good heavens, where are you from?" asked Minerva, helping Meggie down from the steps. "Aren't there any fairies there? They're crazy for human hair, particularly when it's as pretty as yours. If you don't pin it up you'll soon be bald. And anyway, you're too old to wear it loose, not unless you want to be taken for one of the strolling players."

Minerva was small and stocky, not much taller than Meggie. "My word, how thin you are!" she said. "That dress is almost slipping off your shoulders. I'll take it in for you this evening. Has she had any breakfast?" she asked and shook her head at the sight of Fenoglio's baffled expression. "Dear Lord, surely you didn't forget to give the girl something to eat?"

Fenoglio helplessly raised his hands. "I'm an old man, Minerva!" he cried. "I do forget things! What's the matter with everyone this morning? I was in such a good mood, but you all keep going on like this. Rosenquartz has already been infuriating me."

By way of answer Minerva dumped the baby in his arms and led Meggie off with her.

"And whose baby is this?" inquired Fenoglio, following her. "Aren't there enough children running around the place already?"

"It's my eldest daughter's," was all Minerva replied, "and you've seen it a couple of times before. Are you getting so forgetful that I'll have to introduce my own children to you?"

Minerva's younger children were called Despina and Ivo; Ivo was the boy who had been carrying Fenoglio's torch last night. He smiled at Meggie as she and his mother came into the kitchen. Minerva made Meggie eat a plate of polenta and two slices of bread spread with a paste that smelled of olives. The milk she gave her was so rich that Meggie's tongue felt coated with cream after the first sip. As she ate, Minerva pinned up her hair for her. Meggie scarcely recognized herself when Minerva pushed a bowl of water over to her so that she could see her reflection.

"Where did you get those boots?" asked Ivo. His sister was still inspecting Meggie like some strange animal that had lost its way and wandered into their kitchen. Where indeed? Meggie hastily tried to pull down the dress to hide her boots, but it was too short.

"Meggie comes from far away," explained Fenoglio, who had noticed her confusion. "Very far away. A place where there are people with three legs and others whose noses grow on their chins."

The children stared first at him and then at Meggie.

"Oh, stop it! What nonsense you do talk!" Minerva lightly cuffed the back of his head. "They believe every word you say. One of these days they'll be setting off to look for all the crazy places you tell them about, and I'll be left childless."

Meggie almost choked on the rich milk. She had quite forgotten her homesickness, but Minerva's words brought it back — and her guilty conscience, too. She had been away from home five days now, if she'd been keeping count correctly.

"You and your stories!" Minerva handed Fenoglio a mug of milk. "As if it wasn't enough for you to keep telling them those robber tales. Do you know what Ivo said to me yesterday? When I'm grown-up I'm going to join the robbers, too! He wants to be like the Bluejay! What do you think you're doing, pray? Tell them about Cosimo for all I care, tell them about the giants, or the Black Prince and his bear, but not another word about that Bluejay, understand?"

"Yes, yes, not another word," muttered Fenoglio. "But don't blame me if the boy picks up one of the songs about him from somewhere. Everyone's singing them."

Meggie had no idea what they were talking about, but in her mind she was already up at the castle, anyway. Resa had told her that the birds' nests clustered together on its walls so thickly that sometimes the twittering drowned out the minstrels' songs. And fairies nested there, too, she said, fairies who were pale gray like the stone of the castle walls because they often nibbled human food, instead of living on flowers and fruits like their sisters in the wild. And there were said to be trees in the Inner Courtyard of the castle that grew nowhere else except in the very heart of the Wayless Wood, trees with leaves that murmured in the wind like a chorus of human voices and foretold the future on moonless nights — but in a language that no one could understand.

"Would you like anything else to eat?"

Meggie started and came down to earth again.

"Inky infernos!" Fenoglio rose and handed the baby back to Minerva. "Do you want to fatten her up until she fits into that dress? We must be off, or we'll miss half of it. The prince has asked me to bring him the new song before midday, and you know he doesn't like people to be late."

"No, I don't know any such thing," replied Minerva grumpily, as Fenoglio propelled Meggie toward the door. "Because I don't go in and out of the castle the way you do. What does our fine prince want from you this time — another lament?"

"Yes, I've had enough of them, too, but he pays well. Would you rather I was penniless and you had to look for a new lodger?"

"Very well, very well," grumbled Minerva, clearing the children's empty bowls off the table. "I tell you what, though: This prince of ours will sigh and lament himself to death, and then the Adderhead will send his men-at-arms. They'll settle here like flies on fresh horse dung, on the excuse of just wanting to protect their master's poor fatherless grandson."

Fenoglio turned so abruptly that he almost sent Meggie flying. "No, Minerva. No!" he said firmly. "That won't happen. Not as long as I live — which I hope will be a very long time yet!"

"Oh yes?" Minerva removed her son's fingers from the tub of butter. "And how are you going to prevent it? With your robber songs? Do you think some fool with a feathered mask, playing the hero because he's listened to your songs too often, can keep the men-at-arms away from our city? Heroes end up on the gallows, Fenoglio," she continued, lowering her voice, and Meggie could hear the fear behind her mockery. "It may be different in your songs, but in real life princes hang them, and the finest of words don't change that."

The two children looked uneasily at their mother, and Minerva stroked their hair as if that would wipe away her own words. But Fenoglio merely shrugged. "Oh, come on, you see everything in such dismal hues!" he said. "You underestimate the power of words, believe me! They are strong, stronger than you think. Ask Meggie!"

But before Minerva could do just that, he was pushing Meggie out of the house. "Ivo, Despina, do you want to come?" he called to the children. "I'll bring them home safe and sound. I always do!" he added, as Minerva's anxious face appeared in the doorway. "The best entertainers far and wide will be at the castle today. They'll have come from very far away. Your two can't miss this chance!"

As soon as they stepped out of the alley, they were caught up in the crowd streaming along. People came thronging up from all sides: shabbily dressed peasants, beggars, women with children, and men whose wealth showed not only in the magnificence of their embroidered sleeves but most of all in the servants who roughly forced a path through the crowd for them. Riders drove their horses through the throng without a thought for those they pushed against the walls, litters were jammed in the crush of bodies, however angrily the litter-bearers cursed and shouted.

"Devil take it, this is worse than a market day!" Fenoglio shouted to Meggie above the heads around them. Ivo darted through the crowd, quick as a herring in the sea, but Despina looked so alarmed that Fenoglio finally put her up on his shoulders before she was squashed between baskets and people's bellies. Meggie felt her own heart beat faster, what with all the confusion, the pushing and shoving, the thousands of smells and the voices filling the air.

"Look around you, Meggie! Isn't it wonderful?" cried Fenoglio proudly.

It was indeed. It was just as Meggie had imagined it on all those evenings when Resa had told her about the Inkworld. Her senses were quite dazed. Eyes, ears . . . they could scarcely take in a tenth of all that was going on around her. Music came from somewhere: trumpets, jingles, drums . . . and then the street widened, spewing her and all the others out in front of the castle walls. They towered among the other buildings, tall and massive, as if they had been built by men larger than those now flocking to the gateway. Armed guards stood in front of the gate, with their helmets reflecting the pale morning light. Their cloaks were dark green, like the tunics they wore over their coats of mail. Both bore the emblem of the Laughing Prince. Resa had described it to Meggie: a lion on a green background, surrounded by white roses — but it had changed. The lion wept silver tears now, and the roses twined around a broken heart.

The guards let most of the crowd pass, only occasionally barring someone's way with the shaft of a spear or a mailed fist. No one seemed troubled by that, they went on pressing in, and Meggie, too, finally found herself in the shadow of those foot-wide walls. Of course she had been in castles before, with Mo, but it felt quite different to be going in past guards armed with spears instead of a kiosk selling picture postcards. The walls seemed so much more threatening and forbidding. Look, they seemed to say, see how small you all are, how powerless and fragile.

Fenoglio appeared to feel none of this; he was beaming like a child at Christmas. He ignored both the portcullis above their heads and the slits through which hot pitch could be tipped out on the heads of uninvited guests. Meggie, on the contrary, instinctively looked up as they passed and wondered why the traces of pitch on the weathered stone looked so fresh. But finally the open sky was above her again, clear and blue, as if it had been swept clean for the princely birthday — and Meggie was in the Outer Courtyard of Ombra Castle.

VISITORS FROM THE
WRONG SIDE OF THE
FOREST

Darkness always had its part to play. Without it, how would
we know when we walked in the light? It's only when its
ambitions become too grandiose that it must be opposed,
disciplined, sometimes — if necessary — brought down for a
time. Then it will rise again, as it must.

Clive Barker, *Abarat*

First of all Meggie looked for the birds' nests that Resa had
described, and sure enough, there they were, clinging just
below the battlements like blisters on the walls. Birds with yellow
breasts shot out of the entrance holes. Like flakes of gold dancing
in the sun, Resa had said, and she was right. The sky above
Meggie seemed to be covered with swirling gold, all in honor of
the princely birthday. More and more people surged through the
gateway, although there was already a milling crowd in the courtyard. Stalls had been set up within the walls, in front of the

stables and the huts where the blacksmiths, grooms, and everyone else employed in the castle lived and worked. Today, as the prince was inviting his subjects to celebrate with him the birthday of his grandson and royal heir, food and drink was free. "Very generous, I'm sure," Mo would probably have whispered. "Food and drink from their own fields, won by the labor of their own hands." Mo did not particularly like castles. But that was the way of Fenoglio's world: The land on which the peasants toiled belonged to the Laughing Prince who was now the Prince of Sighs, so a large part of the harvest was his, too, and he dressed in silk and velvet, while his peasants wore much-mended smocks that scratched the skin.

Despina had wound her thin arms around Fenoglio's neck when they passed the guards at the gate, but at the sight of the first entertainers she quickly slipped off his back. One of them had stretched his rope between the battlements, and was walking high up there in the air, moving more lightly than a spider on its silver thread. His clothes were blue as the sky above him, for blue was the color of the tightrope-walkers; Meggie's mother had told her that, too. If only Resa had been here! The Motley Folk were everywhere among the stalls: pipers and jugglers, knife-throwers, strong men, animal-tamers, contortionists, actors, clowns. Right in front of the wall Meggie saw a fire-eater, yes, black and red was their costume, and for a moment she thought it was Dustfinger, but when the man turned he was a stranger with an unscarred face, and the smile with which he bowed to the people around him was not at all like Dustfinger's.

But he must *be here, if he's really back,* thought Meggie, as she looked around for him. Why did she feel so disappointed? As if she didn't know. It was Farid she really missed. And if

Dustfinger wasn't here, she supposed it would be no use looking for Farid, either.

"Come along, Meggie!" Despina pronounced her name as if it was going to take her tongue some time to get used to it. She pulled Meggie over to a stall selling sweet cakes dripping with honey. Even today those cakes had to be paid for. The trader selling them was keeping a close eye on his wares, but luckily Fenoglio had a few coins on him. Despina's thin fingers were sticky when she put them into Meggie's hand again. She looked around, wide-eyed, and kept stopping, but Fenoglio impatiently waved them on, past a wooden platform decked with flowers and evergreen branches, rising above the stalls. The black banners flying from the castle battlements and towers overhead hung here as well, to the right and left of three thrones on the platform. The backs of the seats were embroidered with the emblem of the weeping lion.

"Why three thrones, I ask myself?" Fenoglio whispered to Meggie as he urged her and the children on. "The Prince of Sighs himself won't be showing his face, anyway. Come along, we're late already." With a firm step, he turned his back on the busy scene in the Outer Courtyard and made his way to the Inner Ring of the castle walls. The gate toward which he was moving was not quite as tall as the one in the Outer Ring, but it, too, looked forbidding, and so did the guards who crossed their spears as Fenoglio approached them. "As if they didn't know me!" he whispered crossly to Meggie. "But we have to play the same game every time. Tell the prince that Fenoglio the poet is here!" he said, raising his voice, as the two children pressed close to him and stared at the spears as if looking for dried blood on their points.

"Is the prince expecting you?" The guard who spoke seemed

to still be very young, judging by what could be seen of his face under his helmet.

"Of course he is!" snapped Fenoglio. "And if he has to wait any longer I'll blame it on you, Anselmo. What's more, if you want me to write you a few fine-sounding words, as you did last month" — here the guard cast a nervous glance at his fellow sentry, but the latter pretended not to have heard and looked up at the tightrope-walker — "then," Fenoglio concluded, lowering his voice, "I shall keep you waiting in your own turn. I'm an old man, and God knows I have better things to do than cool my heels here in front of your spear."

All that could be seen of Anselmo's face turned as red as the sour wine that Fenoglio had drunk beside the strolling players' fire. However, he did not move his spear aside. "The fact is, Inkweaver, we have visitors," he said in an undertone.

"Visitors? What are you talking about?"

But Anselmo wasn't looking at Fenoglio anymore.

The gate behind him opened, creaking, as if its own weight were too heavy for it. Meggie drew Despina aside; Fenoglio took Ivo's hand. Soldiers rode into the Outer Courtyard, armed horsemen, their cloaks silvery gray, like the greaves they wore on their legs, and the emblem on their breasts was not the Laughing Prince's. It showed a viper's slender body rearing up in search of prey, and Meggie recognized it at once. This was the Adderhead's coat of arms.

Nothing moved in the Outer Courtyard now. All was silent as the grave. The entertainers, even the blue-clad tightrope-walker high above on his rope, were all forgotten. Resa had told Meggie exactly what the Adderhead's emblem looked like; she had seen it often enough at close quarters. Envoys from the Castle of Night had been welcome guests in Capricorn's fortress. Many of the farms set on fire by Capricorn's men, so rumor said at the time, had been burned down on the Adderhead's orders.

Meggie held Despina close as the men-at-arms rode by them. Their breastplates glinted in the sun. It looked as if not even a bolt from a crossbow could pierce that armor, let alone a poor man's arrow. Two men rode at their head: one was a redhead, in armor like the soldiers following him but resplendent in a cloak of foxtails, while the other was wearing a green robe shot with silver that was fine enough for any prince. However, what everyone noticed about him first was not that robe but his nose; unlike ordinary noses of flesh and blood, it was made of silver.

"Look at that couple! What a team!" Fenoglio whispered to Meggie, as the two men rode side by side through the silent crowd. "Both of them my creations, and both once Capricorn's men. Your mother may have told you about them. Firefox was Capricorn's deputy, the Piper was his minstrel. But the silver nose wasn't my idea. Nor the fact that they escaped Cosimo's soldiers when he attacked Capricorn's fortress and now serve the Adderhead."

It was still eerily silent in the courtyard. There was no sound but the clatter of hooves, the snorting horses, the clank of armor, weapons, and spears — curiously loud, as if the sounds were caught between the high walls like birds.

The Adderhead himself was one of the last to ride in. There was no mistaking him. "He looks like a butcher," Resa had said. "A butcher in princely clothes, with his love of killing written all over his coarse face." The horse he rode was white, heavily built like its master, and almost entirely hidden by a caparison patterned with the snake emblem. The Adderhead himself wore a black robe embroidered with silver flowers. His skin was tanned by the sun, his sparse hair was gray, his mouth curiously small —

a lipless slit in his coarse, clean-shaven face. Everything about him seemed heavy and fleshy: his arms and legs, his thick neck, his broad nose. Unlike those richer subjects of the Laughing Prince who were now standing in the courtyard, he wore no jewelry, no heavy chains around his neck, no rings set with precious stones on his fat fingers. But gems sparkled in the corners of his nostrils, red as drops of blood, and on the middle finger of his left hand, over his glove, he wore the silver ring he used for sealing death warrants. His eyes, narrow under lids folded like a salamander's, darted restlessly around the courtyard. They seemed to linger for a split second, like a lizard's sticky tongue, on everything they saw: the strolling players, the tightrope-walker overhead, the rich merchants waiting beside the empty, flower-decked platform, submissively bowing their heads when his glance rested on them. Nothing seemed to escape those salamander eyes, nothing at all: no child pressing his face into his mother's apron in alarm, no beautiful woman, no man glaring up at him with hostility. Yet he reined in his horse in front of only one person in the crowd.

"Well, well, so here's the king of the strolling players! Last time I saw you, your head was in the pillory in my castle courtyard. And when are you going to honor us with another visit?" The Adderhead's voice rang out through the silent courtyard. It sounded very deep, as if it came from the black interior of his stout body. Meggie instinctively moved closer to Fenoglio's side. But the Black Prince bowed, so deeply that the bow turned to mockery. "I'm sorry," he said, loud enough for everyone to hear, "but I'm afraid my bear didn't care for your hospitality. He says the pillory was rather tight for his neck."

Meggie saw the Adderhead's mouth twist into an unpleasant smile. "Well, I could keep a rope ready for your next visit — a rope that will fit perfectly, and a gallows of oak strong enough even for such a fat old bear as yours," he said.

The Black Prince turned to his bear and pretended to discuss it with him. "Sorry again," he said, as the bear threw its paws around his neck, grunting, "the bear says he likes the south, but your shadow lies too dark over it. He won't come until the Bluejay pays you the honor of a visit, too."

A soft whisper ran through the crowd — and was silenced when the Adderhead turned in his saddle and let his lizardlike gaze move over those standing around him.

"And furthermore," the Prince continued in a loud voice, "the bear would like to know why you don't make the Piper trot along behind your horse on a silver chain, as such a good, tame minstrel should?"

The Piper wrenched his horse around, but before he could urge it toward the Black Prince the Adderhead raised a hand. "I will let you know just as soon as the Bluejay is my guest!" he said, while the silver-nosed man reluctantly rode back to his place. "And believe me, that will be before long. I've already ordered the gallows to be built." Then he spurred his horse, and the men-at-arms rode on again. It seemed an eternity before the last of them had disappeared through the gateway.

"Yes, off you ride!" whispered Fenoglio, as the castle court-yard gradually filled with carefree noise again. "Viewing this place as if it would all soon be his, thinking he can spread his power through my world like a running sore and play a part I never wrote for him. . . ."

The guard's spear abruptly silenced him. "Very well, poet!" said Anselmo. "You can go in now. Off with you!"

"Off with you?" thundered Fenoglio. "Is that any way to speak to the prince's poet? Listen," he told the two children, "you'd better stay here. Don't eat too much cake. And don't go too close to the fire-eater, because he's useless at his job, and leave the Black Prince's bear alone. Understand?"

The two of them nodded and ran straight to the nearest cake stall. But Fenoglio took Meggie's hand and strode past the guards with her, his head held high.

"Fenoglio," she asked in a low voice as the gate closed behind them and the noise of the Outer Courtyard died away, "who is the Bluejay?"

It was cool behind the great gate, as if winter had built itself a nest here. Trees shaded a wide courtyard, the air was fragrant with the scent of roses and other flowers whose names Meggie didn't know, and a stone basin of water, round as the moon, reflected the part of the castle in which the Laughing Prince lived.

"Oh, he doesn't exist!" was all Fenoglio would say, as he impatiently beckoned her on. "But I'll explain all that later. Come along now. We must take the Laughing Prince my verses at last, or I won't be his court poet anymore."

THE PRINCE OF SIGHS

The man couldn't very well tell the king, "No, I won't go," for he had to earn his bread.
   Italo Calvino, "The King in the Basket," *Italian Folk Tales*

The windows of the hall where the Prince of Sighs, once the Laughing Prince, received Fenoglio were hung with black draperies. The place smelled like a crypt, of dried flowers and soot from the candles. The candles were burning in front of statues that all had the same face, sometimes a good likeness, sometimes less good. *Cosimo the Fair,* thought Meggie. He stared down at her from countless pairs of marble eyes as she walked toward his father with Fenoglio.

The throne in which the Prince of Sighs sat enthroned stood between two other high-backed chairs. The dark green upholstery of the chair on his left was occupied only by a helmet with a plume of peacock feathers, its metal brightly polished as if it were waiting for its owner. A boy of about five or six sat in the chair on his right. He wore a black brocade doublet embroidered all over with pearls as if it were covered in tears. This must be the birthday boy: Jacopo, grandson of the Prince of Sighs, but the Adderhead's grandson, too.

The child looked bored. He was swinging his short legs restlessly, as if he could hardly prevent himself from running outside to the entertainers, and the sweet cakes, and the armchair waiting for him on the platform adorned with prickly bindweed and roses. His grandfather, on the other hand, looked as if he never intended to rise from his chair again. He sat there as powerless as a puppet, in black robes that were too large for him now, as if hypnotized by the eyes of his dead son. Not particularly tall but fat enough for two men, that was how Resa had described him; seldom seen without something to eat in his greasy fingers, always rather breathless because of the weight his legs, which were not especially strong, had to carry, and yet always in the best of tempers.

The prince whom Meggie saw now, sitting in his dimly lit castle, was nothing like that. His face was pale and his skin hung in wrinkled folds, as if it had once belonged to a larger man. Grief had melted the fat from his limbs, and his expression was fixed, as if it had frozen on the day when they brought him the news of his son's death. Only his eyes still showed his horror and bewilderment at what life had done to him.

Apart from his grandson and the guards standing silent in the background, there were only two women with him. One kept her head humbly bent like a maidservant, although she wore a dress fit for a princess. Her mistress stood between the Prince of Sighs and the empty chair on which the plumed helmet lay. *Violante*, thought Meggie. *The Adderhead's daughter and Cosimo's widow.* Her Ugliness, as people called her. Fenoglio had told Meggie about her, emphasizing the fact that she was indeed one of his creations, but that he had never intended her to be more than a minor character: the unhappy child of an unhappy mother and a very bad father. "It's absurd to marry her to Cosimo the Fair!" Fenoglio had said. "But as I told you, this story is getting out of hand!"

Violante wore black, like her son and her father-in-law. Her dress, too, was embroidered with pearly tears, but their precious luster didn't suit her particularly well. Her face looked as if someone had drawn it on a stained piece of paper with a pencil too pale for the purpose, and the dark silk of her dress made her look even plainer. The only thing you noticed about her face was the purple birthmark, as big as a poppy, disfiguring her left cheek.

When Meggie and Fenoglio came across the dark hall, Violante was just bending down to her father-in-law, speaking to him quietly. The prince's expression did not change but finally he nodded, and the boy slipped down from his chair in relief.

Fenoglio signaled to Meggie to stay where she was. His head respectfully bent, he stepped aside, and unobtrusively signaled to Meggie to do the same. Violante nodded to Fenoglio as she passed him, her head held high, but she didn't even look at Meggie. She ignored the stone statues of her dead husband, too. Her Ugliness seemed to be in a hurry to escape this dark hall — in almost as much of a hurry as her son. The maid who followed her passed so close to Meggie that the servant girl's dress almost touched her. She didn't seem much older than Meggie herself. Her hair had a reddish tinge, as if firelight were falling on it, and she wore it loose, as only the women among the strolling players usually did in this world. Meggie had never seen lovelier hair.

"You're late, Fenoglio!" said the Prince of Sighs as soon as the doors had closed behind the women and his grandson. His voice still came out of his mouth with an effort, like a very fat man's. "Did you run short of words?"

"I won't run short of words until my last breath, My Prince," replied Fenoglio, with a bow. Meggie wasn't sure whether to copy him. In the end she decided on a clumsy curtsy.

At close quarters the Prince of Sighs looked even more fragile. His skin resembled withered leaves, the whites of his eyes like yellowed paper. "Who's the girl?" he asked, bending his weary gaze on her. "Your maid? Too young to be your lover, isn't she?"

Meggie felt the blood rise to her face.

"Your Grace, what an idea!" said Fenoglio, dismissing it and putting an arm around her shoulders. "This is my granddaughter who's come to visit me. My son hopes I shall find her a husband, and what better place for her to look for one than at the wonderful festivities you're holding today?"

Meggie blushed more than ever, but she forced herself to smile.

"You have a son, do you?" The voice of the Prince of Sighs sounded envious, as if he begrudged any of his subjects the luck of having a living son. "It's not wise to let your children go too far away," he murmured, without taking his eyes off Meggie. "Only too likely that they may never come back!"

Meggie didn't know where to look. "I'll be going home soon," she said. "My father knows that." *I hope,* she added in her mind.

"Yes. Yes, of course. She'll be going back. When the time comes." Fenoglio's voice sounded impatient. "But now we come to the reason for my visit." He took the roll of parchment so carefully sealed by Rosenquartz from his belt and climbed the steps to the princely chair with his head respectfully bent. The Prince of Sighs seemed to be in pain. He tightened his lips as he leaned forward to take the parchment, and cool though it was in the hall, sweat stood out on his forehead. Meggie remembered what Minerva had said: *This prince of ours will sigh and lament himself to death.* Fenoglio seemed to think so, too.

"Aren't you feeling well, My Prince?" he asked with concern.

"No, I am not!" snapped the prince, annoyed. "Unfortunately, the Adderhead noticed it today, too." He leaned back, sighing, and struck the side of his chair with his hand. "Tullio!"

A servant clad in black, like the prince, shot out from behind the chair. He would have looked like a rather short human being but for the fine fur on his face and hands. Tullio reminded Meggie of the brownies in Elinor's garden who had turned to ashes, although he clearly had more of the human being about him.

"Go and get me a minstrel — one who can read!" ordered the prince. "He can sing me Fenoglio's song." And Tullio scurried off, as willing as a puppy.

"Did you send for Nettle, as I advised?" Fenoglio's voice sounded urgent, but the prince just waved away the idea angrily.

"Nettle? What for? She wouldn't come, or if she did it would probably just be to poison me, because I had a couple of oaks felled for my son's coffin. How can I help it if she'd rather talk to trees than human beings? None of them can help me, not Nettle nor any of the physicians, stonecutters, and bone-knitters whose evil-smelling potions I've swallowed. No herb grows that can cure grief." His fingers trembled as he broke Fenoglio's seal, and all was so still in the darkened hall as he read that Meggie heard the candle flames hiss as the wicks burned down.

Almost soundlessly, the prince moved his lips as his clouded eyes followed Fenoglio's words. *"He will awake no more, oh nevermore,"* Meggie heard him whisper. She looked sideways at Fenoglio, who flushed guiltily when he noticed her glance. Yes, he had stolen the lines, and certainly not from any poet of this world.

The Laughing Prince raised his head and wiped a tear from his clouded eyes. "Fair words, Fenoglio," he said bitterly, "yes, you know all about those. But when will any of you poets find the words to open the door through which Death takes us?"

Fenoglio looked around at the statues. He stared at them, lost in thought, as if he were seeing them for the first time. "I am sorry, but there are no such words, My Prince," he said. "Death is all silence. Even poets have no words once they have passed the door Death closes behind us. If I may, then, I would humbly beg your leave to go. My landlady's children are waiting outside, and if I don't catch them again soon they may well run off with the strolling players, for like all children they dream of taming bears and dancing between heaven and hell on a tightrope."

"Yes, yes, go away!" said the Prince of Sighs, wearily waving his beringed hand. "I'll send to let you know when I want words again. They are sweet-tasting poison, but still, they're the only way to make even pain taste bittersweet for a few moments."

He will awake no more, oh nevermore . . . Elinor would certainly have known who wrote those lines, thought Meggie as she walked back down the dark hall with Fenoglio. The herbs scattered on the floor rustled under her boots. Their fragrance hung in the cool air as if to remind the sad prince of the world waiting for him out there. But perhaps it reminded him only of the flowers in the crypt where Cosimo lay.

At the door, Tullio came to meet them with the minstrel, hopping and leaping in front of the man like a trained, shaggy animal. The minstrel wore bells at his waist and had a lute on

his back. He was a tall, thin fellow with a sullen set to his mouth
and so garishly clothed that he would have put a peacock's tail to
shame.

"That fellow can actually read, can he?" Fenoglio whispered
to Meggie as he pushed her through the door. "I don't believe it!
What's more, his singing sounds as sweet as the cawing of a crow.
Let's be off before he gets his great horsey teeth into my poor
lines of verse!"

TEN YEARS

Time is a horse that runs in the heart, a horse
Without a rider on a road at night.
The mind sits listening and hears it pass.
> **Wallace Stevens, "The Pure Good of Theory"**

Dustfinger was leaning against the castle wall, behind the stalls where people were crowding. The aroma of honey and hot chestnuts rose to his nostrils, and high above him went the tightrope-walker whose blue figure, from a distance, reminded him so much of Cloud-Dancer. He was holding a long pole with tiny birds sitting on it, birds as red as drops of blood, and when the dancer changed direction — stepping lightly, as if standing on a swaying rope was the most natural thing in the world — the birds flew up and fluttered around him, twittering shrilly. The marten on Dustfinger's shoulder looked up at them and licked his lips. He was still very young, smaller and more delicate than Gwin, not half as likely to bite, and most important of all he didn't fear fire. Absently, Dustfinger tickled his horned head. He had caught him behind the stable soon after his arrival at Roxane's house, when the marten was trying to stalk her chickens, and had called him Jink, because of the way he jinked as he moved, dodging and darting before jumping up at Dustfinger so suddenly that he almost knocked him over. *Are you crazy?* he had asked himself when he lured the animal to him with a fresh egg. *He's a marten. How do you know that it makes any difference to Death what name he bears?* But he'd kept Jink all the same. Perhaps he had left all his fears behind in the other world: his fears, his loneliness, his ill fortune . . .

Jink learned fast; he was soon leaping through the flames as if he'd been doing it all his life. It would be easy to earn a few coins with him at the markets — with him and the boy.

The marten nuzzled Dustfinger's cheek. Some acrobats were building a human tower in front of the empty platform that still awaited the birthday boy. Farid had tried persuading Dustfinger to perform, too, but he didn't want people staring at him today. He wanted to stare himself, see his fill of all he'd missed for so long. So he was not in fire-eater's costume, either, but wore Roxane's dead husband's clothes, which she had given him. They had obviously been almost the same size. Poor fellow: Neither Orpheus nor Silvertongue could bring him back from where he was now.

"Why don't *you* earn the money today for a change?" he had asked Farid. The boy had turned first red and then white as chalk with pride — and shot away into the turmoil. He was a quick learner. Only a tiny morsel of the fiery honey, and Farid was talking to the flames as if he'd been born with their language on his tongue. Of course, they didn't yet spring from the ground when the boy snapped his fingers as readily as for Dustfinger himself, but when Farid called to the fire in a low voice it would speak to him — condescendingly, sometimes with mockery, but still it answered him.

"Oh, but he *is* your son!" Roxane had said when Farid had drawn a bucket of water from the well early in the morning, cursing, to cool his burned fingers. "He's not," Dustfinger had replied — and had seen in her eyes that she didn't believe him.

Before they set off for the castle, he had practiced a couple of tricks with Farid, and Jehan had watched. But when Dustfinger beckoned the boy closer, he ran away. Farid had laughed out loud at him for it, but Dustfinger put his hand over Farid's mouth. "The fire devoured his father, have you forgotten?" he had whispered, and Farid bowed his head, ashamed.

How proudly he stood there among the other entertainers! Dustfinger pushed his own way past the stalls to get a better view. Farid had taken off his shirt as Dustfinger himself sometimes did — burning cloth was more dangerous than a small burn on the skin, and you could easily protect your naked body against the licking tongues of fire with grease. The boy put on a good act, such a good one that even the traders stared at him spellbound, and Dustfinger took his chance to free a few fairies from the cages where they had been imprisoned, to be sold to some fool as lucky charms. *No wonder Roxane suspects you of being his father,* he told himself. *Your chest swells with pride when you look at him.* Next to Farid, a couple of clowns were exchanging broad jokes, to his right the Black Prince was wrestling with his bear, but all the same more and more people stopped to look at the boy standing there playing with fire, oblivious of all around him. Dustfinger watched as Sootbird lowered his torches and looked enviously their way. He'd never learn. He was still as poor a fire-eater as he'd been ten years ago.

Farid bowed, and a shower of coins fell into the wooden bowl that Roxane had given him. He glanced proudly at Dustfinger, as hungry for praise as a dog for a bone, and when Dustfinger clapped his hands he flushed red with delight. What a child he still was, even though he had proudly shown Dustfinger the first stubble on his chin a few months ago!

Dustfinger was making his way past two farmers haggling over a couple of piglets when the gate to the Inner Castle opened again — this time not, as before, for the Adderhead, when Dustfinger himself had only just managed to hide from the Piper's searching glance behind a cake stall. No. Obviously, the birthday boy himself was finally appearing at his own festivities — and his mother would accompany the child, with her maidservant. How fast his foolish heart was suddenly beating! "She has your hair," Roxane had said, "and my eyes."

The prince's pipers made the most of their big scene. Proud as turkey-cocks they stood there, long-stemmed trumpets held aloft in the air. The strolling players, being their own masters, disapproved without exception of musicians who sold their art to a single lord. In exchange, the pipers were better dressed, not in Motley array like the players on the road, but in their prince's colors. For the pipers of the Prince of Sighs, that meant green and gold. His daughter-in-law wore black. Cosimo the Fair had been dead for barely a year, but his young widow would certainly have been courted by several suitors already, in spite of the mark, dark as a burn, that disfigured her face. The crowd came thronging around the platform as soon as Violante and her son had taken their seats. Dustfinger had to climb on an empty barrel to catch a glimpse of her maidservant beyond all those heads and bodies.

Brianna was standing behind the boy. Despite her bright hair, she was like her mother. The dress she wore made her look very grown-up, yet Dustfinger still saw in her face traces of the little girl who had tried to snatch burning torches from his hand or stamped her foot angrily when he wouldn't let her catch the sparks he brought raining down from the sky.

Ten years. Ten years he'd spent in the wrong story. Ten years in which Death had taken one of his daughters, leaving behind nothing but memories as pale and indistinct as if she had never lived at all, while his other daughter had grown up, laughing and weeping through all those years, and he had not been there. *Hypocrite!* he told himself, unable to take his eyes from Brianna's face. *Are you trying to tell yourself you were a devoted father before Silvertongue lured you into his story?*

Cosimo's son laughed out loud. His stubby finger pointed first at one, then at another of the entertainers, and he caught the flowers that the women players threw him. How old was he? Five? Six?

Brianna had been the same age when Silvertongue's voice had enticed him away. She had only come up to his elbow, and she'd weighed so little that he scarcely noticed when she climbed up on his back. When he forgot time yet again and stayed away for weeks on end, in places with names she had never heard, she used to hit him with her little fists and throw the presents he brought her at his feet. Then she would slip out of bed the same night to retrieve them after all: colored ribbons as soft as rabbit fur, fabric flowers to put in her hair, little pipes that could imitate the song of a lark or the hoot of an owl. She had never told him so, of course, she was proud — even prouder than her mother — but he always knew where she put the presents — in a bag among her clothes. Did she still have it?

She had kept his presents, yes, but they could never bring a smile to her face when he had stayed away for a long time. Only fire could do that, and for a moment — a seductive moment — Dustfinger was tempted to step out of the gaping crowd, take his place among the other entertainers performing tricks for the prince's grandson, and summon fire just for his daughter's sake. But he stood where he was, invisible behind the throng, watching her smooth back her hair with the palm of her hand in the same way as her mother did so often, unobtrusively rubbing her nose and shifting from foot to foot, as if she'd much rather be dancing down there than standing stiffly here.

"Eat him, bear! Eat him up this minute! So he really is back, but do you think he's planning to go and see an old friend?"

Dustfinger spun around so suddenly that he almost fell off the barrel where he was still standing. The Black Prince was looking up at him, with his bear behind him. Dustfinger had hoped to meet him here, surrounded by strangers, rather than in the strolling players' camp, where there were too many who would ask where he had been. . . . The two of them had known each other since they were the same age as the prince's grandson enthroned in his chair on the platform — the orphaned sons of strolling players, adult before their time, and Dustfinger had missed that black face almost as much as Roxane's.

"So will he really eat me if I get off this barrel?"

The Prince laughed. His laughter sounded almost as carefree as in the old days. "Maybe. After all, he's noticed that I really do have a grudge against you for not coming to see me. And didn't you scorch his fur last time you two met?"

Jink crouched on Dustfinger's shoulder as he jumped off the barrel, chattering excitedly in his ear. "Don't worry, the bear doesn't eat your sort!" Dustfinger whispered to him — and hugged the Prince as hard as if a single embrace could make up for ten years.

"You still smell more of bear than man."

"And you smell of fire. Now tell me, where've you been?" The

Black Prince held Dustfinger at arm's length and looked at him as if he could read in his face everything that had happened during his friend's absence. "So the fire-raisers didn't string you up, then, as many folk say. You look too healthy for that. What about the other story — that the Adderhead locked you up in his dankest dungeon? Or did you turn yourself into a tree for a while, as some songs say, a tree with burning leaves deep in the Wayless Wood?"

Dustfinger smiled. "I'd have liked that. But I assure you, even you wouldn't believe the real story."

A whisper ran through the crowd. Looking over all the heads, Dustfinger saw Farid, red in the face, acknowledging their applause. Her Ugliness's son was clapping so hard that he almost fell off his chair. But Farid was searching the throng for Dustfinger's face. He smiled at the boy — and sensed that the Black Prince was looking at him thoughtfully.

"So the boy really is yours?" he said. "No, don't worry, I'll ask no more questions. I know you like to have your secrets, and I don't suppose that has changed much. All the same, I want to hear the story you spoke of, sometime. And you owe us a performance, too. We can all do with something to cheer us up. Times are bad, even on this side of the forest, though it may not seem so today. . . ."

"Yes, so I've heard already. And the Adderhead obviously doesn't love you any better than before. What have you done, to make him threaten you with the gallows? Did the bear take one of his stags?" Dustfinger stroked Jink's bristling fur. The marten never took his eyes off the bear.

"Oh, believe me, the Adderhead scarcely guesses half of what I do, or I'd have been dangling from the battlements of the Castle of Night long ago!"

"Oh yes?" The tightrope-walker was sitting on his rope above them, surrounded by his birds and swinging his legs, as if the milling crowd down below had nothing to do with him. "Prince, I don't like that look in your eye," said Dustfinger, looking up at the men walking the rope. "You'd do better not to provoke the Adderhead anymore, or he'll have you hunted down just as he's hunted others. And then you won't be safe on this side of the forest, either!"

Someone was pulling at his sleeve. Dustfinger turned so abruptly that Farid flinched back in alarm. "I'm sorry!" he stammered, nodding rather uncertainly to the Prince. "But Meggie's here. With Fenoglio!" He sounded as excited as if he had met the Laughing Prince in person.

"Where?" Dustfinger looked around, but Farid had eyes only for the bear, who had affectionately placed his muzzle on the Black Prince's head. The Prince smiled and pushed the bear's muzzle away.

"Where?" Dustfinger repeated impatiently. For Fenoglio was the very last person he wanted to meet.

"Over there, just behind the platform!"

Dustfinger looked the way Farid's finger was pointing. Sure enough, there was the old man, with two children, just as he had first seen him. Silvertongue's daughter stood beside him. She had grown tall — and even more like her mother. Dustfinger uttered a quiet curse. What were those two after, here in *his* story? They had as little to do with it as he had to do with theirs. *Oh yes?* mocked a voice inside him. *The old man won't see it that way. Did you forget he claims to have created everything here?*

"I don't want to see him," he told Farid. "Bad luck clings to that old man, and worse than bad luck, too, mark my words."

"Is the boy talking about the Inkweaver?" The Prince came so close to Dustfinger's side that the marten hissed at him. "What do you have against him? He writes good songs."

"He writes other things as well." *And who knows what he's already written about you,* Dustfinger added in his mind. *A few well-chosen words, Prince, and you're a dead man!*

Farid was still looking at the girl. "What about Meggie? Don't you want to see her, either?" His voice sounded husky with disappointment. "She asked how you were."

"Give her my regards. She'll understand. Off you go, then! I can see you're still in love with her. How was it you once described her eyes? Little pieces of the sky!"

Farid blushed scarlet. "Stop it!" he said angrily.

But Dustfinger took him by the shoulders and turned him around. "Go on!" he said. "Give her my regards, but tell her to keep my name out of her magic mouth, understand?"

Farid cast a last glance at the bear, nodded — and strolled back to the girl very slowly, as if to show that he wasn't in any hurry to reach her. She was going to great pains herself not to look his way too often, as she fidgeted awkwardly with the sleeves of her dress. She looked as if she belonged here, a maidservant from a not particularly prosperous home, perhaps the daughter of a farmer or a craftsman. Well, her father was indeed a craftsman, wasn't he? If one with special talents. Perhaps she was looking around rather too freely. Girls here usually kept their heads bent — and sometimes they were already married by her age. Did his daughter Brianna have anything like that in mind? Roxane hadn't said so.

"That boy's good. Better than Sootbird already." The Prince put out his hand to the marten — and withdrew it when Jink bared his tiny teeth.

"That's not difficult." Dustfinger let his eyes wander to

Fenoglio. So they called him Inkweaver here. How contented he looked, the man who had written Dustfinger's death. A knife in the back, plunged so deep that it found his heart, that was what Fenoglio had planned for him. Dustfinger instinctively reached to touch the spot between his shoulder blades. Yes, he had read them already, after all, Fenoglio's deadly words, one night in the other world when he had been lying awake, trying in vain to conjure up Roxane's face in his memory. *You can't go back!* He had kept hearing Meggie's voice saying those words. *"One of Capricorn's men is waiting for you in the book. They want to kill Gwin, and you try to help him, so they kill you instead."* He had taken the book out of his backpack with trembling fingers, had opened it and searched the pages for his death. And then he'd read what it said there in black and white, over and over again. After that he had decided to leave Gwin behind if he should ever come back here. . . . Dustfinger stroked Jink's bushy tail. No, perhaps it had not been a good idea to catch another marten.

"What's the matter? You look as if the hangman had given you the nod all of a sudden." The Black Prince put an arm around his shoulders, while his bear sniffed curiously at Dustfinger's backpack. "The boy must have told you how we picked him up in the forest? He was in a state of great agitation, said he was here to warn you. And when he said of whom, many of my men's hands went to their knives."

Basta. Dustfinger ran a finger over his scarred cheek. "Yes, he's probably back, too."

"With his master?"

"No, Capricorn's dead. I saw him die myself."

The Black Prince put his hand in his bear's mouth and tickled its tongue. "Well, that's good news. And there wouldn't be much for him to come back to, just a few charred walls. Only old Nettle sometimes goes there. She swears you can't find better yarrow anywhere than in the fire-raisers' old fortress."

Dustfinger saw Fenoglio glancing his way. Meggie was looking in the same direction, too. He quickly turned his back on them.

"We have a camp near there now — you'll remember the old brownies' caves," the Prince went on, lowering his voice. "Since Cosimo smoked out the fire-raisers those caves have made a good shelter again. Only the strolling players know about them. The old and frail, cripples, women tired of living on the road with their children — they can all stay and rest there for a while. I tell you what, the Secret Camp would be a good place for you to tell me your story! The one you say is so hard to believe. I've often been there for the bear's sake. He gets grouchy when he spends too long between city walls. Roxane can tell you how to find the place; she knows her way around the forest almost as well as you by now."

"I know the old brownie caves," said Dustfinger. He had hidden from Capricorn's men there many times, but he wasn't sure that he really wanted to tell the Prince about the last ten years.

"Six torches!" Farid was beside him again, wiping soot off his fingers on his trousers. "I juggled with six torches and I didn't drop one. I think she liked it."

Dustfinger suppressed a smile. "Very likely." Two of the strolling players had drawn the Prince aside. Dustfinger wasn't sure whether he knew them, but he turned his back, to be on the safe side.

"Did you know everyone's talking about you?" Farid's eyes were round as coins with excitement. "They're all saying you're back. And I think some of them have recognized you."

"Oh, have they?" Dustfinger looked uneasily around. His daughter was still standing behind the little prince's chair. He hadn't told Farid about her. It was bad enough having the boy jealous of Roxane.

"They say there was never a fire-eater to match you! The other one there, Sootbird they call him" — Farid put a piece of bread in Jink's mouth — "he asked about you, but I didn't know if you wanted to meet him. He's really bad at it, he doesn't know how to do anything — but he says he knows you. Is that right?"

"Yes, but all the same I'd rather not meet him." Dustfinger turned. The tightrope-walker had come down from his rope at last. Cloud-Dancer was talking to him and pointing Dustfinger's way. Time to disappear. He would be happy to see them all again, but not here, and not today. . . .

"I've had enough of this," he told Farid. "You stay and earn us a few more coins. I'll be at Roxane's if you want me."

Up on the platform, Her Ugliness was handing her son a gold-embroidered purse. The child put his plump hand into it and threw the entertainers some coins. They hastily bent to pick them out of the dust. But Dustfinger cast a last look at the Black Prince and went away.

What would Roxane say when she heard that he hadn't exchanged a single word with his daughter? He knew the answer. She would laugh. She knew only too well what a coward he could be.

COLD AND WHITE

I am like a goldsmith hammering day and night
Just so I can extend pain
Into a gold ornament as thin as a cicada's wing
Xi Murong, "Poetry's Value,"
Anthology of Modern Chinese Poetry

There they were again. Mo felt them coming closer, he saw them even though his eyes were closed — White Women, their faces so pale, their eyes colorless and cold. That was all there was in the world, white shadows in the dark and the pain in his breast, red pain. Every breath brought it back. Breathing. Hadn't it once been perfectly easy? Now it was difficult, as difficult as if they had buried him already, heaping earth on his breast, on the pain burning and throbbing there. He couldn't move. His body was useless, a burning prison. He wanted to open his eyes, but his lids weighed down as heavily as if they were made of stone. Everything was lost. Only words remained: *pain, fear, death*. White words. No color in them, no life. Only the pain was red.

Is this death? Mo wondered. *This void, full of faint shadows?*

Sometimes he thought he felt the fingers of the pale women reaching into his agonized breast as if to crush his heart. Their breath wafted over his hot face, and they were whispering a name, but it was not the name he remembered as his own. *Bluejay,* they whispered.

Their voices seemed to be made of cold yearning, nothing but cold yearning. *It's easy,* they whispered, *you don't even have to open your eyes. No more pain, no darkness. Stand up,* they whispered, *it's time to go,* and they entwined their white fingers with his. Their fingers were wonderfully cool on his burning skin.

But the other voice wouldn't let him go. Indistinct, barely audible, as if it came from far, far away, it penetrated the whispering. It sounded strange, almost discordant among the whispering shadows. *Be quiet,* he wanted to tell it with his tongue of stone. *Be quiet, please, let me go!* For nothing but that voice kept him imprisoned in the burning house that was his body. But the voice went on.

He knew it, but where from? He couldn't remember. It was long ago that he had last heard it, too long ago. . . .

IN ELINOR'S CELLAR

The lofty bookshelves sag
Under thousands of sleeping souls
Silence, hopeful —
Every time I open a book, a soul is awakened.
        Xi Chuan, "Books," *New Generation*

I ought to have furnished my cellar more comfortably, thought Elinor, watching Darius pump up the air mattress he had found behind one of the storage shelves for her. But how could she have guessed that some dreadful day she'd have to sleep down here, while a bespectacled, moon-faced man sat up in her wonderful library with his slobbering dog, playing master of the house? The wretched animal had almost eaten the fairy who had slipped out of Orpheus's words. A blue fairy and a lark fluttering in panic against the windowpanes, that was all that had come out of the book — to replace four people! "Look at that!" Orpheus had triumphantly announced. "Two for four! There are fewer and fewer coming out, and one day I'll manage not to let anything out of a book at all." Conceited pig! As if anyone was interested in who or what came out of the book, when Resa and Mortimer had gone! And Mortola and Basta . . .

Quick, Elinor, think of something else!

If only she could have hoped that someone useful would soon come knocking on her front door! But unfortunately, such a visitor was highly improbable. She had never had much to do with her neighbors, certainly not since Darius had taken over the care of her books and Mo, Resa, and Meggie had moved in. What more did she need in the way of company?

Her nose began to prickle ominously. *That's the wrong way to think, Elinor,* she warned herself — as if she'd been able to think of anything else these last few hours. *They're all right!* she kept telling herself. *You'd have sensed it if anything had happened to them. Wasn't that what all the stories said? You felt it, like a pang in your heart, when something happened to someone you loved?*

Darius smiled hesitantly at her as his foot went tirelessly up and down on the pump. The air mattress already looked like a caterpillar, a huge, squashed caterpillar. How was she supposed to sleep on that thing? She'd roll off and land on the cold cement floor.

"Darius!" she said. "We must do something! We can't simply let them shut us up here while Mortola . . ."

Oh God, how that old witch had looked at Mortimer. *Don't think about it, Elinor! Just don't think about it! Or about Basta and his rifle. Or Meggie wandering through the Wayless Wood all alone. I'm sure she's alone! A giant will have stepped on that boy and crushed him by now. . . .* It was a good thing Darius didn't know the silly way her thoughts were getting all mixed up, making the tears start to come all the time. . . .

"Darius!" Elinor whispered, for the man built like a wardrobe would certainly be on guard outside the door. "Darius, it's all up to you! You must read them back!"

Darius shook his head so vigorously that his glasses almost slipped off his nose. "No!" His voice was trembling like a leaf in the wind, and his foot began pumping again as if that stupid mattress were the most important thing in the world. Then, very suddenly, he stopped and hid his face in his hands. "You know what will happen!" Elinor heard him say in a stifled voice. "You know what will happen to them if I read while I'm afraid."

Elinor sighed.

Yes, she knew. Distorted faces, stiff legs, a lost voice . . . and of course he was afraid. Probably even more afraid than she was, for Darius had known Mortola and Basta considerably longer. . . .

"Yes. Yes, I know. All right," she murmured and began abstractedly straightening a few cans on the shelves — tomato sauce, ravioli (not a particularly nice brand), red kidney beans — Mortimer loved red kidney beans. There it came again, that prickling in her nose.

"Very well!" she said, turning around resolutely. "Then that Orpheus will have to do it." *How composed and sure of herself she sounded! She was obviously a gifted actress*, thought Elinor; she'd realized that before, back in Capricorn's church when all had seemed lost . . . indeed, now that she came to think of it, everything had seemed gloomier then, if anything.

Darius stared at her, bewildered.

"Don't look at me like that, for God's sake!" she hissed. "I don't know how we can make him do it, either. Not yet."

She began pacing up and down, up and down, between the shelves full of cans and preserving jars.

"He's vain, Darius!" she whispered. "Very vain. Did you see how he changed color when he realized that Meggie had done something he's tried and failed to do for years? I'm sure he'd like to ask her —" She stopped suddenly and looked at Darius.

"— how she managed it." Darius stopped pumping.

"Yes! But Meggie would have to be here herself to tell him that." They looked at each other.

"That's how we'll do it, Darius!" Elinor whispered. "We'll get Orpheus to bring Meggie back, and then she can read Mortimer and Resa back, too, with the same words he used for her! That ought to work!" She began pacing up and down again like the caged panther in the poem she liked so much . . . except that the look in her eyes was no longer hopeless. She must lay her plans well. That man Orpheus was clever. *And so are you, Elinor,* she told herself. *Just try it!*

She couldn't help it, she started thinking of the way Mortola had looked at Mortimer again. Suppose it was much too late by the time she . . . ?

Oh, stop it!

Elinor thrust out her chin, pulled back her shoulders — and marched firmly toward the cellar door. She hammered on the white-painted metal with the flat of her hand. "Hey!" she called. "Hey, you, wardrobe-man! Open this door! I have to speak to that man Orpheus! At once."

But nothing stirred on the other side of the door — and Elinor let her hand drop again. For a moment she entertained the dreadful thought that the two men had gone and left them alone down here, locked in . . . and without so much as a can opener, thought Elinor. What a ridiculous way to die. Starving among piles of canned food. She was just raising both hands to hammer on the door again when she heard footsteps outside. Footsteps going away, up the stairs leading from the cellar to the entrance hall.

"Hey!" she shouted, so loudly that Darius, standing behind her, jumped. "Hey, come back, you hulking great wardrobe! Open this door! I want to talk to Orpheus!"

But all was quiet on the other side of the door. Elinor fell to her knees in front of it. She felt Darius come up beside her and put a hand hesitantly on her shoulder. "He'll be back," he said quietly. "At least they're still here, aren't they?" Then he returned to the air mattress.

But Elinor sat there, her back against the cold cellar door, listening to the silence. You couldn't even hear the birds down here, not the smallest chirp of a cricket. *Meggie will fetch them back,* she thought. *Meggie will fetch them back! But suppose by now her mother and father are both . . .*

Not the way to think, Elinor. Not the way to think.

She closed her eyes and heard Darius begin pumping again.

I'd have sensed it, she thought. *Yes, I would. I'd have sensed it if anything had happened to them. It says so in all the stories, and surely they can't* all *be lying!*

THE CAMP IN THE FOREST

I thought it said in every tick:
I am so sick, so sick, so sick;
O death, come quick, come quick, come quick.
                    Frances Cornford, "The Watch," *Collected Poems*

Resa didn't know how long she had been sitting there, just sitting in the dimly lit, dark cave where the strolling players slept, holding Mo's hand. One of the women players brought her something to eat, and now and then one of the children crept in, leaned against the cave wall, and listened to what she was telling Mo in a quiet voice — about Meggie and Elinor, Darius, the library and its books, the workshop where he cured books of sickness and wounds as bad as his own . . . How strange the strolling players must find her stories of another world that they had never seen. And how very strange they must think her, to talk to someone who lay so still, his eyes closed as if he would never open them again.

Just as the fifth White Woman appeared on the steps, the old woman had returned to Capricorn's fortress with three men. It had not been so very far for her to go. Resa had seen guards standing among the trees as they entered the camp. The people these men were guarding were the cripples and the old folk, women with small children, and obviously there were also some in the camp who were simply resting from the stress and strain of life on the open road.

When Resa asked where food and clothing for all these people came from, one of the strolling players who had come to fetch Mo replied, "From the Prince." And when she asked what prince he meant, he had put a black stone into her hand by way of answer.

She was known as Nettle, the old woman who had so suddenly appeared at the gate of Capricorn's fortress. Everyone treated her with respect, but a little fear was mingled with it, too. Resa had to help her when she cauterized Mo's wound. She still felt sick when she thought of it. Then she had helped the old woman to bind up the wound again and memorized all her directions. "If he's still breathing in three days' time he may live," she had said before leaving them alone again, in the cave that offered protection from wild beasts, the sun, and the rain, but not from fear or from black, despairing thoughts.

Three days. It grew dark and then light again outside, light and then dark again, and every time Nettle came back and bent over Mo, Resa sought her face desperately for some sign of hope. But the old woman's features remained expressionless. The days went by, and Mo was still breathing, but he still wouldn't open his eyes.

The cave smelled of mushrooms, the brownies' favorite food. Very likely a whole pack of them had once lived here. Now the mushroom aroma mingled with the scent of dead leaves. The strolling players had strewn the cold floor of the cave with them:

dead leaves and fragrant herbs — thyme, meadowsweet, wood-ruff. Resa rubbed the dry leaves between her fingers as she sat there cooling Mo's forehead, which was not cold anymore but hot, terribly hot. . . . The scent of thyme reminded her of a fairy tale he had read to her long, long ago, before he found out that his voice could bring someone like Capricorn out of the words on the page. *Wild thyme should not be brought indoors*, the story had said, *bad luck comes with it*. Resa threw away the hard stems and brushed the scent off her fingers onto her dress.

One of the women brought her something to eat again, and sat beside her for a while in silence, as if hoping that her presence would bring a little comfort. Soon after that three of the men came in, too, but they stayed standing at the entrance of the cave, looking at her and Mo from a distance. They whispered to one another as they glanced at the pair of them.

"Are we welcome here?" Resa asked Nettle on one of her silent visits. "I think they're talking about us."

"Let them!" was all the old woman said. "I told them you were attacked by footpads, but of course that doesn't satisfy them. A beautiful woman, a man with a strange wound, where do they come from? What happened? They're curious. And if you're wise, you won't let too many of them see that scar on his arm."

"Why not?" Resa looked at her, baffled.

The old woman scrutinized her as if she wanted to see into her heart. "Well, if you really don't know, then that's just as well," she said at last. "And let them talk. What else are they to do? Some come here to wait for death, others for life to begin at last, others again live only on the stories they are told. Tightrope-walkers, fire-eaters, peasants, princes — they're all the same, flesh and blood and a heart that knows it will stop beating one day."

Fire-eaters. Resa's heart leaped when Nettle mentioned them. Of course. Why hadn't she thought of it before?

"Please!" she said, when the old woman reached the entrance of the cave again. "You must know many strolling players. Is there one who calls himself Dustfinger?"

Nettle turned as slowly as if she were still deciding whether to answer this. "Dustfinger?" she finally replied, in unforthcoming tones. "You'll scarcely find one of the strolling players who doesn't know of him, but no one's seen him for years. Although there are rumors that he's back. . . ."

Oh yes, he's back, thought Resa, *and he will help me just as I helped him in the other world.*

"I must send him a message!" She heard the desperation in her own voice. "Please!"

Nettle looked at her without any expression on her brown face. "Cloud-Dancer is here," she said at last. "His leg is aching again, but as soon as it's better he'll be on his way. See if he'll ask around for you and deliver your message."

Then she had gone.

Cloud-Dancer.

Darkness was falling again outside, and with the fading light men, women, and children came into the cave and lay down on the dead leaves to sleep — away from her, as if Mo's stillness might be catching. One of the women brought her a torch. It cast quivering shadows on the rocky walls, shadows that made faces and passed black fingers over Mo's pallid face. The fire did not keep the White Women away, although it was said that they both desired and feared it. They appeared in the cave again and again, like pale reflections with faces made of mist. They came closer and disappeared again, presumably driven away by the sharp and bitter smell of the leaves that Nettle had scattered around the place where Mo was lying. "It will keep them off," the old woman had said, "but you must watch carefully all the same."

One of the children was crying in his sleep. His mother stroked his hair to comfort him, and Resa couldn't help thinking of Meggie. Was she alone, or was the boy still with her? Was she happy, sad, sick, in good health . . . ? How often she had asked herself these questions, as if she hoped for an answer sometime, from somewhere. . . .

A woman brought her fresh water. She smiled gratefully and asked the woman about Cloud-Dancer. "He prefers to sleep in the open," she said, pointing. It was some time since Resa had seen any more White Women, but all the same she woke one of the women who had offered to relieve her during the night. Then she climbed over the sleeping figures and went out.

The moon was shining through the dense canopy of leaves, brighter than any torch. A few men were sitting around a fire. Unsure of herself, Resa went toward them, in the dress that wasn't right for this place at all. It ended too far above her ankles even for one of the strolling players, and it was torn, too.

The men stared at her, both suspicious and curious.

"Is one of you Cloud-Dancer?"

A thin little man, toothless and probably not nearly as old as he looked, nudged the man sitting next to him in the ribs.

"Why do you ask?" This man's face was friendly, but his eyes were wary.

"Nettle says he might carry a message for me."

"A message? Who to?" He stretched his left leg, rubbing the knee as if it hurt him.

"To a fire-eater. Dustfinger is his name. His face . . ."

Cloud-Dancer drew one finger over his cheek. "Three scars. I know. What do you want with him?"

"I want you to take him this." Resa kneeled down by the fire and put her hand into the pocket of her dress. She always had paper and a pencil with her; they had done duty as her tongue for years. Now her voice was back, but a wooden tongue was more useful for sending Dustfinger a message. Fingers trembling, she began to write, taking no notice of the suspicious eyes following her hand as if she were doing something forbidden.

"She can write," remarked the toothless man. There was no mistaking the disapproval in his tone. It was a long, long time ago that Resa had sat in the marketplaces of towns on the far side of the forest, dressed in men's clothes and with her hair cut short, because writing was the only way she knew to earn her living — and writing was a craft forbidden to women in this world. Slavery was the punishment for it, and it had made her Mortola's slave. For it was Mortola who had discovered Resa's disguise, and as a reward she was allowed to take her away to Capricorn's fortress.

"Dustfinger won't be able to read that," pointed out Cloud-Dancer equably.

"Yes, he will. I taught him how."

They looked at her incredulously. Letters. Mysterious things, rich men's tools, not meant for strolling players and certainly not for women. . . .

Only Cloud-Dancer smiled. "Well, imagine that. Dustfinger can read," he said softly. "Fine, but I can't. You'd better tell me what you've written, so that I can tell him the words even if your note gets lost. Which can easily happen with written words, much more easily than with words in your head."

Resa looked Cloud-Dancer straight in the face. *You trust people far too easily* . . . How often Dustfinger had told her that, but what choice did she have now? In a low voice, she repeated what she had written. *"Dear Dustfinger, I am in the strolling players' camp with Mo, deep in the Wayless Wood. Mortola and Basta brought us here, and Mortola"* — her voice failed as she said it — *"Mortola shot Mo. Meggie is here, too, I don't know exactly where, but please look for her and bring her to me! Protect her as you tried to protect me. But beware of Basta. Resa."*

"Mortola? Wasn't that what they called the old woman who lived with the fire-raisers?" The man who asked this question had no right hand. A thief — you lost your left hand for stealing a loaf, your right hand for a piece of meat.

"Yes, they say she's poisoned more men than the Adderhead has hairs on his head!" Cloud-Dancer pushed a log of wood back into the fire. "And it was Basta who slashed Dustfinger's face all that time ago. He won't like to hear those two names."

"But Basta's dead!" remarked the toothless minstrel. "And they've been saying the same about the old woman, too!"

"That's what they tell the children," said a man with his back to Resa, "so they'll sleep better. The likes of Mortola don't die. They only bring death to others."

They're not going to help me, thought Resa. *Not now that they've heard those two names.* The only one looking at her in anything like a friendly way was a man wearing the black and red of a fire-eater. But Cloud-Dancer was still inspecting her as if he wasn't sure what to make of her — her and her mysterious message.

Finally, however, and without a word, he took the note from her fingers and put it in the bag he wore at his belt. "Very well, I'll take Dustfinger your message," he said. "I know where he is."

He was going to help her after all. Resa could hardly believe it.

"Oh, thank you." Swaying with exhaustion, she straightened up again. "When do you think he'll get the message?"

Cloud-Dancer patted his knee. "My leg must get better first."

"Of course." Resa bit back the words she wanted to shout, begging him to hurry. She mustn't press him too hard, or he might change his mind, and then who would find Dustfinger for her? A piece of wood broke apart in the flames, spitting out glowing sparks at her feet. "I have no money to pay you," she said, "but perhaps you'll accept this." And she took her wedding ring off her finger and offered it to Cloud-Dancer. The toothless man looked at the gold ring as avidly as if he would like to put his own hand out for it, but Cloud-Dancer shook his head.

"No, forget it," he said. "Your husband is sick. It's bad luck to give away your wedding ring, I've heard."

Bad luck. Resa was quick to put the ring back on her finger. "Yes," she murmured. "Yes, you're right. Thank you. Thank you with all my heart!"

She turned to go.

"Hey, you!" The minstrel whose back had been turned to her was looking at her. He had only two fingers on his right hand. "Your husband — he has dark hair. Dark as the fur of a mole. And he's tall. Very tall."

Bewildered, Resa looked at him. "So?"

"And then there's the scar. Just where the songs say. I've seen it. Everyone knows how he got it: The Adderhead's dogs bit him there when he was poaching near the Castle of Night, and he took a stag, one of the White Stags that only the Adderhead himself may kill."

What on earth was he talking about? Resa remembered what Nettle had said: *And if you're wise, you won't let too many of them see that scar on his arm.*

The toothless man laughed. "Listen to Twofingers, will you! He thinks it's the Bluejay lying there in the cave. Since when did you believe in old wives' tales? Was he wearing his feathered mask?"

"How should I know?" snapped Twofingers. "Did I bring him here? But I tell you, that's him!"

Resa sensed that the fire-eater was examining her thoughtfully. "I don't know what you're talking about," she said. "I don't know any Bluejay."

"You don't?" Twofingers picked up the lute lying on the grass beside him. Resa had never before heard the song that he now sang in a soft voice:

> *Bright hope arises from the dark*
> *And makes the mighty tremble.*
> *Princes can't fail to see his mark,*
> *Nor can they now dissemble.*
> *With hair like moleskin smooth and black,*
> *And mask of blue jay feathers,*
> *He vows wrongdoers to attack,*
> *Strikes princes in all weathers.*
> *He hunts their game*
> *He robs their gold —*
> *And him they would have slain.*
> *But he's away, he will not stay,*
> *They seek the Jay in vain.*

How they were all looking at her! Resa took a step backward.

"I must go to my husband," she said. "That song . . . it has nothing to do with him. Believe me, it doesn't."

She felt their eyes on her back as she returned to the cave. *Forget them,* she told herself. *Dustfinger will get your message, that's all that matters, and he'll find Meggie and bring her here.*

The woman who had taken her place rose without a word and lay down with the others again. Resa was so exhausted that she swayed as she knelt on the dead leaves covering the floor. And the tears came once more. She wiped them away with her sleeve, hid her face in the fabric of her dress that smelled so familiar . . . of Elinor's house, of the old sofa where she used to sit with Meggie — telling her about this world. She began to sob, so loudly that she was afraid she might have woken one of the sleeping company. Alarmed, she pressed her hand to her mouth.

"Resa?" It was hardly more than a whisper.

She raised her head. Mo was looking at her. Looking at her.

"I heard your voice," he whispered.

She didn't know whether to laugh or weep first. She leaned over him and covered his face with kisses. And then she both laughed and wept.

FENOGLIO'S PLAN

All I need is a sheet of paper
and something to write with, and then
I can turn the world upside down.
  Friedrich Nietzsche, *Die Weisse und die Schwarze Kunst*

Two days had passed since the festivities at the castle, two days that Fenoglio had spent showing Meggie every nook and cranny of Ombra. "But today," he said, before they set off again after eating breakfast with Minerva, "today I'll show you the river. It's a steep climb down, not very easy for my old bones, but there's nowhere better to talk in peace. And what's more, if we're in luck you may see some water-nymphs down there." Meggie would have loved to see a water-nymph. She had come upon only one so far, in a rather muddy pond in the Wayless Wood, and as soon as Meggie's reflection had fallen on the water the nymph had darted away. But what exactly did Fenoglio want to talk about in peace? It wasn't hard to guess.

What was he going to ask her to read here this time? Or,

rather, *who* was he going to ask her to read here — and where from? From another story written by Fenoglio himself?

The path down which he led her wound its way along steeply sloping fields where farmers were working, bent double in the morning sun. How hard it must be growing enough to eat to allow you to survive the winter. And then there were all the creatures who secretly attacked your few provisions: mice, mealworms, maggots, wood lice. Life was much more difficult in Fenoglio's world, yet it seemed to Meggie that with every new day his story was spinning a magic spell around her heart, sticky as spiders' webs, and enchantingly beautiful, too. . . .

Everything around her seemed so real by now. Her homesickness had almost disappeared.

"Come on!" Fenoglio's voice startled her out of her thoughts. The river lay before them, shining in the sun, with faded flowers drifting on the water by its banks. Fenoglio took her hand and led her down the bank, to a place where large rocks stood. Meggie hopefully leaned over the slowly flowing water, but there were no river-nymphs in sight.

"Well, they're timid. Too many people around!" Fenoglio looked disapprovingly at the women doing their washing nearby. He waved to Meggie to walk on until the voices died away and only the rippling of the water could be heard. Behind them the roofs and towers of Ombra rose against the pale blue sky. The houses were crowded close inside the walls, like birds in a nest too small for them, and the black banners of the castle fluttered above them as if to inscribe the Laughing Prince's grief on the sky itself.

Meggie clambered up onto a flat rock over the water's edge. The river was not broad but seemed to be deep, and its water was darker than the shadows on the opposite bank.

"Can you see one?" Fenoglio almost slipped off the wet rock as he joined her. Meggie shook her head. "What's the matter?" Fenoglio knew her well after the days and nights they had spent together in Capricorn's house. "Not homesick again, are you?"

"No, no." Meggie kneeled down and ran her fingers through the cold water. "I just had that dream again."

The previous day, Fenoglio had shown her Bakers' Alley, the houses where the rich spice and cloth dealers lived, and every gargoyle, every carved flower, every richly adorned frieze with which the skillful stonemasons of Ombra had ornamented the buildings of the city. Judging by the pride Fenoglio displayed as he led Meggie past every corner of Ombra, however remote, he seemed to consider it all his own work. "Well, perhaps not *every* corner," he admitted, as she once tried getting him to go down an alley she hadn't seen yet. "Of course Ombra has its ugly sides, too, but there's no need for you to bother your pretty head about them."

It had been dark by the time they were back in his room under Minerva's roof, and Fenoglio quarreled with Rosenquartz because the glass man had spattered the fairies with ink. Even though their voices rose louder and louder, Meggie nodded off on the straw mattress that Minerva had sent up the steep staircase for her and that now lay under the window — and suddenly there was all that red, a dull red, shining, wet red, and her heart had started beating faster and faster, ever faster, until its violent thudding woke her with a start. . . .

"There, look!" Fenoglio took her arm.

Rainbow scales shimmered under the watery surface of the river. At first Meggie almost took them for leaves, but then she saw the eyes looking at her, like human eyes yet very different, for they had no whites. The nymph's arms looked delicate and fragile, almost transparent. Another glance, and then the scaly tail flicked in the water, and there was nothing left to be seen but a shoal of fish gliding by, silvery as a snail track, and a flock of fire-elves like the elves she and Farid had seen in the forest. Farid. He had made a fiery flower blossom at her feet, a flower just for her. Dustfinger had certainly taught him many wonderful things.

"I think it's always the same dream, but I can't remember. I just remember the fear — as if something terrible had happened!" She turned to Fenoglio. "Do you think it really has?"

"Nonsense!" Fenoglio brushed aside the thought like a troublesome insect. "We must blame Rosenquartz for your bad dream. I expect the fairies sat on your forehead in the night because he annoyed them! They're vengeful little things, and I'm afraid it makes no difference to them who they avenge themselves on."

"I see." Meggie dipped her fingers in the water again. It was so cold that she shivered. She heard the washerwomen laugh, and a fire-elf settled on her wrist. Insect eyes stared at her out of a human face. Meggie quickly shooed away the tiny creature.

"Very sensible," Fenoglio said. "You want to be careful of fire-elves. They'll burn your skin."

"I know. Resa told me about them." Meggie watched the elf go. There was a sore, red mark on her arm where it had settled.

"My own invention," explained Fenoglio proudly. "They produce honey that lets you talk to fire. Very much sought after by fire-eaters, but the elves attack anyone who comes too close to their nests, and few know how to set about stealing the honey without getting badly burned. In fact, now that I come to think of it, probably no one but Dustfinger knows."

Meggie just nodded. She had hardly been listening. "What did you want to talk to me about? You want me to read something, don't you?"

A few faded red flowers drifted past on the water, red as dried blood, and Meggie's heart began beating so hard again that she put her hand to her breast. What was the matter with her?

Fenoglio undid the bag at his belt and tipped a domed red stone out into his hand. "Isn't it magnificent?" he asked. "I went to get it this morning while you were still asleep. It's a beryl, a reading stone. You can use it like spectacles."

"I know. What about it?" Meggie stroked the smooth stone with her fingertips. Mo had several like it, lying on the window-sill of his workshop.

"What about it? Don't be so impatient! Violante is almost as blind as a bat, and her delightful son has hidden her old reading stone. So I bought her another, even though it was a ruinous price. I hope she'll be so grateful that in return she'll tell us a few things about her late husband! Yes, yes, I know I made up Cosimo myself, but it was long ago that I wrote about him. To be honest, I don't remember that part particularly well, and what's more . . . who knows how he may have changed, once this story took it into its head to go on telling itself?"

A horrible foreboding came into Meggie's mind. No, he couldn't be planning to do that. Not even Fenoglio would think up such an idea. Or would he?

"Listen, Meggie!" He lowered his voice, as if the women doing their washing upstream could hear him. "The two of us are going to bring Cosimo back!"

Meggie sat up straight, so abruptly that she almost slipped and fell into the river. "You're crazy. Totally crazy! Cosimo's dead!"

"Can anyone prove it?" She didn't like Fenoglio's smile one little bit. "I told you — his body was burned beyond recognition. Even his father wasn't sure it was really Cosimo! He waited six months before he would have the dead man buried in the coffin intended for his son."

"But it *was* Cosimo, wasn't it?"

"Who's going to say so? It was a terrible massacre. They say the fire-raisers had been storing some kind of alchemical powder in their fortress, and Firefox set it alight to help him get away. The flames enveloped Cosimo and most of his men, and later no one could identify the dead bodies found among the ruins."

Meggie shuddered. Fenoglio, on the other hand, seemed greatly pleased by this idea. She couldn't believe how satisfied he looked.

"But it was him, you know it was!" Meggie's voice sank to a whisper. "Fenoglio, we can't bring back the dead!"

"I know, I know, probably not." There was deep regret in his voice. "Although didn't some of the dead come back to life when you summoned the Shadow?"

"No! They all fell to dust and ashes again only a few days later. Elinor cried her eyes out — she went to Capricorn's village, even though Mo tried to persuade her not to, and there wasn't anyone there, either. They'd all gone. Forever."

"Hmm." Fenoglio stared at his hands. They looked like the hands of a farmer or a craftsman, not hands that wielded only a pen. "So we can't. Very well!" he murmured. "Perhaps it's all for the best. How would a story ever work if anyone could just come back from the dead at any time? It would lead to hopeless confusion; it would wreck the suspense! No, you're right: The dead stay dead. So we won't bring Cosimo back, just — well, someone who looks like him!"

"Looks like him? You *are* crazy!" whispered Meggie. "You're a total lunatic!"

But her opinion did not impress Fenoglio in the slightest. "So what? All writers are lunatics! I promise you, I'll choose my words very carefully, so carefully that our brand-new Cosimo will be firmly convinced he *is* the old one. Do you see, Meggie? Even if he's only a double, he mustn't know it. On no account is he to know it! What do you think?"

Meggie just shook her head. She hadn't come here to change this world. She'd only wanted to see it!

"Meggie!" Fenoglio placed his hand on her shoulder. "You saw the Laughing Prince! He could die any day, and then what? It's not just strolling players that the Adderhead strings up! He has his peasants' eyes put out if they catch a rabbit in the forest. He forces children to work in his silver mines until they're blind and crippled, and he's made Firefox, who is a murderer and arsonist, his own herald!"

"Oh yes? And who made him that way? You did!" Meggie angrily pushed away his hand. "You always did like your villains best."

"Well, yes, maybe." Fenoglio shrugged, as if he were powerless to do anything about it. "But what was I to do? Who wants to read a story about two benevolent princes ruling a merry band of happy, contented subjects? What kind of a story would that be?"

Meggie leaned over the water and fished out one of the red flowers. "You like making them up!" she said quietly. "All these monsters."

Even Fenoglio had no reply to that. So they sat in silence while the women upstream spread their washing on the rocks to dry. It was still warm in the sun, in spite of the faded flowers that the river kept bringing in to the bank.

Fenoglio broke the silence at last. "Please, Meggie!" he said. "Just this once. If you help me to get back in control of this story I'll write you the most wonderful words to take you home again — whenever you like! Or if you change your mind because you like my world better, then I'll bring your father here for you, and your mother . . . and even that bookworm woman, though from all you tell me she sounds like a frightful person!"

That made Meggie laugh. *Yes, Elinor would like it here,* she thought, and she was sure Resa would like to see the place again. But not Mo. No, never.

She suddenly stood up and smoothed down her dress. Looking up at the castle, she imagined what it would be like if the Adderhead with his salamander gaze ruled up there. She hadn't even liked the Laughing Prince much.

"Meggie, believe me," said Fenoglio, "you'd be doing something truly good. You'd be giving a son back to his father, a husband back to his wife, a father back to his child — yes, I know he's not a particularly nice child, but all the same! And you'd be helping to thwart the Adderhead's plans. Surely that's an honorable thing to do? Please, Meggie!" He looked at her almost imploringly. "Help me. It's my story, after all! Believe me, I know what's best for it! Lend me your voice just once more!"

Lend me your voice . . . Meggie was still looking up at the castle, but she no longer saw the towers and the black banners. She was seeing the Shadow, and Capricorn lying dead in the dust.

"All right, I'll think about it," she said. "But now Farid is waiting for me."

Fenoglio looked at her with as much surprise as if she had suddenly sprouted wings. "Oh, is he indeed?" There was no mistaking the disapproval in his voice. "But I was going to go up to the castle with you to take Her Ugliness the beryl. I wanted you to hear what she has to say about Cosimo. . . ."

"I promised him!" They had agreed to meet outside the city gates so that Farid wouldn't have to pass the guards.

"You promised? Well, never mind. You wouldn't be the first girl to keep a suitor waiting."

"He is not my suitor!"

"Glad to hear it! Since your father isn't here, it's up to me to keep an eye on you, after all." Fenoglio looked at her gloomily. "You really have grown! The girls here marry at your age. Oh, don't look at me like that! Minerva's second daughter has been married for five months, and she was just fourteen. How old is that boy? Fifteen? Sixteen?"

Meggie did not reply, but simply turned her back on him.

VIOLANTE

There is no frigate like a book
To take us lands away,
Nor any courser like a page
Of prancing poetry.
This traverse may the poorest take
Without oppress of toll;
How frugal is the chariot
That bears a human soul!

Emily Dickinson, *The Poems of Emily Dickinson*

Fenoglio simply persuaded Farid to go up to the castle with them. "This will work out very well," he whispered to Meggie. "He can entertain the prince's spoiled brat of a grandson and give us a chance to get Violante to talk in peace."

The Outer Courtyard lay as if deserted that morning. Only a few dry twigs and squashed cakes showed that there had been festivities here. Grooms, blacksmiths, stable lads were all going about their work again, but an oppressive silence seemed to weigh down on everyone within the walls. On recognizing Fenoglio, the guards of the Inner Castle let them pass without a word, and a group of men in gray robes, grave-faced, came toward them beneath the trees of the Inner Courtyard. "Physicians!" muttered Fenoglio, uneasily watching them go. "More than enough of them to cure a dozen men to death. This bodes no good."

The servant whom Fenoglio buttonholed outside the throne room looked pale and tired. The Prince of Sighs, he told Fenoglio in a whisper, had taken to his bed during his grandson's celebrations and hadn't left it since. He would not eat or drink, and he had sent a messenger to the stonemason carving his sarcophagus telling him to hurry up with it.

But they were allowed in to visit Violante. The prince would see neither his daughter-in-law nor his grandson. He had sent away even the physicians. He would have no one near him but his furry-faced page, Tullio.

"She's where she ought not to be, again!" The servant was whispering, as if he could be heard by the sick prince in his apartments as he led them through the castle. A carved likeness of Cosimo looked down on them in every corridor. Now that Meggie knew about Fenoglio's plans, the stony eyes made her even more uncomfortable. "They all have the same face!" Farid whispered to her, but before Meggie could explain why, the servant was beckoning them silently up a spiral staircase.

"Does Balbulus still ask such a high price for letting Violante into the library?" asked Fenoglio quietly as their guide stopped at his door, which was adorned with brass letters.

"Poor thing, she's given him almost all her jewelry," the servant whispered back. "But there you are, he used to live in the Castle of Night, didn't he? Everyone knows that those who live on the other side of the forest are greedy folk. With the exception of my mistress."

"Come in!" called a bad-tempered voice when the servant

knocked. The room they entered was so bright that it made Meggie blink after walking through all those dark passages and up the dark stairs. Daylight fell through high windows onto several intricately carved desks. The man standing at the largest of them was neither young nor old, and he had black hair and brown eyes that looked at them without any cordiality as he turned to them.

"Ah, the Inkweaver!" he said, reluctantly putting down the hare's foot he held in his hand. Meggie knew what it was for; Mo had told her often enough. Rubbing parchment with a hare's foot made it smooth. And there were the colors whose names Mo had repeated over and over to her. *Tell me again!* How often she had plagued Mo with that demand! She never tired of the sound of them: lapis lazuli, orpiment, violet, malachite green. What makes them still shine like that, Mo? she had asked. After all, they're so old! What are they made of? And Mo had told her — told her how you made them, all those wonderful colors that shone even after hundreds of years as if they had been stolen from the rainbow, now protected from air and light between the pages of books. To make malachite green you pounded wild iris flowers and mixed them with yellow lead oxide; the red was made from murex shells and cochineal insects . . . They had so often stood together looking at the pictures in one of the valuable manuscripts that Mo was to free from the grime of many years. Look at those delicate tendrils, he had said, can you imagine how fine the pens and brushes must be to paint something like that, Meggie? He was always complaining that no one could make such implements anymore. And now she saw them with her own eyes, tiny pens as fine as hairs and brushes, whole sets of them standing in a glazed jug: brushes that could conjure up flowers and faces no bigger than a pinhead on parchment or paper. You moistened them with a little gum arabic to make the paint cling better. Her fingers itched to pick a brush out of the set and take it away with her for Mo. . . . *He ought to have come just for this,* she thought, *to stand here in this room.*

An illuminator's workshop . . . Fenoglio's world seemed twice, three times as wonderful. *Elinor would have given one of her little fingers to be standing here now,* thought Meggie. She was about to move toward one of the desks to take a closer look at it all, the brushes, the pigments, the parchment, but Fenoglio held her back.

"Balbulus!" He sketched a bow. "And how is the master today?" There was no mistaking the mockery in his voice.

"The Inkweaver wants to see the Lady Violante," said the servant in a low voice.

Balbulus pointed to a door behind him. "Well, you know where the library is. Or perhaps we had better rename it the Chamber of Forgotten Treasures." He lisped slightly, his tongue touching his teeth as if it didn't have enough room in his mouth. "Violante is just looking at my latest work, or what she can see of it. I finished copying out the stories for her son last night. I'd rather have used the parchment for other texts, I must admit, but Violante insisted."

"Well, I'm sorry you had to waste your art on such frivolities," replied Fenoglio, without so much as glancing at the work Balbulus had before him at the moment. Farid did not seem interested in the picture, either. He looked at the window, where the sky outside shone a brighter blue than any of the paints sticking to the fine brushes. But Meggie wanted to see how good Balbulus was at his art, and whether his haughty attitude was justified. Unobtrusively, she took a step forward. She saw a picture framed in gold leaf, showing a castle among green hills, a forest, magnificently dressed riders among the trees, fairies fluttering around them, and a White Stag turning to flee. Never before had she seen such a picture. It glowed like stained glass — like a window placed on the parchment. She would have loved to look at it more closely, see the faces, the horses' harnesses, the flowers and clouds, but Balbulus cast her such an icy glance that she retreated, blushing.

"That poem you brought yesterday," said Balbulus in a bored voice, as he bent over his work again, "it was good. You ought to write such things more often, but I know you prefer writing stories for children or songs for the Motley Folk. And why? Just for the wind to sing your words? The spoken word is nothing, it hardly lives longer than an insect! Only the written word is eternal."

"Eternal?" Fenoglio made the word sound as if there could be nothing more ridiculous in the world. "Nothing's eternal — and what happier fate could words have than to be sung by minstrels? Yes, of course they change the words, they sing them slightly differently every time, but isn't that in itself wonderful? A story wearing another dress every time you hear it — what could be better? A story that grows and puts out flowers like a living thing! But look at the stories people press in books! They may last longer, yes, but they breathe only when someone opens the book. They are sound pressed between the pages, and only a voice can bring them back to life! Then they throw off sparks, Balbulus! Then they go free as birds flying out into the world. Perhaps you're right, and the paper makes them immortal. But why should I care? Will I live on, neatly pressed between the pages with my words? Nonsense! We're none of us immortal; even the finest words don't change that, do they?"

Balbulus had listened to him without any expression on his face. "What an unusual opinion, Inkweaver!" he said. "For my part, I think highly of the immortality of my work and very poorly of minstrels. But why don't you go in to Violante? She'll probably have to leave soon, to hear some peasant's woes or listen to a merchant complaining of the highwaymen who make the roads unsafe. It's almost impossible to get hold of acceptable parchment these days. Robbers steal it and offer it for sale in the markets at outrageous prices! Have you any idea how many goats must be slaughtered for me to write down one of your stories?"

"About one for each double spread," said Meggie, earning another icy look from Balbulus.

"Clever girl," he said, in a tone that made his words sound more like blame than praise. "And why? Because those fools the goatherders drive them through thorns and prickly bushes, without stopping to think that their skins will be needed for parchment!"

"Oh, come, I keep telling you!" said Fenoglio, steering Meggie and Farid toward the library door. "Paper, Balbulus. Paper is the material of the future."

"Paper!" she heard Balbulus mutter scornfully. "Good heavens, Inkweaver, you're even crazier than I thought."

Meggie had visited more libraries with Mo than she could count. Many had been larger than the Laughing Prince's, but few were more beautiful. You could still see that it had once been its owner's favorite place. The only trace of Cosimo here was a white stone bust; someone had laid roses in front of it. The tapestries on the high walls were finer than those in the throne room, the sconces heavier, the colors warmer, and Meggie had seen enough in Balbulus's workshop to guess what treasures surrounded her here. They stood chained to the shelves, not spine beside spine like the books in Elinor's library, but with the cut edge facing forward, because that was where the title was. In front of the shelves were rows of desks, presumably reserved for the latest precious acquisitions. Books lay on them, chained like sisters in the shelves, and closed so that no harmful ray of light could fall on Balbulus's pictures. In addition all the library windows were hung with heavy fabric; obviously the Prince of Sighs knew what damage sunlight did to books. Only two windows let in the light that might harm them. Her Ugliness stood in front of one window, bending so low over a book that her nose almost touched the pages.

"Balbulus is getting better and better, Brianna," she said.

"He's greedy! A pearl, just for letting you into your father-in-law's library!" Her maidservant was standing at the other window looking out, while Violante's son tugged at her hand.

"Brianna!" he whined. "Come on! This is boring. Come on out into the courtyard. You promised."

"He uses the money from the pearls to buy new pigments! How else would he get them, when no one in this castle will pay gold for anything but statues of a dead man?" Violante jumped when Fenoglio closed the door behind him, guiltily hiding the book behind her back. Only when she saw who it was did her face relax. "Fenoglio!" she said, pushing her mousy brown hair back from her forehead. "Must you scare me like that?" The mark on her face was like a paw-print.

Fenoglio smiled and put his hand to the bag at his belt. "I've brought you something."

Violante's fingers closed greedily on the red stone. Her hands were small and rounded like a child's. She quickly reopened the book she had hidden behind her back and held the beryl up to one of her eyes.

"Come on, Brianna, or I'll tell them to cut off your hair!" Jacopo took a handful of the maid's hair and pulled it so hard that she screamed. "That's what my grandfather does. He shaves them bald, the minstrel girls and the women who live in the forest. He says they turn into owls by night and screech outside your windows till you're dead in your bed."

"Don't look at me like that!" Fenoglio whispered to Meggie. "I didn't invent this little horror. Here, Jacopo!" He dug his elbow imperatively into Farid's ribs as Brianna went on trying to free her hair from the child's small fingers. "Look, I've brought someone to see you."

Jacopo let go of Brianna's hair and examined Farid with little enthusiasm. "He doesn't have a sword," he pointed out.

"A sword! Who needs a sword?" Fenoglio wrinkled his nose. "Farid is a fire-eater."

Brianna raised her head and looked at Farid. But Jacopo was still inspecting him as unenthusiastically as ever.

"Oh, this stone is wonderful!" his mother murmured. "My old one wasn't half so good. I can make them all out, Brianna, every character. Did I ever tell you how my mother taught me to read by making up a little song for each letter?" She began to chant quietly: "*A brown bear bites off a big bit of B* . . . I didn't see particularly well even then, but she traced them on the floor very large for me, laying them out with flower petals or little stones. *A, B, C, the minstrel plays for me.*"

"No," said Brianna. "No, you never told me."

Jacopo was still staring at Farid. "He was at my party!" he said. "He threw torches."

"That was nothing, just a children's game." Farid was looking patronizingly at the boy, as if he himself and not Jacopo were the prince's son. "I can do other tricks, too, but I don't think you're old enough for them."

Meggie saw Brianna hide a smile as she took the comb out of

her pale red hair and pinned it up again. She did it very prettily. Farid was watching her, and for the first time in her life Meggie wished that she had such lovely hair, although she wasn't sure that she could manage to put a comb in it so gracefully. Luckily, Jacopo attracted Farid's attention again by clearing his throat and folding his arms. He had probably copied the mannerism from his grandfather.

"Show me or I'll have you whipped." The threat sounded ridiculous, uttered in such a shrill voice — yet at the same time it was more terrible than if it had come from an adult mouth.

"Oh, will you?" Farid's face gave nothing away. He had obviously learned a thing or two from Dustfinger. "And what do you think I'd do to you then?"

This left Jacopo speechless, but just as he was about to appeal to his mother for support Farid reached out his hand to the boy. "Very well, come along, then."

Jacopo hesitated, and for a moment Meggie was tempted to take Farid's hand herself and follow him into the courtyard, instead of listening to Fenoglio trying to follow a dead man's trail, but Jacopo moved faster. His pale, stubby fingers gripped Farid's brown hand tightly, and when he turned in the doorway his face was that of a happy, perfectly ordinary little boy. "He's going to show me tricks, did you hear?" he said proudly, but his mother didn't even look up.

"Oh, what a wonderful stone," was all she whispered. "If only it wasn't red, if only I had one for each eye —"

"Well, I'm working on a way around that, but I'm afraid I haven't found the right glassmaker yet." With a sigh, Fenoglio dropped into one of the chairs invitingly arranged among the reading desks. They all bore the old coat of arms on their leather upholstery, the one where the lion was not shedding tears, and the leather of some was so worn that you could clearly tell how many hours the Laughing Prince had once spent here — until grief sapped his pleasure in books.

"A glassmaker? Why a glassmaker?" Violante gazed at Fenoglio through the beryl. It looked almost as if her eye was made of fire.

"Glass can be ground to make your eyes see better, much better than through a stone, but there isn't a glazier in Ombra who knows what I'm talking about!"

"Oh, I know, only the stonemasons are good for anything in this place! Balbulus says there's not a single decent bookbinder in all Lombrica."

I could tell you the name of a good one, thought Meggie instinctively, and for a moment she wished Mo were here, so much that it hurt. But Her Ugliness was looking at her book again. "There are good glaziers in my father's realm," she said, without glancing up. "He's had several windows in his castle filled in with glass. He had to sell off a hundred of his peasants to go for soldiers to pay for it." Violante seemed to consider the price well worth paying.

I don't think I like her, thought Meggie, as she went slowly from desk to desk. The bindings of the books lying on them were beautiful, and she would have loved to hide at least one of them under her dress, so that she could look at it in Fenoglio's room at her leisure, but the chips holding the chains in place were firmly riveted to the wooden covers of the books.

"You're welcome to look at them." Her Ugliness spoke to Meggie so suddenly that she jumped. Violante was still holding the red stone up to her eye, and Meggie was reminded of the bloodred jewels at the corners of the Adderhead's nostrils. His daughter resembled her father more than she probably knew.

"Thank you," murmured Meggie, and opened one. She remembered the day when Mo had shown her how to open an old book without using her fingers. He had handed her a book with two brass clasps holding its wooden covers together. She had looked at him, baffled, and then, smiling at her, he had struck the front of the book with his fist so hard that the clasps snapped open like little mouths, and the book was opened as if by a ghostly hand.

But the book that Meggie opened in the Laughing Prince's library showed no sign of age, as that other book had done. No speck of mold disfigured the parchment, no beetles or bookworms had nibbled it, like some of the manuscripts she had seen when Mo restored them. The years were not kind to parchment and paper; a book had many enemies, and in time it withered like a human body. "Which tells us, Meggie," Mo always said, "that a book is a living thing!" If only she could have shown him this one!

Very, very carefully she turned the pages — yet her mind was not entirely on what she was doing, for the wind blew Farid's voice into the room like the memory of another world. Meggie listened to what was going on outside as she snapped shut the clasps of the book again. Fenoglio and Violante were still talking about useless bookbinders. Neither of them was taking any notice of her, and Meggie stole over to one of the darkened windows and peered through the gap in the curtains. Her glance fell on a walled garden, beds full of brightly colored flowers, and Farid standing among them letting flames lick their way up his bare arms, just as Dustfinger had done the first time Meggie saw him breathing fire back in Elinor's garden, before he betrayed her. . . .

Jacopo was laughing exuberantly. He clapped — and then stumbled back in alarm as Farid sent the torches whirling through the air like Catherine wheels. Meggie couldn't help smiling; Dustfinger had certainly taught him a lot, even if Farid couldn't yet breathe fire quite so high in the air as his teacher.

"Books? No, I told you, Cosimo never came in here!" Violante's voice suddenly sounded considerably sharper, and Meggie turned around. "He thought nothing of books, he loved dogs, good boots, a fast horse . . . there were days when he even loved his son. But I don't want to talk about him."

Laughter drifted up from outside again. Brianna joined Meggie at the window. "The boy's a very good fire-eater," she said.

"Really?" Her shortsighted mistress looked at her. "I thought you didn't like fire-eaters. You're always saying they're feckless folk."

"This one's good. Much better than Sootbird." Brianna's voice sounded husky. "I noticed him at the celebrations."

"Violante!" Fenoglio sounded impatient. "Could we forget about that fire-breathing boy for a moment? Very well, so Cosimo didn't like books. These things happen. But surely you can tell me a little more about him!"

"Why?" Her Ugliness raised the beryl to her eye again. "Let Cosimo rest in peace, he's dead! The dead don't want to linger here. Why won't anyone understand that? And if you want to know some secret about him — well, he had none! He could talk about weapons for hours on end. He liked fire-eaters and knife-throwers and wild rides through the night. He had the smiths show him how to forge a sword, and he fenced for hours with the guards down in the courtyard until he'd mastered every trick they knew, but when the minstrels struck up their songs he began yawning after the first verse. He wouldn't have cared for any of the songs you've written about him. He might have liked the robber songs, but as for the idea that words can be like music, making the heart beat faster . . . he had no ear for that! Even executions interested him more than words, although he never enjoyed them the way my father does."

"Really?" Fenoglio sounded surprised but by no means disappointed. "Wild rides through the night," he murmured. "Fast horses. Yes, why not?"

Her Ugliness wasn't listening to him. "Brianna!" she said. "Take this book. If I praise Balbulus enough for his new pictures, perhaps he'll leave it with us for a while." Her maid took the book from her, an abstracted expression on her face, and went to the window again.

"But the people loved him, didn't they?" Fenoglio had risen from his chair. "Cosimo was good to them . . . to the peasants, the poor . . . the strolling players."

Violante stroked the mark on her cheek. "Yes, they all loved him. He was so handsome that you just had to love him. You couldn't help it. But as for the peasants" — and she wearily rubbed her shortsighted eyes — "do you know what he always said about them? 'Why are they so ugly?' he asked. 'Ugly clothes, ugly faces . . .' When they brought their disputes to him he really did try to do justice fairly, but it bored him to tears. He could hardly wait to get away again, back to his father's soldiers, his horse and his hounds. . . ."

Fenoglio said nothing. He looked so baffled that Meggie almost felt sorry for him. *Isn't he going to make me read aloud after all?* she wondered. And for a strange moment she felt something like disappointment.

"Come along, Brianna!" ordered Her Ugliness, but her maid did not stir. She was gazing down at the courtyard as if she had never seen a fire-eater before in her life.

Frowning, Violante went over to her. "What are you staring at?" she asked, squinting through the window with her short-sighted eyes.

"He . . . he's making flowers from fire," stammered Brianna. "They start like golden buds and then they unfold like real flowers. I once saw something like that . . . when I was very little. . . ."

"Yes, very nice, but come along now." Her Ugliness turned and made for the door. She had an odd way of walking, with her head slightly bent, yet carrying herself very upright. Brianna took a last look out the window before hurrying after her.

Balbulus was grinding colors when they entered his workshop: blue for the sky, russet and umber for the earth. Violante whispered something to him. Presumably, she was softening him up. She pointed to the book that Brianna was carrying for her.

"I'll be off now, Your Highness," said Fenoglio.

"Yes, you can go!" she told him. "But next time you visit me don't ask questions about my late husband; bring me one of the songs you write for the minstrels instead. I like them very much, particularly those songs about the robber, the man who makes my father so angry. What's his name? Oh yes — the Bluejay!"

Fenoglio paled slightly under his sunburn. "How do you know I wrote those songs?"

Her Ugliness just laughed. "I'm the Adderhead's daughter, have you forgotten? Of course I have my spies! They're good, too! Are you afraid I'll tell my father who wrote the songs? Don't worry, we say only the bare minimum to each other. And he's more interested in what the songs are about than in the man who wrote them. Although if I were you I'd stay this side of the forest for now!"

Fenoglio bowed, forcing a smile. "I shall take your advice to heart, Highness," he said.

The door with brass letters on it latched heavily into place as Fenoglio pulled it shut. "Curse it!" he muttered. "Curse it, curse it."

"What's the matter?" Meggie looked at him with concern. "Is it what she said about Cosimo?"

"No, nonsense! But if Violante knows who writes the songs about the Bluejay, then so does the Adderhead! He has many more spies than she does, and suppose he doesn't keep to his own side of the forest much longer? Well, there's still time to do something about it . . . Meggie," he whispered, as they went down the steep spiral staircase. "I told you I had a model for the Bluejay. Do you want to guess who it was?" He looked expectantly at her. "I like to base my characters on real people," he whispered in conspiratorial tones. "Not every writer does that, but in my experience it makes them more lifelike. Facial expressions, gestures, the way someone walks, a voice, perhaps a birthmark or a scar — I steal something here, something there, and then they begin to breathe, until anyone hearing or reading about them thinks they can touch them! I didn't have a wide choice for the Bluejay. My model couldn't be too old, nor too young, either, and not fat or short, of course, heroes are never short, fat, or ugly — in real life, maybe, but never in stories . . . no, the Bluejay had to be tall and good-looking, attractive to other people —"

Fenoglio fell silent. Footsteps were coming down the stairs, quick footsteps, and Brianna appeared on the massive steps above them.

"Excuse me," she said and looked around guiltily, as if she had stolen away without her mistress's knowledge. "That boy — do you know who taught him to play with fire like that?" She looked at Fenoglio as if she wanted to hear the answer more than anything, and yet as if at the same time there was nothing she feared hearing more. "Do you know?" she asked again. "Do you know his name?"

"Dustfinger," replied Meggie, speaking for Fenoglio. "Dustfinger taught him." And only when she spoke the name for the second time did she realize who Brianna reminded her of, her face and the shimmer of her red hair.

THE WRONG WORDS

If all you have of me is your red hair
and my wholehearted laughter
what else in me was good or ill may fare
like faded flowers drifting in the water.

> Paul Zech, after François Villon,
> "The Ballade of Little Florestan"

Dustfinger was just chasing Jink out of Roxane's henhouse when Brianna came riding into the yard. The sight of her almost stopped his heart. The dress she wore made her look like a rich merchant's daughter; since when did maidservants wear such clothes? And the horse she was riding didn't suit this place, either, with its expensive harness, its gold-studded saddle, and the deep black coat that shone as if three grooms had spent all day brushing it. A soldier in the Laughing Prince's livery rode with her. He scrutinized the simple house and the fields, his face expressionless. But Brianna looked at Dustfinger. She thrust out her chin just as her mother so often did, straightened the comb in her hair — and looked at him.

He wished he could have made himself invisible. How hostile

her glance was, her expression both adult and that of an injured child! She was so like her mother. The soldier helped her to dismount and then took his horse to drink at the well, acting as if he had neither eyes nor ears.

Roxane came out of the house. Brianna's arrival obviously surprised her as much as him. "Why didn't you tell me he was back?" Brianna snapped. Roxane opened her mouth — and shut it again.

Go on, say something, Dustfinger, he told himself. The marten leaped off his shoulder and disappeared behind the stable.

"I asked her not to." How hoarse his voice sounded. "I thought I'd rather tell you myself." *But your father is a coward,* he added to himself, *afraid of his own daughter.*

She was looking at him so angrily, in exactly her old way. Except that now she was too grown-up to hit him.

"I saw that boy," she said. "He was at the festival, and today he was breathing fire for Jacopo. He did it just like you."

Dustfinger saw Farid appear. He stayed behind Roxane, but Jehan pushed past him, glanced anxiously at the soldier, and then ran to his sister. "Where did you get that horse?" he asked.

"Violante gave it to me. As thanks for taking her with me by night to see the strolling players."

"You take her with you?" Roxane sounded concerned.

"Why not? She loves their shows! And the Black Prince says it's all right." Brianna didn't look at her mother.

Farid went over to Dustfinger. "What does she want here?" he whispered. "She's Her Ugliness's maid."

"And my daughter, too," replied Dustfinger.

Farid stared incredulously at Brianna, but she took no notice of him. It was on her father's account that she had come.

"Ten years!" she said accusingly. "You stayed away for ten

years, and now you come back just like that? Everyone said you were dead! They said you'd moldered away in the Adderhead's dungeons! They said the fire-raisers had handed you over to him because you wouldn't tell them all your secrets!"

"I did tell them," said Dustfinger tonelessly. "Almost all my secrets." *And they used them to set another world on fire,* he added in his thoughts. *A world without a door to let me out again, so that I could come back.*

"I dreamed of you!" Brianna's voice rose so high that her horse shied away. "I dreamed the men-at-arms tied you to a stake and burned you! I could smell the smoke and hear you trying to talk to the fire, but it wouldn't obey you and the flames devoured you. I had that dream almost every night! I still do! I was afraid of going to sleep for ten whole years, and now here you are, hale and hearty, as if nothing had happened! Where — have — you — *been?*"

Dustfinger glanced at Roxane — and saw the same question in her eyes. "I couldn't come back," he said. "I couldn't. I tried, believe me, I tried."

The wrong words. They were true a hundred times over, yet they sounded like a lie. Hadn't he always known it? Words were useless. At times they might sound wonderful, but they let you down the moment you really needed them. You could never find the right words, never, and where would you look for them? The heart is as silent as a fish, however much the tongue tries to give it a voice.

Brianna turned her back on him and buried her face in her horse's mane, while the soldier went on standing by the well, acting as if he were nothing but thin air.

And that's what I wish I was, too, thought Dustfinger. *Just thin air.*

"But it's the truth! He couldn't come back!" Farid stationed himself protectively in front of Dustfinger. "There wasn't any way! It's exactly like he says — he was in an entirely different world, but it's as real as this one. There are many, many worlds, they're all different, and they're written down in books!"

Brianna turned to him. "Do I look like a little girl who still believes in fairy tales?" she asked scornfully. "Once, when he stayed away so long that my mother's eyes were red with crying every morning, the other strolling players told me stories about him. They said he was talking to the fairies, or he'd gone to see the giants, or he was down at the bottom of the sea looking for a fire that even water can't put out. I didn't believe the stories even then, but I liked them. Now I don't. I'm not a little girl anymore. Not by any means. Help me mount my horse!" she ordered the soldier.

He obeyed without a word. Jehan stared at the sword hanging from his belt.

"Stay and eat with us!" said Roxane.

But Brianna just shook her head and turned her horse in silence. The soldier winked at Jehan, who was still gazing at his sword. They rode away on their horses, which seemed much too large for the narrow, stony path leading to Roxane's farm.

Roxane took Jehan indoors with her, but Dustfinger stayed out by the stable until the two riders had disappeared into the hills. Farid's voice quivered with indignation when he finally broke the silence. "But you really couldn't come back!"

"No . . . but you must admit your story didn't sound very convincing."

"It's exactly what happened, all the same!"

Dustfinger shrugged and looked at the place in the distance where his daughter had disappeared. "Sometimes even I think I only dreamed it all," he murmured.

A chicken squawked angrily behind them.

"Where the devil is Jink?" With a curse, Dustfinger opened the stable door. A white hen fluttered past him into the open; another fowl lay in the straw, her feathers bloody. A marten was sitting beside her.

"Jink!" Dustfinger scolded. "Damn it, didn't I tell you to leave the chickens alone?"

The marten looked at him.

Feathers were sticking to the animal's muzzle. He stretched, raised his bushy tail, came to Dustfinger, and rubbed against his legs like a cat.

"Well, what do you know?" whispered Dustfinger. "Hello, Gwin."

His death was back.

29

NEW MASTERS

Tyrants smile with their last breath
For they know that at their death,
Tyranny just changes hands,
Serfdom lives on in their lands.

Heinrich Heine, "King David"

The Prince of Sighs, once the Laughing Prince, died scarcely
a day after Meggie had been to the castle with Fenoglio. He
died at dawn, and the men-at-arms rode into Ombra three days
later. Meggie was in the marketplace with Minerva when they
came. After her father-in-law's death Violante had ordered the
guard at the city gate to be doubled, but there were so many men-
at-arms that the guards let them in without offering any
resistance. The Piper rode at their head, his silver nose like a beak
in the middle of his face, as shiny as if he had polished it up
specially for the occasion. The narrow streets echoed with the
snorting of horses, and it was quiet as the mounted men appeared
among the buildings. The street cries of traders, the voices of

women crowding around the stalls, all fell silent when the Piper reined in his horse and disapprovingly scrutinized the crowd.

"Make way!" he called. His voice sounded oddly strained, but what else would you expect of a man who had no nose? "Make way for the envoy of the Adderhead. We are here to pay his last respects to your dead prince and ensure that his grandson takes his rightful place as his heir."

The silence continued, but then a single voice was raised. "Thursday's market day in Ombra, always was, so if you gentlemen would like to dismount, we can get on with it!"

The Piper looked for the speaker among the faces staring up at him, but the man was hidden by the crowd. A murmur of agreement rose in the marketplace.

"Oh, so that's it!" cried the Piper through the confused voices. "You think we rode right through that accursed forest just to dismount here and make our way through a rabble of stinking peasants. As soon as the cat's dead the mice dance on the table. But I have news for you. There's a cat in your miserable town again, a cat with sharper claws than the old one!"

Without another word, he turned in the saddle, raised his black-gloved hand — and gave his men a signal.

Then he rode his horse straight into the crowd.

The silence that had been weighing down so heavily on the marketplace was torn like rending cloth. Screams rose in its enclosed space. More and more horsemen rode in from among the houses around it, so heavily armed they looked like iron reptiles, their helmets drawn so far down that you could see only their mouths and their eyes between noseguard and rim. There was a clinking of spurs, a clashing of greaves, and breastplates so brightly polished that they reflected the crowd's horrified faces. Minerva pushed her children out of the way. Despina stumbled, and Meggie was going to her aid when she herself tripped over a couple of cabbages and fell flat. A stranger pulled her to her feet just before the Piper rode her down. Meggie heard his horse snorting above her, felt his gleaming spurs brush her shoulder. She took shelter behind a potter's overturned stall, although she cut her hands on his broken pots. Trembling, she crouched among the shards, surrounded by smashed barrels and sacks that had burst open, watching helplessly as others, less lucky, fell under the horses' hooves. The mounted men struck out at many in the crowd with their feet or the shafts of their spears. Horses shied, reared, and kicked at pots and people's heads.

Then, just as suddenly as they had come, the men-at-arms were gone. Only the sound of their horses' hooves could still be heard as they rode fast up the street to the castle. The marketplace was left looking as if a strong wind had blown through it, an ill wind breaking jugs and pots as well as human bones. There was a smell of fear in the air as Meggie crawled out from behind the barrels. Peasants were gathering up their trampled vegetables, mothers wiped tears from their children's faces and blood from their knees, women stood looking at the broken earthenware dishes they had hoped to sell — and all was quiet in the marketplace again. Very quiet. The voices cursing the horsemen did so in undertones, and even the weeping and groaning were muted. Minerva came over to Meggie, concern in her face, with the sobbing Despina and Ivo beside her.

"Yes, I think we have a new master now," she said bitterly, helping Meggie to her feet. "Can you take the children home? I'll stay here and see what I can do to help. There must be many broken bones, but luckily a few physicians can always be found here on market day."

Meggie just nodded. She didn't know how she felt. Afraid?

Angry? Desperate? There didn't seem to be any word to describe the state of her heart. Silently, she took Despina and Ivo by the hand and set off home with them. Her knees hurt, and she was limping, but nonetheless she hurried along the alleys so fast that the children could hardly keep up.

"Now!" She uttered just that one word as she hobbled into Fenoglio's room. "Let me read it now. At once." Her voice shook, and she had to lean against the bare wall because her grazed knees were trembling. Indeed, everything in her and about her was trembling.

"What's happened?" Fenoglio was sitting at his desk. The parchment lying before him was covered with words. Rosenquartz stood beside him with a dripping pen in his hand, looking at Meggie in astonishment.

"We must do it now!" she cried. "This minute! They just rode into the middle of the crowd — into all those people!"

"Ah, so the soldiers are here already. Well, I told you we must hurry. Who was leading them? Firefox?"

"No, it was the Piper." Meggie went over to the bed and sat down on it. Suddenly, she felt only fear, as if she were back kneeling among the toppled stalls again, and her fury had run out of steam. "There are so many of them!" she whispered. "It's too late! What could Cosimo do against them?"

"You just leave that to me!" Fenoglio took the pen from the glass man's hand and began writing again. "The Laughing Prince has many soldiers, too, and they'll follow Cosimo once he's back. Of course, it would have been better if you'd read him here while his father was still alive. The Laughing Prince was in too much of a hurry to die, but that can't be helped now! Other things can be, though." With his brow furrowed, he read through what he had written, crossed out a word here, added one there, and then waved his hand to the glass man. "Sand, Rosenquartz, hurry up!"

Meggie pulled up her skirt and looked at her injured knees. One of them was beginning to swell. "But are you sure it will really be any better with Cosimo?" she asked in a low voice. "From what Her Ugliness said about him, it didn't sound like it."

"Of course it will be better! What kind of question is that? Cosimo is one of the good characters and always was, never mind what Violante says. Anyway, when you read this aloud you'll be bringing a new version of him here. An improved version, we might say."

"But . . . but why does there have to be a new prince here at all?" Meggie passed her sleeve over her tearstained face. The clank of armor was still echoing in her ears, the snorting and whinnying, the screaming — the screams of people who wore no armor.

"What can be better than a prince who does what we want?" Fenoglio took another sheet of parchment. "Just a few more lines," he murmured. "I've almost finished. Oh, curse it, how I hate writing on parchment. I hope you ordered more paper, Rosenquartz."

"Of course I did, long ago," replied the glass man huffily. "But there haven't been any deliveries for ages. The paper mill's on the other side of the forest, remember?"

"Yes, a pity." Fenoglio wrinkled his nose. "Very inconvenient, to be sure."

"Fenoglio, listen to me, will you? Why don't we read that robber here instead of Cosimo?" Meggie pulled down her skirt over her knees again. "You know — the robber in your songs! The Bluejay!"

Fenoglio laughed out loud. "The Bluejay? Good heavens! I'd like to see your face if — but joking aside, no — absolutely not! A robber's not fit to rule, Meggie. Robin Hood didn't become king! Robbers are good for stirring up trouble, that's all. I couldn't even put the Black Prince on the throne here. This world is ruled by royalty, not robbers, entertainers, or peasants. That's the way I made it, and I assure you it's a royal prince we need."

Rosenquartz sharpened another quill and dipped it in the ink, and Fenoglio began writing again. "Yes," Meggie heard him whispering. "Yes, this will sound wonderful when you read it aloud. What a surprise for the Adderhead! He thinks he can do what he likes in my world, do exactly as he pleases, but he's wrong. He'll play the part I give him and no other!"

Meggie rose from the bed and limped over to the window. It had begun to rain again; the sky was weeping as silently as the people in the marketplace. And the Adderhead's banner was already being hoisted above the castle.

30

COSIMO

"Yes," said Abhorsen. "I am a necromancer, but not of the common kind. Where others of the art raise the dead, I lay them back to rest . . ."

Garth Nix, *Sabriel*

It was dark when Fenoglio finally put aside his pen. All was still in the alley below. It had been quiet there all day, as if the people had fled indoors like mice hiding from the cat.

"Have you finished?" asked Meggie, as Fenoglio leaned back and rubbed his weary eyes. Her voice sounded faint and afraid, not like a voice that could awaken a prince and bring him to life, but after all, she had already made a monster rise from Fenoglio's words, even if that was long ago — and Mo, not she, had read the very last words.

Mo. After what had happened in the marketplace, she missed him more than ever.

"Yes, I've finished!" Fenoglio sounded as pleased with himself as he had in Capricorn's village, when he and Meggie between them first planned a way to alter his story. All had ended well that time, but now . . . now she was in the story herself. Did that make Fenoglio's words stronger or weaker? Meggie had told him about Orpheus's rule — that it was better to use only words that were in the story already — but Fenoglio had just dismissed the idea. "Nonsense. Remember how we wrote a happy ending before for the Steadfast Tin Soldier? Did I stop to make sure I was using only words out of his own story? No, I didn't. Perhaps that rule applies to people like this man Orpheus, people who venture to mess around with other writers' stories, but surely not for an author setting out to change his own!"

Meggie hoped he was right.

Fenoglio had crossed out a good deal, but his handwriting had indeed become more legible. Meggie looked along the lines. Yes, this time they were Fenoglio's own words, not stolen from any other writer. . . .

"Good, isn't it?" He dipped a piece of bread in the soup that Minerva had brought up for them hours ago and looked expectantly at Meggie. Of course the soup was cold. Neither of them could have even thought of eating until now, and Rosenquartz was the only one who had drunk some of the soup. It had made his whole body change color, until Fenoglio firmly took his tiny spoon away from him and asked if he wanted to kill himself.

"Leave that alone, Rosenquartz!" he now added sternly, as the glass man reached a transparent finger out to his dish again. "You've had quite enough! You know you can't digest human food. Do you want me to have to take you back to that physician who almost broke off your nose last time?"

"Eating sand all the time is so boring!" complained the glass man, withdrawing his finger with an injured air. "And the sand you bring me isn't particularly tasty, either."

"You ungrateful creature!" thundered Fenoglio. "When I go down to the river for it specially! And last time the river-nymphs thought it would be fun to pull me in. I nearly drowned, all because of you."

The glass man seemed unimpressed. Still looking injured, he sat down beside the jug full of quills, closed his eyes, and pretended to be asleep.

"Two of them have already died on me that way!" Fenoglio whispered to Meggie. "They just can't resist our food. Stupid creatures."

But Meggie was only half listening. She sat down on the bed with the parchment and read through it all again, word by word. Rain came in through the window, as if to remind her of another night — the night when she first heard of Fenoglio's book and saw Dustfinger standing outside in the rain. Dustfinger had looked happy in the castle courtyard. Fenoglio was happy, too, and Farid, and Minerva and her children. And it must stay that way. *I'll read this for all of them*, thought Meggie. For the strolling players, so that the Adderhead won't hang them just for singing a song, for the peasants in the marketplace whose vegetables were trampled by those horses. What about Her Ugliness? Would it make Violante happy to have a husband again? Would she notice that this was a different Cosimo? But the words would come too late for the Prince of Sighs. He would never hear of his son's return.

"Well, say something!" Fenoglio's voice sounded unsure of itself. "Don't you like it?"

"Oh yes. Yes, I do. It's lovely."

Relief spread over his face. "Then what are you waiting for?"

"About the mark on her face — oh, I don't know — it sounds like magic, like an inkspell."

"Oh, come on. I think it's romantic, and that never hurts."

"If you say so. It's your story." Meggie shrugged her shoulders. "But there's one more thing. Who's going to disappear when he arrives?"

Fenoglio went pale. "Heavens, I'd entirely forgotten about that. Rosenquartz, go and hide in your nest!" he told the glass man. "Luckily, the fairies are out."

"That's no use," said Meggie quietly, as the glass man made his way up to the empty fairies' nest, where he used to sulk and sometimes sleep. "Hiding is no use at all."

The sound of a horse's hooves rose to them from the street outside. One of the men-at-arms was riding by. Obviously, the Piper wasn't going to let the people of Ombra forget who their new master truly was, even in their sleep.

"Well, there's a sign for us!" Fenoglio whispered to Meggie. "If that man disappears, he's no loss. Anyway, how do you know anyone will disappear at all? I think it happens only if you read someone here who leaves a gap to be filled in his own story. But our new Cosimo has no story of his own! He was born here, today, from these words!"

Well, he might be right.

The clatter of the hooves mingled with the sound of Meggie's voice. "*It was a quiet night in Ombra, very quiet,*" she read. "*The wounds inflicted by the men-at-arms had not yet healed, and many never would.*" And suddenly she forgot about the fear she had felt in the morning and again thought only of her anger. She had felt so angry with men who encased themselves in armor and kicked women and children in the back with their iron shoes. The anger made her voice strong and full, ready to awaken new life. "*Doors and shutters were bolted, and behind them the children cried, as quietly as if fear itself kept their mouths shut, while their parents peered out into the night, fearfully wondering how dark the future would be under their new master. But suddenly, hoofbeats echoed down the alley where the cobblers and saddlers lived."* How easily the words came now! They flowed over Meggie's tongue as if they had been just waiting to be read aloud, to be brought to life this very night. *"People hurried to their windows. They looked out in fear, expecting to see one of the men-at-arms or even the Piper himself with his silver nose, but someone else came riding up to the castle, and the sight of him, familiar as it was, yet turned their faces pale. For the new arrival who came riding through sleepless Ombra bore the face of their dead prince, Cosimo the Fair, who had been resting in his crypt so long.*

"His likeness rode down the street on a white horse, and he was as handsome as all the songs about the fair Cosimo said. He rode through the castle gateway with the Adderhead's banner flying above it, reined in his horse in the quiet nocturnal courtyard, and for all who saw him there in the moonlight, sitting erect on his white horse, it was as if Cosimo had never been away. Then all the weeping was over, the weeping and the fear. The people of Ombra rejoiced, and others came from the most remote villages to see the man who bore a dead prince's face, and they whispered, 'Cosimo is back. Cosimo the Fair has come back to take his father's place and protect Ombra from the Adderhead.'

"And so it was. The savior of the city ascended the throne, and the birthmark on Her Ugliness's face faded. Cosimo the Fair had his father's court poet summoned and asked his advice, for he had been told how wise a man he was, and now a great new age began."

Meggie lowered the parchment. *A great new age . . .*

Fenoglio hurried to the window. Meggie had heard the sound, too — hoofbeats — but she did not rise to her feet.

"That must be him!" whispered Fenoglio. "He's coming, oh, Meggie, he's coming! Listen!"

But Meggie still sat there looking at the written words on her lap. It seemed to her that they were breathing. Paper made flesh, ink made blood . . . Suddenly she was tired, so tired that it seemed much too far to walk to the window. She felt like a child who had climbed down into the cellar all alone and now felt scared. If only Mo were here. . . .

"Any moment now! He'll be riding by any moment now!" Fenoglio leaned so far out of the window that he was in danger of falling headfirst into the alley. At least *he* was still here — he hadn't disappeared the way he did when she summoned the Shadow. But where else would he have gone? Meggie wondered. There seemed to be only one story left, this story, Fenoglio's story. And it seemed to have no beginning and no end.

"Come on, Meggie!" In great excitement, he beckoned her over. "You read it wonderfully, oh yes, wonderfully well! But I suppose you know that. Some of the phrases weren't among the best I've ever written, it was a little clumsy here and there, a little more dramatic color wouldn't have hurt, but never mind, it worked! It definitely worked!"

There was a knock.

A knock on the door. Rosenquartz peered out of his nest, his face anxious, and Fenoglio turned, both alarmed and annoyed.

"Meggie?" whispered a voice. "Are you there, Meggie?"

It was Farid.

"What does he want here?" Fenoglio uttered a less than delicate curse. "Send him away. We really can't do with having him around just now. Oh — oh, look! Here he comes! Meggie, you're an enchantress!"

The hoofbeats were louder now. But Meggie did not go to the window; she walked to the door instead. Farid was standing outside, his face downcast. He looked almost as if he'd been crying. "It's Gwin, Meggie . . . Gwin's back," he stammered. "I don't know how he found me! I even threw stones to make him go away."

"Meggie!" Fenoglio's voice sounded worse than merely irritated. "Where are you?"

Without a word, she took Farid's hand and drew him over to the window with her.

A white horse was coming up the narrow alley. Its rider had black hair, and his face was as young and handsome as the face of the statues in the castle, but his eyes were not stony white; instead, they were bright and as dark as his hair. He was looking around as if he had just woken from a dream, and one that didn't entirely fit in with what he now saw.

"Cosimo!" whispered Farid, bewildered. "The dead Cosimo."

"Not exactly," Fenoglio whispered back. "First, he isn't dead, as you can see for yourself, and second, he's not *that* Cosimo. He's a new one, a brand-new one, and Meggie and I have made him between us. Of course no one else will notice."

"Not even his wife?"

"Well, maybe she will! But who cares about that? She hardly ever leaves the castle."

Cosimo reined in his horse just a foot or two from Minerva's house. Instinctively, Meggie stepped back from the window. "What about *him*?" she whispered. "Who does he himself think he is?"

"What a question! He thinks he's Cosimo, of course!" replied Fenoglio impatiently. "Don't get me confused, for heaven's sake! All we've done is make sure the story goes on the way I originally planned it, no more and no less!"

Cosimo turned in his saddle and stared back down the street the way he had come — as if he had lost something but forgotten what it was. Then he clicked his tongue softly and urged his horse on, past Minerva's husband's workshop and the narrow house where the physician lived. Fenoglio often complained of the man's lack of skill in pulling teeth.

"That's not a good idea." Farid retreated from the window as if the Devil himself had gone riding by. "It's bad luck to summon the dead."

"He never *was* dead, damn it all!" snapped Fenoglio. "How often do I have to explain? He was born this very day, from my words and Meggie's voice, so don't talk such nonsense. What are you doing here, anyway? Since when do people come visiting decent girls in the middle of the night?"

Farid's face flushed dark red. Then he turned without a word and went to the door.

"Leave him alone! He can visit me whenever he likes!" Meggie told Fenoglio sharply. The stairs were slippery with rain, and she didn't catch up with Farid until he had reached the last step. He looked so sad.

"What did you tell Dustfinger? Did you tell him how Gwin followed us?"

"No, I didn't dare." Farid leaned against the wall of the house and closed his eyes. "You should have seen his face when he saw the marten. Do you think he'll have to die now, Meggie?"

She put out her hand and touched his face. He really had been crying. She could feel the dried tears on his skin.

"That's what Cheeseface said!" She could hardly make out the words he was whispering. "He said I'd bring him bad luck."

"What are you talking about? Dustfinger should be glad to have you!"

Farid looked up at the sky. Rain was still falling. "I must go back," he said. "That's why I came. To tell you I must stay with him now. I have to look after him — do you understand? If I keep close by him, then nothing bad will happen. You can visit me, though, at Roxane's farm! We're there most of the time. Dustfinger is crazy about her, he hardly ever leaves her side. Roxane this, Roxane that . . ." There was no mistaking the jealousy in his voice.

Meggie knew how he felt. She still clearly remembered those first few weeks back at Elinor's house, and her troubled heart when Mo spent hours going for walks with Resa and didn't even ask if she would like to come, too. She remembered what it felt like to stand outside a closed door and hear her father's laughter on the other side, laughter meant not for her but for her mother. "Why do you look like that?" Elinor had asked once, when she found Meggie watching the two of them in the garden. "Half his heart still belongs to you. Isn't that enough?" She had felt so ashamed. At least Farid was only jealous of a stranger. She'd been jealous of her own mother.

"Please, Meggie! I must stay with him. Who else is going to look after him? Roxane? She doesn't know anything about the marten, and anyway . . ."

Meggie turned her head away so that he wouldn't see her disappointment. Bother Gwin! She traced small circles on the damp ground with her toe.

"You will come, won't you?" Farid took her hands. "There are wonderful plants growing in Roxane's fields, and she has a goose who thinks she's a watchdog, and an old horse. Jehan, that's her son, says there's a linchetto living in the stable, don't ask me what a linchetto is, but Jehan says if you fart at it, it runs away. Well, Jehan's still just a baby, but I think you'd like him. . . ."

"Is he Dustfinger's son?" Meggie tucked her hair back behind her ear and tried to smile.

"No, but guess what? Roxane thinks I am. Imagine that! Please, Meggie! Come to Roxane's, do!" He put his hands on her shoulders and kissed her full on her mouth. His skin was wet with rain. When she didn't pull away, he took her face between his hands and kissed her again, on her forehead, on her nose, on her mouth once more. "You will come, won't you? Promise!" he whispered.

Then he ran away, fleet-footed as always, ever since the day Meggie had first set eyes on him. "You must come!" he called back to her once more, before disappearing into the dark passage leading out to the street. "Maybe you'd better stay with us for a while — Dustfinger and me, I mean! That old man is crazy. You don't go playing games with the dead!"

Then he had gone, and Meggie was leaning against the wall of Minerva's house, where Farid had been standing a moment ago. She passed her fingers over her mouth, as if she must make sure that Farid's kiss had not changed it in some way.

"Meggie?" Fenoglio was standing at the top of the stairs, a lantern in his hand. "What are you doing down there? Has the boy gone? What did he want? Standing around in the dark there with you!"

Meggie did not reply. She didn't want to talk to anyone. She just wanted to listen to what her bewildered heart was telling her.

ELINOR

Out in the world not much happened. But here in the special night, a land bricked with paper and leather, anything might happen, always did.

Ray Bradbury, *Something Wicked This Way Comes*

Elinor spent a couple of miserable days and nights in her cellar. The man built like a wardrobe brought them something to eat morning and evening — at least, they assumed it was morning and evening, always supposing that Darius's watch was still keeping time. When the bulky figure first appeared with bread and a plastic bottle of water, she had thrown the bottle at his head. Or rather, she'd tried to, but the colossus ducked just in time and the bottle burst against the wall.

"Never again, Darius!" Elinor whispered when the wardrobe-man, grunting contemptuously, had locked them in once more. "I was never going to let myself be locked up again, that's what I swore back in that stinking cage, when those arsonists walked past the bars with their rifles and flicked burning cigarette butts in my face. And now here I am locked up in my own cellar!"

283

On the first night, she'd gotten up from the air mattress, which made all her bones ache, and thrown cans of food against the wall. Darius just crouched there on the blanket he had spread out over the cushion for the garden bench, looking at her wide-eyed. By the afternoon of the second day — or was it the third? — Elinor was breaking jars, sobbing when she cut her fingers on the glass. Darius was just sweeping up the broken pieces when the wardrobe-man came to fetch her. Darius tried to follow, but the wardrobe-man pushed his thin chest so roughly that he stumbled and fell among the olives, preserved tomatoes, and all the other things that had spilled out of the jars when Elinor smashed them.

"Bastard!" she snapped at the colossus, but he just grinned, pleased as a child who has knocked down a tower of building bricks, and hummed to himself as he led Elinor to her library. *Who says bad people can't be happy, too?* she thought as he opened the door and jerked his head, indicating that she should go in.

Her library was a shocking sight. There were dirty mugs and plates strewn around everywhere — on the windowsill, on the carpet, even on the glass cases containing her greatest treasures — and that wasn't the worst of it. Her books were the worst. Hardly any of them were still in their right places. They were stacked on the floor among the unwashed coffee mugs, they were scattered in front of the windows. Many even lay flat on the floor, open, their spines upward. Elinor couldn't bear to look! Didn't the monster know that was the way to break a book's neck?

If he did, it didn't bother him. Orpheus was sitting in her favorite armchair, his dreadful dog beside him holding something between its paws that looked suspiciously like one of her gardening shoes. Its master had draped his plump legs over one arm of the chair and was holding a beautifully illustrated book about fairies that Elinor had bought in an auction only two months ago, paying such a high price that it had made Darius bury his head in his hands.

"That," she said, her voice trembling slightly, "that is a very, very valuable book."

Orpheus turned his head to her and smiled. It was the smile of a naughty boy. "I know!" he said in his velvety voice. "You have very, very many valuable books, Signora Loredan."

"Yes, indeed," replied Elinor icily. "That's why I don't stack them any old way, like egg cartons or slices of cheese. Each has its own place."

This observation only made Orpheus smile even more broadly. He closed the book, after dog-earing one of the pages. Elinor drew in her breath sharply.

"Books aren't glass vases, dear lady," said Orpheus as he sat up in the chair. "They're not as fragile or as decorative. They're just books! It's their contents that matter, and their contents won't fall out if you stack them in a pile." He ran his hand over his smooth hair, as if afraid his parting might have slipped. "Sugar says you wanted to speak to me?"

Elinor cast an incredulous glance at the wardrobe-man. "Sugar?"

The giant smiled, revealing such an extraordinary collection of bad teeth that Elinor didn't have to wonder how he got his nickname.

"I certainly do. I've been wanting to speak to you for days. I insist on being let out of the cellar — and my librarian, too! I'm sick of having to pee in a bucket in my own house, and not knowing whether it's day or night. I order you to bring my niece and her husband back. They're in the greatest danger, and it's all your fault, and I order you to keep your fat fingers off my books, damn it!"

Elinor shut her mouth — and cursed herself with every curse she could call to mind. Oh no! What was Darius always telling her? What had she told herself hundreds of times, lying down there on that horrible air mattress? *Control yourself, Elinor, be cunning, Elinor, watch your tongue* — all useless. She had burst like a balloon blown up too far.

But Orpheus still sat there, with his legs crossed and that impudent smile on his face. "I could probably bring them back. Yes, probably!" he said, patting his dog's ugly head. "But why should I?" His fat fingers stroked the cover of the book he had just so cruelly dog-eared. "A handsome cover, isn't it? Rather sentimental, perhaps, and I don't think of fairies quite like that, but all the same . . ."

"Yes, yes, I know it's handsome, but I'm not interested in the cover just now!" Elinor was trying not to raise her voice, but she simply couldn't keep it down. "If you can really bring them back, then for heaven's sake get a move on and do it! Before it's too late. The old woman is going to kill him, didn't you hear her? She's going to kill Mortimer!"

His expression indifferent, Orpheus straightened his crumpled tie. "Well, *he* killed Mortola's son, as far as I can make out. An eye for an eye, a tooth for a tooth, as another — not entirely unknown — book so forcibly puts it."

"Her son was a murderer!" Elinor clenched her fists. She wanted to rush at the moon-face and snatch her book from his hands, hands that looked as soft and white as if they had never in their life done anything but turn the pages of a book. However, Sugar barred her way.

"Yes, yes, I know." Orpheus heaved a heavy sigh. "I know all about Capricorn. I've read the book telling his story more times than I can count, and I have to say he was a very good villain, one of the best I ever met in the realm of the written word. Just killing someone like that — well, if you ask me, it's almost a crime. Although I'm glad of it for Dustfinger."

Oh, if only she could have hit him just once, on his broad nose, on his smiling mouth!

"Capricorn had Mortimer abducted! He captured his daughter and kept his wife a prisoner for years on end!" Tears of rage and helplessness came into Elinor's eyes. "Please, Mr. Orpheus or whatever your real name is!" She put all her strength and self-control into sounding reasonably friendly. "Please! Bring them back, and while you're at it please bring Meggie back, too, before she gets trodden on by a giant or impaled on a spear in that story."

Orpheus leaned back and looked at her as if she were a picture on an easel. How naturally he had taken over her armchair — as if Elinor herself had never sat there with Meggie beside her, or with Resa on her lap when she was still tiny, so many years ago. Elinor bit back her fury. *Control yourself, Elinor,* she thought, as she kept her eyes fixed on Orpheus's pale, bespectacled face. *Control yourself! For the sake of Mortimer, and Resa, and Meggie!*

Orpheus cleared his throat. "I don't know what's bothering you," he said, examining his fingernails, which were bitten like a schoolboy's. "I envy all three of them!"

It was a moment before Elinor realized what he was talking about. Only when he went on did it become clear.

"What makes you think they want to come back?" he asked softly. "If I were there I never would! There's nowhere in this world I've ever wanted to be half as much as on the hill where the Laughing Prince's castle lies. I've walked through Ombra market countless times, I've looked up at the towers and the banners with the lion emblem. I've imagined what it would be like to wander through the Wayless Wood and watch Dustfinger stealing honey from the fire-elves. I've pictured the minstrel woman he loves, Roxane. I've stood in Capricorn's fortress smelling the potions that Mortola brewed from monkshood and hemlock. The Adderhead's castle often figures in my dreams, even today. Sometimes I'm in one of its dungeons, sometimes I'm stealing in through the gate with Dustfinger and looking up at the heads of minstrels set there on pikes by the Adderhead for singing the wrong song . . . By all the words and letters in the world, when Mortola told me her name I thought she was crazy! Yes, she and Basta did look like the characters they claimed to be, but could it really be true that someone had brought them here out of my favorite book? Were there other people who could read aloud the way I can? I didn't believe it until Dustfinger came up to me in that musty, ramshackle library. Oh God, how my heart beat when I saw his face with the three pale scars left by Basta's knife! It beat faster than on the day I first kissed a girl. It really was him, the melancholy hero of my very favorite book. And I helped him to disappear into it again, but what about me? Hopeless." He laughed, a sad and bitter laugh. "I just hope he doesn't have to die the death that idiot of an author intended for him. No, he can't! He'll be all right, I'm sure he will. After all, Capricorn is dead and Basta's a coward. Do you know, I wrote to that Fenoglio, the author, when I was twelve, telling him he must change his story, or at least write a sequel in which Dustfinger comes back? He never answered my letter, any more than *Inkheart* ever had a sequel. Oh well." Orpheus sighed deeply.

Dustfinger, Dustfinger . . . Elinor compressed her lips. Who cared what happened to the matchstick-eater? *Keep calm, Elinor, don't go off the deep end again, you must be clever now, clever, go carefully.* . . . Easier said than done.

"Listen, if you'd like to be in that book so much" — and this time she really did manage to make her voice sound as if what she was saying didn't matter all that much to her — "then why not just bring Meggie back? She knows how you can read yourself into a story. She's done it! I'm sure she can tell you how to do it or read you over there, too."

Orpheus's round face darkened so suddenly that Elinor immediately knew she had made a bad mistake. How could she have forgotten what a vain, conceited creature he was?

"No one," said Orpheus softly, rising slowly and menacingly from her chair, "no one can tell me anything about the art of reading. Certainly not a little girl!"

Now he'll put you straight back in the cellar, thought Elinor. *What am I going to do? Think, Elinor, try to find the right answer in your silly head! Do something! Surely you can think up something!* "Oh, of course not!" she stammered. "No one but you could have read Dustfinger back. No one. But —"

"No buts. You watch out." Orpheus posed as if he were about to sing an aria onstage and picked up the book lying on the chair where he had so carelessly put it down. He opened it right where the dog-ear disfigured the creamy white page, ran the tip of his tongue over his lips as if he had to smooth them so that the words would flow freely — and then his voice filled Elinor's library again, the captivating voice that did not suit his outward appearance in the least. Orpheus read as if he were letting his favorite food melt in his mouth, relishing it, greedy for the sound of the letters, pearls melting on his tongue, words like seeds from which he was making life emerge.

Perhaps he really was the greatest master ever of his art. He certainly practiced it with the utmost passion.

"There is a tale of a certain shepherd, Tudur of Llangollen, who came across a troop of faeries, dancing to the tune of a tiny fiddler."

A faint chirping sound arose behind Elinor, but when she turned around there was no one to be seen but Sugar, listening to Orpheus's voice with a bewildered expression on his face. *"Tudur tried to resist the enchanting strains, but finally, throwing his cap in the air and shouting, 'Now for it, then, play away, old devil!' he joined in."*

The fiddling grew shriller and shriller, and when Elinor turned around this time she saw a man standing in her library, surrounded by small creatures dressed in leaves and prancing around on his bare feet like a dancing bear, while a step or so away a tiny little thing with a bellflower on its head was playing a fiddle hardly larger than an acorn.

"Immediately, a pair of horns appeared on the fiddler's head and a tail sprouted from beneath his coat!" Orpheus let his voice swell until he was almost singing. *"The dancing sprites turned into goats, dogs, cats, and foxes, and they and Tudur spun around in a dizzying frenzy."*

Elinor pressed her hands to her mouth. There they were, emerging from behind the armchair, leaping over the stacks of books, dancing on the open pages with their muddy hooves. The dog jumped up and barked at them.

"Stop it!" Elinor cried to Orpheus. "Stop it at once!"

He closed the book with a triumphant smile.

"Chase them out into the garden!" he told Sugar, who was standing there transfixed. Confused, the man groped his way over to the door, opened it — and let the whole troop dance past him, fiddling, screeching, barking, bleating, on down Elinor's corridor and past her bedroom, until the noise gradually died away.

"No one," repeated Orpheus, and now there was not the smallest trace of a smile to be seen on his round face, "no one can teach Orpheus anything about the art of reading. And did you notice? Nothing disappeared! Maybe a few bookworms if there are any in your library, maybe a couple of flies. . . ."

"Maybe a couple of motorists down on the road," added Elinor in a hoarse voice, but unfortunately there was no hiding the fact that she was impressed.

"Maybe!" said Orpheus, carelessly shrugging his round shoulders. "But that wouldn't make any difference to my mastery, would it? And now I hope *you* understand something about the art of cooking, because I'm sick and tired of what Sugar serves up. And I'm hungry. I'm always hungry when I've been reading aloud."

"Cooking?" Elinor practically choked on her rage. "You expect me to act as your cook in my own house?"

"Well, of course. Make yourself useful. Or do you want to give Sugar the idea that you and your stammering friend are superfluous to requirements? He's in a bad mood, anyway, because he hasn't yet found anything worth stealing in your house. No, we really don't want to put any stupid notions into his head, do we?"

Elinor took a deep breath and tried to control her trembling knees. "No. No, we don't," she said, turned — and went into the kitchen.

32

THE WRONG MAN

> So she placed the healing herb
> In his mouth — he slept straightaway.
> She covered him most carefully.
> He still slept on the livelong day.
>
> **Wolfram von Eschenbach**, *Parsifal*

Resa and Mo were alone in the cave when they came in: two women and four men. Two of the men had been sitting by the fire with Cloud-Dancer: Sootbird the fire-eater and Twofingers. His face was no friendlier by daylight, and the others, too, were looking so hostile that Resa instinctively moved closer to Mo. Only Sootbird seemed to feel awkward.

Mo was asleep. He had slept this uneasy, fevered sleep for many days now, and it made Nettle shake her head anxiously. The six strolling players stopped only a few paces away from him. They loomed between Resa and the daylight coming in from outside. One of the women stepped out in front of the rest of them. She wasn't particularly old, but her fingers were crooked like a bird's claws.

"He must go!" she said. "Today. He's not one of us, and nor are you."

"What do you mean?" Hard as Resa was trying to sound calm, her voice shook. "He can't go anywhere. He's still too weak."

If only Nettle had been there! But she had gone away muttering something about sick children — and the root of an herb that might perhaps cure Mo's fever. The six would have felt afraid of Nettle, they'd have been respectful and timid, but to the strolling players Resa was only a stranger, a desperate stranger with a mortally sick husband — even if none of them guessed just *how* much of a stranger she was in this world.

"It's the children . . . you must see how we feel!" The other woman was still very young, and she was pregnant. She placed one protective hand on her belly. "A man like him puts our children in danger, and Martha's right, you don't even belong to us. This is the only place where they let us stay. No one drives us away, but once they hear the Bluejay is here, that will be over. They'll say we were hiding him."

"But he isn't this Bluejay! I told you so before. And who do you mean by 'they'?"

Mo whispered something in his fever, his hand clutching Resa's arm. She soothingly stroked his forehead and forced a little of the decoction that Nettle had made between his lips. Her visitors watched in silence.

"As if you didn't know!" said one of them, a tall, thin man shaken by a dry cough. "The Adderhead's looking for him. He'll send his men-at-arms here. He'll have us all hanged for hiding him."

"I'm telling you again!" Resa took Mo's hand and held it very tight. "He's not a robber or anyone else out of your stories! We've

293

only been here a few days! My husband is a bookbinder, that's his trade, he isn't anything else!"

The way they were looking at her!

"I've seldom heard a worse lie!" The two-fingered man's mouth twisted. He had an unpleasant voice. Judging by his brightly patterned clothing, he was one of the players who put on comic shows in marketplaces, loud, coarse farces to make the spectators laugh all their troubles away. "What would a book-binder be doing in Capricorn's old fortress in the middle of the Wayless Wood? People never go there of their own free will, what with the White Women and the other horrors haunting the ruins. And why would Mortola bother with a bookbinder? Why would she shoot him with some witchy weapon no one's ever heard of before?"

The others nodded agreement — and took another step toward Mo. What was she to do? What could she say? What use was it having a voice if no one would listen to her? "Don't let it worry you, not being able to speak," Dustfinger had often told her. "People tend not to listen, anyway, right?"

Perhaps she could call for help, but who was going to come? Cloud-Dancer had set off early in the morning with Nettle, when the leaves had still been tinged red by the light of the rising sun, and the women who brought Resa food and sometimes kept watch beside Mo for her, to let her get a few hours' sleep, had gone down to the nearby river with the children. There were only a few old men outside the cave, and they had come here because they were tired of other people and were waiting to die. They weren't likely to help her.

"We won't hand him over to the Adderhead; we'll just take him back to where Nettle found you. To that accursed fortress." It was the man with the cough again. He had a raven sitting on his shoulder. Resa knew such ravens from the days when she had sat in marketplaces writing documents and petitions — their owners trained them to steal a few extra coins while they were performing their own tricks.

"The songs say that the Bluejay protects the Motley Folk," the raven's owner went on. "And those he's supposed to have killed threatened our women and children. We appreciate that, we've all sung the songs about him, but we're not ready to be strung up for his sake."

They'd made up their minds long ago. They were going to take Mo away. Resa wanted to shout at them, but she simply had no strength left for shouting. "It will kill him if you take him back there!" Her voice was hardly louder than a whisper.

They didn't care about that; Resa saw it in their eyes. *Why should they?* she thought. What would she do if the children out there were hers? She remembered a visit that the Adderhead had paid to Capricorn's fortress, to see an enemy of theirs executed. Since that day she had known what someone who enjoyed inflicting pain on others looked like.

Before Resa could stop her, the woman with the clawlike fingers kneeled down beside Mo and pushed up his sleeve. "There, see that?" she said triumphantly. "He has the scar, just as the songs describe it — where the Adder's dogs bit him."

Resa hauled her away so violently that the woman fell at her companions' feet. "Those dogs weren't the Adderhead's. They belonged to Basta!"

The name made them start nervously, but all the same they didn't leave. Sootbird helped the woman to her feet, and Twofingers went closer to Mo. "Come on!" he told the others. "Let's pick him up."

They all joined him; only the fire-eater hesitated.

"Oh please, believe me!" Resa pushed their hands away. "How can you think I'd lie to you? What thanks would that be for all your help?"

No one took any notice of her. Twofingers pulled away the blanket that Nettle had given them to cover Mo. It was cold in the cave at night.

"Well, fancy that! Visiting our guests. How kind of you."

How they spun around! Like naughty children caught in the act. A man was standing in the entrance to the cave. For a moment Resa thought it was Dustfinger and wondered, in bewilderment, how Cloud-Dancer could possibly have brought him so quickly. But then she saw that the man the six of them were staring at so guiltily was black. Everything about him was black: his long hair, his skin, his eyes, even his clothes. And beside him, almost a head taller, stood a bear as black as his master.

"These must be the visitors Nettle told me about, I expect?" The bear ducked his head, grunting, as he followed the man into the cave. "She says they know an old friend of mine, a very good friend. Dustfinger. Of course, you've all heard of him, haven't you? And I'm sure you know that his friends have always been my friends, too. The same applies to his enemies, of course."

The six moved aside with some haste, as if to give the stranger a better view of Resa. The fire-eater laughed nervously. "Why, what are you doing here, Prince?"

"Oh, this and that. Why are there no guards outside? Do you think the brownies have lost their taste for our provisions?" He walked slowly toward them. His bear dropped to all fours and lumbered after him, puffing and snorting, as if he didn't like the cramped cave.

Prince! They called him "Prince." Of course. The Black

Prince! Fenoglio's book had told Resa his story, and she had heard his name in the Ombra market, too, from the maids in Capricorn's fortress, even from Capricorn's men. Yet she had never seen him face-to-face. When Fenoglio's story had first swallowed her up he had been a knife-thrower, a bear-tamer . . . and Dustfinger's friend since the two of them had been barely half as old as Meggie was now.

The others drew aside as he stepped up to them with his bear, but the Prince ignored them. He looked down at Resa. There were three knives in his brightly embroidered belt: slender, shiny knives, although no strolling player was allowed to carry weapons. "That's to make it easier to skewer them," Dustfinger had often said mockingly.

"Welcome to the Secret Camp," said the Black Prince, his glance going to Mo's bloodstained bandages. "Dustfinger's friends are always welcome here — even if it may not look like it just now." He looked ironically at the others standing around there. Only the two-fingered man defiantly returned his gaze, but then he, too, bent his head.

The Prince went on looking down at Resa. "Where did you meet Dustfinger?"

What was she to say? In another world? The bear was sniffing the bread lying beside her. His hot breath, the breath of a beast of prey, made her shudder. *Tell the truth, Resa,* she thought. *You don't have to say what world it happened in.*

"I worked as a maid for the fire-raisers for several years," she said. "I ran away, but a snake bit me. Dustfinger found me and helped me. I'd have died but for him." *Yes, he hid me,* she continued the story in her mind, *but Basta and the others soon found me, and they half killed Dustfinger.*

"What about your husband? I hear he's not one of us." The

black eyes explored her face. They seemed to be well versed in detecting lies.

"She says he's a bookbinder, but we know better!" The two-fingered man spat out his words contemptuously.

"So what do you know?" The Prince looked at them, and they fell silent.

"He *is* a bookbinder! Give him paper, glue, and leather, and once he's better he'll show you." *Don't cry, Resa,* she told herself. *You've cried quite enough these last few days.*

The thin man coughed again.

"Very well, you heard her." The Prince crouched down beside her on the ground. "These two stay here until Dustfinger arrives to confirm their story. He'll soon tell us if this is only a harmless bookbinder or that robber you're always going on about. Dustfinger knows your husband, too, doesn't he?"

"Oh yes," replied Resa softly. "He's known him longer than he's known me."

Mo turned his head and whispered Meggie's name.

"Meggie? Is that your name?" The Prince pushed the bear's muzzle away as the animal sniffed the bread again.

"It's our daughter's name."

"You have a daughter? How old is she?" The bear rolled on his back for his belly to be scratched, as if he were a dog.

"Thirteen."

"Thirteen? Almost the same age as Dustfinger's daughter."

Dustfinger's daughter? He'd never said anything to her about any daughter.

"So why are you all still standing around?" the Prince snapped at the others. "Bring fresh water! Can't you see he's feverish?"

The two women hurried away, relieved, or so it seemed to

Resa, to have a good reason to leave the cave. But the men stood around indecisively.

"Suppose it really *is* him, though, Prince?" asked the thin man. "And suppose the Adderhead hears about him before Dustfinger gets here?" He coughed so hard that he had to press his hand to his chest.

"Suppose he's who? The Bluejay? Nonsense! There's probably no such man, and even if there is, since when have we given up people who are on our own side? And suppose the songs are true, and he's protected your women and your children . . ."

"Songs are never true." The two-fingered man's eyebrows were as dark as if he had blackened them with soot. "He's probably no better than any other highwayman, a murderer greedy for gold, nothing more. . . ."

"Perhaps, or perhaps not," retorted the Prince. "I see only an injured man and a woman asking for our help."

The men did not reply, but the glances they cast Mo were still hostile.

"Now get out, and hurry up about it!" the Prince said angrily. "How's he to get better with you staring at him like that? Or do you think his wife likes your ugly mugs? Go and make yourselves useful, there's plenty of work outside."

And they did go, sullenly slouching away like men who had not done what they came to do.

"He isn't the Bluejay!" Resa whispered, when they had left.

"Very likely not!" The Prince stroked his bear's round ears. "But I'm afraid our friends out there are convinced he is. And the Adder has put a high price on the Bluejay's head."

"A high price?" Resa looked at the entrance to the cave. Two of the men were still standing there. "They'll come back," she whispered, "and try to take him away after all."

299

But the Black Prince shook his head.

"Not while I'm here. And I'll stay until Dustfinger arrives. Nettle said you'd sent him a message, so I expect he'll soon be here to tell them you're not lying, won't he?"

The women came back with a basin of water. Resa dipped a scrap of fabric in it to cool Mo's brow. The pregnant woman leaned over her and put a few dried flowers in her lap. "Here," she whispered. "Put this on his heart. It brings luck."

Resa stroked the dried flower heads. "They obey you," she said to the Prince, when the women had gone again. "Why?"

"Oh, because they've chosen me as their leader," replied the Prince. "And because I'm a very good knife-thrower."

33

FAIRYDEATH

The wind this evening, so eagerly playing
Sounds like blades that someone is swinging —
On the instrument of the trees densely growing . . .

Montale, *Poems*

At first Dustfinger didn't believe Farid when he told him what he had seen and heard in Fenoglio's room. Even the old man couldn't be crazy enough to meddle with Death's handiwork. But then, that same day, a couple of women buying herbs from Roxane had the same story to tell as the boy: Cosimo the Fair had come back, they said, back from the dead.

"Women say the White Women fell so deeply in love with him that at last they let him go," said Roxane. "And men say he'd just been hiding from his ugly wife for a while."

Crazy stories, thought Dustfinger, *but not half as crazy as the truth.*

The women had nothing to say about Brianna. He didn't like to think of her up at the castle. No one knew what might happen there next. It seemed that the Piper was still in Ombra with half a dozen men-at-arms. Cosimo had sent the rest of them out of the city, and they were waiting outside the walls for their own lord's arrival. For there was a widespread rumor that the Adderhead would come in person to see this prince who had risen from the dead. He wasn't going to accept the idea of Cosimo's taking the throne from his grandson again so easily.

"I'll ride to Ombra myself and see how she is," said Roxane. "They probably wouldn't even let you through the Outer Gate. But there's something else you can do for me."

The women had not come just for the herbs and to pass on the gossip about Cosimo. They had brought Roxane an order from Nettle, who was in Ombra treating two sick children in the dyers' quarter. She needed a root of fairydeath, dangerous medicine that killed as often as it cured. The old woman hadn't said for what poor devil she needed the root. "Just that it's a man at the Secret Camp who's injured, and Nettle is going back there this evening," said Roxane. "And another thing . . . Cloud-Dancer was with her. It seems he's carrying a message for you."

"A message? For me?"

"Yes, from a woman." Roxane looked at him for a moment, and then went into the house to get the root.

"You're going to Ombra?" Farid was there behind Dustfinger so suddenly that he jumped.

"I am, and Roxane is riding to the castle," he said. "So you stay here to keep an eye on Jehan."

"And who's going to keep an eye on you?"

"Me?"

"Yes." What a look Farid was giving him! And the marten, too. "To stop it from happening." Farid spoke so softly that Dustfinger could hardly hear him. "Stop what it says in the book."

"Oh, that." The boy was watching him as anxiously as if he

might fall down dead any minute. Dustfinger had to suppress a smile, although it was his own death they were discussing. "Did Meggie tell you about it?"

Farid nodded.

"Very well. Forget it, do you hear me? The words are written. Maybe they'll come true, maybe not."

But Farid shook his head so vigorously that his black hair fell over his forehead. "No!" he said. "No, they won't come true! I swear it. I swear it by the djinns that howl in the desert and the ghosts that eat the dead, I swear it by everything I fear!"

Dustfinger looked thoughtfully at him. "You crazy boy!" he said. "But I like your oath. We'd better leave Gwin here, then, and you can keep him!"

Gwin did not approve. He bit Dustfinger's hand when he was put on his chain, snapped at his fingers, and chattered even more angrily when Jink got into his master's backpack.

"You're taking the new marten with you and the old one must be put on the chain?" asked Roxane, when she came back to them with the root for Nettle.

"Yes. Because someone said he'd bring me bad luck."

"Since when have you believed that kind of thing?"

Indeed, since when? *Since I met an old man who claims to have made up you and me,* thought Dustfinger. Gwin was still hissing; he had seldom seen the marten so angry. Without a word he took the chain off Gwin's collar again. And ignored Farid's look of alarm.

All the way to Ombra Gwin sat on Farid's shoulders, as if to show Dustfinger that he hadn't forgiven him yet. And the moment Jink put his nose out of the backpack, Gwin bared his teeth and snarled so menacingly that Farid had to hold his muzzle shut a couple of times.

The gallows outside the city gates were empty; only a few ravens were perched on the wooden beams. Even though Cosimo was back, Her Ugliness was still administering justice in Ombra, just as she had done in his father's lifetime, and she did not think well of hangings — perhaps because, as a child, she had seen too many men dangling from a rope with their tongues blue and their faces bloated.

"Listen," Dustfinger said to Farid as they stopped beneath the gallows, "while I take Nettle the root and ask Cloud-Dancer for the message I'm told he has for me, you go and find Meggie. I must talk to her."

Farid went red, but he nodded. Dustfinger looked at his face with amusement. "What's all this? Did something besides Cosimo's return from the dead happen on the evening when you went to see her?"

"None of your business!" muttered Farid, blushing more deeply than ever.

A farmer, swearing profusely, was driving a cart laden with barrels toward the city gates. The oxen blocked the gateway, and the guards impatiently grabbed the reins. Dustfinger took this chance to get himself and Farid past them. "Bring Meggie here, all the same," he said as they parted on the other side of the gates. "And don't get so lovesick you lose your way."

He watched the boy until he had disappeared among the houses. No wonder Roxane thought Farid was his son. Sometimes he suspected his own heart of thinking the same.

CLOUD-DANCER'S MESSAGE

Yes, my love,
This world of ours bleeds
With more pain than just the pain of love.
> Faiz Ahmed Faiz, "The Love I Gave You Once,"
> *An Elusive Dawn*

There could hardly be a worse smell in the world than the odor rising from the dyers' vats. The acrid stench rose to Dustfinger's nostrils even as he was making his way along the alley where the smiths plied their trade — tinkers mending pots and pans, blacksmiths shoeing horses, and on the other side of the road the armorers, who were considered superior to the other smiths and were arrogant as befitted their status. The sound of all the hammers beating on red-hot iron was almost as bad as the smell in the alley. The dyers had their hovels in the most remote part of Ombra; their stinking vats were never tolerated in the better parts of any town. But just as Dustfinger was approaching the gate separating their quarter from the rest of Ombra, a man coming out of an armorer's workshop collided with him.

The Piper. He was easily recognizable by his silver nose, although Dustfinger could remember the days when he had a nose of flesh and blood. *Just your luck again, Dustfinger,* he told himself, turning his head aside and trying to slip past Capricorn's minstrel quickly. *Of all the men in this world, that bloodhound has to cross your path.* He was beginning to hope that the Piper hadn't noticed who he had bumped into, but just as he thought he was safely past him the silver-nosed man seized his arm and swung him around.

"Dustfinger!" he said in the strained voice that had once sounded so different. It had always reminded Dustfinger of oversweet cakes. Capricorn had loved to listen to it more than any other voice, and the same was true of the songs it sang. The Piper wrote wonderful songs about fire-raising and murder, so wonderful that they almost made you believe there was no nobler occupation than cutting throats. Did he sing the same songs for the Adderhead — or were they too coarse-grained for the silver halls of the Castle of Night?

"Well, fancy that! I'm inclined to think just about everyone's coming back from the dead these days," said the Piper, while the two men-at-arms with him looked covetously at the weapons displayed outside the armorers' workshops. "I really thought Basta had sliced you up and then buried you years ago. Did you know he's back, too? He and the old woman, Mortola. I'm sure you remember her. The Adderhead was delighted to welcome her to his castle. You know how highly he always thought of her deadly concoctions."

Dustfinger hid the fear pervading his heart behind a smile. "Why, if it isn't the Piper!" he said. "Your new nose suits you much better than the old one. It tells everyone who your new master is and shows that it belongs to a minstrel who can be bought for silver."

The Piper's eyes had not changed. They were pale gray like the sky on a rainy day, and they stared at him with as fixed a gaze as the eyes of a bird. Dustfinger knew from Roxane how he had lost his nose, cut off by a man whose daughter he had seduced with his dark songs.

"You always did have a dangerously sharp tongue, Dustfinger," he said. "It's about time someone finally cut it out. Indeed, wasn't that tried once, and you got away only because the Black Prince and his bear protected you? Are they still looking after you? I don't see them anywhere." He looked around, his eye searching the scene.

Dustfinger cast a quick glance at the two men-at-arms. They were both at least a head taller than him. *What would Farid say if he could see me now?* he wondered. *That I ought to have had him with me so that he could keep his vow?* The Piper had a sword, of course, and his hand was already on the hilt. He obviously thought as little as the Black Prince did of the law forbidding strolling players to carry weapons. *A good thing the smiths are hammering so loudly,* thought Dustfinger, *or no doubt everyone would hear my heart beating with fear.*

"I must be on my way," he said, as casually as possible. "Give Basta my regards when you see him, and as for burying me, he hasn't done it yet." He turned — it was worth a try — but the Piper held his arm tightly.

"Of course, and there's your marten, too!" he hissed.

Dustfinger felt Jink's damp muzzle against his ear. *It's the wrong marten,* he thought, trying to calm his racing heart. *The wrong marten.* But had Fenoglio ever mentioned Gwin's name when he staged Dustfinger's death? With the best will in the world he couldn't remember. *I'll have to ask Basta to give me back the book so that I can look it up,* he thought bitterly. He signaled to Jink to get back into the backpack. *Better not think about that.*

The Piper was still holding his arm. He wore pale leather gloves, finely stitched like a lady's. "The Adderhead will soon be here," he told Dustfinger in an undertone. "He didn't care at all for the news of his son-in-law's strange return to life. He thinks the whole business is a wicked masquerade designed to cheat his defenseless grandson of the throne."

Four guards came down the street wearing the Laughing Prince's colors: Cosimo's colors now. Dustfinger had never in his life been so glad to see armed men. The Piper let go of his arm.

"We'll meet again soon," he hissed in his noseless voice.

"I daresay," was all that Dustfinger replied. Then he quickly pushed between a couple of ragged boys standing there and staring wide-eyed at a sword, made his way past a woman showing her battered cooking pot to one of the smiths, and disappeared through the dyers' gate.

No one followed him. No one seized him and hauled him back. *You have too many enemies, Dustfinger,* he thought. He didn't slow down until he came to the tubs from which the vapors of the liquid muck used by the dyers rose. The same miasma hung over the stream that carried the stinking brew under the city wall and down to the river. No wonder the river-nymphs were found only above the place where it flowed into the main waterway.

In the second house Dustfinger tried, they told him where to find Nettle. The woman he had been sent to had eyes red with weeping and was carrying a baby. Without a word, she beckoned him into her house, if a house it could be called. Nettle was bending over a little girl with red cheeks and glazed eyes. At the sight of Dustfinger she straightened up, looking grumpy.

"Roxane asked me to bring you this!"

She glanced briefly at the root, compressed her narrow lips, and nodded.

"What's wrong with the girl?" he asked. The child's mother had sat down by the bed again.

Nettle shrugged. She seemed to be wearing the same moss-green garment as she did ten years ago — and obviously she still liked him as little as ever.

"A high fever, but she'll survive," she replied. "It's not half as bad as the one that killed your daughter . . . while her father was off jaunting around the world!" She looked him in the face as she said that, as if to make sure that her words went home, but Dustfinger knew how to hide pain. He was almost as good at hiding pain as he was at playing with fire.

"The root is dangerous," he said.

"Do you think you have to tell me that?" The old woman looked at him as if he had insulted her. "The wound it's to heal is dangerous, too. He's a strong man or he'd be dead by now."

"Do I know him?"

"You know his wife."

What was the old woman talking about? Dustfinger glanced at the sick child. Her small face was flushed with fever.

"I heard that Roxane's let you back into her bed again," said Nettle. "You can tell her she's more of a fool than I thought. And now go around behind the house. Cloud-Dancer's there. He can tell you more about the other woman. She gave him a message for you."

Cloud-Dancer was standing beside a stunted oleander bush that grew near the dyers' huts.

"That poor child, did you see her?" he asked as Dustfinger came over to him. "I can't bear to see them so sick. And the

309

mothers . . . you'd think they'd weep their eyes away. I remember how Roxane —" But here he broke off abruptly. "Sorry," he murmured, putting his hand into the breast of his dirty tunic, "I was forgetting she was your child, too. Here, this is for you." He brought out a note on fine, pure white paper such as Dustfinger had never seen in this world before. "A woman gave me this for you. Nettle found her and her husband in the forest, in Capricorn's old fortress, and took them to the Secret Camp. The man's wounded, quite badly."

Hesitantly, Dustfinger unfolded the paper. He recognized the writing at once.

"She says she knows you. I told her you can't read, but —"

"I can read now," Dustfinger interrupted him. "She taught me."

How did she come to be here? That was all he could think of as Resa's words danced before his eyes. The paper was so crumpled that it was difficult to decipher them. Not that reading had ever come easily to him. . . .

"Yes, she said so, too: 'I taught him,' she told me." Cloud-Dancer looked at him curiously. "Where did you get to know the woman?"

"It's a long story." He put the note in his backpack. "I must be off," he said.

"We're going back this evening, Nettle and I!" Cloud-Dancer called after him. "Shall I tell the woman anything?"

"Yes. Tell her I'll bring her daughter to her."

Cosimo's soldiers were still standing in Smiths' Alley, assessing the merits of a sword, something an ordinary man-at-arms could never afford. There was no sign of the Piper. Brightly colored strips of fabric hung from the windows: Ombra was celebrating the return of its dead prince, but Dustfinger was in no mood to celebrate. The words in his backpack weighed heavily on him, even if he had to admit that it gave him bitter satisfaction to see that Silvertongue obviously had even less luck in this world than he, Dustfinger, had known in Silvertongue's. Did he know what it felt like to be in the wrong story now? Or hadn't he had time to feel anything before Mortola shot him?

People were thronging the street leading up to the castle as if it were market day. Dustfinger looked up at the towers, from which black banners still flew. What did his daughter think of the return of her mistress's husband? *Even if you were to ask Brianna, she wouldn't tell you,* he thought, turning back to the gate. It was time to get out of here before he encountered the Piper again. Or even his master . . .

Meggie was already waiting with Farid under the empty gallows. The boy whispered something to her, and she laughed. *By fire and ashes,* thought Dustfinger, *see how happy those two look, and you have to be the bearer of bad news yet again! Why is it always you? Simple,* he answered himself. *Bad news suits your face better than good news.*

INK-MEDICINE

The memory of my father is wrapped up in
White paper, like sandwiches taken for a day of work.
Just as a magician takes towers and rabbits
Out of his hat, he drew love from his small body.
Yehuda Amichai, "My Father," Isibongo

Meggie stopped laughing as soon as she saw Dustfinger approaching her. Why was his face so grave? Farid had said he was happy. Was it the sight of her that made him look so grim? Was he angry with her because she had followed him into his story, and her face reminded him of years that he surely wanted to forget? "What does he want to talk to me about?" she had asked Farid.

"Probably Fenoglio," Farid had said. "And probably Cosimo, too. He wants to know what the old man is planning!" As if she could have told Dustfinger that . . .

When he stopped in front of her, there was not a sign on his face of the smile that she had always found so hard to interpret.

"Hello, Meggie," he said. A marten blinked sleepily out of his backpack, but it wasn't Gwin. Gwin was sitting on Farid's shoulders and hissed as the other marten's nose showed above Dustfinger's shoulder.

"Hello," she said awkwardly. "How are you?" It was strange to see him again. She felt both pleased and distrustful.

Behind them, people were flowing ceaselessly toward the city gate: peasants, tradesmen, entertainers, beggars, everyone who had heard of Cosimo's return. Although there were no telephones or newspapers in this world, and only the rich wrote letters, news traveled fast here.

"Fine! Yes, I'm really fine!" Now he was smiling after all and not in his usual enigmatic way. Farid had told the truth. Dustfinger was happy. It almost seemed to embarrass him. His face looked so much younger, in spite of the scars; but suddenly it turned grave again.

The other marten jumped down on the ground when his master took the backpack off his shoulders and brought out a piece of paper. "I'd meant to talk to you about Cosimo, our prince who has so surprisingly come back from the dead," he said, unfolding the crumpled piece of paper. "But I think I'd better show you this first."

Baffled, Meggie took the note. When she saw the handwriting, she looked at Dustfinger with incredulity. How had he come by a letter from her mother? Here, in this world?

But all he said was: "Read it." And Meggie read it. The words were like a noose going around her neck, drawing tighter with every word, until she could scarcely breathe.

"What is it?" asked Farid uneasily. "What does it say?" He looked at Dustfinger, but Dustfinger did not answer.

As for Meggie, she was staring at Resa's words. "Mortola — Mortola shot Mo?"

Behind them, people were pushing forward to see Cosimo, the brand-new Cosimo, but why should she be interested? Nothing else mattered to her now. There was just one thing she wanted to know.

"How . . ." she said, and looked at Dustfinger in desperation, "how come they're here? And how is Mo? It's not too bad, is it?"

Dustfinger avoided her eyes. "All I know is what it says there," he said. "Mortola shot your father, Resa is with him in the Secret Camp, and she asked me to look for you. A friend brought me her note. He's going back to the camp this morning, with Nettle. She —"

"Nettle? Resa told me about her!" Meggie interrupted him. "She's a healer, a very good one. . . . She'll make Mo better, won't she?"

"Of course," said Dustfinger, but he still didn't look at her.

Farid's gaze moved from him to Meggie in confusion. "Mortola shot Silvertongue?" he stammered. "Then the root's for him! But you said it was dangerous!"

Dustfinger cast him a warning glance, and Farid fell silent.

"Dangerous?" whispered Meggie. "What's dangerous?"

"Nothing, nothing at all. I'll take you to them right away." Dustfinger slung the backpack over his shoulder. "Go to Fenoglio and tell him you'll be away for a few days. Tell him Farid and I will be with you. I don't suppose the news will relieve his mind very much, but that's too bad. Don't say where we're going, and don't say why! News travels fast in these hills, and it would be better," he added, lowering his voice, "if Mortola doesn't find out that your father is still alive. The camp where he is now is known only to the strolling players, and they've all had to swear an oath never to let anyone who isn't one of us know about the place. But all the same . . ."

". . . oaths are made to be broken!" Meggie finished his sentence for him.

"You said it." Dustfinger looked at the city gate. "Go now. It won't be easy to get through that crowd, but hurry all the same. Tell the old man there's a minstrel woman who lives on that hill, he —"

"He knows who Roxane is," Meggie interrupted.

"Of course!" This time Dustfinger's smile was bitter. "I keep forgetting he knows all about me. Right, tell him to let Roxane know I must be away for a few days. And ask him to keep an eye on my daughter. I suppose he knows who she is, too?"

Meggie just nodded.

"Good," Dustfinger went on. "Then tell the old man something else: If a single one of his accursed words harms Brianna, he'll rue the day he ever thought up a man who can summon fire."

"I'll tell him!" Meggie whispered. Then she ran off, pushing and shoving her way through the crowds of people trying to get into the city. *Mo,* she thought. *Mortola shot Mo.* And her dream came back to her, her red, red dream.

Fenoglio was standing at the window when Meggie stumbled into his room.

"Good heavens, what do you think you look like?" he exclaimed. "Didn't I tell you not to go out while all these people are thronging the streets? But that boy only has to whistle and you go running to him like a well-trained puppy!"

"Stop that!" snapped Meggie, so abruptly that Fenoglio actually did fall silent. "You have to write something for me. And fast!"

She hauled him over to his desk, where Rosenquartz was quietly snoring away.

"Write what?" Confused, Fenoglio dropped into his chair.

"It's my father," faltered Meggie, taking one of the freshly sharpened quill pens out of the jug with shaking fingers. "He's here, but Mortola's shot him. He's very sick! Dustfinger didn't want to say so, but I could tell from the way he looked, so please write something, anything that will make him well again. He's in the forest in the strolling players' Secret Camp. Please, hurry!"

Fenoglio looked at her in bewilderment. "Shot your father? And he's here? But why? I don't understand!"

"You don't have to understand!" cried Meggie desperately. "You just have to help him. Dustfinger's going to take me to him. And I'll read him better, understand? I mean, he's in your story now, you can even bring back the dead, so why can't you heal a wound, too? Please!" She dipped the pen in the inkwell and put it into his hand.

"Heavens, Meggie!" murmured Fenoglio. "This is bad, but . . . but with the best will in the world I don't know what to write. I don't even know where he is. If at least I knew what the place looks like . . ."

Meggie stared at him. Suddenly, the tears she had been holding back all this time were flowing. "Please!" she whispered. "Just try! Dustfinger's waiting. Outside by the gate."

Fenoglio looked at her and gently took the pen from her hand.

"I'll try, then," he said hoarsely. "You're right, this is my story. I couldn't have helped him in the other world, but perhaps I can here. Go to the window," he told her, when she had brought him two sheets of parchment. "And look out of it, look at the people in the streets or the birds in the sky, occupy your mind somehow. Just don't look at me or I won't be able to write."

Meggie obeyed. She saw Minerva and her children down in the crowd, and the woman who lived opposite; she watched pigs grunting as they pushed past the people, soldiers with the Laughing Prince's emblem on their chests — yet she wasn't really seeing any of it. She just heard Fenoglio dip his pen in the inkwell, heard it scratching over the parchment, pausing, and writing on again. *Please*, she thought, *please let him find the right words. Please.* The pen fell silent for a painfully long time, while down in the street a beggar pushed a child aside with his crutch. Time passed slowly, like a shadow spreading. People thronged the streets, one dog barked at another, trumpets sounded from the castle, ringing out above the rooftops.

Meggie couldn't have said how much time had passed when, with a sigh, Fenoglio put down his pen. Rosenquartz was still snoring, stretched out straight as a ruler behind the sandbox. Fenoglio reached into the box and sprinkled sand over the wet ink.

"Did you — did you think of something?" Meggie hesitantly asked.

"Yes, yes, but don't ask me if I got it right."

He handed her the parchment, and her eyes skimmed the words. There weren't many of them, but if they were indeed the right words, they would be enough.

"I didn't make him up, Meggie!" said Fenoglio in a soft voice. "Your father isn't one of my characters, like Cosimo and Dustfinger and Capricorn. He doesn't belong here. So don't hope for too much, will you?"

Meggie nodded as she rolled up the parchment. "Dustfinger wants you to keep an eye on his daughter while he's gone."

"His daughter? Dustfinger has a daughter? Did I write that? Oh yes — indeed, weren't there two of them?"

"You know one of them, anyway. She's Brianna, Her Ugliness's maid."

"Brianna?" Fenoglio looked at her in astonishment.

"Yes." Meggie picked up the leather bag that she had brought with her from the other world and went to the door. "Look after her. I'm to say that if you don't, you'll rue the day you ever thought up someone who can call on fire."

"He said that?" Fenoglio pushed back his chair and laughed. "You know something? I like him better and better. I believe I'll write another story about him, a story where he's the hero, and he doesn't —"

"Die?" Meggie opened the door. "I'll tell him, but I think he's had more than enough of being in one of your stories."

"But he *is* in one. He came back into my story of his own free will!" Fenoglio called after her as she hurried down the steps. "We're all in it, Meggie, up to our necks in it! When are you coming back? I want you to meet Cosimo!"

Meggie did not reply. How was she to know when she'd be coming back?

"You call that hurrying?" asked Dustfinger, when she was standing before him again, out of breath and putting Fenoglio's parchment in her bag. "What's that parchment for? Did the old man give you one of his songs for nourishment along the way?"

"Something like that," replied Meggie.

"Just so long as my name's not in it," said Dustfinger, turning toward the road.

"Is it far?" called Meggie, as she hurried after him and Farid.

"We'll be there by evening," said Dustfinger, over his shoulder.

36

SCREAMS

I want to see thirst
In the syllables,
Touch fire
In the sound;
Feel through the dark
For the scream.

Pablo Neruda, "Word," *Five Decades*

The White Women were still there. Resa didn't seem to see them anymore, but Mo felt their presence like shadows in sunlight. He didn't tell her about them. She looked so tired. The one thing that still kept her going was her hope that Dustfinger would soon arrive — with Meggie.

"You wait and see, he'll find her," Resa kept whispering to him when he shook with fever. How could she be so sure? As if Dustfinger had never let them down, never stolen the book, never betrayed them . . . Meggie. The need to see her once again was even stronger than the enticing whispers of the White Women, stronger than the pain in his breast . . . and who could say, perhaps this accursed story might yet take a turn for the better? Although Mo remembered Fenoglio's preference for unhappy endings only too well.

"Tell me what it looks like outside," he sometimes whispered to Resa. "It's ridiculous to be in a whole different world and see nothing of it but a cave." And Resa described what he couldn't see — the trees, so much taller and older than any trees he had ever set eyes on, the fairies like swarms of gnats among the branches, the glass men in the tall bracken, and the nameless terrors of the night. Once she caught a fairy — Dustfinger had told her how to do it — and took it to him. She held the little creature in the hollow of her hands and put it close to his ear, so that he could hear the fairy's chirping, indignant voice.

It all seemed so real, however often he told himself it was made of nothing but paper and ink. The hard ground where he lay, the dry leaves that rustled when he tossed and turned in his fever, the bear's hot breath — and the Black Prince, whom he had last seen in the pages of a book. Now the man himself sometimes sat beside him, cooling his brow and talking quietly to Resa. Or was it all just a fevered dream?

Death felt real in this Inkworld, too. Very real. It was strange to encounter death here in a world out of a book. But even if the dying was made only of words — even if, perhaps, it was nothing but a game played by the letters on the page — his body thought it was real. His heart felt fear, his flesh felt pain. And the White Women had not gone away, even if Resa couldn't see them. Mo felt them near him, every minute, every hour, every day, and every night. Fenoglio's angels of death. Did they make dying easier than it was in the world he came from? No. Nothing could make it easier. You lost what you loved. That was death, here as well as there.

It was light outside when Mo heard the first scream. At first he thought the fever was taking hold of him again. But then he saw from Resa's face that she could hear it, too: the clash of weapons and screaming. Cries of fear — death cries. Mo tried to sit up, but the pain pounced on him like an animal digging its teeth into his chest. He saw the Black Prince standing outside the cave, his sword drawn; he saw Resa jump up. Fever made her face blur before his eyes, but then Mo suddenly saw another picture: He saw Meggie sitting in Fenoglio's kitchen staring at the old man in horror as, full of pride, he told her of the fine death scene he had written for Dustfinger. Oh yes, Fenoglio liked sad stories. And perhaps he had just written another.

"Resa!" Mo cursed the way his tongue felt, heavy with fever, "Resa, go and hide — hide somewhere in the forest."

But she stayed with him as she always had — except for that one day, the day when his own voice had banished her.

37

BLOODSTAINED STRAW

Goblins burrowed in the earth, elves sang songs in the trees: Those were the obvious wonders of reading, but behind them lay the fundamental marvel that, in stories, words could command things to be.

Francis Spufford, *The Child That Books Built*

Meggie had often felt frightened in the Wayless Wood with Farid, but it was different with Dustfinger. The trees seemed to rustle more loudly when he passed them, the bushes seemed to reach their branches out to him. Fairies settled on his backpack like butterflies on a flower, pulling his hair until he brushed them away, talking to them. Other creatures, too, appeared and disappeared, beings whose names Meggie didn't know either from Resa's stories or from any other source, some of them no more than a pair of eyes among the trees.

Dustfinger led them as purposefully as if he could see their road laid out like a red guideline before him. He never even stopped to rest, but took them on and on, uphill and downhill, going deeper into the forest every hour. Away from human beings. When at last he stopped, Meggie's legs were shaking with exhaustion. It must be late in the afternoon. Dustfinger passed his hand over the snapped twigs of a bush, bent down, examined the damp ground, and picked up a handful of berries that had been trodden underfoot.

"What's the matter?" asked Farid anxiously.

"Too many feet. And above all, too many boots."

Dustfinger swore quietly and began to go faster. Too many boots . . . Meggie realized what he meant when the camp appeared among the trees. She saw tents that had been torn down, a trampled campfire . . .

"You two stay here!" Dustfinger ordered, and this time they obeyed. They watched anxiously as he stepped out of the shelter of the trees, looked around, raised tent panels, reached his hand into cold ashes — and turned over two bodies lying motionless near the fireplace. Meggie was going to follow him when she saw the corpses, but Farid held her back. When Dustfinger disappeared into a cave and came out again, pale-faced, Meggie tore herself away and ran to him.

"Where are my parents? Are they in there?" She recoiled as her foot struck another dead body.

"No, there's no one left in there. But I found this." Dustfinger held out a strip of fabric. Resa had a dress with that pattern. The fabric was bloodstained. "Do you know it?"

Meggie nodded.

"Then your parents really were here. The blood is probably your father's." Dustfinger passed a hand over his face. "Perhaps someone got away — someone who can tell us what happened here. I'll take a look around. Farid!"

Farid hurried to his side. Meggie was going to thrust her way past the two of them, but Dustfinger held her back. "Listen,

Meggie!" he said, putting his hands on her shoulders. "The fact that your parents aren't here is a good sign. It probably means they're still alive. There's a bed in the cave; I expect your mother was nursing your father there. And I've found a bear's paw prints, which means the Black Prince was here. Perhaps all this was a plan to capture him, although I don't know why they would have taken the others . . . no, that I don't understand."

Before setting off with Farid in search of survivors, Dustfinger told Meggie to wait in the cave. The entrance was tall and broad enough for a man to stand in it upright. The cave beyond it led deep into the mountain. The ground was strewn with leaves, and blankets and beds of straw were arranged side by side there, some of them just the right size for a child.

It was not difficult to see where Mo had been lying. The straw in that place was bloodstained, like the blanket beside it. A bowl of water, an overturned wooden mug, a bunch of dried flowers . . . Meggie picked them up and ran her fingers over the petals. She kneeled down and stared at the bloodstained straw. Fenoglio's parchment was close to her breast, but Mo was gone. How could Fenoglio's words help him now?

Try, something inside her whispered. *You can't tell how powerful his words are in this world. It's made of them, after all.*

She heard footsteps behind her. Farid and Dustfinger were back, and Dustfinger was holding a child in his arms, a little girl. She stared at Meggie, wide-eyed, as if she were in a bad dream and couldn't wake up.

"She wouldn't talk to me, but luckily Farid inspires rather more confidence," said Dustfinger, carefully putting the child down on her feet. "She says her name is Lianna and she's five years old. And there were a lot of men: silver men with swords, and snakes on their breasts. Not so very surprising, if you ask me. They obviously killed the guards and some of those who defended themselves, and then took the rest away, even the women and children. As for the wounded" — he glanced briefly at Meggie — "they were clearly loaded onto some kind of cart. The men had no horses with them. The girl is here only because her mother told her to hide among the trees."

Gwin scurried into the cave, followed by Jink. The little girl jumped when the martens leaped up at Dustfinger. Then she watched, fascinated, as Farid took Gwin off Dustfinger's shoulder and put him on his own lap.

"Ask her if there were other children here," said Dustfinger softly.

Farid held up five fingers and showed them to the girl. "How many children, Lianna?"

The child looked at him and tapped first Farid's forefinger, then his second and third fingers. "Merle. Fabio. Tinka," she whispered.

"Three," said Dustfinger. "Probably no older than she is."

Timidly, Lianna put out her hand to stroke Gwin's bushy tail, but Dustfinger held her fingers in a firm grip. "Better not," he said gently. "He bites. Try the other one."

"Meggie?" Farid came over to her. But Meggie did not answer him. She wound her arms tightly around her knees and buried her face in her skirt. She didn't want to see the cave anymore. She didn't want to see any of Fenoglio's world anymore, not even Farid and Dustfinger or the girl who didn't know where her own parents were, either. She wanted to be in Elinor's library, sitting in the big armchair where Elinor liked to read, and she wanted to see Mo put his head around the door and ask what the book on her lap was. But Mo wasn't here, perhaps he was gone forever, and Fenoglio's story held her fast in its black, inky arms, whispering terrible things to her — about armed men who dragged away children, old people, the sick . . . mothers and fathers.

"Nettle will soon be here with Cloud-Dancer," she heard Dustfinger say. "She'll look after the child."

"What about us?" asked Farid.

"I'll follow them," said Dustfinger. "To find out how many are still alive and where they're being taken. Although I think I know."

Meggie raised her head. "To the Castle of Night."

"Good guess."

The girl put her hand out to Jink; she was still small enough to find comfort for her grief in stroking an animal's fur. Meggie envied her.

"What do you mean, *you'll* follow them?" Farid shooed Gwin off his lap and stood up.

"Exactly what I said." Dustfinger's face was as uncommunicative as a closed door. "*I* will follow them while you two wait here for Cloud-Dancer and Nettle. Tell them I'm trying to follow the trail, and Cloud-Dancer is to take you back to Ombra. He's not fast enough to follow me with his stiff leg. Then tell Roxane what's happened, so she doesn't think I've vanished again, and Meggie will stay with Fenoglio." His face was as well controlled as ever when he looked at her, but in his eyes Meggie saw all that she herself was feeling: fear, anxiety, anger . . . helpless anger.

"But we have to help them!" Farid's voice shook.

"How? The Black Prince might have been able to save them, but they've obviously caught him, and I don't know anyone else ready to risk his life for a few strolling players."

"What about that robber everyone's talking about, the Bluejay?"

"There's no such person." Meggie's voice was little more than a whisper. "Fenoglio made him up."

"Really?" Dustfinger looked at her thoughtfully. "I've heard otherwise, but still . . . well, as soon as you're in Ombra, get Cloud-Dancer to go to the strolling players and tell them what's happened. I know the Prince has men at his command, men who are devoted to him and probably well armed as well, but I've no idea where they are. Perhaps one of the strolling players may know. Or Cloud-Dancer himself. He must try to get word to them somehow. There's a mill in Argenta called the Spelt-Mill, It's always been one of the few places south of the forest where people can meet or exchange news without the risk that it will come to the Adderhead's ears at once. The miller is so rich he doesn't even have to fear the men-at-arms. So if anyone wants to see me, or has any idea of how we can help the prisoners, let him send news there. I'll drop in now and then to ask if any messages have come. Understand?"

Meggie nodded. "The Spelt-Mill," she repeated quietly, unable to look anywhere but at the bloodstained straw.

"Right, Meggie can do all that, but I'm going with you." Farid's voice sounded so defiant that the little girl, still kneeling silently beside Meggie, was upset and reached for her hand.

"I'm warning you, don't start on about looking after me again!" Dustfinger's voice was so sharp that Farid lowered his eyes. "I'm going alone, and that's that. You take care of Meggie and the child until Nettle comes, and then get Cloud-Dancer to take you to Ombra."

"No!" Meggie saw the tears in Farid's eyes, but Dustfinger just walked toward the cave entrance without another word. Gwin scuttled in front of him.

"If it gets dark before they arrive," he added, looking over his shoulder at Farid, "then light a fire. Not because of the soldiers. They have what they came for, but wolves and Night-Mares are always hungry: the wolves for your flesh, the Night-Mares for your fear."

Then he was gone, and Farid stood there, his eyes blurred with tears. "That bloody bastard!" he whispered. "That thrice-accursed son of a bitch! But he'll soon see. I'm going to follow him. I *will* look after him! I swore I would." Abruptly, he kneeled down in front of Meggie and took her hand. "You will go to Ombra, won't you? Please. I have to go after him. I know you understand!"

Meggie said nothing. What was there to say? That she wasn't going back any more than he was? He'd only have tried to persuade her not to go on. Jink rubbed against Farid's legs, and then scurried outside. The little girl ran after the marten but stopped at the entrance to the cave — a small, forlorn figure, all alone. *Like me,* thought Meggie.

Without looking at Farid, she took Fenoglio's parchment out of her belt. The letters could scarcely be made out in the twilight that filled the cave.

"What's that?" Farid straightened up.

"Words. Only words, but better than nothing."

"Wait, I'll give you a light." Farid rubbed his fingertips together and whispered. A tiny flame appeared on his thumb-nail. He blew gently on the little flame, until it grew like the flame of a candle, and then held his thumb above the parchment. The flickering light made the letters shine as if Rosenquartz had retraced them with fresh ink.

Useless, something whispered in Meggie. *The words will be useless! Mo isn't here, he's far away, he may not even be alive any-more. Shut up!* she snapped at this internal voice. *I'm not listening.*

This is all I can do, there's nothing else, nothing at all! She picked up the bloodstained blanket, placed the parchment on it, and ran her fingers over her lips. The little girl was still standing outside the cave, waiting for her mother to come back.

"Read it, Meggie!" Farid nodded at her encouragingly.

And she read it, her fingers clutching the blanket stained with Mo's dried blood. *"Mortimer felt the pain. . . ."* She thought she felt it herself, in the sound of every letter on her tongue, in every word that passed her lips. *"The wound was burning. It burned like the hatred in Mortola's eyes when she had shot him. Perhaps it was her hatred that was sucking the life out of him, making him weaker and weaker. He felt his own blood wet and warm on his skin. He felt Death reaching out to him. But all of a sudden there was something else, too: words. Words that relieved the pain, cooled his brow, and spoke of love, nothing but love. They made his breathing easier again and healed the place where death had been flowing in. He felt the sound of them on his skin and deep in his heart. They echoed ever louder, ever more clearly through the darkness that threatened to swallow him up, and suddenly he knew the voice speaking the words: It was his daughter's voice, and the White Women withdrew their pale hands as if they had burned themselves on her love."*

Meggie buried her face in her hands. The parchment rolled up on her lap of its own accord, as if it had served its purpose. Straw pricked her through her dress, as it had in the shed where Capricorn had once imprisoned her and Mo. She felt someone stroking her hair, and for a moment, a crazy moment, she thought Fenoglio's words had brought Mo back, back to the cave safe and sound, and everything was all right again. But when she raised her head, it was only Farid standing beside her.

"That was beautiful," he said. "I'm sure it helped. You wait and see."

But Meggie shook her head. "No!" she whispered. "No. Those were only beautiful words, but my father isn't made of Fenoglio's words. He's made of flesh and blood."

"So? What difference does that make?" Farid removed her hands from her tearstained face. "Perhaps everything's just made of words. Look at me, for instance. Pinch me. Am I made of paper?"

No, he wasn't. And Meggie had to smile when he kissed her, although she was still shedding tears.

Dustfinger had not been gone long when they heard footsteps among the trees. Farid had taken Dustfinger's advice and made a fire, and Meggie was sitting close to him with the little girl's head on her lap. Nettle said not a word as she emerged from the darkness and saw the wrecked camp. Silently, she went from one dead body to another, looking for life where none was left, while Cloud-Dancer, his face unmoving, listened to the message Dustfinger had left for him. It was only when Meggie asked Cloud-Dancer to take a message, not just to Roxane and the strolling players but to Fenoglio, too, that Farid fully realized she didn't intend to go back to Ombra any more than he did. His expressionless face didn't show whether he was angry or glad.

"I've written my message for Fenoglio." With a heavy heart, Meggie had torn a page for it out of the notebook that Mo had given her. On the other hand, what better use could she put it to than saving him? If it was still possible to save him. "You'll find Fenoglio in Minerva's house, in Cobblers' Alley. And it's very important that no one else reads the message."

"I know the Inkweaver!" Cloud-Dancer watched Nettle draw a ragged cloak over the face of another dead man. Then he frowned at the sheet of paper with Meggie's writing on it.

"There've been messengers who were hanged for the words they carried. I hope these aren't that kind? No, don't tell me!" he said defensively as Meggie was about to answer. "Usually, I ask the sender to tell me the words of any message I carry, but with this one I have a feeling I'd better not know."

"What do you suppose she's written?" asked Nettle bitterly. "No doubt she was thanking the old man for writing the songs that will bring her father to the gallows! Or is he to write a dirge for him, the Bluejay's last song? I scented misfortune the moment I saw that scar on his arm. I always thought the Bluejay was just a legend, like all the noble princes and princesses in other songs. Well, you were wrong there, Nettle, said I to myself, and you're certainly not the first to notice the scar. So the Inkweaver had to go and describe it in detail! Curse the old fool and his silly songs! Men have been hanged before because they were taken for the Bluejay, but now it seems the Adderhead has the right man in his hands, and the game of playing heroes is over. Protecting the weak, robbing the strong . . . Yes, it all sounds very fine, but heroes aren't immortal except in songs, and your father will find only too soon that a mask doesn't protect you from death."

Meggie just sat there and stared at the old woman. What was she talking about?

"Why are you looking at me like that, so surprised?" asked Nettle. "Do you think the Adderhead sent his men here for a few old strolling players and pregnant women, or for the Black Prince? Nonsense. The Black Prince never hid from the Adder yet. No. Someone slipped off to the Castle of Night and whispered in the Adderhead's ear that the Bluejay was lying wounded in the strolling players' Secret Camp and could easily be picked up, along with the poor players who were hiding him.

It will have been someone who knows the camp and has surely been paid good silver for his treachery. The Adderhead will make a great spectacle of the execution, the Inkweaver will write a touching song about it, and perhaps someone else will soon wear the feathered mask, for they'll go on singing those songs long after your father's dead and buried behind the Castle of Night."

Meggie heard her own blood surging through her veins.

"What scar are you talking about?" Her voice was little more than a whisper.

"Why, the scar on his left arm! Surely you must know it? The songs say that the Adderhead's hounds bit the Bluejay there when he was hunting their master's White Stags. . . ."

Fenoglio. What had he done?

Meggie covered her mouth with her hand. She once again heard Fenoglio's voice on the spiral staircase as they were going down from Balbulus's workshop: *"I like to base my characters on real people. Not every writer does that, but in my experience it makes them more lifelike! Facial expressions, gestures, the way someone walks, a voice, perhaps a birthmark or a scar — I steal something here, something there, and then they begin to breathe, until anyone hearing or reading about them thinks they can touch them! I didn't have a wide choice for the Bluejay. . . ."*

Mo. Fenoglio had taken her father as his model.

Meggie stared at the sleeping child. She, too, had often slept like that, with her head in Mo's lap.

"Meggie's father is the Bluejay?" Farid, beside her, uttered an incredulous laugh. "What nonsense! Silvertongue can't even bring himself to kill a rabbit. You mark my words, Meggie, the Adderhead will soon realize that, and then he'll let him go. Come on!" He rose to his feet and offered her his hand. "We must start out or we'll never catch up with Dustfinger!"

"You're going after him now?" Nettle shook her head at such folly, while Meggie laid the little girl's head down on the grass.

"Keep going south if you miss his trail in the dark," said Cloud-Dancer. "Due south, and then you'll reach the road sometime. But beware of wolves. There are many wolves in these parts."

Farid just nodded. "I have fire with me," he said, making a spark dance on the palm of his hand.

Cloud-Dancer grinned. "Well done! Perhaps you really are Dustfinger's son, as Roxane suspects!"

"Who knows?" was all Farid would reply, and he led Meggie away with him.

She followed him into the dark trees, feeling numb. A robber! She could think of nothing else. He had made Mo into a robber, a part of his story! At that moment she hated Fenoglio just as much as Dustfinger did.

An Audience for Fenoglio

"Lady Cora," he said, "sometimes one has to do things which are unpalatable. When great issues are involved one can't toy with the situation in silk gloves. No. We are making history."
Mervyn Peake, *Titus Groan*

Fenoglio was pacing up and down his room. Seven steps to the window, seven back to the door. Meggie had gone, and there was no one who could tell him if she'd found her father still alive. What an appalling muddle! Whenever he began to hope he was getting things under control again, something happened that did not remotely suit his plans. Perhaps another man really did exist somewhere — a diabolical storyteller who was continuing his tale, giving it new twists and turns, unpredictable and unpleasant developments, moving his characters as if they were chessmen, or simply placing new ones who had nothing to do with his own story on the chessboard!

And still Cosimo had sent no messenger. *Well, I must exercise a little more patience*, Fenoglio told himself. *He's only just ascended his throne, and I'm sure he has a great deal to do. All his subjects wanting to see him, petitioners, widows, orphans, his administrators, gamekeepers, his son, his wife* . . . "Oh, nonsense! I'm the one he should have sent for first of all!" Fenoglio uttered the words so angrily that he was startled by the sound of his own voice. "I, the man who brought him back to life, who made him in the first place!"

He went to the window and looked up at the castle. The Adderhead's banner flew from the left-hand tower. Yes, the Adderhead was in Ombra and must have ridden like the devil to see in person his son-in-law, newly back from the dead. He hadn't brought Firefox with him this time; no doubt the man was busy looting or murdering elsewhere on his master's behalf, but the Piper was still abroad in the streets of Ombra, always with a few men-at-arms in his wake. What did they want here? Did the Adderhead still seriously hope to place his grandson on the throne?

No, Cosimo would never allow it.

For a moment Fenoglio forgot his dark mood, and a smile stole over his face. Ah, if he could only have told the Adderhead who had wrecked his fine plans! A writer! How that would have angered him! They had given him an unpleasant surprise — he with his words, Meggie with her voice. . . .

Poor Meggie . . . poor Mortimer . . .

How pleadingly she had looked at him. And what a farcical performance he had put on for her! Yet how could the poor thing have thought for a moment that he could help her father, when he himself hadn't even brought Mortimer here? Quite apart from the fact that Mortimer wasn't one of his creations in the first place. But that look of hers! He simply had not the heart to let her leave without any hope at all!

Rosenquartz was sitting on the desk with his transparent legs crossed, throwing bread crumbs at the fairies.

"Stop that!" Fenoglio snapped. "Do you want them to grab you by the legs and try throwing you out of the window again? I won't save you this time, believe you me. I won't even sweep you up when you're a little pile of broken glass down there in the pigs' muck. The garbage collector can shovel you into his barrow instead."

"That's right, take your bad temper out on me!" The glass man turned his back on Fenoglio. "It won't make Cosimo summon you any sooner, though!"

Here, unfortunately, he was right. Fenoglio went to the window. In the streets below, the excitement over Cosimo's return had died down, and perhaps the Adderhead's presence had cast a damper on it, too. People were going about their business again, the pigs were rooting about among the trash, children were chasing one another around the close-packed houses, and now and then an armed soldier made his way through the crowd. There were clearly more soldiers around than usual in Ombra now. Cosimo was obviously having them patrol the city, perhaps to prevent the men-at-arms from riding his subjects down again just because they were in the way. *Yes, Cosimo will see to everything,* thought Fenoglio. *He'll be a good prince, insofar as any princes are good. Who knows, perhaps he'll even allow the strolling players back into Ombra on ordinary market days soon.*

"That's it. That will be my first piece of advice. To let the players back again," murmured Fenoglio. "And if he doesn't send for me by this evening I'll go to him unasked. What's the ungrateful fellow thinking of? Does he suppose men get brought back from the dead every day?"

"I thought he'd never been dead at all." Rosenquartz

clambered up to his nest. He was out of reach there, as he very well knew. "What about Meggie's father, then? Do you think he's still alive?"

"How should I know?" replied Fenoglio irritably. He didn't want to be reminded of Mortimer. "Well, at least no one can blame me for *that* mess!" he growled. "I can't help it if they're all knocking my story around, like a tree that just has to be thoroughly pruned to make it bear fruit."

"Pruned?" Rosenquartz piped up. "No, they're adding things. Your story is growing — growing like a weed! And not a particularly pretty one, either, if you ask me."

Fenoglio was just wondering whether to throw the inkwell at him when Minerva put her head around the door.

"A messenger, Fenoglio!" Her face was flushed, as if she had run too fast. "A messenger from the castle! He wants to see you! Cosimo wants to see you!"

Fenoglio hurried to the door, smoothing down the tunic that Minerva had made him. He had been wearing it for days, it was badly crumpled, but there was no helping that now. When he had tried to pay Minerva for it she had just shaken her head, saying he'd paid already — with the stories he told her children day after day, evening after evening. It was a fine tunic, though, even if fairy tales for children had paid for it.

The messenger was waiting down in the street outside the house, looking important and frowning impatiently. He wore the black mourning cloak, as if the Prince of Sighs were still on the throne.

Oh well, it will all be different now, thought Fenoglio. *It will most definitely be different. From now on I, and not my characters, will be telling this story again.*

His guide didn't even look around at him as he hurried along the streets after the man. *Surly oaf!* Fenoglio thought. But this character probably really was a product of his, Fenoglio's, pen — one of the many anonymous people with whom he had populated this world so that his main characters wouldn't be rattling around it on their own.

A number of men-at-arms were loafing around outside the stables in the Outer Courtyard of the castle. Fenoglio wondered, with annoyance, what they were doing there. Cosimo's men were pacing back and forth up on the battlements, like hounds set to keep watch on a pack of wolves. The men-at-arms stared up at them with hostility. *Yes, you look at that,* thought Fenoglio. *There'll be no leading part in my story for your dark lord, only a death fit for a thoroughgoing villain.* Perhaps he'd invent another one sometime, for stories soon get boring without a proper villain, but it was unlikely that Meggie would lend him her voice to call such a character to life.

The guards at the Inner Gate raised their spears.

"What's all this?" Fenoglio heard the Adderhead's voice the moment he set foot in the Inner Courtyard. "Are you telling me he's still keeping me waiting, you lousy fur-faced creature?"

A softer voice answered, apprehensive and scared. Fenoglio saw the Laughing Prince's dwarfish servant, Tullio, facing the Adderhead. He only came up to the prince's silver-studded belt. Two of the Laughing Prince's guards stood behind him, but the Adderhead was at the head of at least twenty heavily armed men: an intimidating sight, even if Firefox wasn't with them, nor was there any sign of the Piper.

"Your daughter will receive you, sir." Tullio's voice shook like a leaf in the wind.

"My daughter? If I want Violante's company I'll summon her to my own castle. No, I want to see this dead man who's come to life! So you will now take me to Cosimo at once, you stinking brownie bastard!"

The unfortunate Tullio began trembling. "The Prince of Ombra," he began again, in a thread of a voice, "will not receive you!"

These words made Fenoglio stumble back as if he had been struck in the chest — right into the nearest rosebush, where the thorns caught in his new tunic. What was going on? Cosimo wouldn't receive the Adderhead? Was that part of his own plan?

The Adderhead thrust out his lips as if he had a bad taste in his mouth. The veins at his temples stood out, dark on his blotched and ruddy skin. His lizardlike eyes stared down at Tullio. Then he took the crossbow from the nearest soldier's hand and, as Tullio ducked like a frightened rabbit, aimed at one of the birds in the sky above. It was a good shot. The bird fell right at the Adderhead's feet, its yellow feathers red with blood. A gold-mocker: Fenoglio had invented them especially for the castle of the Prince of Sighs. The Adderhead bent and pulled the arrow out of its tiny breast.

"Here, take that!" he said, pressing the dead bird into Tullio's hand. "And tell your master that he has obviously left his common sense behind in the realm of the dead. I'll allow that to be some excuse this once, but should he send you to me with such an outrageous message when next I visit him, he'll get not a bird back but you with an arrow in *your* breast. Will you tell him that?"

Tullio stared at the bloodstained bird he was holding and nodded.

As for the Adderhead, he turned on his heel and waved to his men to follow him. Fenoglio's guide bent his head timorously as they marched past. *Look him straight in the eye!*

339

Fenoglio told himself as the Adderhead passed so close to him that he thought he could smell his sweat. *You invented him!* But instead he hunched his head between his shoulders, like a tortoise sensing danger, and did not move until the Inner Gate had closed behind the last of the men-at-arms.

Tullio was still waiting at the door that had shut behind the Adderhead, staring at the dead bird in his hand. "Should I show it to Cosimo?" he asked, looking distressed, as they came up to him.

"Oh, have it roasted in the kitchen and eat it if you like!" Fenoglio's guide snarled at him. "But get out of my way."

The throne room hadn't changed since Fenoglio's last visit. The windows were still hung with black. The only light came from candles, and the blank eyes of the statues stared at everyone who approached the throne itself. But now their living, breathing model sat on the throne, resembling his stone copies so much that the dark hall seemed to Fenoglio like a house of mirrors.

Cosimo was alone. Neither Her Ugliness nor her son was to be seen. There were only six guards standing in the background, almost invisible in the dim light.

Fenoglio stopped at a suitable distance from the steps up to the throne and bowed. Although it was his opinion that no one in this or any other world deserved to have him — Fenoglio — bow his head to them, certainly not those whom his own words had called to life, nevertheless he, too, had to observe the rules of the game in this world of his own creation. Here it was as natural to bow to nobles dressed in silk and velvet as it had been to shake hands in his old world.

Go on, then, old man, bow, even if it hurts your back, he thought, bending his head a little more humbly. *You fixed it this way yourself.*

Cosimo examined him as if he were not sure whether he remembered his face. He was dressed entirely in white, which emphasized his likeness to the statues even more.

"You are the poet Fenoglio, also known as the Inkweaver, is that so?" Fenoglio had imagined that the voice would be rather fuller. Cosimo looked at the statues, letting his eyes wander from one to another. "Someone recommended me to summon you. I believe it was my wife. She says you have the cleverest mind to be found between this castle and the Adderhead's, and she thinks I shall need clever minds. But that's not why I called for you."

Violante? Violante had recommended him? Fenoglio tried to hide his surprise. "No? Why then, Your Grace?" he asked.

Cosimo's eyes rested on him as abstractedly as if he were looking straight through him. Then he glanced down at himself, plucked at the magnificent tunic he wore, and adjusted his belt. "My clothes don't fit anymore," he observed. "They're all a little too long or too wide, as if they'd been made for those statues and not for me."

He smiled at Fenoglio rather helplessly. It was the smile of an angel.

"You . . . er . . . you've been through a difficult time, Your Grace," said Fenoglio.

"Yes. Yes, so I'm told. You see, I don't remember. There's very little I can remember at all. My head feels strangely empty." He passed a hand over his brow and looked at the statues again. "That's why I summoned you," he said. "They say you're a master of words, and I want you to help me remember. I'm giving you the task of writing down everything there is to say about Cosimo. Get my soldiers to tell you, my servants, my old nurse, my . . . wife." He hesitated for a moment before saying that last word. "Balbulus will write your stories out and illuminate them, and then I'll have them read to me, to fill the empty space in my head and heart with words and images again. Do you think you can do it?"

Fenoglio hastily nodded. "Oh yes, of course, Your Grace. I'll write it all down. Stories of your childhood, when your worthy father was still alive, tales of your first rides through the Wayless Wood, everything about the day your wife came to this castle, and the day your son was born."

Cosimo nodded. "Yes, yes!" he said, and there was relief in his voice. "I see you understand. And don't forget my victory over the fire-raisers and the time I spent with the White Women."

"I certainly will not." Fenoglio examined the handsome face as unobtrusively as possible. How could this have happened? He had been meant not just to believe that he was the real Cosimo, but to share all the dead man's memories, too. . . .

Cosimo rose from the throne occupied by his father not so long ago and began pacing up and down. "I've already been told several stories myself. By my wife."

Her Ugliness again. Fenoglio looked around for her. "Where is your wife?"

"Looking for my son. He ran away because I wouldn't receive his grandfather."

"If I may make so bold, Your Grace — why wouldn't you receive him?"

The heavy door opened behind Fenoglio's back, and Tullio scurried in. He was no longer holding the dead bird as he crouched on the steps at Cosimo's feet, but fear still lingered on his face.

"I do not intend ever to receive him again." Cosimo stopped in front of the throne and patted the emblem of his house. "I have told the guards at the gate not to let my father-in-law into this castle another time, or any who serve him."

Tullio looked up at him in alarm and incredulity, as if he already felt the Adderhead's arrow in his own furry breast.

But Cosimo, unmoved, was continuing. "I have had myself informed of what went on in my realm while I" — and he hesitated for a moment again before going on — "while I was away. Yes, let's call it that: away. I have listened to my administrators, head foresters, merchants and peasants, my soldiers, and my wife. In the process I have learned some very interesting things. Alarming things. And just imagine, poet: My father-in-law had something to do with almost every bad tale that I hear. Tell me, since I believe you go in and out of the strolling players' tents: What do the Motley Folk say about the Adderhead?"

"The Motley Folk?" Fenoglio cleared his throat. "Well, what everyone says. They say he's very powerful, perhaps rather too powerful."

Cosimo uttered a mirthless laugh. "Oh yes. He is indeed. And?"

What was he getting at? *You should know, Fenoglio,* he told himself uneasily. *If you don't know what's going on in his head, then who does?* "Well, they say the Adderhead rules with an iron fist," he went on hesitantly. "There's no law in Argenta but his own word and his seal. He is vengeful and vain, he extorts so much from his peasants that they go hungry, he sends rebellious subjects to his silver mines, even children, until they're spitting blood down in the depths. Poachers caught in his part of the forest are blinded, thieves have their right hands cut off — I am glad to say your father abolished that custom some time ago — and the only minstrel who can safely approach the Castle of

Night is the Piper — when he's not plundering villages with Firefox." *Good heavens, did I write all this?* thought Fenoglio. *I suppose I did.*

"Yes, I've heard all that, too. What else?" Cosimo folded his arms over his chest and began pacing up and down, up and down. He really was as beautiful as an angel. *Perhaps I ought to have made him a little less beautiful,* thought Fenoglio. *He looks almost unreal.*

"What else?" Fenoglio frowned. "The Adderhead was always afraid of death, but as he gets older they say it's become almost an obsession. He is said to spend the night on his knees, sobbing and cursing, shaking with fear that the White Women will come for him. They also say that he washes several times a day, for fear of sickness and infection, and he sends envoys to distant lands, with chests full of silver to buy him miracle cures for old age. And the women he marries are younger and younger. He hopes that a son will be born to him at long last."

Cosimo had stopped pacing. "Yes!" he said softly. "Yes, I have heard all that, too. But there are even worse stories. When are you coming to those — or must I tell them myself?" And before Fenoglio could answer he went on. "They say the Adderhead sends Firefox over the border by night to extort goods from my peasants. They say he claims the whole Wayless Wood for himself, he has my merchants plundered when they come ashore in his harbors, demands high tolls from them for the use of his streets and bridges, and pays footpads to make my roads unsafe. They say he has the timber for his ships chopped down in my part of the forest and keeps his informers in this castle and in every street in Ombra. They say he even paid my own son to tell him everything my father discussed with his councillors in this hall. And finally" — Cosimo paused for effect before he went on — "I am assured that the messenger who warned the fire-raisers of my forthcoming attack on them was sent by my father-in-law. I'm told he ate quails covered in silver leaf to celebrate my death, and sent my father a letter of sympathy on parchment so cleverly painted with poison that every character on it was deadly as snake's venom. So do you still wonder why I wouldn't receive him?"

Poisoned parchment? Good heavens, who'd think up something like that? thought Fenoglio. *Not I, for one!*

"Are you at a loss for words, poet?" asked Cosimo. "Well, I can tell you I felt the same when I was told all these terrible things. What can one say of such a neighbor? What do *you* think of the rumor that the Adderhead had my wife's mother poisoned because she liked listening to a minstrel too much? What do you think of his sending Firefox his own men-at-arms as reinforcements, to make quite sure that I never returned from the fire-raisers' fortress? My father-in-law tried to do away with me, poet! I have forgotten a year of my life, and everything before it is as vague in my mind as if someone else had lived it. They say I was dead. They say the White Women took me away. They ask: Where have you been, Cosimo? And I don't know the answer! But now I know who wanted my death, and I know who to blame for the way I feel now: empty like a gutted fish, younger than my own son. Tell me, what's the appropriate punishment for crimes of such a monstrous kind against both me and others?"

But Fenoglio could only look at him. *Who is he?* he asked himself. *For heaven's sake, Fenoglio, you know what he looks like, but who is he?* "You tell me!" he replied at last, hoarsely.

And Cosimo gave him that angelic smile again. "Why, there's only one appropriate punishment, poet!" he said. "I will go to war. I'll wage war against my father-in-law until the Castle of Night is razed to the ground and his name is forgotten."

Fenoglio stood there in the darkened hall, hearing his own blood roaring in his ears. *War? I must have misheard,* he thought. *I never wrote anything about war.* But a voice began whispering inside him: *"A great new age, Fenoglio! Didn't you write something about a great new age?"*

"He has the impudence to ride to my castle with men in his retinue who have already pillaged and burned for Capricorn; he's made Firefox, whom I rode out to defeat, his herald; he's sent the Piper here as protector of my son! The audacity of it! Perhaps he could deride my father in that way, but not me. I'll show him he's not dealing with a prince who's either shedding tears or overeating now." A faint flush had risen to Cosimo's face. Anger made him even more handsome.

War. Think, Fenoglio. Think. War! Is that what you wanted? He felt his old knees beginning to tremble.

As for Cosimo, he laid his hand almost lovingly on his sword. He slowly drew it from the scabbard. "It was for this alone that death spared me, poet," he said, cutting the air with the long, slender blade. "So that I could bring justice to this world and turn the Devil himself off his throne. That's worth fighting for, don't you think? Even worth dying for." He was a fine sight standing there with the drawn sword in his hand. And yes, wasn't he right? Perhaps war really was the only way to put the Adderhead in his place.

"You must help me, Inkweaver! That's what they call you, don't they? I like the name!" Cosimo gracefully sheathed the sword again. Tullio, who was still sitting on the steps at his feet, shuddered as the sharp blade scraped the leather scabbard. "You will write a speech for me, calling my people to arms. You will explain our cause to them, you'll plant enthusiasm for that cause and hatred for our enemy in every heart. And we'll use the strolling players, too — you're a friend of theirs. Write them fiery songs, poet! Songs that will make men want to fight. You forge the words, I'll have the swords forged. Many, many swords."

He stood there like an avenging angel, lacking nothing but the wings, and for the first, the very first time in his life Fenoglio felt something like affection for one of his inky creations. *I'll give him wings,* he thought. *I will indeed. With my words.*

"Your Highness!" When he bowed his head this time it wasn't difficult, and for a wonderful moment he felt almost as if he had written himself the son he'd never had. *Don't go turning sentimental in your old age,* he told himself, but this warning made no difference to the unaccustomed softening of his heart.

I ought to ride with him, he thought. *Yes, indeed. I'll go to war against the Adderhead with him, old as I may be.* Fenoglio, a hero in the world of his own creation, a poet and a warrior, too. It was a role he'd like. As if he had written himself the perfect part to play.

Cosimo smiled again. Fenoglio would have bet everything he had that there was no more delightful smile in this or any other world. Tullio seemed to have succumbed to Cosimo's charm, too, despite the fear the Adderhead had put into his heart. Enchanted, he stared up at the master who had come back to him, his little hands in his lap as if they were still holding the bird with the bloody breast.

"I hear your words already!" said Cosimo, returning to the throne. "My wife loves written words, you know, words that stick to parchment and paper like dead flies, and it seems my father felt the same — but I want to *hear* words, not read them! Remember that, when you're looking for the right words: You must ask yourself what they *sound* like! Glowing with passion, dark with sorrow, sweet with love, that's what I want. Write words quivering with all our righteous anger at the Adderhead's evil deeds, and soon that anger will be in every heart. You will write my accusation, my fiery accusation, and we'll have it read out in every marketplace and spread abroad by the strolling players: *Beware, Adderhead!* Let it be heard all the way to his own side of the forest. *Your wicked days are numbered!* And soon every peasant will want to fight under my banner, every man young or old, your words will bring them flocking here to the castle! I've heard that when the Adderhead doesn't like what books say he'll sometimes have them burned in the fireplaces of his castle, but how will he burn words that everyone is singing and speaking?"

He could always burn the man who speaks them, thought Fenoglio. *Or the man who wrote them.* It was an uncomfortable thought that cooled the ardor of his heart slightly, but Cosimo seemed to have picked it up.

"I shall, of course, take you under my personal protection immediately," he said. "In the future you will live here at the castle, in apartments suitable for a court poet."

"At the castle?" Fenoglio cleared his throat, so awkward did this offer make him feel. "That . . . that's very generous of you. Yes, indeed." New times were coming, new and wonderful times. A great new age . . .

"You will be a good prince, Your Grace!" he said, his voice much moved. "A good and great prince. And my songs about you will still be sung in centuries to come, when the Adderhead is long forgotten. I promise you that."

Footsteps sounded behind him. Fenoglio turned, annoyed by the interruption at such an emotional moment. Violante came hurrying through the hall, holding her son's hand, with her maid behind her.

"Cosimo!" she cried. "Listen to him. Your son wants to say he's sorry."

Fenoglio didn't think that Jacopo looked at all sorry. Violante was having to drag him along behind her, and his face was dark as thunder. He didn't seem particularly pleased by his father's return. His mother, on the other hand, was radiant as Fenoglio had never seen her before, and the mark on her face was not much darker than a shadow cast by the sun.

"The birthmark on Her Ugliness's face faded." Oh, thank you, Meggie, he thought. *What a pity you're not here. . . .*

"I won't say sorry!" announced Jacopo, as his mother propelled him none too gently up the steps to the throne. "He's the one who ought to say sorry to my grandfather!"

Unobtrusively, Fenoglio took a step back. Time for him to go.

"Do you remember me?" he heard Cosimo ask. "Was I a stern father?"

Jacopo merely shrugged.

"Oh yes, you were very stern!" Her Ugliness replied on the child's behalf. "You took away his hounds when he acted like this. And his horse."

She was clever, cleverer than Fenoglio had expected. He went quietly toward the door. It was a good thing he'd soon be living at the castle. He must keep an eye on Violante, or she'd soon be filling the blank of Cosimo's memory to her own liking — as if stuffing a newly prepared turkey. When the servants opened the great door he saw Cosimo abstractedly smiling at his wife. *He's grateful to her,* thought Fenoglio, *grateful to her for filling his emptiness with her words, but he doesn't love her.*

And of course that's another thing you never thought of, Fenoglio, he told himself reproachfully as he walked through the Inner Courtyard. *Why didn't you write a word about Cosimo loving his wife? Didn't you tell Meggie the story, long ago, about the flower maiden who gave her heart to the wrong man? What are stories for if we don't learn from them?* Well, at least Violante loved Cosimo. You only had to look at her to see it. That was something, after all. . . .

On the other hand . . . Violante's maid, the girl with the beautiful hair, Brianna, who Meggie said was Dustfinger's daughter — hadn't she seemed equally enraptured when she looked at Cosimo? And Cosimo himself — hadn't he looked at the maid more often than at his wife? *Oh, never mind,* thought Fenoglio. *There'll soon be more important matters at stake than love. Far more important matters . . .*

39

ANOTHER MESSENGER

**The strongest memory is weaker
than the palest ink.**

Chinese proverb

The Adderhead and his men-at-arms had disappeared when
Fenoglio came out of the gate of the Inner Castle. *Good,*
thought Fenoglio. *He'll be fuming with rage on his long ride home!*
The thought of it made him smile. A number of men were waiting in the Outer Courtyard. It was easy to guess their trade from
their blackened hands, even though no doubt they had scrubbed
them thoroughly for their prince. The entire population of
Smiths' Alley in Ombra seemed to have come up to the castle.
*You forge the words, I'll have the swords forged. Many, many
swords.* Had Cosimo's preparations for his war begun already? *If
so, it's time I set to work on my words,* Fenoglio told himself.

As he turned into Cobblers' Alley he thought for a moment
that he heard steps behind him, but when he turned there was
only a one-legged beggar hobbling laboriously past him. At

351

every other step the beggar's crutch slipped in the filth lying among the houses — pig dung, vegetable refuse, stinking puddles of whatever fluids people tipped out of their windows. *Well, there'll soon be cripples enough,* thought Fenoglio as he walked on toward Minerva's house. *You could call war a cripple factory. . . .* What kind of idea was that? Were doubts of Cosimo's plans stirring in his elated mind? *Oh, let it alone. . . .*

By all the letters of the alphabet, I'm certainly not going to miss this climb once I'm living in the castle, he thought as he toiled up the stairway to his room. *I must just remember to ask Cosimo not, on any account, to give me quarters in one of the towers. The climb up to Balbulus's workshop was bad enough!* "Oh, so these few steps *are too steep for you, but you trust yourself to go to war in your old age, do you?"* said a quiet, mocking voice inside him. It always spoke up at the most inappropriate moments, but Fenoglio had plenty of practice in ignoring it.

Rosenquartz wasn't there. Presumably he had climbed out of the window again to visit the glass man working for the scribe who lived over the road in Bakers' Alley. The fairies all seemed to have flown away, too. It was quiet in Fenoglio's room, unusually quiet. He sat down on his bed, sighing. He didn't know why, but he couldn't help thinking of his grandchildren and the way they used to fill his house with noise and laughter. *So what?* he thought, feeling angry with himself. Minerva's children make just the same kind of noise, and think how often you've sent them packing down to the yard because it was too much for you!

Footsteps came up the stairs. *Well, speak of the devil . . . !* He didn't feel like telling stories, not at the moment. He had to pack his things and then break the news gently to Minerva that she must look around for a new lodger.

"Go away!" he called to whoever was at the door. "Go and tease the pigs or chickens in the yard! The Inkweaver doesn't have time just now. He's moving to the castle."

The door swung open all the same, but not to reveal two children's faces. A man stood there — a man with a blotched face and slightly protuberant eyes. Fenoglio had never seen him before, yet he seemed strangely familiar. His leather trousers were patched and dirty, but the color of his cloak made Fenoglio's heart beat faster. It was the Adderhead's silvery gray.

"What's the idea?" he asked brusquely, getting to his feet, but the stranger was already through the doorway. He stood there with his legs spread, his grin as ugly as his face itself, but it was the sight of his companion that made Fenoglio's old knees feel weak. Basta was smiling at him like a long-lost friend. He, too, wore the silver of the Adderhead.

"Bad luck again! Talk about terrible luck!" said Basta, looking around the room. "The girl's not here. And there we go stalking you all the way from the castle, quiet as cats, thinking we'll catch two birds with one stone, and now it's just one ugly old raven in our trap. Never mind, at least one is something. Can't expect too much of Lady Fortune, can we? After all, she sent you to the castle at just the right time. I recognized your ugly tortoise face at once, but you didn't even see me, did you?"

No, Fenoglio hadn't seen him. Should he have looked closely at every man standing behind the Adderhead? *Yes — if you'd had your wits about you, Fenoglio,* he told himself, *that's exactly what you'd have done! How could you forget that Basta's back? Wasn't what happened to Mortimer warning enough?*

"Well, what a surprise! Basta! How did you escape the Shadow?" he said out loud, moving unobtrusively backward until he could feel the bed behind him. Ever since a man in the house next door had his throat cut in his sleep, he had slept with a knife under his pillow, although he wasn't sure if it was still there.

"Sorry, but he must have overlooked me, shut up in that cage as I was," purred Basta in his catlike voice. "Capricorn wasn't so lucky, but Mortola is still around, and she's told our old friend the Adderhead about the three birds we're after. Dangerous sorcerers who kill with words." Basta slowly came toward Fenoglio. "Who do you think those birds are?"

The other man kicked the door shut with his boot.

"Mortola?" Fenoglio tried to make his voice mocking and supercilious, but it sounded more like the croak of a dying raven. "Wasn't it Mortola who had you put in the cage to be fed to the Shadow?"

Basta just shrugged his shoulders and flung back his silver-gray cloak. Of course, he had his knife. A brand-new one, it seemed, finer than any he'd ever had in the other world and undoubtedly just as sharp.

"Yes, not very nice of her," he said as his fingers caressed the handle of the knife. "But she's *really* sorry. Come on, then, do you know what birds we're after? Let me help you a little. We've already wrung the neck of one of them — the one that sang loudest."

Fenoglio let himself drop onto the bed, without — or so he hoped — any expression on his face. "I assume you mean Mortimer," he said, slowly pushing his hand under the pillow.

"Quite right!" Basta smiled. "You should have been there when Mortola shot him. Just the way she used to shoot the crows who stole the seed from her fields." The memory made his smile even nastier. How well Fenoglio knew what was going on in his black heart! After all, he had made up Basta, just as he had made up Cosimo and his angelic smile. Basta had always liked describing his own and other people's abominable deeds in detail. His companion didn't seem to be so talkative. He was looking around Fenoglio's room with a bored expression. A good thing the glass man wasn't there; it was so easy to smash him.

"But we're not going to shoot you." Basta came a little closer to Fenoglio, his face as intent as that of a stalking cat. "We'll probably hang you until your tongue is sticking out of your poor old mouth."

"How very imaginative!" said Fenoglio, moving his fingers farther and farther under the pillow. "But you know what will happen then. You'll die, too."

Basta's smile disappeared as suddenly as a mouse scurrying into its hole. "Oh yes!" he hissed unpleasantly, as his hand instinctively went to the amulet at his throat. "I almost forgot. You believe you made me up, right? And what about him?" He pointed to the other man. "That's Slasher. Did you make him up, too? He sometimes worked for Capricorn, after all. Many of the old fire-raisers wear the Adder's silver now, although some of us think it was more fun under Capricorn. All those fine folk in the Castle of Night . . . !" He spat scornfully at Fenoglio's feet. "It's no coincidence that the Adderhead has a snake on his coat of arms. He wants you to crawl on your belly to him, that's what our noble lord and master likes. But never mind, he pays well! Hey, Slasher!" he addressed his still-silent companion. "What do you think, does the old fellow look as if he made you up?"

Slasher's ugly face twisted. "If so, he made a bad job of it, eh?"

"You're right there." Basta laughed. "I'd say he deserves a taste of our knives just for the face he gave you, right?"

Slasher. Yes, indeed, he'd invented Slasher, too. Fenoglio felt sick to his stomach when he remembered why he'd given the man that name.

"Out with it, old man!" Basta leaned so close that Fenoglio smelled his peppermint-scented breath. "Where's the girl? Tell us and we may let you live a little longer. We'll send the child after her father first. I'm sure she's longing to see him. They were so fond of each other, those two. Come on, where is she? Spit it out!" He slowly drew the knife from his belt. Its blade was long and slightly curved. Fenoglio swallowed as if to force down his fear. He pushed his hand yet farther under the pillow, but all his fingertips met was a piece of bread, probably hidden there by Rosenquartz. *Just as well,* he thought. *What good would a knife have done? Basta would have run me through before I even got a proper hold on it, not to mention Slasher.* He felt the sweat running into his eyes.

"Hey, Basta, I know you like the sound of your own voice, but let's get going and take him with us." Slasher spoke in croaking tones, like the toads in the hills by night. Of course, that was how Fenoglio had described him: Slasher, the man with the voice of a toad. "We can question him later. We have to follow the others now," he urged Basta. "Who knows what this dead prince will do next? Suppose he doesn't let us out of his accursed gate? Suppose he sends his soldiers after us? The others must be miles ahead by now!"

With a regretful sigh, Basta put the knife back in his belt. "Yes, very well, you're right," he said in surly tones. "I need to take my time with this sort of thing. Questioning people is an art, a real art." He roughly seized Fenoglio's arm, pulled him to his feet, and pushed him toward the door. "Just like old times, eh?" he snarled in his ear. "I took you out of your own house once before, remember? Put on as good an act as you did then and you'll go on breathing a little longer. And if we pass that woman feeding pigs in the yard, tell her we're taking you to see an old girlfriend of yours, understand?"

Fenoglio just nodded. Minerva wouldn't believe a word of it, but perhaps she might fetch help.

Basta's hand was already on the door handle when footsteps came upstairs again. The old wood creaked and groaned. The children. For heaven's sake! But it was not a child's voice that spoke outside the door.

"Inkweaver?"

Basta cast an anxious glance at Slasher, but Fenoglio had recognized the voice: It was Cloud-Dancer, the former tightrope-walker, who had brought him messages from the Black Prince many times before. He'd be no help, not with his stiff leg! But what news brought him here? Had the Black Prince heard anything of Meggie?

Basta waved Slasher over to the left of the door and stationed himself to the right. Then he gave Fenoglio a sign and drew the knife from his belt again.

Fenoglio opened the door. It was so low that he always had to duck his head coming in. There stood Cloud-Dancer, rubbing his knee. "Bloody stairs!" he swore. "Steep and falling apart. I'm just glad you're in and I don't have to climb them again. Here." He looked around as if the old house had ears and reached into the leather bag that had carried so many letters from place to place. "The girl who's staying with you sends you this." He held out a piece of paper folded several times. It looked like a page from Meggie's notebook. Meggie hated to tear pages out of a book, and she'd have been reluctant to take one out of this notebook in particular; her father had bound it for her. So the message must be very important — and Basta would take it from him at once.

"Well, here you are, then!" Cloud-Dancer impatiently held the folded paper in front of his nose. "Any idea how fast I hurried to bring you this?"

Reluctantly, Fenoglio put out his hand. He knew just one thing: Basta must not see Meggie's message. Never. His fingers closed around the paper so tightly that none of it was visible.

"And listen!" Cloud-Dancer went on quietly. "The Adderhead has attacked the Secret Camp. Dustfinger —"

Fenoglio shook his head, almost imperceptibly. "Fine. Thank you very much, but the fact is I have visitors just now," he said, desperately trying to convey what he couldn't say in words with his eyes. He rolled them to right and left, as if they could act as fingers pointing to where Basta and Slasher were waiting behind the door.

Cloud-Dancer took a step back.

"Run!" cried Fenoglio and leaped out of the doorway. Cloud-Dancer almost fell downstairs as Fenoglio made his way past him, but then he stumbled. Fenoglio was sliding, rather than running, down the stairs. He didn't turn until he had reached the bottom. He heard Basta cursing behind him, and Slasher's croaking voice. He heard the children in the yard screaming with fright, and from somewhere came Minerva's voice, but by then he was running past the sheds and the lines where her freshly washed laundry hung. A pig ran between his legs, making him stumble and fall in the mud, and when he got up he saw that Cloud-Dancer hadn't been as fast as he was. How could he be, with his stiff leg? Basta had taken him by the collar, while Slasher pushed Minerva aside as she tried to bar his way with a rake. Fenoglio ducked down, first behind an empty barrel, then behind the pigs' trough, and crawled over to one of the sheds on all fours.

Despina.

She was staring at him in astonishment. He laid his finger on his lips, crawled on, forced his way past a couple of planks, and squeezed into the place where Minerva's children had their hide-out. He only just fitted in — the place wasn't meant for old men who were beginning to put on weight around the hips. The two children came here when they didn't want to go to bed or weren't keen to work. They hadn't shown their hiding place to anyone but Fenoglio, as proof of friendship — and in return for a good ghost story.

He heard Cloud-Dancer scream, he heard Basta roaring something, and Minerva weeping. He almost crawled back to them, but fear paralyzed him. And what could he do against Basta's knife and the sword that hung from Slasher's belt? He leaned against the wooden wall of the shed, heard the pigs grunting and rooting about in the ground. Meggie's message swam before his eyes; the sheet of paper was dirty with the mud he'd crawled through, but he could still decipher what she had written.

"I don't know!" he heard Cloud-Dancer scream. "I don't know what she wrote on it. I can't read!" Brave Cloud-Dancer. He probably did know, all the same. He usually had people tell him what their messages said.

"But you can tell me where she is, can't you?" That was Basta's voice. "Out with it. Is she with Dustfinger? You whispered his name to the old man!"

"I don't know!" He screamed again, and Minerva wept louder than ever and shouted for help, her voice echoing back from the narrow houses.

"The Adderhead's men have taken them all away, my parents and the strolling players," Fenoglio read. *"Dustfinger is following . . . the Spelt-Mill . . ."* The letters blurred as he looked at them. Yet again he heard screaming out there. He bit his knuckles so hard

that they began to bleed. *"Write something, Fenoglio. Save them. Write . . ."* It was as if he could hear Meggie's voice. Another scream. No. No, he couldn't just sit here. He crawled out, on and on, until he could rise to his feet.

Basta was still holding Cloud-Dancer in a firm grip, pressing him back against the wall of the house. The old tightrope-walker's shirt was slit and bloody, and Slasher was standing in front of him with a knife in his hand. Where was Minerva? She was nowhere to be seen, but Despina and Ivo were there, in hiding near the sheds, watching what one man can do to another. With a smile on his lips.

"Basta!" Fenoglio took a step forward. He put all his rage and all his fear into his voice and held Meggie's close-written sheet of paper up in the air.

Basta turned with assumed surprise. "Oh, there you are!" he called. "With the pigs. I might have known it. You'd better bring us that letter before Slasher finishes slicing up your friend here."

"You'll have to fetch it yourselves."

"Why?" Slasher laughed. "You can read it to us, can't you?"

Yes. He could. Fenoglio stood there at his wits' end. Where were all the lies, the clever lies that usually sprang to his lips so easily? Cloud-Dancer was staring at him, his face twisted with pain and fear — and suddenly, as if he couldn't stand the fear a moment longer, he tore himself away from Basta and ran toward Fenoglio. He ran fast in spite of his stiff knee, but Basta's knife was faster — so much faster. It went straight into Cloud-Dancer's back, just as the Adderhead's arrow had pierced the gold-mocker's breast. The tightrope-walker fell in the mud, and Fenoglio, standing there, began to tremble. He was trembling so much that Meggie's letter slipped out of his hand and fluttered to the ground. But Cloud-Dancer lay there unmoving, his face in the dirt. Despina came out of hiding, hard as Ivo tried to haul her back, and stared wide-eyed at the motionless figure lying before Fenoglio's feet. It was quiet in the yard, very quiet.

"Read it out, scribbler!"

Fenoglio raised his head. Basta stood there in front of him, holding the knife that had been sticking into Cloud-Dancer's back just now. Fenoglio stared at the blood on the bright blade and at Meggie's message. In Basta's hand. Without thinking, he clenched his fists. He struck Basta in the chest as if neither the knife nor Slasher existed. Basta staggered back, anger and astonishment on his face. He fell over a bucket full of weeds that Minerva had been pulling out of her vegetable plots. Cursing, he got to his feet. "Don't do that again, old man!" he spat. "I'm telling you for the last time, read that out!"

But Fenoglio had snatched Minerva's pitchfork from the dirty straw piled up outside the pigsty. "Murderer!" he whispered, pointing the crudely forged prongs at Basta. What had happened to his voice? "Murderer, murderer!" he repeated, louder and louder, and he thrust the pitchfork at the place in Basta's breast where his black heart beat.

Basta retreated, his face distorted with rage.

"Slasher!" he roared. "Slasher, come here and get that damn fork away from him!"

But Slasher had gone beyond the houses, sword in hand, and was listening. Horses' hooves were clattering along the alley outside. "We must go, Basta!" he called. "Cosimo's guards are on their way!"

Basta stared at Fenoglio, his narrowed eyes full of hate. "We'll meet again, old man!" he whispered. "And next time you'll be lying in the dirt in front of me, like him." He stepped heedlessly over the motionless Cloud-Dancer. "As for this," he said, tucking Meggie's letter under his belt, "Mortola will read it to me.

Who'd have thought that the third little bird would write telling us where to find her in her own fair hand? And we'll pick up the fire-eater for free into the bargain!"

"Come on, quickly, Basta!" Slasher beckoned impatiently.

"What are you bothered about? You think they'll string us up because there's one less strolling player in the world?" replied Basta calmly, but he turned away from Fenoglio. He waved to him one last time before disappearing among the houses.

Fenoglio thought he heard voices, the clink of weapons, but perhaps it was something else. He kneeled down beside Cloud-Dancer, turned him gently on his back, and put his ear to his chest — as if he hadn't seen death in his face some moments ago. He sensed the two children coming up beside him. Despina put her hand on his shoulder. It was slim and light as a leaf.

"Is he dead?" she whispered.

"You can see he is," said her brother.

"Will the White Women come to fetch him now?"

Fenoglio shook his head. "No, he's going to them of his own accord," he answered quietly. "You can see that. He's gone already. But they'll welcome him to their White Castle. It's built of bones but very beautiful. There's a courtyard in that castle, full of fragrant flowers, with a tightrope made of moonlight stretched across it just for Cloud-Dancer. . . ." The words came easily: beautiful, comforting words, but were they really true? Fenoglio didn't know. He had never taken any interest in what came after death, either in this world or the other one. Probably just silence, silence without a single word of comfort.

Minerva came stumbling back from the alley, a cut on her forehead. The physician who lived on the corner was with her, and two other women, their faces pale with fear. Despina ran to her mother, but Ivo stayed beside Fenoglio.

"No one would come." Minerva sobbed as she fell to her knees beside the dead man. "They were all afraid. Every one of them!"

"Cloud-Dancer," murmured the physician. Bone-knitter, he was often called, Stonecutter, Piss-Prophet, and sometimes, when he had lost a patient, Angel of Death. "Only a week ago he was asking if I knew anything that would do the pain in his knee good."

Fenoglio remembered seeing the physician with the Black Prince. Should he tell him what Cloud-Dancer had said about the Secret Camp? Could he trust him? No, it was better to trust no one. Nothing and no one. The Adderhead had many spies. Fenoglio straightened up. Never before had he felt so old, so very old that it seemed as if he couldn't survive another single day. The mill that Meggie had mentioned in her letter, where the devil was it? The name had sounded familiar. . . . Well, of course it did; he himself had described it in one of the last chapters of *Inkheart*. The miller was no friend to the Adderhead, even though his mill stood near the Castle of Night, in a dark valley south of the Wayless Wood.

"Minerva," he asked, "how long does it take a mounted man to get from here to the Castle of Night?"

"Two days for sure, if he's not going to ruin his horse," replied Minerva quietly.

Two days, if not less, before Basta found out what was in Meggie's letter. If he rode to the Castle of Night with it, that was. *But he's sure to do that,* thought Fenoglio. *Basta can't read, so he will take the letter to Mortola, and the Magpie is sure to be at the Castle of Night. Yes, there were probably two days to go before Mortola would read what Meggie had said and send Basta to the mill. Where Meggie might already be waiting. . . .* Fenoglio sighed. Two days. Perhaps that would be enough to get a warning to her, but not to write the words she hoped he would send — words to save her parents.

Write something, Fenoglio. Write . . .

As if it were so simple! Meggie, Cosimo, they all wanted words from him. It was easy for them to talk. You needed time to find the right words, and enough time was exactly what he didn't have!

"Minerva, tell Rosenquartz I have to go to the castle," said Fenoglio. Suddenly, he felt dreadfully tired. "Tell him I'll fetch him later."

Minerva stroked Despina's hair — the girl was sobbing into her skirt — and nodded. "Yes, you go to the castle!" she said huskily. "Go and tell Cosimo to send soldiers after those murderers. By God, I'll be in the front row to watch them hang!"

"Hang? What are you talking about?" The physician ran a hand through his sparse hair and looked sadly down at the dead man. "Cloud-Dancer was one of the strolling players. No one gets hanged for stabbing a strolling player. There's a harsher penalty for killing a hare in the forest."

Ivo looked incredulously at Fenoglio. "Will they really not punish them?"

What was he to tell the boy? No, it was a fact. No one would punish them. Perhaps the Black Prince might someday, or the man who had taken to wearing the Bluejay's mask, but Cosimo wouldn't send a single soldier after Basta. The Motley Folk were all outlaws, in Lombrica and Argenta alike. Subject to none, protected by none. *But Cosimo will give me a horseman if I ask him,* thought Fenoglio, *a fast horseman who can warn Meggie of Basta. "Write something, Fenoglio. Save them! Write something that will set them all free and kill the Adderhead. . . ."* Yes, by God, he would. He'd write rousing songs for Cosimo and powerful words for Meggie. And then her voice could help this story to find a good ending at last.

40

No Hope

> The mustard-pot got up and walked over to his plate on thin silver legs that waddled like the owl's. . . . "Oh, I love the mustard-pot!" cried the Wart. "Wherever did you get it?"
> T. H. White, *The Sword in the Stone*

Luckily, Darius was a good cook, or Orpheus would probably have locked up Elinor in the cellar again after the very first meal and read himself food to eat out of her books. Thanks to Darius's cooking, however, they were able to spend time upstairs more often — although under the watchful eye of Sugar — for Orpheus liked his food, and plenty of it, and he enjoyed what Darius cooked.

Fearing that otherwise Orpheus might let only Darius upstairs, they pretended that Elinor had concocted all those delicacies with their appetizing aromas and Darius was just her assistant, tirelessly chopping, stirring, and tasting; but as soon as Sugar, getting bored, left the kitchen to stare at the bookshelves, Darius took over the wooden spoon and Elinor the chopping — not that she was much better at chopping than cooking.

Now and then some bewildered figure, looking around as if lost, stumbled into the kitchen. Sometimes the visitor was human, sometimes furry or feathered, once it was even a talking mustard-pot. Elinor could usually work out, from the appearance of each one, which of her poor books Orpheus had in his pale hands at that moment. Tiny men with old-fashioned hairstyles were presumably from *Gulliver's Travels*. The mustard-pot was very probably from Merlin's cottage, and the enchanting and extremely confused faun who tripped in one lunchtime on delicate goat's hooves must have come from Narnia.

Naturally, Elinor wondered anxiously if all these creatures were in her library when they didn't happen to be standing glassy-eyed in the kitchen, and finally she asked Darius to go and find out, on the pretext of asking what Orpheus wanted to eat. He came back with the reassuring news that her Holy of Holies was still in dreadful disorder, but apart from Orpheus, his horrible dog, and a rather pale gentleman who looked to Darius suspiciously like the Canterville Ghost, no one was pawing, soiling, sniffing, or otherwise damaging Elinor's books.

"Thank God!" she sighed, relieved. "He obviously makes them all disappear again. I must say that appalling man really does know his trade. And it looks as if he can read them out of a book by now without making someone else disappear into it!"

"No doubt about that," remarked Darius — and Elinor thought she heard a trace of envy in his gentle voice.

"He's a monster all the same," she said, in a clumsy attempt to console him. "It's just a pity this house is so well stocked with provisions, or he'd have had to send the wardrobe-man shopping, and then he'd be alone facing the two of us."

As it was, however, days passed by, and there was nothing they could do about either their own imprisonment or the fact that Mortimer and Resa were probably in deadly danger. Elinor tried not even to think of Meggie. And Orpheus, the one person who could obviously have put everything right with such ease, sat in her library like a pale, fat spider, playing with her books and the characters who populated them, as if they were toys to be taken out and put away again.

"How much longer is he planning to go on like this, I ask myself?" she said for about the hundredth time as Darius was putting rice in a serving dish — rice cooked just long enough, of course, so that it was soft but the grains were all separate. "Is he planning to keep us cooking and cleaning for him as unpaid servants for the rest of his life, while he amuses himself with my poor books? In *my* house?"

Darius did not reply. Instead, and without a word, he piled food onto four plates — this was a meal that certainly wasn't going to send Orpheus out of the house.

"Darius!" whispered Elinor, putting a hand on his thin shoulder. "Won't you just have a try? I know he always keeps the book close to him, but perhaps we can get our hands on it somehow. You could put something in his food. . . ."

"He gets Sugar to taste everything he's going to eat."

"Yes, I know. Right, so we must try something else, anything, and then you can read us into the book! If this repulsive creature won't bring them out for us, then we'll simply go after them!"

But Darius shook his head, as he had done every time Elinor had suggested the same thing, although in slightly different words. "I can't do it, Elinor!" he whispered, and his glasses clouded over, whether with the steam of cooking or tears rising to his eyes she thought it better not to inquire. "I've never read anyone into a book, only out of it, and you know what happened then."

"Oh, all right, then read someone here, someone strong and heroic who'll chase those two out of my house! Who cares if his nose has been flattened or he's lost his voice like Resa, just so long as he has plenty of muscles!"

As if on cue, Sugar put his head around the door. Elinor was constantly amazed to see that it was not much wider than his neck. "Orpheus wants to know where dinner is."

"Just ready," replied Darius, handing him one of the steaming plates.

"Rice again?" growled Sugar.

"Yes, sorry about that," said Darius, as he pushed past him with Orpheus's plate.

"And you see about the dessert!" Sugar ordered Elinor as she was about to put the first forkful into her own mouth.

No, this just couldn't go on. Acting the kitchen maid in her own house, with a horrible man in her library throwing her books on the floor, treating them like boxes of chocolates, nibbling something from one book here, another there.

There must be a way to do it, she thought, spooning walnut ice cream into two dishes with a gloomy expression on her face. *There must. There must.* Why couldn't her stupid brain work it out?

THE CAPTIVES

"Then you don't think he's dead, then?"

He put on his hat. "Now I may be wrong, of course, but I think he's very alive. Shows all the symptoms of it. Go have a look at him, and when I come back we'll get together and decide."

Harper Lee, *To Kill a Mockingbird*

Night had fallen long ago when Meggie and Farid set out to follow Dustfinger. Go south, keep going south, Cloud-Dancer had told them, but how did you know you were going south when there was no sun to show you the way, no stars shining through the black leaves? The darkness seemed to have devoured everything: the trees, even the ground before their feet. Moths fluttered into their faces, attracted by the fire that Farid was nursing in his fingers like a little animal. The trees seemed to have eyes and hands, and the wind carried voices to their ears, soft voices whispering words to Meggie that she didn't understand. On any other night a point would probably have come when she just stopped or ran back to where Cloud-Dancer and Nettle might still be sitting by the fire; but tonight she knew only that she must find Dustfinger and her parents, for neither night nor the forest could hold any terrors for her greater than the fear that had taken root in her heart when she saw Mo's blood on the straw.

At first, and with the fire to help him, Farid kept finding traces: a print left by one of Dustfinger's boots, a broken twig, a marten's trail . . . but the time came when he stood there at a loss, not sure which way to go. Tree grew beside tree in the pale moonlight whichever way you looked, so close together that you couldn't make out any path between their trunks, and Meggie saw eyes: eyes above her, behind her, beside her . . . hungry eyes, angry eyes, so many of them that she wished the moon wouldn't shine so brightly through the leaves.

"Farid!" she whispered. "Let's climb a tree and wait for sunrise. We'll never find Dustfinger's trail again if we just go on like this."

"My own opinion exactly!" Dustfinger appeared among the trees without a sound, as if he had been standing there for some time already. "I've been able to hear you plowing through the forest behind me like a herd of wild boar for the last hour," he said, as Jink pushed past his legs. "This is the Wayless Wood, and not the safest part of it, either. You can think yourselves lucky I managed to convince the elves in the ash trees that you weren't breaking their branches just for fun. And how about the Night-Mares? Do you think they don't pick up your scent? If I hadn't sent them packing you'd probably be lying stiff as dead wood among the trees by now, caught in bad dreams like two flies in a spider's web."

"Night-Mares?" whispered Farid, as the sparks at his fingertips went out. Night-Mares. Meggie came closer to him. She was remembering a story that Resa had told her. What a good thing it hadn't come into her mind earlier. . . .

370

"Yes, did I never tell you about them?" Jink ran to Dustfinger as he walked toward them and greeted Gwin with a delighted chatter. "They may not eat you alive like those desert ghosts you kept telling me about, but they're not exactly friendly, either."

"I'm not going back," said Meggie, looking at him resolutely. "Whatever you say I'm not going back."

Dustfinger looked at her. "No, I know," he said. "Your mother all over." That was all.

All night they followed the broad track left by the men-at-arms as they had marched through the forest — all night and the following day. Dustfinger let them stop for a brief rest only when he saw that Meggie was staggering with exhaustion. When the sun was once again so low in the sky that it touched the treetops they reached the crest of a hill, and Meggie saw the dark ribbon of a road running through the green of the forest down below. A collection of buildings stood beside it: a long, low house, with stables around a yard.

"The only inn close to the border," Dustfinger whispered to them. "They probably left their horses there. You can move considerably faster on foot in the forest. Everyone who wants to go south and down to the sea stops to rest at this inn: couriers, traders, even a few of the strolling players, though everyone knows that the landlord is one of the Adderhead's spies. If we're lucky we'll be there before the party we're following, because they won't be able to get down the slopes with the handcart and the prisoners. They'll have to go the long way around, but we can take the direct route and wait for them at the inn."

"And then what?" For a moment Meggie thought she saw the same anxiety in his eyes that had driven her into the woods by night. But who was he anxious about? The Black Prince, the other strolling players . . . her mother? She still clearly remembered that day in Capricorn's crypt when he had begged Resa to escape with him and leave her daughter behind. . . .

Perhaps Dustfinger had remembered it, too. "Why are you looking at me like that?" he asked.

"Oh, it's nothing," she murmured, bending her head. "I'm just worried."

"And for good reason," he said, abruptly turning his back on her.

"But what are we going to do when we've caught up with them?" Farid was hurrying unsteadily after him.

"I don't know," was all Dustfinger said as he began looking for a way down the slope, keeping in the cover of the trees. "I thought one of you might have some idea, since you were so keen to come along."

The route he took led downhill so steeply that Meggie could hardly keep her footing, but then she suddenly saw the road — stony and rutted with channels where water had once flowed down from the hills. On the other side were the stables and the house she had seen from the top of the hill. Dustfinger waved her over to a place by the roadside where the undergrowth would shield her from curious eyes.

"No, they don't seem to be here yet, but they must arrive soon!" he said quietly. "They may even stay the night, fill their bellies, and get drunk to forget the terrors of the forest. I can't show my face over there while it's still light. Given my luck, one of Capricorn's fire-raisers who's working for the Adderhead now will cross my path. But you," he said, placing a hand on Farid's shoulder, "you can go over there safely. If anyone asks where you're from, just say your master's sitting in the inn drinking. Count the soldiers, count the prisoners, and see how many children are among them. Understand? Meanwhile I'll take a look farther along the road. I have a kind of idea."

Farid nodded and lured Gwin over to him.

"I'll go with him!" Meggie expected Dustfinger to forbid her to go with Farid, but he just shrugged his shoulders.

"As you like. I can't keep you here. I just hope your mother doesn't give herself away when she recognizes you. And another thing!" He took hold of Meggie's arm as she was about to follow Farid. "Don't take it into your head that we can do anything for your parents. Perhaps we can free the children, even a few of the adults if they run fast enough. But your father won't be able to run, and your mother will stay with him. She won't leave him on his own, any more than she would leave you behind that other time. We both remember it, don't we?"

Meggie nodded and turned her face away, so that he wouldn't see her tears. But Dustfinger gently turned her around and wiped them from her cheeks. "You really are very like your mother," he said softly. "She never wanted anyone to see her cry, either — however good her reasons for tears." His face looked strained as he scrutinized the two of them again. "Well, you're dirty enough," he commented. "Anyone would take you for a stable boy and a kitchen maid. We'll meet behind the stables as soon as it's dark. Now, off you go."

They didn't have long to wait.

Meggie and Farid had been hanging around the stables for barely an hour when they saw the procession of prisoners come down the road — women, children, old men, hands tied behind their backs and soldiers on both sides of them. These men were not armed, no helmets hid their sullen features, but they all wore their master's snake emblem on their breasts, silver-gray cloaks, and swords at their belts. Meggie recognized their leader at once: It was Firefox. And judging by his face, he didn't seem to like traveling on foot very much.

"Don't stare at them like that!" whispered Farid, as Meggie stood there rooted to the spot. He dragged her behind one of the carts standing around the yard. "Your mother's not hurt. Did you see her?" Meggie nodded. Yes, Resa was walking between two other women, one of them pregnant. But where was Mo?

"Hey!" bellowed Firefox, as his men drove the prisoners into the yard. "Whose are those carts? We need more room."

The soldiers pushed the carts aside, handling one of them so roughly that its load of sacks slipped off. A man hurried out of the inn — probably the cart's owner — a protest already on his lips, but when he saw the soldiers he bit it back and shouted at the grooms, who quickly righted the cart again. Traders, farmers, servants — more and more people came crowding out of the stables and the main building to see the cause of all the noise in the yard. A fat, perspiring man made his way through the turmoil to Firefox, faced him with a hostile expression, and let fly a torrent of angry words.

"All right, all right!" Meggie heard Firefox growl. "But we need space. Can't you see we have prisoners with us? Would you rather we drove them into your stables?"

"Yes, yes, use one of the stables!" cried the fat man in relief, beckoning to a couple of his servants who were standing there staring at the prisoners, some of whom had fallen to their knees just where they were, their faces pale with exhaustion and fear.

"Come on!" Farid whispered to Meggie, and side by side they pushed their way past the muttering farmers and traders, past the servants still clearing the burst sacks out of the yard, past the soldiers casting hopeful glances at the inn. No one seemed to be taking very much notice of the prisoners, but it was hardly necessary: None of them looked as if they still had the strength to escape. Even the children, whose legs might have been fast enough for them to run, were clinging to their mothers' skirts, empty-eyed, or staring in fear at the armed men who had brought them here. Resa was supporting the pregnant woman. Yes, her mother was uninjured; Meggie could see that much, although she avoided coming too close to her, in case Dustfinger was right to fear that Resa would give herself away if she recognized her. How desperately she was looking around! She took the arm of a soldier, whose beardless face made him look only a boy, and then —

"Farid!" Meggie couldn't believe it. Resa was talking. Not with her hands but with her mouth. Her voice could hardly be heard in all this noise, but it *was* her voice. How could it be possible? The soldier didn't listen to her but pushed her roughly away, and Resa turned. The Black Prince and his bear were pulling a cart into the yard. They had been harnessed to it like oxen. A chain was wound around the bear's black muzzle, another around his throat and chest. But Resa had eyes for neither the bear nor the Prince — she kept looking at the cart, and Meggie immediately realized what that meant.

Without a word, she took off. "Meggie!" Farid called after her, but she wasn't listening. No one could stop her. The cart was a ramshackle thing. First she saw only the man with the injured leg, one of the strolling players holding a child on his lap. Then she saw Mo.

She thought her heart would never beat again. He was lying there with his eyes closed, under a dirty blanket, but all the same Meggie saw the blood. His shirt was soaked in it, the shirt he liked best to wear, although the sleeves had worn thin. Meggie forgot everything: Farid, the soldiers, Dustfinger's warning, where she was, why she was here. She just stared at her father and his still face. The world was suddenly an empty place, very empty, and her heart was a cold, dead thing.

"Meggie!" Farid reached for her arm. He hauled her away with him, ignoring her resistance, and held her close when she began to sob.

"He's dead, Farid! Did you see him? Mo . . . he's dead!" She kept stammering that terrible word. Dead. Gone. Forever.

She pushed Farid's arm away. "I must go to him." *Bad luck clings to this book, Meggie, nothing but bad luck, even if you don't believe me.* Hadn't he told her that in Elinor's library? How much every one of those words hurt now. Death had been waiting in the book. His death.

"Meggie!" Farid was still holding her firmly. He shook her as if he had to wake her up. "Meggie, listen. He's not dead! Do you think they'd be dragging him along with them if he was?"

Would they? She wasn't sure of anything anymore.

"Come with me. Come on!" Farid pulled her away with him. He pushed his way casually through the crowd, as if none of the hurry and bustle interested him. Finally, with an indifferent expression on his face, he stopped by the stable into which the soldiers were herding the prisoners. Meggie wiped away her tears and tried to look equally indifferent, but how could she when her heart, coming back to life, felt as if someone had cut it in two?

"Do you have enough for us to eat there?" she heard Firefox ask. "We're ravenous after our journey through that accursed forest."

Meggie saw them push Resa into the dark stable with the other women, while two soldiers released the Black Prince and his bear.

"Of course I have enough!" said the fat landlord indignantly. "And you won't recognize your horses, their coats are so glossy!"

"So I should hope," replied Firefox. "Otherwise the

Adderhead will make sure you're not landlord of this hovel much longer. We ride at daybreak tomorrow. My men and the prisoners can stay in the stable, but I want a bed — and a bed to myself, too, not one I have to share with a crowd of snoring, farting strangers."

"Of course, of course!" The landlord nodded eagerly. "But what about that monster?" He pointed anxiously at the bear. "He'll scare the horses. Why didn't you kill him and leave him in the forest?"

"Because the Adderhead wants to hang him along with his master," replied Firefox, "and because my men believe all the nonsense they hear about him — folk say he's a Night-Mare who likes to take the shape of a bear, so it's a bad idea to fire an arrow into his coat."

"A Night-Mare?" The landlord chuckled nervously. He obviously seemed to think the story not impossible. "Never mind what he is, he's not going into my stable. Tie him up behind the bakehouse if you like. Then perhaps the horses won't smell him." The bear growled in a low tone as one of the soldiers pulled him along on his chain, but as they were forced away behind the main building the Black Prince spoke to him soothingly, in a quiet voice, as if comforting a child.

The cart with Mo and the injured old man on it was still in the yard. A few servants were standing around, gossiping to one another, presumably trying to work out exactly who had been captured on the Adderhead's orders. Was the rumor already spreading that the man lying as if dead on the cart was the Bluejay? The soldier with the beardless face shooed away the servants, took the child off the cart and pushed him toward the stable, too. "What about the wounded prisoners?" he called to Firefox. "Do we just leave those two on the cart where they are?"

"And find that they're dead in the morning, or gone? What

are you thinking of, you fool? One of them's the reason why we went into that damned forest, right?" Firefox turned to the landlord again. "Is there a physician among your guests?" he asked. "I have a prisoner who must be kept alive because the Adderhead plans a magnificent execution for him. It's no real fun with a dead man, if you see what I mean."

Must be kept alive . . . Farid pressed Meggie's hand and smiled triumphantly at her.

"Oh yes, of course, of course!" The landlord looked curiously at the cart. "It's a nuisance, for sure, if condemned men die before their execution. I hear that's happened twice this year already. However, I can't offer you a physician. I do have a moss-woman helping out in the kitchen, though. She's set many of my guests to rights in her time."

"Good! Send for her!"

The landlord impatiently beckoned to a snotty-nosed boy leaning by the stable door. Firefox called two of his soldiers to him. "Go on, get the wounded men into the stable, too!" Meggie heard him say. "Double guards outside the door, and four of you keep watch on the Bluejay tonight, understand? No wine, no mead, and anyone who falls asleep will be sorry for it!"

"The Bluejay?" The landlord stared in amazement. "You have the Bluejay on that cart?" When Firefox cast him a warning glance, he quickly put his fat fingers to his mouth. "Not a word!" he uttered. "No one will hear a word of it from me."

"I should hope not," growled Firefox, and looked around as if to make sure that no one else had heard what he said.

When the soldiers lifted Mo off the cart, Meggie instinctively took a step forward, but Farid dragged her back. "Meggie, what's the matter with you?" he hissed. "If you carry on like this they'll shut you up, too. Do you think that will help anyone?"

Meggie shook her head. "He really is still alive, Farid, isn't he?" she whispered. She was almost afraid to believe it.

"Yes, of course. I told you so. Don't look so sad. Everything will turn out all right, you wait and see!" Farid caressed her forehead and kissed the tears from her eyelashes.

"Hey, you two lovebirds, get away from the horses!"

The Piper was standing before them. Meggie bent her head, although she was sure he wouldn't recognize her. She had been just a girl in a dirty dress when he almost rode her down in the Ombra marketplace. Today he was once again more splendidly clothed than any of the strolling players Meggie had yet seen. His silken garments shimmered like a peacock's tail, and the rings on his fingers were genuine silver, like the nose on his face. Obviously, the Adderhead paid well for songs that pleased him.

The Piper looked hard at them again, and then strolled over to Firefox. "Well, so you're back from the forest!" he called from some way off. "And with rich booty, so I've heard. Looks as if one of your spies wasn't lying for a change. Good news for the Adderhead at last."

Firefox replied, but Meggie wasn't listening. The snotty-nosed boy came back with the moss-woman, a short little creature who hardly came up to his shoulder. Her skin was gray as beech bark, her face as wrinkled as a shriveled apple. Moss-women, healers . . . Before Farid realized what she meant to do, Meggie had slipped away from him. The moss-woman would know how Mo really was. She made her way as close as she could to the little woman, until only the boy stood between them. The moss-woman's smock was stained with meat juices from the spit, and her feet were bare, but she inspected the men standing around her with fearless eyes.

"Sure as I live, a genuine moss-woman," growled Firefox, while his men retreated from the tiny woman as if she were as dangerous as the Black Prince's bear. "I thought they never came out of the forest. But yes, apparently they know something about healing. Don't folk say that old witch Nettle's mother was a moss-woman?"

"Yes, but her father was useless." The little woman scrutinized Firefox as intently as if she were trying to find out what kind of blood flowed in his veins. "You drink too much," she observed. "Just look at your face. Carry on like this and your liver will soon burst like an overripe pumpkin."

A ripple of laughter ran through the onlookers, but a glance from Firefox silenced them. "Listen, you're not here to give me advice, she-gnome!" he snapped at the moss-woman. "I want you to look at one of my prisoners. He has to reach the Adderhead's castle alive."

"Yes, I know all that," replied the moss-woman, still examining his face with disapproval. "So that your master can kill him by all the rules of the executioner's trade. Fetch me water. Hot water and clean towels. And I want someone to help me."

Firefox nodded to the boy. "If you want a helper, pick one for yourself," he growled, and surreptitiously felt his stomach, where he presumably supposed his liver was located.

"One of your men? No, thank you." The moss-woman wrinkled up her little nose scornfully and looked around until her eye fell on Meggie. "That one will do," said the little creature. "She doesn't look too stupid."

And before Meggie knew it, one of the soldiers took her roughly by the shoulder. The last thing she saw before she stumbled into the stable after the moss-woman was the expression of alarm on Farid's face.

A Familiar Face

Believe me. Sometimes when life looks to be at its grimmest, there's a light hidden at the heart of things.

Clive Barker, *Abarat*

Mo was conscious as the moss-woman kneeled down beside him. He sat leaning back against the damp wall, his eyes searching all the prisoners crouching in the dimly lit stable, looking for Resa's face. He didn't see Meggie until the little woman impatiently beckoned her over. Of course he realized at once that even a smile would have given her away, but it was so hard for him not to take her in his arms, so hard to hide the joy and fear that struggled for his heart at the sight of her.

"What are you standing around for?" the old woman snapped at Meggie. "Come here, you stupid thing!" Mo could have shaken her, but Meggie just kneeled down quickly beside her and took the bloodstained bandages that the old woman was none too gently cutting away from his chest. *Don't stare at her,* thought Mo, forcing his eyes to look anywhere else: at the old woman's hands, at the other prisoners, not at his daughter. Had Resa seen her, too? *She's all right,* he thought. Yes, definitely. She wasn't any thinner than usual, and she didn't seem to be sick or injured, either. If only he could at least have exchanged a word with her!

"By fairy spit, what's the matter with you?" asked the little woman roughly as Meggie almost spilled the water she was handing her. "I might just as well have taken one of the soldiers." She began feeling Mo's injuries with her barklike fingers. It hurt, but he clenched his teeth so that Meggie wouldn't notice.

"Are you always so hard on her?" he asked the old woman.

The little moss-woman muttered something incomprehensible without looking at him, but Meggie ventured a quick glance, and he smiled at her, hoping she wouldn't notice the concern in his eyes, his alarm at seeing her again in this of all places, among all the soldiers. *Be careful, Meggie,* he tried to tell her with his eyes. How her lips were quivering, probably with all the words that she couldn't say aloud, any more than he could! But it was so good to see her. Even in this place. In all those days and nights of fever, he had so often felt sure that he would never see her face again!

"Hurry up, can't you?" Suddenly, Firefox was standing right behind Meggie, and at the sound of his voice she quickly bowed her head and held out the bowl of water to the little old woman again.

"This is a nasty wound!" remarked the moss-woman. "I'm surprised you're still alive."

"Yes, strange, isn't it?" Mo was as much aware of Meggie's glance as if it were the pressure of her hand. "Perhaps the fairies whispered a few words of healing in my ear."

"Words of healing?" The moss-woman wrinkled up her nose. "What kind of words would those be? Fairies' gossip is as stupid and useless as fairies themselves."

"Well, then someone else must have whispered them to me."

Mo saw how pale Meggie turned as she helped the moss-woman rebandage his wound, the wound that hadn't killed him. *It's nothing, Meggie,* he wanted to say, *I'm fine* — but all he could do was look at her again, only in passing, as if her face meant no more to him than any other.

"Believe it or not," he told the old woman, "I did hear the words. Beautiful words. At first I thought it was my wife's voice, but then I realized it was my daughter's. I heard her voice as clearly as if she were sitting here beside me."

"Yes, yes, folk hear all kinds of things in a fever!" replied the moss-woman brusquely. "I've heard of those who swore the dead spoke to them. The dead, angels, demons . . . A fever will summon up whole troops of them." She turned to Firefox. "I have an ointment that will help him," she said, "and I'll brew up something for him to drink. I can't do any more." When she turned her back on them, Meggie quickly put her hand on Mo's fingers. No one noticed, nor did they notice the gentle pressure he gave her hand in return. He smiled at her again, and only when the moss-woman turned again did he quickly look aside. "You ought to look at his leg, too!" he said, nodding toward the strolling player lying asleep beside him on the straw, exhausted.

"No, she oughtn't!" Firefox interrupted. "It's all one to me whether he lives or dies. You're different."

"Oh, I see! You still think I'm that robber." Mo leaned his head against the wall and closed his eyes for a moment. "I suppose it's no good if I tell you yet again that I'm not?"

By way of answer, Firefox just cast him a contemptuous glance. "Tell the Adderhead. Perhaps he'll believe you," he said. Then he pulled Meggie roughly to her feet. "Go on, off with you both! That'll do!" he shouted at her and the moss-woman. His men pushed them both toward the stable door. Meggie tried to look around again, her eyes searching for her mother, sitting somewhere among the other prisoners, and looking toward Mo yet again, but Firefox grabbed her arm and forced her out of the door — leaving Mo wishing he had words at his command, words like those that had killed Capricorn. His tongue longed to taste them, longed to send them after Firefox and see him fall in the dust like his former master. But there was no one here to write the words for him. Only Fenoglio's story was everywhere, surrounding them with horror and darkness — and presumably his own death was already planned for one of the next chapters.

PAPER AND FIRE

"Good, well, if that's decided," came a weary voice from the opposite end of the dank hold. It was the gnokgoblin, still manacled and quite forgotten. "Then will someone please release *me*."

Paul Stewart, *Midnight Over Sanctaphrax*

Dustfinger saw the windows of the inn glowing like dirty yellow eyes as he stole across the road. Jink scurried ahead of him, little more than a shadow in the darkness. There was no moon tonight, and it was so dark in the yard and around the stables that even his own scarred face would just look like a pale patch.

There were guards outside the stable where the prisoners had been shut up, four guards, but they didn't notice him. They were staring into the night, their faces bored, hands on their sword hilts, looking longingly again and again at the lighted windows opposite. Loud, drunken voices came from the inn — and then the sound of a lute, its strings well plucked, followed by singing in a curiously strained voice. Ah, so the Piper was back from

Ombra, too, and singing one of his songs, drunk with blood and the intoxication of killing. The presence of the man with the silver nose was yet another reason why he had to stay out of sight. Meggie and Farid were waiting behind the stables, as agreed, but they were arguing in such loud voices that Dustfinger came up behind the boy and put his hand over his mouth.

"What do you think you're doing?" he said angrily, his voice low. "Do you want them to put you two in with the others?"

Meggie bowed her head. She had tears in her eyes again.

"She wants to go into the stable!" Farid whispered. "She thinks they'll all be asleep! As if —"

Dustfinger closed the boy's mouth with his hand again. Voices rang out over the yard. Obviously, someone had brought the guards outside the stable something to eat. "Where's the Black Prince?" he whispered, when all was still again.

"Between the bakehouse and the main building. Tell her she can't go back into that stable! There are at least fifteen soldiers in there."

"How many guarding the Prince?"

"Three."

Three. Dustfinger glanced up at the sky. No moon. It was hidden behind the clouds, and the darkness was black as a cloak.

"Are you going to free him? Three aren't many!" Farid sounded excited. Not a trace of fear in his voice. That fearlessness would be the death of him yet. "We can cut their throats before they make a sound. It'll be easy." He often said such things. Dustfinger kept wondering if it was just talk, or if he'd actually done something of the kind in the past.

"I can tell you're ready for anything!" he said softly. "But you know very well I'm no good at cutting throats. How many prisoners are there?"

"Eleven women, three children, nine men not counting Silvertongue."

"How is he?" Dustfinger looked at Meggie. "Have you seen him? Can he walk?"

She shook her head.

"What about your mother?" She cast him a quick glance. She didn't like it when he mentioned Resa. "Come on, is she all right?"

"I think so." She put one hand to the stable wall, as if she could feel her parents behind it. "But I didn't get a chance to talk to her. Please!" How pleadingly she was looking at him! "I'm sure they're all asleep. I'll be very careful!"

Farid cast a despairing glance up at the stars, as if such stupidity would make them break their eternal silence.

"The guards won't sleep," said Dustfinger. "So think up a good lie for them. Do you have anything to write with?"

Meggie looked at him incredulously, and for a moment Dustfinger saw her mother's eyes. Then she quickly put her hand into the bag that she carried with her. "I have some paper with me," she whispered, hastily tearing a page out of her little marbled notebook.

Like mother, like daughter. Never without the means of writing.

"You're letting her do it?" Farid looked at him in astonishment.

"Yes."

Meggie looked at him expectantly.

"Write that there'll be a fallen tree lying across the road they take tomorrow. When it catches fire, everyone strong and young enough must run into the forest to the left. To the left: That's important! Write that we'll be waiting there to hide them. Did you get that down?"

Meggie nodded. Her pencil hurried over the paper. He could

only hope that Resa would be able to decipher the tiny handwriting in the darkness of the stable, because he wouldn't be there to make fire for her.

"Have you thought what you're going to tell the guards?" he asked.

Meggie nodded. For a moment she looked almost like the little girl she had still been not much more than a year ago, and Dustfinger wondered whether it was a mistake, after all, to let her go — but before he could change his mind she was off. She raced over the yard and disappeared into the inn. When she came back, she was carrying a jug.

"Please, the moss-woman sent me!" they heard her clear voice telling the guards. "I'm to take the children milk."

"Look at that. Clever as a jackal!" whispered Farid as the guards moved aside. "And brave as a lioness." There was so much admiration in his voice that Dustfinger couldn't help smiling. The boy was definitely in love.

"Yes, she's probably cleverer than both of us put together," he whispered back. "And certainly braver, at least as far as I'm concerned."

Farid just nodded. He was staring at the open stable door — and smiled with relief when Meggie came out again.

"See that?" she whispered to him when she was back beside Farid. "It was perfectly easy."

"Good!" said Dustfinger, beckoning Farid over to his side. "Then let's cross our fingers and hope that what we have to do now is as easy. What about it, Farid? Do you feel like playing with fire?"

The boy carried out his task with as cool a head as Meggie. Apparently lost to the world but in a spot where the men guarding the Prince had a clear view of him, he began making fire dance as naturally as if he were standing in some peaceful marketplace, not in front of an inn that sheltered Firefox and the Piper. The guards nudged each other, laughed, glad of something to pass the time this sleepless night. *Seems that I'm the only one here whose heart is beating faster*, thought Dustfinger as he stole past heaps of stinking offal and rotting vegetables. It looked as if the fat landlord's cooks simply threw everything they couldn't serve to the guests out here behind the house. A few rats scurried off when they heard Dustfinger's footsteps, and the hungry eyes of a brownie glowed among the bushes. They had tied up the Prince next to a mountain of carcasses, and his bear just far enough away to keep him from reaching the bones. He squatted there, snorting unhappily through his muzzle, which was bound, now and then uttering a miserably muted howl.

The guards had stuck a torch in the ground not far away, but the flame went out at once when the wind carried Dustfinger's quiet voice to it. Nothing was left but a faint glow — and the Black Prince raised his head. He knew at once who must be slinking around in the dark when the fire so suddenly died down. A few more quick and silent steps, and Dustfinger took cover behind the bear's furry back.

"That boy's really good!" whispered the Prince without turning around. A sharp knife would soon deal with the ropes binding him.

"Yes, very good. And afraid of nothing, unlike me." Dustfinger examined the padlocks on the bear's chains. They were rusty but not particularly difficult to open. "What do you say to a little walk in the forest? But the bear must be quiet, quiet as an owl. Can he do it?" He ducked when one of the guards turned, but the man had obviously just heard the maid who was coming out of the kitchen to tip a bucket of refuse onto the garbage heaps behind the building. She disappeared again, with a curious look at the bound Prince — and took with her the noise that had come spilling out of the doorway.

"What about the others?"

"Four guards outside the stable, another four told off by Firefox to guard Silvertongue, and there must be ten more guarding the other prisoners. It's unlikely that we can distract the attention of all of them, certainly not for long enough to get the injured and crippled to safety."

"Silvertongue?"

"Yes, the man they were looking for in your camp. What do you call him?" A padlock sprang open. The bear growled; perhaps Jink was making him uneasy. The second chain had better stay where it was for now, or he'd probably eat the marten. Dustfinger set about cutting the ropes tying up the Black Prince. He had to hurry, for they must be gone before Farid's arms tired. The second padlock clicked. Another quick glance at the boy . . . *By the fire of the elves!* thought Dustfinger. *He throws the torches almost as high as I do now!* But just as the Prince was throwing off his ropes, a fat man marched up to Farid with a maid and a soldier behind him. He shouted at the boy and pointed indignantly to the flames. Farid just smiled, skipped back while Gwin leaped around his legs, and went on juggling the burning torches. Oh yes, he was as clever as Meggie! Dustfinger signed to the Prince to go with him. The bear groped his way along after them, following his master's low voice. A pity he really was only a bear and not a Night-Mare. There'd have been no need to tell one of those to keep quiet. But at least he was black, as black as his master, and the night swallowed them up as if they were a part of it.

"We'll meet down on the road by the fallen tree." The Prince nodded and disappeared into the darkness. As for Dustfinger, he set off in search of the boy and Resa's daughter.

The soldiers were all shouting in confusion in the yard now that it was clear that the Black Prince had escaped; even the Piper had come out of the inn. But neither Farid nor the girl could be seen. The soldiers began searching the outskirts of the forest and the slope behind the house, carrying torches. Dustfinger whispered words into the night until the fire felt sleepy, and torch after torch was extinguished as if the slight breeze had blown them out. The men stopped in the middle of the road, feeling uneasy, and looked around with eyes full of fear — fear of the dark, fear of the bear, fear of everything else that roamed the woods by night.

None of them dared go as far as the place where the fallen tree was blocking the road. The forest and the hills were as quiet as if no human foot had ever trodden there. Gwin was perched on the tree trunk, and Farid and Meggie were waiting on the other side under the trees. The boy had a bleeding lip, and the girl had laid her head wearily against his shoulder. Embarrassed, she straightened up as Dustfinger emerged in front of them.

"Is he free?" asked Farid.

Dustfinger put a hand under his chin and looked at the split lip. "Yes. Whatever happens tomorrow, the Prince and his bear will lend us a hand. How did you do that?" The two martens scurried past him and disappeared into the forest side by side.

"Oh, it's nothing. One of the soldiers tried to grab me, but I got away. Well, tell me, was I good?" As if he didn't know the answer.

"So good that I'm beginning to worry. If you carry on like this I'll soon be out of a job."

Farid smiled. How sad Meggie looked, though. She seemed as

lost as the child they had found in the looted camp. It wasn't difficult to imagine how she was feeling, even if, like Dustfinger himself, you had never known your parents. Acrobats, some of the women among the strolling players, a traveling physician . . . he had had many substitutes for them. Any of the Motley Folk who looked after abandoned children were like their parents. *Well, say something to her, Dustfinger, anything,* he thought. You often used to cheer up her mother. Though usually it was just for a short time . . . stolen time.

"Listen." He kneeled down in front of Meggie and looked at her. "If we really manage to free some of them tomorrow, the Black Prince will take them to safety — but the three of us will follow the others."

She looked at him as distrustfully as if he were a worn tightrope that she must walk high in the air.

"Why?" she asked quietly. When she spoke in a low tone you didn't guess at the power that her voice could exert. "Why do you want to help them?" She didn't have to spell it out: *Last time you didn't. Back in Capricorn's village.* What could he say? That it was easier to stand by and watch in a strange world than in your own?

"Let's say I may have something to make up for," he said at last. He knew he didn't have to explain what he meant. They both remembered that night, in another tale, when he had betrayed her to Capricorn. *And there's something else, too,* he almost added, *I think your mother has been a captive long enough.* But he didn't say that. He knew that Meggie wouldn't have liked it.

A good hour later the Black Prince joined them, uninjured and with his bear.

THE BURNING TREE

Do you see the tongues of fire
Darting, flickering higher and higher?
Do you see the flames all dancing,
Flaring, off the dry wood glancing?

James Krüss, "Fire"

Resa's feet were bleeding. The road was stony and wet with the morning dew. They all had their hands bound again, except the children. She had been terrified that the soldiers wouldn't let them walk with the other prisoners but would load them onto the cart instead. "Cry if they try to make you get up there!" she had whispered to the little ones. "Cry and scream until they let you walk with us." But luckily that hadn't been necessary. How scared the three children looked — two girls and a boy, not counting the baby still inside Mina's belly.

The elder girl, who was just six, was walking between Resa and Mina. Whenever Resa glanced at her she wondered what Meggie had looked like at that age. Mo had shown her photographs, wonderful photographs taken in all the years she herself had missed, but those weren't her own memories but his. And Meggie's.

Brave Meggie. Resa's heart still contracted when she remembered how her daughter had passed her the sheet of paper in the stable. Where was she now? Was she watching them from somewhere in the forest?

Only when the hue and cry over the Black Prince had broken out had she been able to read the note, by the light of the torch left burning overnight in the stable. None of the others could read, so she had been able to pass on Dustfinger's news to the women sitting near her only in whispers. After that, there had been no chance to tell the men, too, but the ones who could walk would run, anyway. Resa was to look after the children, and they knew what they were to do.

The other girl and the boy were walking between their mother and the woman with clawlike fingers who had wanted to take Mo back to Capricorn's fortress. Resa had said nothing to her about Dustfinger's news, and every glance the woman cast her said: *I was right, too!* But Mina smiled when she looked at Resa, Mina with her round belly, who could have thought she had good reason to hate her for what had happened. Perhaps the flowers she gave Resa in the cave really had brought luck. Mo was better, much better — after she had thought for so many endless hours that every breath he drew would be his last. Now that the Prince had escaped, a horse was pulling the cart with Mo on it. The bear had set the Prince free, they whispered, which finally proved that he was indeed a Night-Mare. His ghostly glance had made the chains disappear, and he had turned himself into a human being and cut his master's bonds. Resa wondered whether that human being had a scarred face.

When all the noise had begun in the night she had been so

scared for Dustfinger, Meggie, and the boy, but next morning the fury on the soldiers' faces told her that they had gotten away.

But where was the fallen tree Meggie had mentioned in her note?

The little girl beside her was clinging to her dress. Resa smiled at the child — and sensed the Piper looking down at her from his horse. She quickly turned her head away. Luckily, neither he nor Firefox had recognized her. She had often enough listened to the Piper's bloodthirsty songs in Capricorn's fortress — the minstrel still had a human nose on his face in those days — and she had polished Firefox's boots, but fortunately he had not been one of those who chased her and the other maids.

Up above the prisoners' heads the soldiers were describing, at the tops of their voices, what their master would do to the Black Prince once he'd caught him and his enchanted bear again. Now that they were on horseback once more their tempers had clearly improved. From time to time the Piper turned in his saddle and contributed some particularly cruel idea. Resa would have liked to put her hands over the ears of the little girl beside her. The child's mother was not among the prisoners but was wandering the country with some of the other strolling players, happy in the belief that her daughter was safe in the Secret Camp.

The girl would run. So would the other children with their mother. The claw-fingered woman would probably try to escape, too, and Sootbird and most of the other men. The minstrel with the injured leg who was on the cart with Mo would stay, like Twofingers, because he was afraid of the soldiers' crossbows, and so would the old stilt-walker, who no longer trusted his legs. Benedicta, who could hardly see where she was going, would stay behind, too, and Mina, whose child would soon be coming into the world . . . and Mo.

The road went ever more steeply downhill. Overhead, the branches of the trees were intertwined. It was a still, windless morning, cloudy and damp, but Dustfinger's fires burned even in rain. Resa peered past the horses. How close together the trees stood, nothing but darkness showing between them even in broad daylight. The plan was for them to run to the left. Did Meggie expect her to try and escape, too? How often she had asked herself that — and she always came to the same conclusion: No, Meggie knows that I won't leave her father alone. She loves him just as much.

Resa's pace slowed. There it was, the fallen tree, its trunk green with moss. The little girl looked up at her, wide-eyed. They had feared that one of the children would talk, but they had been silent as the grave all morning.

Firefox swore when he saw the tree. He reined in his horse and told the first four horsemen to dismount and clear the obstacle out of the way. They obeyed, looking sullen, handed their horses' reins to other men and strode toward the tree trunk. Resa dared not look at the roadside, for fear that any glance of hers might give away Dustfinger or Meggie. She thought she heard fingers snapping and then a whisper, barely audible. Not human words, but fire-words. Dustfinger had once spoken them for her in the other world, where they didn't work, where fire was deaf and dumb. "They sound much better when I say them there," he had said, and he told her about the fire-honey he took from the elves. She remembered the sound very well, all the same — as if flames were biting their way through black coal, as if they were hungrily devouring white paper. No one else heard the whisper through the rustle of the leaves, the steady rain, the twittering of birds, and the chirping of crickets.

The fire licked up from beneath the bark of the tree like a nest full of snakes. The men didn't notice. Only when the first flame shot up, hot and greedy, rising so high that it almost brought down the leaves of the trees, did they stumble back in alarm and disbelief. The riderless horses reared and tried to break free as the fire hissed and danced.

"Run!" whispered Resa, and the little girl ran for it, fleet-footed as a fawn. Children, women, men, they all ran toward the trees — Sootbird, the claw-fingered woman — past the shying horses they ran, and into the shelter of the dark forest. Two soldiers shot arrows after them, but their own horses were rearing in fear of the fire, and the arrows buried themselves in the bark of trees instead of in human flesh. Resa saw fugitive after fugitive disappear among the trees while the soldiers shouted at one another, and it hurt her to stay standing there, it hurt badly.

The tree went on burning, its bark turned black. . . . *Run, thought Resa, run, all of you!* Yet she herself still stood there although her feet longed to run, too, run away, run to her daughter waiting somewhere in the trees. Yet she stayed there. She stood still. There was just one thing she must not think of: that they would shut her up again. For if she did she would run in spite of Mo. She'd run and run and never stop again. She had been a prisoner too long, she had lived on nothing but memories too long, memories of Mo, memories of Meggie . . . She had fed on them all those years when she served first Mortola, then Capricorn.

"Don't get any silly ideas, Bluejay!" she heard one of the soldiers call back. "Or I'll put an arrow through you!"

"What kind of ideas did you have in mind?" replied Mo. "Do I look stupid enough to run away from your crossbow?" She could almost have laughed. He'd always been able to make her laugh so easily.

"What are you waiting for? Fetch them back!" roared the

Piper. His silver nose had slipped out of place, and his horse was still shying hard as he pulled on the reins. Some of the men obeyed, stumbling halfheartedly into the forest but retreating again as a shadow stirred in the undergrowth, growling.

"The Night-Mare!" one of them shouted, and the next moment they were all back in the middle of the road, pale-faced and with trembling hands, as if the swords they held could do nothing to defend them from the horror lurking in the trees.

"Night-Mare? This is broad daylight, you fools!" Firefox yelled at them. "That's a bear, nothing but a bear!"

Hesitantly, they moved toward the forest again, keeping close together like a brood of chicks hiding behind their mother. Resa heard them swearing as they used their swords to cut a path through the twining wild vines and brambles, while their horses stood in the road snorting and trembling. Firefox and the Piper put their heads together, while the soldiers still standing in the road to guard the remaining prisoners stared at the forest wide-eyed, as if the Night-Mare that looked so deceptively like a bear would leap out at any moment and swallow them up, skin and hair and all, in the usual manner of ghosts.

Resa saw Mo glance at her, saw the relief in his face when he saw her — and his disappointment that she was still there, too. He was still pale, but no longer as pale as if the hand of Death had touched his face. She took a step toward the cart, wanting to go to him, take his hand, see if it was still hot with the fever, but one of the soldiers roughly pushed her back.

The tree was still burning. The flames crackled as if they were singing a mocking song about the Adderhead, and when the men who had gone into the forest came back, they brought not a single one of the escaped prisoners with them.

45

POOR MEGGIE

"Hello," said a soft, musical voice, and Leonardo looked up. In front of him stood the most beautiful young girl he had ever seen, a girl who might have frightened him but for the sad expression in her blue eyes. He knew about sadness.

Eva Ibbotson, *The Mystery of the Seventh Witch*

Meggie did not say a word. However hard Farid tried to cheer her up she just sat there among the trees, her arms wrapped around her legs, perfectly silent. Yes, they had set many of the captives free, but her parents were not among them.

Not one of those who managed to escape had been injured. One of the children had twisted his ankle, that was all, and he was small enough for the grown-ups to carry him. The forest had swallowed them up so quickly that after only a few steps the Adderhead's men had found themselves chasing shadows. Dustfinger hid the children inside a hollow tree, the women crawled underneath a thicket of wild vine and nettles, while the Prince's bear kept the soldiers at a distance. The men had climbed trees and perched high up among the leaves; Dustfinger and the Prince were the last to hide, after leading the soldiers astray in different directions.

The Black Prince advised the freed captives to go back to Ombra and, for the time being, to join the strolling players still encamped there. He himself had other plans. Before he left he spoke to Meggie, and she did not look quite so hopeless after that.

"He said he won't let anyone hang my father," she told Farid. "He says he knows that Mo is not the Bluejay, and he and his men will make the Adderhead realize that he's caught the wrong man." And she looked so hopeful as she said this that Farid just nodded and murmured, "That's great!" — although he could think only that the Adderhead would execute Silvertongue all the same.

"What about the informer the Piper mentioned? Will the Prince look for him?" he asked Dustfinger, as they set out again.

"He won't have to look for long," Dustfinger said. "He just has to wait until one of the strolling players suddenly has his pockets full of silver."

Silver. Farid had to admit that he was curious to see the silver towers of the Castle of Night. Even the battlements were said to be lined with silver. But they would not choose the same route as Firefox. "We know where they're going," said Dustfinger, "and there are shorter and safer ways to the Castle of Night than the road."

"What about the Spelt-Mill?" asked Meggie. "The mill in the forest that you mentioned? Aren't we going there first?"

"Not necessarily. Why?"

Meggie didn't answer at once. Obviously, she guessed that the reply would not please Dustfinger. "I gave Cloud-Dancer a letter for Fenoglio," she said at last, reluctantly. "I asked him to write something to save my parents and to send it to the mill."

"A letter?" Dustfinger's voice was so cutting that Farid instinctively put his arm around Meggie's shoulders. "Oh, wonderful! And suppose the wrong eyes read it?"

Farid ducked his head, but Meggie did not. Instead, she returned Dustfinger's glance. "Nobody but Fenoglio can help them now," she said. "You know that. You know it perfectly well."

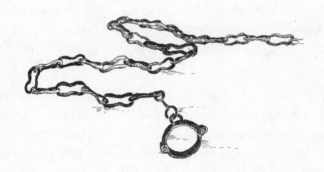

46

A KNOCK ON THE DOOR

Lancelot considered his cup.

"He is inhuman," he said at last. "But why should he be human? Are angels supposed to be human?"

T. H. White, *The Ill-Made Knight*

The horseman Fenoglio had sent after Meggie had been gone for days now. "You must ride like the wind," he had told the man, saying that the life or death of a young and, of course, beautiful girl was at stake. (After all, he wanted to be sure that the man would really do his best.) "But I'm afraid you won't be able to persuade her to come back with you. She's very obstinate," he had added, "so decide on a new meeting place with her — a safe one this time — and tell her you'll be back as soon as possible with a letter from me. Can you remember that?"

The soldier, a fresh-faced youth, had repeated his instructions without any trouble and galloped away, saying he would be back in three days' time at the latest. Three days. If the lad kept his word, he'd soon be back — but Fenoglio would have no letter for him to take to Meggie. For the words that were to put the whole story right again — save the good, punish the bad — simply would not come.

Fenoglio sat day and night in the room that Cosimo had given him, staring at the sheets of parchment that Minerva had brought him, in the company of the terrified Rosenquartz. But there seemed to be a jinx on it: Whatever he began to write seeped out of his head like ink running on damp paper. Where were the words he wanted? Why did they stay as dead as dry leaves? He argued with Rosenquartz, told him to send for wine, roast meat, sweetmeats, different ink, a new pen — while the smiths were hammering and forging metal out in the castle courtyards, the castle gates were reinforced, the pans for pitch were cleaned and spears sharpened. Preparing for war was a noisy business. Particularly when you were in a hurry.

And Cosimo was in a great hurry. The words for him had almost written themselves: words full of righteous anger. Cosimo's criers had already gone out proclaiming them in every marketplace and every village. Ever since then volunteers had been flocking to Ombra, soldiers recruited for the fight against the Adderhead. But where were the words with which Cosimo's war would be won and Meggie's father saved from the gallows at the same time?

How he racked his old brains! But nothing occurred to him. The days went by, and despair entered Fenoglio's heart. Suppose the Adderhead had hanged Mortimer long ago? Would Meggie still read what he had written then? If her father was dead, wouldn't what happened to Cosimo and this world itself be a matter of indifference to her? "Nonsense, Fenoglio," he muttered, as he crossed out sentence after sentence after hours of work. "And I tell you what: If you can't think of any words, they'll have to do without them for once. Cosimo will just have to rescue Mortimer!"

"Oh yes? Suppose they storm the Adderhead's castle, and everyone in the dungeons dies as the building burns?" a voice inside him whispered. *"Or suppose Cosimo's troops are dashed to pieces on the steep and towering walls of the Castle of Night?"*

Fenoglio put down his pen and buried his face in his hands. It was dark again outside, and his head was as empty as the parchment in front of him. Cosimo had sent Fenoglio an invitation, brought by Tullio, to dine at his table — but he had no appetite, although he liked to watch Cosimo listening with shining eyes to the songs he had written about him. Her Ugliness claimed that their words bored her husband, but this version of Cosimo loved what Fenoglio wrote for him: wonderful fairy tales about his heroic deeds in the past, the time he had spent with the White Women, and the battle at Capricorn's fortress.

Yes, he was in high favor with the handsome prince, just as he himself had written — while Her Ugliness was more and more often refused admittance to her husband's presence. So Violante spent even more time in the library than she had before Cosimo's return. Since her father-in-law's death, she no longer had to steal into it secretly or bribe Balbulus with her jewels, for Cosimo didn't mind whether or not she read books. All that interested him was whether she was writing letters to her father or trying to make contact with the Adderhead in some other way. As if she ever had!

Fenoglio felt sorry for Violante, lonely as she was, but he consoled himself by remembering that she had always been solitary by nature. Even her son hadn't changed that. And yet — she had probably never before wanted any human being's company as much as she wanted Cosimo's. The mark on her face had faded, but something else burned there now — love, just as pointless as the birthmark, for Cosimo did not return her love. On the contrary, he was having his wife watched. For some time Violante had been followed by a sturdy, bald-headed man who used to train the Laughing Prince's hounds. Now he shadowed Her Ugliness as if he had turned himself into a dog, a sniffer dog trying to pick up the scent of all her thoughts. Apparently, Violante asked Balbulus to write letters to Cosimo, pleading letters assuring him of her loyalty and devotion, but people said he didn't read them. One of his courtiers even claimed that Cosimo had forgotten how to read.

Fenoglio took his hands away from his face and looked enviously at the sleeping Rosenquartz, lying beside the inkwell and snoring peacefully. He was just picking up his pen again when there was a knock at the door.

Who could it be so late at night? Cosimo usually went out riding at this hour.

It was his wife standing at the door. Violante was wearing one of the black dresses she had put away when Cosimo returned. Her eyes were reddened, as if sore with weeping, but perhaps she was just using the beryl too often.

"Cosimo has taken Brianna with him again!" she said in a broken voice. "She's allowed to ride with him, eat with him, she even spends the nights with him. She tells him stories now instead of me, she reads to him, sings for him, dances for him the way she once did for me. And I'm left alone."

Fenoglio rose from his chair. "Come in!" he said. "Where's your shadow?"

"I bought a litter of puppies and told him to train them, as a surprise for Cosimo. Since then he disappears on occasion."

She was clever, oh yes, in fact very clever. Had he known that? No, he hardly even remembered making her up.

"Sit down!" He gave her his own chair — there was no other — and sat on the chest under the window where he kept his clothes. Not his old, moth-eaten garments but the new ones that Cosimo had given him, magnificent clothes made for a court poet.

"Can't you talk to her?" Violante passed nervous hands over her black dress. "Brianna loves your songs, she might listen to you! I need her. I have no one else in this castle except for Balbulus, and all he wants is for me to give him gold to buy more pigments."

"What about your son?"

"He doesn't like me."

Fenoglio did not reply, for she was right. Jacopo didn't like anyone except his sinister grandfather, and no one liked Jacopo, either. He wasn't easy to like.

Night came in from outside, and the hammering of the smiths. "Cosimo is planning to reinforce the city walls," Violante went on. "He's going to fell every tree from here to the river. They say Nettle cursed him for it. They say she said she'd go to the White Women and tell them to fetch him back again."

"Don't worry. The White Women don't do as Nettle says."

"Are you sure?" She rubbed her sore eyes. "Brianna is supposed to read to *me*! He has no right to take her away. I want you to write to her mother. Cosimo has all my letters read, but *you* can ask her to come. He trusts you. Write and tell Brianna's mother that Jacopo wants to play with her son, and say she's to bring him to the castle about midday. I know she used to be a minstrel woman, but I'm told she grows herbs now; all the physicians in the city go to her. I have some very rare plants in my garden. Write and tell her she can take anything from the garden that she likes: seeds, root runners, cuttings, anything at all if only she will come."

Roxane. She wanted Roxane to come here.

"Why do you want to talk to her mother and not Brianna herself? She's not a little girl anymore."

"I tried! She won't listen. She just looks at me in silence, murmurs excuses — and goes back to him. No, I have to speak to her mother."

Fenoglio said nothing. From all he knew of Roxane, he wasn't sure that she would come. After all, he himself had given her a proud nature and a dislike of royal blood. On the other hand — hadn't he promised Meggie to keep an eye on Dustfinger's daughter? If he couldn't keep any other promise, because his words had failed him so pitifully, perhaps he should at least try with this one. . . . *Heavens,* he thought. *I wouldn't like to be anywhere near Dustfinger when he hears that his daughter is spending her nights with Cosimo!*

"Very well, I'll send Roxane a messenger," he said. "But don't expect too much. I've heard that she isn't particularly happy to have her daughter living at court."

"I know!" Violante rose and glanced at the paper waiting on his desk. "Are you writing a new story? Is it about the Bluejay? You must show it to me first!" For a moment she was very much the Adderhead's daughter.

"Of course, of course," Fenoglio hastily assured her. "You'll get it before even the strolling players. And I'll write it the way you like a story best: dark, hopeless, sinister. . . ." *Cruel, too,* he added silently. For Her Ugliness loved stories full of darkness. She didn't want to be told tales of good fortune and beauty, she liked to hear about death, ugly things, secrets heavy with tears. She wanted her very own world, and it had never heard of beauty and good fortune.

She was still gazing at him, with the same arrogant look that her father turned on the world. Fenoglio remembered the words he had once written about her kindred: *Noble blood — for centuries the Adderhead's kin firmly believed that the blood flowing in their veins made them bolder, cleverer, stronger than all who were their subjects.* The same look in their eyes for hundreds and hundreds of years, even in those of Her Ugliness, whom her noble family would happily have drowned at birth in the castle moat, like a puppy born deformed.

"The servants say Brianna's mother can sing even better than she does. They say her mother knew how to make stones weep and roses blossom with her voice." Violante patted her face, just where the birthmark had been such a fiery red only a short time ago.

"Yes, I've heard much the same." Fenoglio followed her to the door.

"They even say she sang in my father's castle, but I don't believe that. My father never let any strolling players though his gate. The nearest they came was to be hanged outside it." *Yes, because there was once a rumor that your mother betrayed him with a minstrel,* thought Fenoglio as he opened the door for her.

"Brianna says her mother doesn't sing anymore because she believes her voice brings great misfortune to everyone she loves. It seems that happened to Brianna's father."

"I've heard that story, too."

Violante went out into the corridor. Even at close quarters her birthmark was barely visible now. "You'll send the messenger to her tomorrow morning?"

"If that's what you want."

She looked down the dark corridor. "Brianna will never talk about her father. One of the cooks says he was a fire-eater. The way that cook tells the story, Brianna's mother was deeply in love with him, but then one of the fire-raisers fell in love with her himself and slashed the fire-eater's face."

"Yes, I've heard that one as well!" Fenoglio looked at her thoughtfully. Dustfinger's bittersweet story was certainly very much to Violante's taste.

"She took him to a physician, the cook says, and stayed with him until his face was healed." How far away her voice sounded, as if she had lost herself among the words. Fenoglio's words. "But he left her all the same." Violante turned her face away. "Write that letter!" she said abruptly. "Write it tonight." Then she hurried away in her black dress, in such haste that it looked as if she were suddenly ashamed of coming to see him.

"Rosenquartz," said Fenoglio, closing the door behind her. "Do you think I'm only any good at making up characters who are sad or bad?"

But the glass man was still asleep beside the quill, from which ink dripped onto the empty sheet of parchment.

47

ROXANE

My mistress' eyes are nothing like the sun;
Coral is far more red than her lips' red.
If snow be white, why then her breasts are dun;
If hairs be wires, black wires grow on her head.

William Shakespeare, *Sonnets*, No. 130

Fenoglio waited for Roxane in a room in the castle where petitioners were usually received, ordinary folk who came here to tell Cosimo's administrators their troubles while a scribe recorded their words on paper (parchment being far too valuable for such purposes). Then they were sent away hoping that their prince would put his mind to their concerns sometime. But under the Laughing Prince that had not been very often, except at Violante's persuasion, so his subjects had usually settled their quarrels among themselves, with or without violence, depending on their temperament and their influence in the community. It was hoped that Cosimo would change all that soon. . . .

"What am I doing here?" murmured Fenoglio, looking around the high-ceilinged, narrow room. He had still been in bed (in much more comfort than at Minerva's house) when Her Ugliness's messenger had appeared. Violante sent her apologies, said the man, and since he was better with words than anyone else she knew, she asked him to talk to Roxane on her behalf. That was how the powerful acted — offloading the less pleasant tasks in life onto other people. But on the other hand . . . he had always hoped to meet Dustfinger's wife someday. Was she really as beautiful as his description of her?

With a sigh, he dropped into the armchair generally used by one of Cosimo's administrators. Since Cosimo's return, so many petitioners had flocked to the castle that in the future they were going to be allowed to come and put their cases on only two days of the week. Their prince had weightier matters on his mind just now than the troubles of a farmer whose neighbor had stolen his pig, a cobbler who had bought poor quality leather from a dealer, or a seamstress whose husband beat her every night when he came home drunk. Of course, there was a judge in every town of any size to settle such quarrels, but most of them had a poor reputation. Folk said, on both sides of the Wayless Wood, that you'd get your rights only if you filled the judges' pockets with gold. So those who had no gold went up to the castle to appeal to their angel-faced prince, without realizing that he had more than enough to do preparing for his war.

When Roxane entered the room she had two children with her: a girl of about five and an older boy, probably Brianna's brother, Jehan — the lad who had the dubious honor of playing with Jacopo now and then. She frowned as she scrutinized the tapestries on the walls celebrating the Laughing Prince's exploits in his youth. Unicorns, dragons, White Stags . . . Clearly nothing had been safe from his royal spear.

"Why don't we just go into the garden?" suggested Fenoglio,

noticing her expression of disapproval and quickly rising from the princely chair. If anything, she was even more beautiful than his description of her. But after all, he had sought the most wonderful of words for her when he wrote the scene in *Inkheart* where Dustfinger saw her for the first time. Yet all at once, now that she so suddenly stood before him in the flesh, he felt as lovelorn as a silly boy. *Oh, for goodness' sake, Fenoglio!* he reproached himself. *You made her up, and now you're staring at her as if this was the first time in your life you'd ever seen a woman!* Worst of all, Roxane seemed to notice it.

"Yes, let's go into the garden! I've heard a great deal about it, but I've never seen it," she said with a smile that cast Fenoglio into total confusion. "But first, please tell me why you want to speak to me. Your letter said only that it was about Brianna."

Why he wanted to speak to her? Huh! He cursed Violante's jealousy, Cosimo's faithless heart, and himself, too. "Let's go into the garden first," he said. Perhaps it would be easier to tell her what Her Ugliness had instructed him to say in the open air.

But of course it was not.

The boy set off in search of Jacopo as soon as they were outside, but the girl stayed with Roxane, clinging to her hand as she went from plant to plant — and Fenoglio found he couldn't utter a word.

"I know why I was summoned," said Roxane, just as he was trying for the tenth time to find the right words. "Brianna didn't tell me herself, she'd never do that. But the maid who takes Cosimo his breakfast every morning often comes to me for advice about her sick mother, and she's told me that Brianna seldom leaves his room. Not even at night."

"Yes. Yes, that's it . . . Violante is concerned. And she hopes that you . . ." Oh, damn it, how his voice was faltering! He didn't know how to go on. This wretched confusion. His story clearly had too many characters in it. How was he to foresee everything they'd think of? It was downright impossible, particularly when a young girl's heart was involved. No one could expect him to understand anything about that.

Roxane scrutinized his face as if she were still waiting for the end of his sentence. *You stupid old fool, surely you're not going to blush,* Fenoglio thought — and felt the blood shoot into his wrinkled face as if to drive age out of it.

"The boy has told me about you," said Roxane. "Farid. He's in love with the girl who's staying with you — Meggie, isn't that right? When he speaks her name he looks as if he had a pearl in his mouth."

"Yes, I'm beginning to think that Meggie likes him, too."

What exactly, wondered Fenoglio uneasily, *has the boy been saying about me? Telling her I made her up, and the man she loves, too — only to kill him off again?*

The little girl was still clutching Roxane's hand. With a smile, she put a flower in the child's long, dark hair. *You know something, Fenoglio?* he thought. *All this is nonsense! What makes you think you invented her? She must always have been here, long before you wrote your story. A woman like her can't possibly be made of nothing but words! You've been wrong all this time! They were here already, all of them: Dustfinger and Capricorn, Basta and Roxane, Minerva, Violante, the Adderhead . . . you merely wrote their story, but they didn't like it, and now they're writing it for themselves.*

The little girl felt the flower with her fingers and smiled.

"Is she Dustfinger's daughter?" asked Fenoglio.

Roxane looked at him in surprise. "No," she said. "Our second daughter died long ago. But how do you come to know Dustfinger? He's never mentioned you to me."

You fool, Fenoglio, you stupid fool.

"Oh, I certainly know Dustfinger!" he stammered. "In fact, I know him very well. I often visit the strolling players, you see, when they pitch their tents here outside the city wall. That's where — er — where I met him."

"Really?" Roxane ran her fingers over a plant with feathery leaves. "I didn't know he'd been back there already." Her face thoughtful, she moved on to another flower bed. "Wild mallow. I grow it in my own fields. Isn't it beautiful? So useful, too. . . ." She did not look at Fenoglio as she went on. "Dustfinger has gone. Yet again. All I had was a message to say he's following men of the Adderhead's troops who have kidnapped some of the strolling players. Her mother," she added, putting her arm around the girl, "is one of them. And the Black Prince, a good friend of his."

They'd captured the Prince, too? Fenoglio tried to hide his alarm. Obviously, matters were even worse than he'd thought — and what he was writing down on parchment was still no use.

Roxane felt the seed heads of a lavender bush. Their sweet scent immediately filled the air. "I'm told that you were there when Cloud-Dancer was killed. Did you know his murderer? I heard that it was Basta, one of the fire-raisers from the forest."

"I'm afraid what you heard was right." Not a night passed when Fenoglio did not see Basta's knife flying through the air. It pursued him into all his dreams.

"The boy told Dustfinger that Basta was back. But I hoped he wasn't telling the truth. I'm anxious" — she spoke so softly that Fenoglio could hardly make out her words — "so anxious that I keep finding myself just standing and staring at the forest, as if he might appear among the trees again at any moment, the way he did on the morning he came back." She picked a dried lavender head and shook some of the tiny seeds into her hand. "May I take these with me?"

"You can take anything you want," replied Fenoglio. "Seeds, runners, cuttings, so Violante told me to tell you — anything, if you'll persuade your daughter to keep Violante herself company in the future and not her husband."

Roxane looked at the seeds in her hand and then let a few of them fall lightly to the flower bed. "It won't work. My daughter hasn't listened to me for years. She loves the life up here, although she knows that I don't, and she's loved Cosimo ever since she first saw him ride out of the castle gate on his wedding day. She was barely seven then, and after that her heart was set on coming here to the castle, even if it meant working as a maid. If Violante hadn't once heard her singing down in the kitchen she'd probably still be emptying chamber pots, feeding kitchen scraps to the pigs, and sometimes stealing upstairs in secret to feast her eyes on the statues of Cosimo. Instead, she became like Violante's little sister . . . wore her clothes, looked after her son, sang and danced for her like one of the strolling players, like her own mother. Not with Motley skirts and dirty feet, not sleeping by the roadside and carrying a knife to defend herself against vagrants trying to creep in under her blanket by night, but in silken clothes and with a soft bed to sleep in. She wears her hair loose, all the same, just as I did, and she loves too much, exactly as I did. No," she said, placing the seeds in Fenoglio's hand. "Tell Violante that much as I would like to help her, I can't."

The little girl looked at Fenoglio. Where was her mother now?

"Listen," he told Roxane. Her beauty took his breath away. "Take as many seeds as you like. They'll grow and thrive in your fields much better than within these gray walls. Dustfinger has gone off with Meggie. I sent her a messenger. As soon as the man is back you'll hear everything he has to tell: where they are now, how long they'll stay away, everything!"

Roxane took the lavender from him again, picked a handful more, and carefully put them in the bag hanging from her belt. "Thank you," she said. "But if I don't hear from Dustfinger soon I shall set off in search of him myself. I've stayed here too often just waiting for him to come back safe and sound, and I can't get it out of my mind that Basta is back!"

"But how will you find him? The last news I heard from Meggie was that they were making for a mill known as the Spelt-Mill. It's on the far side of the forest in Argenta. That's dangerous country!"

Roxane smiled at him, like a woman explaining the way of the world to her child. "It will soon be dangerous here, too," she said. "Do you think the Adderhead won't have heard by now that Cosimo is having swords forged day and night? Perhaps you should look around for some other place to do your writing, before the fiery arrows come raining down on your desk."

Roxane's mount was waiting in the Outer Courtyard of the castle. It was an old black horse, thin and going gray around the muzzle. "I know the Spelt-Mill," she said, lifting the little girl up on the horse's back. "I'll ride past it, and if I don't find them there I'll try the Barn Owl's place. He's the best physician I know on either side of the forest, and he looked after Dustfinger as a boy. Perhaps he may have heard news of him."

Of course, the Barn Owl! How could Fenoglio have forgotten him? If Dustfinger ever had anything like a father, it was this man. He had been one of the physicians who went around with the strolling players from place to place, from market to market. Unfortunately, Fenoglio didn't know much more about him. *Damn it all,* he thought, *how can you forget your own stories? And don't try making your age an excuse.*

"If you see Jehan, send him home," said Roxane, as she swung herself up behind the girl on the horse. "He knows the way."

"Are you planning to ride through the Wayless Wood on that old nag?"

"This old nag will still carry me as far as I want," she said. The girl leaned back against Roxane's breast as she gathered up the reins. "Good-bye," she said, but Fenoglio held the horse back by the bridle. An idea had come to him, an idea born of desperation, but what else could he do? Wait for the mounted messenger he had sent, until it was too late?

"Roxane," he said, low-voiced, as he looked up at her, "I have to get a letter to Meggie. I've sent a horseman after her to tell me where she is and whether she's well, but he isn't back yet, and by the time I've sent him off again with the letter . . . *(Don't tell her anything about Basta and Slasher, Fenoglio, it would only upset her unnecessarily!)* . . . well, what I'm getting at is . . . *(For heaven's sake, Fenoglio, don't stare at her like that, stammering like an old dotard!)* . . . what I mean is, if you really do ride after Dustfinger, would you take my letter to Meggie with you? You'd probably find her sooner than any messenger I could send now." *"What kind of a letter?"* an inner voice mocked him. *"A letter telling her that nothing has occurred to you?"* But as usual, he ignored the voice. "It's a very important letter!" If he could have spoken even more softly he would have done so.

Roxane wrinkled her brow. Even that was a beautiful sight. "The last time you had anything to do with a letter, it cost Cloud-Dancer his life. Still, very well, bring it to me if you like. As I said, I'm not going to wait much longer."

The castle courtyard seemed strangely empty to Fenoglio when she had gone. Rosenquartz was waiting in his room beside the parchment, which was still blank, looking reproachful. "You know something, Rosenquartz?" Fenoglio said to the glass man, sitting down on his chair again with a sigh. "I think Dustfinger would wring my old neck if he knew how I gazed at his wife. But what does that matter — he'd like to wring my neck, anyway, one reason more or less makes no difference. He doesn't deserve Roxane, anyway, leaving her alone so often!"

"Someone's in a truly princely temper again!" remarked Rosenquartz.

"Be quiet!" growled Fenoglio. "This parchment is about to be covered with words. And I just hope you've stirred the ink properly!"

"The ink's not to blame if the parchment is still blank!" retorted the glass man.

Fenoglio didn't throw the pen at him, although his fingers itched to do so. The words that had passed Rosenquartz's pale lips were only the truth. How could the glass man help it if the truth was unpleasant?

48

THE CASTLE BY THE SEA

It was a page he had
Found in the handbook
Of heartbreak.
> Wallace Stevens, "Madame la Fleurie,"
> *Collected Poems*

It was exactly as Mo had imagined the Castle of Night: mighty towers, round and heavily built, crenellations like black teeth below the silver rooftops. Mo thought he was seeing Fenoglio's words before his eyes when the exhausted captives staggered through the castle gateway ahead of him. Black words on paper white as milk: *The Castle of Night, a dark growth by the sea, every stone of it polished with screams, its walls slippery with tears and blood.* Yes, Fenoglio was a good storyteller. Silver rimmed the battlements and gateways and wound over the walls like snail trails. The Adderhead loved that metal; his subjects called it moonspit, perhaps because an alchemist had once spun him a tale that it could keep away the White Women, who hated it because it reflected their pale faces. Or so Fenoglio had written, anyway.

Of all places in the Inkworld, this was the last where Mo

would have chosen to be. But he wasn't choosing his own way through this story, that much was certain. It had even given him a new name — the Bluejay. Sometimes he felt as if the name were really his. As if he had been carrying it around in him like a seed that only now had begun to grow in this world of words.

He was feeling better. The fever was still there, like opaque glass in front of his eyes, but the pain was a tame kitten by comparison with the beast of prey that had still been tearing at him in the cave. He could sit up if he gritted his teeth, he could look around to find Resa. He seldom took his eyes off her, as if, in that way, he could protect her from the glances of the soldiers, their kicks and blows. The sight of her hurt more than his wound. By the time the gates of the Castle of Night closed behind her and the other prisoners, she could barely keep on her feet for exhaustion. She stood still and looked up at the walls surrounding her, like a mouse examining the trap it has fallen into. One of the soldiers pushed her on with the shaft of his spear, and Mo longed to put his hands around the man's neck and press hard. He tasted the hatred on his tongue and in his heart like a shivering sensation, and cursed his own weakness.

Resa looked at him and tried to smile, but she was too exhausted, and he saw her fear. The soldiers reined in their horses and surrounded the prisoners, as if they could possibly have escaped from those steeply towering walls. The vipers' heads supporting the roofs and ledges left no one in any doubt who the lord of this castle was. They looked down on the forlorn little troop from everywhere, with forked tongues in their narrow mouths, eyes of red gemstone, silver scales shimmering like fish skin in the moonlight.

"Put the Bluejay in the tower!" Firefox's voice was almost lost in the huge expanse of the castle courtyard. "And take the others to the dungeons." So they were going to be separated. Mo saw Resa, moving painfully on her sore feet, turn to Firefox. One of the mounted men kicked her back so roughly with his boot that she fell to the ground. And Mo felt a dragging sensation in his breast, as if his hatred had given birth to something, something that wanted to kill. A new heart, cold and hard.

A weapon. If only he had a weapon, one of the ugly swords they all wore at their belts, or one of those sharp, shiny knives. There seemed to be nothing more desirable in the world than such a sharp piece of metal — more desirable than all the words Fenoglio could write. They hauled him off the cart. He could hardly keep his footing, but somehow or other he stood upright. Four soldiers surrounded him and seized him, and he imagined himself killing them one by one. While that new, cold heart in his breast beat time.

"Hey, go a bit more carefully with him, will you?" Firefox snapped at them. "You think I brought him this whole damn way just for you fools to kill him now?"

Resa was crying. Mo heard her call his name again and again. He turned, but he couldn't see her anywhere, he only heard her voice. He called her name, tried to break free, kicked out at the soldiers who were dragging him away toward one of the towers.

"You just try that again!" snarled one of them. "What's biting you, then? You two will soon be reunited. The Adderhead likes wives to watch an execution."

"That's right, he can't get enough of their weeping and wailing," mocked another man. "You'll see, he'll keep her alive a little longer just for that. And you'll get a magnificent execution, Bluejay, you mark my words."

Bluejay. A new name. A new heart. Like ice in his breast, with edges as sharp as a blade.

THE MILL

"We rode and rode and nothing happened. Wherever we went, it was calm, peaceful, and beautiful. You could call it a quiet evening in the mountains, I thought, if that hadn't been so wrong."

Astrid Lindgren, *The Brothers Lionheart*

It took Dustfinger over three days to reach the Spelt-Mill with Meggie and Farid. Three long, gray days during which Meggie hardly spoke a word, although Farid did his best to cheer her up. Most of the time it was raining, a fine drizzle, and soon none of them could remember what it felt like to sleep in dry clothes. Only when, at last, the dark valley where the mill stood opened out before them, did the sun break through the clouds. Low in the sky above the hills, it shed golden light on the river and the shingle roofs. There wasn't another dwelling to be seen far and wide — only the miller's house, a few outhouses, and the mill itself, with its great wooden wheel dipping deep into the water. Willows, poplars, and eucalyptus bushes lined the bank of the river on which it stood, together with alders and wild pear trees. There was a cart standing at the foot of the steps leading into the mill. A broad-shouldered man, dusty with flour, was just loading it up with sacks. There was no one else in sight except a boy who, on seeing them approach, ran over to the house. All looked peaceful — peaceful and quiet, apart from the rushing of the water, which drowned out even the chirping of the cicadas.

"You'll see!" Farid whispered to Meggie. "Fenoglio's written something. I'm sure he has. Or if not, we'll just wait until —"

"We'll do no such thing," Dustfinger brusquely interrupted him, looking distrustfully around. "We'll ask about the letter and then go on. Many people come to this mill, and after what happened on the road the first of the soldiers will soon be putting in an appearance. If it was up to me, we wouldn't show our faces here until everything had calmed down a bit, but if you must . . ."

"Suppose the letter hasn't come yet?" Meggie looked at him with anxiety in her face. "When I wrote to Fenoglio I told him I'd wait for it here!"

"Yes, and I don't remember saying you could write to him at all, did I?"

Meggie made no answer, and Dustfinger glanced at the mill again. "I just hope Cloud-Dancer delivered the letter safely, and the old man hasn't been showing it around. I don't have to tell you what damage the words on a page can do."

He looked around for the last time before moving out of the cover of the trees. Then he signaled to Farid and Meggie to follow him and strode toward the buildings. The boy who had run to the house was sitting on the steps outside the door of the mill again, and a few chickens ran away, squawking, as Gwin shot toward them.

"Farid, catch that damn marten!" ordered Dustfinger, as he

whistled Jink to his side, but Gwin hissed at Farid. He didn't bite him (he never bit Farid), but he wasn't letting himself be caught, either. He slipped through Farid's legs and bounded after one of the chickens. Cackling, it fluttered up the steps of the mill, but the marten wasn't to be shaken off that way. He shot past the boy, who was still sitting on the steps apparently taking no interest in anything, and disappeared through the open door in pursuit of the chicken. A moment later the cackling stopped abruptly — and Meggie glanced anxiously at Dustfinger.

"Oh, wonderful!" he murmured, making Jink jump back into his backpack. "A marten in the flour and a dead chicken, that's going to make us very popular here! Speak of the devil . . ."

The man loading up the cart wiped his floury hands on his trousers and came toward them.

"Excuse me, please!" Dustfinger called to him. "Where's the miller? I'll pay for the chicken, of course. But we're really here to collect something. A letter."

The man stopped in front of them. He was a full head taller than Dustfinger. "I'm the miller now," he said. "My father's dead. A letter, you say?" He inspected them one by one. His eyes lingered longest on Dustfinger's face.

"Yes, a letter from Ombra," replied Dustfinger, glancing up at the mill. "Why isn't it grinding? Don't the farmers bring you their grain anymore, or have you run out of miller's men?"

The miller shrugged. "Someone brought us damp spelt to grind yesterday. The bran gummed up the millstones. My man spent hours cleaning them. What kind of letter is it? And who's it to? Don't you have a name?"

Dustfinger looked at him thoughtfully. "So *is* there a letter here?"

"It's for me," said Meggie, stepping forward beside him. "Meggie Folchart. That's my name."

The miller inspected her at length — her dirty dress, her matted hair — and then he nodded. "Yes, I have it inside," he said. "I'm only asking because a letter can be dangerous in the wrong hands, can't it? Go on in, I'll just load up this last sack."

"Fill the water bottles," Dustfinger whispered to Farid, slinging his backpack over the boy's shoulders. "I'll catch that damn marten, pay for the chicken, and as soon as Meggie has the letter we'll be off out of here."

Before Farid could protest, he had disappeared into the mill. With Meggie. The boy passed his arm over his dirty face and watched them go.

"Fill the water bottles!" muttered Farid as he climbed down the bank to the river. "Catch the marten! Does he think I'm his servant?" The mill boy was still sitting on the steps as Farid stood in the cold river, holding their gourds under water. There was something about that boy that he didn't like. Something in his face. Fear. Yes, that was it. He was afraid. What of? *It's hardly likely to be me,* thought Farid, looking around. Something was wrong, he could smell it. He'd always been able to smell it, even back in his other life when he had to stand guard, spy out the land, follow people unseen, go scouting ahead — oh yes, he knew what danger smelled like. He put the water bottles in the backpack with Jink and scratched the sleepy marten's head.

He didn't see the body until he was about to wade back to the bank. The dead man was still young, and Farid had a feeling that he'd seen his face before. Hadn't the man thrown a copper coin into his bowl in Ombra, during the celebrations at the castle? The body was caught in the branches bending low above the water, but the wound in its chest was clearly visible. A knife. Farid's heart began to race so suddenly that he could hardly breathe. He looked at the mill. The boy sitting outside it was clutching his own shoulders as if he feared he might fall apart with terror. But the miller had disappeared.

No sound could be heard from the mill, but that meant nothing. The rushing water would have drowned out everything — screams, the clash of swords . . .

Come on, Farid, he told himself sharply. *Slink up there and find out what's going on. You've done it a hundred times — no, even more often.* Ducking low, he waded through the river and climbed up onto the bank behind the mill wheel. His heart was in his mouth as he leaned against the wall of the mill, but that was nothing new, either. A thousand times or more he had slunk up to a building, a window, a closed door, with his heart beating hard. He leaned Dustfinger's backpack with the sleeping marten in it against the wall.

Gwin. Gwin had run inside the mill. And Dustfinger had gone after him. That wasn't good. Not good at all. Meggie was with him, too. Farid looked up at the mill. The nearest window was a good way above his head, but luckily the wall was rough-textured. "Keep silent as a snake," he whispered to himself as he hauled himself up. The windowsill was white with flour dust. Holding his breath, Farid peered in. The first thing he saw was a pudgy fellow with a foolish face, probably the miller's man. Farid had never seen the other man beside him before, but unfortunately he couldn't say the same of his companion.

Basta. The same thin face, the same vicious smile. Only the clothes were different. Basta was no longer wearing his white shirt and black suit with the flower in his buttonhole. No, Basta now wore the Adderhead's silvery gray, and he had a sword at his side. With a knife in his belt, too, of course. But he was holding a dead chicken in his left hand.

Only the millstone stood between him and Dustfinger — the millstone and Gwin, who was crouching in the middle of the round stone, staring longingly at the chicken as the tip of his tail twitched restlessly up and down. Meggie was standing close to Dustfinger. Was she thinking the same as Farid? Did she remember Fenoglio's deadly words? Perhaps, for she was trying to entice Gwin over to her, but the marten took no notice.

What am I to do? Farid wondered. *What on earth am I to do? Climb in?* Nonsense, what use would that be? His silly little knife couldn't prevail against two swords, and then there'd be the miller and his man to deal with, too. The miller was standing right beside the door. "Well, are these the folk you were waiting for?" he asked Basta. How pleased with himself and his lies he looked. Farid would have loved to use his knife to peel that sly smile off his lips.

"Yes, they are!" purred Basta. "The little witch and the fire-eater in the bargain. It was well worth the wait. Even though I'll probably never get that damn flour out of my lungs again."

Think, Farid. Go on. He looked around, let his eyes wander, as if they could find him a way of escape through the solid masonry. There was another window, but the miller's man was standing in front of it, and a wooden staircase led to the loft, where they probably stored the grain. They would tip it through the wooden hopper sticking up through the floor of the loft, and then it would fall on the millstone. The hopper! Yes, it rose through the ceiling of the mill like a wooden mouth right above the stone. Suppose he . . .

Farid looked up at the mill. Was there another window higher up? Yes, there was, hardly more than a hole in the wall, but he had crawled through narrower openings before. His heart was still in his mouth as he hauled himself farther up the wall. The river flowed fast to his left, and a crow stared at him from a willow as suspiciously as if it were about to give him away to the miller at any moment. Farid was breathing heavily as he forced his shoulders through the narrow aperture in the wall. As he set foot on the wooden floorboards of the loft, they creaked treacherously, but the river drowned out that telltale sound. On his stomach, Farid inched over to the hopper and peered down through it. Right below him stood Basta. And Dustfinger must be standing opposite him on the other side of the stone, with Meggie. Farid couldn't see him, but he could imagine only too well what Dustfinger was thinking of: Fenoglio's words telling the tale of his death.

"Grab that marten, Slasher!" Basta told the man beside him. "Go on, do it."

"Do it yourself. You think I want to catch rabies?"

"Come here, Gwin!" That was Dustfinger's voice. What was he doing? Trying to laugh his own fear in the face, the way he sometimes did when the fire bit his skin? Gwin leaped off the stone. He would be sitting on Dustfinger's shoulder, staring at Basta. Stupid Gwin. He didn't know about the words. . . .

"Fine new clothes, Basta!" said Dustfinger. "When the servant finds a new master he must wear new clothes, mustn't he?"

"Servant? Who's a servant here? Just listen to him. As bold as if he'd never felt my knife! Have you forgotten how you screamed when it cut your face?" Basta set one boot on the millstone. "Don't you dare move so much as a finger. Hands up! Go on, up in the air! I know what you can do with fire in this world. One little whisper from you, one snap of your fingers, and my knife goes into the little witch's breast."

A snap of the fingers. *Yes, get on with it, Farid!* He looked around, searching for what he needed, quickly twisted some straw together to make a torch, and began whispering. "Come along!" he lured the fire, clicking his tongue and hissing the way Dustfinger had shown him after he put a little fire-honey in his mouth for the first time. They had practiced every evening behind Roxane's house, practiced the language of fire, its crackling words . . . Farid whispered them all until a tiny flame came licking up out of the straw.

"Ooh dear! See how the little witch is staring at me, Slasher?" asked Basta below him, with pretended terror. "What a pity she needs written words for her witchcraft! But there's no book anywhere here. Wasn't it nice of her to write to us in person and tell us where to find you?" Basta disguised his voice to make it sound shrill and girlish. *"The Adderhead's men have taken them all away, my parents and the strolling players! Write something for me, Fenoglio!* Or something like that. You know, I was really disappointed to hear that your father's still alive. Oh, don't look so disbelieving, little witch, I still can't read and I don't intend to learn, but there are enough fools around the place who can, even in this world. A scribe ran into our arms right outside the city gates of Ombra. It took a little while for him to decipher your scribble , but we still had a good enough start to get here ahead of you. We were even on the spot in time to kill the old man's messenger, who was supposed to warn you."

"You're even more talkative than you used to be, Basta." Dustfinger's voice sounded as if he found this tedious. How well he could hide his fear! Farid always admired him for that, almost more than for his skill with fire.

Slowly, very slowly, Basta drew his knife from his belt. Dustfinger didn't like knives. He generally kept his in his backpack, and his backpack was leaning against the wall outside. Farid had so often begged him to keep the knife in his belt, but no, he wouldn't hear of it.

"Talkative? Well, well." Basta looked at his reflection in the bright blade of the knife. "No one could say the same of you. But I tell you what! Since we've known each other so long, I'll carry the news of your death to your wife in person! What do you say to that, fire-eater? Do you think Roxane will be glad to see me again?" Caressingly, he ran two fingers along the blade. "And as for you, little witch . . . I thought it was really nice of you to entrust your letter to an old tightrope-walker. With his stiff leg, he wasn't half as fast as my knife."

"Cloud-Dancer? You killed Cloud-Dancer?"

There was no boredom in Dustfinger's voice now. *Stand still, please,* whispered Farid. *Please, please stand still.* He was hastily feeding more straw to the flames.

"Ah, so you didn't know that yet!" Basta's voice became soft with contentment. "Yes, there'll be no more dancing for your old friend. Ask Slasher, he was there."

"You're lying!" Meggie's voice shook. Farid bent cautiously forward. He saw Dustfinger push her roughly behind him, his eyes searching for a way out, but there was none. Sacks full of flour were stacked behind him and Meggie, Slasher was barring their way to their right, on their left was the man with the silly grin, and in front of the window through which Farid had peered stood the miller. But there was straw lying on the floor at their feet, a great deal of straw, and it would burn almost as well as paper.

Basta laughed. With one bound, he leaped up on the millstone and looked down at Dustfinger. He was standing very close to the outlet of the hopper now. *Hurry up, come on,* whispered

Farid, kindling a second bundle of straw from the first and holding them both above the funnel. He hoped its wood wouldn't catch fire. He hoped the straw would slide through. He hoped so. His fingers were scorched as he stuffed the burning bundles in, but he took no notice. Dustfinger was in a trap, and Meggie was in it with him. What did a couple of burned fingers matter?

"Yes, poor Cloud-Dancer was far too slow," purred Basta, as he tossed his knife from one hand to the other. "You're faster than him, I know, fire-eater, but you won't get away all the same. And this time I'm not just going to cut your face, this time I'll slice your skin off in strips from head to foot."

Now! Farid let the burning straw drop. The hopper swallowed it like a sack of corn and spat it out on Basta's boots.

"Fire! Where's that fire coming from?" It was the miller's voice. His man was bellowing like an ox when it sees the butcher's hatchet.

Farid's fingers hurt, his skin was beginning to blister, but the fire was dancing, dancing up Basta's boots, licking close to his arms. Terrified, he stumbled, fell backward off the millstone, and cracked open his head against the edge of it. Blood flowed. Basta feared fire, feared it more than the bad luck against which his amulets were supposed to protect him.

As for Farid, he raced down the steps to the floor of the mill, pushed aside the miller's man, who was staring at him as if he were a ghost, ran to Meggie, and pulled her away with him toward the window through which he had first looked.

"Jump!" he called to her. "Quick, jump out!" Meggie was trembling. Her hair was full of flour, and she closed her eyes before she jumped, but jump she did.

Farid looked around at Dustfinger. He was talking to the

flames, making them sing and grow, while the miller and his man beat desperately at the burning straw with empty sacks, but the fire danced on. It was dancing for Dustfinger.

Farid crouched in the open window. "Come on!" he called to Dustfinger. "Hurry up!"

Where was Basta?

Dustfinger pushed the miller aside and ran to him through the smoke and flames. Farid swung himself out of the window and clung to the sill outside as he watched the dazed Basta hauling himself up by the millstone. His hand was bloody when he put it to the back of his head. "Get him!" he shouted to Slasher. "Hold the fire-eater fast!"

"Quick!" cried Farid, as his toes tried to find a foothold on the outside of the wall, but Dustfinger stumbled over an empty sack as he ran. Gwin jumped off his shoulder and scurried toward Farid; when Dustfinger got to his feet again Slasher was standing between him and the window, coughing, his sword in his hand.

"Come on!" Farid heard Meggie shouting. She was standing right under the window, her eyes wide with fear, staring up at him. But Farid wriggled his way back into the burning mill.

"What are you doing? Get out!" Dustfinger shouted at him as he struck out with a burning sack at Slasher, whose trousers had caught fire. Slasher swayed as he lashed out with his sword, first at the flames, then at Dustfinger. His sharp blade slit open Dustfinger's leg just as Farid jumped down into the burning straw again. Dustfinger stumbled back against the wall, pressing his hand to his thigh, while Slasher raised his sword again, half mad with rage and pain.

"No!" Farid's own voice rang in his ears as he jumped at the man. He bit his shoulder and kicked him until he dropped the sword that he had been pointing at Dustfinger's chest. Then

Farid pushed Slasher into the flames. The man was more than a head taller than Farid himself, but desperation lent him strength. Farid was about to attack Basta, too, as he emerged from the smoke, coughing, but Dustfinger pulled him back and hissed at the flames until they made for Basta like angry vipers. Farid heard Basta scream but did not turn to look. He just stumbled toward the window, with Dustfinger beside him, cursing as he pressed his fingers to his bleeding leg. But he was alive. He was really alive. While the fire was devouring Basta.

THE BEST OF ALL NIGHTS

"Eat," said Merlot.

"I couldn't possibly," said Despereaux, backing away from the book.

"Why?"

"Um," said Despereaux, "it would ruin the story."

Kate DiCamillo, *The Tale of Despereaux*

Later, none of them knew how they had gotten away from the mill. All Farid could remember were images: of Meggie's face as she stumbled down to the river, of the blood in the water when Dustfinger jumped in, of the smoke they could see still rising into the sky after they had been wading through the cold water for more than an hour. But no one came after them: not Slasher or the miller or his man, and not Basta, either. Only Gwin appeared on the bank at some point. Stupid Gwin.

It was the middle of the night when Dustfinger clambered out of the water, his face pale with exhaustion. As he let himself drop onto the grass, Farid anxiously listened into the darkness, but all he heard was a loud and steady roar like the breathing of a gigantic animal.

434

"What's that?" he whispered.

"The sea. Don't you know what the sea sounds like?"

The sea. Gwin jumped on Farid's back as he was looking at Dustfinger's leg, but he shooed the marten away. "Get out!" he snapped. "Go hunting! You've done enough harm for one day." Then he let Jink out of the backpack, too, and looked for something to bind up the wound. Meggie wrung out her wet dress and crouched beside them.

"Is it bad?"

"No, I'm fine," said Dustfinger, but he winced as Farid cleaned the deep gash. "Poor Cloud-Dancer!" he murmured. "He escaped death once, and now the Grim Reaper's come for him after all. Who knows? Perhaps the White Women don't like people to slip through their fingers like that."

"I'm sorry." Meggie spoke so quietly that Farid could hardly hear her. "I'm so very sorry. It's all my fault, and he died for nothing. Because where is Fenoglio going to find us now, even if he's written something for me?"

"Fenoglio." Dustfinger spoke as if it were the name of some disease.

"Did you feel them, too?" Meggie looked at him. "I thought I could feel his words on my skin. I thought: They're going to kill Dustfinger, and there's nothing we can do about it!"

"But there was," said Farid defiantly.

Dustfinger, however, leaned back and looked up at the stars. "Really? We'll see. Perhaps the old man's thought up some different fate for me by now. Perhaps death is waiting just around another corner."

"Let it wait!" was all Farid would say, fishing a bag out of Dustfinger's backpack. "A little fairy dust can never hurt," he murmured as he trickled the glittering powder into the wound.

Then he pulled his shirt over his head, cut off a strip with his knife, and tied it carefully around Dustfinger's leg. It wasn't easy with his burned fingers, but he did his best, although the pain twisted his face.

Dustfinger reached for his hand and looked at it, frowning. "Heavens, your fingers are covered with as many blisters as if fire-elves had been dancing on them," he commented. "I guess we both need a physician. What a pity Roxane isn't here." Sighing, Dustfinger lay down on his back again and looked up at the dark sky. "You know what, Farid?" he said, as if talking to the stars. "There's one really strange thing about all this. If Meggie's father hadn't plucked me out of my own story, I don't suppose I'd ever have found such a fabulous watchdog as you." He winked at Meggie. "Did you see him biting? I'll bet Slasher thought it was the Black Prince's bear gnawing his shoulder."

"Oh, stop it!" Farid didn't know where to look. Embarrassed, he picked a blade of grass with his bare toes.

"Yes, but Farid is cleverer than the bear," said Meggie. "Much cleverer."

"Indeed. Cleverer than me, too," Dustfinger pointed out. "And as for what he can do with fire, I'm beginning to get seriously worried."

Farid couldn't help it; he had to grin. He felt so proud that the blood shot all the way to his ears, but in the dark no one, luckily, would see him blushing.

Dustfinger felt his leg and cautiously rose to his feet. The first step he took made his face contort with pain, but then he limped up and down the riverbank a few times. "There we are," he said. "A little slower than usual, but it will do. It must." Then he stopped in front of Farid. "I believe I owe you a debt," he said.

"How am I to repay you? Perhaps I could show you something new? A game with fire that only I can play? How about that?"

Farid held his breath. "What kind of a game is it?" he asked.

"I can't show you except by the sea," replied Dustfinger, "but we must go there, anyway, because we both need a physician. And the best physician I know lives by the sea. In the shadow of the Castle of Night."

They decided to take turns keeping watch. Farid said he would take the first watch, and while Meggie and Dustfinger slept behind him, under the branches of a durmast oak that dipped low to the ground, he sat in the grass and looked up at the sky, where more stars shone than there were fireflies hovering above the river. Farid tried to remember a night, any night, when he had felt as he did now, so entirely at ease with himself, but he couldn't. This was the best of all nights for him — in spite of all the terrors that lay behind him, in spite of his burned fingers, which still hurt although Dustfinger had put fairy dust on them and the cooling ointment that Roxane had made for him.

He felt so much alive. As alive as the fire.

He had saved Dustfinger. He had been stronger than the words. Everything was all right.

The two martens were squabbling behind him, no doubt over prey of some kind. "Wake me when the moon is above that hill," Dustfinger had said, but when Farid went to him he was sleeping deeply, with such peace in his face that Farid decided to let him sleep on and returned to his place under the stars.

Soon afterward, when he heard steps behind him, it was not Dustfinger but Meggie he saw there. "I keep waking up," she said. "I just can't stop thinking."

"Wondering how Fenoglio is going to find you now?"

She nodded.

She still believed in words so much. Farid believed in other things: in his knife, in courage and cunning. And in friendship. Meggie leaned her head against his shoulder, and they both remained as silent as the stars above them. After a while a wind rose, cold and gusty, salty as seawater, and Meggie sat up and clasped her arms around her knees, shivering.

"This world," she said. "Do you really like it?"

What a question! Farid never asked himself such things. He was glad to be with Dustfinger again and didn't mind where that was.

"It's a cruel world, don't you think?" Meggie went on. "Mo often told me I forget how cruel it is too easily."

With his burned fingers, Farid stroked her fair hair. It shone even in the dark. "They're all cruel," he said. "The world I come from, the world you come from, and this one, too. Maybe people don't see the cruelty in your world right away, it's better hidden, but it's there all the same."

He put his arm around her, sensed her fear, her anxiety, her anger . . . It was as if he could hear her heart whispering as clearly as the voice of fire.

"You know a funny thing?" she asked. "Even if I could go back at this moment, I wouldn't. Now that's crazy, isn't it? It's almost as if I'd always wanted to come here, to somewhere like this. But why? It's a terrible place!"

"Terrible and beautiful," said Farid, and kissed her. Kissing her tasted good. Much better than Dustfinger's fire-honey. Much better than anything he had ever tasted before. "You can't go back, anyway," he whispered to her. "As soon as we have your father free, we'll explain that to him."

"Explain what?"

"Why, that we're afraid he'll have to leave you here. Because you belong with me now, and I'm staying with Dustfinger."

She laughed and pressed her face to his shoulder in embarrassment. "I'm sure Mo won't agree to that."

"Well? So tell him the girls here marry when they're your age."

She laughed again, but then her face grew grave. "Perhaps Mo will stay, too," she said softly. "Perhaps we'll all stay . . . Resa and Fenoglio, too. And we'll go and fetch Elinor and Darius as well, and then we'll all live happily ever after." The sad note had crept back into her voice. "They can't hang Mo, Farid!" she whispered. "We'll save him, won't we? And my mother and the others. It's always like that in stories: Bad things happen, but then it all ends happily. And this is a story."

"Of course!" said Farid, although with the best will in the world he couldn't imagine that happy ending. He felt good, though, all the same.

After a while, Meggie dropped off to sleep beside him. And he sat there and kept watch over her — her and Dustfinger — all night long. It was the best of all nights.

THE RIGHT WORDS

There's nothing ill can dwell in such a temple.
If the ill spirit have so fair a house,
Good things will strive to dwell with't.
                         William Shakespeare, *The Tempest*

The groom was a fool and took forever to saddle up the wretched horse. *I never invented a character like that,* thought Fenoglio. *Lucky that I'm in a good mood.* For he was indeed in the best of moods. He had been whistling quietly to himself for hours, because he had done it. He had found the solution! Yes, at last the words had flowed onto the parchment as if they'd just been waiting for him to fish them out of the sea of letters. The right words. The only right words. Now the story could go on and all would end well. He was an enchanter, after all, a conjuror with words, one of the very first quality. No one could hold a candle to him — well, one or two, maybe, but in his own world, not this one. If only this dolt of a groom would hurry up! It was high time he went to Roxane's house or she would ride away without the letter — and then how was he going to get it to

Meggie? For there was still no sign of life from the young hot-head he had sent after her. That callow youth had probably gotten lost in the Wayless Wood.

He felt for the letter under his cloak. A good thing that words weighed light, light as a feather, even the most important of them. Roxane wouldn't have a heavy load to carry when she took Meggie the Adderhead's death warrant. And she would take something else to the principality by the sea with her — the certainty of Cosimo's victory.

Just so long as Cosimo didn't set out before Meggie even had a chance to read his words! Cosimo was burning with impatience, longing for the day when he would lead his soldiers to the other side of the forest. *"Because he wants to find out who he is!"* whispered the quiet voice in Fenoglio's head (or was it in his heart?). *"Because your fine avenging angel is empty, like a box with nothing inside it. A few borrowed memories, a few stone statues — that's all the poor lad has, and your stories of his heroic deeds. He searches his empty heart in desperation for some echo of them. You ought to have tried to bring back the real Cosimo, after all, straight back from the realm of the dead, but you didn't dare!"* Hush! Fenoglio shook his head in annoyance. Why did these troublesome thoughts keep returning? Everything would be all right once Cosimo sat on the Adderhead's throne. Then he'd have memories of his own, and he'd gather more of them every day. And soon the emptiness would be forgotten.

His horse was saddled at last. The groom helped him to mount, his mouth twisted in a mocking smile. The fool! Fenoglio knew he didn't cut a very good figure on a horse, he'd never get used to riding — but so what? These horses were alarming beasts, much too strong for his liking, but a poet living at his prince's court didn't travel on foot like a peasant. And he would go much faster on horseback — assuming the animal wanted to go the same way as he did. What a business it was to get the creature moving!

The hooves clattered over the paved courtyard, past the barrels of pitch and iron spikes that Cosimo was having set on the walls. The castle still resounded at night to the hammering of the smiths, and Cosimo's soldiers slept in the wooden huts along the wall, crammed close together like larvae in an ants' nest. He had certainly brought a warrior angel into being, but hadn't angels always been warlike? *The fact is, I'm just no good at making up peaceful characters,* thought Fenoglio as he trotted across the yard. *The good ones either have bad luck like Dustfinger or they fall among thieves like the Black Prince.* Could he ever have made up a character like Mortimer? Probably not.

As Fenoglio was riding toward the Outer Gate it swung open, so that for a moment he actually assumed the guards were finally showing a little respect for their prince's poet. But when he saw how low they bent their heads he realized that it couldn't possibly be for him.

Cosimo came riding toward him through the wide gateway, on a horse so white that it looked a little unreal. In the dark he looked almost more beautiful than by day, but wasn't that the case with all angels? Only seven soldiers followed him; he never took more as guards on his nocturnal rides. But someone else rode at his side, too: Brianna, Dustfinger's daughter, no longer wearing a dress that had belonged to her mistress, poor Violante, as so often in the past, but in one of the gowns that Cosimo had given her. He heaped presents upon her, while he no longer allowed his wife even to leave the castle, or their son, either. But in spite of all these proofs of love, Brianna didn't look particularly happy. And why should she? What girl would be cheerful if her lover was planning to go to war? The prospect didn't seem to cloud Cosimo's mood. Far from it; he looked as light at heart as if the future could bring nothing but good. He went riding every night. He seemed to need very little sleep, and Fenoglio had heard he rode at such a breakneck pace that hardly any of his bodyguards could keep up — like a man who had been told that death had no power over him. What difference did it make, anyway, when he could remember neither his death nor his life?

Day and night, Balbulus was painting the most wonderful pictures to illustrate stories about that lost life. More than a dozen scribes supplied him with the handwritten pages. "My husband still won't enter the library," Violante had commented bitterly, last time Fenoglio saw her. "But he fills all the reading desks with books about himself."

Unfortunately, it was only too clear that the words from which Fenoglio and Meggie had made him did not satisfy Cosimo. There were simply not enough of them. Everything he heard about himself seemed to have to do with another man. Perhaps that was why he loved Dustfinger's daughter so much: because she had nothing to do with the man he seemed to have been before his death. Fenoglio had to keep writing new and ardent love songs to Brianna for him. He generally stole them from other poets; he had always had a good memory for verse, and Meggie wasn't here now to catch him in the act of theft. Tears always came to Brianna's eyes when one of the minstrels, who were now welcomed to the castle again, sang her one of those songs.

"Fenoglio!" Cosimo reined in his horse, and Fenoglio bent his head in the most natural way in the world, as he did only for the young prince. "Where are you going, poet? Everything's ready for us to march out!" He sounded as impatient as his horse, which was prancing back and forth, and threatened to infect Fenoglio's horse with its restlessness. "Or would you rather stay here and sharpen your pens for all the songs you'll have to write about my victory?"

March out? Ready?

Fenoglio looked around in confusion, but Cosimo laughed. "Do you think I'd assemble the troops here in the castle? There are far too many for that. No, they're encamped down by the river. I'm only waiting for one more company of mercenaries recruited for me in the north. They may arrive tomorrow!"

As soon as that? Fenoglio cast Brianna a quick glance. So that was why she looked so sad. "Please, Your Grace!" Fenoglio could not conceal the anxiety in his voice. "It's much too soon! Wait a little longer!"

But Cosimo only smiled. "The moon is red, poet! The sooth-sayers think that's a good sign. A sign that we mustn't miss the moment, or all may come to grief."

What nonsense! Fenoglio bowed his head to keep Cosimo from seeing the annoyance in his face. Cosimo knew, anyway, that his love of soothsayers and fortune-tellers irritated Fenoglio, who thought them all a set of avaricious frauds. "Let me say it once again, Your Grace!" He had repeated this warning so often that it was beginning to sound flat. "The only thing that will bring you bad luck is setting out too soon!"

But Cosimo merely shook his head indulgently.

"You're an old man, Fenoglio," he said. "Your blood flows slowly, but I'm young! What should I wait for? For the Adderhead to recruit mercenaries, too, and barricade himself in the Castle of Night?"

He probably did that long ago, thought Fenoglio. *And that's why you must wait for the words, my words, and for Meggie to read them, the way she read you here. Wait for her voice!* "Just one or two weeks more, Your Grace!" he said urgently. "Your peasants must bring in their harvest. What else will they have to live on in winter?"

But Cosimo didn't want to hear about such things. "That truly is old man's talk!" he said angrily. "Where are your fiery words now? They'll live on the Adderhead's stores of provisions, on the good fortune of our victory, on the silver from the Castle of Night. I'll have it distributed in the villages!"

They can't eat silver, Your Grace, thought Fenoglio, but he did not say so aloud. Instead, he looked up at the sky. Dear God, how high the moon had risen already! But Cosimo still had something on his mind.

"There's a question I've been meaning to ask you for some time," he said, just as Fenoglio was about to take his leave with some stammered excuse. "You're so friendly with the strolling players. Everyone's talking about that fire-eater, the one they say can talk to the flames. . . ."

Out of the corner of his eye, Fenoglio saw Brianna bend her head.

"You mean Dustfinger?"

"Yes, that's his name. I know he's Brianna's father," said Cosimo, casting her a loving glance, "but she won't talk about him. And she says she doesn't know where he is now. But perhaps you do?" Cosimo patted his horse's neck. His face seemed to burn with beauty.

"Why? What do you want of him?"

"Isn't that obvious? He can talk to fire! They say he can make the flames grow to a great height without burning him."

Fenoglio understood even before Cosimo explained. "You want Dustfinger for your war." He couldn't help it, he laughed aloud.

"What's so funny about that?" Cosimo frowned.

Dustfinger the fire-dancer as a weapon. Fenoglio shook his

head. "Oh no," he said. "I know Dustfinger very well" — he saw Brianna give him a look of surprise as he said so — "and he is many things but certainly not a warrior. He'd laugh in your face."

"He had better not." There was no mistaking the anger in Cosimo's voice. But Brianna was looking at Fenoglio as if she had a thousand questions on the tip of her tongue. Well, this was no time for them! "Your Highness," he said hastily, "please excuse me now! One of Minerva's children is ill, and I promised to get a few herbs from Brianna's mother for her."

"Oh, I see. Of course. Yes, of course, ride on, and we'll talk later." Cosimo gathered up his reins again. "If the child doesn't improve let me know, and I'll send a physician."

"Thank you," said Fenoglio, but before he finally went on his way there was one question he himself had to ask. "I've heard your wife isn't well, either?" Balbulus, who at present was the only visitor allowed to see Violante, had told him so.

"Oh, she's just in a temper." Cosimo took Brianna's hand as if to comfort her for the fact that they were talking about his wife. "Violante loses her temper easily. She gets it from her father. She simply will not understand why I won't let her leave the castle, yet it's obvious that her father's informers are everywhere, and who would they try to pump for information first? Violante and Jacopo." It was hard not to believe every word that those beautiful lips uttered, particularly when they spoke with so much genuine conviction.

"Well, I expect you're right! But please don't forget that your wife hates her father."

"You can hate someone and obey him all the same. Isn't that so?" Cosimo looked at Fenoglio with that naked expression in his eyes, like the eyes of a very young baby.

"Yes, yes, probably," he replied uncomfortably. Every time

Cosimo looked at him like that, Fenoglio felt as if he had found an empty page in a book, a moth hole in the finely woven carpet of words.

"Your Highness!" he said, bowing his head again, and he finally, if not very elegantly, got his horse to trot out of the gateway.

Brianna had given him a good description of the way to her mother's farmhouse. He had asked her about it after Roxane's visit, apparently in all innocence, saying that he was plagued by aching bones. Dustfinger's daughter was a strange child. She wanted nothing to do with her father and obviously not much with her mother, either. Luckily, she had warned him about the goose, so he was holding the horse's reins firmly when the cackling bird came toward him. Roxane was sitting outside her house when he rode into the yard. It was a poor place. Her beauty seemed to fit into it as little as a jewel in a beggar's hut. Her son was sleeping in the doorway beside her, curled up like a puppy, his head on her lap.

"He wants to come with me," she said as Fenoglio slid clumsily off the horse. "The little girl cried, too, when I told her I had to go away. But I can't take them, not to Argenta. The Adderhead's had children hanged before now. A friend is going to look after the girl for me, and Jehan, and the plants and animals, too."

She stroked her son's dark hair, and for a moment Fenoglio didn't want her to ride away. But what would become of his words then? Who else would find Meggie? Should he ask Cosimo for another horseman who might not come back, either? *"Well, who knows, maybe Roxane won't come back,"* the insidious voice inside him whispered. *"And then your precious words will be lost."* "Nonsense!" he said angrily, out loud. "I made a copy, of course."

"What did you say?" Roxane looked at him in surprise.

"Oh, nothing, nothing!" Heavens above, now he was talking to himself. "There's something else I have to tell you — don't ride to the mill! A minstrel who sings for Cosimo has brought me news from the Black Prince."

Roxane pressed her hand to her mouth.

"No, no. It's not so bad!" Fenoglio quickly reassured her. "The fact is, Meggie's father has obviously been taken prisoner by the Adderhead, but to be honest I feared as much. As for Dustfinger and Meggie — well, to be brief, the mill where Meggie was going to wait for my letter seems to have burned down. Apparently, the miller is telling everyone that a marten made fire rain down from the roof, while a wizard with a scarred face spoke to the flames. It seems this wizard had a demon with him in the shape of a dark-skinned boy who saved him when he was wounded and helped him and a girl to escape."

Roxane looked at him with a thoughtful expression, as if she had to search for the meaning of what he said. "Wounded?"

"Yes, but they escaped! That's the main thing. Roxane, do you really think you can find them?"

She passed a hand over her forehead. "I'll try."

"Don't worry," said Fenoglio. "You heard what they're saying. Dustfinger has a demon protecting him now. In any case, hasn't he always managed very well on his own?"

"Oh yes, indeed he has!"

Fenoglio cursed every wrinkle on his old face, she was so beautiful. Why didn't he have Cosimo's good looks? Although would she like that? She liked Dustfinger, who ought to have been dead by now if the story had gone the way he had once written it. *Fenoglio,* he told himself, *this is going too far. You're behaving like a jealous lover!*

But Roxane was taking no notice of him, anyway. She looked

down at the boy sleeping in her lap. "Brianna was furious when she heard I was going to ride after her father," she said. "I only hope Cosimo will look after her and won't begin his war before I get back."

Fenoglio made no reply to that. Why tell her about Cosimo's plans? To make her even more anxious? No. He took out the letter for Meggie from under his cloak. Written words that could become sound, a mighty sound . . . He had never before made Rosenquartz seal a letter so carefully.

"This letter can save Meggie's parents," he said urgently. "It can save her father. It can save us all, so take good care of it!"

Roxane turned the sealed parchment this way and that, as if it seemed to her too small for such great claims. "I never heard of a letter that could open the dungeons of the Castle of Night," she said. "Do you think it's right to give the girl false hopes?"

"They aren't false," said Fenoglio, rather hurt to find that she had so little faith in his words.

"Very well. If I find Dustfinger, and the girl is still with him, she'll get your letter." Roxane stroked her son's hair again, very gently, as if to brush away a leaf. "Does she love her father?"

"Yes. Yes, she loves him very much."

"My daughter loves hers, too. Brianna loves him so much that she won't speak a word to him now. When he went away in the old days, when he just used to go into the forest or down to the sea, anywhere that fire or the wind happened to lure him, she would try to run after him on her little feet. I don't think he even noticed, he always disappeared so fast, quick as a fox that has stolen a chicken. But she loved him all the same. Why? That boy loves him, too. He even thinks Dustfinger needs him, but he needs no one, only fire."

Fenoglio looked thoughtfully at her. "You're wrong," he said.

"He was wretchedly unhappy when he was away. You should have seen him."

She eyed him incredulously. "You know where he was?"

Now what? Old fool that he was, what had he said this time? "Well, yes," he stammered. "Yes. Yes, I was there myself." He needed some lies, and where were they? The truth wasn't going to be much use this time. A few good lies were needed to explain everything. Why shouldn't he find a few good words for Dustfinger for a change — even if he envied him his wife?

"He says he couldn't come back." She didn't believe it, but you could tell from Roxane's voice how much she wished she did.

"That's exactly how it was! He had a bad time! Capricorn set Basta on him, they took him far, far away and tried to make him tell them how to talk with fire." Here came the lies now, and they might even be close to the truth, who could say? "Believe me, Basta took his revenge for your preference for Dustfinger! They shut him away for years, and he finally escaped, but they soon found him and beat him half to death." Meggie had told him that part. A little of the truth couldn't hurt, and Roxane didn't have to know that it was because of Resa. "It was dreadful, dreadful!" Fenoglio felt the pleasure of storytelling run away with him, the pleasure of watching Roxane's eyes widen as she hung on his lips, waiting eagerly for his next words. Should he make Dustfinger a little villainous after all? No, he'd killed him once already, he'd do him a favor today. He would make his wife forgive him, once and for all, for staying away those ten years. *Sometimes I can be a truly benevolent person,* thought Fenoglio.

"He thought he'd die. He thought he'd never see you again, and that was the worst of it for him." Fenoglio had to clear his throat. He was moved by his own words — and so was Roxane. Oh yes, he saw the distrust disappear from her eyes, he saw them soften with love. "After that he wandered in strange lands, like a dog turned out of doors, looking for a way that would take him not to Basta or Capricorn but to you." The words were coming as if of their own accord now. As if he really knew what Dustfinger had felt all those years. "He was forlorn, truly forlorn, his heart was cold as a stone from loneliness. There was no room in it for anything but longing — longing for you. And for his daughter."

"He had two daughters." Roxane's voice was almost inaudible.

Damn it, he'd forgotten that. Two daughters, of course! But Roxane was so rapt with his words that his mistake didn't break the spell.

"How do you know all this?" she asked. "He never told me you knew each other so well."

Oh, no one knows him better, thought Fenoglio. *I can assure you, my beauty, no one knows him better.*

Roxane pushed her black hair back from her face. Fenoglio saw a trace of gray in it, as if she had combed it with a dusty comb. "I shall ride early in the morning," she said.

"Excellent." Fenoglio drew his horse to his side. Why was it so difficult to get onto these creatures with anything like elegance? "Look after yourself," he said, when he was finally on the horse's back. "And the letter, too. And give Meggie my love. Tell her everything will be all right. I promise."

As he rode away she stood beside her sleeping son, looking thoughtful, and watched him go. He really did hope she would find Dustfinger, and it wasn't just that he wanted Meggie to get his words. No. A little happiness in this story couldn't hurt, and Roxane was not happy without Dustfinger. That was the way he'd fixed it.

He doesn't deserve her, all the same, thought Fenoglio again as he rode toward the lights of Ombra, which were neither as bright

451

nor as many as the lights of his old world but were at least equally inviting. Soon the houses behind the protecting walls would be without their menfolk. They would all be going with Cosimo, including Minerva's husband — although she had begged him to stay — and the cobbler whose workshop was next to his. Even the rag-collector who went around every Tuesday was going to fight the Adderhead. *Would they follow Cosimo as willingly if I'd made him ugly?* Fenoglio wondered. *Ugly as the Adderhead with his butcher's face?* No, people find it easier to believe that a man with a handsome face has good intentions, so he had done well to put an angel on the throne. Yes, that was clever, extremely clever. Fenoglio caught himself humming quietly as the horse carried him past the guards. They let him in without a word, their prince's poet, the man who put their world into words and had made it out of words. *Bow your heads to Fenoglio!*

The guards would go with Cosimo, too, and the soldiers up in the castle, and the grooms who were hardly as old as the boy who went around with Dustfinger. Even Minerva's son Ivo would have gone if she had let him. *They'll all come back,* thought Fenoglio, as he rode toward the stables. *Or most of them, at least. It will end well, I know it will. Not just well, but very well indeed!*

52

ANGRY ORPHEUS

All words are written in the same ink,
"flower" and "power," say, are much the same,
and though I might write "blood, blood, blood"
all over the page, the paper would not be stained
nor would I bleed.

              Philippe Jaccottet, "Chant d'en Bas"

Elinor lay on her air mattress staring at the ceiling. She had quarreled with Orpheus again, even though she knew she'd be punished with the cellar. *Sent to bed early, Elinor!* she thought bitterly. That was how her father used to punish her as a child when he caught her yet again with a book that he didn't think she should be reading at her age. Sent to bed early, sometimes at five in the afternoon. It had been particularly bad in summer, when the birds were singing and her sister was playing outside under the window — her sister who didn't care for books at all, but liked nothing so much as telling tales on Elinor when, instead of playing with her, she buried her head in a book that her father had said she mustn't read.

"Elinor, please don't quarrel with Orpheus!" Darius had

tried drumming that into her so often, but no, she just couldn't control her temper! How could she be expected to, when his wretched dog slobbered all over some of her most valuable books because his master never thought of putting them back on their shelves when he'd had his fun with them?

Recently, however, he hadn't been taking any more books off the shelves, not one. That at least was a small comfort. "He just reads *Inkheart*," Darius had whispered to her as they were washing the dishes together in the kitchen. Her dishwasher had broken down. As if it wasn't bad enough to be working as a kitchen maid in her own house, now her hands were all swollen with washing-up water! "He seems to be looking for words," Darius whispered. "Then he puts them together differently, writes them down, writes and writes; the wastepaper basket is brimming over. He keeps on trying, and then he reads what he's written out loud, and when nothing happens . . ."

"Yes? Then what?"

"Oh, nothing," Darius had said evasively, scrubbing away industriously at a pan encrusted with fat, but Elinor knew that if it was "nothing" he wouldn't have turned so embarrassed and silent.

"Then what?" she repeated — and Darius, blushing to his ears, had finally told her. Then Orpheus threw her books, her wonderful books, at the walls. He flung them on the floor in his rage — now and then one even sailed out of the window — and all because he couldn't do what Meggie had done. *Inkheart* was closed to him, however lovingly he cooed and implored in his velvety voice, reading and rereading the sentences he so longed to slip between.

Of course, she had run straight off when she next heard him shouting. She'd gone to save her printed children. "No!"

Orpheus had yelled, so loudly that you could hear him in the kitchen. "No, no, no! Let me in, you thrice-accursed thing! I sent Dustfinger back into you! Can't you understand that? What would you be without him? I gave you back Mortola and Basta! I've earned my reward, haven't I?"

The man built like a wardrobe wasn't standing outside the library door to stop Elinor. He was probably roaming the house yet again, to see if he could find something worth stealing after all. Not in a hundred years would it have occurred to him that the books were by far the most valuable things in the place. Later, Elinor couldn't remember the names she had called Orpheus. She remembered only the book he was holding in his raised hand, a beautiful edition of the poems of William Blake. And for all her furious insults, he threw it out of the window, while the wardrobe-man grabbed her from behind and dragged her to the cellar stairs.

Oh, Meggie! thought Elinor as she lay on the air mattress, staring up at the crumbling plaster on her cellar ceiling. *Why didn't you take me with you? Why didn't you at least ask if I'd like to come, too?*

53

THE BARN OWL

And every doctor must know that God has set a great mystery
in the plants, if only because of the spirits and wild fancies that
cast men into despair, and this aid comes not from the Devil
but from Nature.

Paracelsus, *Works*

The sea. Meggie hadn't seen it since the day they drove back
from Capricorn's village to Elinor's house with the fairies
and brownies who were nothing but ashes now. "This is where
the physician whom I told you about lives," said Dustfinger,
when the bay appeared beyond the trees. It was beautiful. The
sun made the water shimmer like green glass, foaming glass
constantly shaped by the wind into new folds. It was a strong
wind, driving veils of cloud over the blue sky, and it carried a
scent of salt and distant islands. It would have gladdened the
heart but for the bare hill in the distance rising above the wooded
slopes, and the castle on the top of the hill, broad and heavy as its
master's face, in spite of its silvered rooftops and battlements.

"Yes, there it is," said Dustfinger when he saw Meggie's look of alarm. "The Castle of Night. And the hill where it stands is called Mount Adder, what else? Bare as an old man's bald head, so no one can come close under the cover of trees. But don't worry, it's not quite as close as it looks."

"The towers," said Farid. "Are they really all pure silver?"

"Oh yes," said Dustfinger. "Dug from the mountains, this one and others. Roast fowls, young women, fertile land . . . and silver . . . the Adderhead has a hearty appetite for many things."

A broad, sandy beach edged the bay. Where it joined the trees a long wall and a tower rose, sand-colored and inconspicuous. There was not a soul to be seen on the beach, no boat was drawn up on the pale sand, only that building — the low tower and the long, tiled rooftops hardly visible behind the wall. A path wound toward it like a viper's trail, but Dustfinger led them around to the back of the building under cover of the trees. He beckoned impatiently to them before disappearing into the shadow of the wall. The wood of the door outside which he was waiting for them was weathered, and the bell hanging above it was rusty with the salty wind. Wildflowers grew near the door, faded blossoms and brown seed heads with a fairy nibbling at them. She had paler skin than her woodland sisters.

It all seemed so peaceful. The buzz of a wasp reached Meggie's ear, mingling with the roaring of the sea, but she remembered only too well how peaceful the mill had looked. Dustfinger had not forgotten it, either. He stood there listening intently before he finally put out his hand and pulled the chain of the rusty bell. His leg was bleeding again — Meggie saw him press his hand to it — but nonetheless he had kept urging them to make haste on the way to this place. "There's no better physician," was all he would say when Farid asked where he was taking them, "and none we can trust more. In addition, it's not far from there to the Castle of Night, and that's where Meggie still wants to go, doesn't she?" He had given them some leaves to eat, downy and bitter. "Get them down inside you," he said when they made faces of disgust. "You can stay where we're going only if you have at least five of them in your belly."

The wooden door opened just a crack, and a woman peered through. "By all good spirits!" Meggie heard her whisper, and then the door opened and a thin, wrinkled hand beckoned them in. The woman who quickly closed it behind them again was just as wrinkled and thin as her hand, and she stared at Dustfinger as if he had fallen straight from heaven.

"Yesterday! He said so yesterday!" she exclaimed. "You wait and see, Bella, he's back, that's what he said. Who else would have set the mill ablaze? Who else talks to fire? He didn't get a wink of sleep all night. He was worried, but you're all right, aren't you? What's the matter with your leg?"

Dustfinger put a finger to his mouth, but Meggie saw that he was smiling. "It could be better," he said quietly. "And you talk as fast as ever, Bella, but could you take us to the Barn Owl now?"

"Yes, yes, of course!" Bella sounded slightly injured. "I suppose you have that horrible marten in there?" she inquired, with a distrustful look at Dustfinger's backpack. "Don't you go letting him out."

"Of course not," Dustfinger assured her, casting a glance at Farid, which obviously warned him to say nothing about the second marten asleep in his own backpack.

Without another word, the old woman beckoned them to follow her down a dark, unadorned colonnade. She took small, hasty footsteps, as if she were a squirrel wearing a long dress of coarsely woven fabric. "A good thing you came around the back way," she said in a lowered voice as she led them past a series of closed doors. "I'm afraid the Adderhead has ears even here now, but luckily he doesn't pay his informers well enough for them to work in the wing where we treat infectious cases. I hope you gave those two enough of the leaves?"

"Yes, indeed." Dustfinger nodded, but Meggie saw that he looked around uneasily and inconspicuously put another of the leaves that he had given them into his own mouth. Not until they passed the fragile figures sunning themselves in the courtyard around which the colonnade ran did Meggie realize just where Dustfinger had brought them. It was an infirmary. Farid put his hand to his mouth in horror when they met an old man who looked as pale as if Death had come for him long ago, and he replied to the man's toothless smile with only a frightened nod.

"Don't look as if you were about to fall down dead!" Dustfinger whispered to him, although he didn't look particularly comfortable here, either. "Your fingers will be well tended here, and moreover we'll be relatively safe, which is more than can be said for many places on this side of the forest."

"Yes, if there's one thing the Adderhead fears," added Bella in knowing tones, "it's death and the diseases that lead to it. All the same, you shouldn't let either the patients or the nurses here see more of you than they must. If there's one thing I've learned in life it's never to trust anyone. Except the Barn Owl, of course."

"And what about me, Bella?" asked Dustfinger.

"You least of all!" was her only reply. She stopped at a plain wooden door. "It's a pity your face is so unmistakable," she told Dustfinger, low-voiced, "or you could have put on a show for our patients. Nothing does the sick more good than a little pleasure." Then she knocked on the door and, with a nod, stepped aside.

The room on the other side of the door was dark, for the only window was half hidden behind stacks of books. It was the kind of room Mo would have loved. He liked books to look as if someone had only just put them down. Quite unlike Elinor, he saw nothing wrong in leaving them lying there open, waiting for the next reader. The Barn Owl seemed to feel the same. He could hardly be spotted among all those piled books — a small man with shortsighted eyes and broad hands. He looked to Meggie like a mole, except that his hair was gray.

"Didn't I say so?" He knocked two books off their stacks as he hurried toward Dustfinger. "He's back," I said, but they wouldn't believe it. Obviously, the White Women are letting more and more of the dead come back to life these days!"

The two men embraced. Then the Barn Owl took a step back and looked Dustfinger thoroughly up and down. The physician was an old man, older than Fenoglio, but his eyes were as young as Farid's. "You look all right," he commented, pleased. "Except for your leg. What's the matter with it? Did you get that injury at the mill? One of my women healers was taken up to the castle yesterday to tend two men bitten by fire. She brought back a strange story about an ambush and a horned marten that spits fire. . . ."

Up to the castle? Instinctively, Meggie moved toward the physician. "Did she see the prisoners, too?" she interrupted him. "They would just have been taken there — strolling players, men and women. My mother and father are with them."

The Barn Owl looked at her sympathetically. "Are you the girl that the Black Prince's men told me about? Your father —"

"— is the man they take for the Bluejay." Dustfinger finished the sentence. "Do you know how he and the other prisoners are?"

Before the Barn Owl could answer, a girl put her head around the door. She stared at the strangers in alarm. Her eyes lingered on Meggie so long that finally the Barn Owl cleared his throat.

"What is it, Carla?" he asked.

The girl bit her pale lips nervously. "I'm to ask if we have any eyebright left," she said timidly.

"Of course. Go to Bella and she'll give you some, but now leave us alone."

The girl disappeared with a hasty nod, but she left the door open. Sighing, the Barn Owl closed it and then bolted it, too. "Where were we? Oh yes, the prisoners. The physician responsible for the dungeons is looking after them. He's useless at his job, but who else could stand it up there? Instead of healing the sick he has to preside over whippings and lashings. Luckily, they're not letting him near your father, and the Adderhead's own physician isn't going to soil his fingers on a prisoner, so my best woman healer goes up to the castle every day to tend him."

"How is my father?" Meggie tried not to sound like a little girl holding back her tears with difficulty, but she didn't entirely succeed.

"He's badly wounded, but I think you know that?"

Meggie nodded. And the tears came again, flowing and flowing as if to wash it all out of her heart: her grief, her longing, her fear. Farid put his arm around her shoulders, but that just reminded her of Mo even more — of all the years he had protected her and held her close. And now that he was in trouble, she wasn't with him.

"He's lost a great deal of blood, and he's still weak, but he's doing well — much better, anyway, than we let the Adderhead know." You could tell from the Barn Owl's voice that he often had to talk to people who were anxious about those they loved. "My healer has advised him not to let anyone notice, to give us more time. But at the moment there really is nothing for you to worry about."

Meggie's heart soared. *It will be all right*, something inside her said — for the first time since Dustfinger had given her Resa's note. *Everything will be all right!* Feeling embarrassed, she wiped the tears off her face.

"The weapon that wounded your father — my healer says it must be a terrible thing," the Barn Owl continued. "I hope the Adderhead's armorers are not working on some diabolical invention in secret!"

"No, that weapon was from a very different place." And nothing good comes from that place, said Dustfinger's face, but Meggie didn't want to think of what a rifle could do to this world just now. Her thoughts were with Mo.

"My father," she told the Barn Owl, "would like this room very much. He loves books, and yours are really beautiful. Although he'd probably tell you that some of them needed rebinding, and that one won't live much longer if you don't soon do something about the beetles eating it."

The Barn Owl picked up the book she had pointed out and caressed the pages just as Mo always did. "The Bluejay loves books?" he asked. "Unusual for a robber."

"He's not a robber," said Meggie. "He's a doctor like you, only he heals books instead of people."

"Really? Then is it true that the Adderhead had captured the wrong man? In that case, I suppose when they say your father killed Capricorn, that isn't true, either?"

"Oh yes, that's true." Dustfinger looked out of the window as if he saw the scene of Capricorn's festivities outside. "And all he needed to do it was his voice. You ought to get him or his daughter to read to you sometime. Afterward, I assure you, you'll see your books in a very different light. You might well close and padlock them."

"Really?" The Barn Owl looked at Meggie with great interest, as if he would like to hear more about Capricorn's death, but there was another knock. This time a man's voice came through the bolted door. "Will you come, master? We've prepared everything, but it will be better if you make the incision."

Meggie saw Farid turn pale. "Just coming!" said the Barn Owl. "You go ahead. I hope I can welcome your father to this room someday," he said to Meggie as he went to the door. "For you're right: My books could certainly do with a doctor. Does the Black Prince have any plans for the prisoners?" He looked inquiringly at Dustfinger.

"No. No, I don't think so. Have you heard anything about the other captives? Meggie's mother is among them." It gave Meggie a pang that Dustfinger, and not she, had been the one to ask about Resa.

"No, I don't know anything about the others," replied the Barn Owl. "But now you must excuse me. I am sure Bella's already told you that you had better keep to this part of the building. The Adderhead is spending more and more of his silver on informers. No place in Argenta is safe from them, not even this one."

"I know." Dustfinger picked up one of the books lying on the Barn Owl's table. It was an herbal. Meggie could imagine how Elinor would have looked at it — full of longing to own it — and Mo would have run a finger over the painted pages as if he could feel the brush that had conjured up the fine lines of the pictures on paper. But what was Dustfinger thinking of? The herbs in Roxane's fields? "Believe me, I wouldn't have come here but for what happened at the mill," he said. "No one would want to bring danger to this place, but we'll be gone again this very day."

However, the Barn Owl wouldn't hear of it. "Nonsense, you

must stay until your leg and the boy's fingers are better," he said. "You know how glad I am you came. And I'm glad you have the boy with you, too. Did you know," he asked, turning to Farid, "he's never had a pupil before? I was always telling him that a master must pass on his art, but he wouldn't listen to me. I pass mine on to many, and that's why I must leave you now. I have to show a pupil how to cut off a foot without killing the man it's attached to."

Farid stared at him, horrified. "Cut it off?" he whispered. "How do you mean, cut it off?" But the Barn Owl had already closed the door behind him.

"Didn't I tell you?" said Dustfinger, feeling his injured thigh. "The Barn Owl is a first-class sawbones. But I think we'll be allowed to keep our own fingers and feet."

After Bella had treated Farid's blisters and Dustfinger's leg, she took them to a remote room, close to the door through which they had entered the building. Meggie liked the prospect of sleeping under a roof again, but Farid was not at all comfortable with the idea. Looking unhappy, he squatted on the lavender-strewn floor, chewing one of the bitter leaves with determination. "Can't we sleep on the beach tonight? I should think the sand would be nice and soft," he asked Dustfinger, who was stretching out on one of the straw mattresses. "Or in the forest?"

"If you like," replied Dustfinger. "But let me sleep now. And stop looking as if I'd brought you among cannibals, or I won't show you what I promised tomorrow night."

"Tomorrow?" Farid spat out the leaf into his hand. "Why not tonight?"

"Because it's too windy now," said Dustfinger, turning his back on him, "and because my damn leg hurts. . . . Do you need any more reasons?"

Remorsefully, Farid shook his head, put the leaf back in his mouth, and stared at the door as if Death in person might walk in any moment. But Meggie just sat there in the bare room, repeating to herself, over and over, what the Barn Owl had said about Mo: *He's doing well — much better, anyway, than we let the Adderhead know. . . . At the moment there really is nothing for you to worry about.*

When twilight fell, Dustfinger limped outside. He leaned against a column and looked up at the hill where the Castle of Night stood. Never moving, he gazed at the silver towers — and Meggie asked herself, for what was surely the hundredth time, if he was helping her only for her mother's sake. Perhaps Dustfinger himself didn't know.

IN THE DUNGEON OF THE CASTLE OF NIGHT

They say:
Speak for us (to whom?)
Some say: Avenge us (on whom?)
Some say: Take our place.
Some say: Witness
Others say (and these are women)
Be happy for us.

Margaret Atwood, "Down," Eating Fire

Mina was crying again. Resa took the other woman in her arms as if she were still a child, hummed a tune, and rocked her as she sometimes rocked Meggie, although by now her daughter was almost as tall as Resa herself.

A girl came twice a day, a thin, nervous little thing, younger than Meggie, to bring them bread and water. Sometimes there was porridge, too, cold and sticky, but it filled the stomach — and reminded Resa of the days when Mortola had locked her up for something she had or hadn't done. The porridge had tasted just like this. When she asked the girl about the Bluejay, the child just ducked her head in fright and left Resa in fear — the fear that Mo was dead by now, that they had hanged him, up there in the huge courtyard, and the last thing he had seen in this world was not her face but the silver vipers' heads with their tongues licking down from the walls. Sometimes she saw it all so clearly in her mind's eye that she put her hands over her eyes, but the pictures were still there. And the darkness around her made her think it could all have been a dream: that moment at Capricorn's festivities when she had suddenly seen Mo standing beside Meggie, the year in Elinor's house, all that happiness — just a dream.

At least she was not alone. Even if the glances of the others were often hostile, their voices brought her out of her dark thoughts for a brief while. Now and then someone told a story, to keep them from hearing the weeping from the other cells, the scurrying of rats, the screams, the stammering voices that had long since ceased to make sense. Usually, it was the women who told stories. Stories of love and death, betrayal and friendship, but they all ended happily, lights in the darkness, like the candles in Resa's pocket with wicks that had now become damp. Resa told fairy tales that Mo had read aloud to her long, long ago, when Meggie's fingers were still soft and tiny, and the written word held no terrors for any of them yet. As for the strolling players, they told tales of the world around them: of Cosimo the Fair and his battle with the fire-raisers, of the Black Prince and how he found his bear, and his friend the fire-dancer, the man who made sparks rain down and fiery flowers blossom in the darkest night. Benedicta sang a song about him in a soft voice, a beautiful song, and in the end even Twofingers joined in, until the warder banged his stick against the bars and told them to keep quiet.

"I saw him once," whispered Benedicta when the warder had

gone away again. "Many years ago, when I was a little girl. It was wonderful. The fire was so bright that even my eyes could see it. They say he's dead."

"No, he isn't," said Resa quietly. "Who do you think made the tree across the road burn?" They looked at her so incredulously! But she was too tired to tell them any more. She was too tired to explain anything. Let me go to my husband, that was all she wanted to say. Let me go to my child. Don't tell me any more stories; tell me how they are. Please.

Someone did at last give her news of Meggie and Mo, but Resa would rather have heard it from any other mouth.

The others were asleep when Mortola came. She had two soldiers with her. Resa was awake, because she was seeing those pictures again, pictures of Mo being brought into the courtyard, having the rope put around his neck . . . *He's dead, and she has come to tell me!* That was her first thought when the Magpie stood before her with a triumphant smile.

"Well, well, here's our faithless maid!" said Mortola as Resa got to her feet with difficulty. "You seem to be as much of a witch as your daughter. How have you kept him alive? Perhaps I took aim a little too hastily. Never mind. A few more weeks and he'll be strong enough for his execution!"

Alive.

Resa turned her head away so that Mortola wouldn't see the smile that stole over her lips, but the Magpie was not looking at her face. She was enjoying the sight of her torn dress and bleeding, bare feet.

"The Bluejay!" Mortola lowered her voice. "Of course, I haven't told the Adderhead that he's going to execute the wrong man — why should I? It's all working out just as I wanted. And I shall get my hands on your daughter, too."

Meggie. The sense of happiness that had briefly warmed Resa's heart disappeared as suddenly as it had come. Beside her, Mina sat up, woken by Mortola's hoarse voice.

"Oh yes, I have powerful friends in this world," continued the Magpie, with a self-satisfied smile. "The Adderhead has caught me your husband, why wouldn't he catch me your witch of a daughter, too? Do you know how I've convinced him that she's a witch? By showing him a photograph of her. Yes, Resa, I let Basta take the photos of your little darling with him, all those pretty silver-framed photographs standing around the book-worm woman's house. Of course the Adderhead thinks they're magic pictures, mirror images captured on paper. His soldiers are afraid to touch them, but they're showing them around all over the place. A pity we can't duplicate them as we could in your world! But fortunately your daughter has joined forces with Dustfinger, and there's no need for any magic picture of him. Every peasant has heard of him — him and his scars."

"He'll protect her!" said Resa. She had to say something.

"Oh yes? The way he protected *you*?"

Resa dug her fingers into the fabric of her dirty dress. There was no one, in either this or the other world, whom she hated as much as the Magpie. Not even Basta. It was Mortola who had taught her how to hate. "Everything is different here," she managed to say. "Fire obeys him here, and he's not alone as he was in the other world. He has friends."

"Friends! Ah, I suppose you mean the other mountebanks: the Black Prince, as he calls himself, and the rest of that rabble!" Contemptuously, the Magpie scanned the other prisoners. They had almost all woken up. "Look at them, Resa!" said Mortola spitefully. "How are they going to help you out of here? With a few brightly colored balls or a couple of sentimental songs? One of them gave you away, did you know that? And as for Dustfinger, what could he do? Unleash fire to save you? It would burn you, too, and he certainly won't risk that, besotted with you as he always was." She leaned forward with a smile. "Did you ever tell your husband what good friends you two were?"

Resa did not reply. She knew Mortola's games. She knew them very well.

"What do you think? Shall I tell him?" Mortola whispered, ready to pounce, like a cat waiting by a mouse hole.

"Do that," Resa whispered back. "Tell him. You can't tell him anything he doesn't know already. I've given him back the years you stole from us, word for word, day after day. And Mo knows, too, that your own son made you live in his cellar and let everyone think you were only his housekeeper."

Mortola tried to hit her in the face, as she had so often done before, as she had done to all her maids — right in the middle of the face — but Resa caught her hand before it landed.

"He's alive, Mortola!" she whispered to the Magpie. "This story isn't over yet, and his death isn't written anywhere in it — but my daughter will whisper yours in your ear when she hears what you did to her father. You'll see one day. And then I shall watch *you* die."

This time she didn't manage to catch Mortola's hand, and her cheek was still burning long after the Magpie had gone away. She felt the eyes of the other prisoners like fingers feeling her face when she was sitting on the cold ground again. Mina was the first to say something. "Where did you meet the old woman? She mixed poisons for Capricorn."

"I know," said Resa tonelessly. "I belonged to her. For many long years."

A LETTER FROM FENOGLIO

Is there then a world
Where I rule absolutely on fate?
A time I bind with chains of signs?
An existence become endless at my bidding?
Wislawa Szymborska, "The Joy of Writing,"
View with a Grain of Sand

Dustfinger was asleep when Roxane arrived. It was already growing dark outside. Farid and Meggie had gone out to the beach, but he was lying down because his leg was hurting. When he saw Roxane standing in the doorway he thought at first his imagination was playing tricks on him, as it so often did by night. After all, he had once been here with her, very long ago. The room they had then had looked almost the same, and he had been lying on a straw mattress just like this, his face slashed and sticky with his own blood.

Roxane was wearing her hair loose. Perhaps that was why she woke the memory of that other night. His heart always seemed to miss a beat at the mere thought of it. He had been mad with pain and fear, had crawled away like a wounded animal, until Roxane found him and brought him here. At first the Barn Owl had hardly recognized him. He had given him something to drink that made him sleep, and when he woke again Roxane had been standing in the doorway, just as she was standing now. When the cuts would not heal, for all the physician's skill, she had gone into the forest with him, deeper and deeper into the forest to find the fairies — and she had stayed with him until his face was healed well enough for him to venture among other people again. There could be few men whose love for a woman had been written on his face with a knife.

But what was his greeting when she suddenly appeared? "What are you doing here?" he asked. Then he could have bitten off his tongue. Why didn't he say how much he had missed her, so much that he had almost turned back a dozen times?

"Yes, indeed, what am I doing here?" Roxane asked back. Once she would have turned her back on him for such a question, but now she just smiled, so mockingly that he felt as awkward as a boy.

"Where have you left Jehan?"

"With a friend." She kissed him. "What's the matter with your leg? Fenoglio told me you were wounded."

"It's getting better. What do you have to do with Fenoglio?"

"You don't like him. Why not?" Roxane stroked his face. How beautiful she looked. So very beautiful.

"Let's just say he had plans for me that I didn't care for in the least. Has the old man by any chance given you something for Meggie? A letter, for instance?"

Without a word, she brought it out from under her cloak. There the words were — words that wanted to come true. Roxane offered him the sealed parchment, but Dustfinger shook his head. "You'd better give that to Meggie," he said. "She's down on the beach."

Roxane glanced at him in surprise. "You look almost as if you were afraid of a piece of parchment."

"Yes," said Dustfinger, reaching for her hand. "Yes, I am. Particularly when Fenoglio's been writing on it. Come on, let's go and look for Meggie."

Meggie smiled awkwardly at Roxane when she gave her the parchment and for a moment looked curiously from her to Dustfinger, but then she had eyes only for Fenoglio's letter. She broke the seal so hastily that she almost tore the parchment. There were three closely written sheets. The first was a letter to her. When she had read it Meggie put it away under her belt, paying it no further attention. The words she had been so eagerly waiting for filled the other two sheets. Meggie's eyes traveled over the lines so fast that Dustfinger could hardly believe she was really reading them. Finally, she raised her head, looked up at the Castle of Night — and smiled.

"Well, what does the old devil say?" asked Dustfinger.

Meggie offered him the two sheets. "It's different from what I expected. Quite different, but it's good. Here, read it for yourself."

Gingerly, he took the parchment in his fingertips, as if he might burn himself on it more easily than on a flame. "When did you learn to read?" Roxane's voice sounded so surprised that he had to smile.

"Meggie's mother taught me." Fool; why was he telling her that? Roxane gave Meggie a long look as he labored to decipher Fenoglio's handwriting. Resa had usually written in capital letters, to make it easier for him.

"It could work, couldn't it?" Meggie was looking over his shoulder.

The sea roared as if to agree with her. Yes, perhaps it really would work. . . . Dustfinger followed the written words like a dangerous path. But it *was* a path, and it led right into the middle of the Adderhead's heart. However, Dustfinger didn't like the part the old man intended Meggie to play. After all, her mother had asked him to take care of her.

Farid looked unhappily at the letters. He still couldn't read. Sometimes Dustfinger felt that he suspected those tiny black signs of witchcraft. What else would he think of them, indeed, after all his experiences? "Come on!" Farid shifted impatiently from foot to foot. "What's he written?"

"Meggie will have to go to the castle. Straight into the Adder's nest."

"What?" Horrified, the boy looked first at him and then at the girl. "But that's impossible!" He took Meggie by the shoulders and turned her roughly around to face him. "You can't go there. It's much too dangerous!"

Poor boy. Of course she would go. "That's the way Fenoglio has written it," she said, removing Farid's hands from her shoulders.

"Leave her alone," said Dustfinger, giving Meggie the sheets of parchment back. "When are you going to read it aloud?"

"Now."

Of course. She didn't want to lose any time, and why should she? The sooner the story took a new turn, the better. It could hardly get worse.

Or could it?

"What's all this about?" Roxane looked from one to another of them, baffled. She scrutinized Farid without much friendliness; she still didn't like him. Dustfinger thought that wouldn't change until something convinced her that Farid was not his son.

"Explain!" she said. "Fenoglio said this letter could save her parents. But what can a letter do for someone in a dungeon in the Castle of Night?"

Dustfinger stroked her hair back. He liked to see her wearing it loose again. "Listen," he said. "I know it's difficult to believe, but if anything can open the dungeon doors in the Castle of Night, it's this letter — and Meggie's voice. She can make ink live and breathe, Roxane, just as you can bring a song to life. Her father has the same gift. If the Adderhead knew that, then I imagine he'd have hanged him long ago. The words that Meggie's father used to kill Capricorn looked just as harmless as these."

The way she was looking at him! As incredulously as she used to when he had yet again tried to explain where he had been for weeks on end. "You mean magic, an inkspell?" she whispered.

"No. I mean reading aloud."

She didn't understand a word of this, of course, which was not surprising. Perhaps she would if she heard Meggie read, if she saw the words suddenly trembling in the air, if she could smell them, feel them on her skin. . . .

"I'd like to be alone when I read it," said Meggie, looking at Farid. Then she turned and went back to the infirmary with Fenoglio's letter in her hand. Farid wanted to follow her, but Dustfinger detained him.

"Let her!" he said. "Do you think she'll disappear into the words? That's nonsense. We're all up to our necks in the story she's going to read, anyway. She only wants to make sure the wind changes, and it will — if the old man has written the right words!"

56

THE WRONG EARS

Song lies asleep in everything
That dreams the day and night away,
And the whole world itself will sing
If once the magic word you say.
              Joseph von Eichendorff, "The Divining Rod"

Roxane brought Meggie an oil lamp before leaving her alone in the room where they would be sleeping. "Written words need light, that's the awkward thing about them," she said. "But if these words are really as important as you all say, I can understand that you want to read them alone. I've always thought my singing voice sounds best when I'm on my own, too." She was already in the doorway when she added, "Your mother — do she and Dustfinger know each other well?"

Meggie almost replied: I don't know. I never asked my mother. But at last she said, "They were friends." She did not mention the resentment she still felt when she thought of how Dustfinger had known where Resa was, all those years, and hadn't told Mo.

But Roxane asked no more questions, anyway. "If you need any help," was all she said before she left the room, "you'll find me with the Barn Owl."

Meggie waited until her footsteps along the dark corridor had died away. Then she sat down on one of the straw mattresses and put the sheets of parchment on her lap. What would it be like, she couldn't help thinking as the words lay spread out before her, simply to do it for fun, just once? What would it be like to feel the magic of the words on her tongue when it wasn't a matter of life or death, good or bad luck? Once, in Elinor's house, she had been almost unable to resist that temptation, when she had seen a book that she'd loved as a small child — a book with mice in frilly dresses and tiny suits making jam and going for picnics. She had stopped the first word from forming on her lips by closing the book, though, because she'd suddenly seen some dreadful pictures in her mind. One of the dressed-up mice in Elinor's garden surrounded by its wild relations, who would never in a million years dream of making jam. And an image of a little frilly dress, complete with a gray tail, in the jaws of one of the cats that regularly roamed among Elinor's rhododendron bushes. Meggie had never brought anything out of the words on the page just for fun, and she wasn't going to do it this evening, either.

"The whole secret, Meggie," Mo had once told her, "is in the breathing. It gives your voice strength and fills it with your life. And not just yours. Sometimes it feels as if when you take a breath you are breathing in everything around you, everything that makes up the world and moves it, and then it all flows into the words." She tried it. She tried to breathe as calmly and deeply as the sea — the sound of the surf came into the room from outside — in and out, in and out, as if she could capture its power in her voice. The oil lamp that Roxane had brought in filled the bare room with warm light, and outside one of the women healers walked softly by.

"I'm just going on with the story!" whispered Meggie. "I'm going on with the story. That's what it's waiting for. Come on!" She pictured the massive figure of the Adderhead pacing sleeplessly up and down in the Castle of Night, never guessing that there was a girl who planned to whisper his name in Death's ear this very night.

She took the letter that Fenoglio had written her from her belt. It was as well that Dustfinger hadn't read it.

Dear Meggie, it said, *I hope that what I'm sending won't disappoint you. It's odd, but I have found that obviously I can write only what doesn't contradict anything I wrote about the Inkworld earlier. I have to keep the rules I made myself, even though I often made them unconsciously.*

I hope your father is all right. From what I hear he is now a prisoner in the Castle of Night — and I must admit that I am not entirely blameless there. Yes, I admit it. After all, as you will have found out by now, I used him as a living model for the Bluejay. I am sorry, but I really did think it was a good idea at the time. He made an excellent and noble robber in my imagination, and how could I guess that he would ever really come into my story? Well, be that as it may, he's here, and the Adderhead won't set him free just because I write a new passage saying so. I didn't make him that way, Meggie. The story must be true to itself, that's the only way to do it, so I can only send you these words. At first they may do no more than delay your father's execution, but I hope they will ultimately lead to his freedom after all. Trust me. I believe the words I enclose are the only possible way of bringing this story to a truly happy ending, and you like stories with happy endings, don't you?

Go on with my story, Meggie, before it goes on with itself!

I would have liked to bring you the words myself, but I have to keep an eye on Cosimo. I am rather afraid that in his case we made it a little too easy for ourselves. Take care of yourself, give my good wishes to your father when you see him again (which I hope will be soon) and to the boy who worships the ground under your feet, too — oh yes, and tell Dustfinger, though I don't suppose he'll like it, that his wife is much too beautiful for him.

Love and kisses,

Fenoglio

P.S. Since your father is still alive, I have wondered whether perhaps the words I gave you for him in the forest worked after all? If so, Meggie, then that could be only because I made him one of my characters, in a way — which would mean that some good came of the whole Bluejay story, don't you think?

Oh, Fenoglio. What a master he was in the art of turning everything to his own advantage!

A breath of wind came through the window as Meggie reread the letter, making the sheets of parchment move as if the story itself were impatient and wanted to hear the new words. "Yes, all right. Here I go," whispered Meggie.

She had not often heard her father read aloud, but she remembered exactly how Mo gave every word the right sound, every single word. . . .

It was quiet in the room, very quiet. The whole Inkworld — every fairy, every tree, even the sea — seemed to be waiting for her voice. *"Night after night,"* Meggie began, *"the Adderhead could get no rest. His wife slept soundly and deeply. She was his fifth wife, and younger than his three eldest daughters. Her body, pregnant with his child, was a mound under the bedclothes. It must be a boy this time; she had already borne him two daughters. If this child was another girl he would disown her, just as he had repudiated his other wives. He would send her back to her father or to some lonely castle in the mountains.*

Why could she sleep, although she feared him, while he paced up and down the magnificent bedchamber like an old dancing bear in its cage?

Because he alone felt the truly great fear. The fear of Death.

Death waited outside the windows, outside the glass panes paid for by selling his strongest peasants. Death pressed its ugly face against them as soon as darkness swallowed up his castle like a snake swallowing a mouse. He had more torches lit every night, more candles, yet still the fear came — to make him shake and fall on his knees because they trembled so much, to show him his future: the flesh falling from his bones, the worms eating him, the White Women leading him away. The Adderhead pressed his hands to his mouth so that the guards outside the door would not hear him sobbing. Fear. Fear of the end of all his days, fear of the void, fear, fear, fear. Fear that Death was already in his body somewhere, invisible, growing and flourishing and eating him away — the one enemy he could never defeat, never burn or stab or hang, the one enemy from whom there was no escaping.

One night, blacker and more endless than any that had gone before, the fear was particularly terrible, and he had them all woken, as he quite often did, all who were sleeping peacefully in their beds instead of trembling and sweating like him: his wife, the useless physicians, the petitioners, scribes, administrators, his herald, the silver-nosed minstrel. He had the cooks driven into the kitchen to prepare him a banquet, but as he was sitting at his table, his fingers dripping with fat from the freshly roasted meat, a girl came to the Castle of Night. She walked fearlessly past the guards and offered him a deal: a bargain with Death.

That was how it would be. Because she was reading it. How the words made their way out through Meggie's lips. As if they were weaving the future. Every sound, every character a thread. . . . Meggie forgot everything around her: the infirmary, the straw mattress she was sitting on, even Farid and his unhappy face as he watched her go. She went on spinning Fenoglio's story; that was why she was here, spinning it out of threads of sound with her breath and her voice — to save her father and her mother. And this whole strange world that had enchanted her.

When Meggie heard the agitated voices she thought at first that they were coming out of the words, but they grew louder and louder. Reluctantly, she raised her head. She hadn't read it all yet. There were still a few sentences waiting, waiting for her to teach them to breathe. *Look at the words on the page, Meggie,* she told herself. *Concentrate!*

She gave a start when a dull knocking resounded through the infirmary. The voices grew louder, she heard hasty footsteps, and Roxane appeared in the doorway. "They've come from the Castle of Night!" she whispered. "They have a picture of you, a strange picture. Quick, come with me!"

Meggie tried to put the parchment in her sleeve until she could read those last few sentences, but then thought better of it and pushed it down the neck of her dress. She hoped it would not show under the firm fabric. She could still taste the words on her tongue, she still saw herself standing before the Adderhead just as she had read it, but Roxane reached for her hand and pulled her along. A woman's voice came down the colonnade, Bella's voice, and then the voice of a man, loud and commanding. Roxane did not let Meggie's hand go but led her on, past the doors behind which the patients slept or else lay awake listening to their own heavy breathing.

The Barn Owl's room was empty. Roxane took Meggie in with her, bolted the door, and looked around. The window was barred, and the steps were coming closer. Meggie thought she heard the Barn Owl's voice, and another voice, rough and threatening. Then, suddenly, there was silence. They had stopped outside the door. Roxane put her arm around Meggie's shoulders.

"They're going to take you with them!" she whispered as the Barn Owl talked to the intruders on the other side of the door. "We'll send word to the Black Prince. He has spies in the castle. We'll try to help you, understand?"

Meggie just nodded.

Someone was hammering on the door. "Open up, little witch, or do we have to come and get you?"

Books, books everywhere. Meggie retreated among the stacks of volumes. There wasn't a single book here she could have gone to for help, even if she'd wanted to. The knowledge in them could give her no aid. She'd have needed a story for that, but she remembered looking for a suitable story in vain in Capricorn's house. She glanced at Roxane in search of help — and saw the same helplessness on Roxane's face, too.

What would happen if they took her away with them? So many sentences were still unread. Meggie tried desperately to remember just where she had been interrupted. . . .

More hammering on the door. The wood groaned; it would soon splinter and break. Meggie went to the door, pushed back the bolt, and opened it. She couldn't count the soldiers standing out in the narrow corridor, but there were a great many of them.

They were led by Firefox; Meggie recognized him in spite of the scarf he had tied over his mouth and nose. They all had such scarves wound around their faces, and their eyes above the cloth were terrified. *I hope you've all caught the plague here,* thought Meggie. *I hope you die like flies.* The soldier beside Firefox stumbled back as if he had heard her thoughts, but it was Meggie's face that frightened him. "Witch!" he exclaimed, staring at what Firefox held in his hand. Meggie recognized the narrow silver frame at once. It was her photograph, from Elinor's library.

A murmur arose among the men-at-arms. But Firefox put his hand roughly under her chin, making her turn her face to him. "I thought so. You're the girl from the stable," he said. "I'll admit you didn't look to me like a witch there!" Meggie tried to turn her head away, but Firefox's hand did not let go. "Well done!" he said to a girl who was standing among the men-at-arms looking lost. Her feet were bare, and she wore the same plain tunic as all the women who worked in the infirmary. Carla, wasn't that her name?

She bent her head and looked at the piece of silver that the soldier pressed into her hand as if she'd never seen such a beautiful, shiny coin before. "He said I'd get work," she whispered almost inaudibly. "In the castle kitchen. The minstrel with the silver nose said so."

Firefox shrugged scornfully. "You've come to the wrong man here," he said, turning his back to her heedlessly. "And this time I'm to take you, too, sawbones," he said to the Barn Owl. "You've let the wrong sort of visitors through your gate once too often. I told the Adderhead it was high time to light a fire here, a great fire. I can still do that kind of thing extremely well, but he wouldn't hear of it. Someone's told him his death will come out of a fire. Since then he won't let us light anything but candles."

There was no missing his contempt for his master's weakness.

The Barn Owl looked at Meggie. *I'm sorry*, said his eyes. And she read a question in them, too: *Where's Dustfinger?* Yes, where?

"Let me go with her." Roxane went up to Meggie and tried to put an arm around her shoulders again, but Firefox pushed her roughly back.

"Only the girl in the witch picture," he said, "and the physician."

Roxane, Bella, and a few of the other women followed them to the gate leading out to the sea. The surf shone in the moonlight, and the beach lay there deserted, except for a few footprints that no one, luckily, examined closely. The soldiers had brought horses for their prisoners. Meggie's laid its ears back when one of the soldiers put her on its back. Only when it was trotting toward the mountains with her did she dare to look surreptitiously around. But there was no sign of Dustfinger and Farid. Except for the footprints in the sand.

57

FIRE AND WATER

And what is word knowledge but a shadow of wordless knowledge?

Khalil Gibran, *The Prophet*

All was quiet behind the walls of the infirmary when Dustfinger gestured to Farid to come out from among the trees. No weeping, no cursing the men who had come from the Castle of Night. Most of the women had gone back to the sick and dying. Only Roxane still stood on the beach, looking at the path the soldiers had taken.

She went to Dustfinger, her footsteps weary.

"I'll go after them!" stammered Farid beside him, his fists clenched. "At least there's no missing that accursed castle!"

"What do you think you're talking about, damn it?" Dustfinger snapped at him. "Do you believe you can just walk through the gates? That is the Castle of Night, where they stick chopped-off heads on the battlements."

Farid ducked his head and stared up at the silver towers. They rose to the sky as if to impale the stars.

"But . . . but Meggie," he stammered.

"Yes, all right, we'll follow her," said Dustfinger, irritation in his voice. "My leg's already looking forward to the climb. But we're not stumbling off just like that. You have something to learn yet."

The relief in the boy's face when he looked at him — as if he were delighted at the prospect of creeping into the Adder's nest! Dustfinger could only shake his head at such idiocy.

"Something to learn? What?"

"What I was going to show you anyway." Dustfinger went toward the water. He wished his leg would hurry up and heal.

Roxane followed him. "You two are going after them? What are you talking about?" Fear and rage were mingled on her face as she came between him and the boy. "You can't go to the castle! There's no more you can do! Either for the girl, or for the Barn Owl, or for any of the others. Your wonderful letter came to nothing, nothing at all!"

"We'll see," was all Dustfinger would reply. "It depends whether Meggie read it out loud, and if so, how far she got."

He tried to move her aside, but Roxane pushed his hands away. "Let's send a message to the Black Prince!" There was desperation in her voice. "Have you forgotten all the fire-raisers up there at the castle? You'll be dead before the sun rises! What about Basta? What about Firefox and the Piper? Someone is bound to recognize your face!"

"Who says I'm going to show my face?" he replied.

Roxane flinched back. She cast Farid such a hostile glance that the boy turned away. "But that's our secret. You've never shown anyone but me before. And you yourself said you're the only one who can do it!"

"The boy will be able to do it, too!"

The sand crunched under his feet as he walked toward the waves. He did not stop until the surf was washing around his boots.

"What's she talking about?" asked Farid. "What are you going to show me? Is it very difficult?"

Dustfinger looked around. Roxane was walking slowly back to the infirmary. She disappeared behind the plain wooden gate without once turning.

"What is it?" Impatiently, Farid tugged at his sleeve. "Tell me."

Dustfinger turned his back to him. "Fire and water," he said, "don't really mix. You could say they're incompatible. But when they do love each other, they love passionately."

It was a long time since he had last spoken the words he now whispered. But the fire understood. A flame licked up between the wet pebbles that the sea had washed up on the sand. Dustfinger bent and enticed it into the hollow of his hand as if it were a young bird, whispered, told it what he wanted, promised it a nocturnal game such as it had never played before . . . and when it answered, crackling, flaring up, so hot that it burned his skin, he threw it into the foaming sea, fingers outstretched as if he still held the fire on invisible strings. The water snapped at the flame like a fish snapping at a fly, but the fire only burned brighter, while Dustfinger, standing on the shore, spread his arms wide.

Hissing and flaring, the fire imitated him, moving to left and right along the sea wave, farther and farther, until the surf, now rimmed with flames, rolled toward the shore, and a band of fire was washed up at Dustfinger's feet like a love token. He plunged both hands into the blazing foam, and when he straightened up again he held a fairy fluttering in his fingers, as blue as her forest sisters but surrounded by a fiery luster, and her eyes were as red as the flames from which she was born. Dustfinger held her in his hands like a rare moth, waited for the prickling of his skin, the heat running up his arms as if he suddenly had liquid fire instead of blood in his veins. Not until it had burned its way right up to his armpits did he let the tiny creature fly away, chattering and swearing crossly, as they always did when you lured them to you by making the sea play with fire.

"What's that?" asked Farid in alarm, looking at Dustfinger's blackened hands and arms.

Dustfinger took a cloth from his belt and carefully rubbed the soot into his skin. "That," he said, "is something that will get us into the castle. But the soot works only if you get it from the fairies for yourself. So it's your turn now."

Farid looked at him incredulously. "But I can't do that!" he stammered. "I don't know how you did it."

"Nonsense!" Dustfinger stepped back from the water and sat down on the damp sand. "Of course you can do it! Just think of Meggie!"

Undecided, Farid looked up at the castle, while the waves licked his bare toes as if inviting him to play.

"Won't they see the fire up there?"

"The castle is farther away than it looks. Believe me, your feet will show you that when we start climbing. And if the guards up there do see anything they'll think it's lightning, or fire-elves dancing over the water. When did you start thinking so hard before you began to play? All I can say is, if you wait much longer I shall certainly start remembering what a crazy notion going up there is."

That convinced Farid.

The flame went out three times when he threw it into the breakers. But on the fourth attempt the waves were rimmed with fire for him as he had demanded — perhaps not quite such bright fire as they had made for Dustfinger, but the sea burned for Farid, too. And for the second time that night, fire and water played together.

"Well done," said Dustfinger, as the boy looked proudly at the soot on his arms. "Spread it well over your chest and legs and face."

"Why?" Farid looked at him, wide-eyed.

"Because it will make us invisible," replied Dustfinger, rubbing soot into his own face. "Until sunrise."

58

INVISIBLE AS THE WIND

"So sorry, your bloodiness, Mr. Baron, sir," he said greasily.
"My mistake, my mistake — I didn't see you — of course I
didn't, you're invisible — forgive old Peevsie his little joke, sir."
J. K. Rowling, *Harry Potter and the Sorcerer's Stone*

It was an odd feeling, being invisible. Farid felt all-powerful and lost at the same time. As if he were nowhere and everywhere. The worst of it was that he couldn't see Dustfinger. He had to rely on his hearing. "Dustfinger?" he kept whispering as he followed him through the night, and every time a quiet reply came back: "I'm here, right in front of you."

The soldiers who had taken Meggie and the Barn Owl with them would have to follow a road — a bad one, almost entirely overgrown in many places — that wound up into the hills, bending and curving. Dustfinger, on the other hand, was making his way across country and up slopes too steep for horses, especially when they had to carry armed riders. Farid tried not to think how much it must be hurting Dustfinger's leg. Now and then he heard him swearing quietly, and he kept stopping, invisible, nothing but a breathing in the night.

The castle was indeed farther away than it had looked from the beach, but finally its walls towered to the sky right in front of them. By comparison with this fortress, the castle of Ombra seemed to Farid like a toy, built by a prince who liked to eat and drink but had no intention of going to war. In the Castle of Night, every stone seemed to have been set in place with war in mind, and as Farid followed the sound of Dustfinger's gasping breaths, he pictured to himself, with horror, what it must be like to storm up the steep slope with hot pitch raining down on you from the battlements above and bolts from crossbows flying your way.

Morning was still far off when they reached the castle gate. They still had a few precious hours of invisibility left, but the gate was shut, and Farid felt tears of disappointment fill his eyes. "It's closed!" he whispered. "They've taken them into the castle already! Now what?" Every breath hurt him, they had traveled so fast. But what good did it do them now to be as transparent as glass, as invisible as the wind?

He sensed Dustfinger's body beside him, warm in the windy night. "Of course it's closed!" his voice whispered. "What did you expect? Did you think the two of us would overtake them? We wouldn't have done that even if I wasn't hobbling like an old woman! But you wait: They're sure to open the gate for someone else tonight. Even if it's only one of their informers."

"Or maybe we could climb in?" Farid looked up hopefully at the pale gray walls. He saw the guards on the battlements, armed with spears.

"Climb in? You really do seem to be head over heels in love.

Can't you see how smooth and high these walls are? Forget it —
we'll wait."

Six gallows towered in front of them. Dead men hung from four
of them. Farid was thankful that in the darkness they just looked
like bundles of old clothes. "Damn it!" he heard Dustfinger murmur. "Why doesn't the fairy venom make your fear go away as
well as your body?" The same thing had occurred to Farid, too, but
he was not afraid of the guards, Basta, or Firefox. His fear, his terrible fear, was for Meggie. Being invisible only made it worse. There
seemed to be nothing left of him but the pain in his heart.

A chilly wind was blowing tonight, and Farid was just
breathing on his invisible fingers to warm them when hoofbeats
echoed through the dark.

"There, now!" whispered Dustfinger. "Looks like we're in
luck for a change! Remember, whatever happens, we must be out
of here before daybreak. The sun will make us visible again
almost as fast as you can summon fire."

The hoofbeats grew louder, and a horseman emerged from the
darkness — not in the Adderhead's pale silver but clothed in red
and black. "Well, would you believe it?" whispered Dustfinger.
"Sootbird, no less!"

One of the guards called something down from the battlements, and Sootbird replied.

"Come on!" Dustfinger hissed to Farid as the gate swung
open, creaking. They followed so close to Sootbird that Farid
could have touched his horse's tail. *Traitor,* he thought, *filthy
traitor!* He would have liked to drag him down from the saddle,
put a knife to his throat, and ask what news he was bringing to
the Castle of Night — but Dustfinger thrust him on, through the
gigantic gate and into the courtyard. He led Farid onward as
Sootbird rode to the castle stables. They were swarming with

men-at-arms. Obviously, the Castle of Night was as wakeful as its master was said to be.

"Listen!" whispered Dustfinger, drawing Farid under an arch. "This castle is the size of a city and as full of nooks and crannies as a labyrinth. Mark the way you go with soot. I don't want to have to search for you later because you're lost like a child in the forest, understand?"

"But what about Sootbird? He gave away the Secret Camp, didn't he?"

"Very likely. But forget him for now. Think of Meggie."

"But he was among the prisoners!" A troop of soldiers marched past them. Farid flinched back in alarm. He still couldn't believe that they really did not see him.

"So?" Dustfinger's voice sounded like the wind itself speaking. "It's the oldest disguise in the world for traitors. Where do you hide your informer? Among your victims. I expect the Piper told him once or twice what a magnificent fire-eater he was, and then they were best friends. Sootbird's always had peculiar taste in friends. Well, come on, or we'll still be standing here when the sun melts our invisibility off us."

That made Farid instinctively look up at the sky. It was a dark night. Even the moon seemed lost in all the blackness, and he could not take his eyes off the silver towers.

"The Adder's nest!" he whispered — and felt Dustfinger's invisible hand drawing him on again, none too gently.

59

THE ADDERHEAD

Thoughts of death
Crowd over my happiness
Like dark clouds
Over the silver sickle of the moon.
Sterling Allen Brown, *Poems to Read*

The Adderhead was at table when Firefox brought Meggie to him. Exactly as she had read it in the story. The hall where he was feasting was so magnificent that the Laughing Prince's throne room seemed plain as a farmhouse by comparison. The tiles over which Firefox dragged Meggie to his master were strewn with white rose petals. A sea of candles burned in claw-footed candelabra, standing between columns covered with silver scales. The light of the candles made them shimmer like snakeskin. Countless servants hurried around between the scaly pillars, soundlessly, heads bent. Maidservants waited in respect-ful rows for a sign from their master. They all looked tired, torn from sleep, just as Fenoglio had described it. Some were leaning their backs surreptitiously against the tapestries on the walls.

Beside the Adderhead, at a table that seemed to be laid for a hundred guests, sat a woman as pale as a porcelain doll, with such a childlike face that Meggie would have thought her the Adderhead's daughter if she didn't know better. The Silver Prince himself ate greedily, as if by swallowing the food that stood in countless dishes on the table covered with black cloth, he could swallow his own fear, too. But his wife touched nothing. It seemed to Meggie that the sight of her husband eating so greedily nauseated her; she kept passing her ringed hands over her swollen belly. Oddly enough, her pregnancy made her look even more like a child: a child with a thin, bitter mouth and cool eyes.

The silver-nosed Piper stood behind the Adderhead, one foot on a stool, his lute supported on his thigh, singing softly as his fingers slowly plucked the strings. But Meggie's eyes did not linger on him long. At the end of the table she had seen someone she knew only too well. Her heart faltered like an old woman's feet when Mortola returned her glance, with a smile so full of triumph that Meggie's knees began to tremble. The man who had wounded Dustfinger in the mill sat beside Mortola. His hands were bandaged, and above his forehead the fire had burned a pathway into his hair. Basta was in an even worse state. He was sitting close to Mortola, his face so red and swollen that Meggie almost failed to recognize him. But he had escaped death once again. Perhaps the good-luck charms he always wore worked after all.

Firefox clutched Meggie's arm tightly as he walked toward the Adderhead in his heavy fox-fur cloak — as if to prove that he personally had caught this little bird. He roughly pushed her in front of the table and threw the framed photograph down among the dishes.

The Adderhead raised his head and looked at her, with

bloodshot eyes in which Meggie could still see the traces of the bad night Fenoglio's words had given him. When he raised his greasy hand, the Piper fell silent behind him and propped his lute against the wall.

"There she is!" announced Firefox, as his master wiped the grease from his fingers and lips with an embroidered napkin. "I wish we had a witch-picture like this of everyone we're after. Then the informers wouldn't keep bringing us the wrong people."

The Adderhead had picked up the photograph. Appraisingly, he compared it with Meggie. She tried to bend her head, but Firefox forced up her face.

"Remarkable!" commented the Adderhead. "My best painters couldn't have produced anywhere near as good a likeness of the girl." With a bored expression, he reached for a little silver toothpick and prodded his teeth with it. "Mortola says you're a witch. Is it true?"

"Yes!" replied Meggie, looking him straight in the eye. Now they'd find out whether Fenoglio's words would come true again. If only she had been able to read to the end! She had read a great deal of it, but she could feel the rest of the words still waiting under her dress. *Forget them, Meggie,* she told herself. *You must make the words you* have *already read come true — and hope that the Adderhead plays his part just as you do.*

"Yes?" repeated the Adderhead. "So you admit it? Don't you know what I usually do to witches and magicians? I burn them." The same words. He was speaking Fenoglio's words. Exactly as Fenoglio had put them into his mouth. Exactly as she had read them out loud in the infirmary a few hours ago.

She knew what she must answer. The words came into her mind of their own accord, as if they were hers and not Fenoglio's.

Meggie looked at Basta and the other man from the mill. Fenoglio hadn't written about them personally, but the answer was still right. "The last to burn," she said calmly, "were your own men. Only one man commands fire in this world, and he's not you."

The Adderhead stared at her — watchful as a fat tomcat not yet certain how to play his game most satisfactorily with the mouse he has caught. "Ah," he said in his heavy, thick voice. "I suppose you mean that fire-dancer. He likes to go around with poachers and footpads. You think he'll come and try to rescue you, eh? Then, at last, I could feed him to the fire that you claim obeys him so well."

"I don't need anyone to rescue me," replied Meggie. "I would have come to you myself in any case, even if you hadn't had me brought here."

There was laughter among the silver columns. The Adderhead leaned across the table and examined her with unconcealed curiosity.

"Well, well!" he said. "Really? Why? To plead with me to let your father go? Because that robber is your father, isn't he? At least, Mortola says so. She even says we've caught your mother, too."

Mortola! Fenoglio had never thought of her. He hadn't written a word about her, but there she sat with her magpie gaze. *Don't think about it, Meggie. Be cold. Cold to your very heart, as you were on the night when you summoned the Shadow.* But where was she to get the right words from now? *Improvise, Meggie,* she told herself, *like an actress who's forgotten her lines. Go on! Make up your own words and then just mix them into the words Fenoglio wrote for you, like an extra spice.*

"The Magpie is right," she replied to the Adderhead. And sure enough, her voice sounded calm and steady, as if her heart wasn't thudding in her breast like a small, hunted animal. "You took my father captive when she'd almost killed him, and you're holding my mother prisoner in your dungeons. However, I'm not here to ask for leniency. I have a deal to offer you."

"Listen to the little witch!" Basta's voice shook with hatred. "Why don't I just slice her up nice and thin, and you can feed her to your dogs?"

However, the Adderhead ignored him. He kept his eyes fixed on Meggie's face, as if seeking it for what she *wasn't* saying. *Be like Dustfinger,* she told herself. *You can never tell what Dustfinger is thinking or feeling from the way he looks. Try! It can't be all that difficult.*

"A deal?" The Adderhead took his wife's hand, as casually as if he had just found it lying beside his plate by chance. "What do you plan to sell me that I can't simply take for myself?"

His men laughed. Meggie tried not to notice that her fingers were numb with terror. Once again it was Fenoglio's words that passed her lips. Words that she had read aloud.

"My father," she continued, in a carefully controlled voice, "is no robber. He's a bookbinder and an enchanter. He is the only man alive who doesn't fear Death. Haven't you seen his wound? Didn't the physicians tell you that injury ought to have killed him? *Nothing* can kill him. Mortola tried, and did he die? No. He has brought Cosimo the Fair back to life, although the White Women had already delivered him up to Death, and if you let him and my mother go then you need not fear Death, either, for my father," said Meggie, taking her time over the last few words, "my father can make you immortal."

All was very quiet in the great hall.

Until Mortola's voice broke the silence. "She's lying!" she cried. "The little witch is lying! Don't believe a word of it. It's her tongue, her bewitched tongue. That's her only weapon. Her father can die, all right, indeed he can! Bring him here and I'll prove it. I'll kill him myself before your eyes, and this time I'll do it properly!"

No! Meggie's heart began to race as if it would leap out of her breast. What had she done? The Adderhead was staring at her, but when at last he spoke it seemed as if he hadn't even heard what Mortola had said.

"How?" was all he asked. "How could your father do what you promise?" He was thinking of the night to come now. Meggie saw it in his eyes. He was thinking of the fear waiting for him: It would be even worse than in the night just gone, even more merciless. . . .

Meggie leaned forward over the laden table. She spoke the words as if she were reading them aloud again. "My father will bind you a book!" she said, so quietly that apart from the Adderhead no one, except perhaps his doll-like wife, could hear her. "He will bind it for you with my help, a book with five hundred blank pages. He will cover it with wood and leather, he will give it brass clasps, and you will write your name on the first page in your own hand. In token of thanks, however, you will let him go, and with him all whose lives he asks for, and you will hide the book in a place known only to you, for hear this: As long as that book exists you will be immortal. Nothing will be able to kill you, no disease, no weapon — as long as the book remains intact."

"Indeed!" The Adderhead's bloodshot eyes were staring at her. His breath smelled sweetish, as if he had been drinking wine that was too heavy. "And suppose someone burns it or tears it up? Parchment doesn't last like silver."

"You will have to take good care of it," replied Meggie quietly — *and it will kill you all the same,* she added in her thoughts. She felt as if she were hearing her own voice reading Fenoglio's words again (and how good they had tasted!): *But there was that one thing the girl did not tell the Adderhead: The book not only made him immortal but could kill him, too, if someone only wrote three words on its white pages, and those words were: heart, spell, death.*

"What's she whispering?" Mortola had risen to her feet. She leaned her bony hands on the table. "Don't listen to her!" she told the Adderhead. "She's a witch and a liar! How often do I have to tell you? Kill her — her and her father — before they kill you! The old man probably wrote all her words for her, the old man I told you about!"

For the first time the Adderhead turned to look at Mortola, and Meggie briefly feared that he might believe her after all. But then she saw the anger in his face. "Be quiet!" he snapped at the Magpie. "Capricorn may have listened to you, but he's gone, like the Shadow who made him powerful, and you are tolerated at this court only because you have rendered me certain services! But I don't want to hear any more of your drivel about silver tongues and old men who can bring written words to life. Not another word out of you, or I'll send you back to where you once came from — in the kitchen with the maids."

Mortola turned as white as if she had no blood left in her veins. "I warned you!" she said hoarsely. "Don't forget it!" Then, stony-faced, she sat down again. Basta cast her an anxious glance, but Mortola took no notice of him. She just stared at Meggie with such venom that she felt those eyes were burning a hole in her face.

The Adderhead, however, speared one of the tiny roasted birds lying on a silver platter in front of him with his knife and put it between his lips with relish. Obviously, his angry exchange with Mortola had given him an appetite. "Did I understand you correctly? You yourself would help your father with the work?" he asked, as he spat out the little bones into the hand of a servant who hastily stepped forward. "Does that mean he has taught a daughter his craft, as a master craftsman usually teaches his sons? Surely you know that such a thing is forbidden in my realm?"

Meggie looked at him fearlessly. Even these words had been written by Fenoglio, every one of them, and she knew what the Adderhead was going to say next, because she had read that, too.

"If a craftsman of Argenta breaks that law, my pretty child," he went on, "I usually have his right hand chopped off. But, very well, I'll make an exception in your case, since it's to my own advantage."

He's going to do it, thought Meggie. *He's going to let me see Mo just as Fenoglio planned.* Happiness emboldened her. "My mother," she said, although Fenoglio had not written anything about that, "she could help, too. Then it would be done even faster."

"No, no!" The Adderhead smiled with delight, as if the disappointment in Meggie's eyes tasted better than all the delicacies on silver dishes before him. "Your mother stays in her dungeon, as a little incentive for the two of you to work quickly." He signaled impatiently to Firefox. "What are you waiting for? Take her to her father! And tell the librarian to set to work this very night, to provide everything a bookbinder needs for his work."

"Take her to her father?" Firefox gripped Meggie's arm, but he did not take a step. "You surely don't believe her witchy nonsense?"

Meggie almost forgot to breathe. She had not read these words aloud; not one of them was written by Fenoglio. What would happen now? Not a foot moved in the hall; even the servants stood still exactly where they were, and you could feel the silence. But Firefox went on. "A book to hold Death captive in its pages? Only a child would believe such a story, and this child has thought it up to save her father. Mortola's right. Hang him now, before we become the laughingstock of the peasants! Capricorn would have done it long ago."

"Capricorn?" The Adderhead spat out the name like one of the delicate bones he had spat into the servant's hand. He did not look at Firefox as he spoke, but his thick fingers clenched into a fist on the table. "Since Mortola came back I've heard that name very often. But as far as I know Capricorn is dead — even his personal witch and poisoner couldn't prevent that — and you, Firefox, have obviously forgotten who your new master is. I am the Adderhead! My family has ruled this land for more than seven generations, while your old master was only the bastard son of a soot-blackened smith! You were a fire-raiser, a murderer, no more, and I've made you my herald. A little more gratitude is called for, I think, or do you want to look for a new master?"

Firefox's face turned almost as red as his hair. "No, Your Grace," he said almost inaudibly. "No, I don't."

"Good!" The Adderhead impaled another bird on his knife. They were waiting in their silver dish, piled up like chestnuts. "Then do as I said. Take the girl to her father and make sure he soon sets to work. Have you brought that physician, as I ordered? The Barn Owl?"

Firefox nodded, without looking at his master.

"Good. Let him visit her father to tend him twice a day. We want our prisoner to be fit and well, understand?"

"I understand," said Firefox hoarsely.

He looked neither to right nor left as he led Meggie out of the hall. All eyes followed her — and avoided her own eyes when they met theirs. Witch. That was what they had called her before, back in Capricorn's village. Perhaps it was true. At that moment she felt powerful, as powerful as if the whole Inkworld obeyed her voice. *They are taking me to Mo,* she thought. *They are taking me to him, and that will be the beginning of the end for the Adderhead.*

But when the servants had closed the doors of the hall behind them, a soldier barred Firefox's way.

"Mortola has a message for you," he said. "You're to search the girl for a sheet of paper or anything else with writing on it. She says you should look in her sleeves first. She hid something there once before."

Before Meggie fully realized what was happening, Firefox took hold of her and roughly pushed up her sleeves. Finding nothing there, he was about to put his hands inside her dress, but Meggie pushed them away and took out the parchment herself. Firefox tore it from her fingers, stared at the written letters for a moment with the baffled look of a man who couldn't read, and then, without a word, handed the parchment to the soldier.

Meggie felt dizzy with fear as he led her on. Suppose Mortola showed the letter to the Adderhead? Suppose, suppose . . . ?

"Get moving!" growled Firefox, pushing her up a flight of stairs. As if numbed, Meggie stumbled up the steep steps. *Fenoglio,* she thought, *Fenoglio, help me. Mortola knows about our plan.*

"Stop!" Firefox brutally grabbed her by the hair. Four men-at-arms were on guard outside a door with three bolts over it. A nod of the head from Firefox told them to open it.

Mo, thought Meggie. *They really are taking me to him.* And that thought extinguished any others. Even thoughts of Mortola.

FIRE ON THE WALL

Lo, on the whiteness of the wall,
Behold, appeared a human hand,
Which wrote and wrote, in letters tall,
A fiery message for the land.

Heinrich Heine, "Belshazzar"

All was quiet in the wide, dark corridors as Dustfinger and Farid stole into the Castle of Night. Only wax dripped from a thousand candles on the stone flags that all bore the Adderhead's coat of arms. Servants hurried past them in soft-soled shoes, and maids scuttled by with bent heads. Guards stood in endless passages and outside doorways so high that they seemed to have been made for giants, not ordinary humans. Every one of them bore the emblematic creature of the Adderhead — the snake striking at its prey — in scales of silver, and huge mirrors hung beside the doors. Farid kept stopping in front of them to look into the polished metal and reassure himself that he really was invisible.

Dustfinger made an acorn-sized flame dance on his hand so

that the boy could follow him. Servants were carrying delicious things to eat out of one of the halls they passed. Their aroma reminded Dustfinger painfully of his invisible stomach, and when he pushed his way past the servants as soundlessly as the Adderhead's snake, he heard them talking in muted tones about a young witch and a deal that was to save the Bluejay from the gallows. Dustfinger, as invisible as their voices, listened to them and did not know which of his emotions was the stronger: relief that Fenoglio's words were obviously coming true again, or fear of those words and the invisible threads spun by the old man, threads to catch even the Adderhead and make him dream of immortality, although Fenoglio had recorded his death in writing long ago. But had Meggie really read those deadly words before they took her away? "Now what?" Farid whispered. "Did you hear that? They've shut up Meggie with Silvertongue in one of the towers! How do I get there?" His voice was shaking — heavens, what a plague love was! Anyone who claimed otherwise had never yet felt that wretched trembling of the heart.

"Forget it!" Dustfinger whispered to the boy. "The dungeons in the tower have strong doors. Even invisible you wouldn't get through them. And the place will be swarming with guards. After all, they still think they've caught the Bluejay. You'd do better to steal into the kitchen and listen to the maids and the menservants — you always learn something interesting that way. But be careful! I repeat: Invisible doesn't mean immortal."

"How about you?"

"I'm going to venture down to the dungeons under the castle, where the less valuable prisoners are held, to find the Barn Owl and Meggie's mother. See that fat marble statue there? Must be some ancestor of the Adderhead. We'll meet there. And don't even think of following me! Farid?"

But the boy had already gone. Dustfinger suppressed a soft curse. He just hoped no one heard the boy's lovesick heart thudding!

It was a long, dark way to the dungeons. One of the women healers who worked for the Barn Owl had told him where the entrance lay. None of the guards he passed even turned their heads as Dustfinger slipped by them. Two were lounging around at the mouth of the damp corridor, lit only by a single torch, with the door to the dungeons at the end of it. Beyond that door the way went on down, down into the deadly entrails of the Castle of Night, which digested human beings like a stony stomach, now and then excreting a few dead bodies. There was another snake on the door that no one ever wished to enter, but here the silver adder was coiled around a skull.

The guards were quarreling — it was something to do with Firefox — but Dustfinger had no time to eavesdrop. He was only glad that all their attention was on each other as he slipped past. The door creaked slightly when he opened it, just wide enough to get through — his heart almost stopped as he did it — but the guards didn't turn around. What wouldn't he give for a fearless heart like Farid's, even if it made you reckless! It was so dark beyond the door that, for a moment, he had to summon fire before his invisible feet made their way down the steps, and just in time. They were steep and well trodden, worn away by the people whom the dungeons had swallowed up. Fear and desperation rose to greet him like vapors from the depths. The steps were said to lead as far down under the hill as the castle towers rose to the sky above it, but Dustfinger had never met anyone who could confirm this tale. Of those he had known who were taken down here, he had never seen a single one alive again.

Dustfinger, Dustfinger, he thought before starting on the downward climb, *this is a dangerous path to take just to pass the time of day with two old friends, and your visit won't even do them much good.* However, he had run after the Barn Owl for years just as Farid was now running after him, and as for Resa — perhaps he recalled her name last to convince himself that he was certainly not climbing down this damned stairway on her account.

Unfortunately, even invisible feet make sounds, but luckily he only met guards once. Three warders passed him at such close quarters that he could smell the garlic on their breath, and he only just managed to press close to the wall in time to stop the fattest of them from bumping into him. During the rest of the dark downward climb, he met no one. There was a torch burning every few feet along the rough-hewn walls, so different from the finely chiseled masonry in the castle above. Dustfinger twice passed a room where more guards were sitting, but they never even raised their heads as he stole by, more quietly than a breath of air and equally invisible.

When the stairs finally came to an end, he almost collided with a warder pacing up and down a candlelit corridor with a bored expression on his face. Soundlessly, he slipped past the man. He peered into dungeons scarcely larger than holes, too low for anyone to stand up in. Others were large enough to take fifty men. It would certainly be easy simply to forget a prisoner down here, and Dustfinger's heart contracted as he imagined how Resa must be feeling in this darkness. She had been a prisoner before, for so many years, and after that her freedom had lasted barely a year.

He heard voices, and followed them along another corridor until they grew louder. A small, bald-headed man came toward him. He passed so close that Dustfinger held his breath — but the man didn't notice him, just muttered something about stupid women and disappeared around the corner. Dustfinger pressed his back against the damp wall and listened. Someone

was weeping — a woman, and someone else was speaking soothingly to her. There was only one cell at the end of the corridor: a
dark, barred cavern with a torch burning beside it. How was he
to get past those damned bars? He went close to them. There sat
Resa, stroking another woman's hair to comfort her, while
Twofingers sat beside them playing a sad tune on a little flute.
No one could have done it half as well with all ten fingers as he
did with seven. Dustfinger didn't know the others: neither the
women with Resa nor the other men. There was no sign of
the Barn Owl. Where had they taken him? Had he perhaps
been imprisoned with Silvertongue?

He looked around, listened. Somewhere a man laughed,
probably one of the warders. Dustfinger held a finger in the
burning torch, whispered fire-words until a flame leaped from
his fingertip like a sparrow picking up crumbs. When he had
first shown Farid how to write his name on a wall in fire, the
boy's black eyes had almost popped out of his head. Yet it was
perfectly easy. Dustfinger put his hand between the bars and
passed his finger over the rough stone. *Resa*, he wrote, and saw
Twofingers lower his flute and stare at the burning letters. Resa
turned. Heavens, how sad she looked! He should have come
sooner. A good thing her daughter couldn't see her like this.

She rose, took a step toward her name, and hesitated. Still
with his finger, Dustfinger drew a fiery line like an arrow pointing
his way. She came close to the bars and stared at the empty air,
incredulous and baffled.

"I'm sorry," he whispered. "You won't see my face today, but
it's still as scarred as ever."

"Dustfinger?" She reached into the air, and his invisible fingers
took her hand. She was actually speaking! The Black Prince had
told him she could speak again, but he hadn't believed him.

"What a beautiful voice!" he whispered. "I always imagined it would be something like that. When did you get it back?"

"When Mortola shot Mo."

Twofingers was still staring at her. The woman Resa had been comforting turned to them, too. Just so long as they didn't say anything . . .

"How are you?" she whispered. "How is Meggie?"

"Well. Better off than you, for sure. She and the writer got together to change this story for the better."

Resa was clinging to the bars with one hand and to his own hand with the other. "Where is she now?"

"Probably with her father." He saw the horror in her face. "Yes, I know, he's up in the tower, but that's what she wanted. It's all part of the plan Fenoglio has thought up."

"How is he? How's Mo?"

Jealousy still gave him a pang. The heart was a stupid thing. "Said to be better, and thanks to Meggie he's not going to be hanged for the time being, so don't look so sad. Your daughter and Fenoglio have thought of a very clever way to save him. Him, and you, and all the others. . . ." Steps approached. Dustfinger let go of Resa's hand and moved back, but the footsteps went past and away again.

"Are you still there?" Her eyes searched the darkness.

"Yes." He took hold of her fingers once more. "We only ever seem to meet in dungeons now! How long does it take your husband to bind a book?"

"Bind a book?"

He heard footsteps again, but this time the sound died away more quickly.

"Yes. It's a crazy story, but since Fenoglio has written it and your daughter has read it, no doubt it will come true."

She put her other hand through the bars until her fingers met his face. "You really are invisible! How do you do it?" She sounded as curious as a little girl. She was curious about everything she didn't know. He had always liked that in her.

"Only an old fairy trick!" Her fingers stroked his scarred cheek. *Why can't you help her, Dustfinger?* he thought. *She'll go mad down here!* Suppose he struck one of the warders down? But there was still that endless staircase to climb, and after it the castle, the wide courtyard, the bare hilltop — nowhere to hide her, no tree to conceal her. Only stones and soldiers.

"What about your wife?" Her voice was beautiful. "Did you find her?"

"Yes."

"What did you tell her?"

"About what?"

"The time you were away."

"Nothing."

"I've told Mo everything."

Yes, no doubt she had. "Well, Silvertongue knows what you're talking about, but I don't think Roxane would have believed me, do you?"

"No, probably not." For a moment she bent her head as if she were remembering — remembering the time he couldn't tell Roxane about. "The Black Prince told me you have a daughter, too," she whispered. "Why didn't you ever tell me about her?"

Twofingers and the woman with the tearstained face were still staring at them. With luck they believed by now that they had imagined the fiery letters. There was only a faint trace of soot left on the wall, and it was not unusual, after all, for people to begin talking to the empty air in dungeons.

"I had two daughters." Dustfinger jumped as someone

screamed somewhere. "The elder is around Meggie's age, but she's angry with me. She wants to know where I was for those ten years. Perhaps you know a pretty story I can tell her?"

"What about the other one?"

"She's dead."

Resa just pressed his hand. "I'm sorry."

"Yes. So am I." He turned. One of the warders was standing at the end of the corridor. He called something to another warder, and then walked on, looking sullen.

"Three weeks, maybe four!" Resa whispered. "That's how long Mo would need, depending on the thickness of the book."

"Good, then that's not so bad." He put his hand through the bars and stroked her hair. "A couple of weeks are nothing to all those years in Capricorn's house, Resa! Remember that every time you feel like beating your head against these bars. Promise me."

She nodded. "Tell Meggie I'm well!" she whispered. "And tell Mo, too, please. You'll be talking to him as well, won't you?"

"Yes, of course!" lied Dustfinger. What harm did it do to promise her that? For what else could he do to help her? The other woman began sobbing again. Her weeping echoed back from the moldering walls, louder and louder.

"Damn it all, shut your gob there!"

Dustfinger pressed close to the wall as the warder approached. He was a fat fellow, a hulk of a man, and Dustfinger held his breath as he stopped right beside him. For a terrible moment Twofingers was staring straight at Dustfinger as if he could see him, but then his eyes moved on, searching the darkness, perhaps for more fiery letters on the wall.

"Don't cry!" Resa tried to calm the woman as the warder struck the bars with his stick. Dustfinger could hardly find a corner to retreat into. The weeping woman buried her face in

Resa's skirt, and the warder turned with a grunt and trudged away again. Dustfinger waited until the sound of his footsteps had died away before returning to the bars. Resa was kneeling beside the woman, whose face was still buried in her dress, and talking to her softly.

"Resa!" he whispered. "I must go. Did they bring an old man down here tonight? A physician, he calls himself the Barn Owl."

She came back to the bars. "No," she whispered, "but the warders were talking about a physician they've arrested. He has to treat all the sick people in the castle before they shut him up with us."

"That'll be him. Give him my greetings." It was hard for him to leave her alone in the dark like this. He would have liked to free her from her cage, just as he set fairies free in marketplaces, but Resa wouldn't be able to fly away.

At the foot of the stairs, two warders were joking about the hangman whose work Firefox was only too keen to take over. Dustfinger slipped past them, quick as a lizard, but all the same one of them turned his way with a confused expression. Perhaps the smell of fire that Dustfinger wore like a second coat had risen to his nostrils.

In the Tower of the Castle of Night

You never came out the way you came in.
    Francis Spufford, *The Child That Books Built*

Mo was asleep when they brought Meggie to him. It was only the fever that made him sleep, numbing the thoughts that kept him awake hour after hour, day after day, while he listened to his own heartbeat in the draughty cell where they had put him, high in one of the silver towers. The moon was still shining through the barred windows when the approaching footsteps roused him.

"Wake up, Bluejay!" The light of a torch fell into the cell, and Firefox pushed a slender figure through the door.

Resa? What kind of dream was this? A good one, for a change?

But it was not his wife they had brought. It was his daughter.

With difficulty, Mo sat up. He tasted Meggie's tears on his

face as she hugged him so hard that he drew in his breath sharply
with pain.

Meggie. They had caught her, too.

"Mo? Say something!" She took his hand and looked at his
face with concern. "How are you?" she whispered.

"Well, fancy that!" mocked Firefox. "The Bluejay really does
have a daughter. I expect she's about to tell you she's here of her
own free will, as she tried to make the Adderhead believe. She's
done a deal with him, and it's supposed to save your neck. You
should have heard the fairy tales she told. You could always sell
her and her angel's tongue to the strolling players."

Mo didn't even ask what he was talking about. He drew
Meggie close as soon as the guard had bolted the door behind
Firefox, kissed her hair, her forehead, took her face between his
hands. He had been so sure that he'd seen that face for the last
time in the stable in the forest. "Meggie, for God's sake," he said,
leaning his back against the cold wall, since he could still hardly
stand. He was so glad to see her there. So glad and so dismayed,
too. "How did they catch you?"

"Never mind that. Everything will be all right, believe me!"
She put her hand on his shirt where there was still dried blood on
it. "You looked so sick in the stable . . . I thought I'd never see you
again."

"I thought the same when I found that letter on your pillow."
He stroked the tears off her lashes as he had so often done before
over the years. How tall she was, hardly a child anymore,
although he could still clearly see the child in her. "Oh, heavens,
it's so good to see you, Meggie. I know I shouldn't say so. A good
father would say: Dear daughter, do you have to get yourself
locked up every time I do?"

She had to laugh, but he saw the concern in her eyes. She

passed her fingers over his face as if she were finding shadows that hadn't been there before. Perhaps the White Women had left their fingerprints behind, even though they hadn't taken him away with them.

"Don't look at me like that! I'm better, much better, and you know why." He brushed the hair back from her forehead; it was so like her mother's. The thought of Resa hurt like a sharp thorn. "Those were powerful words. Did Fenoglio write them for you?"

Meggie nodded. "And he wrote more for me, too," she whispered in his ear. "Words that will save you. You and Resa and all the others."

Words. His whole life seemed to be woven from words. His life, and his death, too.

"They took your mother and the others to the dungeons under the castle." He remembered Fenoglio's description only too well: *The dungeons under the Castle of Night, where fear clung to the walls like mold, and no ray of sun ever warmed the black stones.*

"Mo?" Meggie put her hand on his shoulder. "Do you think you can work?"

"Work? Why?" He couldn't help smiling, for the first time in a long, long while. "Do you think the Adderhead will forget he wants to hang me if I restore his books for him?"

But he didn't once interrupt as she told him, in a low voice, Fenoglio's idea for rescuing him. He sat on the straw mattress where he had lain these last few days and nights, counting the notches carved in the walls by other unfortunates, and listened to Meggie.

And the more of the story she told, the crazier Fenoglio's plan seemed, but when she had finished Mo shook his head and smiled.

"Not a bad idea!" he said quietly. "No, the old fox is no fool, he knows his story." *It's just a pity that Mortola presumably knows the altered version now, too,* he added to himself. *And that you were interrupted before you had read it to the end.* As so often, Meggie seemed to see what he was thinking from his face. He saw it in her eyes. He stroked the bridge of her nose with his forefinger, as he always used to when she was little, so little that her hand could hardly close around his finger. Little Meggie, big Meggie, brave Meggie . . .

"You're so much braver than I am," he said. "Bargaining with the Adderhead. I'd really have liked to see that."

She put her arms around his neck and stroked his tired face. "You will see it, Mo!" she whispered. "Fenoglio's words always come true, much more so in this world than in our own. They made you well again, didn't they?"

He just nodded. If he had said anything, she would have known from his voice that he found it difficult to believe, as she did, in a happy ending. Even when Meggie was younger she had always known at once if he was troubled in some way, but then it had been easy to take her mind off it with a joke, a pun, a story. It wasn't so simple now. No one could see into Mo's heart as easily as Meggie, except her mother. Resa had the same way of looking at him.

"I expect you've heard why they dragged me here, haven't you?" he asked. "I'm supposed to be a famous robber. Remember when we used to play Robin Hood?"

Meggie nodded. "You always wanted to be Robin."

"And you wanted to be the Sheriff of Nottingham. The baddies are stronger, Mo, you kept telling me. Clever child. Do you know what they call me? You'll like it."

"The Bluejay." Meggie almost whispered the name.

"Yes, exactly. What do you think? I don't suppose there's

much hope the real Bluejay will come wanting his name back before my execution, do you?"

How gravely she was looking at him. As if she knew something he didn't.

"There isn't any other Bluejay, Mo," she said quietly. "You *are* him." Without another word she took his arm, turned up his sleeve, and let her finger trace the scar that Basta's dogs had left. "That wound was just healing when we were in Fenoglio's house. He gave you an ointment to help the scar tissue form better, remember?"

He didn't understand. Not a word. "So?"

"*You* are the Bluejay!" She repeated it. "No one else. Fenoglio wrote the songs about him. He made him up because he thought his world needed a robber — and he used you as his model! *He was a noble robber in my imagination*, that's what he wrote to me."

It was some time before Mo's mind could take in the meaning of her words. Suddenly, he had to laugh. So loudly that the guard opened the barred flap in the door and stared in suspiciously. Mo wiped the laugh off his face and stared back until the guard disappeared again, cursing. Then he leaned his head against the wall behind him and closed his eyes.

"I'm sorry, Mo," whispered Meggie. "So sorry. Sometimes Fenoglio is a terrible old man!"

"Well, yes."

Perhaps that was why Orpheus had found it so easy to read him here. Because he was already in this story, anyway. "What do you think?" he asked. "Do I feel honored, or do I wring Fenoglio's old neck?"

Meggie put her hand on his forehead. "You're all hot! Lie down. You must rest."

How often had he said the same to her; how many nights had

he spent sitting beside her bed? Measles, chicken pox, scarlet fever . . . "Lord, Meggie," he had groaned when she caught whooping cough, too, "can't you leave out at least one childhood illness?"

The fever was pouring hot lead into his veins, and when Meggie bent over him, he thought for a moment that Resa was sitting beside him. But Meggie's hair was fairer.

"Where are Dustfinger and Farid? They were with you, weren't they? Have they been captured, too?" The fever made his tongue heavy.

"No, I don't think so. Did you know Dustfinger has a wife?"

"Yes, it was because of her that Basta cut his face. Have you met her?"

Meggie nodded. "She's very beautiful. Farid is jealous of her."

"Really? I thought he was in love with you."

She went red, bright red.

"Meggie?" Mo sat up. When on earth was this fever finally going to go away? It made him as weak as an old man. "Oh no!" he said quietly. "I see I've missed something. My daughter falls in love and I fail to notice! One more reason to curse that damned book. You should have stayed with Farid. I'd have been all right."

"You wouldn't! They'd have hanged you!"

"They may yet. The boy must be worried out of his mind about you now. Poor fellow. Has he kissed you?"

"Mo!" She turned her face away, embarrassed, but she was smiling.

"I have to know. I think I even have to give my permission, don't I?"

"Mo, stop it!" She nudged him in the ribs with her elbow, as usual when he was teasing her, and was horrified to see his face twist with pain. "Oh, I'm sorry," she whispered.

"Well, so long as it hurts, I'm still alive."

The wind carried the sound of horses' hooves up to them. Weapons clashed, and voices rang through the night.

"I tell you what," said Mo quietly. "Let's play our old game. We'll imagine we're in another story. In Hobbiton, maybe, that's quite a peaceful place, or with Wart and the wild geese. What do you think?"

She did not reply for some time. Then she took his hand and whispered, "I'd like to imagine us in the Wayless Wood together. You and me and Resa. Then I could show you the fairies, and the fire-elves, and the whispering trees, and — no, wait! Balbulus's workshop! That's it. I'd like to be there with you. He's an illuminator, Mo. In the Castle of Sighs in Ombra! The best of all illuminators. You could see his brushes and pigments. . . ."

Suddenly, she sounded so excited! She could still forget everything, like a child — she could forget the bolted door and the gallows in the courtyard. The mere thought of a couple of fine paintbrushes would do it. "Very well," said Mo, stroking her fair hair again. "Anything you say. Let's imagine we're in the castle of Ombra. I really would like to see those brushes."

62

WHERE TO?

I dreamt a limitless book,
A book unbound,
Its leaves scattered in fantastic abundance
On every line there was a new horizon drawn,
New heavens supposed;
New states, new souls.

Clive Barker, *Abarat*

Farid was waiting by the statue, as they had agreed. He had hidden behind it — obviously he still found it hard to believe that he was invisible — and he hadn't managed to get a sight of Meggie. Dustfinger could tell from his voice; it was husky with disappointment. "I got into the tower, I even saw the cell, but it's just too well guarded. And in the kitchen they were saying she's a witch and she'll be killed along with her father!"

"Well, what did you expect they'd be talking about? Did you hear anything else?"

"Yes, something about Firefox. They said he'll send Cosimo back to the dead."

"Ah. Nothing about the Black Prince?"

"Only that there are people looking for him, but they haven't found him. They say he and his bear can exchange shapes, so that sometimes the bear is the Prince and the Prince is the bear. And they say he can fly and make himself invisible, and that he's going to rescue the Bluejay!"

"Really?" Dustfinger laughed quietly. "The Prince will like that. Right, come on. It's time for us to be off."

"Be off?" Dustfinger felt Farid's fingers clutching his arm. "Why? We could hide. The castle's so big, no one would find us."

"You think so? What would you do here anyway? Meggie wouldn't go with you even if you could magic her through locked doors. Have you forgotten the deal she was offering the Adderhead? Resa says it will take Silvertongue a few weeks to bind a book, and the Adderhead won't hurt a hair of his head or Meggie's until he has that book, will he? So come on! It's time we looked for the Prince. We must tell him about Sootbird."

Outside, it was still as dark as if morning would never come. This time they slipped through the castle gate together with a troop of men-at-arms. Dustfinger would have liked to know where they were going so late at night. *Let's hope they're not hunting the Prince,* he thought, cursing Sootbird for his treacherous heart.

The men-at-arms galloped off down the road leading away from Mount Adder into the mountains. Dustfinger was standing there watching them go when something furry suddenly jumped up at him. Taken by surprise, he stumbled into the structure of one of the gallows. Two feet were swinging back and forth above him. But Gwin clung to his arm as naturally as if his master had always been invisible.

"Damn it all!" His heart was in his mouth as he seized the marten. "You'll be the death of me yet, you little beast, won't you?" he hissed at him. "Where did you spring from?"

As if in answer, Roxane stepped out of the shadow of the castle walls. "Dustfinger?" she whispered as her eyes searched for his invisible face. Jink appeared behind her and raised his nose, sniffing.

"Yes, who did you think?" He guided her on with him, pressing her close to the wall so that the sentries on the battlements couldn't see her. This time he didn't ask why she had followed them. He was too glad that she was there. Even if the expression on her face reminded him for a moment of Resa and her sadness. "There's nothing we can do here for the moment," he whispered. "But did you know that Sootbird is a welcome guest in the Castle of Night?"

"Sootbird?"

"Yes. It's bad news. You ride back to Ombra and see to Jehan and Brianna. I'll go and look for the Black Prince and warn him of this cuckoo in the nest."

"And how are you going to find him?" Roxane smiled, as if she could see his baffled face. "Shall I take you to him?"

"You?"

"Yes." Up above, the guards called something to one another. Dustfinger drew Roxane even closer to the wall. "The Prince cares for his Motley Folk very well," she whispered. "And as I'm sure you can imagine, he doesn't always earn the money he needs for cripples and old folk, widows and orphans, by doing tricks in marketplaces. His men are skillful poachers and the terror of tax-gatherers, they have hiding places all over the forest, in Argenta and Lombrica alike, and there are often sick or wounded men there. . . . Nettle will have nothing to do with robbers, nor will the moss-women, and they don't trust most physicians. So some time ago they began coming to me. I'm not afraid of the forest, I've been in its darkest corners with you. Arrow wounds, broken bones, a bad cough — I know how to cure all those, and the Prince trusts me. I was always Dustfinger's wife to him, even when I was married to another man. Perhaps he was right."

"Was he?" Dustfinger spun around. Someone was clearing his throat in the darkness.

"Didn't you say we must be gone before the sun rises?" Farid's voice sounded reproachful.

By fire and fairies, he'd forgotten the boy! And Farid was right. Morning couldn't be far away, and the shadow of the Castle of Night was not the best place to discuss dead husbands.

"Very well. Catch the martens!" Dustfinger whispered into the night. "But don't, for heaven's sake, scare me to death like that again, understand? Or I'll never let you make yourself invisible again."

THE BADGER'S EARTH

"Oh, Sara. It is like a story."

"It is a story . . . everything is a story. You are a story — I am
a story. Miss Minchin is a story."

Frances Hodgson Burnett, *The Little Princess*

Farid followed Dustfinger and Roxane through the night with
an expression that must surely be as dark as the sky above
them. It hurt to leave Meggie behind in the castle, however
sensible it was. And now here was Roxane coming with them,
too. Although he had to admit that she seemed to know exactly
where she was going. They soon came upon the first hiding
place, well concealed behind thorny undergrowth, but it was
deserted. In the next they found two men who distrustfully drew
their knives and did not put them back in their belts until Roxane
had spoken to them at length. Perhaps they sensed the presence
of Dustfinger and Farid, in spite of their invisibility. Fortunately,
Roxane had once cured a nasty ulcer for one of them, and he
finally told her where she would find the Prince.

The Badger's Earth. Farid thought he heard those words

twice. "Their main hideout," was all that Roxane said. "We must be there by daybreak. But they warned me that there are said to be soldiers on the move, a great many of them."

From then on Farid sometimes thought he heard the clink of swords in the distance, the snorting of horses, voices, marching footsteps — but perhaps he was only imagining it. Soon the first rays of sunlight penetrated the leaf canopy above them, gradually turning their bodies visible again, like reflections on dark water. It was good not to have to keep looking for his own hands and feet, and to see Dustfinger again. Even if he was walking beside Roxane.

Now and then Farid sensed her looking at him, as if she were still searching his dark face for some similarity to Dustfinger. At her farm she had once or twice asked him questions about his mother. Farid would have liked to tell her that his mother had been a princess, much, much more beautiful than Roxane, and that Dustfinger had loved her so dearly that he stayed with her for ten years until death took her from him, leaving him only with their son, their dark-skinned, black-eyed son who now followed him like a shadow. But his age wasn't quite right for this tale, and moreover Dustfinger would probably have been furious if Roxane had asked him for the truth behind it, so in the end Farid told her only that his mother was dead — which was probably correct. If Roxane was stupid enough to think Dustfinger had come back to her only because he had lost another woman, all the better. Every glance that Dustfinger cast her filled Farid's heart to the brim with jealousy. Suppose he decided to stay with her forever, at the farm with the fragrant fields of herbs? Suppose he stopped wanting to go from one marketplace to the next but preferred to live with her, kissing her and laughing with her as he already did only too often, forgetting fire and Farid?

The forest became denser and denser, and the Castle of Night might have been only a bad dream, when they suddenly saw more than a dozen men standing among the trees around them. Armed men in ragged clothes. They appeared so silently that even Dustfinger hadn't heard them. They surrounded them with hostile expressions on their faces, knives and swords in their hands, and stared at the two figures who were still almost transparent around the chests and arms.

"Hey, Snapper, don't you know me?" asked Roxane, going up to one of them. "How are your fingers doing?"

The man's face cleared. He was a heavily built fellow with a scar on his neck. "Ah, the herb-witch," he said. "Of course. Why are you roaming the forest here so early? And what are those ghosts with you?"

"We're not ghosts. We're looking for the Black Prince." As Dustfinger moved to Roxane's side all the men's weapons turned his way.

"What are you doing?" Roxane asked the men angrily. "Look at his face. Did you never hear of the fire-dancer? The Prince will set his bear on you if he hears that you threatened him."

The men put their heads together and scrutinized Dustfinger's scarred face uneasily.

"Three scars as pale as cobwebs," whispered Snapper. "Oh yes, we've all heard about him, but only in songs. . . ."

"Who says songs can't be believed?" Dustfinger breathed into the cool morning air and whispered fire-words until a flame consumed his steaming breath. The robbers flinched back and stared at him, as if this only reinforced their certainty that he was a ghost. However, Dustfinger raised both hands in the air and put the flame out between them as if nothing could be easier. Then he bent down and cooled the palms of his hands on the dewy grass.

"Did you see that?" Snapper looked at the others. "That's just what the Prince has always told us about him — he catches fire as you might catch a rabbit; he speaks to it like a lover."

The robbers took the three into their midst. Farid looked uneasily at the men's faces as he walked along beside them. They reminded him of other faces, faces from an earlier life, from a world that he did not like to remember, and he stayed as close as he could to Dustfinger's side.

"Are you sure these are the Prince's men?" Dustfinger asked Roxane in an undertone.

"Oh yes," she whispered back. "He can't choose who will follow him."

Farid did not think this answer very reassuring.

The robbers in Farid's old life had claimed caves full of treasure as their own, caverns more magnificent than the halls of the Castle of Night. The hideout where Snapper took them could not be compared with those caves. Its entrance, hidden in a crevice in the ground among tall beech trees, was so narrow that you had to squeeze your way in, and even Farid had to duck his head in the passage beyond it. The cave it led to was not much better. Other passages branched off, obviously leading even deeper underground. "Welcome to the Badger's Earth!" said Snapper, while the men sitting on the floor of the cave looked at them suspiciously. "Who says that only the Adderhead can dig deep into the ground? There are several men among us who toiled in his mines for years. They found out how you can nest far down in the earth and not have it fall on your head."

The Prince was alone in a cave to one side of the others, only the bear was with him, and he looked tired. But at the sight of Dustfinger his face brightened, and the news they brought was not so much of a surprise to him as they had expected.

"Ah yes, Sootbird!" he said, and Snapper drew a finger across his throat at the mention of that name. "I ought to have asked myself much sooner how he could afford the alchemists' powders he uses in his fire-eating shows. The few coins he earns in marketplaces wouldn't pay for it. But unfortunately I didn't have him watched until after the attack on the Secret Camp. He soon parted from the other prisoners we freed and met the Adderhead's informers on the border. While those he betrayed are in the dungeons of the Castle of Night, and there's nothing I can do for them! Here I am stuck in a forest swarming with soldiers. The Adderhead is assembling them up on the road that leads to Ombra."

"Cosimo?" It was Roxane who spoke the name, and the Prince nodded.

"Yes. I sent him three messengers with three warnings. One came back, but only to say that Cosimo laughed in his face. I'll admit I don't remember him as being quite so stupid. The year he spent away seems to have robbed him of his reason. He's planning to make war on the Adderhead with an army of peasants. It's as if we were to march against the Adderhead ourselves."

"We'd have a better chance," said Snapper.

"Yes, I expect we would." The Black Prince sounded so discouraged that Farid's heart failed him. Secretly, he had always put far more trust in the Prince than in Fenoglio's words, but what could this troop of ragged men digging themselves holes in the forest like rabbits do against the Castle of Night?

The men brought them something to eat, and Roxane looked at Dustfinger's leg. She treated the wound with an ointment that made it smell like spring in the cave for a moment. And Farid couldn't help thinking of Meggie. He remembered a story that he had heard by a fire on a cold night in the desert. It was the tale of a thief who fell in love with a princess; he still remembered it very well. The two were so deeply in love that they could speak to each other over a distance of many miles. Each could hear the other's thoughts even if walls separated them, each knew whether the other was sad or happy . . . but intently as Farid listened to his own feelings, he could sense nothing. He couldn't even have said whether Meggie was still alive. She seemed to have gone away, gone away from his heart, from the world. When he brushed the tears from his eyes, he felt Dustfinger looking at him.

"I'll have to rest this wretched leg or it will never heal," he said quietly. "But we'll go back. When the time comes . . ."

Roxane frowned, but she said nothing. The Prince and Dustfinger began talking so quietly that Farid had to move close to them to make out anything. Roxane put her head on Dustfinger's lap and was soon asleep. But Farid curled up like a puppy beside him, closed his eyes, and listened to the two men.

The Black Prince wanted to know all about Silvertongue — whether the day of the execution was fixed, where he was held prisoner, how his wound was doing. Dustfinger told him what he knew. And he told him about the book that Meggie had offered the Adderhead as a ransom for her father.

"A book to hold Death prisoner?" The Prince laughed incredulously. "Has the Adderhead taken to believing in fairy tales?"

Dustfinger did not reply to that. He said nothing about Fenoglio, he did not say they were all part of a story that an old man had written. In his place Farid wouldn't have said so, either. The Black Prince probably wouldn't believe there were words that could decide even his own fate, words like invisible paths from which you could not turn aside. The bear grunted in his sleep, and Roxane turned her head restlessly. She was holding Dustfinger's hand as if she wanted to take him into her dreams.

"You told the boy you'd go back," said the Prince. "You can come with us."

"Are you going to the Castle of Night? Why? Do you plan to storm it with these few men? Or tell the Adderhead that he's caught the wrong man? With this on your nose?" Dustfinger put his hand among the blankets lying on the floor and brought out a bird mask. Blue jay feathers sewn to cracked leather. He put the mask on his scarred face.

"Many of us have worn that mask before," said the Prince. "And now they're going to hang another innocent man for the deeds we've done. I can't allow that! This time it's a book-binder. Last time, after we attacked one of the silver transports, they hanged a charcoal-burner just because he had a scar on his arm. His wife is probably still mourning him."

"It's not just the deeds you did. Fenoglio invented most of them!" Dustfinger sounded irritated. "Damn it, Prince, you can't save Silvertongue. You'll only die, too. Or do you seriously think the Adderhead will let him go just because you've turned yourself in?"

"No, I'm not such a fool as that. But I must do something." The Prince put his hand in his bear's mouth, as he so often did, and as always that hand, as if miraculously, came back intact from between the bear's teeth.

"Yes, yes, very well." Dustfinger sighed. "You and your unwritten rules. You don't even know Silvertongue! How can you want to die for someone you don't know?"

"Who would you die for?" the Prince asked in return.

Farid saw Dustfinger look at Roxane's sleeping face — and then turn to him. He quickly closed his eyes.

"You'd die for Roxane," he heard the Prince say.

"Perhaps," said Dustfinger, and through his lashes Farid saw him trace Roxane's dark brows with his finger. "Or perhaps not. Do you have many informers in the Castle of Night?"

"Yes, indeed. Kitchen maids, stable boys, even a few of the guards — although they come very expensive — and most useful of all, a falconer who sends me a message now and then by one of his clever birds. I shall hear at once when they've fixed the day of the execution. You know the Adderhead doesn't have such things done in a marketplace or in front of the common people in the castle courtyard anymore, not since you spoiled my punishment so thoroughly for him. He was never a friend of such spectacles, anyway. An execution is a serious matter to the Adderhead. The gallows outside the castle will do for a poor minstrel, there'll be no trouble about that, but the Bluejay will die inside the gate."

"Yes. If his daughter's voice doesn't open that gate for him," replied Dustfinger. "Her voice and a book — a book full of immortality."

Farid heard the Black Prince laugh. "That sounds almost like some new song by the Inkweaver!"

"Yes," replied Dustfinger in a husky voice. "It sounds just like him, doesn't it?"

ALL IS LOST

'Tis war! 'Tis war! God's angel stand by ye
And guide your hand.
'Tis war, alas, and guiltless I would be
Of what betides this land.

Matthias Claudius, "War Song"

After a few days' rest, Dustfinger's leg was much better, and Farid was just telling the two martens how they'd soon all be stealing into the Castle of Night to rescue Meggie and her parents when bad news came to the Badger's Earth. One of the men who had been watching the road to Ombra brought it. His face was covered with blood and he could hardly keep on his feet.

"They're killing them!" he kept stammering over and over again. "They're killing them all."

"Where?" asked the Prince. "Where exactly?"

"Not two hours from here," the messenger managed to say. "Keep going north."

The Prince left ten men at the Badger's Earth. Roxane tried to persuade Dustfinger to stay, too. "You must spare your leg, or it will never heal," she said. But he would not listen to her, so she, too, came on the fast, silent march through the forest.

They heard the sound of battle long before they could see anything. Screams reached Farid's ears, cries of pain, and the whinnying of horses, shrill with fear. A moment came when the Prince signaled to them to go more slowly. A few more paces, bending low, and the ground in front of them dropped steeply to the road that ended, many miles farther on, at the gates of Ombra. Dustfinger made Farid and Roxane get down on the ground, although no one was looking their way. Hundreds of men were fighting among the trees down below, but there were no robbers among them. Robbers do not wear shirts of chain mail, breastplates, and helmets decked with peacock feathers, they seldom have horses, and never coats of arms embroidered on silken surcoats.

Dustfinger held Roxane close when she began to sob. The sun was sinking behind the hills as the Adderhead's soldiers cut down Cosimo's men one by one. It looked as if the battle had been raging for a long time; the road was covered with dead bodies lying side by side. Only a small troop was still on horseback amid all this death. Cosimo himself was among them, his beautiful face distorted by rage and fear. For a moment it looked almost as if those few mounted men would be able to carve themselves a breach in the enemy ranks, but then Firefox came among them with a company of men gleaming like deadly beetles in their armor. They mowed down Cosimo and his retinue like dry grass as the sun sank right behind the hills, as red as if all the blood that had been shed was reflected in the sky. Firefox himself struck Cosimo from his horse, and Dustfinger buried his face in Roxane's hair, as if he were tired of seeing Death at work. But Farid did not turn his head away. His face unmoving, he looked at the slaughter and thought of Meggie — Meggie, who perhaps still believed that a little ink could cure anything in this world. Would she believe it if her eyes saw what his were seeing now?

Few of Cosimo's men survived their prince. Barely a dozen fled into the trees. No one went to the trouble of pursuing them. The Adderhead's soldiers broke into cries of triumph and began plundering the corpses like a flock of vultures in human form. They did not get Cosimo's body, however. Firefox himself drove his soldiers off and had that beautiful corpse loaded onto a horse and taken away.

"Why are they doing that?" asked Farid.

"Why? Because his corpse is the proof that he really is dead this time," said Dustfinger bitterly.

"Yes, he is indeed," whispered the Black Prince. "I suppose you think yourself immortal if you've come back from the dead once. But he wasn't, any more than his men, and now almost all the people of Lombrica will be widows and orphans."

It was many hours before the Adderhead's soldiers finally moved away, laden with what they could rob from the dead. Darkness was coming on again when silence fell at last among the trees, the silence that is felt only in the presence of Death.

Roxane was the first to find a way down the slope. She was no longer weeping. Her face was fixed and rigid, but whether with anger or pain Farid could not have said. The robbers hesitated before following her, for the first White Women were already standing there among the dead.

LORD OF THE STORY

Iron helmets will not save
Even heroes from the grave.
Good men's blood will drain away
While the wicked win the day.

Heinrich Heine, "Valkyries"

Fenoglio was wandering among the dead when the robbers found him. Night fell, but he did not know what night it was. Nor could he remember how many days had passed since he rode out of the gates of Ombra with Cosimo. He knew only one thing: They were all dead. Minerva's husband, his neighbor, the father of the boy who had so often begged him for a story. All dead. And he himself would very likely have been dead, too, if his horse hadn't shied and thrown him. He had crawled away into the trees, to hide there like an animal and watch the slaughter.

Since the departure of the Adderhead's soldiers he had been stumbling from one corpse to the next, cursing himself, cursing his story, cursing the world he had created. When he felt the hand on his shoulder he actually thought for a moment that

Cosimo had risen from the dead yet again, but it was the Black Prince standing behind him.

"What are you doing here?" he snarled at him and the men with him. "Do you want to die, too? Go away and hide, and leave me in peace." He struck his brow. His damned head that had invented them all, and with them all the misfortune they were wading through like black, stinking water! He fell on his knees beside a dead man whose open eyes were staring at the sky, and blamed himself furiously — himself, the Adderhead, Cosimo and his haste — and then suddenly fell silent when he saw Dustfinger standing next to the Prince.

"You!" he stammered and got to his feet again, swaying. "You're still alive! You're not dead yet, even though I wrote it that way." He took Dustfinger's arm and clutched it tightly.

"Yes, disappointing, isn't it?" replied Dustfinger, shaking off Fenoglio's hand roughly. "Is it any comfort to you that no doubt, but for Farid, I'd have been lying as dead and cold as these men? After all, you didn't foresee him."

Farid? Oh yes, the boy plucked by Mortimer from his desert story. He was standing beside Dustfinger and staring at Fenoglio with murder in his eyes. No, the boy really did not belong here. Whoever had sent him to protect Dustfinger, it hadn't been him, Fenoglio! But that was the wretched part of the whole business! With everyone interfering in his story, how could it turn out well?

"I can't find Cosimo!" he muttered. "I've been looking for him for hours. Have any of you seen him?"

"Firefox has had his body taken away," the Prince replied. "I expect they'll put it on public display so that this time no one can claim he's still alive."

Fenoglio stared at him until the bear began to growl. Then he shook his head again and again. "I don't understand it!" he stammered. "How could it happen? Didn't Meggie read what I wrote for her? Didn't Roxane find her?" He looked despairingly at Dustfinger. How well he remembered the day he had described his death! A good scene, one of the best he'd ever written.

"Oh yes, Roxane gave Meggie the letter. Ask her yourself if you don't believe me. Although I don't think she'll feel much like talking at the moment." Dustfinger pointed to the woman walking among the corpses. Roxane. The beautiful Roxane. She bent over the dead, looked into their faces, and finally kneeled down beside a man whom a White Woman was approaching. She quickly put her hands over his ears, bent over his face, and gestured to the two robbers who were following her with torches in their hands. No, she would certainly not feel much like talking just now.

Dustfinger looked at him. Why that reproachful expression? Fenoglio wanted to snap at him. After all, I invented your wife, too! But he bit back the words. "Very well. So Roxane gave Meggie the letter," he said instead. "But did Meggie *read* it?"

Dustfinger looked at him with great dislike. "She tried to, but the Adderhead had her taken to the Castle of Night that very evening."

"Oh God!" Fenoglio looked around. The dead faces of Cosimo's men stared at him. "So that's it!" he cried. "I thought all this had happened only because Cosimo wanted to set off too soon, but no! The words, my wonderful words . . . Meggie can't have read them, or everything would have been all right!"

"Nothing would have been all right!" Dustfinger's voice was so cutting that Fenoglio involuntarily flinched. "Not a man of all these lying here would be dead if you hadn't brought Cosimo back!"

The Prince and his men stared at Dustfinger, unable to make anything of this. Of course, they had no idea what he was talking about. But obviously Dustfinger knew only too well. Meggie had told him about Cosimo. Or had it been the boy?

"Why are you staring at him like that?" Farid challenged the robbers, ranging himself at Dustfinger's side. "It was exactly as he says! Fenoglio brought Cosimo back from the dead. I was there myself."

How the fools flinched away! Only the Black Prince looked thoughtfully at Fenoglio.

"What nonsense!" Fenoglio said. "No one comes back to this world from the dead! Think what a crowd there'd be! I made a new Cosimo, a brand-new one, and everything would have turned out well if Meggie hadn't been interrupted while she read! My Cosimo would have been a wonderful ruler, a —"

Before he could say any more, the Prince's black hand came down over his mouth. "That's enough," he said. "Enough talking while the dead lie here around us. Your Cosimo is dead, wherever he came from, and the man they take for the Bluejay because of your songs may well be dead soon, too. You seem to enjoy playing with Death, Inkweaver."

Fenoglio tried to protest, but the Black Prince had already turned to his men. "Go on looking for the wounded!" he told them. "And hurry! It's time we got off this road."

They found barely two dozen survivors. Two dozen among hundreds of dead. When the robbers set off again with the wounded men, Fenoglio staggered after them in silence without asking where they were going. "The old man is following us!" he heard Dustfinger tell the Prince. "Where else would he go?" was all the Prince replied — and Dustfinger said nothing. But he kept well away from Fenoglio, as if he were Death itself.

BLANK PAPER

We make for your sake such things as stand fast,
Through the ages these pages forever will last.
On blank paper the printer sets down what is heard,
Giving life to what's rife with the power of the word.

Michael Kongehl, "On the White Art,"
Die Weisse und die Schwarze Kunst

When Mortola had Mo's cell unlocked, Meggie was just telling him about the Laughing Prince's festivities, the tightrope-walker and the Black Prince and Farid's juggling with the torches. Mo put his arm protectively around her as the bolts outside were shot back and Mortola came into the cell, flanked by Basta and the Piper. The sunlight falling into the room made Basta's face look like boiled lobster.

"Look at that, what an idyll! Father and daughter reunited," sneered Mortola. "Truly touching!"

"Hurry up!" the guard told her through the door, low-voiced. "If the Adderhead hears that I let you in to see him, they'll put me in the pillory for three days!"

"And if they do I've paid you well enough, haven't I?" was all Mortola replied, while Basta went up to Mo with a vicious smile.

"Well, Silvertongue," he purred, "didn't I say you'd all fall into our trap yet?"

"You look more as if it was you who fell into Dustfinger's trap," replied Mo, quickly putting Meggie behind him when, by way of answer, Basta snapped open his knife.

"Basta! Stop that!" Mortola snapped at him. "We don't have time for your games."

Meggie came out from behind Mo's back as Mortola moved toward her. She wanted to show the old woman that she wasn't afraid of her (even if, of course, that was only a brave lie).

"Those were interesting words that you had hidden in your clothing," Mortola said to her, low-voiced. "The Adderhead was particularly interested in the part about three very special words. Oh, see how pale she's gone around her pretty little nose! Yes, the Adderhead knows about your plans, little pigeon, and he knows now that Mortola isn't as stupid as he thought. But unfortunately he still wants the book you promised him. The fool really does believe that you two can keep his death imprisoned in a book." The Magpie wrinkled her nose at such princely stupidity and came yet closer to Meggie. "Yes, he's a gullible fool, like all princes!" she whispered. "We both know that, don't we? For the words you carried with you also say that Cosimo the Fair will conquer this castle and kill the Adderhead, with the aid of the book your father is to bind for him. But how can that be so? Cosimo is dead, and for good this time. Oh, how alarmed you look, you little witch!" Her bony fingers pinched Meggie's cheeks hard. Mo went to strike her hand away, but Basta faced him with the knife. "Your tongue has lost its magic power, my little darling!" said the Magpie. "The words are only words. The book your father is to bind for the Adderhead will be nothing but a blank book — and once the Silver Prince finally realizes that, nothing will save you two from the hangman. And Mortola will be avenged at last."

"Leave her alone, Mortola!" Mo reached for Meggie's hand in spite of Basta's knife, and Meggie clasped his fingers firmly in hers as thoughts raced through her mind in confusion. Cosimo was dead? For the second time? What did that mean? *Nothing,* she thought. *Nothing at all, Meggie. Because you never read the words that were to protect him.*

Mortola seemed to notice her relief, for the Magpie's eyes became as narrow as her lips. "Ah, so that doesn't trouble you? Do you think I'd lie to you? Or do you believe in that book of immortality yourself? Let me tell you something." The Magpie's thin fingers dug into Meggie's shoulder. "It's a book, no more, and I am sure you and your father remember what my son used to do with books! Capricorn would never have been fool enough to entrust his life to one, even if you'd promised him immortality for it! And furthermore . . . those three words that it seems must not be written in the book . . . I know them now, too."

"What do you mean by that, Mortola?" asked Mo quietly. "Do you by any chance dream of putting Basta here on the Adderhead's throne? Or even yourself?"

The Magpie cast a quick glance at the guard outside the cell door, but he had his back to them, and she turned to Mo again, her face expressionless. "Whatever I intend to do, Silvertongue," she hissed at him, "you won't live to see it. This story is over for you. Why isn't he in chains?" she snapped at the Piper. "He's still a prisoner, isn't he? At least tie his hands while you move him."

Meggie was about to protest, but Mo cast her a warning glance.

"Believe me, Silvertongue," said Mortola in a low voice as the Piper roughly tied Mo's hands behind his back, "even if the

Adderhead sets you free after you've made him his book, you won't get far. And Mortola's word is worth more than the words of a poet. Take the pair of them to the Old Chamber!" she ordered as she went to the door again. "But watch them closely, and make sure that not a single book falls into their hands."

The Old Chamber lay in the most remote part of the Castle of Night, far from the halls where the Adderhead held court. The corridors down which Basta and the Piper led them were dusty and deserted. No silver adorned the columns and doors here, there was no glass in the draughty windows. The room whose door the Piper finally opened, with a mocking bow to Mo, seemed to have been unoccupied for a long time. The pink fabric of the bed hangings was moth-eaten. The bunches of flowers standing in pitchers in the window niches were long dried up; dust was caught in the withered blossoms, and lay thick and dirty white on the chests that stood under the windows. In the middle of the chamber there was a table: a long wooden surface laid on trestles. A man stood behind it, as pale as paper, with white hair and inkstains on his fingers. He gave Meggie only a quick glance, but he studied Mo as thoroughly as if someone had asked him to deliver an expert opinion on him.

"Is this the man?" he asked the Piper. "He looks as if he'd never held a book in his hand in his life, let alone had the faintest idea how to bind one."

Meggie saw a smile steal over Mo's face. Without a word he went over to the table and examined the tools lying on it.

"My name is Taddeo, and I am the librarian here," the stranger went on, sounding annoyed. "I don't suppose that a single one of these objects means anything to you, but I can assure you that the paper you see there alone is worth more than your wretched robber's life. The finest product of the best paper mill for a thousand miles around, enough to bind more than two books of five hundred pages. Although a genuine bookbinder, of course, would prefer parchment to any paper, however good."

Mo held out his bound hands to the Piper. "There could be two opinions about that," he said, as the silver-nosed minstrel, his expression sullen, undid his bonds. "You should be glad I asked for paper. Parchment for this book would cost a fortune. Quite apart from the hundreds of goats that would have to give their lives for it. And as for the quality of these sheets, it's by no means as good as you claim. The texture is coarse, but if there's no better available it will have to do. I hope at least it's well sized. As for the rest of this" — Mo's expert fingers passed over the tools lying ready — "it looks serviceable."

Knives and bone folders, hemp, strong thread and needles to stitch the pages, glue and a pot to heat it in, beechwood for the back and front covers, leather to go over them — Mo picked them all up, as he did in his own workshop, before he set to work. Then he looked around. "What about the press and the sewing frame? And what am I going to heat the glue with?"

"You . . . you'll have everything you need before evening," replied Taddeo, in some confusion.

"The clasps are all right, but I shall need another file, and leather and linen for the tapes."

"Of course, of course. Anything you say." The librarian nodded, very ready to oblige now, while an incredulous smile spread over his pale face.

"Good." Mo leaned on the table, supporting himself with both hands. "I'm sorry, but I'm not very strong on my legs yet. I hope the leather is more flexible than the parchment, and as for the glue," he added, picking up the pot and sniffing, "well, we'll see if it's good enough. And bring me some paste, too. I'll use glue only for the covers. Bookworms like the flavor too much."

Meggie relished the sight of the surprised faces. Even the Piper was staring at Mo in disbelief. Only Basta remained unmoved. He knew that he had brought the librarian a book-binder, not a robber.

"My father needs a chair," said Meggie, with an imperious glance at the librarian. "Can't you see he's injured? Is he supposed to work standing up?"

"Standing up? No . . . no, of course not! By no means. I'll have an armchair brought at once," answered the librarian distractedly. He was still staring at Mo. "You . . . er . . . you know a remark-able amount about books for a highwayman."

Mo gave him a smile. "Yes, don't I?" he said. "Perhaps the highwayman was once a bookbinder? Don't they say that all kinds of professions are to be found among the outlaws? Farmers, cobblers, physicians, minstrels —"

"Never mind what he once was," the Piper interrupted. "He's a murderer, anyway, so don't fall for his soft voice, bookworm. He kills without batting an eyelid. Ask Basta if you don't believe me."

"Yes, very true!" Basta rubbed his burned skin. "He's more dangerous than a nest of vipers. And his daughter's no better. I hope those knives won't give you any silly ideas," he said to Mo. "The guards will be counting them regularly, and they'll cut off one of your daughter's fingers for every knife that goes missing. And the same applies to any other stupid tricks you try. Do you understand?"

Mo did not answer him, but he looked at the knives as if to count them for safety's sake. "Oh, do get him a chair!" said Meggie to the librarian impatiently as Mo leaned on the table again.

"Yes, of course! At once!" Taddeo hurried away, but the Piper gave an ugly laugh.

"Listen to the little witch! Ordering people around like a prince's brat! Well, not surprising, is it, since she claims to be the daughter of a man who can keep Death a prisoner between two wooden covers! What about you, Basta? Do you believe her story?"

Basta put his hand to the amulet hanging around his neck. It was not a rabbit's paw, as he had worn in Capricorn's service, but something that looked suspiciously like a human finger bone. "Who knows?" he muttered.

"Yes, who knows?" agreed Mo, without turning to look at the two of them. "But I can summon Death, anyway, can't I, Basta? So can Meggie."

The Piper cast Basta a swift glance.

Basta had pale blotches on his burned skin. "All I know," he growled, his hand still on his amulet, "is that you should have been dead and buried long ago, Silvertongue. And the Adderhead would do better to listen to Mortola instead of your witchy daughter. He ate out of her hand, did the Silver Prince. He fell for her lies."

The Piper straightened his back, as ready to attack as the viper on his master's coat of arms. "Fell for her lies?" he said, in his curiously strained voice. He was a good head taller than Basta. "The Adderhead falls for nothing anyone says. He is a great ruler, greater than any other. Firefox sometimes forgets that, and so does Mortola. Don't go making the same mistake. And now get out. The Adderhead's orders are that no one who ever worked for Capricorn is to be on guard in this room. Could that mean that he doesn't trust you?"

Basta's voice turned to a hiss. "You worked for Capricorn once yourself, Piper!" he said through compressed lips. "You'd be nothing but for him."

"Oh yes? You see this nose?" The Piper stroked his silver nose. "I once had a nose like yours, an ordinary nose of flesh and blood. It hurt losing it, but the Adderhead had a better one made for me, and since then I don't sing for drunken fire-raisers, I sing only for him — a real prince whose family is older than the towers of this castle. If you don't want to serve him, then go back to Capricorn's fortress. Maybe his ghost is haunting those burned-out walls — oh, but you're afraid of ghosts, aren't you, Basta?"

The two men were standing so close that the blade of Basta's knife wouldn't have fitted between them.

"Yes, I am afraid of ghosts," he hissed. "But at least I don't spend every night on my knees, whimpering because I'm afraid the White Women might fetch me away, like your fine new master."

The Piper struck Basta in the face so hard that his head hit the door frame. Blood ran down his burned cheek in a trail of red. He wiped it away with the back of his hand. "Take care to avoid dark corridors, Piper!" he whispered. "You don't have a nose anymore, but one can always find something else to cut off."

When the librarian came back with the chair Basta had gone, and the Piper left, too, after posting two guards outside the door. "No one comes in or goes out except the librarian!" Meggie heard him ordering brusquely before he left. "And check up regularly to make sure the Bluejay is working."

Taddeo smiled awkwardly at Mo as the Piper's footsteps died away outside, as if he felt he should apologize for the soldiers guarding the door. "Excuse me," he said quietly, placing the chair at the table for him, "but I have a few books that are showing strange signs of damage. Could you maybe take a look at them?"

Meggie had to suppress a smile, but Mo acted as if the librarian had asked him the most natural question in the world. "Of course," he said.

Taddeo nodded and glanced at the door. One of the guards was pacing up and down outside, looking sullen. "But Mortola mustn't know, so I'll come back when it's dark," he whispered to Mo. "Luckily, she goes to bed early. There are wonderful books in this castle, but sad to say no one here can appreciate them. It was different in the past, but the past is over and forgotten. I've heard matters aren't much better at the Laughing Prince's castle these days, but at least they have Balbulus there. We were all very sorry when the Adderhead gave his daughter our best illuminator to take with her as her dowry! Since then I'm not allowed to employ more than two scribes and one illuminator of only average talent. The only copies I can commission are of manuscripts about the Adderhead's ancestors, the mining and working of silver, or the art of war. Last year, when wood ran short again, Firefox even heated the small banqueting hall with my finest books." Tears came to Taddeo's clouded eyes.

"Bring me the books whenever you like," said Mo.

The old librarian passed the hem of his dark blue tunic over his eyes. "Oh yes!" he murmured. "Oh yes, I will. Thank you."

Then he was gone. Sighing, Mo sat down in the chair that Taddeo had brought him. "Very well," he said. "Let's get down to work. A book to keep Death at bay — what an idea! It's just a pity it's for this butcher. You'll have to help me, Meggie, with the folding and stitching, the pressing. . . ." She just nodded. Of course she would help him. There were few things she liked doing better.

It felt so familiar, watching Mo at work again — setting the paper straight, folding it, cutting and stitching it. He worked more slowly than usual, and his hand kept going to his chest and the place where Mortola had wounded him. But Meggie could tell that carrying out the familiar movements did him good, even if some of the tools were not like those he was used to. The actions had been the same for hundreds of years, in both this world and the other one.

After only a few hours the Old Chamber had something curiously familiar about it, like a refuge and not just another prison. When twilight began to fall outside, the librarian and a servant brought them a couple of oil lamps. The warm light almost made the dusty room look full of life, for the first time in ages.

"It's a long while since any lamps were lit in this room," said Taddeo, putting a second one on the table for Mo.

"Who lived in this room last?" asked Mo.

"Our first princess," replied Taddeo. "Her daughter Violante married the Laughing Prince's son. I wonder if Violante knows that Cosimo has died for the second time." He looked sadly out the window. A moist wind was blowing in, and Mo weighted the paper down with a piece of wood. "Violante came into the world with a birthmark that disfigured her face," the librarian went on, in an abstracted voice, as if he were telling this story not to them but to some distant hearer. "Everyone said it was a punishment, a curse from the fairies because her mother had fallen in love with a minstrel. The Adderhead had her mother banished to this part of the castle as soon as the baby was born, and she lived here with her daughter until she died . . . died very suddenly."

"That's a sad story," said Mo.

"Believe me," replied Taddeo bitterly, "if all the sad stories these walls have seen were written down in books, we could fill every room in the castle with them."

Meggie looked around as if she could see all those books of sad stories. "How old was Violante when she was betrothed to Cosimo and sent to Ombra?" she asked.

"Seven. And the daughters of our present princess were only six when they were betrothed and sent away. We all hope she'll have a son this time!" Taddeo let his eyes linger on the paper that Mo had cut to size, the tools . . . "It's good to see life in this room again," he said quietly. "I'll come back with the books as soon as I'm sure that Mortola is asleep."

"Six, seven years old — my God, Meggie," said Mo when Taddeo had gone, "here you are, thirteen already, and I still haven't sent you away, let alone betrothed you to anyone!"

It felt good to laugh, even if the sound echoed strangely in this high-ceilinged room.

Taddeo did not come back until hours later. Mo was still working, although he put his hand to his chest more and more often, and Meggie had already tried persuading him once or twice to lie down and sleep. "Sleep?" was all he said. "I haven't slept properly for a single night in this castle. And anyway, I want to see your mother again, and I won't be able to do that until this book is finished."

The librarian brought him two volumes. "Look at this!" he whispered, pushing the first over to Mo. "See those places where the binding is eaten away? And inside it looks almost as if the ink were rusting. These are holes in the parchment. You can hardly read some of the words now. What can have caused it? Worms, beetles? I never used to concern myself with these things. I had an assistant who knew all about these sicknesses that books suffer, but one morning he disappeared. They say he joined the robbers in the forest."

Mo picked up the book, opened it, and passed his hand over the pages. "Good heavens!" he said. "Who painted this? I've never seen such beautiful illuminations."

"Balbulus," replied Taddeo. "The illuminator who was sent away with Violante. He was very young when he painted this book. Look, his script was still a little awkward, but now his mastery is impeccable."

"How do you know?" asked Meggie.

The librarian lowered his voice. "Violante has a book sent to me now and then. She knows how much I admire the craftsmanship of Balbulus, and she knows there's no one else left in the Castle of Night who loves books. Not since her mother died. Do you see the chests there?" He pointed to the heavy, dusty wooden chests by the door and under the windows. "Violante's mother kept her books in them, hidden among her clothes. She would take them out only in the evening and show them to the little girl, although I suppose the child hardly understood a word of what her mother read her at the time. But then, soon after Capricorn had disappeared, Mortola came here. The Adderhead had asked her to train the maids in the kitchen — no one said what exactly they were to be trained to do. Then Violante's mother asked me to hide her books in the library, because Mortola had her room searched at least twice a day — she never found out what for. This," he said, pointing to the book that Mo was still leafing through, "was one of her favorites. The little girl would point to a picture and then her mother told her a story about it. I was going to give it to Violante when they sent her away, but she left it behind in this room. Perhaps because she didn't want to take any memories of this sad place to her new life with her. All the same, I'd like to save it as a memento of her mother. You know, I think that a book always keeps something of its owners between its pages."

"Yes, I think so, too," said Mo. "I'm sure of it."

"And?" The old man looked at him hopefully. "Do you know how it can be preserved from further harm?"

Mo carefully closed the book. "Yes, but it won't be easy. Woodworm, the corrosive effect of the ink, who knows what else. . . . Does the second book look the same?"

"Oh, that one" — the librarian cast another nervous look at the door — "Well, it's not in such a bad way yet. But I thought you might like to see it. Balbulus completed it not long ago, for Violante. It contains," he said, looking uncertainly at Mo, "it contains all the songs that the strolling players sing about the Bluejay. As far as I know there are only two copies. Violante owns one, and the other is before you and is a copy that she had specially made for me. They say the man who wrote the songs didn't want them written down, but any minstrel will sing them to you for a few coins. That was how Violante collected them and had them written out by Balbulus. The strolling players, you see — well, they're like walking books here, where real books are so few and far between! You know," he whispered to Mo as he opened the volume, "I sometimes think this world would have lost its memory long ago but for the Motley Folk. Unfortunately, the Adderhead is only too fond of hanging them! I've often suggested sending a scribe to see them before they're executed, to get all those beautiful songs written down before the words die with them, but no one in this castle listens to an old librarian."

"No, very likely not," murmured Mo, but Meggie could tell from his voice that he hadn't been listening to anything Taddeo had said. Mo was immersed in the letters, the beautiful written characters flowing over the parchment in front of him like a delicate river of ink.

"Forgive my curiosity." Taddeo cleared his throat, embarrassed.

"I've heard that you deny being the Bluejay . . . but if you will allow me . . ." He took the book from Mo's hand and opened it at a page that Balbulus had illuminated lavishly. A man stood between two trees, so wonderfully painted that Meggie thought she could hear the rustle of the leaves. He wore a bird mask over his face. "That's how Balbulus painted the Bluejay," whispered Taddeo, "just as the songs describe him, dark-haired, tall . . . doesn't he look like you?"

"I don't know," said Mo. "He's wearing a mask, isn't he?"

"Yes, yes, indeed." Taddeo was still looking intently at him. "But did you know that they say something else about the Bluejay? They say he has a very beautiful voice, not at all like the bird that shares his name. It's said that he can tame bears and wolves with a few words. Forgive me for being so forward, but" — he lowered his voice to a conspiratorial tone — "*you* have a very beautiful voice. Mortola tells strange tales of it. And then, when you have the scar, too . . ." He stared at Mo's arm.

"Oh, you mean this, don't you?" Mo placed his finger under a line beside which Balbulus had painted a pack of white dogs, and read: "*'High on his left arm he will bear the scar to his dying day.'* Yes, I do have a scar like that, but I didn't get it from the dogs in this song." He put his hand to his arm, as if remembering the day when Basta had found them in the tumbledown hut full of broken pots and tiles.

However, the old librarian took a step back. "So you *are* him!" he breathed. "The hope of the poor, the terror of butchers, avenger and robber, as much at home in the forest as the bears and wolves?"

Mo shut the book and pressed the metal clasps into the leather-covered binding. "No," he said. "No, I'm not, but thank you very much for the book, all the same. It's a long time since I had one in my hands, and it will be good to have something to read again, won't it, Meggie?"

"Yes," was all she said, taking the book from his hand. Songs about the Bluejay. What would Fenoglio have said if he'd known that Violante had had them written down in secret? And they might offer so much help! Her heart leaped as she thought of the possibilities, but Taddeo immediately dashed her hopes.

"I'm very sorry," he said, taking the book gently but firmly from her hands again. "But I can't leave either of the books here with you. Mortola has been talking to me — to everyone who has anything to do with the library. She's threatened to have anyone who so much as brings a book into this room blinded. Blinded, imagine it! What a threat, when only our eyes reveal the world of words to us! I've already risked far too much coming here with them at all, but I love those books so much that I had to ask your advice. Please, tell me what I must do to save them!"

Meggie was so disappointed that she would have turned down his request point blank, but of course Mo saw things differently. Mo thought only of the sick books. "Of course," he said to Taddeo. "I'd better write it down for you. It will take time — weeks, months — and I don't know if you'll be able to get all the materials you need, but it's worth a try. I'm not happy about suggesting this, but I'm afraid you'll have to take apart at least the first book, because if you're to save it, the pages must bleach in the sun. If you don't know how to go about it — and it must be done with the utmost care — I'll be happy to do it for you. Mortola can watch if she wants, to make sure I'm not doing anything dangerous."

"Oh, thank you!" The old man bowed deeply as he put the two books firmly under his thin arm. "Many, many thanks. I really do most fervently hope the Adderhead will let you live, and if he doesn't that he grants you a quick death."

Meggie would very much have liked to give him the answer this remark deserved, but Taddeo scurried away too fast on his grasshopper legs.

"Mo, don't you help him!" she said when the guard outside had bolted the door again. "Why should you? He's a miserable coward!"

"Oh, I can understand him," said Mo. "I wouldn't like to do without my eyes, either, even though we have useful inventions like Braille in our own world."

"All the same, I wouldn't help him." Meggie loved her father for his strangely soft heart, but her own could not summon up any sympathy for Taddeo. She imitated his voice. "'I hope he grants you a quick death!' How can anyone say such a thing?"

But Mo wasn't listening. "Have you ever seen such beautiful books, Meggie?" he asked, lying down on the bed.

"You bet I have!" she said indignantly. "Any book I'm allowed to read is more beautiful, right?"

But Mo did not reply. He had turned his back to her and was breathing deeply and peacefully. Obviously, sleep had found its way to him at last.

67

KINDNESS AND MERCY

Here are we five or six strung up, you see,
And here the flesh that all too well we fed,
Bit by bit eaten and rotten, rent and shred,
And we the bones grow dust and ash withal.
François Villon, "Ballade of the Hanged Men"

"When are we going back?" Farid asked Dustfinger this question several times a day, and every time he got the same answer: "Not yet."

"But we've been here so long." It was almost two weeks since the bloodbath in the forest, and he was sick and tired of hanging around in the Badger's Earth. "What about Meggie? You promised we'd go back!"

All Dustfinger said to that was, "If you go on pressing me so hard I shall forget that promise." Then he went to Roxane. She was busy day and night, nursing the wounded they had found among the dead, in the hope that at least these few would return to Ombra, but some of them she tended in vain. *He will stay with her,* thought Farid every time he saw Dustfinger sitting beside her. *And I'll have to go back to the Castle of Night alone.* The thought hurt like fire biting him.

On the fifteenth day, when Farid felt he would never be able to wash the smell of mouse droppings and pale mushrooms off his skin, two of the Black Prince's informers brought identical news: The Adderhead's wife had borne him a son. To celebrate this event, so his criers were announcing in every marketplace, in exactly two weeks' time he would show his great kindness and mercy by setting free all the prisoners held in the dungeons of the Castle of Night. Including the Bluejay.

"Nonsense!" said Dustfinger, when Farid told him about it. "The Adderhead has a roast quail where other people have a heart. He would never set anyone free out of mercy, however many sons were born to him. No, if he really intends to let them go it's because Fenoglio wrote it that way, and for no other reason."

Fenoglio seemed to share this opinion. Ever since the blood-bath he had spent most of his time sitting in some dark corner of the Badger's Earth, looking gloomy and scarcely saying a word, but now he started defiantly announcing to anyone who would listen that the good news was due solely to him. No one took any notice of him, no one knew what he was talking about — except for Dustfinger, who was still avoiding him like the plague in human form. "Listen to the old man! How he boasts and brags!" he said to Farid. "Cosimo and his men are hardly cold in the ground and he's forgotten them already. I hope he drops dead himself!"

The Black Prince, of course, believed in the Adderhead's mercy as little as Dustfinger did, in spite of Fenoglio's assurances that exactly what the informers had said would really happen. The robbers sat together until late into the night, discussing what to do. They would not let Farid join this council, but Dustfinger was with them.

"What's their plan? Tell me!" Farid asked him, when he finally came back from the cave where the robbers had been putting their heads together for hours on end.

"They're going to set out in a week's time."

"Where for? The Castle of Night?"

"Yes." Dustfinger didn't seem half as pleased as he was. "Good heavens, you're fidgeting like fire when the wind blows into it," he snapped at Farid irritably. "We'll see if you're still so happy once we get there. We'll have to crawl underground like worms, and go much deeper there than here."

"Even deeper?"

But of course. Farid pictured Mount Adder before him: There wasn't anywhere to hide, not a bush, not a tree.

"There's an abandoned mine at the foot of the north slope." Dustfinger made a face, as if the mere thought of the place turned his stomach. "Some ancestor of the Adderhead must have dug too deep there, and several galleries fell in, but that's so long ago that obviously not even the Adderhead himself remembers the mine. Not a pleasant place, but a good hideout, and the only one on Mount Adder. The bear found the entrance."

A mine. Farid swallowed. The thought of it left him struggling for air. "Then what?" he asked. "What do we do when we get there?"

"Wait. Wait to see if the Adderhead really keeps his promise."

"Wait? Is that all?"

"You'll learn everything else soon enough."

"Then we're going, too?"

"Did you have anything else in mind?"

Farid hugged him more tightly than he had for a long time. Even though he knew that Dustfinger did not particularly like to be hugged.

*   *   *

"No," said Roxane when the Black Prince offered to have her escorted back to Ombra by one of his men before they set out. "I'm coming with you. If you can spare a man, then send him to my children to tell them I'll be home soon."

Soon! Farid wondered exactly when that was going to be, but he said nothing. Although the time when they would set out was now fixed, the days still passed terribly slowly, and almost every night he dreamed of Meggie. Those were bad dreams, full of darkness and fear. When the day of their departure finally came, half a dozen robbers stayed in the Badger's Earth to go on tending the wounded. The rest set out on the road to the Castle of Night: thirty men in ragged clothing, but well armed. And Roxane. And Fenoglio.

"You're taking the old man, too?" Dustfinger asked the Prince in astonishment when he saw Fenoglio among the men. "Are you crazy? Send him back to Ombra. Take him anywhere else, straight to the White Women for preference, but send him away!"

However, the Prince wouldn't hear of it. "What do you have against him?" he asked. "He's a harmless old man. And don't start telling me again how he can bring the dead to life! Even my bear likes him. He's written us some fine songs, and he can tell wonderful stories, even if he has no appetite for them just now. And he doesn't want to go back to Ombra, anyway."

"I'm not surprised, considering all the widows and orphans he's made there," said Dustfinger bitterly, and when Fenoglio looked his way he cast him so icy a glance that the old man quickly turned his head again.

It was a silent march. The trees whispered above their heads, as if warning them not to take a step farther south, and once or twice Dustfinger had to summon fire to chase away beings that none of them could see, although they sensed them. Farid was tired, tired to death, his face and his arms all scratched with thorns, by the time the silver towers finally appeared above the treetops. "Like a crown on a bald head!" whispered one of the robbers, and for a moment Farid felt he could physically grasp the fear that these ragged men felt at the sight of the mighty fortress. No doubt they were all glad when the Prince led them to the north slope of Mount Adder, and the tops of the towers disappeared again. The earth fell in folds like a crumpled garment on this side of the hill, and the few trees cowered low, as if they heard the sound of axes too often. Farid had never seen such trees before. Their leaves seemed as black as night itself, and their bark was prickly like a hedgehog. Red berries grew on the branches. "Mortola's berries!" Dustfinger whispered to him as he picked a handful in passing. "She's said to have scattered them everywhere at the foot of this hill, until they were sprinkled all over the ground. The trees grow very fast, they shoot up from the earth like mushrooms and keep all other trees away. Bitterberry trees, they're called. Everything about them is poisonous — their berries and their leaves. And their bark burns the skin worse than fire." Farid dropped the berries, and wiped his hand on his trousers.

A little later, when it was pitch dark, they almost ran into one of the patrols that the Adderhead regularly sent out, but the bear warned them in time. The mounted men appeared among the trees like silver beetles. Moonlight was reflected on their breast-plates, and Farid hardly dared to breathe as he ducked down into a crevice in the ground with Dustfinger and Roxane, waiting for the hoofbeats to die away. They stole on, like mice under the eyes of a cat, until they had finally reached their goal.

Wild vines and rubble hid the entrance. The Prince was the first to force his way down into the bowels of the earth. Farid hesitated when he saw how steep the climb down into the darkness looked. "Come on!" whispered Dustfinger impatiently. "The sun will soon rise, and the Adder's soldiers aren't going to mistake you for a squirrel."

"But it smells like a burial vault," said Farid, and he looked longingly up at the sky.

"The boy has a good nose!" said Snapper, before pushing his way past him, grim-faced. "Yes, there are many dead men down there. The mountain devoured them because they dug too deep. You don't see them, but you smell them. People say they stop up the galleries like a cargo of dead fish."

Horrified, Farid looked at him, but Dustfinger just pushed him in the back. "Look, how often do I have to tell you it's not the dead but the living you should fear? Come on, make a few sparks dance on your fingertips to give us a light."

The robbers had settled in those galleries that were not buried in rubble. They had given the roofs and walls additional props, but Farid didn't trust the beams now braced against the stone and the ground. How could they support the weight of a whole mountain? He thought he heard it sighing and groaning, and while he made himself as comfortable as he could on the dirty blankets that the robbers had spread on the hard ground, he suddenly remembered Sootbird again. But the Prince only laughed when he anxiously asked about him. "No, Sootbird doesn't know about this place or any of our hideouts. He's often tried to get us to take him along, but who's going to trust such a wretched fire-eater? The only reason he knew about the Secret Camp was because he's one of the strolling players."

All the same, Farid did not feel safe. Almost a week yet to go before the Adderhead freed his prisoners! It would be a long wait. He was already wishing himself back among the mouse droppings in the Badger's Earth. During the night he kept staring at the rubble closing off the galleries where they were sleeping. He thought he heard pale fingers scraping at the stones. "Put your hands over your ears, then!" was all Dustfinger said when Farid shook him awake to say so, and he put his arms around Roxane again. Dustfinger was having bad dreams, the kind he had often had in the other world, but now it was Roxane who calmed him and whispered him back to sleep. Her quiet voice, soft with love, reminded Farid of Meggie's, and he missed Meggie so much that he felt ashamed of his weakness. In this darkness, surrounded by the dead, it was difficult to believe that she was missing him, too. Suppose she had forgotten him, the way Dustfinger often forgot him now that Roxane was here? Only Meggie had made him forget his jealousy, but Meggie wasn't with him now.

On the second night a boy came to the mine. He worked in the stables of the Castle of Night and had been spying for the Black Prince ever since the Piper had his brother hanged. He said that the Adderhead would let the prisoners go along the road leading down to the harbor, on condition that they boarded a ship there and never returned.

"The road to the harbor. Ah," was all the Prince said when the informer had gone again — and he set out with Dustfinger that same night. Farid didn't ask if he could go, too. He simply followed them.

The road was little more than a footpath leading through the trees. It ran straight down Mount Adder, as if in a hurry to slip under the canopy of leaves. "The Adderhead pardoned a troop of prisoners once before and let them go along this road," said the Prince, when they were under the trees at the roadside. "And they did reach the sea without mishap, just as he had promised, but the ship waiting for them was a slave ship, and they say the

Adderhead got a particularly fine silver bridle for those prisoners, a scant dozen of them."

Slaves? Farid remembered markets where people were sold, and buyers gaped at them and felt them as if they were cattle. Girls with blonde hair had been in great demand.

"Don't look as if Meggie had been sold already!" said Dustfinger. "The Prince will think of something — won't you?"

The Black Prince tried to smile, but he couldn't conceal the fact that he was eyeing the road with great concern. "They must never reach that ship," he said. "And we can only hope that the Adderhead doesn't send too many soldiers to escort them. We must hide them quickly — in the mine at first, that will be best, until everything's quieted down again. And very likely," he added almost as an afterthought, "we shall need fire."

Dustfinger blew on his fingers until flames as delicate as butterfly wings were dancing there. "What do you think I'm still here for?" he asked. "Fire there shall be. But I will not take a sword in my hand, in case that's what you're hoping. You know I'm no good with such things."

68

A VISIT

"If I cannot get me forth out of this house," he thought, "I am a dead man!"

Robert Louis Stevenson, *The Black Arrow*

When Meggie woke, she didn't know for a moment where she was. *In Elinor's house?* she wondered. *With Fenoglio?* But then she saw Mo bending low over the big table, binding a book. *The* book. Five hundred blank pages. They were in the Castle of Night, and Mo was to have the book finished tomorrow. . . . A flash of lightning illuminated the soot-blackened ceiling, and the thunder that followed sounded menacingly loud, but it wasn't the storm that had woken Meggie. She had heard voices. The guards. There was someone at the door. Mo had heard it, too.

"Meggie, he mustn't work such long hours. It could bring back the fever," the Barn Owl had told her that very morning, before they took him down to the dungeons again. But what could she do about it? Mo sent her to bed the moment she began yawning too often. ("That was the twenty-third yawn, Meggie.

Go on, bed for you, or you'll be dead on your feet before this damned book is finished.") Then it would be ages before he went to sleep himself. He stayed up cutting, folding, and stitching until it was nearly dawn. He'd done that tonight as well.

When one of the guards opened the door, Meggie thought for a dreadful moment that Mortola had come to kill Mo after all, before the Adderhead let him go. But it was not the Magpie. The Adderhead stood in the doorway, breathing heavily. Two servants stood behind him, their faces pale with exhaustion, carrying silver candelabras from which wax dripped to the floorboards. Their master, treading heavily, approached the table at which Mo worked and stared at the book. It was almost finished.

"What are you doing here?" Mo still had the paper knife in his hand. The Adderhead stared at him. His eyes were even more bloodshot than on the night when Meggie had made her bargain with him.

"How much longer?" he demanded. "My son is crying. He cries all night. He feels the White Women coming close, just as I do. Now they want to fetch him away, too, him and me at the same time. Folk say they're particularly hungry on stormy nights."

Mo put down the knife. "The book will be finished tomorrow, as agreed. It would have been ready sooner, but the leather to cover it was full of tears and holes made by thorns, so that held us up, and the paper wasn't as good as it might have been, either."

"Yes, yes, very well, the librarian has passed on your complaints!" The Adderhead's voice sounded as if he had been shouting himself hoarse. "If Taddeo had his way, you'd spend the rest of your life in this room, rebinding *all* my books. But I will let you go — you, your daughter, your wife, and those good-for-nothing strolling players. They can all go, I just want the book! Mortola has told me about the three words that your daughter so cunningly failed to mention, but never mind that — I shall take good care that no one writes them in its pages! I want to be able to laugh in the Cold Man's face at last — laugh at him and his pale women! Another night like this and I shall be beating my head against the wall, I shall kill my wife, I shall kill my child, I shall kill all of you. Do you understand, Bluejay or whatever your name is? You must finish the book before dark falls again! You must!"

Mo stroked the wooden boards that he had covered with leather only the day before. "I'll be finished by the time the sun rises. But you must swear to me on your son's life that then you will let us go at once."

The Adderhead looked at him as if the White Women were there standing behind him. "Yes, yes, I swear by whomever and whatever you like! By sunrise, that sounds good!" He walked ponderously over to Mo and stared at his chest. "Show me!" he whispered. "Show me where Mortola wounded you. With the magic weapon that my master-at-arms took apart so thoroughly that now no one can put it together again. I had the fool hanged for that."

Mo hesitated, but finally he opened his shirt.

"So close to the heart!" The Adderhead put his hand on Mo's chest as if to make sure that the heart in it was really still beating. "Yes," he said. "Yes, you must indeed know a way to cheat death or you wouldn't be alive now."

He turned abruptly and waved the two servants over to the door. "Very well, I shall have you fetched soon after sunrise, you and the book," he said over his shoulder.

"Now get me something to eat in the hall!" Meggie heard him shouting outside the door as the guards bolted it again. "Wake the cooks, wake the maids and the Piper. Wake them all! I want to eat and listen to a few dark songs. And the Piper must sing them so loudly that I don't hear the child crying."

Then his footsteps retreated, and only the rolling of the thunder remained. A flash of lightning made the pages of the almost-finished book shine as if they had a life of their own. Mo had gone over to the window. He stood there motionless, looking out.

"By sunrise! Can you do it?" asked Meggie anxiously.

"Of course," he said, without turning. Lightning was flickering over the sea like a distant light being switched on and off by someone — except that no such light existed in this world. Meggie went over to Mo, and he put his arm around her. He knew she was afraid of thunderstorms. When she was very small and had crept into bed with him, he always told her the same story: Thunderstorms were because the sky longed to be united with the earth, and reached out fiery fingers to touch it on such nights.

But Mo didn't tell that story today.

"Did you see the fear in his face?" Meggie whispered to him. "Exactly as Fenoglio described it."

"Yes, even the Adderhead must play the part that Fenoglio has written for him," replied Mo. "But so must we, Meggie. How do you like that idea?"

THE NIGHT BEFORE

True, I talk of dreams,
Which are the children of an idle brain,
Begot of nothing but vain fantasy,
Which is as thin of substance as the air.
                    William Shakespeare, *Romeo and Juliet*

It was the last night before the day when the Adderhead would
show his clemency. In a few hours, just before dawn, they
would all be in position by the road. None of the informers had
been able to say exactly when the prisoners were to come down it —
they knew only that this would be the day. The robbers were sitting together, telling one another tales of old adventures in loud
voices. Presumably that was their means of keeping fear at bay,
but Dustfinger did not feel like either talking or listening. He
kept waking suddenly from sleep, but not because of the voices
that came to his ears. Pictures in his mind woke him, terrible
pictures that had been robbing him of sleep for days.

This time they had been particularly bad, and so real that he
started up as if Gwin had jumped on his chest. His heart was still

thudding hard as he sat there staring into the dark. Dreams — in the other world they had often kept him from sleeping, too, but he couldn't remember any of them as bad as this one. "It's the dead. They bring bad dreams," Farid always said. "They whisper terrible things to you, and then they lie on your breast to feel your racing heart. It makes them feel alive again!"

Dustfinger liked this explanation. He feared death but not the dead. But suppose it was quite different, suppose the dreams were showing him a story already waiting for him somewhere? Reality was a fragile thing; Silvertongue's voice had shown him that once and for all.

Roxane stirred in her sleep beside him. She turned her head and murmured the names of her children, the dead as well as the living. There was still no news from Ombra. Even the Black Prince had heard nothing for a long time, either from the castle or the city, no word of what had happened after the Adderhead sent Cosimo's body back to his daughter, with the news that hardly any of the men who had followed him would come back, either.

Roxane whispered Brianna's name again. Every day she stayed here with him cut her to the heart, Dustfinger knew that only too well. So why didn't he simply go back with her? Why not turn his back on this infernal hill and return at last to a place where you didn't have to hide underground like an animal? *Or like a dead man,* he added in his thoughts.

You know why, he told himself. *It's the dreams. The accursed dreams.* He whispered fire-words to banish the darkness in which dreams put forth such dreadful blossoms. A flame licked up sleepily from the ground beside him. He held out his hand and let it dance up his arm, lick his fingers and his forehead, in the hope that it would simply burn away the horrible pictures. But even the pain did not rid him of them, and Dustfinger extinguished the flame with the flat of his hand. His skin was sooty and hot afterward, as if the fire had left its black breath behind, but the dream was still there, a terror in his heart, too black and strong even for the fire.

How could he simply go away when he saw such images by night — pictures of the dead, again and again, nothing but blood and death? The faces changed. Sometimes it was Resa's face he saw, sometimes Meggie's, then at other times the face of the Barn Owl. He had seen the Black Prince, too, with blood on his breast. And today — today it had been Farid's face. Just like the night before. Dustfinger closed his eyes when the pictures came back, so plain and clear. . . . Of course he had tried to persuade the boy to stay with Roxane tomorrow, when he set off with the robbers — along the road they were to come down, Resa and Silvertongue, Meggie, the Barn Owl, and all the others. (Just how many there would be, even the Prince's informers could not say.) But it was hopeless.

Dustfinger leaned back against the damp stone into which hands long gone had cut the narrow galleries, and looked at the boy. Farid had curled up like a small child, knees drawn up against his chest, with the two martens beside him. They slept at Farid's side more and more often when they came back from hunting, perhaps because they knew that Roxane did not like them.

How peacefully the boy lay there, not at all as Dustfinger had just seen him in his dreams. A smile even flickered across his dark face. Perhaps he was dreaming of Meggie, Resa's Meggie, as like her mother as one flame is like another and yet so different. "You do think she's all right, don't you?" Farid asked that question heaven knows how many times a day. Dustfinger still clearly remembered the feeling of being in love for the first time. How vulnerable his heart had suddenly been! Such a trembling, quivering thing, happy and miserably unhappy at once.

A cold wind blew through the galleries, and Dustfinger saw the boy shivering in his sleep. Gwin raised his head when he rose and took the cloak off his shoulders, covering Farid with it. "Why are you looking at me like that?" he whispered to the marten. "He's crept into your heart just as he crept into mine. How could it happen to us, Gwin?"

The marten licked his paw and looked at him from dark eyes. When he dreamed it was surely only of hunting, not of dead boys.

Suppose the old man was sending the dreams? The idea made Dustfinger shudder as he lay down beside Roxane on the hard ground again. Yes, Fenoglio could be sitting in some corner, as he had often done these last few days, spinning bad dreams for him. That was exactly what he had done with the Adderhead's fears! *Nonsense*, thought Dustfinger angrily, putting his arm around Roxane. *Meggie isn't here. Without her, the old man's words are nothing but ink. Now try to get some sleep, or you'll be nodding off as you wait among the trees with the others tomorrow.*

But it was a long time before he could close his eyes.

He just lay there and listened to the boy's breathing.

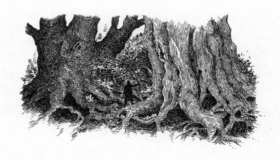

THE PEN AND THE SWORD

"Of course not," said Hermione. "Everything we need is here on this paper."

J. K. Rowling, *Harry Potter and the Sorcerer's Stone*

Mo worked all night, while the storm raged outside as if Fenoglio's world could not accept that soon immortality would arrive in it. Meggie had tried to stay awake, but finally she had nodded off again, head on the table, and he had put her to bed as he had done so many times before. Marveling yet again to see how big she was now. Almost grown-up. Almost.

Meggie woke as he snapped the clasps shut. "Good morning," he said as she raised her head from the pillow — and hoped it would really be a good morning. Outside, the sky was turning red like a face with the blood streaming back into it. The clasps held well. Mo had filed them so that no part of them pricked or dug into the fingers. They held the blank pages together as firmly as if Death were already between them. The leather he had been given for the binding had a reddish tinge, and it surrounded the wooden boards of the covers like their natural skin. The back was gently rounded, the stitching firm, the quires carefully planed. But the fact was that none of that mattered with this book. No one would read it. No one would keep it beside his bed to leaf through its pages again and again. The book was eerie for all its beauty, even Mo felt that, although it was the work of his own hands. It seemed to have a voice that whispered barely perceptible words, words that were not to be found on its blank pages. But they existed. Fenoglio had written them, in a place far away, where women and children now wept for their dead husbands and fathers. Yes, the clasps were important.

Heavy footsteps echoed along the corridor outside the door. Soldiers' footsteps. They came closer and closer. Outside, the night was fading. The Adderhead was taking Mo at his word. *By the time the sun rises . . .*

Meggie quickly got out of bed, passed her hand over her hair, and smoothed down her creased dress.

"Is it finished?" she whispered.

He nodded and took the book from the table. "Do you think the Adderhead will like it?"

The Piper opened the door, with four men following him. His silver nose sat on his face as if it had grown from the flesh.

"Well, Bluejay? Have you finished?"

Mo inspected the book from all sides. "Yes, I think so," he said, but when the Piper put out his hand he hid it behind his back. "Oh no," he said. "I'm keeping this until your master has kept his side of the bargain."

"You are?" The Piper smiled in derision. "Don't you think I know ways of taking it from you? But hold on to it for a while. Fear will make you weak at the knees soon enough."

It was a long way from the part of the Castle of Night where the ghosts of forgotten women lived to the halls where the

Adderhead held court. The Piper walked behind Mo all the way with his curiously arrogant gait, stiff as a stork, so close behind that Mo felt his breath on the nape of his neck. Mo had never been in most of the corridors along which they marched, yet he felt as if he had walked down them all before — in the days when he read Fenoglio's book over and over again as he tried to bring Resa back. It was a strange feeling to be here himself, behind the words on the page — and looking for her again.

He had read about the hall whose mighty doors opened for them, too, and when he saw Meggie's look of alarm he knew only too well what other dreadful place it reminded them both of. Capricorn's red church had not been half as magnificent as the Adderhead's throne room, but thanks to Fenoglio's description Mo had recognized the model at once. Red-washed walls, column ranged beside column on both sides, except that, unlike those in Capricorn's church, these were faced with scales of silver. Capricorn had even taken the idea of a statue from the Adderhead, but the sculptor who immortalized the Silver Prince clearly knew his trade better.

Capricorn had not tried to imitate the Adderhead's throne. It was in the shape of a nest of silver vipers, two of them rearing up with their mouths fixed and wide open, so that the Adderhead's hands could rest on their heads. The lord of the Castle of Night was magnificently clad, despite the early hour, as if to welcome his immortality with due honor. He wore a cape of silvery-white heron feathers over garments of black silk. Behind him, like a flock of birds with bright plumage, stood his court: administrators, ladies' maids, servants — and among them, dressed in the ashen gray of their guild, a number of physicians.

Mortola was there, too, of course. She stood in the background, almost invisible in her black dress. If Mo had not been looking out for her he would have missed her. There was no sign of Basta, but Firefox was standing next to the throne, arms crossed under his fox-fur cloak. He was staring their way with hostility, but to Mo's surprise his dark looks were aimed not at him but mainly at the Piper.

It's a game, thought Mo as he walked past the silver columns. *Fenoglio's game.* If only it hadn't felt so real. How quiet it was in the red hall, in spite of all the people. Meggie looked at him, her face so pale under her fair hair, and he gave her the most encouraging smile his lips could manage — feeling thankful that she couldn't hear how fast his heart was beating.

The Adderhead's wife sat beside him. Meggie had described her perfectly: an ivory porcelain doll. Behind them stood the nurse with the eagerly awaited son. Mo had never wanted a son, only a daughter. Resa had teased him about it when they didn't yet know what their baby would be. The child's crying sounded strangely lost in the great hall. Even the rain beating against glazed windows high above them drowned out the shrill little voice.

It's a game, thought Mo once more when he was standing before the steps of the throne, *only a game.* If only he'd known more about the rules. There was someone else present whom they knew. Taddeo the librarian, head humbly bent, stood right behind the Adderhead's throne and gave Mo an anxious smile.

The Adderhead looked even more exhausted for lack of sleep than he had on their last meeting. His face was blotched and full of shadows, his lips colorless. Only the rubies in the corners of his nostrils shone red. Who could say how many sleepless nights he had spent? For a moment it seemed to Mo as if all his life had gone into the rubies at the corners of his nose.

"Good, so you have really finished," he said. "Of course,

you're in a hurry to see your wife again, I'm sure. I've been told she asks about you every day. That's love, I expect, isn't it?"

A game, only a game . . . It didn't feel like that. Nothing had ever seemed more real than the hatred that Mo felt at this moment, as he looked at that coarse and arrogant face. And he felt something else beating in his breast again: his new, cold heart. Or was it just his old heart, burned out with hatred?

The Adderhead made a sign to the Piper, and the silver-nosed man stepped commandingly toward Mo. He found it hard to put the book into the man's gloved hands. After all, there was nothing else that could save them now. The Piper noticed his reluctance, smiled scornfully at him — and took the book up the steps to his master. Then, with a brief glance at Firefox, he stationed himself right beside the throne with an arrogant air, as if there were no more important man in the hall.

"Beautiful. Beautiful indeed!" The Adderhead caressed the white pages of the book. "Whether or not he's a robber, he knows something about bookbinding, don't you agree, Firefox?"

"There are men of many trades among the robbers," was all that Firefox replied. "Why not an accursed bookbinder, too?"

"How true, how true. Did you all hear that?" The Adderhead looked at his colorfully clad retinue, inviting approval. "It seems to me that my herald still thinks I'd have let a little girl trick me. Yes, he believes I'm a credulous fool by comparison with his old master, Capricorn."

Firefox was about to protest, but the Adderhead silenced him with a gesture. "Do not speak!" was all he said, loud enough for everyone to hear. "In spite of my very obvious folly, I have thought of a way to prove which of the two of us is wrong." With a nod of the head, he summoned Taddeo to his side. Eager to oblige, the librarian approached him, taking pen and ink from the folds of his flowing robe.

"It's perfectly simple, Firefox!" You could tell that the Adderhead liked the sound of his own voice. "You, and not I, will be the first to write your name in this book! Taddeo here has assured me that the letters can be removed again with a scraper that Balbulus once designed specially for that purpose, leaving no trace. No one will be able to see even a shadow of your writing on the pages. So you write your name — which I know you are able to do — we give the Bluejay a sword, and he runs it through your body. Isn't that a fabulous idea? Won't it prove beyond doubt whether or not this book can do what his daughter promised me?"

A game. Mo saw fear spread over Firefox's face like a rash.

"Well, come along!" the Adderhead derided him, opening the book and leafing through the blank pages, as if lost in thought. "Why do you suddenly look so pale? Isn't such a game precisely to your taste? Come along, write your name in it. Not the name you've given yourself, but the one you were born with."

Think. Mo saw one of the guards surrounding him and Meggie draw his sword. *What are you going to do? What?* He felt Meggie's horrified gaze, felt her fear like a chill beside him.

Firefox looked around as if searching for a face that might offer help, but no one stepped forward, not even Mortola. She stood there with her lips compressed so tightly that they were almost white, and if her glance could have killed as her poisons often did, the book would not have helped the Adderhead. As it was, however, he just smiled at her and put the pen in his herald's hand. Firefox stared at the sharpened quill as if he were not sure what to do with it. Then he dipped it ceremoniously in the ink — and wrote.

"Excellent!" The Piper took the book from his hand the moment he had finished. The Adderhead waved to one of the servants waiting with dishes full of fruit and cakes at the foot of the silver columns. "Well, what are you waiting for, Firefox? Try your luck!" Honey dripped from his fingers as he pushed one of the cakes between his lips.

Firefox, however, stood there, still staring at the Piper, whose long arms were wound around the book as if he were holding a baby. He responded to Firefox's glance with a nasty smile. Firefox abruptly turned his back to him and the Adderhead and came down the steps.

Mo removed Meggie's hand from his arm and pushed her gently aside, although she resisted. The men-at-arms standing around retreated, with incredulity on their faces, as if clearing a stage. Except for the one who had drawn his sword and now held it out to Mo. Was this still Fenoglio's game? It would be like him. When Mo had entered the hall just now he'd have given one of his eyes for a sword, but he didn't want this one. He wanted it as little as the roles some other people wanted him to play, whether Fenoglio or the Adderhead. He had always hated games like this, games played by the strong with someone weaker, the cat with the helpless mouse. . . . He hated them, even when the mouse was a murderer and fire-raiser.

When Firefox stopped at the foot of the steps, hesitating as if he were wondering whether there might not be some way out for him after all, one of the men-at-arms went up to him and took his sword from its sheath.

"Here, Bluejay, take it." The soldier who was holding his sword out to Mo was getting impatient, and Mo remembered the night when he had picked up Basta's sword and chased him and Capricorn out of his house. He still remembered just how heavy the weapon had felt in his hand, how the bright blade caught the light. . . .

"No, thank you," Mo said, stepping back. "Swords are not among the tools of my trade. I thought I'd proved that with the book."

The Adderhead wiped the honey off his fingers, removed a few cake crumbs from his lips, and looked him up and down. "Oh, come on, Bluejay!" he said in a tone of mild surprise. "You heard. We don't expect any great skill in swordplay. All you have to do is run it through his body. It really isn't difficult!"

Firefox was staring at Mo. His eyes were clouded with hatred. *Look at him, you fool,* Mo told himself. *He'd run you through with that sword on the spot, so why don't you do it to him?* Meggie understood why not. He saw it in her eyes. Perhaps the Bluejay might take that sword, but not her father.

"Forget it, Adder," he said out loud. "If you have an account to settle with your bloodhound, see to it yourself. Ours is a different agreement."

The Adderhead looked at him with as much interest as if some exotic animal had wandered into his hall. Then he laughed. "I like your answer!" he cried. "Indeed I do. And do you know something? It finally shows me I've caught the right man. You are the Bluejay, without any doubt. He's said to be a sly fox. But all the same I'll keep my bargain."

And so saying, he nodded to the man-at-arms who was still offering Mo the sword. Without hesitation, the man turned and thrust the long blade through the body of his master's herald, so fast that Firefox did not even manage to flinch back.

Meggie screamed. Mo drew her close and hid her face against his chest. But Firefox stood there, staring in bewilderment at the sword sticking out of his body as if it were a part of him.

With a self-satisfied smile, the Adderhead looked around, enjoying the silent horror in the hall around him. Firefox took the sword sticking out of his body and pulled out the blade very slowly, his face distorted, but without swaying on his feet. And the great hall became as still as if all present had stopped breathing.

As for the Adderhead, he applauded. "Well, look at that!" he cried. "Is there anyone here in this hall who thinks he could have survived that sword stroke? He's just a little pale, that's all — am I right, Firefox?"

His herald did not reply, but just stood there staring at the bloodstained sword in his hands.

But the Adderhead went on, in a voice of high good humor, "Well, I think that proves it! The girl wasn't lying, and the Adderhead is not a gullible fool who fell for a child's fairy tale, is he?"

He placed his words as carefully as a beast of prey places its paws. Nothing but silence answered him. Even Firefox, his face white with pain, said not a word as he wiped his own blood from the sword blade.

"Excellent!" remarked the Adderhead. "That's done, then — and now I have an immortal herald. It's time I was able to say the same of myself. Piper," he said, turning to the man with the silver nose. "Empty the hall for me. Get everyone out — servants, women, physicians, clerks, all of them. I want just ten men-at-arms to stay, the librarian, you and Firefox, and the two prisoners. You go away, too!" he snapped at Mortola, who was about to protest. "Stay with my wife and get that baby to stop crying at last."

"What's he going to do, Mo?" whispered Meggie as the hall emptied around them. But he could only shake his head. He didn't know, either. He only felt that the game was far from over yet.

"What about us?" he called to the Adderhead. "My daughter and I have fulfilled our part of the bargain, so fetch the prisoners from your dungeons and let us go."

But the Adderhead only raised his hands in a conciliatory gesture. "Yes, of course, of course, Bluejay," he graciously replied. "As you have kept your word, I keep mine. The Adder's word of honor. I've already sent men down to the dungeons, but it's a long way from there to the gate, so give us the pleasure of your company a little longer. Believe me, we shall provide you with entertainment."

A game. Mo looked around and saw the huge doors close behind the last servants. Once empty, the hall only seemed larger.

"Well, how are you doing, Firefox?" The Adderhead ran a cool eye over his herald. "What does it feel like to be immortal? Fabulous? Reassuring?"

Firefox said nothing. He was still holding the sword that had run him through. "I'd like my own sword back," he said hoarsely, without taking his eyes off his master. "This one is no good."

"Nonsense. I'll have a new sword forged for you, a better one, in gratitude for the service you've done me today!" replied the Adderhead. "But first we have one small thing to do so that we can remove your name from my book without any damage."

"Remove it?" Firefox's eyes wandered to the Piper, who opened the book again and held it out to the librarian.

"Remove it, yes. You remember that originally the book was to make *me* immortal, not you, and for that to happen the scribe must write three more words in it."

"What for?" Firefox wiped the sweat from his brow with his sleeve.

Three words. Poor devil. Did he hear the trap snapping shut? Meggie reached for Mo's hand.

"To make room, one might say. To make room for me," replied the Adderhead. "And do you know what?" he went on, as Firefox looked at him uncomprehendingly. "As a reward for your unselfish proof of how reliably this book really does protect one from death, as soon as the scribe has written those three words you may kill the Bluejay. If he can be killed, that is. Well, is it a fair offer?"

"What? What are you talking about?" Meggie's voice was shrill with fear, but Mo quickly put his hand over her mouth. "Meggie, please!" he said, low-voiced. "Have you forgotten what you said about Fenoglio's words? Nothing will happen to me. Do you hear me?"

But she wouldn't listen. She sobbed and held him tightly until two men-at-arms roughly dragged her away.

"Three words!" Firefox was advancing on him. And hadn't he just been feeling sorry for him? *You're a fool, Mortimer,* thought Mo.

"Three words! Count them well, Bluejay!" said Firefox, raising his sword. "On four I shall strike, and it will hurt, I promise you, even if it may not kill you. I know what I'm talking about."

The sword blade shone like ice in the candlelight. It looked long enough to run three men through at once, and here and there Firefox's blood still clung to the bright metal like rust.

"Come now, Taddeo," said the Adderhead. "You remember the words I told you? Write them one by one, but don't say them aloud. Just count them for us."

The Piper opened the book and held it out to the old man. With trembling fingers, Taddeo dipped his pen in the jar of ink. "One," he whispered, and the pen scratched over the parchment.

"Two."

Firefox, smiling, set the point of the sword against Mo's chest.

Taddeo raised his head, dipped his pen in the ink again, and looked uncertainly at the Adderhead.

"Have you forgotten how to count, old man?" he asked.

Taddeo just shook his head and lowered the pen to the paper again. "Three!" he whispered.

Mo heard Meggie call his name and stared at the point of the sword. Words, nothing but words protected him from that sharp, bright blade. . . .

In Fenoglio's world, words were enough.

Firefox's eyes widened in mingled astonishment and horror. Mo saw him try with his last breath to thrust the sword into him, to take him to wherever pen and ink were sending him, too, but the sword dropped from his hands. Firefox collapsed like a bundle of empty clothes and fell at Mo's feet.

The Piper stood there staring down at the dead man in silence, while Taddeo lowered his pen and retreated from the book in which he had just been writing as if it might kill him as well, with a quiet voice, with a single word.

"Take him away," ordered the Adderhead. "Before the White Women come to fetch him from my castle. Get on with it!"

Three men-at-arms carried Firefox out. The foxtails on his cloak dragged on the tiles as they hauled him away, and Mo stood there staring at the sword lying at his feet. He felt Meggie put her arms around him. Her heart was beating like a frightened bird's.

"Who wants an immortal herald?" remarked the Adderhead as the dead Firefox was removed. "If you'd been a little cleverer you'd have seen that for yourself." The jewels that adorned his nostrils looked more than ever like drops of blood.

"Shall I remove his name, Your Grace?" Taddeo's voice was so hesitant that it was barely audible.

"Of course. His name and the three words, you understand. And do a thorough job of it. I want the pages white as newly fallen snow again."

The librarian obediently set to work. The scraping sound was curiously loud in the empty hall. When Taddeo had finished, he passed the flat of his hand over the parchment, which was blank again now. Then the Piper took the book from his hands and offered it to the Adderhead.

Mo saw the man's stout fingers shaking as they dipped the pen in the ink. And before he began to write, the Adderhead looked up once more. "I am sure you weren't stupid enough to bind any kind of extra magic into this book, were you, Bluejay?" he asked warily. "There are ways of killing a man — and not just a man, but his wife and daughter, too — that make dying a very long and very painful business. It can take days — many days and many nights."

"Magic? No," replied Mo, still staring at the sword at his feet. "I don't know anything about magic. Let me say it again: Bookbinding, and nothing else, is my trade. And all I know about it has gone into that book. No more and no less."

"Very well." The Adderhead dipped the pen in the ink again — and stopped once more. "White," he murmured, staring at the blank pages. "See how white they are. White as the women who bring death, white as the bones the Cold Man leaves behind when he's had his fill of flesh and blood."

Then he wrote. Wrote his name in the blank book and closed it. "That's done!" he cried triumphantly. "That's done, Taddeo! Lock him in the book, the soul-swallower, the enemy who can't be killed. Now he can't kill me, either. Now we're equals. Two Cold Men ruling the world together, for all eternity."

The librarian obeyed, but as he was engaging the clasps he looked at Mo. *Who are you?* his eyes seemed to ask. *What's your part in this game?* But even if Mo had wanted to, he couldn't have given him the answer.

The Adderhead, however, seemed to think he knew it. "You

know, I like you, Bluejay," he said, never taking his lizardlike gaze off Mo. "Yes, you'd make a good herald, but that's not the way the parts are shared out, is it?"

"No, indeed not," said Mo. *But you don't know who shares them out, and I do,* he added in his thoughts.

The Adderhead nodded to the men-at-arms. "Let him go," he ordered. "And the girl, and anyone else he wants to take."

They stepped aside, if reluctantly.

"Come on, Mo!" whispered Meggie, pressing his hand.

How pale she was. Pale with fear, and so defenseless. Mo looked past the men-at-arms and thought of the walled court-yard waiting for them out there, the silver vipers staring down, the openings for boiling pitch above the gate. He thought of the crossbows of the guards on the battlements, too, the spears of the guards at the gate — and the soldiers who had pushed Resa down in the dirt. Without a word, he bent down and picked up the sword that had fallen from Firefox's hand.

"Mo!" Meggie let go of his hand and looked at him in horror. "What are you doing?"

But he just pulled her close to him without a word, while the men-at-arms all drew their weapons. Firefox's sword weighed heavy, heavier than the one he had used to chase Capricorn out of his house.

"Well, fancy that!" said the Adderhead. "You don't seem to trust my word, Bluejay!"

"Oh, I trust it," said Mo, without lowering the sword. "But everyone here except me has a weapon, so I think I'll keep this masterless sword. You keep the book, and if we're both lucky we'll never see each other again after this morning."

Even the Adderhead's laughter sounded as if it were made

of silver — dark, tarnished silver. "Well, now," he said. "It's a pleasure to play games with you, Bluejay. You're a good opponent. Which is why I'll keep my word. Let him go," he told the men-at-arms again. "Tell the guards at the gate the Adderhead is letting the Bluejay go because he need never fear him again. For the Adderhead is immortal!"

The words echoed in Mo's ears as he took Meggie's hand. Taddeo was still holding the book, holding it as if it might bite him. Mo thought he could still feel its paper between his fingers, the wood of the boards, the leather covering it, the thread stitching the pages. Then he saw Meggie's gaze. She was staring at the sword in his hand as if it made a stranger of him.

"Come on," he said. "Let's join your mother!"

"Yes, go, Bluejay, take your daughter and your wife and all the others," the Adderhead called after them. "Before Mortola reminds me how stupid it is to let you go free!"

Only two men-at-arms followed them on their long journey through the castle. The courtyard was almost empty at this early hour of the morning. The sky above the Castle of Night was gray, and fine rain was falling like a veil before the face of the dawning day. The few servants already at work retreated in alarm from the sight of the sword in Mo's hand, and the men-at-arms waved them aside without a word.

The other prisoners were already waiting at the gate, a forlorn little troop guarded by a dozen soldiers. At first Mo couldn't see Resa, but suddenly one figure moved away from the others and ran toward him and Meggie. No one stopped her. Perhaps the soldiers had heard of Firefox's fate. Mo felt their eyes on him, full of horror and fear — the man who bound Death between white pages and was a robber in the bargain! Didn't the sword in his hand prove that for all time? He didn't care what they thought. Let them be afraid of him. He had felt more than enough fear for one lifetime in all those days and nights when he thought he had lost everything — his wife, his daughter — and there was nothing left for him but a lonely death in this world made of words.

Resa hugged him and Meggie in turn, she almost crushed them, and his face was wet with her tears when she let go of him again.

"Come on, let's go through the gate, Resa!" he urged in a low voice. "Before the lord of this castle changes his mind! We all have a great deal to tell one another, but for now let's go!"

The other prisoners joined them in silence. They watched incredulously as the gate opened for them, as its ironbound wings swung open and let them go free. Some of them stumbled over their own feet in their haste as they crowded out. But still no one from the castle followed them. The guards just stood there, swords and spears in their hands, staring as the prisoners stumbled uncertainly away, their legs stiff from weeks in the dungeons. Only one man-at-arms came out of the gate with them, wordlessly indicating the path they should take. *Suppose they shoot at us from the battlements?* Mo thought, when he saw that there was not a single tree or bush to give them cover as they followed the road down the bare slope. He felt like a fly on the wall ready to be swatted. But nothing happened. They walked through the gray morning, through the rain now pouring down, with the castle crouched menacingly behind them like a monster — and nothing happened.

"He's keeping his promise!" Mo heard the others whispering these words more and more often. "The Adderhead is keeping his word." Resa asked anxiously about his wound, and he replied quietly that he was all right, while he waited to hear footsteps behind them, soldier's footsteps. But all was still. It seemed as if they had been going down the bare hillside for an eternity when trees suddenly appeared in front of them. The shade that their branches cast on the road was as dark as if night itself had taken refuge under them.

ONLY A DREAM

One day a young man said, "This tale about everybody
having to die doesn't sit too well with me. I will go in search of
the land where one never dies."
Italo Calvino, "The Land Where One Never Dies,"
Italian Folk Tales

Dustfinger was lying among the trees, drenched to the skin
by the rain, with Farid beside him. The boy's black hair
clung to his forehead, and he kept shivering. The others were
certainly in no better shape. They had been waiting for hours;
they'd taken up their positions before sunrise, and it had been
raining ever since. It was dark under the trees, as dark as if day had
never dawned. And quiet, as quiet as if the waiting men were not
alone in holding their breath. Only the noise of the rain splashed
and dripped onto the trees and branches, falling and falling. Farid
wiped his wet nose on his sleeve, and someone sneezed somewhere. *Stupid fool, hold your nose,* thought Dustfinger — then
started when he heard something rustling on the other side of the
road. But it was only a rabbit scuttling out of the thickets. It

stopped in the middle of the road, sniffing the air, ears twitching, eyes wide open. *It's probably not half as scared as I am,* thought Dustfinger, wishing himself back with Roxane in the dark underground galleries of the mine. They smelled like a crypt, but at least they were dry.

He was pushing his dripping hair back from his forehead for about the hundredth time when Farid, beside him, suddenly raised his head. The rabbit raced away among the trees, and footsteps sounded through the rushing of the rain. Here they came at last, a forlorn little troop, almost as wet as the robbers waiting for them. Farid was going to jump up, but Dustfinger seized him and pulled him roughly back to his side. "Stay where you are, understand?" he hissed. "I didn't leave the martens with Roxane only to have to catch you instead!"

Silvertongue led the way, with Meggie and Resa behind him. He was holding a sword in his hand, as he had on the night when he turned Capricorn and Basta out of his house. The pregnant woman he had seen in the dungeon was stumbling down the road beside Resa. She kept looking back, up to the Castle of Night, which still towered menacing and huge behind them, even though it was so far away now. There were more prisoners than he had seen at the inn in the forest. Obviously, the Adderhead really had emptied his dungeons. Some were swaying as if they could hardly keep on their feet, others blinking as if even the dim light of this dark day was too much for their eyes. Silvertongue seemed to be all right, in spite of his bloodstained shirt, and Resa did not look quite as pale as in the dungeon, but perhaps that was just his imagination.

He had just seen the Barn Owl among the others — how old and fragile he looked! — when Farid clutched his arm in sudden fright and pointed at the men who had appeared on the road.

They emerged so soundlessly that they might have been growing out of the rain, more and more of them, and at first Dustfinger thought the Black Prince had managed to get reinforcements after all. But then he saw Basta.

He was holding a sword in one hand and a knife in the other, and bloodlust was written all over his scorched face. None of the men with him wore the Adderhead's coat of arms, but that meant nothing. Perhaps Mortola had sent them, perhaps the Adderhead wanted to be able to protest innocence when his prisoners were found dead in the road. There were a great many men; that was all that mattered. Dozens and dozens of them. Far more than the robbers lying in wait in the trees with the Black Prince. Basta raised a hand, smiling, and they advanced down the road with drawn swords, going at a comfortable pace as if they wanted to enjoy the fear on the prisoners' faces for a while before they struck.

The Black Prince was the first to leap out of the trees, with the bear at his side. The two of them took up their position in the road as if they alone could stop the slaughter. But his men were quick to follow, silently forming a wall of bodies between the prisoners and the men who had come to kill them. Cursing quietly, Dustfinger rose to his feet, too. This was going to be a day of bloodshed. The rain wouldn't fall fast enough to wash all the blood away, and he would have to provoke the fire to great anger, for it didn't like rain. Damp made it sleepy — and it would have to bite hard, very hard.

"Farid!" He breathed the boy's name and was just in time to haul him back by the arm. He wanted to go to Meggie, of course, but he would have to take fire with him. They would need to make a circle of it — a ring of flames around those who had nothing but their hands against all those swords. He picked up a strong branch, enticed fire from its damp bark — hissing, steaming fire — and threw the burning wood to the boy. The barrier of human flesh wouldn't hold for long; it was fire that must save them.

Basta's voice came through the gloom, derisive, bloodthirsty, while Farid made sparks rain down on the ground. He scattered them over the wet earth like a farmer sowing his seed, while Dustfinger followed him and made them grow. The flames were flaring up as Basta's men attacked. Sword clashed against sword, screams filled the air, bodies collided as Dustfinger and Farid lured fire into being and nursed it until it almost surrounded the company of prisoners. Dustfinger left only a narrow path free, a way of escape into the forest in case the flames stopped obeying even him and their anger finally made them bite everyone, friend and foe alike.

He saw Resa's face and the fear in it, he saw Farid leap over the flames to join the freed prisoners, in line with their plan. A good thing Meggie was there, or very likely Farid would not have left his side. Dustfinger himself still stood outside the fire. He drew his knife — it was always better to have a knife in your hand when Basta was around — and whispered to the fire, insistently, almost lovingly, to keep it from doing what it wanted and becoming an enemy instead of a friend. As the robbers were forced farther and farther back, they came closer and closer to the troop of freed prisoners. Among them all, only Silvertongue had a weapon.

Three of Basta's men were attacking the Prince, but the bear was protecting his master with teeth and claws. Dustfinger felt almost sick at the sight of the wounds those black paws inflicted. The fire crackled at him, wanted to play, wanted to dance, didn't understand anything about the fear all around, neither smelled nor tasted it. Dustfinger heard cries, one as clear as a

boy's voice. He pushed his way through the fighting bodies —
and picked up a sword lying in the mud. Where was Farid?

There, thrusting about him with his knife, swift as an adder
striking. Dustfinger seized his arm, hissing at the flames to let
them pass, and dragged him away. "Damn it all! I ought to have
left you with Roxane," he shouted as he pushed Farid through
the fire. "Didn't I tell you to stay with Meggie?" He could have
wrung the boy's thin neck, but he was so relieved to see him
uninjured.

Meggie ran to Farid and took his hand. They stood there side
by side, staring at the blood and the turmoil, but Dustfinger tried
to hear nothing, see nothing. The fire alone was his concern. The
rest was up to the Prince.

Silvertongue was striking out well with his sword, far better
than Dustfinger himself could have managed, but his face looked
exhausted and wet with rain. Dustfinger glanced at Resa. She
was standing beside Meggie, and she was still unhurt. For now.
The damned rain was running down his face and the back of
his neck, drowning out his voice with its rushing. The water
was singing a lullaby to the flames, an ancient lullaby, and
Dustfinger raised his voice, called louder and louder to wake it
again, to make it roar and bite. He went very near the ring of fire,
saw the fighting men come closer and closer. Some were already
almost stumbling into the flames.

Farid, too, had seen what the rain was doing. He ran nimbly
to where the flames were dying down, and Meggie ran after him.
A man fell dead in the ring of fire where the boy was standing,
extinguishing the flames there with his lifeless body, and a
second man stumbled over him. Cursing, Dustfinger made for
the deadly breach in the ring, called Silvertongue to help — and
saw Basta appear among the flames. Basta, with his face singed

and hatred in his eyes — hatred and fear of the fire. Which would prove stronger? He was staring through the flames, blinking at the smoke, as if in search of one particular face; Dustfinger could well imagine whose. Instinctively, he took a step back. Another man fell dead in the flames; two more, swords drawn, leaped over his body and attacked the prisoners. Screams rang in Dustfinger's ears. He saw Silvertongue place himself in front of Resa, while Basta set a foot on the dead men as if they were a bridge. More flames were needed. Dustfinger was making for the fire, so that it could hear him better at close quarters, but someone seized his arm and swung him around. Twofingers.

"They'll kill us!" he stammered, his eyes wide with fear. "They were going to kill us all along! And if they don't get us, the flames will burn us alive!"

"Let me go!" Dustfinger shouted at him. The smoke was stinging his eyes and making him cough.

Basta. He was staring at him through the smoke as if an invisible bond united them. The flames licked up at him in vain, and he raised his knife. Who was he aiming at? And why was he smiling like that?

The boy.

Dustfinger pushed the two-fingered man aside. He shouted Farid's name, but the noise all around drowned out his voice. The boy was still holding Meggie's hand with one of his own, while his other held the knife, the knife that Dustfinger had given him in another life, in another story.

"Farid!" The boy did not hear him — and Basta threw.

Dustfinger saw the knife go into that thin back. He caught the boy before he fell to the ground, but he was already dead. And there stood Basta with his foot on another dead body, smiling. Why not? He had hit his target, and it was the target he had been aiming for all along: Dustfinger's heart, his stupid heart. It broke in two as he held Farid in his arms, it simply broke in two, although he had taken such good care of it all these years. He saw Meggie's face, heard her sobbing Farid's name, and put the boy's body into her arms. His legs were trembling so much that he had difficulty straightening up. Everything about him was trembling, even the hand holding the knife that he had pulled out of the boy's back. He wanted to get at Basta, through the fire and the fighting men, but Silvertongue was faster. Silvertongue, who had plucked Farid from his own story and whose daughter sat there weeping as if her own heart had had a knife driven into it, like the boy. . . .

Mo ignored the flames moving toward him. He thrust his sword through Basta's body as if he had never done anything else in his life, as if from now on his trade was killing. Basta died with an expression of surprise still on his face. He fell into the fire, and Dustfinger stumbled back to Farid, who was still held in Meggie's arms.

What had he expected — that the boy would come back to life just because his killer was dead? No, the black eyes were still empty, empty as a deserted house. There was none of the joy in them now that had always been so difficult to banish. And Dustfinger kneeled there on the trodden earth, while Resa comforted her weeping daughter, and men were fighting, killing, and being killed around them, and he no longer had any idea what he was doing here, what was going on, why he had ever come beneath these trees, the same trees that he had seen in his dream.

In the worst of all dreams.

And now it had come true.

An Exchange

The blue of my eyes was extinguished tonight
The red gold of my heart

Georg Trakl, "By Night," *Poems*

They almost all escaped. The fire saved them, the fury of the
bear, the Black Prince's men — and Mo, who practiced
killing that gray morning as if he meant to become a master of the
craft. Basta was left dead under the trees, along with Slasher and
so many of their men that the ground was covered with their
corpses as if with dead leaves. Two of the strolling players had
been killed, too — and Farid.

Farid.

Dustfinger himself was pale as death when he carried him
back to the mine. Meggie walked beside him all the long, dark
way. She held Farid's hand, as if that could help, feeling as sore
inside herself as if it would never get better.

She was the only one whom Dustfinger did not send away
when he had laid Farid down on his cloak in the most remote of
the galleries. No one dared approach him as he bent over the

dead boy and wiped the soot from his brow. Roxane did try to talk to him, but when she saw the expression on his face she left him alone. He allowed only Meggie to sit beside Farid, as if he had seen his own pain in her eyes. So they both sat with him in the depths of Mount Adder, as if they had come to the end of all stories. Without a single word still left to say.

Perhaps night had fallen outside by the time Meggie heard Dustfinger's voice. It came to her as if from far away, through the fog of pain that enveloped her as if she would never find her way out.

"You'd like him back, too, wouldn't you?"

It was difficult for her to turn her eyes away from Farid's face. "He'll never come back," she whispered, and looked at Dustfinger. She didn't have the strength to speak any louder. All her strength was gone, as if Farid had taken it away with him. He had taken everything away with him.

"There's a story." Dustfinger looked at his hands, as if what he was talking about was written there. "A story about the White Women."

"What kind of story?" Meggie didn't want to hear any more stories ever again. This one had broken her heart for all time. Nonetheless, there was something in Dustfinger's voice. . . .

He bent over Farid and wiped some soot from his cold forehead. "Roxane knows it," he said. "She'll tell it to you. Just go to her and . . . and tell her I've had to go away. Tell her I'm going to find out if the story is true." He spoke with a strange kind of hesitation, as if it were infinitely difficult to find the right words. "And remind her of my promise — that I'll always find a way back to her, wherever I am. Will you tell her that?"

What was he talking about? "Find out?" Meggie's voice was husky with tears. "Find out what exactly?"

"Oh, people say this and that about the White Women. Much of it's just superstition, but there's sure to be some truth in it somewhere. Stories are always like that, aren't they? No doubt Fenoglio could tell me more, but to be honest I don't want to ask him. I'd rather ask them in person."

Dustfinger straightened up. He stood there looking around him, as if he had forgotten where he really was.

The White Women. "They'll be coming soon, won't they?" Meggie asked him anxiously. "Coming for Farid."

But Dustfinger shook his head, and for the first time since Farid's death he smiled, that strangely sad smile that Meggie had never seen on any face but his, and that she had never entirely understood. "No, why should they? They're sure of him already. They come only if you're still clinging to life, if they have to lure you to them with a look or a whispered word. Everything else is superstition. They come while you're still breathing, but very close to death. They come when your heart is beating more and more faintly, when they can smell fear, or blood, as in your father's case. If you die as quickly as Farid you go to them entirely of your own accord."

Meggie caressed Farid's fingers. They were colder than the stone where she was sitting. "Then I don't understand," she whispered. "If they aren't coming at all, how will you ask them anything?"

"I shall summon them," replied Dustfinger. "But you had better not be here when I do it, so will you go to Roxane and tell her what I have said to you?"

She was going to ask more questions, but he put a finger on his lips. "Please, Meggie!" he said. He didn't often call her by her name. "Tell Roxane what I have told you — and say . . . say I'm sorry. Now, off you go."

Meggie sensed that he was afraid, but she did not ask him what of, because her heart was asking other questions. How could it be true that Farid was dead, and how would it feel to have him dead in her heart forever? She caressed his still face one last time before she got to her feet. When she looked back once more at the entrance to the gallery, Dustfinger was looking down at Farid. And, for the first time since she had known him, his face showed all that he usually hid: affection, love — and pain.

Meggie knew where to look for Roxane, but she lost her way twice in the dark galleries before she finally found her. Roxane was tending the injured women, while the Barn Owl was looking after the men. Many of them had been hurt, and although the fire had saved their lives it had burned many of them badly. Mo was nowhere to be seen, and nor was the Prince; they were probably on guard at the entrance to the mine, but Resa was with Roxane. She was just bandaging an arm that had suffered burns, and Roxane was treating a cut on an old woman's forehead with the same ointment she had once used on Dustfinger's wounds. Its springlike fragrance did not suit this place.

When Meggie came out of the dark passage, Roxane raised her head. Perhaps she had been hoping it was Dustfinger's footsteps that she had heard. Meggie leaned back against the cold wall of the gallery. *This is all a dream,* she thought, *a terrible, terrible dream.* She felt dizzy with weeping.

"What's that story?" she asked Roxane. "A story about the White Women . . . Dustfinger says you're to tell me. And he says he has to go away because he wants to find out if it's true."

"Go away?" Roxane put down the ointment. "What are you talking about?"

Meggie wiped her eyes, but there were no tears left in them. She supposed she had used them all up. Where did so many tears come from? "He says he's going to summon them," she murmured. "And he says you're to remember his promise. That he'll always come back, he'll find a way wherever he is. . . ." The words still made no sense to her when she repeated them. But they obviously meant something to Roxane.

She straightened up, and so did Resa.

"What are you talking about, Meggie?" asked her mother, with concern in her voice. "Where's Dustfinger?"

"With Farid. He's still with Farid." It hurt so much to speak his name. Resa took her in her arms. But Roxane just stood there, staring at the dark gallery from which Meggie had come. Then she suddenly pushed Meggie aside, made her way past her, and disappeared into the darkness. Resa hurried after her, without letting go of Meggie's hand. Roxane was only a little way ahead of them. She trod on the hem of her dress, fell over, picked herself up again, and ran on. Faster and faster. But still she came too late.

Resa almost stumbled into Roxane, for she was standing rooted to the spot at the entrance of the gallery where Farid lay. Roxane's name burned on the wall in fiery letters, and the White Women were still there. They withdrew their pale hands from Dustfinger's breast as if they had torn out his heart. Perhaps Roxane was the last thing he saw. Perhaps he just had time to see Farid move before he himself collapsed without a sound, as the White Women vanished.

Yes, Farid was moving — like someone who has slept too long and too deeply. He sat up, his gaze blurred, with no idea who was suddenly lying there motionless behind him. Even when Roxane made her way past him he did not turn. He stared into space, as if there were pictures in front of him that no one else could see.

Hesitantly, as if he were a stranger, Meggie went to him. She didn't know what to feel. She didn't know what to think.

But Roxane stood beside Dustfinger, her hand pressed firmly to her mouth, as if she had to hold back her pain. Her name was still burning on the wall of the gallery as if it had stood there forever, but she took no notice of the letters of fire. Without a word she sank to her knees and took Dustfinger's head on her lap, as carefully as if she feared to break what was already broken, and she bent over him until her black hair surrounded his face like a veil.

Resa began to weep. But Farid still sat there as if numbed. Only when Meggie was right in front of him did he seem to notice her.

"Meggie?" he murmured, his tongue heavy.

It couldn't be true. He was really back.

Farid. Suddenly, his name did not taste of pain. He put his hand out to her and she took it, quickly, as if she had to hold on tight to prevent him from going away again, so far away. Was Dustfinger in that place now? How warm Farid's face felt again. Her fingers couldn't believe it. She kneeled beside him and put her arms around him, much too tight, felt his heart beating against her, beating strongly.

"Meggie!" He looked as relieved as if he had woken from a bad dream. There was even a smile stealing over his lips. But then Roxane, behind them, began sobbing very quietly, so quietly that you could hardly hear it through her curtain of hair — and Farid turned around.

For a moment he seemed unable to take in what he saw.

Then he tore himself away from Meggie, stood up, stumbled over the cloak as if his legs were still too weak for him to walk. He crawled over to Dustfinger's side on his knees and touched the still face with incredulous horror.

"What happened?" He was shouting at Roxane as if she were

the cause of all misfortune. "What have you done? What did you do to him?"

Meggie kneeled down beside him, trying to soothe him, but he wouldn't let her. He pushed her hands away and bent over Dustfinger again, putting his ear to his chest, listening — and sobbing as he pressed his face to the place where no heart beat anymore.

The Black Prince entered the gallery. Mo was with him, and more and more faces appeared behind them.

"Go away!" Farid shouted at them. "Go away, all of you! What have you done to him? Why isn't he breathing? There's no blood anywhere, no blood at all."

"No one did anything to him, Farid!" whispered Meggie. *You'd like him back, too, wouldn't you?* Meggie heard Dustfinger saying. She kept hearing the words in her head, over and over again. "It was the White Women. We saw them. He summoned them himself."

"You're lying!" Farid was almost shouting at her. "Why would he do a thing like that?"

But Roxane ran her finger over Dustfinger's scars, fine, pale lines, as fine as if a glass man's pen, and not a knife, had drawn them. "There's a story that the strolling players tell their children," she said, without looking at any of them. "About a fire-eater whose son the White Women took. In his despair he remembered something that was said about them: They fear fire, yet long for its warmth. So he decided to summon them by his art and ask them to give him back his son. It worked. He summoned them with fire, he made it dance and sing for them, and they did not deliver his son to death but gave him back his life. However, they took the fire-eater with them, and he never came back. The story says he must live with them forever, until the end of time, and make fire dance for them." Roxane picked up Dustfinger's lifeless hand and kissed the soot-blackened fingertips. "It's only a story," she went on. "But he loved to hear it. He always said it was so beautiful that there must be a grain of truth in it. Whether that's so or not — he's made it come true himself now, and he'll never return. In spite of his promise. Not this time."

Farid stared at her in horror. Watching his face, Meggie saw memory return: the memory of Basta's knife. He reached around to his back, and when he withdrew his hand his own blood was sticking to his fingers. His tunic was still damp with it.

"You were dead, Farid!" Meggie whispered. "And Dustfinger brought you back." She closed her eyes so as not to see that motionless figure anymore. She wanted to see other pictures: Dustfinger breathing fire for her in Elinor's garden, or guiding her and Mo through the hills away from Capricorn's dreadful village, and his happiness when she first saw him in his own world. He had both betrayed and rescued her — and now he had given her Farid back. Tears were running down her face, and she hardly noticed when her mother kneeled down beside her.

It was a long night.

Roxane and the Prince kept watch by Dustfinger's side, but Farid had climbed out of the mine to where the moon was showing through black clouds, and mist rose from the ground that was wet with rain. He had pushed aside the guards who tried to stop him and thrown himself down on the moss. He lay there now under Mortola's venomous trees, sobbing — while the two martens scuffled in the darkness as if they still had a master to quarrel over.

Of course Meggie went to him, but Farid sent her away, so she set off to find Mo. Resa was asleep beside him, her face wet with tears, but Mo was awake. He sat there with his arm around her sleeping mother and looked into the darkness as if a story was written there — a story that he didn't yet understand. For the first time, Meggie couldn't read in his face what he was thinking. There was something strange and closed in it, hard as the scab over a wound, but when he noticed her inquiring look he smiled at her, and all the strangeness was gone.

"Come here," he said softly, and she sat down beside him and pressed her face into his shoulder. "I want to go home, Mo!" she whispered.

"No, you don't," he whispered back, and she sobbed into his shirt, as she had done so often when she was a little girl. She had been able to unload all her grief onto him, however heavily it weighed. Mo had brushed it away simply by stroking her hair, putting his hand on her brow, and whispering her name, and that was what he did now in this sad place, on this sad night. He couldn't take away all the pain, there was too much of it, but he could help just by holding her close. No one could do it better. Not Resa. Not even Farid.

Yes, it was a long night, as long as a thousand nights, darker than any that Meggie had ever known. And she didn't know how long she had been sleeping beside Mo when Farid was suddenly shaking her awake. He led her off with him, away from her sleeping parents, into a dark corner that smelled of the Prince's bear.

"Meggie," he whispered, taking her hand between his and pressing it so hard that it hurt. "I know how we can make everything right again. You go to Fenoglio! Tell him to write something that will bring Dustfinger back to life! He'll listen to you!"

Of course. She might have known he would think up this idea. He was looking at her so pleadingly that it hurt, but she shook her head.

"No, Farid. Dustfinger is dead. Fenoglio can't do anything for him. And even if he could — haven't you heard what he keeps muttering to himself? He says he'll never write another word, not after what happened to Cosimo."

Fenoglio had indeed changed. Meggie had hardly recognized him when she saw him again. Once, his eyes had always reminded her of a little boy's. Now they were an old man's eyes. His gaze was suspicious, uncertain, as if he didn't trust the ground under his feet anymore, and since Cosimo's death he cared nothing for shaving himself, combing his hair, or washing. He had asked only about the book that Mo had bound. But not even Meggie's assurance that its blank pages did indeed ward off death had wiped the bitterness from his face. "Oh, wonderful!" he had muttered. "The Adderhead's immortal and Cosimo's dead as a doornail. Nothing goes right with this story anymore." And he had gone off again, far from all the others. No, Fenoglio wouldn't help anyone anymore, not even himself. All the same, when Farid set off in search of him, Meggie went, too.

Fenoglio was spending most of his time these days in one of the deepest galleries of the mine, a place almost entirely filled with rubble, to which no one else climbed down. He was asleep when they clambered down the steep ladder, the fur that the robbers had given him drawn up to his chin, his old forehead wrinkled as if he were thinking hard even in his dreams.

"Fenoglio!" Farid roughly shook him awake.

The old man turned over on his back with a grunt that would have done the Prince's bear credit. Then he opened his eyes and stared at Farid as if seeing his dark face for the very first time. "Oh, it's you!" he growled, dazed with sleep, and propped himself on his elbows. "The boy who came back from the dead.

Something else that I never wrote! What do you want? Do you know I was just having my first good dream for days?"

"You must write us something!"

"Write something? I'm never going to write again. Haven't we seen what comes of it? I have this fabulous idea about the book of immortality that will set the good characters free and bring the Adderhead to his death in the most subtle way. And what happens? The Adder is immortal now, and the forest is full of corpses again! Robbers, strolling players, the two-fingered man — dead! Why do I keep making them up if this story is only going to kill them? Oh, this thrice-accursed story! It's in love with Death!"

"But you must bring him back!" Farid's lips were trembling. "You made the Adderhead immortal, so why not him?"

"You're talking about Dustfinger, aren't you?" Fenoglio sat up and rubbed his face, sighing heavily. "Yes, he's dead now, too, dead as a doornail, but I'd planned that a long way back, as you perhaps remember. Be that as it may, Dustfinger is dead, you were dead . . . Minerva's husband, Cosimo, the boys who rode with him, they're all dead! Can't this story think of anything else? I'll tell you something, my boy. I'm not its author anymore. No, the author is Death, the Grim Reaper, the Cold Man, call him what you like. It's his dance, and never mind what I write he'll take my words and make them serve him!"

"Nonsense!" Farid was no longer even wiping away the tears that streamed down his face. "You must fetch him back. It wasn't his death at all, it was mine! Make him breathe again! It will only take a few words. After all, you did it for Cosimo and for Silvertongue."

"Just a moment — Meggie's father wasn't dead yet," Fenoglio soberly pointed out. "And as for Cosimo, he only looked like

Cosimo — how many more times do I have to explain that? Meggie and I made a brand-new Cosimo, and unfortunately it went terribly wrong. No!" He reached into his belt, produced something resembling a handkerchief, and blew his nose noisily. "This is not a story in which the dead come to life! All right, I admit I brought immortality into it, yes. But that's different from bringing back the dead. No, when someone is dead here, he stays dead! It's the same in this world as in the one I come from. Dustfinger got around that rule very cleverly on your behalf. Perhaps I wrote the sentimental story that gave him the idea myself . . . I really don't remember, but never mind, there are always gaps. And he paid for your life with his own. That's always been the only trade-off that Death will accept. Who'd have thought it? Dustfinger, of all people, gets so fond of a good-for-nothing boy that he ends up dying for him. I admit it's a much better idea than the one about the marten, but it isn't mine. Oh no! So if you're looking for someone to blame, then blame yourself. Because one thing is certain, my boy" — and so saying he jabbed his finger roughly into Farid's thin chest — "and it's that you don't belong in this story! And if you hadn't taken it into your head to wangle your way into it, Dustfinger would still be alive —"

Farid punched Fenoglio in the face before Meggie could pull him back.

"How can you say a thing like that?" she shouted at Fenoglio as Farid, sobbing, put his arms around her. "Farid saved Dustfinger at the mill. He's protected him ever since he arrived here —"

"Yes, yes, all right!" growled Fenoglio, feeling his nose. It hurt. "I'm a heartless old man, I know. But although you may not believe it, I felt dreadful when I saw Dustfinger lying there. And then Roxane's tears, appalling, really appalling. All the wounded men, Meggie, all the dead, so many dead . . . No, Meggie, the words don't obey me anymore. Except when it suits them. They've turned against me like snakes."

"Exactly. You're a failure, a miserable failure!" Farid shook Meggie off. "You don't know your own trade. But someone else does. The man who brought Dustfinger here. Orpheus. He"ll get him back, you wait and see. Write him here! You can at least do that! Yes, write Orpheus here at once or . . . or . . . I'll tell the Adderhead you were going to kill him, I'll tell all the women in Ombra it's your fault their menfolk are dead . . . I'll . . . I'll . . ."

He stood there with his fists clenched, quivering with rage and despair. But the old man just looked at him. Then, with difficulty, he rose to his feet. "Do you know something, my boy?" he said, putting his face very close to Farid's. "If you'd asked me nicely I might have tried, but not this way. No, no! Fenoglio must be asked, not threatened. I still have that much pride left."

At this Farid looked like going for him again, but Meggie held him back. "Fenoglio, stop it!" she shouted at the old man. "He's desperate, can't you see that?"

"Desperate? So what? I'm desperate, too!" Fenoglio snapped at her. "My story is foundering in misfortune, and these hands here," he said, holding them out to her, "don't want to write anymore! I'm afraid of words, Meggie! Once they were like honey, now they're poison, pure poison! But what is a writer who doesn't love words anymore? What have I come to? This story is devouring me, crushing me, and I'm its creator!"

"Fetch Orpheus!" said Farid hoarsely. Meggie could hear how much trouble he was taking to control his voice, to banish the rage from it. "Bring him here, and let him write it for you! Teach him what you know, the way Dustfinger taught me everything! Let him find the right words for you. He loves your story, he told Dustfinger so himself! He even wrote you a letter when he was a boy."

"Did he?" For a moment Fenoglio sounded almost like his old inquisitive self.

"Yes, he admires you! He thinks this is the best of all stories, he said so!"

"Really?" Fenoglio sounded flattered. "Well, it isn't bad. That is to say, it *wasn't* bad." He looked thoughtfully at Farid. "A pupil. A pupil for Fenoglio," he murmured. "A writer's apprentice. Hmm. Orpheus . . ." He spoke the name as if he had to taste it. "The only poet who ever challenged Death . . . appropriate."

Farid was looking at him so hopefully that it went to Meggie's heart again. But Fenoglio smiled, even though it was a sad smile.

"Look at him, Meggie!" he said. "He has the same pleading look as my grandchildren could turn on to wheedle anything out of me. Does he look at you the same way when he wants something from you?"

Meggie felt herself blushing. However, Fenoglio turned back to Farid. "You know we'll need Meggie's help, don't you?"

Farid nodded, and looked at her.

"I'll read it," she said quietly. "If Fenoglio writes it, I'll read it." *And get the man who helped Mortola to bring my father here and almost kill him into this story,* Meggie added in her thoughts. She tried not to think of what Mo would say about the deal.

However, Fenoglio already seemed to be searching for words in his mind. The right words — words that would not betray and deceive him. "Very well," he muttered abstractedly, "let's get down to work one last time. But where am I going to find paper and ink? Not to mention a pen and a helpful glass man? Poor Rosenquartz is still in Ombra."

"I have paper," said Meggie, "and a pencil."

"That's very beautiful," said Fenoglio when she put her notebook in his lap. "Did your father bind it?"

Meggie nodded.

"There are some pages torn out."

"Yes, for a message I gave my mother and the letter I sent you. The one that Cloud-Dancer brought you."

"Oh. Oh yes. Him." For a moment Fenoglio looked dreadfully tired. "Books with blank pages," he murmured. "They seem to be playing more and more of a part in this story, don't you think?" Then he asked Meggie to leave him alone with Farid so that the boy could tell him about Orpheus. "To be honest," he whispered to Meggie, "I think he vastly overestimates the man's abilities! What has this fellow Orpheus done? Put my own words together in a different order, that's all. But I'll admit I'm curious to meet him. It takes a fair amount of megalomania to give yourself a name like that, and megalomania is an interesting character trait."

Meggie did not share his opinion, but it was too late to go back on her promise. She would read again. For Farid this time. She went quietly back to her parents, laid her head on Mo's chest, and fell asleep hearing his heartbeat in her ear. Words had saved him, why shouldn't they do the same for Dustfinger? Even if he had gone far, far away . . . didn't the words of this world rule even the land of silence?

73

THE BLUEJAY

The world existed to be read. And I read it.
L. S. Schwartz, Ruined by Reading

Resa and Meggie were asleep when Mo woke, but he felt as if he couldn't breathe among all the stones and the dead a moment longer. The men guarding the entrance of the mine greeted him with a nod as he came climbing up to them. Pale morning light was seeping through the crevice that led to the outside world; the air smelled of rosemary, thyme, and the berries on Mortola's poisonous trees. Mo's senses were constantly confused by the way the familiar mingled with the strange in Fenoglio's world — and by the fact that the strange features often struck him as more real than the others.

The guards were not the only men Mo met at the entrance to the mine. Five more were leaning against the walls of the gallery, among them Snapper and the Black Prince himself.

"Ah, here comes the most wanted robber between Ombra and the sea!" said Snapper, low-voiced, as Mo came toward them. They examined him like some new kind of animal, of which they had heard the strangest stories. And Mo felt more than ever like an actor who had stepped onstage with the unpleasant feeling that he knew neither the play nor his part in it.

"I don't know how the rest of you feel," said Snapper, glancing around at the others, "but I always thought some writer had made up the Bluejay. And that the only man who might lay claim to that feathered mask was our own Black Prince, even if he doesn't entirely match the description in the songs. So when folk said the Bluejay was a prisoner in the Castle of Night, I thought they just wanted to hang some other poor fellow because he happened to have a scar on his arm. But then," he said, looking Mo up and down as extensively as if assessing him by every line of every song he had ever heard about the Bluejay, "then I saw you fight in the forest . . . *'and his sword-blade flashes through them like a needle through the pages,'* isn't that what one of the songs says? A good description, indeed!"

Oh yes, Snapper? thought Mo. *Suppose I were to tell you that the Bluejay was really made up by a writer just like you?*

How furtively they were all looking at him.

"We must get away from here," said the Prince into the silence. "They're combing the forest all the way down to the sea. They've already found two of our hiding places and smoked them out — they haven't yet come upon the mine, but only because they don't expect us to be so close to their own back door." The bear grunted, as if amused by the stupidity of the men-at-arms. The gray muzzle in the furry black face, the clever little amber eyes — Mo had liked the bear even in the book, although he had imagined him slightly larger. "Tonight half of us will take the injured to the Badger's Earth," the Black Prince continued, "and the others will go to Ombra with me and Roxane."

"And where does *he* go?" Snapper was looking at Mo. Then

they all looked at him. Mo felt as if their eyes were fingering his skin. Eyes full of hope, but what for? What had they heard about him? Were people already telling stories about what had happened at the Castle of Night, about the book full of blank pages and Firefox's death?

"He has to get away from here, what else do you think? A long way away!" The Prince picked a dead leaf out of the bear's coat. "The Adderhead will be looking for him, even though he's spreading word everywhere that Mortola was responsible for the attack in the forest." He nodded to a thin boy, at least a head shorter than Meggie, who was standing among the men. "Tell us again what the crier announced in your village."

"*This,*" began the boy in a hesitant voice, "*this is the Adderhead's promise: If the Bluejay ever ventures to show his face in Argenta again, he will die the slowest death that the executioners of the Castle of Night have ever given anyone. And the man who brings him in will be rewarded with the Bluejay's weight in silver.*"

"Better start starving yourself, then, Bluejay," mocked Snapper, but none of the others laughed.

"Did you really make him immortal?" It was the boy who asked this question.

Snapper laughed out loud. "Listen to the lad! I expect you think the Prince can fly, too, eh?"

But the boy took no notice of him. He was still looking at Mo. "They say you yourself can't die," he said in a low voice. "They say you made yourself a book like that, too, a book of white pages with your death held captive in it."

Mo had to smile. Meggie had so often looked at him wide-eyed, just like that. *Is it a true story, Mo? Come on, tell me!* They were all waiting for his answer, even the Black Prince. He saw it in their faces.

"Oh, I can die all right," he said. "Believe me, I have come very close. As for the Adderhead, however — yes, I have made him immortal. But not for long."

"What do you mean by that?" The smile had long since frozen on Snapper's coarse-featured face.

Mo was looking not at him but at the Black Prince when he answered. "I mean that at present nothing can kill the Adderhead. No sword, no knife, no disease. The book I have bound for him protects him. But the same book will be his undoing, for he will have only a few weeks to enjoy it."

"Why's that?" It was the boy again.

Mo lowered his voice when he replied, just as he did when he was sharing a secret with Meggie. "Oh, it's not particularly difficult to ensure that a book doesn't live long, you know. Particularly not for a bookbinder. And that's my trade, although so many people seem to think differently. Normally, it's not my job to kill a book — on the contrary, I'm usually called in to save the lives of books — but in this case I'm afraid I had to do it. After all, I didn't want to be guilty of letting the Adderhead sit on his throne for all eternity, passing the time by hanging strolling players."

"Then you *are* a wizard!" Snapper's voice was hoarse.

"No, really, I'm not," replied Mo. "Let me say it once again: I'm a bookbinder."

They were staring at him again, and this time Mo wasn't sure whether there might not be some fear mingled with the respect in their eyes.

"Off you all go now!" The Prince's voice broke the silence. "Go and make litters for the injured." They obeyed, although every one of them cast a last glance at Mo before they walked away. Only the boy gave him a bashful smile, too.

As for the Black Prince, he signaled to Mo to go with him.

"A few weeks," he repeated when they were in the gallery

where he and the bear slept, away from the others. "How many exactly?"

How many? Even Mo couldn't tell for sure. If they didn't notice what he had done for the time being, it would all be quite quick. "Not very many," he replied.

"And they won't be able to save the book?"

"No."

The Prince smiled. It was the first smile Mo had seen on his dark face. "That's consoling news, Bluejay. It saps one's courage to fight an immortal enemy. But you do know, don't you, that he'll only hunt you down all the more pitilessly when he realizes that you've tricked him?"

So he would, indeed. That was why Mo hadn't told Meggie, had done what had to be done in secret, while she was asleep. He hadn't wanted the Adderhead to see the fear in her face.

"I don't intend to come back to this side of the forest," he told the Prince. "Perhaps there'll be a good hiding place for us some-where near Ombra."

The Prince smiled again. "I'm sure there will be," he said and looked at Mo as intently as if he meant to see straight into his heart. *Go on, try it,* thought Mo. *Look into my heart and tell me what you find there, because I don't know myself anymore.* He remembered reading about the Black Prince for the first time. *What a fabulous character,* he had thought, but the man now standing before him was considerably more impressive than the image of him that the words had conjured up. Perhaps a little smaller, though. And a little sadder.

"Your wife says you're not the man we take you for," said the Prince. "Dustfinger said the same. He told me that you come from the country where he spent all those years when we thought he was dead. Is it very different from here?"

Mo couldn't help smiling. "Oh yes. I think so."

"How? Are people happier there?"

"Perhaps."

"Perhaps! Hmm." The Prince bent and picked up something lying on the blanket under which he'd slept. "I've forgotten what your wife calls you. Dustfinger had a strange name for you: Silvertongue. But Dustfinger is dead, and to everyone else you will be the Bluejay now. Even I find it difficult to call you anything else, after seeing you fight in the forest. So this belongs to you here in the future. Unless you decide to go back after all . . . back to the country where you came from, and where I suppose you have another name."

Mo had never before seen the mask that the Prince was holding out to him. The leather was dark and damaged here and there, but the feathers shone brightly: white, black, yellowish-brown, blue. The colors of a blue jay.

"This mask has been celebrated in many songs," said the Black Prince. "I allowed myself to wear it for a while, and several of us have done so, too, but now it is yours."

In silence, Mo turned the mask this way and that in his hands. For a strange moment he felt an urge to put it on, as if he had done so many times before. Oh yes, Fenoglio's words were powerful, but words they were, nothing but words — even if they had been written for him. Any actor, surely, could choose the part he played?

"No," he said, handing the mask back to the Prince. "Snapper is right; the Bluejay is a fantasy, an old man's invention. Fighting, I assure you, is not my trade."

The Prince looked at him thoughtfully, but he did not take the mask. "Keep it all the same," he said. "It's too dangerous for anyone to wear it now. And as for your trade — none of us here was born a robber."

Mo said nothing to that. He just looked at his fingers. It had taken him a long time to wash off all the blood on them after the fight in the forest.

He was still standing there holding the mask, alone in the dark gallery that smelled of the long-forgotten dead, when he heard Meggie's voice behind him.

"Mo?" She looked at his face with concern. "Where have you been? Roxane is setting out soon, and Resa wants to know if we're going with her. What do you say?"

Yes, what did he say? Where did he want to go? *Back to my workshop,* he thought. *Back to Elinor's house.* Or did he?

What did Meggie want? He had only to look at her to know the answer. Of course. She wanted to stay because of the boy, but he was not the only reason. Resa wanted to stay, too, in spite of the dungeon where they had put her, in spite of all the pain and darkness. What was it about Fenoglio's world that filled the heart with longing? Didn't he feel it himself? Like sweet poison that worked on you only too quickly. . . .

"What do you say, Mo?" Meggie took his hand. How tall she had grown. And how pleadingly she looked at him!

"What do I say?" He listened as though, if he concentrated hard, he could hear the words whispering in the walls of the gallery or in the weave of the blanket under which the Black Prince slept. But all he heard was his own voice. "How would you like it if I said: Show me the fairies, Meggie? And the water-nymphs. And that illuminator in Ombra castle. Let's find out how fine those brushes really are."

Dangerous words. But Meggie hugged him harder than she had since she was a little girl.

74

FARID'S HOPE

And now he was dead, his soul fled down to the Sunless Country and his body lying cold in the cold mud, somewhere in the city's wake.

Philip Reeve, *Mortal Engines*

When the men on guard raised the alarm for the second time, just before sunset, the Black Prince ordered everyone to climb deep down into the mine, where there was water in the narrow passages and you thought you could hear the earth breathing. But one man did not join them: Fenoglio. When the Prince gave the all clear, and Meggie climbed up again with the others, her feet wet and her heart still full of fear, Fenoglio came toward her and drew her aside. Luckily, Mo happened to be talking to Resa and didn't notice.

"Here you are. But I'm not guaranteeing anything," Fenoglio whispered to her as he gave her back the notebook. "This is very likely another mistake in black and white just like the others, but I'm too tired to worry about it. Feed this damned story, feed it with new words, I'm not going to listen. I'm going to lie down and sleep. That was the last thing I will ever write in my life."

Feed it.

Farid suggested that Meggie should read Fenoglio's words in the place where he and Dustfinger had slept. Dustfinger's backpack was still lying beside his blanket, and the two martens had curled up to the right and left of it. Farid crouched down between them and hugged the backpack to him as if Dustfinger's heart were beating inside. He looked expectantly at Meggie, but she remained silent. She looked at the words and said nothing. Fenoglio's writing swam before her eyes as if, for the first time, it did not want her to read it.

"Meggie?" Farid was still looking at her. There was such sadness in his eyes, such despair. *For him,* she thought. *Just for him.* And she kneeled down on the blanket where Dustfinger used to sleep.

Even as she read the first few words, she sensed that Fenoglio had done his work well yet again. She felt it like breath on her face. The letters on the page were alive, the story was alive. It wanted to take those words and grow. That was what it wanted. Had Fenoglio felt the same when he wrote them?

"One day, when Death had taken much prey again," began Meggie, and it was almost as if she were reading a familiar book that she had only just laid aside, *"Fenoglio the great poet decided to write no more. He was tired of words and their seductive power. He had had enough of the way they cheated and scorned him and kept silent when they should have spoken. So he called on another, younger man, Orpheus by name — skilled in letters, even if he could not yet handle them with the mastery of Fenoglio himself — and decided to instruct him in his art, as every master does at some time. For a while Orpheus should play with words in his place, seduce and*

*lie with them, create and destroy, banish and restore — while
Fenoglio waited for his weariness to pass, for his pleasure in words
to reawaken, and then he would send Orpheus back to the world
from which he had summoned him, to keep his story alive with new
words never used before."*

Meggie's voice died away. It echoed underground as if it had
a shadow. And just as silence was spreading around them, they
heard footsteps.

Footsteps on the damp stone.

ALONE AGAIN

"Hope" is the thing with feathers.

Emily Dickinson,
The Poems of Emily Dickinson

Orpheus disappeared right in front of Elinor's eyes. She was standing only a few steps from him, holding the bottle of wine he had demanded, when he simply vanished into thin air — into less than thin air, into nothing — as if he had never been there at all, as if she had only dreamed him. The bottle slipped from her hand, fell on the wooden floorboards of the library, and broke among the books that Orpheus had left open there.

The dog began to howl so horribly that Darius came racing out of the kitchen. The wardrobe-man didn't bar his way. He was simply staring at the place where Orpheus had been standing a moment ago. His voice trembling, he had been reading from a sheet of paper lying on one of Elinor's glass display cases right in front of him and clutching *Inkheart* to his breast, as if he could force the book to accept him at last in that way. Elinor had stopped as if turned to stone when she realized what he was trying to do for the hundredth, even the thousandth time. *Perhaps they'll come back out of the book to replace him,* she had thought, *or at least one of them: Meggie, Resa, Mortimer.* Each of the three names tasted so bitter on her tongue, as bitter as all that is lost. But now Orpheus had gone, and none of the three had come back. Only the damned dog refused to stop howling.

"He's done it," whispered Elinor. "Darius, he's done it! He's over there . . . they're all over there. All except for us!"

For a moment she felt infinitely sorry for herself. Here she was, Elinor Loredan, among all her books, and they wouldn't let her in, not one of them would let her in. Closed doors enticing her, filling her heart with longing, and then letting her go no farther than the doorway. Accursed, blasted, heartless things! Full of empty promises, full of false lures, always making you hungry, never satisfying you, never!

But you once saw it quite differently, Elinor! she reminded herself, wiping the tears from her eyes. So what? Wasn't she old enough to change her mind, to bury an old love that had betrayed her miserably? They had not let her in. All the others were between their pages now, but she wasn't. Poor Elinor, poor, lonely Elinor! She sobbed so loudly that she had to put her hand over her mouth.

Darius cast her a sympathetic glance and hesitantly came to her side. Well, at least he was still with her, that was one good thing. And of course he could read her thoughts in her face, as always. But he couldn't help her, either.

I want to be with them, she thought despairingly. *They're my family: Resa and Meggie and Mortimer. I want to see the Wayless Wood and feel a fairy settle on my hand again, I want to meet the Black Prince even if it means smelling his bear, I want to hear Dustfinger talking to fire even if I still can't stand the man! I want, I want, I want . . .*

"Oh, Darius!" sobbed Elinor. "Why didn't the wretched fellow take me, too?" But Darius just looked at her with his wise, owl-like eyes.

"Hey, where did he go? That bastard still owed me money!" Sugar went to the place where Orpheus had disappeared and looked all around him, as if Orpheus might be stuck among the bookshelves somewhere. "Damn it, what does he think he's doing, just vanishing like that?" He bent down and picked up a sheet of paper.

The sheet of paper that Orpheus had been reading from! Had he taken the book with him but left behind the words that had opened the door for him? If so, then all was not lost after all. . . . With determination, Elinor snatched the sheet of paper from Sugar's hand. "Give me that!" she demanded, clutching it to her breast just as Orpheus had clutched the book. The wardrobe-man's face darkened.

Two very different feelings seemed to be struggling with each other on his face: anger at Elinor's boldness, and fear of the written words that she was pressing to her breast so passionately. For a moment Elinor wasn't sure which would get the upper hand. Darius came up behind her, as if he seriously intended to defend her if necessary, but luckily Sugar's face cleared again, and he began to laugh.

"Well, fancy that!" he mocked her. "What do you want that scrap of paper for? Do you want to disappear into thin air, too, like Orpheus and the Magpie and your two friends? Feel free, but first I want the wages Orpheus and the old woman still owe me!" And he looked around Elinor's library as if he might see something in it that would do instead of payment.

"Your wages, yes, of course, I understand!" said Elinor quickly, leading him to the door. "I still have some money hidden in my room. Darius, you know where it is. Give it to him, all that's left, just so long as he goes away."

Darius did not look very enthusiastic, but Sugar gave such a broad smile that you could see every one of his bad teeth. "Well, that sounds like sense at last!" he grunted and stomped after Darius who, resigned to this development, led him to Elinor's room.

But Elinor stayed behind in the library.

How quiet it suddenly was there. Orpheus had indeed sent all the characters he had read out of their books back into them again. Only his dog was still there, tail drooping as it sniffed the spot where its master had been standing only a few minutes before.

"So empty!" Elinor murmured. "So empty." She felt desolate. Almost more so than on the day when the Magpie had taken Mortimer and Resa away. The book into which they had all disappeared was gone. What happened to a book that disappeared into its own story?

Oh, forget the book, Elinor! she thought as a tear ran down her nose. *How are you ever going to find them again now?*

Orpheus's words. They swam before her eyes as she looked at the paper. Yes, they must have taken him over there, what else? Carefully, she opened the glass case on which the paper had been lying before Orpheus disappeared, took out the book inside it — a wonderfully illustrated edition of Hans Christian Andersen's fairy tales signed by the author himself — and put the sheet of paper in its place.

A NEW POET

The joy of writing
The power of preserving,
Revenge of a mortal hand.
> Wislawa Szymborska, "The Joy of Writing,"
> *View with a Grain of Sand*

At first Orpheus could hardly be seen in the shadows filling the gallery like black breath. He stepped hesitantly into the light of the oil lamp by whose light Meggie had been reading. She thought she saw him put something under his jacket, but she couldn't make out what it was. Perhaps a book.

"Orpheus!" Farid ran to him, still holding Dustfinger's backpack in his arms.

So he was really here. Orpheus. Meggie had imagined him very differently . . . as much more impressive. This was just a man who was rather too stout, still very young, in an ill-fitting suit, and he looked as out of place in the Inkworld as a polar bear or a whale. In addition, he seemed to have lost his tongue. He stood there in a daze, looking at Meggie, at the dark gallery down which he had come, and finally at Farid, who had obviously entirely forgotten that the man he now greeted with such a radiant smile had stolen from him and betrayed him to Basta at their last meeting. Orpheus didn't even seem to recognize Farid, but when he finally did it brought back his voice.

"Dustfinger's boy! How did you get here?" he faltered. And yes, Meggie had to admit that his voice was impressive, much more impressive than his face. "Well, never mind that. This must be the Inkworld!" he went on, taking no more notice of Farid. "I knew I could do it! I knew I could!" A self-satisfied smile spread over his face. Gwin leaped up, hissing, as he almost trod on his tail, but Orpheus didn't even notice the marten. "Fantastic!" he murmured as he ran the palm of his hand over the gallery walls. "I suppose this is one of the passages that lead to the princely tombs under the castle of Ombra."

"No, it's not," said Meggie coldly. Orpheus — in league with Mortola — a magic-tongued deceiver. How empty his round face looked! *No wonder,* she thought with great dislike, as she rose from the place where Dustfinger had slept. He has no conscience, no sympathy, no heart. Why had she brought him here? As if there weren't enough of his sort in the Inkworld. *I did it for Farid,* replied her heart, *for Farid. . . .*

"How are Elinor and Darius? If you've done anything to them . . ." Meggie didn't finish her sentence. If he had, then what?

Orpheus turned, with as much surprise as if he hadn't seen her at all before. "Elinor and Darius? Oh, are you that girl who apparently read herself here?" His eyes became watchful. Obviously, he remembered what he had done to her parents.

"My father almost died because of you!" Meggie was angry with herself for the way her voice shook.

Orpheus blushed childishly red, whether in annoyance or

embarrassment Meggie couldn't have said, but whichever it was he quickly recovered. "Well, how can I help it if Mortola had a score to settle with him?" he replied. "And from what you say I take it that he's still alive, so there's nothing to get upset about, is there?" Shrugging, he turned his back to Meggie. "Strange!" he murmured, glancing at the rubble at the end of the gallery, the narrow ladders and the props supporting the roof. "Will someone explain exactly where I am? This looks almost like a mine, but I didn't read anything about a mine. . . ."

"Never mind what you read. I'm the one who brought you here."

Meggie's voice was so sharp that Farid cast her a glance of alarm.

"You?" Orpheus turned and examined her so condescendingly that the blood rushed to Meggie's face. "You obviously don't know who you're talking to. But why am I bothering with you, anyway? I'm tired of looking at this unattractive mine. Where are the fairies? The men-at-arms? The strolling players?" He roughly pushed Meggie aside and went to the ladder, but Farid barred his way.

"You stay where you are, Cheeseface!" he snapped. "Do you want to know why you're here? Because of Dustfinger."

"Oh yes?" There was derision in Orpheus's laughter. "Haven't you found him yet? Well, perhaps he doesn't want to be found, or not by a persistent fellow like you. . . ."

"He's dead," Farid interrupted brusquely. "Dustfinger is dead, and the only reason why Meggie read you here is for you to write him back!"

"She — did — not — read — me — here! How many more times do I have to tell you?" Orpheus made for the ladder again, but Farid simply took his hand without a word and led him over to the place where Dustfinger was.

Roxane had hung his cloak in front of the gallery where he was still lying, motionless, as if the earth had crushed him. She and Resa had placed burning candles around him — dancing fire instead of the flowers usually laid beside corpses.

"Good heavens!" exclaimed Orpheus when he saw him lying there. "Dead! He really is dead! But this is terrible!"

Meggie was amazed to see that there were tears in his eyes. His fingers shook as he took his misted-up glasses off his nose and polished them on his jacket. Then, hesitantly, he went up to Dustfinger, bent, and touched his hand.

"Cold!" he whispered and retreated. His eyes blurred with tears, he looked at Farid. "Was it Basta? Come on, tell me! No, wait, how did it go? Was Basta even there? '*Some of Capricorn's men,*' yes, that was it, they were going to kill the marten and Dustfinger tried to save him! I wept my eyes out when I read that chapter, I threw the book at the wall! And now I get here at last and —" He was struggling for breath. "I only sent him back because I thought he'd be safe here now! Oh God. Oh God, oh God, oh God! Dead!" Orpheus sobbed — and then fell silent. He bent over Dustfinger's body again. "Wait a moment. *Stabbed. Stabbed,* that's what it says in the book. So where's the wound? '*Stabbed for the marten's sake,*' yes, that's what it said." He turned abruptly and stared at Gwin, who was perched on Farid's shoulders, hissing at him. "He left the marten behind. He left him and you both behind. So how is it possible that —"

Farid said nothing, as the marten affectionately licked his ear. Meggie felt so sorry for him, but when she put out her hand he drew back.

"What's that marten doing here? Tell me! Have you lost your tongue?" There was a metallic edge to Orpheus's beautiful voice.

"He didn't die for Gwin," whispered Farid.

"No? Who did he die for, then?"

"For me."

This time Farid did not withdraw his hand when Meggie took it. But before he could tell Orpheus any more, they heard another voice behind them. Abrupt and angry.

"Who's this? What is a stranger doing here?"

Orpheus spun around as if caught in some guilty act. There stood Roxane, with Resa beside her. Orpheus stared at her in amazement. "Roxane!" he whispered. "The beautiful minstrel woman! May I introduce myself? My name is Orpheus. I was a — a friend of Dustfinger's. Yes, I think one could say that."

"Meggie!" said Resa in a faltering voice. "How did he get here?"

Meggie instinctively hid the notebook containing Fenoglio's words behind her back.

"So how is Elinor?" Resa asked Orpheus sharply. "And Darius? What have you done to them?"

"Nothing!" replied Orpheus. In his confusion he obviously didn't notice that the woman who had been able to speak only with her fingers had a voice again. "Far from it. I went to a lot of trouble to help them feel more relaxed about books. They keep them like butterflies pinned in a case, each in its own place, imprisoned in their cells! But books want to breathe and sing, they want to feel air between their pages and a reader's fingers tenderly stroking them —"

Roxane took Dustfinger's cloak from the prop over which she had draped it. "You don't look like a friend of Dustfinger's to me," she interrupted Orpheus. "But if you want to say good-bye to him, do it now, because I'm going to take him with me."

"Take him with you? What do you mean?" Farid barred her way. "Orpheus is here to bring him back!"

"Get out of my sight!" Roxane snapped at him. "The very first time I saw you coming to my farm, I knew you brought bad luck. *You* ought to be dead, not Dustfinger. That's how it is and that's how it stays."

Farid flinched as if Roxane had struck him. He did not resist as she pushed him aside, and stood there with his shoulders drooping as she bent over Dustfinger.

Meggie couldn't think of any way to comfort him, but her mother kneeled down beside Roxane. "Listen!" she said quietly. "Dustfinger brought Farid back from the dead by making the words of a story come true. Words, Roxane! In this world they make strange things happen, and Orpheus knows a lot about words."

"Oh yes, I do!" Orpheus quickly went to Roxane's side. "I made him a door of words so that he could come back to you. Did he never tell you?"

Roxane looked at him disbelievingly, but the magic of his voice worked on her, too. "Yes, believe me, I did it!" Orpheus went on. "And I'll write something to bring him back from the dead. I'll find words as precious and intoxicating as the scent of a lily, words to beguile Death and open the cold fingers he has closed around Dustfinger's warm heart!" A delighted smile lit up his face, as if he were already relishing his great achievements to come.

But Roxane just shook her head, as if to free herself from the magic of his voice, and blew out the candles standing around Dustfinger. "Now I understand," she said, covering Dustfinger with his cloak. "You're an enchanter. I only went to an enchanter once. After our younger daughter died. People who go to enchanters are desperate, and they know it. They live on false hopes like ravens preying on carrion. His promises sounded just as wonderful as yours. He promised me what I most desperately wanted. They all do. They promise to bring back what's lost forever: a child, a friend — or a husband." She drew the cloak over Dustfinger's still face. "I'll never believe such promises again. They only make the pain worse. I'll take him back to Ombra with me and find a place there where no one will disturb him, not the Adderhead, not the wolves, not even the fairies. And he will still look as if he were only sleeping long after my hair is white, for I know from Nettle how you go about preserving the body even when the soul is long gone."

"You'll tell me where that is, won't you?" Farid's voice trembled, as if he knew Roxane's answer already. "You'll tell me where you're taking him?"

"No," said Roxane. "You least of all."

WHERE NOW?

The Giant rested back in his chair. "You've some stories left,"
he said. "I can smell them on your skin."
Brian Patten, *The Story Giant*

Farid watched as they laid the injured on litters under cover of
night. The injured and the dead. Six robbers were standing
among the trees listening for any sound that might mean danger.
Only the tops of the silver towers were to be seen in the distance,
bright in the starlight, yet it seemed to them all as if the
Adderhead could see them. Could he sense it up in his castle
when they stole soft-footed over Mount Adder? Who could tell
what the Adderhead might be able to do now? Now that he was
immortal and as invincible as Death itself?

But the night was still, as still as Dustfinger, who was to be
taken back to Ombra on a cart drawn by the Black Prince's bear.
Meggie was going there, too, for the time being, to the other side of
the forest, with Silvertongue and her mother. The Black Prince had
told them of a village too poor and remote from any road to interest
princes. He would hide them there, or on one of the nearby farms.

Should he go with them?

Farid saw Meggie looking at him. She was standing with her mother and the other women. Silvertongue was with the robbers, and hanging from his belt was the sword with which he had apparently killed Basta — and not just Basta. Almost a dozen men had died at his hands, so several of the robbers had told Farid, their voices lowered in respect. Amazing. Back in the hills around Capricorn's village, Silvertongue couldn't have killed a blackbird when they were in hiding together, let alone a human being. On the other hand, how had he himself learned to kill? The answer was not hard to find. Fear and rage. And there was enough of those in this story.

Roxane was with the robbers, too. She turned her back on Farid when she noticed him looking at her. She treated him like air — as if he had never returned to the land of the living, as if he were only a ghost, an ill-intentioned ghost who had devoured her husband's heart. "What was it like being dead, Farid?" Meggie had asked him. But he couldn't remember. Or perhaps he didn't want to remember.

Orpheus was standing barely two paces away from him, shivering in the thin shirt he wore. The Prince had told him he must change his light-colored suit for a dark cloak and woolen trousers. But in spite of the clothes he still looked like a cuckoo among sparrows. Fenoglio was watching Orpheus like an old tomcat keeping a wary eye on a young one who has invaded his territory. "He looks a fool!" Fenoglio had whispered this comment to Meggie just loud enough for everyone to hear it. "Look at him. A callow youth, knows nothing about life, how is he going to be able to write? It might well be best to send him straight back, but never mind. There's no saving this wretched story now, anyway."

He was probably right. But why hadn't he at least *tried* to write Dustfinger back? Didn't he care anything for the characters he had created? Was he just moving them like pawns in a game of chess, enjoying their pain?

Farid clenched his fists in helpless anger. *I would have tried,* he thought. *A hundred times, a thousand times, for the rest of my life.* But he couldn't even read those strange little signs! The few that Dustfinger had taught him would never be enough to bring him back from where he was now. Even if he wrote his name in letters of fire on the walls of the Castle of Night, Dustfinger's face would remain as terribly still as when he last saw it.

No, only Orpheus could try it. But he hadn't written a single word since Meggie read him here. He just stood there — or paced up and down, up and down, while the robbers watched him suspiciously. The glances Silvertongue cast him were not very friendly, either. He had turned pale when he saw Orpheus again. For a moment Farid had thought he would seize Cheeseface and beat him to a pulp, but Meggie had taken his hand and drawn him away. Whatever the two of them had said to each other, she wasn't telling Farid. She had known that her father would not approve if she read Orpheus here, but she had done it all the same. For him. Was Orpheus interested in any of that? Oh no. He was still acting as if his own voice, not Meggie's, had brought him here. Stuck-up, thrice-accursed son of a bitch!

"Farid? Have you made up your mind?" Farid came out of his gloomy thoughts. Meggie was standing in front of him. "You will come with us, won't you? Resa says you can stay with us as long as you like, and Mo doesn't mind, either."

Silvertongue was still standing with the robbers, talking to the Black Prince. Farid saw Orpheus watching the two of them . . . then he began pacing up and down once more, rubbed his forehead, smoothed back his hair, muttered as if talking to himself. *Like a lunatic,* thought Farid. *I've pinned my hopes on a lunatic!*

"Wait here." He turned away from Meggie and went over to Orpheus. "I'm going with Meggie," he said brusquely. "You can go wherever you like."

Cheeseface straightened his glasses. "What are you talking about? Of course I'm coming with you! After all, I want to see everything — the Wayless Wood, the Laughing Prince's castle." He looked up at the hill. "And of course I'd have liked to see the Castle of Night, too, but after what's happened here, I suppose it isn't a good time. Well, this is only my first day here. . . . Have you seen the Adderhead yourself? Is he very terrifying? I'd like to see those silver scales on the columns. . . ."

"You're not here to go sightseeing!" Farid's voice was choked with anger. What on earth was Cheeseface thinking of? How could he stand there looking around him as if he were on a pleasure trip, while Dustfinger would soon be lying in some dark crypt or wherever Roxane planned to take him?

"Oh no?" Orpheus's round face darkened. "Is that any way to talk to me? I'll do as I like. Do you think I've finally arrived where I always wanted to be just to have a snotty boy, who has no business here, anyway, order me around? You think words can simply be plucked from the empty air? This is all about Death, you stupid boy! It could take months for me to get the right idea. Who knows? You don't call up ideas just like that, not even with fire, and we need a brilliant, a divine idea. Which means" — Orpheus inspected his fingernails — "that I shall need a servant! Or do you want me to waste my time washing my own clothes and finding myself something to eat?"

The dog. The accursed dog. "Very well. I'll be your servant, too." Farid brought the words out only with difficulty. "If you will bring him back."

"Excellent!" Orpheus smiled. "Then, for a start, get me some food. It looks as if we're going to be embarking on a long and uncomfortable march."

Farid gritted his teeth, but of course he obeyed. He would have scraped the silver from the towers of the Castle of Night to get Dustfinger breathing again.

"Farid? What is it? Are you coming with us?" Meggie stepped into his path as he ran past her, with bread and dried meat for Cheeseface in his pockets.

"Yes — yes, we're coming with you!" He flung his arms around her neck, but only once he saw that Silvertongue's back was turned to him. You never knew with fathers. "I'll save him, Meggie!" he whispered in her ear. "I'll bring Dustfinger back. This story will have a happy ending. I swear!"

ACKNOWLEDGMENTS

*The author and publisher would like to thank the following for
the permission to use copyrighted material:*

DAVID ALMOND: from *Skellig* (Hodder Children's Books, 1998), reprinted by permission of Hodder & Stoughton Ltd.

YEHUDA AMICHAI: from "The Mother," translated by Azila, from *Isibongo* 2, No. 1 (January 1997), reprinted by permission of the translator.

MARGARET ATWOOD: from "Orpheus 2," from *Poems 1976–86* (Virago Press, 1992), in *Eating Fire: Selected Poetry, 1965–95* (Virago Press, 1998), © 1987 by Margaret Atwood, reprinted by permission of Time Warner Book Group UK, Oxford University Press Canada, and Houghton Mifflin Company; from "Down," from *Morning in the Burned House* (Virago Press, 1995), © 1995 by Margaret Atwood, in *Eating Fire: Selected Poetry, 1965–95* (Virago Press, 1998), reprinted by permission of Curtis Brown Ltd., Houghton Mifflin Company, and McClelland & Stewart Ltd.

CLIVE BARKER: from *Abarat* (Voyager, 2004), text © 2004 by Clive Barker, reprinted by permission of HarperCollins Publishers Inc.

J. M. BARRIE: from *Peter Pan* (Penguin Popular Classics, 1995).

RAY BRADBURY: from *Something Wicked This Way Comes* (Simon & Schuster, 1962).

STERLING ALLEN BROWN: from "Thoughts of Death," from *The Collected Poems of Sterling Allen Brown*, edited by Michael S. Harper (Harper & Row,

PHILIPPE JACCOTTET: from "Songs from Below," from *Selected Poems*, translated by Derek Mahon (Penguin Books, 1987).

RUDYARD KIPLING: from *Just So Stories* (Penguin Popular Classics, 1994), reprinted by permission of A. P. Watt Ltd. on behalf of The National Trust for Places of Historic Interest or Natural Beauty.

HARPER LEE: from *To Kill a Mockingbird* (William Heinemann, 2003), © 1960 by Harper Lee; renewed © 1988 by Harper Lee. Foreword copyright © 1993 by Harper Lee, reprinted by permission of HarperCollins Publishers Inc. and The Random House Group Ltd.

ASTRID LINDGREN: from *The Brothers Lionheart*, translated by Jean Tate (Hodder Children's Books, 1979), reprinted by permission of Hodder & Stoughton Ltd. and Saltkrakan AB.

MICHAEL LONGLEY: from an interview/profile published in *The Observer* (March, 1991), reprinted by permission of LAW Ltd. on behalf of the author.

XI MURONG: "Poetry's Value," from *Anthology of Modern Chinese Poetry*, edited by Michelle Yeh (Yale University Press, 1993), © 1992 Yale University Press, reprinted by permission of the publisher.

PABLO NERUDA: "Word," from *Five Decades: Poems 1925–1970*, translated by Ben Belitt (Grove Press/Atlantic Monthly Press, 1983), English translation © 1974 by Ben Belitt, reprinted by permission of Grove/Atlantic, Inc.; from "The Dead Woman," in *Pablo Neruda: The Captain's Verses*, translated by Brian Cole (Anvil Press Poetry, 1994), reprinted by permission of the publisher.

GARTH NIX: from *Sabriel* (HarperCollins Publishers, 2002), reprinted by permission of the publisher.

BRIAN PATTEN: from *The Story Giant* (Flamingo, 2001), © 2001 Brian Patten, reprinted by permission of the author c/o Rogers, Coleridge & White Ltd., 20 Powis Mews, London W11 1JN.

MERVYN PEAKE: from *Titus Groan* (Vintage, 1998), reprinted by permission of The Random House Group Ltd.

Start reading here for a
sneak preview of the novel
by Nagaru Tanigawa!

AVAILABLE
SPRING 2009

Flip the book over and enjoy
the first manga volume of
The Melancholy of Haruhi Suzumiya!

Prologue

The question of how long someone believed in Santa Claus is a worthless topic that would never come up in idle conversation. Having said that, if you're going to ask me how much of my childhood I spent believing in the old man in a red suit, I can confidently say that I never believed in him to begin with.

I knew that the Santa at the preschool Christmas pageant was just a fake. Digging into my memories, I'm pretty sure that the other kids watching our principal dressed up as Santa didn't think he was real either.

I was a precocious child who didn't need to see Mommy kissing Santa Claus to question the existence of an old man who only worked on Christmas. However, I wouldn't realize that aliens, time travelers, ghosts, demons, espers, and evil organizations and the heroes that battle them in cartoons, monster movies, and comics, were made up until some time later.

No, I had probably already realized the truth. I just didn't want to admit it.

Deep in my heart, I wished that aliens, time travelers, ghosts, demons, evil organizations or espers might just pop up in front of me one day.

Compared to the ordinary world I wake up in every morning, the worlds depicted in cartoons, monster movies, and comics have a certain charm to them.

I wish I could have been born into one of those worlds!

Saving a girl who's been kidnapped by aliens and imprisoned within a huge, transparent pea shell. Repelling a laser-wielding time traveler trying to change history, armed only with my courage and wits. Taking out evil spirits and demons with a single incantation. Engaging in psychic battles with espers from a secret organization. Those were the kinds of things I wanted to do!

Wait a minute. Assuming that aliens, etc. were actually to attack, without having any particular special powers, I would have no way to do battle with them. So I did some brainstorming.

A mysterious transfer student suddenly arrives in my class one day and what if that student turns out to actually be an alien or time traveler or something along those lines with unknown powers. Then, the student is fighting against some evil gang and I just happen to get caught up in that fight. The other student is the main one doing the fighting. I'm just a sidekick. Hey, that sounds cool. Damn, I'm smart.

Or how about this? I'll just go with suddenly waking up one day with special powers—telepathy or psychokinesis or the like. It turns out there are a bunch of other people with special powers. Naturally, there are organizations recruiting such people. Members of a heroic organization come for me and I end up joining them in their battle against evil espers seeking world domination.

However, reality is rather cruel.

Fact is, no one had ever transferred into my class. I'd never seen a UFO. Going to all the local haunted spots yielded nothing in terms of ghosts and demons. Staring intently at the pencil on my desk for two hours didn't even move it a micron. And I'd be more likely to burn a hole in the head of the guy sitting in front of me, before I ever read his mind.

You have to admire how well the laws of physics were written while fighting the urge to laugh at yourself. At some point, I stopped being glued to the TV watching specials on UFOs and stories about psychics. They couldn't possibly exist, though I kind of wished they did. I figured my ability to hold onto my convictions while accepting reality was a sign that I'd matured.

When I graduated from middle school, I also graduated from those childish dreams and became used to the normalcy of the world. 1999 was my last hope and it wasn't like anything was going to happen that year anyway. We'd reached the 21st century without humankind making it beyond the moon. It looked unlikely that travel to Alpha Centauri and back within a day would happen in my lifetime.

Having pushed such thoughts to the corner of my mind, I entered high school without a care in the world—

And met Haruhi Suzumiya.

Chapter 1

My first regret, upon successfully cruising through admission to a local public high school, was that the school was situated atop a rather sizable hill. This meant that I found myself trudging up a winding hill, dripping sweat when it was only spring, feeling like I'd already done enough hiking for a lifetime. The fact that I'd have to embark on this uphill trek every day for the next three years depressed me deeply. Though if I stopped to think for a moment, lying in bed until the last second possible might just be the reason my legs were moving so quickly right then. Which meant that if I were to wake up ten minutes earlier, I'd be able to take a more leisurely pace, and the hike wouldn't be such a pain. Of course, once I factored in how precious those last ten minutes of sleep were, I realized that waking up earlier was simply out of the question. This meant that I would be required to continue the morning workout, which depressed me even more.

During of the school commencement ceremony, held in a gratuitously large gymnasium, I, unlike the other new students whose faces shone with hope and anxiety in anticipation of life at a new school, merely looked gloomy. However a good number of people from my old middle school were here, and I'd been on pretty good terms with a few of them so I wasn't too concerned about making friends.

It seemed like an odd combination to have guys in blazers and girls in sailor uniforms. Maybe Principal Toupee up on the podium putting everyone to sleep with his droning sound waves happened to be a fan of sailor uniforms? While I was thinking about this, the trite, monotonous commencement suddenly ended, and I shuffled into my assigned classroom, 1-5, with the rest of my classmates, whose faces I would be seeing for the upcoming year, whether I liked it or not.

Okabe, our young homeroom teacher, took the podium with a million dollar smile he probably spent an hour practicing in front of the mirror. He then proceeded to inform us that he was a gym teacher, that he was the handball team's advisor, that he played for a handball team back in college which got pretty far in the tournament, that the current school handball team was short on members so you were practically guaranteed a spot as a starter upon joining, and that there was no sport in this world as fun as handball. Having apparently run out of things to say after that long-winded speech, he finished with, "Let's have everyone introduce themselves."

Well, this was the same old way of kicking things off, and I'd expected as much, so it didn't exactly come as a surprise.

Starting from the left side of the seating chart, alternating boy-girl-boy-girl, one by one, people stood up and gave their name, the middle school they went to, and an interesting fact (a hobby, favorite food, etc.) about themselves. Some people just mumbled their way through it. Some people sounded completely relaxed. A few told bad jokes which killed any excitement in the room. And all the while, my turn gradually drew closer. Nerve-racking. *You know what I mean, right?*

Once I had managed to not stumble over the required autobiography I had practiced in my head, I sat back down in my seat, relishing that liberating feeling you get after taking care of business. In turn, the person behind me stood up—*Yes, I'll remember this moment for the rest of my life*—and spoke the words people would be talking about for years to come.

"Haruhi Suzumiya. From East Middle School."

Everything was still normal at this point. Twisting around to look behind me would have been too much of a hassle, which is why I was facing forward as I listened to her energetic voice.

"I have no interest in ordinary humans. If there are any aliens, time travelers, sliders, or espers here, come join me. That is all."

That made me turn around.

I found a girl with long, straight black hair decorated with a flashy hair band adorning her perfectly proportioned face. She stared back at the gawking students with unusually large, black, and determined eyes embellished with long, fringed eyelashes, her soft pink lips tightly pursed.

I was dazzled by Haruhi's snow white skin. A striking beauty stood before me.

Haruhi let her gaze sweep across the classroom, looking like she was trying to pick a fight, before finally glaring at me, gaping at her with my jaw on the floor, then sat down without so much as cracking a smile.

Is this some kind of a joke?

There were probably big question marks in the minds of everyone in the room as they wondered how they were supposed to react. *Are we supposed to laugh?*

In hindsight, it was neither a joke nor a laughing matter. Haruhi, no matter when or where, is never joking. She is always dead serious.

I learned this the hard way later on so there's no doubt about it.

Fairies of silence flittered around the classroom for thirty seconds before gym teacher Okabe hesitantly gestured to the next student and the frozen atmosphere finally returned to normal.

And so we met.

I deeply hope that it was mere coincidence.

••

After capturing the hearts of everyone in the class in every way, Haruhi was relatively quiet for the next few days, playing the role of a seemingly harmless high school girl.

I now understand very well just what people mean by "the calm before a storm."

Well, everyone who came to this particular high school was a student with average grades from one of the four city middle schools, which included East Middle School. This meant that some of these students had gone to middle school with Haruhi, so they realized that her decision to stay in the background was probably an omen of some kind. Unfortunately, I didn't know anyone from East Middle, and nobody in the class ever bothered to enlighten me. This led to what happened right after morning homeroom started, a few days after her crazy introduction. This was a moment I'll never forget. I broke the world record for stupidity and talked to Haruhi Suzumiya.

My domino reaction of misfortune had begun, and I was the one who had knocked the first one down.

But, come on. As long as Haruhi Suzumiya sat still with her mouth shut, anyone looking at her would be convinced that she was just a beautiful high school girl. Who's going to blame me for losing my mind for a moment and assuming that I could use the fact that my seat was right in front of hers to approach her?

Naturally, there was only one topic to talk about.

"Hey," I said, as I nonchalantly turned around with a casual smile on my face. "About the stuff in your introduction earlier. How much of it was serious?"

With her arms crossed and her mouth forming an upside-down V, Haruhi stared into my eyes unflinchingly.

"What stuff earlier?"

"Well, you know. The stuff about aliens and whatever."

"Are you an alien?" She asked this with a dead serious look on her face.

"No, but . . ."

"No, but what?"

" . . . Just forget it."

"Don't talk to me then. You're wasting my time."

The tone of her voice and the look she gave me were frigid enough to almost make me apologize out of reflex. Haruhi Suzumiya then stopped staring at me the way one would stare at Brussels sprouts, and with a "hmph," turned to glare in the direction of the blackboard.

Frozen out of a quick comeback, my pride was saved by the timely entrance of our homeroom teacher, Okabe.

As I dejectedly turned to face the front of the room, I noticed a number of people looking curiously towards me. When our eyes met, each person would half-smile in a knowing way, as if to say, "Thought so." And then nod as if to offer their condolences.

8

That kind of left me feeling uncomfortable. It was only later that I learned they had all gone to East Middle.

••

So, yeah. Given that my first contact with Haruhi would probably fall into the "worst ever" category, I had begun wondering if it would be better not to get involved with her. A week went by without anything happening to prove that idea wrong.

However, there were other people in the class who hadn't grasped the situation or were just plain blind to their surroundings. Those classmates would approach Haruhi, who was always in a foul mood, brow wrinkled and mouth looking like an upside-down V, and attempt to start a conversation about one thing or another.

They were just some nosy girls who saw this girl who had isolated herself from day one and wanted to bring her into their circle of friends. I'm sure they were well-intentioned, but you have to take into account who they were dealing with.

"Did you watch that TV show last night? The one that starts at nine."

"No."

"What—? Why not—?"

"Don't care."

"You should try watching an episode. Oh, but you won't know what's going on if you start now. That's right. In that case, I can fill you in on what's happened so far."

"Shut up."

That's how it went.

It'd be one thing if her response were devoid of emotion, but Haruhi's facial expression and tone of voice were clearly broadcasting irritation, leaving the other person feeling like she'd done something wrong. In the end, all the girl could say was, "Um . . . Well, you know . . ." before slinking away with drooping shoulders. "Did I say something strange?"

Rest assured, you didn't. The only thing strange here is Haruhi's mind.

I don't particularly have a problem with eating alone, but picking at your lunch by yourself while everyone else is chattering at their tables might make people wonder. I'm not saying that's the reason, but when it came time for lunch, I would move my desk next to the tables of Kunikida, someone I'd been relatively close to in middle school, and Taniguchi, a guy from East Middle who happened to sit near me.

That's when the subject of Haruhi Suzumiya came up.

"Hey. You talked to Suzumiya the other day, right?" Taniguchi suddenly asked. "She probably drove you away with some random nonsense."

You got that right.

Taniguchi placed a boiled egg in his mouth and chewed.

"If you're interested in her, I won't mince words. Just let it go. You should be well aware that Suzumiya's a freak."

He mentioned by way of introduction that he'd been in the same class as her for three years in middle school, so he knew what he was talking about.

"She's the strangest girl you'll ever meet. I thought she might calm down after becoming a high school student, but she hasn't changed one bit. You heard her introduction, right?"

"The thing about aliens or whatever?" That was Kunikida, busily picking bones from his grilled fish, cutting in.

"Yep. She said and did a bunch of strange things back in middle school too. The most famous one would be the graffiti incident on school grounds."

"What's that?"

"There's this machine that uses chalk to draw white lines, right? What was it called again? Whatever. Anyway, someone used that to draw some huge, bizarre pictograph on the school grounds. And whoever it was snuck in at night to do it."

Taniguchi grinned as he remembered what happened.

"You'd be amazed. I arrived at school in the morning to find giant circles and triangles scribbled all over the ground. I couldn't tell what it was supposed to be from up close, so I tried looking at it from the fourth floor. I still couldn't tell what it was supposed to be."

"Oh, I remember seeing that. Wasn't that in the local section of the newspaper? They had an aerial photo. It looked like a failed attempt at a Nazca geoglyph." That was Kunikida. I didn't remember any of this.

"It was. Headlined *Mysterious Graffiti Found on Middle School Grounds*. So it came time to figure out who the culprit behind this ridiculous stunt was."

"And she was the one who did it?"

"She admitted to it, so it had to be her. 'Course, they wanted to know why she did it. They even called her to the principal's office. Seems like all the teachers got together to question her."

"Why'd she do it?"

"Dunno."

With that offhand response, Taniguchi began gulping down his white rice.

"Seems like she never 'fessed up. You try dealing with Suzumiya when she refuses to say a word and gives you that killer glare. Can't do a thing about it. According to one account, the drawing was to invite UFOs. Another said it was a summoning circle for evil demons. Yet another said it was to open a gate to another world. A bunch of rumors popped up, but since she never gave a reason, no one can really say. It's still a mystery."

In my mind, I could picture Haruhi Suzumiya drawing white lines in the pitch-black darkness of the school grounds with an earnest expression on her face. The clattering line marker she was dragging around and the heap of bags of lime were probably taken from the gym storeroom beforehand. She might have at least brought a flashlight. I couldn't help but think that in the flickering light, Haruhi Suzumiya's expression seemed filled with an overwhelming sense of tragic heroism. Only in my imagination, though.

Haruhi Suzumiya was probably genuinely trying to invite UFOs or summon demons or open up a gate to another world. She might have spent the whole night toiling away on the middle school grounds. And then finally, after nothing showed up, she must have been really demoralized. Just some baseless speculation on my part.

"She also did a bunch of other stuff."

Taniguchi was in the process of finishing off the remaining bits of his lunch.

"One morning, we showed up at the classroom to find all the desks out in the hall. She drew stars on the roof in paint. She even took a bunch of weird talismans, like the ones they stick on a corpse's head to reanimate it, and stuck them all around school. I really don't get her."

By the way, Haruhi Suzumiya wasn't in the classroom right then. We wouldn't have been able to have this conversation otherwise. Though I got the feeling she wouldn't care, even if she were there. Speaking of Haruhi Suzumiya, she made a habit of leaving the room the moment fourth period ended and not coming back until right before fifth period started. I'd never seen her bring a lunch, so she probably ate in the cafeteria. Still, it can't take an hour to eat lunch. Come to think of it, I could safely say that she was never in the room between classes. I wonder where she wandered off to.

"Even so, she's pretty popular…" Taniguchi was still talking. "It's because she has the looks. Plus she's great at sports and probably gets better grades than most. You can't tell she's a freak when she just stands there and keeps her mouth shut."

"Are there any stories about her love life?" That was Kunikida, who hadn't eaten even half as much as Taniguchi.

"For a while, she kept switching from one guy to another. As far as I know, the longest lasted a week, and apparently the shortest was five minutes after she agreed to go out with him. It was always Suzumiya doing the dumping, without exception. She always used the same line. 'I don't have time to deal with ordinary humans!' Then don't agree to go out in the first place!"

Taniguchi was probably speaking from experience. I guess he noticed me looking at him since he hurriedly went on.

"It's just a story I heard. Really. I don't know why, but apparently, she doesn't turn anyone down. Everyone had it figured out by the third year so there wasn't anybody left trying to ask her out. But I get the feeling that the same thing's going to happen in high school. That's why I'm warning you before you get any weird ideas. Give it up. Consider it a friendly warning from a classmate."

There's nothing to give up on. I'm not even interested.

Taniguchi placed his empty lunch box in his bag and smirked.

"If you ask me, then yeah, that's the best one in the class over there. Ryoko Asakura."

Taniguchi stuck his chin towards a cluster of chatting girls with their desks tightly together. In the center of the cluster with a cheerful smile on her face was Ryoko Asakura.

"As far as I'm concerned, she's gotta be in the top three for our year."

"Did you check out all the freshman girls already or something?"

"Oh, yeah! I assigned them ranks from A to D, and I learned the full names of the ones who ranked A. You only get to live the high school life once. Might as well have fun doing it."

"And Asakura is an A?" Kunikida asked.

"An A+, for sure. Once you've reached my level of expertise, you can tell just by looking at their face. She's definitely a nice person too."

Well, even if you assume that half of Taniguchi's opinionated rambling was a load of bull, Ryoko Asakura was, in fact, a girl who stood out in a different way from Haruhi Suzumiya.

First off, she was a hottie. It was also really sweet how she gave you the feeling she was always smiling. Second, Taniguchi was probably correct in judging that Ryoko was a nice person. By this point, there pretty much wasn't anybody left foolish enough to try to talk to Haruhi Suzumiya. The only human undeterred by the constantly rude reception was Ryoko Asakura. She had the temperament of a class representative. Third, judging by her responses in class, she seemed to be pretty smart too. Every question directed toward her was guaranteed to be answered correctly. She was a student any teacher would love to have. Fourth, she was also popular among girls. It had only been a week since school started, and she'd already succeeded in becoming the ringleader of the girls in the class. She obviously had enough charisma to attract the masses.

If you pit Ryoko Asakura against Haruhi Suzumiya, with her perpetually furrowed brow and incomprehensible thinking pattern, everyone's going to pick Asakura. Myself included, I guess. Regardless, they were both way out of Taniguchi's league.

••

A novel by
Nagaru Tanigawa

AVAILABLE
SPRING 2009

Flip the book over and start reading
from the second to last page
for a sneak preview!

THE MELANCHOLY of HARUHI SUZUMIYA

HEROES IN ANIME AND SANTA CLAUS...

...ONLY EXIST IN DREAMS.

...RIGHT?

I MUST HAVE ALREADY REALIZED THAT.

ONLY I DIDN'T WANT TO ACCEPT IT.

BECAUSE DREAM OR NOT...

...THE ME BACK THEN WAS COMPLETELY ENTHRALLED BY THEM.

...AS IF.

...OR SO I THOUGHT.

...WITH THE MAJORITY OF MY CLASSMATES COMING FROM THE SAME MIDDLE SCHOOL, FOR BETTER OR FOR WORSE, IT WAS A STABLE BEGINNING.

IT'S NOT THAT I'VE GOT NO EXPECTATIONS FOR MY NEW LIFE, BUT...

HARUHI SUZUMIYA FROM HIGASHI MIDDLE SCHOOL.

GATAN (CLATTER)

NAILED IT!

IF THERE ARE ANY *ALIENS*, *TIME TRAVELERS*, *SLIDERS*, OR *ESPERS* HERE, THEN COME JOIN ME.

THAT IS ALL!

BOY, I'LL PROBABLY NEVER FORGET THAT FOR THE REST OF MY LIFE.

GIRO
(GLARE)

I WAS
AWARE OF
JUST HOW
BADLY...

...I WANTED IT TO BE A COINCIDENCE.

HEY, DID YOU CATCH THAT SHOW YESTERDAY?

OH, YOU MEAN THE ONE THAT STARTS AT NINE O'CLOCK?

I'M NOT WATCHING THAT ONE.

THE SERIES SO FAR WENT LIKE THIS—

YOU SHOULD WATCH IT SOMETIME, SUZUMIYA-SAN.

"UGLY CAT-LOVER"

IT'S SO GOOD!

A ROMANTIC SITCOM ABOUT UGLY CATS!

ㅇㅇㅇㅇㅇㅇ

NOT INTERESTED.

THAT'S NONE OF YOUR BUSINESS.

U-UM, YOU'VE GOT A GREAT BODY, SUZUMIYA-SAN!

YEAH, YOU DO! I'M SO JEALOUS!

PA (GLOW)

URK...

BAN (SLAM)

YOU ON A DIET OR SOMETHING?

SO SHE'S WEARING HER HAIR DIFFERENTLY AGAIN TODAY, EH?

HMPH!

GATAN (CLATTER)

BEFORE EVEN A WEEK HAD PASSED SINCE HER SURPRISE-ATTACK SELF-INTRO-DUCTION...

W-WELL... WE SHOULD GET GOING...

ZAWA
(MURMUR)

...THERE WASN'T A PERSON LEFT AT SCHOOL WHO DIDN'T KNOW HARUHI SUZUMIYA'S NAME.

OH, IF IT ISN'T TANIGUCHI AND KUNIKIDA.

MORNING.

QUIT CALLING ME BY THAT NICKNAME ALREADY...

MORNING, KYON!

IF YOU'VE GOT YOUR EYE ON SUZUMIYA, YOU'RE BETTER OFF GIVING IT UP.

PERFECT TIMING.

THERE'S SOMETHING I WANTED TO WARN YOU ABOUT AS A FRIEND.

WH—

JUST QUIT WHILE YOU'RE AHEAD. SHE'S WAY OUT OF YOUR LEAGUE.

I KNOW YOU'RE WATCHING HER OUT OF THE CORNER OF YOUR EYE, RIGHT?

DID YOU THINK YOU COULD FOOL ME? I WENT TO MIDDLE SCHOOL WITH HER.

WHAT!?

YOU KNOW, DON'T YOU? HOW ALL THE GUYS DIG HER.

YOU CAN'T DENY SHE'S GOOD LOOKING. NOT TO MENTION SHE EXCELS AT EVERY SPORT AND HAS TOP GRADES.

YOU COULD RATE HER AS AN A+.

FOR A WHILE THERE, SHE WAS HOPPING FROM ONE GUY TO THE NEXT. BUT AS FAR AS I KNOW...

...THE LONGEST RELATIONSHIP SHE'S HAD LASTED A WEEK, AND THE SHORTEST WAS FIVE MINUTES.

WITHOUT EXCEPTION, SUZUMIYA'S ALWAYS THE ONE TO CUT IT OFF.

KATA (CLATTER)

AND SHE ALWAYS GIVES THE SAME EXCUSE.

I DON'T HAVE TIME TO WASTE WITH ORDINARY HUMANS.

YOU'VE SEEN HER ECCENTRIC BEHAVIOR ALREADY, HAVEN'T YOU?

...THE HEADLINE DURING MIDDLE SCHOOL: "PRANK GRAFFITI ON SCHOOL CAMPUS"!

SHE'S ABNORMAL... THE SUREST PROOF OF IT WAS...

THERE WERE THESE GINORMOUS, BIZARRE CHARACTERS ON THE SCHOOL GROUNDS...

...THAT SHE SCRIBBLED OUT ALL BY HERSELF AFTER SNEAKING INTO THE SCHOOL IN THE DEAD OF NIGHT.

DON'T TELL ME THE FIVE-MINUTE RELATIONSHIP SHE HAD WAS WITH HIM...

W-WE WENT TO THE SAME MIDDLE SCHOOL...

DABA (FLAIL)

DABA

DABA

HOW DO YOU KNOW SO MUCH ABOUT SUZUMIYA?

URK!!

WAI (GAB)

EVEN WHEN QUESTIONED ABOUT IT, SHE REFUSED TO COMMENT.

WHETHER THEY WERE PART OF A CEREMONY TO SUMMON DEMONS OR A MESSAGE TO UFOS... THE DETAILS REMAIN A MYSTERY TO THIS DAY.

WAI

IN ANY CASE, JUST GIVE UP ON SUZUMIYA.

THE GIRL WHO'S REALLY IN SEASON IS...

WAI

RYOUKO ASAKURA!

SHE'S A COMPLETELY DIFFERENT KIND OF GIRL THAN SUZUMIYA!

FIRST OFF, SHE'S A TOTAL **BABE!**

CAN YOU HELP US WITH THIS...?

CLASS PRESIDENT!!

OOH! I GET IT NOW!

YOU SUBSTITUTE THIS IN, AND THEN...

THIS GOES THIS WAY...

QUIET AND LEVEL-HEADED— THE WORKS!

DOUUN (DUUUUN)

BUT...

IN SHORT, **AN AAA RANK!!**

...DESPITE ALL THAT, YOU'RE STILL AIMING FOR SUZUMIYA, EH?

HAA (SIGH)

GOOD LUCK.

WH–

THANKS, CLASS PRESIDENT!

WAAA! (YAAY)

SHE'S AT THE TOP OF HER STUDIES AND POPULAR WITH THE OTHER GIRLS TOO.

THAT'S
NOT
HOW IT
IS...

IN THE BACK
OF MY MIND,
AN IMAGE OF
HARUHI SUZUMIYA
DRAWING A WHITE
LINE ON THE
PITCH-BLACK
CAMPUS WITH
HER SERIOUS
EXPRESSION
POPPED UP.

SMEARING
THE GROUND
WITH THE
LIME SHE'D
SWIPED
FROM THE
SHED AHEAD
OF TIME...

...HER
EXPRESSION
ILLUMINATED
BY THE FAINT
LIGHT...

I'M SUCH A ROMANTIC.

YEAH, RIGHT.

IN ANY CASE...IT'S UNDENIABLE THAT THERE'S A PART OF ME THAT'S JEALOUS OF SUZUMIYA'S APPROACH TO LIFE.

AFTER ALL, SHE'S WAITING FOR THE DAY SHE'LL RUN INTO THE EXTRAORDINARY, WHILE I'VE LONG SINCE GIVEN UP ON THAT.

...WOULD BE ONE OF TRAGEDY AS SHE LOOKED OFF SOMEWHERE, DEEP IN THOUGHT.

SU
(SLIDE)

KOOON
(DOOONG)

KIIN
(DIIING)

AND WHILE THAT WAS GOING ON...

GOLDEN WEEK ENDED... AND A WEEK PASSED.

PLEASE! GO RIGHT AHEAD!

OH! ASAKURA-SAN!

CAN I HAVE A MINUTE?

I CAME UP WITH THIS SINCE THERE ARE STILL SOME PEOPLE IN OUR CLASS WHO HAVEN'T BECOME CLOSE.

WHAT IS IT?

GO!
PAPER: FIRST-CLASS VOLUNTEERING CREATION
第一回 クラス 自主レクリエーション

I'M SORRY FOR INTER-RUPTING.

URKKGH!

AH!

ESPECIALLY THAT... SUZUMIYA-SAN, FOR ONE.

BUT I'M PASSING THIS AROUND.

SEE, HE ALREADY LIKES—

GU
(TUG)

IF IT'S ABOUT HER, LOOK TO KYON.

HEY!

I'M SURE SHE'S STILL JUST A LITTLE SHY.

PAAA (GLOOOW)

SHE REALLY NEEDS SOMEONE TO REACH OUT TO HER!

WHY, THAT'S WONDER-FUL!

......

I'M HOPING SHE CAN TAKE THIS AS AN OPPORTUNITY TO OPEN UP.

MOGA (CLAMP)

SUZUMIYA IS A TOTAL **FREAK.**

I AGREE WHOLE-HEARTEDLY WITH YOU, ASAKURA-SAN, BUT... I THINK THIS IS GOING TO BE A CHALLENGING UNDER-TAKING.

TO CARE ABOUT SUZUMIYA THIS MUCH... IS JUST WHAT YOU'D EXPECT FROM AN AAA.

HMMMMMM.

YOU KNOW HOW SHE STICKS OUT LIKE A SORE THUMB IN CLASS!

HYAH!

AND SHE'S JOINED EVERY CLUB IN SCHOOL FOR ONLY A FEW DAYS EACH!

BUT YOU'VE GOT IT ALL WRO—

MUGU (MMAPH)

PISHAAAN
(SLAAAM)

TO CLARIFY...

FROZEN

...

HEY, KYON?

HEY...

...I DIDN'T DO IT TO IMPRESS ASAKURA.

IS THE WAY YOU CHANGE YOUR HAIRSTYLE EVERY DAY SOME KIND OF *COUNTER-MEASURE* AGAINST ALIENS?

WHEN...

...DID YOU REAL- IZE IT?

I KNOW THAT MOST OF THE TIME IT'S HARD TO PINPOINT THE EXACT CATALYST THAT SETS OFF A CHAIN OF EVENTS...

...BUT I'M PRETTY SURE THAT THIS WAS THE TRIGGER.

...WHY'RE YOU GOING AFTER ALIENS AND STUFF?

SO...

HMM... NOT LONG AGO.

I SEE.

DOOON (BOOM)

BECAUSE THINGS ARE MORE INTERESTING THAT WAY, DUH!!

......

...NO?

A LONG TIME AGO?

HAVE WE MET BEFORE?

OKAY, LET'S START HOMEROOM NOW...

GARA (RATTLE)

SORRY I'M LATE!

KIIIN (DIIING)

KOOON (DOOONG)

SOMETHING CHANGED...

...THE VERY NEXT DAY.

GA (GRAB)

CHII (CHIRP)
CHI
CHI

CHUN (TWEET)

CHUN

DON
(BAM)

YOU CUT YOUR HAIR?

HEY...

ASSIST ME.

KYON, WAS IT?

WHY DIDN'T I REALIZE SOMETHING SO SIMPLE BEFORE?

HUH!?

ZUN ZUN ZUN ZUN

ZUN (DRAG)

...ASSIST YOU WITH WHAT!?

WAIT, THAT'S JUST MY NICKNAME.

NO, I MEAN...

24

SIGN: LITERATURE CLUB

26

KONN
(TAP)

WELL, ISN'T THIS A NICE PLACE WE GOT HERE!

CHA
(CLACK)

SO YOU'RE A MEMBER OF THIS CLUB, EH? PERFECT.

LISTEN UP. STARTING TODAY, THIS CLUB ROOM...

....

...IS FOR THE NEW INTEREST GROUP I'M MAKING.

GOT IT!?

HUH !?

......

DO (SLAM)

DO (STOMP)

DO

WAIT!!

DO

DO

HEY...

I'M GOING TO GO AND GATHER ALL THE THINGS WE NEED NOW.

WELL, WITH THAT SETTLED, WE CAN'T KEEP THE ROOM THIS WAY!

WAIT, SU—

DA (DASH)

UH...

WHAT'S YOUR NAME?

WHAT IN THE WORLD...

FRESH-MAN.

YUKI NAGATO.

UHH...

NAGATO-SAN, OR WHAT-EVER...

......

PARA (FLIP)

PERA

I'M THE ONLY MEMBER OF THIS CLUB, AFTER ALL.

YEAH, BUT IT MIGHT... ERR, MOST DEFINITELY, WILL BE A REAL BOTHER FOR YOU...

I DON'T MIND.

PERARI

THAT GIRL'S TRYING TO TURN THIS ROOM INTO THE CLUBROOM FOR SOME GOD-KNOWS-WHAT CLUB, BUT...

IT'S FINE.

PERARI (FLIP)

I CAN ALREADY TELL THIS GIRL'S SLIGHTLY OFF, BUT...

...NOW THAT I TAKE A GOOD LOOK AT HER, SHE'S GOT A PRETTY FACE.

KA (FLASH)

IT'S UNIQUE.

SUU (LUNGE)

BIKU (JUMP)

OKAY, WHAT DO I DO NOW ...?

SO... IS THAT BOOK INTERESTING?

30

I WILL LEND IT TO YOU.

READ IT.

YURA (FLOAT)

NUVOOOO (CLOOOMO)

UH, WHAT?

WHAT DO YOU MEAN!?

YOU'RE THE UNIQUE ONE HERE!

HEY, HEY!

MOVE IT OR LOSE IT!

BATA (STOMP)

BATA

AH THANKS...

SORRY I'M LATE!

BAAN (BADULUM)

!?

SFX: SUSSUKU (SCRIBBLE) SUSSUKU

WHERE DID YOU GET ALL THAT...?

SOME-WHERE!

MORE IMPORTANTLY, I CAME UP WITH A NAME FOR OUR INTEREST GROUP!

I GOT ALL THE BASICS!

BAND: BRIGADE CHIEF

团長

KYU (SQUEAK)

THE SAVE THE WORLD BY OVER-LOADING IT WITH FUN HARUHI SUZUMIYA BRIGADE! OR FOR SHORT...

°°° THE SOS BRI- GADE !!

DON (BAM)

IS THIS... THE PART WHERE I'M SUPPOSED TO LAUGH?

KOOON (DOOOON)

I'M SHOCKED.

ZA (SCUFF)

I'M TELLING YOU, THAT'S NOT IT!

YEAH, WELL, KYON'S ALWAYS HAD A THING FOR WEIRD GIRLS.

NOT ONLY DO YOU MANAGE CONVERSATION WITH THAT SUZUMIYA, BUT...

I'M IMPRESSED, KYON-KUN.

I WONDER IF YOU COULD *CHANGE* HER?

...YOU GO AND MAKE AN INTEREST GROUP TOGETHER WITH HER TOO!

I SWEAR, BOTH YOU AND SUZU-MIYA—

I DON'T EVEN KNOW WHAT KIND OF CLUB IT'S SUPPOSED TO BE!

WHAT, YOU'RE NOT INTER-ESTED?

I DON'T THINK IT'S ABOUT CHANGE. SHE'S NEVER MADE MUCH SENSE TO BEGIN WITH.

AND JUST FOR THE RECORD, I NEVER SAID ANYTHING ABOUT BECOMING A MEMBER.

THIS IS ALL MOVING TOO FAST FOR ME!

I'M TELLING YOU, QUIT MAKING STUFF UP!

WHAT THE HELL IS AN SOS BRIGADE EVEN SUPPOSED TO BE...?

PACHI
(CLICK)

WELCOME
BACK.

I'M
HOME.

"YOU'RE NOT INTERESTED?"

CHRIST
...

THAT'S
NOT
EVEN
FUNNY.

BOFU
(FOOMPH)

SURE, I
WON'T
DENY
ENVYING
SUZUMIYA.

THAT'S WHY
I STARTED A
CONVERSATION WITH
HER, EVEN KNOWING
HOW IRRATIONAL
SHE IS...BUT...

......

I CAN DO
WITHOUT
THE
TROUBLE.

I'VE GOT MY OWN ROUTINE!

CHUN
(CHIRP)

CHUN

SEE YA!

HAVE A GOOD DAY!

BUT BY THAT TIME...

...MY ROUTINE HAD ALREADY BECOME "BIZARRE."

THE MELANCHOLY OF HARUHI SUZUMIYA I: END

FROM THE TIME I GET UP IN THE MORNING, TO WHEN I GO TO SLEEP AT NIGHT...

...IT'S THE SAME ROUTINE OVER AND OVER AGAIN.

KA (FLASH)

DAAA (ZOOOM)

...I'M SURE YOU HAVE SOME IDEA.

AS FOR WHY, WELL...

GU (YANK)

MORNING!

MORNING!

IT'S HARD NOT TO FEEL OVER-WHELMED BY IT.

OKAY! STARTING FIRST THING TODAY...

...WE'RE GOING ON A SEARCH FOR ALIENS!!

BAAN (BADUUM)

38

BAAN (WHACK)

GOGOGO

GOGO (RUMBLE)

SORRY, NOT A CLUE.

KYON, DO YOU EVEN UNDERSTAND WHY WE HAVE THE SOS BRIGADE?

YEAH, I UNDERSTAND THE WORD, BUT...

ALIENS! A-LI-ENS! YOU KNOW WHAT I'M TALKING ABOUT!

GOGOGO

KOOON (DOOONG)

WA (CHEER)

WA

HUH?

DOOON (BABULIM)

MY GUT TELLS ME SOMETHING'S BOUND TO HAPPEN ANY DAY NOW!!

TO GO IN SEARCH OF THE MYSTERIES OF THE WORLD!!

HARUHI SUZUMIYA.

......

PON (SMACK)

OH, THAT'S RIGHT. I ALMOST FORGOT.

JUST WHAT DO YOU MEAN BY "GO ON A SEARCH"...?

?

I'VE SOMEHOW GOTTEN MIXED UP WITH HER. IF I HADN'T, I'D JUST BE SPENDING MY AFTERNOONS IN PEACE.

INTEREST GROUP REGULATIONS?

PAPER: INTEREST GROUP REGULATIONS

PERARI (FLIP)

CHIRA (GLANCE)

"YOU GUYS"...?

THERE'S A MOUNTAIN OF DUTIES THAT YOU GUYS HAVE TO SORT OUT...SO FOR NOW, JUST WRITE THAT UP.

YEP. OUR FIRST STEP IS TO ESTABLISH OUR-SELVES AS A GROUP.

......

① NAMES OF AT LEAST FIVE MEMBERS.
② NAME OF FACULTY ADVISOR.
③ TITLE.
④ RESPONSIBLE PARTY.
⑤ DESCRIPTION OF ACTIVITIES.

SHE DOESN'T LOOK LIKE SHE'D BE ABLE TO DISOBEY SUZUMIYA.

SFX: DOOON (BADUUM)

USE YOUR BRAIN!

SO YOU MEAN "MAKE IT UP"...

YOU ARE SO ANNOYING...

NO, LIKE I SAID, I CAN'T.

YOU CAN WRITE EVERYTHING BESIDES "NAMES OF AT LEAST FIVE MEMBERS."

I CAN'T FILL IN MOST OF THESE...

I GOTTA GET CHANGED.

THERE'S THE BELL. NEXT IS GYM CLASS, RIGHT?

I...I CAN'T WRITE THIS...

WE'LL DO THE REST LATER, SO JUST LEAVE IT THERE.

KOOON (DOOONG)

KIIIN (DIIING)

記入欄

① 涼宮ハルヒ

②

③ 涼宮ハルヒの団

④ 涼宮ハルヒ

⑤ 涼宮ハルヒによる涼宮ハルヒのため

WE'LL REGROUP AFTER SCHOOL!

SOSO KUSA (VWIP)

I NEVER AGREED TO BE A MEMBER OF THIS...

...NOW SEE HERE!

PHEW...

TO PUT IT BLUNTLY, SHE GIVES ME A HEADACHE...

DESPITE ALL THAT, SHE'S STILL BUSTY...

SHE REALLY DOESN'T PAY ANY ATTENTION TO OTHER PEOPLE'S PERSPECTIVES...

I THINK I CAN UNDERSTAND WHY EVERYTHING STILL ENDS IN CALAMITY EVEN THOUGH SHE'S POPULAR.

...I'VE HAD ENOUGH FOR TODAY. I'M GOING HOME.

SHE TOLD ME TO COME. BUT I'M JUST GONNA IGNORE HER. IGNORE HER!

OH, SHE ALREADY ON THE BRINK OF A CATASTROPHE?

......

TON (TAP)

YOU IDIOT...

HEY, KYON!

YOU'RE "PLAYING CLUB" WITH SUZUMIYA AGAIN TODAY, RIGHT?

THAT REMINDS ME. WHAT DOES NAGATO THINK ABOUT HARUHI?

IT'S THAT BOOK SHE LENT ME YESTERDAY...

SHE'S SO DEADPAN I CAN'T READ HER.

PARA (FLIP)

BOOKMARK: 7 P.M. I'LL BE WAITING IN THE PARK ACROSS FROM KOUYOU PARK STATION.

午後七時。光陽園駅前公園にて待つ。

WHAT NOW?

GACHAN
(CLANK)

MORE IMPORTANTLY...

WHAT DOES SHE WANT?

44

...DIDN'T SHE GIVE ME THE BOOK YESTERDAY?

WE CANNOT SPEAK ABOUT IT AT SCHOOL, SO...

I HAVE TO TALK TO YOU.

HUH?

...WE WILL GO TO MY HOUSE.

YOU NEED NOT WORRY.

WHY AM I BEING INVITED TO HER HOUSE?

WHOA WHOA WHOA... WHAT'S GOING ON HERE?

1 2

ﾞﾞﾞ ｽﾞ

UIIIIN (WHIRRR)

BU (CHOKE)

1 2 3 4 5

THERE IS NO ONE HERE.

CHIIN (DIING)

GAAAAAH!

THIS IS GETTING WEIRDER BY THE SECOND!!

?

WATA

WATA (PANIC)

LIKE... YOUR FAMILY?

SO WHEN YOU SAY NOBODY'S HERE, YOU MEAN THEY'RE OUT?

HUH?

I'VE ALWAYS BEEN THE ONLY ONE HERE.

IT'S THIS ONE.

COME IN.

SHE LIVES BY HERSELF!?

GACHA (CLICK)

46

UHHHH...
....
....

DRINK.

IT CONCERNS HARUHI SUZU- MIYA... AND ME.

I AM GOING TO TELL YOU ABOUT IT.

HOW TO PUT IT? HER PLACE IS SO DREARY...

SO... ANYWAY...

...YOU WANTED TO TALK?

KOTON (THUMP)

HARUHI SUZUMIYA AND I ARE...

...NOT ORDINARY HUMANS.

I KINDA ALREADY KNEW THAT...

THAT'S NOT WHAT I MEAN.

....

YEAH, WELL...

I DO NOT MEAN THAT WE LACK UNIVERSAL PROPERTIES IN OUR PERSON-ALITIES.

...I WILL SAY THAT SHE AND I ARE DIFFERENT FROM THE VAST MAJORITY OF HUMANS, SUCH AS YOURSELF.

IN THE SIMPLEST SENSE...

...IS WHAT I AM.

A HUMANOID INTERFACE MEANT FOR CONTACT WITH ORGANIC LIFE FORMS, CREATED BY THE *DATA INTEGRATION THOUGHT ENTITY* THAT GOVERNS THIS MILKY WAY GALAXY...

THE DATA INTEGRATION THOUGHT ENTITY...

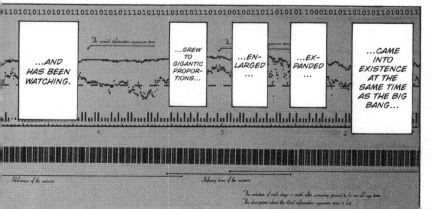

01101010110101011010101010110101011010101110101001101101101010110001010110101011010101

...AND HAS BEEN WATCHING.

...GREW TO GIGANTIC PROPORTIONS...

...EN-LARGED...

...EX-PANDED...

...CAME INTO EXISTENCE AT THE SAME TIME AS THE BIG BANG...

...A HIGHLY INTELLIGENT LIFE FORM OF DATA WITHOUT PHYSICAL BODY, BORN FROM THE SEA OF DATA THAT SPANS THE GALAXY AND BEYOND...TO THE ENTIRE UNIVERSE.

POSSESSING NO PHYSICAL FORM, THE MASS THAT EXISTS ONLY AS DATA...

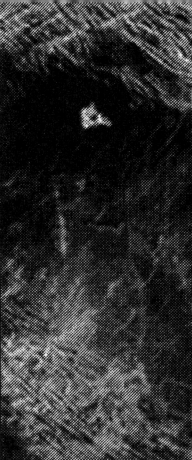

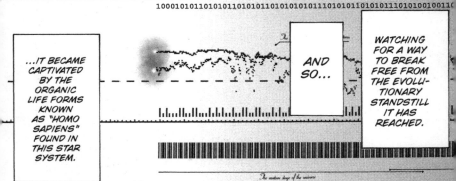

10001010110101011010101101010101011101010110101011101010010011

...IT BECAME CAPTIVATED BY THE ORGANIC LIFE FORMS KNOWN AS "HOMO SAPIENS" FOUND IN THIS STAR SYSTEM.

AND SO...

WATCHING FOR A WAY TO BREAK FREE FROM THE EVOLUTIONARY STANDSTILL IT HAS REACHED.

REGARDING THE OBVIOUS QUESTION OF "WHY HARUHI?"... THAT WILL COME LATER. FOR NOW, I MUST ADD THAT...

...I WAS NOT THE ONLY ONE GIVEN THIS DUTY. I WANT YOU TO UNDERSTAND THAT.

AND FOR THESE THREE YEARS, THERE HAVE BEEN NO UNCERTAIN ELEMENTS IN PARTICULAR. ALL WAS EXTREMELY STABLE.

AT ANY RATE, FOR THE THREE YEARS SINCE MY BIRTH, I HAVE CARRIED OUT THIS TASK.

MY DUTY IS TO OBSERVE HARUHI SUZUMIYA AND REPORT ANY INFORMATION TO THE INTEGRATION THOUGHT ENTITY.

BUT RECENTLY, AN IRREGULAR FACTOR THAT CANNOT BE IGNORED HAS APPEARED BEFORE HARUHI SUZUMIYA.

THAT WOULD BE YOU.

THE TEA.

THANKS FOR IT.

IT WAS DELI-CIOUS.

GACHA
(CLACK)

I BET SUZUMIYA WOULD BE OVER-JOYED IF YOU TOLD HER.

YEAH, IT WAS ALL VERY INTERESTING.

I'M NOT FIN-ISHED TALK-ING.

SHU
(SHFF)

AHHH...

BATAN
(SLAM)

I DEFINITELY DIDN'T SEE THAT COMING.

OH, I SEE... SO IN SHORT, NAGATO-SAN'S AN ALIEN.

I WONDER IF SHE'LL LET ME JOIN THEM TOO?

SUTA
(STRIDE)

SUTA

WOOOW... THIS IS SO EXCITING!

SUTA

OBSERVING SUZUMIYA... RIGHT. BIRDS OF A FEATHER FLOCK TOGETHER, EH?

SUTA

......

WELL, WELL.

GAN
(BANG)

...YEAH,
RIGHT!!

LOOKS
LIKE I
SHOULDN'T
GET MY
HOPES UP.

I DON'T FOLLOW...

...IS
WHAT
ANYBODY
WOULD
THINK,
RIGHT?

FUU
CWHSH)

MORNING!

GOOD
MORNING!

BUT...

AND THAT
INCLUDES
ME.

...I WAS TAKING THIS SITUATION TOO LIGHTLY!

GO

GO (RUMBLE)

GO

GO

GO

...OOO I MUST ADMIT...!

GO

I'LL ASK JUST THIS ONCE. WHAT WAS YOUR REASON FOR SKIPPING OUT!? TELL ME NOW! *OUT WITH IT!!*

GO

WHY DIDN'T YOU COME YESTERDAY? THERE'S A SEVERE PUNISHMENT FOR NOT SHOWING UP TO CLUB MEETINGS.

DOOON! (BADUUM)

NO EXCUS-ES!!

I HAD TO STU—

WHAAT...!?

UM... WELL...

TARA (SWEAT)

BATAN (SLAM)

ZUSAA (DRAAG)

FOR CRYING OUT LOUD! I WAS TOO CONSIDERATE BEFORE!

NO, UH ...!

UM... THIS IS GIVING ME DÉJÀ VU.

SIGN: SOS BRIGADE
UNDER: LITERATURE CLUB

IT WAS TOO DEMANDING TO SUDDENLY SEND YOU ON A SEARCH FOR ALIENS.

ONCE AGAIN, WHERE ARE YOU GETTING THIS STUFF?

FINE! IT WAS ALSO MY FAULT HOW YESTERDAY WENT.

KOTON (THUNK)

SIGN: BRIGADE CHIEF

団長

......

YESTER-DAY...

PERA (FLIP)

FIRST, LET'S LOWER THE HURDLES SOME.

LOWER THEM?

I FEEL LIKE I'M GONNA GET SLUGGED...

WHAT NAGATO SAID...NAH, I WON'T BRING IT UP.

HUH?

I'LL COMPRO-MISE.

IT DOESN'T HAVE TO BE AN ALIEN. SO LONG AS IT'S SOMETHING MYSTERIOUS, I'LL TAKE IT.

BUT...

ゴ GO

放課後
巡回路

→2F

ゴ
GO (RUMBLE)

ゴ
GO

ゴ
GO

LOCATING A PLACE WHERE THERE'S A DISTORTION IN THE SPACE-TIME CONTINUUM OR UNCOVERING AN ALIEN POSING AS AN EARTHLING...

...IS, OF COURSE, THE LEAST OF WHAT I EXPECT FROM YOU.

PON. (PAT)
ぽん

ゴ GO

ゴ GO

PAPER: AFTER-SCHOOL CIRCUIT

ブワッ
HEH HEH HEH

I'LL HAVE TO MAKE HIM REALIZE THAT.

FIFTH TIME AROUND

KYON DOESN'T SEEM LIKE MUCH OF A CLUB MEMBER.

HAA (CHUFF)
はぁ

HAA
はぁ

HAA
はぁ

I-5

HELLO, KYON-KUN.

YUKI?

......?
THAT'S
ODD.

YOU'RE
STILL
HERE?

OH.
HEY
THERE,
ASA-
KURA
...

LAST TIME
I CAME
AROUND,
THERE WAS
NOBODY
HERE.

HUMANS
ARE
ALWAYS
SAYING...

......

...IT'S
BETTER TO
REGRET
WHAT
YOU'VE
DONE THAN
TO REGRET
HAVING
DONE
NOTHING.

KO

KO
(CLACK)

KO

HOW DO
YOU FEEL
ABOUT THAT
STATEMENT?

......?

BUT YOU DIDN'T KNOW WHAT TO DO?

WHAT IF YOU KNEW THAT MAINTAINING A SITUATION YOU WERE IN AS IT WAS WOULD YIELD NO RESULTS?

HOW? WELL, I GUESS IT MEANS WHAT IT SAYS.

WHAT...?

WOULDN'T ANY CHANGE BE GOOD AS LONG AS IT'S CHANGE?

NAGATO-SAN INCLUDED.

THE HIGHER-UPS ARE SO STUBBORN.

WHAT'S SHE TALKING ABOUT? I DON'T SEE WHAT SHE'S GETTING AT.

HYOWAN (SWOOSH)

HUH?

THIS SPACE IS UNDER MY DATA JURIS-DICTION.

...ALL ESCAPE ROUTES HAVE BEEN BLOCKED.

WITH JUST A LITTLE REWORKING OF THE MOLECULAR COMPOSITION...

HEY...!

IT'S GOOD I DODGED HER FIRST ATTACK, BUT...

...COMPLETELY SERIOUS JUST NOW!!

...SHE WAS...

BULIN
(SWING)

GA
(GRAB)

KAAN
(CRACKLE)

...!!?

DON'T
TELL
ME...

... SHE'S
...

BIKI
(TWITCH)

BIKI

BIKI

...AN ALIEN!?

THAT DOESN'T LOOK HUMAN TO ME AT ALL!!

WHAT'S SUZU-MIYA HAVE TO DO WITH ANY-THING!?

I DON'T UNDER-STAND!! WHY ARE YOU DOING THIS!?

WAIT... ASA-KURA!

OH WELL. I SUPPOSE ASKING YOU TO GRASP IT FULLY IS EXPECTING A BIT MUCH.

KOOOOO (WHOOO)

DIDN'T NAGATO-SAN TELL YOU ANYTHING?

DON'T LOSE YOUR HEAD.

I'LL TELL YOU.

FINE.

BASA (FWAP)

THREE YEARS AGO!

GUWAA (BLAST)

THE DATA INTEGRATION THOUGHT ENTITY OBSERVED AN ABNORMAL EXPLOSION OF DATA.

HOMO SAPIENS ARE ABLE TO HANDLE ONLY A LIMITED AMOUNT OF SET DATA.

HOWEVER, AT THE HEART OF THAT FLARE WAS...YOU GUESSED IT...

ZAKA
(SLICE)

BISHA
(SPLAT)

IT'S
NO
USE.

....!!

IF YOU'RE
GOING
TO KEEP
PROTECTING
THAT HUMAN,
YOU STAND
NO CHANCE.

ZA
-(STAND)

ZUSHAA
(SLIIDE)

NAGA-
TO!!

HANG IN
THERE!
I'LL GO
CALL FOR AN
AMBU-
LANCE...

KYON-
KUN.

74

I THOUGHT YOU'D CHANGE HARUHI SUZUMIYA IN SOME WAY...

I HAD HOPES FOR YOU.

...BUT YOU WERE TOO SLOW.

"NOW DIE."

（ガクン）
(COLLAPSE)

カーン
(JOLT)

YOU REALLY ARE GOOD.

BUT IT'S OVER NOW.

する
SURU
(SLIDE)

SURU

THAT'S WHY IT TOOK SO LONG TO INTERRUPT THIS SPACE WITH A PROGRAM.

SURU

する

SURU する

SAAAA
(WHOOOSH)

ARE YOU OKAY!? I'LL GO CALL AN AMBULANCE RIGHT—

H-HEY, NAGATO!!

THE DAMAGE TO MY PHYSICAL BODY IS NOT SERIOUS.

I'M FINE.

I WILL COMMENCE RECOMBINING MOLECULES.

KIN
(SHINE)

HEY...

(VWEEEEEE)

HOW MANY ARE THERE LIKE YOU ON EARTH?

AM I...

...HAVING A DREAM?

THEN I COULD BE ATTACKED BY ANOTHER ONE LIKE ASAKURA...

......

PLENTY.

DON'T WORRY.

I WON'T LET THAT HAPPEN.

I FORGOT TO RECONSTRUCT GLASSES.

OKAY.

IT FELT LIKE THE FIRST TIME...

...WE'D EVER SPOKEN WHERE SHE ACTUALLY LOOKED ME IN THE EYE.

OH.

I THINK YOU LOOK CUTER WITHOUT THEM.

AFTER ALL, I DON'T REALLY HAVE A GLASSES FETISH.

WAIT.

I WILL SUMMON THE DATA NOW—

....

WHAT'S A GLASSES FETISH?

"I'M ACCUSTOMED TO THE MUNDANE DAILY ROUTINE OF LIFE."

THAT'S WHAT PEOPLE THINK ONCE THEY GET BOGGED DOWN IN EVERYDAY HAPPENINGS.

...MAYBE THE SAME THING WAS STARTING TO HAPPEN TO ME, WITH ALL THE MADNESS IN MY LIFE.

THE SCHOOL BUILDING THAT HAD BEEN SO SEVERELY DAMAGED...

......

...WAS RESTORED TO ITS OLD SELF AGAIN, AS IF NOTHING HAD HAPPENED YESTERDAY.

PON (PAT)

MORNING, KYON!

WHY THE LONG FACE SO EARLY IN THE MORNING?

YOU GET REJECTED BY SUZUMIYA OR SOMETHING?

HAHAHA!

HAHAHA!

は は は は は は

THE BIZARRE TALE THAT THIS ORDINARY BUILDING TOLD...

...WAS ENOUGH TO THROW ME INTO SHOCK.

IN SHORT, I WAS TROUBLED.

I HAVE MY ROUTINE.

AND THAT DOESN'T INVOLVE HAVING MY CLASSMATE TRY TO KILL ME OUT OF THE BLUE.

AND A CLASSROOM ISN'T MEANT TO TURN INTO A BATTLE-GROUND.

OH, YEAH... THAT'S RIGHT.

1-5

HA-HA...

THIS IS THE LAME ENDING WHERE I FIND OUT IT WAS ALL A DREAM!

IT WAS A DREAM!!

THE THING IS, I'D REALIZED THE TRUTH BY NOW.

HA...

THEY'RE SAYING SHE SUDDENLY TRANSFERRED SCHOOLS!

ABOUT ASAKURA-SAN?

HEY, DID YOU HEAR?

HA HA HA!

W-WHOA THERE, KYON. WHAT'S GOTTEN INTO YOU?

I JUST DIDN'T WANT TO ACCEPT IT.

BECAUSE WHETHER IT WAS A DREAM OR NOT...

LOOKS LIKE YOU'RE ALREADY A MEMBER, HUH?

...I WAS CLEARLY ALREADY ENTANGLED WITH "THEM."

THE MELANCHOLY OF HARUHI SUZUMIYA II: END

THE MELANCHOLY OF HARUHI SUZUMIYA

HEY, DID YOU HEAR?

THEY SAY ASAKURA-SAN SUDDENLY TRANSFERRED!

NO WAY... EVEN THOUGH SCHOOL ONLY STARTED A MONTH AGO?

AWW, AND I WAS HER BIGGEST FAN...

DOES ANYBODY KNOW WHY?

THING IS...UNTIL YESTER-DAY, NOBODY KNEW THAT SHE WAS EVEN MOVING.

FOR REAL!?

THAT SOUNDS AWFULLY *SUSPICIOUS.*

© THE MELANCHOLY OF HARUHI SUZUMIYA III

YOU SURE SOUND BUSY, KYON.

YOU'RE GOING TODAY AFTER SCHOOL AGAIN, AREN'T YOU?

WHAT ARE YOU TALKING ABOUT?

OH, DON'T PULL THAT ON ME AGAIN!

HM?

YOU'VE GOTTA REPORT IN ABOUT YOUR FINDINGS. 'COS OF...

ОН (NUDGE)

TO THE *GREAT BRIGADE CHIEF!*

THIS BASTARD...

BAN (BAM)

...WHAT IT SAYS RIGHT HERE!

SOS団部員

連絡その他雑用は全てキョン(090-XXX-XXXX)まで!!

WELL, UH...

THERE ISN'T MUCH TO EXPLAIN.

SOS

WHAT IS THE MEANING OF THIS!?

BAN (SLAM)

...AND DISTRIBUTED THEM ALONG WITH MY CELL PHONE NUMBER FROM THE SCHOOL ROOF, OF ALL THINGS!!

JUST THE OTHER DAY SHE MADE FLYERS ABOUT HER MADE-UP MYSTERY GROUP, THE SOS BRIGADE, OR WHATEVER IT IS...

IT'S LIKE I SAID. I HAVEN'T GOTTEN ANY INQUIRES, SUZUMIYA.

AND WHERE DO YOU GET OFF...?

DON'T YOU HAVE ANY COMMON SENSE!?

HOW DARE YOU USE A PERSON'S PHONE NUMBER WITHOUT ASKING!

THAT'S RIGHT.

GO

I COULD NEVER SAY THAT...

GOOD GRIEF...

GO

GO

GO

WHERE DO I GET OFF... WHAT?

GO

GO (RUMBLE)

COULDN'T THERE BE AT LEAST ONE WEIRD ONE!?

BUT IT'S THE SAME AS IN MIDDLE SCHOOL. ALL THE CLUBS ARE COMPLETELY NORMAL!

I THOUGHT THAT ONCE I GOT INTO HIGH SCHOOL THINGS WOULD BE AT LEAST A LITTLE BETTER.

......

PUNSUKA (FUME)

THE KINDS OF CLUBS I LIKE ARE *WEIRD*.

AND JUST WHAT CONSTITUTES "WEIRD" OR "NORMAL"?

AND THOSE I DON'T ARE *ALL NORMAL*.

HA (GASP)

BESIDES, YOU WERE ALWAYS REALLY POPULAR WITH THE GUYS IN MIDDLE SCHOOL, SO SHOULDN'T THAT MAKE YOU HAPPY ENOUGH?

C'MON. THAT'S NOT HOW IT WAS IN MIDDLE SCHOOL OR HIGH SCHOOL.

AH... NO...

WHATEVER.

SIGN: BRIGADE CHIEF

IT'S PROBABLY ALL TRUE, ANYWAY.

I DON'T KNOW WHAT YOU HEARD, BUT...

...IT WAS ALL FROM TANIGUCHI, RIGHT?

ALL OF THEM WERE LAME TO THE POINT OF IDIOCY.

IS THAT ALL THERE IS ANYMORE!?

JIWA

JIWA
(FUME)

NOT GOOD. I FLIPPED SOME KIND OF WEIRD SWITCH OF HERS.

AH...

...JOKE AROUND AND HAVE A DRINK, THEN TOP IT ALL OFF WITH A "SEE YOU TOMORROW!"

THE OLD ROUTINE OF MEETING IN FRONT OF THE STATION ON A SUNDAY, HIT UP A MOVIE, AMUSEMENT PARK, OR STADIUM...

DON'T TELL ME...

IF IT WAS ME, I'D PROBABLY INVITE THE GIRL TO SOME PRIVATE PLACE TO DO IT.

YEAH, I GUESS THAT'S TRUE...

AND ALMOST ALL OF THEM ASKED ME OUT OVER THE PHONE. I MEAN, WHAT IS THAT!?

DON (SLAM)

IF YOU'RE GOING TO SAY SOMETHING SO IMPORTANT, SAY IT TO THE GIRL'S FACE FOR CRYING OUT LOUD!

MAKE UP YOUR MIND.

I DON'T CARE ABOUT THAT!

BISHI (JAB)

THE PROBLEM IS THAT THERE'RE ONLY WORTHLESS GUYS IN THE WORLD!!

I SWEAR, I SPENT MY ENTIRE MIDDLE SCHOOL CAREER SUFFERING FROM IT!

OKAY, THEN...

WHAT KIND OF GUY WOULD BE GOOD?

THAT SHOULD GO WITHOUT SAYING.

AN ALIEN OR SOMETHING LIKE THAT!

THAT WOULD MAKE THINGS MUCH MORE INTERESTING, DUH!!

TH-

THAT...

...MIGHT BE TRUE, YEAH.

AFTER ALL, I CAN'T DENY THE APPEAL OF HARUHI'S POINT OF VIEW.

FOR EXAMPLE, IF THAT IDIOT TANIGUCHI WAS ACTUALLY A TIME TRAVELER FROM THE FUTURE OR SOME OTHER SUCH FANTASTIC THING, HELL, YEAH, IT'D MAKE THINGS INTERESTING...

...OR HAVING A BEAUTIFUL TRANSFER STUDENT BE AN ALIEN OR SOMETHING... BUT FAT CHANCE.

STILL...

...THE FACT THAT IT'S TRUE TROUBLES ME.

AN A-.

SFX: PORO (SWEAT)

HMMM...

...THIS SMELLS FISHY.

IT CAME OUT OF THE BLUE.

I'LL LOOK INTO IT FOR YOU. BY THE WAY...

SHE WAS ALWAYS A VERY MYSTERIOUS STUDENT.

TO BEGIN WITH, SHE TRANSFERRED TO OUR SCHOOL FROM ANOTHER DISTRICT IN THE SUBURBS.

職員室

WHY DO YOU SUDDENLY WANT TO KNOW WHERE ASAKURA TRANSFERRED?

...WHY ALL THIS INTEREST, SUZU-MIYA?

SIGN: FACULTY ROOM

YES, WELL...

...WE WERE FRIENDS.

THE IMPORTANT POINT IN ALL OF THIS IS THAT SHE HAS *THE POWER TO MAKE THAT WHICH SHE IMAGINES BECOME REALITY.*

BUT IN ANY CASE, *THE FLOODS OF DATA THAT HARUHI SUZUMIYA TRANSMITS* CONTINUE IN SHORT BURSTS.

SIGN: SOS BRIGADE

BUT COULDN'T I GO AND TELL SUZUMIYA EVERYTHING I JUST HEARD?

NI (SMIRK)

SHE WOULD NOT TAKE YOUR DATA FEED SERIOUSLY.

...IF THAT'S THE CASE, THEN WHY DON'T YOU TELL ALL THIS TO SUZUMIYA YOURSELF?

THAT WOULD BE EXTREMELY DANGER-OUS.

LOOK...

THAT IS WHAT I WANT YOU TO UNDER-STAND.

BATA

BATA

BATA (STOMP)

BATA

...YOU'RE PROBABLY RIGHT ABOUT THAT.

KYA!? W-WAIT...

!?

DOTA (BAM)

DOTA

DOTA

WHERE AM I?

PIPE DOWN!

DOTAN (SLAM)

KYAAAAA!!

BASUN (BANG)

BAN (BANG)

WHAT IS IT THIS TIME!?

WHY ARE YOU DOING THIS!?

PON (PUSH)

IT TOOK ME A WHILE TO CATCH HER!

YO! SORRY I'M LATE!

!?

THIS IS JUNIOR MIKURU ASAHINA-CHAN!

ALLOW ME TO INTRO-DUCE YOU!

AH... SHE'S CUTE...

HUH?

HUH?

SFX: DOOON (SHOCK)

SUCH A SCARY FACE!

DIDN'T SHE JUST SAY SHE HAD TO "CATCH HER" EARLIER?

RIGHT?

HOW RUDE. SHE CAME OF HER OWN FREE WILL.

WAIT, I MEAN...

WHERE'D YOU KIDNAP HER FROM?

AND ISN'T SHE AN UPPER-CLASSMAN?

HAWAWA...

BUT WHY'D YOU HAVE TO DO THIS TO...

...ASAHINA-SAN?

I'VE WALKED EVERY INCH OF THIS SCHOOL DURING MY BREAKS!!

DRAMATIZATION

IT'S A WHOPPER!

I CAUGHT HER SPACING OUT IN SOME JUNIOR CLASS-ROOM.

NICE BREEZE.

Soon I'll be able to hear the footsteps of early summer approaching.

A **LOLITA** CHARACTER LIKE THIS IS ESSENTIAL.

(GRAPE JUICE)

MOE...

...IS VERY IMPORTANT, I BELIEVE.

AND THAT'S NOT ALL!

I THOUGHT WE COULD USE A **MASCOT** !!

POWAN (SMOOSH)

WAH YAAA AAH!?

CHECK THESE OUT!!

ZAAA (ZSHHH)

EXPERIENCING TECHNICAL DIFFICULTIES.

STOP! WAIT! SAVE ME! AH! NOT UNDER THE SHIRT...!!

STOP IIIIT!

MOMU

MOMU (SQUISH)

HER **RACK** IS BIGGER THAN MINE!!

HOW'S THIS!?

つやーー
TSUYAAA
(GLEEEAM)

WAAH... WAAH...

FIVE MINUTES LATER

WELL, QUIT THAT.

IT'LL CONFLICT WITH OUR CLUB'S ACTIVITIES.

すっ
(BECKON)

UM... THE CALLIGRAPHY CLUB...

I SEE.

MIKURU-CHAN.

ARE YOU IN ANY OTHER CLUBS?

SUZUMIYA, DON'T TELL ME...

うぐぇっ
WAAH...

BUT YES, THAT'S 90% OF IT.

HEY!

はぁ
HAA
(SIGH)

HOW RUDE.

OF COURSE THERE ARE OTHER REASONS.

...THAT ASAHINA-SAN BEING *MOE* AND *BIG-BREASTED*...

...ARE THE ONLY REASONS YOU'RE FORCING HER INTO THE SOS BRIGADE.

WANNA HEAR SOMETHING GOOD?

I FOUND US A "MYSTERY."

DAN (SLAM)

SIGN: COUNTERMEASURES HQ CHIEF

BOARD: ASA-

...FOR THE SOS BRIGADE'S FIRST MISSION...

NOT EVEN THE HOMEROOM TEACHER OKABE KNEW ANYTHING ABOUT IT, SO...

KYU

KYU

KYU

KYU

WHAT'S SHE PLANNING ON STARTING NOW...?

KYU (SQUEAK)

I'LL SAY THIS UP FRONT. THIS IS A DIFFI-CULT CASE.

KYU

...I PRE-SENT TO YOU...

GURU (SPIN)

DON
DON
ドン
ドン…
DON ドン…
(ECHO)

EVEN THOUGH SHE JUST ENTERED OUR SCHOOL, SHE SUDDENLY DISAPPEARED WITHOUT A TRACE.

AND NO-BODY KNOWS WHY!

DON (BADUUN)

...THE SEARCH FOR THE VANISHED TRANSFER STUDENT!!

BOARD: RYOUKO ASAKURA (UPSIDE DOWN)

AND...

SOMETHING IS UP.

KO (TAP)

...ALWAYS END UP INVOLVED IN SOMETHING MYSTERIOUS!

STUDENTS WHO TRANSFER IN AND OUT OF SCHOOL...

...OUR CLUB NEEDS MORE MEMBERS!!

THIS IS TO SOLVE THE CASE!!

KA (FLASH)

ABANDON SHIP!

WE'RE SINKING!

DOKAAAN (CRAAASH)

I'LL JOIN...

UWAAAH!!

KO

YOU DON'T HAVE TO JOIN THAT WEIRD CLUB, YOU KNOW.

AND IF IT'S SUZUMIYA YOU'RE WORRIED ABOUT, DON'T BE...

KO

AH...

KYON-KUN... RIGHT?

ASA-HINA-SAN!

WE'RE NOT EVEN SURE WHAT IT IS SHE WANTS TO DO WITH THIS BRIGADE.

SHE TALKS ABOUT ALIENS AND ALL THIS STUFF, BUT...

...MAYBE SHE HERSELF DOESN'T EVEN KNOW...

...HOW SHE CAN EVER BE SATISFIED.

...YOU DON'T HAVE TO FORCE YOURSELF TO PLAY ALONG.

SO...

SHE ONLY JUMPS AT THE IDEA OF "MYSTERIES" AND "MOE" BECAUSE THEY SEEM INTERESTING.

NO, IT'S OKAY.

I'M GOING TO JOIN!

KURA (FAINT)

THAT MUST BE IT.

YEAAAH!

PERHAPS IT WAS *UNAVOIDABLE* FOR THIS TIME PLANE...

KURURI (TWIRL)

HMMM...

I'LL BE OKAY... AFTER ALL, YOU'LL BE THERE TOO, RIGHT, KYON-KUN?

SHE'S SO ADORABLE IT MAKES ME DIZZY...

AND THERE'S SOMETHING ABOUT NAGATO-SAN BEING HERE THAT I CAN'T IGNORE...

HM?

PLEASE...

...CALL ME MIKU-RU-CHAN.

FUWA (FLOAT)

ASA-HINA-SAN?

OH, UH... NEVER MIND.

I MAY BE A BUMBLING NEWBIE, BUT...

...LET'S GET ALONG!

PAA (GLOW)

AHH...

THE SOS BRIGADE ISN'T ALL BAD.

OR RATHER I SHOULD SAY...I'M A LITTLE RELIEVED.

...OR SO I THOUGHT.

AGAIN, I WAS TOO NAIVE WHEN ASSESSING THE SITUATION.

WELCOME TO THE SOS BRIGADE! ♥

STOP ON BY!! ♥

SHE'S SO DAMN HYPER...

OH! HEY, MISTER, ARE YOU AN ALIEN!?

KYA!

YOU'VE GOT THE WRONG GUY.

PAAN (SLAP)

ZAWA (MURMUR)

ZAWA

COME ON, MIKURU-CHAN! DO YOUR JOB!

KACHA CLICK

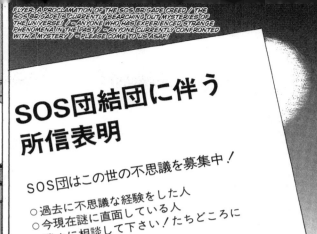

MAYBE THE TITLE "SOS BRIGADE" ALONE IS TOO VAGUE, AND THEY DIDN'T GET WHAT IT WAS ABOUT.

......

THAT GIRL...

SOS団結団に伴う
所信表明

SOS団はこの世の不思議を募集中！

○過去に不思議な経験をした人
○今現在謎に直面している人
○我々に相談して下さい！たちどころに

PASA (FLAP)

HMPH.

JUST BECAUSE SHE ACTUALLY LISTENED TO MY ADVICE DOESN'T MEAN SHE'S GOING TO GET MEMBERS.

KON (KNOCK)

KON

IN ANY CASE, I HOPE SHE AT LEAST BRINGS BACK ONE MORE PERSON.

I DON'T WANT TO BE THE ONLY ONE WHO HAS TO GET YELLED AT.

I SEE. SO SHE'S NOT HERE, EH?

WELL, IT WAS ABOUT ASAKURA'S NEW ADDRESS.

I CAN'T TELL HIM SHE'S DRESSED UP AS A BUNNY GIRL RIGHT NOW!

AH... NO...

GII (CREAK)

SA (FLAP)

SA

SA

?

AH, OKA-BE-SEN-SEI.

IS SUZUMIYA HERE?

HUH...?

TURNS OUT ASAKURA TRANSFERRED TO A SCHOOL IN *CANADA*.

SORRY TO SAY, I DON'T THINK SHE'LL BE SEEING HER AGAIN.

GOOOOOO (WHOOOOO)

GURU (SPIN)

GURU

TELL SUZUMIYA THAT FOR ME.

UH...

WELL...

GURU GURU

THAT'S HOW IT WAS TAKEN CARE OF.

BA (WHIP)

YOU'RE GIVING ME THE JOB OF TAKING AWAY THE "MYSTERY" FROM HARUHI!? THAT'S LIKE STEALING A TOY FROM A SPOILED KID.

WHAT'RE YOU DOING!?

EH?

SHE WAS TAKEN AWAY IN NO TIME.

THE MELANCHOLY OF HARUHI SUZUMIYA III: END

WHY IS IT, I WONDER ...?

PAPER: LETTER OF APOLOGY

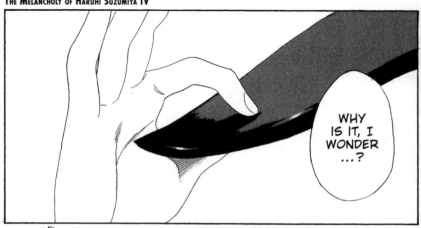

WHY IS IT WE CAN'T DRESS UP AS *BUNNY GIRLS* AT SCHOOL?

BA (FLAP)

IT'S MORE *INTERESTING* THAT WAY!

反省文

HUH?

SURE, IT'S INTERESTING TO YOU, BUT...

...CONSIDERING WHAT YOU DID...

DON'T GIVE ME THAT "CONSIDERING WHAT YOU DID" CRAP!!

BA
(FWAP)

BANNER: WELCOME TO THE SOS BRIGADE

FLYERS: A PROCLAMATION OF THE SOS BRIGADE CREED

NOT ONLY WAS SHE STOPPED HALFWAY THROUGH HER FLYER DISTRIBUTION WHILE DRESSED AS A BUNNY GIRL...

...BUT TODAY ALSO STARTED OFF WITHOUT ANY NEW MEMBERS FOR THE BRIGADE.

NOW ALL WE HAVE LEFT IS THE *MYSTERIOUS TRANSFER STUDENT*...

YOU AGREE, DON'T YOU?

......

SHE'S GOING ON ABOUT THAT AGAIN?

KYU (FOLD) キュ
KYU

ANYONE WHO TRANSFERS SMACK DAB IN THE MIDDLE OF THE SEMESTER'S GOTTA BE MYSTERIOUS.

NI GRIND

EXACTLY.

YOU'RE STARTING TO CATCH ON, HUH?

STILL, THAT'D BE AB-NORMAL!

SUKON (THUNK)

MAYBE IT'S BE-CAUSE HER DAD WAS SUD-DENLY TRANS-FERRED ...

FINE, THEN IF SHE WAS AN *ESPER* OR SOMETHING, THEN THAT'D BE GOOD ENOUGH?

.... I'LL SAY IT AGAIN.

IT'S IMPOSSIBLE.

WAI (CHATTER)

WAI

WAI

THAT'S RIGHT. IMPOSSIBLE.

DOKI (BADMP)

EVEN IF THERE WAS SOMEBODY LIKE THAT, IT'S NOT LIKE HE'D SHOW UP AND INTRODUCE HIMSELF TO US.

RIGHT?

YEAH.

OH, DEAR ME!

AH... I'M SORRY.

KAAA (BLUSH)

ASA-HINA-SAN...

WERE YOU IN THE MIDDLE OF SOMETHING?

JUDGING BY YOUR REACTION... MAYBE YOU'VE MISUNDERSTOOD HERE...

THAT'S IT! ♥ TURN YOUR EYES THIS WAY!

THAT'S GREAT! ♥

▷ PHOTO

HEY... SUZU-MIYA.

I'VE BEEN MEANING TO ASK, BUT...

NOT THAT...

I'M TALKING ABOUT...

OH, LIKE THIS DIGITAL CAMERA?

I BOR-ROWED IT FROM THE PHOTO-GRAPHY CLUB.

...THESE THINGS YOU KEEP BRINGING IN...

WHERE DO YOU GET THEM?

OKAY, I THINK THAT'S ENOUGH...

PIII (BEEEP?)

VERY NICE!

PASHA

PASHA

PASHA

PASHA

YES!

...THIS IS AWE-SOME!

SCREEN: OUT OF SPACE

HUH?

ファイル容量不足

PIII
ピーッ

PIII
ピーッ

PIII
ピーッ

UGH... NOT ANOTHER DEAD-LOCK...

I CAN'T TAKE ANY MORE PHOTOS.

FIX IT NOW!

I'M TELL-ING YOU, I CAN'T.

31/62△ MENU

I GUESS YOU TOOK ALL OF THEM...

I SEE.

ALL YOU CAN DO IS EITHER ERASE SOME OF THE PHOTOS OR MOVE THEM ONTO ANOTHER COMPUTER...

SIGN: COMPUTER RESEARCH SOCIETY

IT'S LIKE I SAID!

FORK OVER A COMPUTER!

FUN (CHMPH)

NOW JUST WHAT ARE YOU TALKING ABOUT?

FIRST YOU BARGE IN HERE UNANNOUNCED, AND THEN YOU DON'T EVEN INTRODUCE YOURSELVES.

SHE'S NOT LISTENING!!

DON (BADUUM)

GASHI (GRAB)

HEY, SUZUMIYA...

YOU'VE ALREADY GOT SO MANY OF THESE THINGS, YOU WON'T MISS ONE, RIGHT?

!?

GA (GRAB)

W-WHAT ARE YOU DOING!?

KA (TAP)

I'M THE SOS BRIGADE CHIEF, HARUHI SUZUMIYA.

MY BRIGADE REQUIRES MANY THINGS RIGHT NOW.

I WANT TO SAVE THESE PHOTOS!

WHAT'S THE BIG DEAL OVER ONE MACHINE!? YOU CHEAPSKATE!

HEY...

STOP IT.

I... I DON'T CARE HOW INFAMOUS YOU ARE AROUND SCHOOL, HARUHI SUZUMIYA...

TH-THIS COMPUTER'S SO VALUABLE, WE HAD TO BUY IT OUT OF OUR OWN POCKETS.

STOP IT, SUZU-MIYA!!

THIS IS GOING TOO FAR, EVEN FOR YOU.

LEARN TO JUST DEAL SOMETIMES.

THINGS CAN'T ALWAYS GO THE WAY YOU WANT THEM TO.

GU
CLENCH

....

THE CLUB PRESIDENT IS RIGHT.

I JUST THOUGHT I'D TRY ASKING.

SORRY TO HAVE BOTHERED YOU.

HUH?

KURU (TWIRL)

HMM. IS THAT SO?

UH...

UMM...

THAT'S WEIRD.

HUH?

SO HOW ABOUT WE MAKE A TRADE?

I UNDERSTAND WHAT YOU'RE ASKING.

IN EXCHANGE FOR LENDING YOU A COMPUTER FROM OUR SOCIETY...

...WE WANT YOU TO HAVE THE GIRL IN THESE PHOTOS JOIN OUR CLUB PART-TIME.

AS YOU CAN ALREADY SEE...OUR COMPUTER SOCIETY LACKS ANY FEMALE MEMBERS ...AND, WELL...

...WE'VE ALWAYS WANTED SOMEONE WHO'D DO THE CLEANING ...

SFX: HERA (FLAIL) HERA

....

...OF COURSE, JUST TEMPORARILY IS FINE...

NO, I MEAN...

WHAT ARE THEY SUGGESTING?

HUH?

WHAAAT!?

I'LL LEASE HER TO YOU.

I ACCEPT YOUR PROPOSAL.

THAT WAS UNEXPECTED. COMPLETELY UNEXPECTED.

WHO MAKES PROPOSALS LIKE THAT? AND MORE TO THE POINT...

...NOT ONLY DID SUZUMIYA ACTUALLY HEAR HIM OUT, BUT TO THINK THAT SHE'D ACTUALLY PARTAKE IN THIS "COMPROMISE"...

OF COURSE.

UM... DO I REALLY HAVE TO WEAR *THIS*?

KYU (TUG)

KYU

HYAH!?

PAN (SLAP)

AS THE EXCHANGE STUDENT FROM THE SOS BRIGADE, THROW YOUR CHEST OUT!

EVEN AFTER GIVING IT MY ALL...

I REALLY JUST CAN'T GET MY HEAD AROUND IT.

CAN YOU REALLY FINISH USING THE COMPUTER SO QUICKLY?

THIRTY MIN-UTES?

HUH?

GOT IT, MIKURU-CHAN?

WHAT ARE YOU TALKING ABOUT?

I HAVE NO INTENTION OF LOSING EITHER MIKURU-CHAN OR THE COMPUTER.

. . . . . .

AFTER THIRTY MINUTES, YOU ARE TO COME RIGHT BACK HERE TO THE SOS BRIGADE.

HYOKO

HYOKO
(WADDLE)
ひょこ

WELL,
ANYWAY,
OFF YOU
GO!

PECHAN
(SPLAT)
ぺちゃん

IS SHE
GOING
TO BE
OKAY
...?

DO YOU
HAVE SOME
KIND OF PLAN
AS TO HOW
YOU'RE GOING
TO HOLD ONTO
BOTH OF
THEM?

LISTEN,
SUZUMIYA
...

SIGN: COMPUTER RESEARCH

OOO
(CHEER)

TH-
THANK
YOU FOR
HAVING
ME.

HMM...

コンピュータ研

142

SCREEN: TRANSFERRING IMAGES FROM USB PORT / 42% COMPLETE

SHE'S LATE.

TOO LATE!!

ZUI (LOOM)

IF YOU JUST RETURNED THE COMPUTER, YOU COULD HAVE HER BACK HERE SOONER.

WHY ARE YOU SAYING SHE'S LATE? IT HASN'T EVEN BEEN TWENTY MINUTES.

IRA IRA IRA (IRKED)

I TOLD HER TO COME BACK RIGHT AWAY...

HOW LONG IS THAT GIRL GOING TO DAWDLE?

QUIT TALKING NONSENSE.

IN THE END, THIS IS ONLY A LEASE ANYWAY.

DON'T YOU GET WHAT THAT MEANS?

DA
(DASH)

HEY, WAIT A SEC!

WHAT ARE YOU DOING?

DAN
(BAM)

I'LL FILL YOU IN ON MY PLAN OF ATTACK.

POI
(TOSS)

WAH!?

WHAT ARE YOU TAL—

BETWEEN THE LENDER AND THE BORROWER...

...THE FORMER ALWAYS HAS THE UPPER HAND, REMEMBER?

DO
(STOMP)

DO

DO

DO A GOOD JOB FOLLOWING THROUGH.

HA HA

WAHA

WHY DON'T YOU STAY HERE AND BECOME A FULL-TIME MEMBER?

I HAVE TO GO BACK SOON...

HA ...HA

UH... UMM...

最高

IT'S HEAVEN!

THIS TEA YOU'VE MADE IS SO DELICIOUS, MIKURU-CHAN!

MOEEE!

萌え 萌え

THIS IS THE BEST! ♥

HOWAAA! ♥

コンビ

BAN (BANG)

...THAT SUGGESTED SHE STAY HERE AND BECOME A FULL-TIME MEMBER?

WHOOO WAS IT...?

ピキ PIKI (TWITCH)

PIKI ピキ

ピキ PIKI

HEY.

DID YOU KNOW ABOUT THIS?

WHAT DO YOU WANT NOW?

SHIN (SILENCE)

OH, PLEASE. IT WAS JUST A JOKE.

S-SUZU-MIYA...

...EVEN IN THE CASE OF LOANS, THE EXCHANGE MUST BE PAID BACK IN FULL.

WHEN AN EXCHANGE OF GOODS HAS OCCURRED, SHOULD THE ALLOTTED TIME TO BE BREACHED BY EVEN A SECOND....

OH WELL. NO MATTER.

PON (PAT)

PERHAPS YOU DON'T QUITE UNDER-STAND.

......

WHAT ABOUT IT?

NYARI
(GRIN)

I FORGOT TO ASK EARLIER...

...WHICH OF THESE COMPUTERS IS THE NEWEST MODEL!

COULD IT BE THIS ONE!?

GA
(GRAB)

GA

DON'T BE SO ROUGH WITH—

HEY!

HUH...?

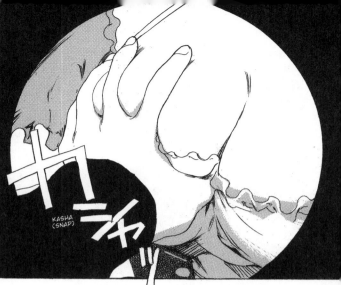

KASHA
(SNAP)

MOUTH: WHA!?

PA
(WHAP)

WHAT ARE YOU—

NOW, THEN.

JIII
(STARE)

I JUST GOT A PERFECT SHOT OF YOU *SEXUALLY HARASSING* HER.

YOU CAN'T DO THAT!!

YOU MADE ME TOUCH HER!!

IF YOU DON'T WANT THAT PHOTO PLASTERED ALL OVER, THEN HAND OVER A COMPUTER!

THE NEWEST MODEL YOU'VE GOT!!

DON (BADUM)

"ALL THE CLUB MEMBERS TEAMED UP TO GANG-RAPE HER!"

S-SO EVIL...

BA (WHIP)

ALL THE MEMBERS HERE WILL VOUCH FOR ME!

DO YOU WANT THAT TO GET AROUND?

NEVER THINK FOR A SECOND THAT ONE OF MY SOS BRIGADE MEMBERS IS WORTH AS LITTLE AS SOME COMPUTER.

SO I'LL ONLY ASK YOU ONE MORE TIME.

LUCKY FOR YOU, YOU HAVE A WHOLE HOUR TO PAY UP.

WHICH IS THE NEWEST MODEL?

SHE... SHE'S CRAZY...

WAAAH ...

HEY— IT'S NOT LIKE THEY WEAR OUT.

GEEZ ...

THAT WAS QUITE A JUSTIFI-CATION YOU GAVE FOR ROBBING THEM.

NOW I CAN NEVER GET MARRIED...

COME ON, MIKURU-CHAN. HOW LONG ARE YOU GOING TO KEEP CRYING!?

ROBBING! AS IF!

IT WAS NEVER A FAIR TRADE IN THE FIRST PLACE.

WHO AM I KIDDING? I CAN'T ARGUE WITH THAT.

BUT LET'S MAKE THIS THE LAST TIME YOU MAKE ME YOUR ACCOMPLICE.

WHAT ARE YOU TALKING ABOUT?

FOR ONCE, I ACTUALLY AGREE.

THEY WON'T QUIT NAGGING ME ABOUT RETURNING THE CAMERA.

NEXT UP IS MESSING WITH THE PHOTOGRAPHY CLUB.

UNBELIEVABLE.

THE MELANCHOLY OF HARUHI SUZUMIYA IV: END

SOS団

世界を大いに盛り上げるための涼宮

SOS団のサイトによVERうこそ

Eメールはこちら

IT'S A LITTLE PREMATURE FOR A GUESTBOOK... I GUESS.

Y style="top : 126px; left : 32
osition : absolute;
-index : 1;
idth : 375px;
eight : 16px;
d="Layer1"><FONT size="+4"><B>
Y style="width : 250px;height
osition : absolute;
-index : 2;
d="Layer2"><FO
Y style="top

盛り上げるための涼宮ハルヒの団</FONT></DIV>

KATA
(CLICK)

HOW COULD SHE ASK FOR A WEBSITE?

GEEZ...

SCREEN: SOS BRIGADE / HARUHI SUZUMIYA'S BRIGADE TO GREATLY ENLIVEN THE WORLD / WELCOME TO THE SOS BRIGADE WEBSITE. / PLEASE E-MAIL US HERE. / HARUHI SUZUMIYA'S BRIGADE TO GREATLY ENLIVEN THE WORLD</FONT></DIV>

あぁ AA
(YAWN)

I DON'T HAVE ANYTHING TO POST!

THIS SHOULD DO...

DOKI
(BADMP)

KYON

MIKURU
ASAHINA

ITSUKI
KOIZUMI

YUKI
NAGATO

© THE MELANCHOLY OF HARUHI SUZUMIYA V

SASH: BRIGADE CHIEF

...OH, IT'S YOU, NAGATO.

....

A FEW DAYS AFTER PLUNDERING A COMPUTER FROM THE COMPUTER RESEARCH SOCIETY...

THIS GIRL IS LIKE A PHANTOM.

WHAT ARE YOU DOING JUST STANDING THERE?

ARE COMPUTERS THAT RARE FOR YOU?

...AND AFTER FINISHING TRANSFERRING THE DIGITAL CAMERA PICTURES...

...THE CONSTRUCTION OF A WEBSITE FOR THE SOS BRIGADE BECAME MY NEWEST JOB.

......

SCREEN: SEARCH OPTIONS / START
COMICS TICKETS TRAVEL / STORE
SPORTS FINANCES / RING TONES
GAMES / AREA MAPS / KIDS / ART-
NET / WORK CHAT / PAGE BUILDER

IT'S BEEN AROUND TWO MONTHS SINCE SCHOOL STARTED...

WHEN YOU CLICK HERE, YOU JUMP TO A NEW LINK.

THIS IS THE INTERNET. GET IT YET?

IF YOU LOOK AT THIS WHILE WORKING, IT SHOULD DO...

KUI
(PULL)

HYOI
(LIFT)

?

GUESS YOU'RE GONNA NEED A MANUAL.

BOOK: THE BLUE BIRD
MAURICE MAETERLINCK (AUTHOR) / SEISHIROU OSHIMA (TRANSLATOR)

OH.

I'M *ITSUKI KOIZUMI.* NICE TO MEET YOU.

I JUST TRANSFERRED INTO THE FRESHMAN CLASS 9.

GO ON, INTRODUCE YOURSELF!

AH, YES...

YIPPEE! I FINALLY FOUND ONE!

HEY, SUZUMIYA, DON'T TELL ME YOU DID IT AGAIN...

THIS IS THE *SOS BRIGADE.*

PAA (GLOW)

HOW MANY TIMES HAVE I SAID IT? I'VE ALWAYS WANTED A *MYSTERIOUS TRANSFER STUDENT* TO SHOW UP AT A WEIRD TIME IN THE SEMESTER!

I'M THE LEADER, HARUHI SUZUMIYA. AND THOSE MEMBERS ARE NUMBERS ONE, TWO, AND THREE.

oooooooooo

HE FILLS THE ROLE PERFECTLY! KOIZUMI-KUN, LISTEN UP!

MYSTERIES OF THIS WORLD!!

LET'S LOCATE ALIENS, TIME TRAVELERS, AND ESPERS AND HANG OUT WITH THEM!

DOOON (BADUUUM)

BANNER: FIRST MYSTERY TOUR

A CITY EXPLORATION IN SEARCH OF MYSTERIES!

PISHAAAN (SPLAASH)

...THIS COMING SATURDAY AKA TOMORROW MORNING AT 9 A.M., WE'RE MEETING IN FRONT OF THE NORTH EXIT OF THE TRAIN STATION!

IF WE LEAVE NO STONE UNTURNED IN OUR EXPLORATION OF THE CITY, THERE'S NO DOUBT AT LEAST ONE PHENOMENON THAT COULD BE CONSIDERED MYSTERIOUS WILL TURN UP!

THAT'S WHY...

MY...MY ONE DAY OFF...

OH, I SEE.

162

THERE'S SOMETHING CREEPY ABOUT THIS GUY, I'M TELLING YOU...

OKAY, THEN. COME EARLY TOMORROW.

SFX: PORI (SCRATCH) PORI

...GEEZ.

SHE SURE LIKES TO WORK ME TO THE BONE.

PON (PLOP)

HM?

YOU FINISH READING THE MANUAL?

KATAN (CLATTER)

WE'RE HEADING HOME NOW.

KYON, THANKS FOR PUTTING EVERYTHING AWAY FOR US!

IT'S AN EXTREMELY PRIMITIVE DATA NETWORK COMPUTER TERMINAL.

KOKI (CRACK)
コキッ

I UNDERSTAND NOW.

....

·青い

OH! HEY, YOU FORGOT YOUR BOOK...

FINE BY ME...

I WAS LOOKING TO ESCAPE A BIT BY READING TONIGHT ANYWAY...

AHAHA...

YOU CAN BORROW IT.

...I NEARLY FORGOT...

MY HIGH SCHOOL LIFE ALREADY HAD AN ALIEN (NAGATO) THROWN INTO THE PICTURE...

I WANNA KNOW WHERE MY BLUE-BIRD IS...

パチン
PACHIN
(CLICK)

REALLY, NOW...

SO THE MESSAGE WAS THAT THE BLUE-BIRD OF HAPPINESS WAS NEAR ALL ALONG, EH?

TO (THUMP)

BREAKING A SWEAT IN SOME FIERCE CLUB ACTIVITIES...

...LANDING MYSELF A GIRL-FRIEND...

...JUST WHAT HAPPENED ALONG THE WAY?

I ALWAYS THOUGHT I'D HAVE THAT KIND OF HIGH SCHOOL LIFE, BUT...

THE NEXT DAY

SHAKO

SHAKO

SHAKO (PEDAL)

BUT WE WERE MEETING AT 9 A.M.

EVEN IF YOU'RE NOT LATE, THE LAST GUY TO COME HAS TO PAY A FINE.

GOOD MORNING!

GACHAN (CLANG)

YOU'RE LATE!!

YOU PAY THE FINE!!

SIGN: CAFÉ

SIGN: DREAM

SO YOU HAVE TO *TREAT US* ALL TO DRINKS.

THANKS!

...THAT I BECAME AWARE OF JUST HOW PECULIAR MY SITUATION WAS.

IT WAS DURING THIS EXCURSION...

WHAT GIVES...?

NOW LISTEN UP. WE'RE GOING TO DRAW STRAWS...

...AND SPLIT UP INTO THREE GROUPS.

WE'LL LOOK FOR ANYTHING STRANGE OR DUBIOUS!

KOI-ZUMI-KUN, YOU SHOW GREAT PROMISE!

EXACTLY!

I SEE.

IN SHORT, WE SHOULD LOOK FOR ALIENS AND THE LIKE...OR ANY EVIDENCE THEY MAY HAVE LEFT BEHIND FROM A VISIT, CORRECT?

COME ON...

...DO YOU REALLY GET IT?

OH, MY.

HM...

KOIZUMI

HARUHI / NAGATO

KYON / MIKURU

THAT'S TOO BAD.

BA (FWAP)

I COULDN'T BE LUCKIER! TALK ABOUT THE PERFECT COMBO!

OOOOOH!

I'D BEEN HOPING TO TAKE ADVANTAGE OF THIS OUTING TO DEEPEN MY FRIENDSHIP WITH A CERTAIN SOMEONE, BUT...

I GOT IT ALREADY.

THIS IS NOT A DATE. GOT IT?

BUT MORE IMPORTANTLY...

YOU HAVE THREE HOURS! IF YOU GOOF OFF...I'LL **KILL** YOU.

伝票

PAPER: BILL

SIGN: LUNCHTIME

172

HOORAY FOR A NORMAL LIFE!

I AM NOT FROM THIS ERA.

I COME FROM FURTHER IN THE *"FUTURE."*

YOU DO REALIZE THAT WE'RE AT THE PARK ACROSS FROM THE STATION?

Meaning no?

HAVE YOU AT LEAST FOUND *A LANDING SITE FOR A UFO* YET?

I figured you'd pull that.

TSULU (DOO)
TSULU

Same café as before. Pronto!

GACHA (CLICK)

HUH!? COME ON...

It was my mistake to let you partner up with Mikuru-chan.

I WAS SENT...

Tell Mikuru-chan that I want her to join my group over here.

...TO OBSERVE WHETHER OR NOT ANY NEW ANOMALIES IN TIME APPEAR AROUND SUZUMIYA-SAN.

I SEE NOW...

SO NAGATO'S AN ALIEN, AND ASAHINA-SAN'S A TIME TRAVELER, IS THAT IT?

NO MATTER WHAT HAPPENS...

...LOOKS LIKE I'LL NEVER BE AN "ORDINARY HIGH SCHOOLER."

OH, BLUE-BIRD OF MINE. WHERE ARE YOU NOW?

...YEAH, RIGHT.

EXCUSE ME.

IS YOUR HUNT FOR THE PARANORMAL GOING WELL?

....

HE REALLY IS CREEPY...

KURU (TURN)

SHE TOLD ME TO PARTNER UP WITH YOU IN THE PARK.

TO BE HONEST, I'M THANKFUL.

I JUST GOT A CALL FROM SUZUMIYA-SAN.

ON MY OWN, I DON'T THINK I CAN FIND ANYTHING.

KOIZUMI.

180

DON'T YOU ALSO HAVE SOMETHING YOU WANT TO SAY TO ME?

....

LIKE, "I'M ACTU-ALLY AN *ESPER*"...

...OR SOME-THING?

LIKE WHAT?

....

I HAVE NO IDEA...

...WHAT YOU'RE TRYING TO DO, BUT...

...I WISH YOU WOULDN'T SPOIL THE SURPRISE.

I WANT TO SAY IT'S A LITTLE DIFFERENT THAN THAT, BUT...

OH WELL...

· · · · · · · ·

THE TRUTH IS, I NEVER MEANT TO START TALKING ABOUT THIS WITH YOU SO QUICKLY, BUT...

...IS SOMETHING THE MATTER?

A DREAM...

PA (TURN)

...YES, I SUPPOSE CALLING ME THAT WOULD BE THE CLOSEST THING.

YES. I'M AN ESPER.

...LEAVE ME ALONE ALREADY!!

AH!

カラ (KARAN (CLINK))

ドン
DON (BAM)

YOU SURE HAVE SOME GALL...

...FALLING ASLEEP HALFWAY THROUGH OUR WRAP-UP MEETING.

OH, THAT'S RIGHT...

COME ON... HE MUST BE TIRED TOO.

HAVING BEEN ON AN EXPEDITION SINCE MORNING.

WERE YOU HAVING A NICE DREAM?

......

BANNER: FIRST MYSTERY

LET'S NOT TALK ABOUT THAT.

AFTER ALL, IT SHOULDN'T BE SOMETHING SO EASY TO DISCOVER IN THE FIRST PLACE.

EVEN THOUGH IT ENDED WITHOUT ANY DISCOVERIES.

WHAT MATTERS IS THAT YOU GUYS UNDERSTAND TODAY...

...WHAT THE *SOS BRIGADE* IS ALL ABOUT!

I REALLY WISH IT WAS ALL A DREAM...

IT WAS QUITE OUTSIDE OUR ESTI-MATIONS...

HAA (PANT) HAA

I'M SURE IT'S NOT SOMETHING SO EASY TO BELIEVE...BUT THE SITUATION HAS CHANGED.

PLEASE, DON'T TAKE OFFENSE.

...HOW QUICKLY ASAHINA-SAN AND NAGATO-SAN...

...CAME TO GATHER AROUND HARUHI SUZUMIYA.

YOU'LL COME TO FIND OUT MORE IN TIME.

WELL, I WON'T GO INTO TOO MUCH DETAIL TODAY.

INCLUDING MORE ABOUT THOSE GIRLS TOO.

I CAN TELL BY LOOKING THAT YOU'RE ALREADY QUITE EXHAUSTED.

AAAH...I'M SERIOUS.

HEY, SUZU-MIYA...

...YOU KNOW WHAT THEY SAY...

BASA (FLAP)

BASA

KYA!?

MAP

OH, MY BLUEBIRD OF HAPPINESS... WHERE ARE YOU NOW?

...SOMETIMES WHAT YOU'RE LOOKING FOR IS CLOSER THAN YOU THINK.

...YOU'RE TREATING.

AS A FINE FOR SLEEPING ON THE JOB...

伝票

BAM BAM

SOMEBODY, TELL ME, PLEASE.

STREET: YOUR ILLEGALLY PARKED BICYCLE HAS BEEN CONFISCATED

放置自転車
撤去しました

......

THE MELANCHOLY OF HARUHI SUZUMIYA V: END

TRANSLATION NOTES

Page 7
An *Esper* is an individual who uses telepathy and other paranormal mental techniques. It is derived from the acronym ESP, meaning extra-sensory-perception.

Page 32
The original Japanese for "Save the World by Overloading it with Fun Haruhi Suzumiya Brigade" is *Sekai wo Ooi ni Moriageru tame no Suzumiya Haruhi no dan*, which is where Haruhi pulls the acronym *SOS* from.

Page 107
Moe is Japanese slang that refers to a fetish or obsession with fictional characters in anime, manga, and video games. Mikuru is archetypical of the type of character that is usually fetishized.

Page 153
Haruhi tells Mikuru, "It's not like they wear out," after she gets groped because there is a Japanese myth that having your breasts touched or rubbed will make them grow larger.

TO BE CONTINUED

LONG TIME NO SEE.

HUH?

FOR SOME REASON, I FELT UNEASY...

HOW LONG DO YOU THINK THE WORLD'S BEEN AROUND?

I'M JUST... A LITTLE TIRED.

IT'S NOTHING.

...LIKE A DISASTER WAS APPROACHING.

YOU CAN STILL GO BACK.

SINCE LONG AGO, HUMANS HAVE GIVEN THAT ENTITY...

...THE NAME "GOD."

......

BUT IT MAY HAVE BEEN TOO LATE BY THE TIME I REALIZED...

...I SWEAR, I'M SO BORED.

THE MELANCHOLY ARC REACHES ITS CLIMAX!!

THE MELANCHOLY OF HARUHI SUZUMIYA

VOLUME 2 ON SALE SOON!!

THE MELANCHOLY OF HARUHI SUZUMIYA

1

Original Story: Nagaru Tanigawa
Manga: Gaku Tsugano
Character Design: Noizi Ito

Translation: Christine Schilling
Lettering: Alexis Eckerman

SUZUMIYA HARUHI NO YUUUTSU Vol. 1 © 2006 NAGARU TANIGAWA, GAKU TSUGANO, NOIZI ITO / Kadokawa. All rights reserved. First published in Japan in 2006 by Kadokawa Co., Ltd. English translation rights arranged with Kadokawa Co., Ltd., and Hachette Book Group USA through Tuttle-Mori Agency, Inc. English translation © 2008 by Hachette Book Group USA, Inc.

Yen Press
Hachette Book Group USA
237 Park Avenue, New York, NY 10017

Visit our Web sites at www.HachetteBookGroupUSA.com and www.YenPress.com.

Yen Press is an imprint of Hachette Book Group USA, Inc. The Yen Press name and logo are trademarks of Hachette Book Group USA, Inc.

First Yen Press Edition: October 2008

ISBN-10: 0-7595-2944-2
ISBN-13: 978-0-7595-2944-1

10 9 8 7 6 5 4 3 2 1

BVG

Printed in the United States of America